AF674547

The Emissary

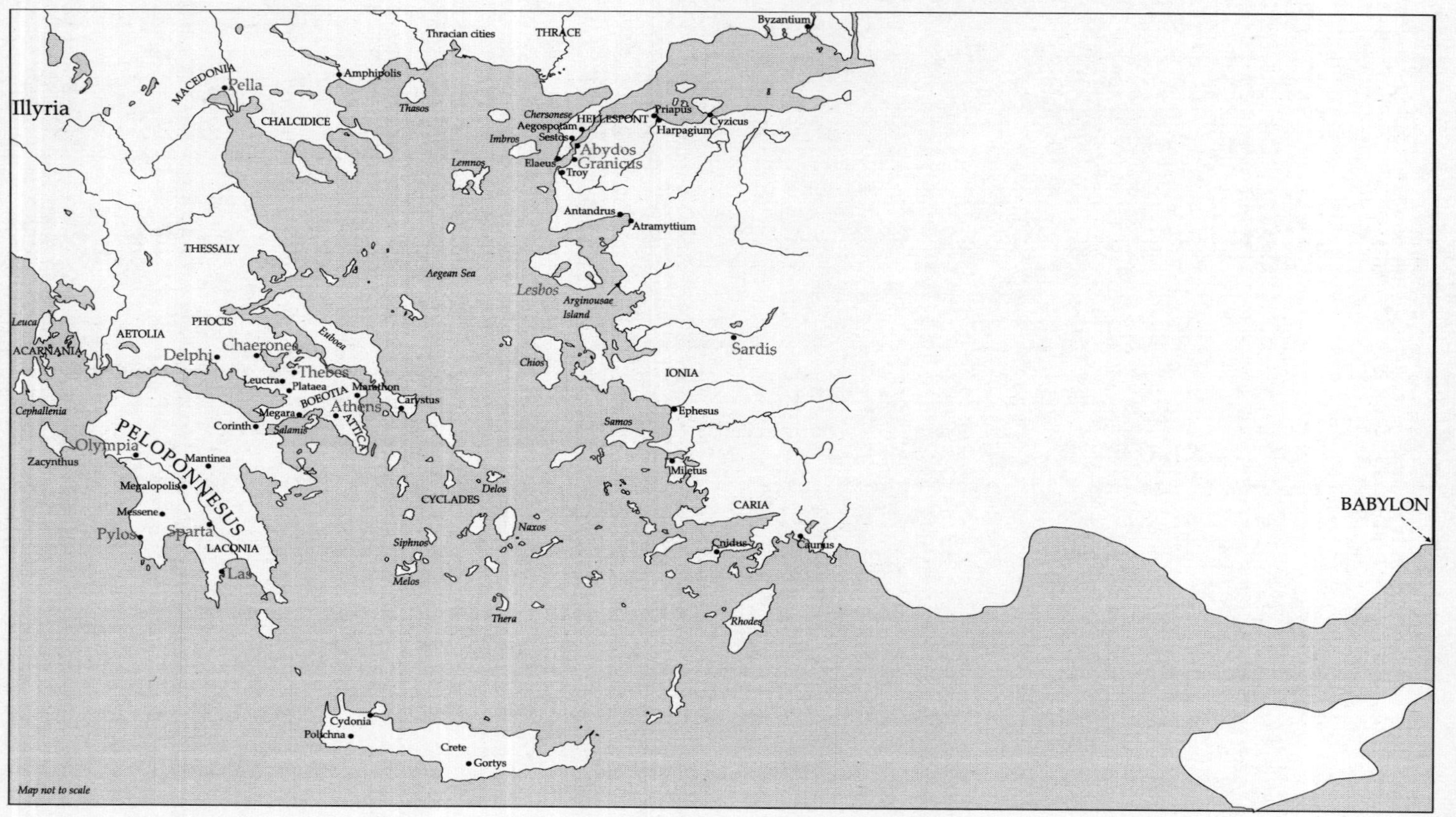
Illyria
MACEDONIA
Pella
CHALCIDICE
Amphipolis
Thasos
Thracian cities
THRACE
Byzantium
Chersonese
HELLESPONT
Aegospotami
Sestos
Imbros
Abydos
Granicus
Elaeus
Troy
Priapus
Harpagium
Cyzicus
Lemnos
Antandrus
Atramyttium
THESSALY
Aegean Sea
Lesbos
Arginousae Island
Leuca
ACARNANIA
AETOLIA
PHOCIS
Euboea
Delphi
Chaeronea
Thebes
Leuctra
Plataea
BOEOTIA
Marathon
Athens
Carystus
ATTICA
Megara
Salamis
Corinth
Cephallenia
Zacynthus
Olympia
PELOPONNESUS
Mantinea
Megalopolis
Messene
Pylos
Sparta
LACONIA
Las
Chios
Sardis
IONIA
Ephesus
Samos
Miletus
Delos
CYCLADES
Naxos
Siphnos
Melos
Thera
CARIA
Cnidus
Caunus
Rhodes
BABYLON
Cydonia
Polichna
Crete
Gortys
Map not to scale

The Emissary

A Tale of Love, Vendetta and War

Aniruddha Bahal

FOURTH ESTATE • *New Delhi*

First published in India in 2010 by Fourth Estate
An imprint of HarperCollins *Publishers*
A-75, Sector 57, Noida, Uttar Pradesh 201301, India
www.harpercollins.co.in

4 6 8 10 9 7 5 3

ISBN: 978-81-7223-998-5

This is a work of fiction with some parts based on historical fact. All situations, incidents, dialogue and characters in this novel, with the exception of some well-known historical and public figures, are products of the author's imagination and are not to be construed as real. They are not intended to depict actual events or people or to change the entirely fictional nature of the work. In all other respects, any resemblance to actual persons, living or dead, is entirely coincidental.

Typeset in Adobe Caslon Pro 11/13.7
InoSoft Systems

Printed and bound at
Replika Press Pvt. Ltd.

To
my parents, Kedar and Meena
for the uncountable blessings

Part One

ONE

I Seleucus, son of Nicanor, begin my account from the time when Kelos, son of Patrimus, was the chief controller of the Games in ,Olympia.

They say that the start of an account is like a dot on a circle: it bridges the past and the future. It is my intention to narrate the story of my life as it happened, without any of the embellishment that authors of my time are inclined to furnish. I will give you accounts of battles and escapes and vendetta which you must not confuse with imaginary tales, for these were real happenings and what I didn't witness myself, I had other witnesses tell me.

I have achieved much in this life. Wealth, women, victory in battle have all been mine. I have also suffered and seen the passing of those whom I have loved. In all this, I have been fortunate to be guided by those amongst us who can see the future – though I call them men, their powers of prophecy are not of this world, and I have often wondered how they see what awaits us in the distance. One of the reasons I write this account is for posterity to know how we lived in the years that I am going to speak of, and learn lessons from the pursuits that obsessed us.

I have deliberated at length about where I should start. I could begin from the time when I was a small child, but when one is talking about important events and people, one should try and avoid bringing too much of oneself into the tale – or people might say that Seleucus is trying to give too much importance to himself.

I am not a man of letters, and that's an advantage, for I will not attempt to dazzle you with words but by the truth of what I say. Nor do I believe in destiny, except for that which I make myself and what I have achieved through pleasing the Gods.

As I narrate my tale, I will tell you occasionally of the circumstances in which I write. Though these personal narrations may be few and far between, they are, I believe, important because they reveal my thoughts as I occupied myself with the process of writing. But one thing I do promise to those who read this account: no compromise has been made with the truth.

My name, as I told you at the very beginning, is Seleucus. But because of the fame of my father, I am better known as the son of Nicanor. I grew up in Olympia in a Macedonian family that made its living by looking after the Macedonians who came to prepare for the annual Games and visit the oracle. At my home, I spoke the Macedonian tongue, but my friends were largely from Olympia.

My father Nicanor was a charioteer and he raised horses for the races. I was twenty-two when Prince Alexander came to Olympia with his entourage and was refused participation in the Games: being a Macedonian, he was considered a foreigner. At every Game, both the annual and the big one that took place every four years, there used to be a debate about whether to admit the Macedonians or not. They spoke a corruption of Greek and some people didn't consider them proper Greeks for this reason.

But Alexander claimed descent from Achilles, and so he was allowed to enter. Actually, the opposition to the participation of the Macedonians was a big sham and organized mostly by the Athenians who used Olympian exiles and other such disgruntled elements to create a fuss; there was never any real intent to stop their involvement. The Athenians just made a lot of noise in order to insult the Macedonians.

That year, Argus, son of Pathos from Pella in Macedonia, was the principal Macedonian participant in the four-horse chariot race, though Pythagoras, son of Melender from Athens, was considered the favourite by most. My father was also favoured by some, as he had been practising for the whole year with his horses. But Argus from Alexander's team had his own diabolical intentions, which he executed ten days before the race. He committed this treachery a week after practising with my father. During that time, on one occasion, my father beat him by the length of one whole stadium in a practice race.

It happened thus: My father refused Argus's appeal to practise jointly in the big ground behind the temple at Olympia as he felt Argus would learn about his techniques and his strategy before the big race. But Argus complained about my father to Polemon, son of Agenor, who was managing the Macedonian delegation. He also spread the lie that my father was conniving with Pythagoras to defeat him. The truth, however, was that Argus was not even a likely contender in the race because his horses were inferior and his judgement so poor that he didn't know which horse to place in which position.

Polemon spoke to my father Nicanor, and I was present when he spoke to him.

Polemon said: 'Don't we always seek your advice, Nicanor, on matters concerning the Games? And we buy your horses to replenish our own, though we could get them from Thessaly, where the finest horses are available. Don't we tell Macedonians to come and do business with you when they visit the oracle, and they come to you with gifts of grain and cloth? Now that we seek some stature at the Games, why are you opposing Argus's request? If you two plan the race jointly, it will benefit Macedonia, as whoever wins, he will be a Macedonian.'

My father Nicanor replied thus: 'I seek no glory apart from Macedonia. But the rules of the Games state that there may be no collusion between participants before the race. Also, Argus and I seek the same glory. I shall give all my help for your delegation to win in other disciplines such as wrestling and sword fighting, but please do not ask for what is not mine to give.'

At this reply of my father, Polemon left angrily and reported the matter to Alexander, who was then only sixteen but behaved as if he were already king. Alexander called my father to the nobleman's house where he was staying and addressed him thus: 'Would it not be good, Nicanor, if two Macedonians could plan the race together and box in Pythagoras so that his chariot is pushed against the parapet of the stadium? In this manner, Polemon tells me, you could defeat Pythagoras. We will offer you two talents for your services if you connive with Argus in this race.'

Alexander was under instructions from King Philip, his father, to win as many crowns as he could for the Macedonian delegation, for Philip wanted to demonstrate in the Games the superiority of Macedonian discipline and how only they could be trusted to teach the Persians a lesson.

The four-horse chariot race was the most famous race at the Games. The individual who won it was assured renown for many years to come in all of Hellas. His fame would extend even to the Greek colonies of Asia. My father had taken part in this race many times but had never won it. For two years running, he had defeated everybody else, but he came second to Pythagoras. Alas, only winning mattered.

That year, he had even sacrificed a bull at the altar of Zeus in Olympia, observing all the proper rituals, and then asked the oracle about the outcome of the race. After examining the entrails of the bull, the Alamid priest signalled with his hands to the interpreters but they were reluctant to tell my father what the priest had conveyed to them; it was a language that only the interpreters understood. I was also present as I was helping my father with the observances that went with a proper bull sacrifice. When my father insisted on knowing, the interpreters told him in private what the oracle had said and my father kept the words to himself. Later, in the evening, I met Pindar, who was the son of one of the interpreters, and he extracted the information from his father and told me. According to Pindar, the oracle said: 'A mighty man will lose the race even before the start of the race.'

Two days after the disclosure by the oracle, news came that Pythagoras's lead horse, a black steed by the name of Amon, had picked up an injury in his foreleg and would not be able to run in the race, so Pythagoras was looking for a replacement. A stable hand by the name of Minos, who worked for Pythagoras, told this to his wife Helen, who, in turn, gave this detail to her father Kostinos, son of Doloros, who, in passing, mentioned it to Kelos, the chief controller of the Games. And Kelos, being a good friend of my father, mentioned it to him.

That night, my father was very happy, thinking that the words of the oracle were coming true. Amon had been the main reason, according to my father, why Pythagoras had won the race for two consecutive years. It would be very difficult for him to find a replacement at the last moment for the outer left position where the horse ran. Pythagoras had announced that he would race only if he was sure to win and my father felt that, without Amon, he could no longer be sure of victory. My father's own horse in that position, Sarissa, would be far superior to anything that Pythagoras might find as replacement. Thus, he thought, the oracle saying that a mighty man would lose the race before the race began meant that Pythagoras would not race at all because of the injury to his horse Amon.

With this assessment at the back of his mind, he agreed to Alexander's request for training with Argus as he estimated that, with Pythagoras not racing, it would make matters less complicated and he could give some tips to the buffoon Argus without hurting his own chances. But when Argus, too, became familiar with the dilemma of Pythagoras, his ambition soared even more and he began thinking of my father as the only obstacle between him and victory.

My father Nicanor had a racing style all his own, and if it hadn't been for the horse Amon, he would have won both times against Pythagoras. For he had a dangerous racing style which allowed him to turn the post faster than the others. He used to wrap the reins of all the four horses around his waist and control their direction by bending from his hips. Thus, his arms would be free to whip Numa, his anchor stallion, who couldn't make up his mind without a whipping, and to stave off dirty tactics from the other drivers.

Samthos, son of Socrates from Corinth, would often throw nails at other charioteers to obstruct them. Clonus, son of Elonas from Sparta, would use his whip on other charioteers on the bend away from the judges as one was not supposed to be dangerous in that way. Once, Clonus hit Pythagoras with his whip, but Pythagoras caught the end and wrested it from him and, in so doing, made him lose his balance and fall from his chariot. His chariot crashed into the bank near the judges and he was lucky no horses ran over him. After this incident, Clonus began whipping the horses rather than the charioteers. He would get in close and whip the anchor horse if he was on the outside, and if he were on the inside, he would whip the lead horse. By doing this, he would rouse the horses of the other charioteers before their time and tire them.

The most dangerous, however, was Samocles from Thebes. He would drive his horses into you from the outside and try to drive you into the post which marked the turn. He was treacherous because he would often do things without considering the outcome. He would use a grapple hook which he hid on the floor of his chariot. He would hide it so well that when the magistrates searched him and his chariot before placing them in the hyspleges (the gates which had been designed by Cleoitas a hundred years back, or so they said), they would find nothing.

He would then take out the grapple hook when the judges were not looking and expertly throw it on the straps that held a charioteer's xystis. When he snapped them loose, the wind got into the charioteer's garment and unbalanced him.

Previously, the charioteers used to race naked like in the other disciplines, but with so many accidents having occured, they changed the rule. They now wore a xystis that came down to the ankles and also covered the hands. This was to keep the dust from the body and also, in case of a bloody crash, the garment could be used as a bandage on the charioteers. Some even wore armour, though it was frowned upon to do so.

Samocles tried this trick on Samthos once, but it reversed on him: though he managed to take the straps off Samthos's xystis, he didn't get ahead. The wind blew Samthos's garment off his back and straight into Samocles's face, blinding him. As a result, his horses lost direction and his chariot crashed into the post on the turn, creating difficulties for the others.

Earlier, the magistrates would stop a race if there was a crash and clean up the tracks, but the rules had changed and charioteers now had to negotiate around the debris of the crash. According to the written records, there was a big debate at Olympia when one of Alcibiades's charioteers, Democles, son of Arnaut, stopped his chariot to help his friend Xanthus from Athens, who had crashed into the post and lay bleeding, having been run over by another chariot. Alcibiades had Democles whipped for stopping and thus spoiling his chances in the race. For this, he received great criticism from the magistrates and they banned his chariots from participating in the next race.

There was also the opposite case of the Spartan woman Cynisca, daughter of Archidamus, who crashed and lay bleeding, but her brother Patromos, who was also participating in the same race, kept going and didn't pay any heed to his sister's plight. This led to comments from many critics that the Spartans were not human. But some Athenian generals praised Patromos for keeping his mind on the job and winning, even though in his heart he wanted to stop.

My father Nicanor had no fear of Samocles's grapple hook, for his xystis was tightly fastened with his straps and so were the four reins, which he wrapped around his waist. He even had the strength to face up to Clonus's whip. However, if he lost his balance and fell from the chariot, he was in danger of being dragged by his own horses unless he cut the reins at his waist with the dagger he carried on his body.

Pythagoras always tried to unbalance my father Nicanor from his chariot. Since my father's strategy in a race was to save the energy of his horses during the first ten laps before he started whipping Numa, his anchor stallion, in the last two laps and speeding to the front, he was always behind Pythagoras. And Pythagoras would control the pace of the race by sometimes slowing down and whipping my father's lead horse Sarissa over his back, hoping my father would lose his balance when Sarissa suddenly slowed down. Pythagoras would do this only after kicking up a lot of dust in the hippodrome, so that the judges and even the spectators would not know that he had whipped Sarissa. He had a big reputation and he wanted the demos to think that he played by the rules.

As for my father, he only played by the rules set by the magistrates because he thought Zeus would not take care of him otherwise. But in the training match with Argus, Zeus did not take care of him.

Argus was strong but he was heavy. As a charioteer, one has to be strong but light, so that the horses have less weight to pull. My father's chariot was very light and functional. He himself was strong and had a wiry frame.

For two days, the practice with Argus went well; I was there. On the third, my father sent me on the task of preparing for the feast that he wanted to give once he won. With the two talents that Alexander was to give him, he planned to start an institution for charioteers who wanted to participate in the Games. He wanted to make this announcement at the feast.

My father was sure of winning, specially after seeing what a buffoon Argus was. Argus had a very poor sense of balance and every bump would see him holding the front end of the chariot desperately, like a clown.

My father told me Argus was too heavy to be a charioteer. In one round of the post, he would fall behind by sixty paces. And by the time the last round came, he would be one whole round behind. Argus too realized this and, like other men whose ambition runs ahead of their talent, he turned evil and began to scheme.

On the day that my father sent me to buy olive oil for the feast, I returned at dusk to find him close to dying. Pindar, the interpreter's son who had earlier told me of the prophecy made to my father, told me what had transpired. Pindar had gone to the Macedonian camp to help Polemon arrange for a sacrifice at the altar of Zeus. It was a long procedure since Polemon was sacrificing forty rams, one for each Macedonian athlete participating in the Games. Polemon wanted the entrails of every ram read by the oracle, to know beforehand the possibility of each athlete's success. It would take the entire day to sacrifice the rams, but everything had to happen before dusk.

It so happened that the ram sacrificed for Argus's success was read by the oracle in the morning itself and the interpreters said that he would lose. Though only Polemon knew what the oracle had said, Argus bribed one of the interpreters with five drachmas and came to know of the prophecy. According to Pindar, Argus turned grey when he heard it. He had been dreaming far beyond his skills. At that moment, he started devising his plot. In front of the entire Macedonian camp, outside the temple premises, where everybody was waiting for Polemon to emerge, he challenged my father. Said Argus to him: 'I think you are good only because of your horses. If I had your chariot, I would do better than you, Nicanor. If you had my chariot, you would do worse than me. To know who is better, you race in my chariot and I will race in yours, and the world will see who wins.'

Saying this, he put down a wager of a hundred drachmas that he would win. My father didn't like the idea, even though he was confident he would win, because he didn't want any harm to come to his horses from Argus's driving. But Alexander, who was also in the assembly, was seized by the idea in a boyish manner, not realizing the larger consequences. He fixed the race for the afternoon without taking my father's view into consideration, and the entire Macedonian delegation assembled at the practice tracks, except for Polemon, who was sacrificing rams at the altar of Zeus.

My father spoke to his horses individually, specially to Sarissa. He told her in her ears that somebody else would be riding the chariot and she was not to worry. He even talked to Numa to try and calm him down, as he was a little flustered that day and would become more so if a stranger rode the chariot.

It was I who used to rub the horses down and feed them and give them their morning exercise, and my father used to make me drive his chariot too, to prepare me for the future. The horses, not seeing me and having Argus ride them, behaved very strangely. Also, they were used to a very light hand on the reins, but Argus pulled the reins very tightly and the horses reacted by moving more than required. Thus, Argus had to count his mistakes often and once, while he was doing this, my father went ahead, even though Argus had initially taken a lead of seventy paces. By the second round, my father had gauged the temperament of Argus's horses and assessed how best to guide them forward. But in the seventh round, after he had overtaken Argus and taken a lead of twenty paces, the axle of the chariot he was riding broke, and he came beneath the wheel. And then Argus ran my father's own horses over him.

When I arrived in the night, he was barely alive. His body was swollen to twice its size and his hands and legs were twisted from the bones being broken. But he had willed himself to live till he saw me, for he had great love for me and I for him. The interpreters from the temple of Zeus were at the house and my mother was praying at the altar of Athena. Many of my father's friends had gathered, even the charioteer Pythagoras.

Alexander never sent an emissary, but Polemon came and my father asked him not to forget the two talents that Alexander had offered to give him if he practised with Argus. Even as he was dying, he wanted to provide for us. But Polemon never said anything. Now that he was dying, the Macedonians didn't feel the need to waste two talents. Since my father, though a Macedonian, lived in Olympia and had married an Olympian girl, some of the Macedonians didn't even consider him Macedonian.

I held my father's hand gently and my mother sent everybody else outside the room, even the medicine man who was applying cakes of opium to relieve his pain.

'Go and appeal to Alexander directly and get the two talents that were promised,' he gasped to me.

'Rest, Father, rest in peace. You will be healthy again and we shall demand what is due to us,' I told him.

'I am dying, my son. Zeus is calling me,' he said.

I took his palm gently.

'I think Argus weakened the axle purposefully,' he said.

'I will not leave him alive. I will avenge you, Father,' I said with tears in my eyes.

There was hatred in his eyes for Argus, more than I had ever seen in them. My father's dreams had been cut short. He said nothing more after that and life ebbed away from him, draining his hand of all strength as it lay in mine.

The next day was the funeral and many people walked in the procession behind the cypress coffin in which Nicanor, my father, lay. Pythagoras, his chief rival at the Games, was one of the people who spoke after his coffin had been buried and all the women in our family – my mother, her sisters, her friends and my father's sister – had wailed. Pythagoras first asked my mother's permission to speak and my mother nodded her head.

So, after my father's brother Nicias had spoken in memory of my father, Pythagoras climbed to the elevated platform and spoke thus: 'Many times did I race with Nicanor at the Games, and also in the matches organized in Athens to celebrate the festival of Athena. Nicanor defeated me there, though at the Games I always triumphed. But Nicanor would come and commend my victory after the race and, for me, his acknowledgement meant more than the palm leaf. We would share many racing tips with each other, specially how to manage horses, and we would compare the qualities of our horses, which many of you might find baffling, to say the least. That is not to say that we weren't in competition and we didn't have our moments of friction with each other. It is destiny which brings us together, and in the position we were in, of being rivals, it was natural to speak ill of the other and think unpleasant things and even, as some of us do, perform sacrifices designed to hurt the other.

'And I must confess that though I never performed any sacrifice designed to hurt my rivals – as we all know, there are many that claim those effects – I did speak ill of my competitors and imagined that they were demons when I first became a charioteer of the races. But meeting Nicanor changed my outlook and, even though there was no dilution in my thirst for victory, I began to feel that it would be enhanced if it came in the spirit of the Games. I was looking forward to our contest in this year's Games, which are to take place in ten days' time. And though my lead horse Amon is injured and I am hampered, my competition with Nicanor was such that I would have raced for the pure enjoyment of it, even though I might have lost. Sadly, that opportunity is no longer there and we will all be the lesser for it.

'At the risk of causing affront to some people, I must also mention that the circumstances surrounding his death were unfortunate. The magistrate of the Games should conduct an inquiry and recommend action to the archon of Olympia if it is found that his death had something to do with some others increasing their chances at the races. For if that indeed is the case, then the matter converts itself beyond the sadness which now engulfs us, and raises the question of the sanctity of the Games. If some nations or individuals seek to achieve victory by deeds such as these, then we must put ourselves on guard and expose them, so that the social acrimony against such cowardly acts serves as a lesson to people who harbour evil designs. If we allow ambition to become a slave to our baser instincts, there will be no difference between us and the Persian armies across the Hellespont who, harbouring a great desire for conquests, become tyrants to their own people and put them through much misery. We must make sure that a dark fate awaits such people in this world itself and that they are recognized for the barbarians they are. Though the occasion is solemn and we all mourn the death of Nicanor, for a brave charioteer he was and unafraid of death, we must raise our voices so that such barbarity never happens again.'

Even before Pythagoras had finished, the Macedonian delegation began making snide comments about his speech, feeling that it was directed at them, and Polemon felt the need to get up and address the gathering because tempers were rising and people were feeling that Nicanor's death had to be investigated.

So Polemon spoke, pushing Pythagoras to the side and uninvited by either my mother or my uncle Nicias, who felt great anger towards the Macedonian delegation, even though my father happened to be Macedonian himself.

'Friends,' he shouted, addressing the angry crowd, 'I will not claim that I feel Nicanor's loss more than you do, for that would be belittling your grief. Nicanor was an esteemed member of our delegation as we prepared for the Games and we greatly valued his advice. His death was an accident we all mourn, including Argus, though some of you may imagine conspiracies where none exists. Nicanor was a Macedonian and glory to him would have meant glory to all of us. For we believe in sharing our joys and our pain and, in so doing, we cultivate a spirit of well-being amongst our people, which holds us together in times of great challenges. One must remember that on occasions such as this, when grief is uppermost in our mind, we become prey to phantoms fed by ignorant people who want nothing more than to exploit an incident, perhaps for their own importance or some other gain.

'All of us pay our condolences to Nicanor's family and pray that they have the fortitude to bear this loss. And you, men and women who knew Nicanor well, let me exhort you to not believe things without evidence, for that is how rumours of the worst kind are spread, causing grievous harm to the population. For it is easy to believe evil things of people, but to exercise discretion and rationality is the need of the hour. And, in so doing, we will value the memory of Nicanor more than by believing the ranting of men who seek to sow discord in a grieving people. And who, by so doing, promote their own interests, whatever they are.'

Thus Polemon finished. Both men had talked of each other without taking names and brought the acrimony to a riot. As my father's son, I took the stand next. It wasn't my intention to speak about the grief we all felt, but to present matters in such a way that Polemon would be hard pressed to oppose them publicly. Through my friend Pindar, I had come to know that it had indeed been a conspiracy on Argus's part to weaken the axle of his chariot by hollowing it considerably from the inside. The task had fallen to Corcyra, son of Kozma, who was the chief metallurgist of the Games and had been appointed thus by the magistrate himself, as many delegates need repairing of their swords, spears and other instruments. Corcyra had detailed to Pindar the kind of work he had done. They had drilled the axle and taken out the iron from the inside to create a hollow. This, Corcyra had done, believing Argus wanted to lighten his chariot to get an advantage, though he had warned him that it would make the axle brittle and liable to break if it received a big jerk or even many small jerks.

When Pindar went again to Corcyra with my request to bring this bit of information to the notice of the magistrate and thus implicate Argus, it was a different Corcyra he encountered. He refused to acknowledge that he had confided any such thing to Pindar and violently sent Pindar away. But Corcyra's assistant, a person by the name of Hagnon, turned out to be a friend of Pindar, being a frequent visitor to the oracle. Hagnon met Pindar away from his place of work and told him that Polemon had come to meet Corcyra and, though he himself didn't know what the matter was, many threats had been issued by Polemon and Corcyra was in great fear. Later, said Hagnon, a bag arrived with three hundred drachmas and though Corcyra didn't tell him from whom it came, he recognized the bearer of the bag as Polemon's servant Zanus, who had some years before been servant to Kelos, son of Patrimus, the chief controller of the Games.

Hagnon then proceeded by flattery to induce Zanus into revealing how many drachmas there were in the bag. Zanus told him there were three hundred in number and he had counted them himself at Polemon's treasury in the nobleman Erasmus's house, where Polemon was staying. Having thus ascertained all the facts, I made Pindar make Kelos, the chief controller of the Games, aware of the circumstances surrounding my father's murder, and Kelos, after summoning his former servant Zanus secretly and ascertaining the truth of the matter from him, also spoke to Hagnon. After doubly convincing himself, he agreed to help me in the manner that I asked.

Ever desirous of showing up the Macedonians as barbarians and wanting to put them down, Kelos entered my name in the chariot race, replacing that of my father Nicanor. Though the date for entries had long since expired, the chief controller of the Games could use his special powers to grant right of participation to anyone he chose, provided the person was of Greek origin.

In a similar manner, the Spartan woman Cynisca, daughter of Archidamus, had been favoured by the controller of the Games a hundred years ago, even though the rules forbade a woman to compete in them.

But her special talent, and the fact that the controller had been enamoured of her, had led to this permission being granted. Or so it was said.

By granting permission to me to take my father's place, the Greeks would be putting the Macedonians down and making sure that Argus didn't race with my father's chariot and horses, which the Macedonian delegation had confiscated and refused to release to Pindar, who had approached them on my mother's behalf. Even the remains of Argus's smashed chariot had mysteriously disappeared from the hippodrome.

Keeping in mind all this, I spoke at my father's funeral with great control and without displaying any animosity. My words went thus: 'I value the sympathy that my family has received from all quarters. It is at moments like this that one knows one's true supporters. To my father, winning was important, but it had to be in the right way. In his memory, I would like to take his place in the four-horse chariot race in the Games. Chief controller Kelos has agreed to my request. In fact, it was his idea, as he feels that my father would have wanted nothing more than for his son to take his place. I will request respected Polemon to extend the same support to me that he extended to my father. By doing so, both of us will honour his memory more. I would like all of you to come to the grounds and bless my chariot and horses, for I feel that with your blessings I will be stronger and recover sooner from my grief. Practising for the race will be my rite of mourning, and it will give peace to the departed soul of my father.'

My friends and relatives who were present cheered me no end and soon, the atmosphere turned from funereal to festive. Everyone left in a procession towards the grounds and Polemon had no option but to follow. He was taken aback by my announcement, but now he followed to hand over the chariot and the horses. By this strategem did I get back what was my father's. If I had waited, Argus might have poisoned the horses out of spite.

In this manner my father's funeral got over. The funeral of Nicanor, to whom the oracle had said that a mighty man would lose the race even before it began.

TWO

The day of the race was one I can never forget. Though I had practised a great deal with my father, I had never actually raced except against him, in a two-horse race.

The hippodrome of the Games was full with twenty thousand people and even though I was of a Macedonian father, the Greeks cheered for me. The story of my father's death had spread and people were calling the Macedonians murderers. When Alexander reached the venue with his delegation to sit in the special area with his bodyguards, the spectators did not cheer him.

To make a show of neutrality, Kelos invited Alexander to pull the draw for the chariot positions. But Alexander sent Polemon to stand in for him. There were twelve chariots, and my place was in the middle lane. The chariot near the barrier started two hundred paces ahead of the chariot in the innermost lane to make sure everybody had the same distance to travel.

The lane nearest the post was the most coveted, as one was protected on one's left. In the middle, you had to worry about the chariots on both sides.

The hippodrome was in the shape of an egg, and in the middle were rocks. The spectators sat above the barriers on the outer side, encouraging the participants from their cities. It was only when you turned the posts that the other side came to know what was happening because the rocks were in the middle, obstructing sight. Some people made a business of gambling on who would turn the post first on their side and who would crash and who would win. They placed bets with each other, the chief organizer of these bets being Zeferino, son of Admes from Olympia. Though the magistrates had banned betting in the hippodrome, they could not enforce the closure of such activities because they were very widespread and Zeferino was a powerful noble, who had won the hand of his wife Fedora, daughter of Lamachus, in a chariot race ten years ago.

He had since used his popularity to begin his own betting business and had prospered manyfold.

This Zeferino had come to my house the day before the races with a proposal. He had come to know that Pindar was my friend and had brought him along. Even though I was meeting him for the first time, he behaved like he was an old friend and kept saying that he knew my father very well, though he had not come to the funeral.

Zeferino started thus: 'There is a lot of sympathy for you amongst the public and they would like to see you win. But I will give you two talents if you do exactly as I say. All you have to do is crash your chariot against Pythagoras's chariot by the fourth round, and so make sure he doesn't win.'

'And how will anybody gain from that?' I asked, listening quietly and not giving my mind away.

'Polemon has bet on Argus winning and I am supporting him. Argus wants to marry Drucilla, daughter of Antos from Hella, who has made it a condition that Argus must win this chariot race. Argus is the son of Damaris, the chief maid of Olympias, who is the queen of Macedonia and Alexander's mother, and it is at Olympias's request that Polemon is promoting Argus. And since Pythagoras is the main contender to win, it is desirable that somebody who has no chance of winning should crash into him. And Argus seems confident of winning against the rest. Polemon has paid me four talents to make sure Pythagoras crashes. And of this I am offering you two,' explained Zeferino.

Zeferino further elaborated that he had thought it wise not to approach Samthos, Clonus or Samocles with the same proposal, as they might reveal the plan to Kelos, who might order an arbitrary disbarment. Besides, Samthos, Clonus and Samocles fancied their own chances this year because Pythagoras's chariot was without his lead horse and they would want to aim for victory instead of a profitable loss. It was not possible for Zeferino to approach the other charioteers because the owners of the chariots were different from the drivers and the owners had the drivers under strict watch.

'But you will make much more through the betting as people will lose to you,' I protested to Zeferino.

'All right, I can pay you three talents but not more, as I have to take care of my establishment,' Zeferino said with great reluctance.

'... and ten amphorae of olive oil,' I added. I needed the oil for a feast that my mother planned to give in memory of my father. 'And I will only do what you ask if I get the talents in advance of the race, and the oil too.

For it could be that I die in the crash and then you will gain everything at my cost.'

After much haggling, Zeferino agreed to deliver three talents that night through Pindar. But the olive oil, he said, would be difficult to arrange before the race as it was a large quantity. He threatened me with dire consequences if, after taking the talents, I did not deliver on my promise. I told him that, as a Macedonian, it would be a pleasure to crash an Athenian, specially one who had been the main rival to my father. Hearing this, Zeferino left, pleased.

Even though I had agreed to Zeferino's proposal, I had no intention of implementing it in a manner that would bring gain to Argus. In fact, I had sworn to kill Argus to avenge the murder of my father. In the night, I sent my mother Stella, daughter of Artemis, to her brother Nicias's house. He was a timber merchant and had his yard outside Olympia. Before she left, I told her about Zeferino's offer and she listened quietly.

'Whatever you do, don't bring disgrace to the name of your father,' she told me.

Once she saw that I would not be dissuaded from my enterprise, she hugged me like a mother might hug a son she was seeing for the last time. The period of defilement was over by now. In Olympia, a decree exists that lays down the proper code of behaviour of friends and family after a death. The mother, wife, sisters and daughters of the dead man and seven other women can be in mourning by tearing their clothes, rubbing sacrificial ash on their bodies, cutting their hair, sleeping on the mud floor and not washing for seven days. No fire can burn in the house for cooking during this time.

After the period of ruination ended, my mother had washed our whole house with sea water and brought new fire from the altar of Zeus. The floor of the house was plastered with fresh mud.

Then she took me to her room and told me something which I shall reveal at a suitable time, but suffice it to say that it had such power of revelation that it was like taking a kick from a horse. For a while, I was in rage with my mother for not having made a disclosure of the matter when my father was still alive. It was my contention that it would have given me an opportunity to tell him that the revelation didn't matter and that I still had the same affection for him.

To console me, my mother took me to the altar of Zeus in our house and both of us knelt down to pray. After we sang the hymn of strength together, which is the prelude to invoking him, she went into a deep trance like she does at festivals and it took her one hour to come out of it. She then began singing in a voice not her own and placed her hands on my face, as if she were blessing me. Then she became normal again.

From the pit where my father himself sacrificed rams at home on festival days, she took some dust, wrapped it in linen and tied it to a leather strap, which she then hung around my neck, saying: 'Let this never leave your neck in love or battle. As long as this is around your neck, Zeus will protect you and I shall never be far away.'

Ever since, I have had the charm around my neck. It has been with me through all the battles that have been my fate to endure, and even while I satisfied my desires with women.

The necklace made me feel invincible at the chariot race and, with no fear left in me, I followed my father's tactic of tying the reins around my waist, of which he had given me sufficient practice. Late in the night, after my mother had left, Pindar and I went to visit the charioteers Samthos, Clonus and Samocles. Each one of them I asked for good wishes to perform well in the race the next day and, moved by my humility, they said that, as Nicanor's son, I had nothing to fear from them.

They kept their promise the next day. As the champion of the previous race, Pythagoras had the privilege of starting in the innermost lane, while the others got their positions from the lots drawn by Polemon from the pitcher. Argus got lucky, for he started second on the innermost side, next only to Pythagoras.

After the chariots turned the first corner, it was no longer necessary to maintain the individual lanes the drivers had started in, so I started manoeuvring to be next to Argus. With Samocles and Clonus to my left, and in between Argus and me, it was taking me time to guide Sarissa in towards Argus's chariot.

I had a plan to push Argus to the post on the turn after Samocles and Clonus had raced ahead of him. I assumed that, by then, Pythagoras would have fallen behind because he was not as fast as when he had Amon.

On the morning of the race, I had gone to the oracle at the Zeus temple to know the best way in which I could win the race. Pindar had arranged for the seer to meet me at the precincts of Pelops, where the Eleans had gathered since early morning. The entrance to the precincts was from the west, and after sacrificing at Pelops, one could go and sacrifice at the altar of Zeus. For the Eleans, Pelops was the foremost amongst all heroes and Zeus was the God they loved more than the others. Since the Games had begun, the Eleans were sacrificing every day, and only after they finished could the Greek envoys begin their rituals. The man who supplied poplar wood for all sacrifices at Pelops knew Pindar and took him straight to the seer, who had sacrificed a black ram and was overseeing the boiling of it in a tripod kettle, which was the proper procedure.

According to Pindar, the seer was more accurate than the one who had spoken to my father at the altar of Zeus. Also, he had agreed to give me some time alone in the inner sanctorum, separate from even the interpreters, because I feared that the interpreters might leak whatever the seer said to me. Pindar had come to know that the Thessalian Spitos, son of Andromenes, who was racing for the first time, was coming to the temple a little while later to sacrifice for success.

The seer knew my father, but he spoke in a strange tongue which neither Pindar nor I could understand. So he wrote down what he had to say after I asked him my question. My question was simple: 'What do I do to win the race, please ask Pelops, the hero of all heroes.'

The seer wrote with ash from the sacrificial pit, on a piece of linen. The words were: 'Save yourself for the last, for as the race progresses, an opportunity will come, which you will have to recognize and make use of. There will also be something which you think is an opportunity but will be a trap. You have to overcome your temptation or it will be your death. And victory will come in great pain.'

Now, as I jostled for space, Spitos the Thessalian, whom nobody knew anything about, started pushing me to the left, before Clonus had moved out of my way. He wanted to get ahead of me from the right. There were changes in the rules from this year at the Games. There would be no stoppage of the race in case of a crash and the tracks would be cleared of obstacles while the chariots were on the other side of the rocks. Kelos, the controller of the Games, had even designated a group of twenty-four boys, twelve on each side of the track, who would water the tracks when the chariots had crossed to keep the dust down so the spectators could see better.

When we turned the post after the first round, one of these water boys was caught in the middle of the tracks, unable to get back to safety. He escaped Pythagoras's chariot as, being the first one, he had the option of going to the left or the right of the boy. He chose the left and, in so doing, gave him no opportunity to run to safety in the middle, where they had cut the rocks to give the boys space to store their sheepskins. Argus, who was next, could not avoid him and hit him with the back of his chariot. The boy stumbled and Argus deliberately whipped him as he went by, to great shouts of anger from the stands.

Since Clonus and I were abreast and proceeding together, there was nothing the boy could do except stand in the middle, but then Spitos the Thessalian started squeezing me from the right, trying to get ahead of me, heedless of the perilous circumstances the boy was in.

Spitos's chariot was heavier than mine and the wheels sharper and bigger. If they collided with my chariot, I would crash against Clonus. But Clonus saw what was happening and he scooped up the boy with his right hand, from the middle of the track, for he had that kind of strength, and this gave me the space to move further to the left. Clonus had more weight on his chariot now, but he got lots of cheers from the crowd. The weight made him drop back, so I was directly behind Argus now and Spitos was next to me. That was when Spitos pulled out a slinger with a lead weight attached at the end, and threw it over my reins, meaning to detach them from my waist and leaving me with no way to control my horses. But I swerved to the left in time and the weight fell in my chariot.

By this time, Samocles had moved to Spitos's right and his attention was diverted from me. Spitos, thinking that he could try the same trick on Samocles, took out another slinger and threw it at Samocles's reins. But Samocles had quick reflexes and he caught the weight in the air and pulled the string from Spitos's hands, nearly plucking Spitos out of his chariot, so that he had no option but to let go. Spitos had picked the wrong person to engage with in this manner, for now Samocles's mettle was up and, before Spitos knew what was happening, Samocles had thrown his grapple hook on his reins and pulled them from his hands. The local crowd and the Thebans, having judged Spitos to be the first aggressor, condemned him loudly for his behaviour. They had earlier shouted insults at him when he squeezed my chariot even though the boy stood transfixed on the track. They called him an impostor, and a fight began in the stands between the Spartans and the Thebans because Samocles was from Thebes.

The charioteers could make out a fight was taking place because most of the stones thrown at Spitos by the Thebans fell on the tracks, posing a danger for all the chariots. Soon Spitos lost control of his chariot, for the reins had slipped out of his hands. And though he tried to use his slinger to recover them, they fell away from him and got entangled in the legs of his horses. Samocles then caused further problems for Spitos by whipping the two horses that were nearest to him – that increased their speed, but being without direction, they ran towards Argus's chariot. When Argus saw them coming his way, he panicked and made to the right, thinking that they would crash on the rocks and he could escape them.

In the meantime, Pythagoras had slowed considerably and Spitos, now hanging desperately to his chariot and not knowing what to do, watched helplessly as his horses cut across in front of my chariot to reach the rocks and then straightened to get behind Pythagoras. Argus was now to the right of Spitos and he couldn't drop back because Samocles was behind him and he was afraid to get ahead of Spitos.

This was the situation just after the bend in the third lap. Pythagoras, who was in front, had no knowledge of what had happened to Spitos. So he didn't increase his speed or get out of the way of Spitos's chariot. Argus, weak in strategy, became possessed by fear and started whipping Spitos's horses, hoping that, by doing so, they would stay away from his chariot.

At this point, Argus, fearing that Spitos's chariot would collide with his, decided to slow down considerably. As Samocles was behind him, he had to slow down as well. This provided me with an opening to overtake Spitos from the right and I nearly acted on my instinct, except I remembered the words of the seer. He had told me to beware of an opportunity that would tempt me but would turn out to be a trap. So, curbing my natural instincts, I, too, slowed and went behind Samocles to the right, emptying the space behind Spitos.

By now, all of us were nearing the post. For some reason, Pythagoras was having problems with his lead horse and he slowed down even further at the post. Spitos's horses then went straight on and collided with Pythagoras's chariot. Fortunately for Pythagoras, he went straight up in the air and landed on the rocks, not in front of Argus's chariot, which overtook the collision from the left, as did Samocles and I.

But Spitos's legs got caught in the wheels of Samocles's chariot and he was dragged around the post, his head hitting the ground as Samocles tried to kick him away. Even from that position, he battled Samocles and used his whip to haul himself into Samocles's chariot and to safety. The Spartans cheered, and while Samocles was thus occupied, I raced past him, finding myself behind Argus.

The situation had changed a great deal since the race began. Zeferino had wanted me to crash into Pythagoras, but Spitos had done the job for me. Clonus had been forced to slow down because of the boy he had saved and Samocles had become entangled with Spitos. Anyhow, Zeferino had never said anything about not racing Argus to the finish.

I was after Argus now and, by the tenth round, I was just a few paces off him and the Eleans were roaring for me. The Spartans and the Thebans were quiet but they had nothing against me. And though Samocles had stopped and let off Spitos and joined the race again, he was far behind and so was Clonus, who had slowed because of the boy but hadn't stopped to let him down. Thus, by a combination of circumstances, Argus ended up taking the lead in the race.

Argus kept looking back to see what I was doing. He was looking more at me than ahead. On the bend where the crash had occurred, we had to go slow, as there were too many things to avoid. The boys had not been able to clear the hippodrome of all the remains of Spitos's chariot. On these bends, I made good advantage over Argus. I had also half-blinded my horses with eye covers, so they could look only straight ahead. This made them less nervous, as they did not get excited by what was happening on either side. The horses harnessed on the right side of a chariot are always more susceptible: sometimes the roaring of the crowds in particular sections makes them run to the left. My father's horses were used to the shouting, as they had run many times in the hippodrome, but Argus's horses were new and they moved three cubits to the left every time they crossed the Elean, Athenian and Spartan sections, where there was much condemnation of the Macedonians – horses can sense hostility. Only in front of the Macedonian section did they move in one line. It could also be that the crowds were affecting Argus and he was communicating his fear through his reins each time he crossed those hostile sections.

The Eleans, the most numerous in the hippodrome, cheered for me, even though I was the son of a Macedonian father. They took to me as they considered me a local child, born and brought up in Olympia, whose father the Macedonians had harmed. So they were eager to adopt me as their own, specially since there were no Eleans in the race. The Macedonians themselves were in doubt about me, though why that was the case I never really examined in detail. Perhaps the friendly attitude of the Elean crowd towards me sowed suspicion among the Macedonians regarding my father and me.

By now I was just a chariot length behind Argus, with only one circle of the hippodrome left. Both Argus and I were so far ahead of the rest of the chariots that we started coming up against them. In this manner, we crossed Hippos, son of Melachos from Corinth, Ajax, son of Pausinias from Athens, and some others whose names I don't remember now. They let us cross without difficulty from the right, as they were in battle with each other and not with us.

But Samocles was different. He blocked Argus. When Argus tried to cross him on his left, he went to the left, and when he tried to go to the right, Samocles moved to the right. He was not violating any rules by behaving in this manner, though the judges could confiscate his chariot if it was proved that he had used a grapple hook while racing. But it always happened that when the drivers were checked after the race, the hook would have mysteriously disappeared. Pindar used to say that Samocles would throw it into the crowds in the last circle of the hippodrome, but I never saw him do it. It was a mystery.

I took the decision that when Argus moved to the left the next time and Samocles moved to close the gap, I would whip my horses and cross both of them from the right. The timing of my acceleration would have to be perfect. Otherwise, when Argus moved to the right again, he would crash into me. If, however, Samocles moved to the right and closed the gap with me, it would leave a gap to his left for Argus to exploit. Argus could take to Samocles's left and beat me on the straight line.

Samocles, however, did not close the gap. I think he did not want Argus to win and did not particularly care if I did. Between Argus and me, it was a battle of wills. He was surprised when I made my move, believing that I would be content with being second. Maybe Zeferino had told him that I would crash Pythagoras and he had assumed I would work towards his victory. By the time he realized I was passing him, my horses were ahead of his, though my chariot hadn't crossed his. He was boxed. If he moved to the right now, he would crash into me and both of us would be out of the race.

He didn't even threaten to move to his right to thwart me, though such a move would surely have dissuaded a person less determined than I was. But all I wanted was to win, even at the risk of my own life, and I grabbed the opportunity with all the skills I had developed with my father's assistance. I was not afraid of the seer's words – that victory would come in great pain. I had to avenge my father's death and, being still in mourning, I felt my victory would give him peace in his grave.

I crossed Argus and quickly came abreast of Samocles who, though he was next to me, was running one circle behind. It was then that Argus used his whip on me from behind, with such force that it wrapped around my right leg, and then he pulled it from under me. As a result, I had one leg on the chariot while my right leg dragged along the ground.

As I told you earlier, all the reins were wrapped around my waist and though I had my dagger at the waist to cut them off if there was a crash, the rules would disqualify me if I wasn't connected to the chariot in some way, even if my chariot crossed the line before the others.

In the Pythian games, a situation had arisen where Neomalus, son of Plato, claimed victory because his chariot had crossed the line before the others, even though he had fallen off it fifty cubits before the finishing line. Since the rules only mentioned chariots and not whether they were empty or with the driver, Neomalus claimed before the judges that victory should be announced in his favour. But the judges ruled otherwise and said, rightly so, that there should be some connection between the chariot and the driver or it could very well be called a race of horses with carts and not of humans.

By the time I had crossed Samocles in this manner, with my right leg dragging on the ground, there was a big force being exerted on my waist from the reins. So I had to cut off the reins of the two horses on the right with my dagger to relieve the pressure and control the chariot with only the horses on the left. Though Argus's whip had fallen away from my right leg by this time, I had lost my balance because of the speed of the chariot and both my legs were dragging along the hippodrome. But I had managed to hold on to the reins of the two horses on the left, and Sarissa was guiding the other horses without losing speed.

In this manner did I cross the line ahead of Argus, my chest ripped open by the many stones on the ground, but my hands still holding the reins.

And thus was the seer's prophecy fulfilled. His name I came to know later. He was Mestacles, son of Agis, and he died of plague within a year of the race. His prophecy concerning me had been: 'Save yourself for the last, for as the race progresses, an opportunity will come, which you will have to recognize and make use of. There will also be something which you think is an opportunity but will be a trap. You have to overcome your temptation or it will be your death. And victory will come in great pain.'

THREE

Argus's chariot was confiscated because the judges saw him use his whip on me. The Macedonians argued that I could not be considered the victor because I was not on the chariot, but the Eleans and even the Athenians, who also supported me, insisted that I had the reins in my hand when the chariot crossed the line, and since the reason for my predicament was the illegal intervention of Argus, it could not be held against me.

While the doctors stitched my chest and the cuts on my face, Zeferino came to meet me. My legs were severely bruised and all the charioteers had come to congratulate me, except Argus and Spitos, who had many injuries too.

Zeferino was very angry and he had his bodyguards around him. He came close to me and, bending, spoke in an angry whisper. He wanted his talents back.

I rose up weakly, in spite of my pain, and addressed my fellow racers, judges and Kelos thus: 'My friends, I speak to you as Nicanor's son. I am still in mourning for him, as you all know. Most of you have raced with him and know that he raced fairly and never violated the rules. It was his burning desire to win the quadregi in these Olympic Games and I will forever mourn the fact that he could not do it while he was alive. But as his son, I felt that it would bring peace to him in his grave if I won the race for him. You, the honourable judges of these Games, have announced me as victor and even if my injuries are untreatable, I shall die peacefully. But I wish to make an announcement regarding a matter between Zeferino and me, even at the risk that you might take my victory away from me or that it might cause a big scandal.

'Zeferino approached me with a proposal to crash into Pythagoras's chariot, for which he offered me three talents and ten amphorae of olive oil. He said that Polemon had instructed him to find a way in which the race could be won for Argus and they thought that the only threat to Argus was Pythagoras. They thought that since I had no chance, being just a boy, I would do their bidding and crash into Pythagoras and thus help Argus win.

'Even though I took the three talents, which I shall now return to him in the presence of everybody here, I had no intention of keeping my promise. I intended to win the race and defeat Argus; crashing into Pythagoras, who spoke so well at my father's funeral, was never a consideration. Some of you might think that if I did not entertain the proposition of crashing into Pythagoras, why did I take the talents at all? The truth is, I was tempted like many men would have been, and I intended to run away with the silver after the race. But you all know what happened during the race. The spirit of my father protected me and even though I lie wounded in front of you all, my chariot did cross the line first. I had no hand in the crashing of Pythagoras's chariot as it was Spitos's horses, unaided by Spitos, who caused the crash.'

To Pythagoras's credit, he didn't take offence at my disclosure. Instead, he said: 'It took great courage on your part to make this confession. I accept your word that you had no intention to harm me. As for Argus and Polemon, may Apollo cause their brains to be eaten by maggots. And as for you, Zeferino, who doesn't think twice before hurting somebody who hasn't harmed you, may disease strike you and waste you.'

I collapsed after hearing these words from Pythagoras and my senses left me. Zeferino was taken into custody by Kelos and the Elean magistrates confiscated the talents. There was a debate among the judges again about whether the victory should stand with me or, in the light of what I had said, it should go to Clonus, who had come in after Argus. And they all went to Mestacles, son of Agis, the seer at Pelops, to know what the Gods desired. Mestacles told them that he had seen a vision that if the victory was snatched from Nicanor's son, great harm would come to the Eleans in the form of an earthquake. The Eleans didn't need much convincing after that and they unanimously let my victory stand. Kelos went so far as to say that, but for my revelations, the Macedonian conspiracy would have remained unexposed and that I deserved an award for exposing the villainy of Polemon. He stopped short of taking Alexander's name, for everyone was afraid of his father Philip, the ruler of Macedonia.

But my words created a big scandal and the Macedonians were ejected from the Games in disgrace. Argus, son of Pathos from Pella, left Olympia with insults in his ears, his dreams of winning Drucilla, daughter of Antos from Hella, of no consequence any more.

Pindar was told by Kelos that when news of their expulsion was communicated to the Macedonian delegation, Alexander flew into a rage and said that he would enslave the Athenians and their allies for this mortification. His rage at the Athenians, in fact, led to his sending a message to his father, King Philip, in advance of his return to Pella, about the misconduct of the Eleans and the Athenians in particular. It angered Philip so much that he vowed to rout Athens and moved against them in battle the next year, at Chaeronea in Boeotia, the year that Gylippus, son of Menecea, was the archon of Athens.

Meanwhile, word spread that Polemon had gambled away on the race some of the talents that Alexander had entrusted him with for other tasks, the principal one being to bribe the orators of Athens, who had been making speeches condemning the rule of Philip and were trying to revive the Delian league which was headed by Athens. Many orators such as Demosthenes, Aeschylus and Timos were in attendance at the Games as part of the Athenian envoy's delegation, and Philip had given Alexander the task of trying to win over Timos in particular. This was because Timos seemed to be the most amenable to being bought, given that Demosthenes had already aligned himself with the Athenian general Chares and, in so doing, had identified himself as being in the camp against the Macedonians.

Since I have no intention of hiding things from which detrimental conclusions about me may be made, I have a confession to make here. When I won the race, I won a sum of six talents by making a fool of Zeferino, even though I returned his three talents. This is how I did it. Having come to know of the manner in which Zeferino made his money by gambling at the race and how he stood to gain by managing a result unknown to all but him and, in this case, me, I arranged for Pindar to place eight hundred drachmas through his friends, who were corn merchants, on Seleucus, son of Nicanor, emerging the victor in the race. Zeferino was offering forty-two times the money if I won the race. When I won instead of Argus, he had to pay six talents to the merchants, who kept two hundred drachmas each for themselves and passed on the rest of the money to Pindar, not knowing who had placed the gamble and who had won.

So, after I won, I was doubly pleased when Pindar told me that the merchants had collected the talents from Zeferino, as the rules were for the bet to be settled within one hour of the race finishing. The Macedonians, specially Polemon, had lost twenty talents because they had all gambled on Argus winning the race, having been assured by Zeferino that Nicanor's son had agreed to crash Pythagoras out of the race.

On my part, though I didn't feel that I had avenged my father Nicanor's death in full, I had made a start. By not keeping the three talents that Zeferino had originally offered me and announcing the illegal transaction, I had exacted a bigger price from the Macedonians in terms of their humiliation and banishment from the Games – far more than anything those three talents could have achieved.

Now, after Pindar brought me home, the doctor, Telos, son of Xenocrates from Olympia, came to enquire about my health. Telos was the foremost physician of our time. Because the cut on my chest was big and wide, he advised that I have it sewn together with hair from a horse's tail. Since I was in great pain, I agreed, and so they made me drink honey with opium to lessen my pain, while Pindar went and cut many strands of hair from Sarissa's tail.

Before sewing my chest up with horse's hair, Telos washed my wounds with warm water and applied some herbs. By the next morning, a fever had come upon me. Pindar brought news at this time that Zeferino had been released and had been instructed by Polemon to teach me a lesson. He had even provided some Macedonian guards to Zeferino, who were strong and not known in Olympia. They spoke the Elean tongue and so were not easily recognizable as outsiders. This information Pindar had got from Kelos, who got it from his old servant Zanus. Zanus was serving as Polemon's servant for the time he was in Elean territory and he now informed Kelos that the men intended to locate me and torture me for the talents that they believed I had made from the betting.

Once the merchants told the Macedonians that it was Pindar who had instructed them to bet in that manner and with a sum that was not their own, their suspicions had been confirmed that I was the party to whom the winnings had returned. They had vowed to hunt me down and had sent their guards everywhere to seek me out. Furious at having been duped, they had decided amongst themselves that after they repossessed the six talents, they would put me to the sword. All this Zanus revealed to Kelos, and he in turn told all to Pindar.

Kelos had also discovered that Alexander was very angry with Polemon for having used up the talents in betting without his authorization and at such great loss. Since the talents had been given by Philip for the specific purpose of managing the orators, that job remained unfinished. In fact, the orator Timos, having secretly been promised a sum of two talents per year by Polemon to speak in laudatory terms about King Philip and his ambition to teach Persia a lesson for all her cruelties against the Greeks, was much in anger because Polemon had no talents to give him.

Telos told me while washing my wounds that Polemon had been summoned by Alexander and told to make good the loss in one month or face the consequences of the matter being reported to Philip. The Macedonian king was known to have little tolerance for such frivolities on the part of his men. Telos had all this information from a personal friend of Alexander, whom he was treating at his place of residence.

A nobleman by the name of Carinus, son of Orinth, this friend of Alexander had a boil on his back and was seeking a surgical procedure. Polemon had urged Carinus to put onc talent on Argus winning and thus make three talents, and he was upset that, instead of the gain promised, he had lost what was his. At Carinus's urging, Alexander had asked Polemon to submit all accounts. Polemon had then claimed that Timos had been paid the talents he had asked for in advance, but Alexander knew this was a lie because he had received a report that Timos had given a long speech against him after the expulsion of Macedonia from the Games. Timos had called Philip a tyrant and Prince Alexander a tyrant in the making and had told the Greeks to beware of the Macedonians because they were more dangerous than the barbarians. He said that while the demos were aware who the barbarians were, as they didn't speak Greek, with the Macedonians because they spoke a corrupt form of Greek, people were fooled into confidence.

Alexander recognized that Timos wouldn't have spoken thus if he had been in possession of a bribe. In the face of this evidence, Polemon admitted to his folly, which was when Alexander gave him thirty days to make good the loss or face Philip. He could have ordered Polemon's execution but he did not want to create another incident in Elean territory.

In the light of my injuries and the fact that Polemon and Zeferino were hunting for me with their guards, Kelos advised me through Pindar to leave for an asclepeion he knew near the ocean, where his nephew Ganymede cured many patients by drawing blood and balancing the humours of blood, yellow bile, black bile and phlegm. He urged me to leave quickly and provided Pindar with a sealed letter of introduction to be given to Ganymede so that he might take better care of us. Ganymede, he said, had learned his craft from Aspasia herself, the famous surgeon from Athens. Kelos said the altar of Asclepios and those of his daughters

Panacea and Hygeia at Ganymede's place had special powers. Once, he had had a growth on his leg which turned into a big tumour, and in his sleep he had had visions of Panacea and Hygeia and he had been cured in one month. Ganymede also made special offerings on behalf of his patients to Artemis and Apollo and thus, by pleasing all the Gods and applying the right herbs and balancing the humours, he cured his patients.

Ganymede's asclepeion was in Pylos in Messenia, by the sea. In Pindar's wagon, it took us fourteen days to journey there. Messenia was adjacent to Sparta and ruled by King Fagus, who had taken as wife an Egyptian Helot and created much scandal amongst his people. Messenia was in alliance with Sparta, but its people had none of the military prowess which Sparta was known for.

Before leaving Olympia, I sent two talents to my mother through my uncle Nicias, the timber merchant outside Olympia, so her needs could be taken care of. And one talent I gave to Pindar for being the friend that he was. He was pleased at this and vowed to do my bidding for as long as I wanted. Two talents I hid in the well in my house for use after my return and with one talent I journeyed to Pylos with Pindar.

By the time we reached Pylos, I was in great torment and swollen from the humours, besides being in delirium. Ganymede took us in with great affection but expressed agitation over the fact that the physician Telos had used horse's hair instead of linen thread to tie up my wounds. He said the hair was unbalancing the humours, and the first thing he did was pull it out which, though very painful, was not dangerous as the wound had closed.

Since my body was in high fever, he gave me opium three times a day, saying the process of healing would start when Asclepios came to me in a dream. For the dream to come soon, he made me perform a ceremony each morning. I had to bathe despite the fever and, after thus purifying myself, I had to pray at the altars of Asclepios and his daughters Panacea and Hygeia after lighting incense. Every second day, I made a sacrifice of a goat and everybody in the asclepeion ate different portions of it. The beggars got the lower part of the legs, the priest took the portion from the chest and Ganymede himself took the upper portion of the legs. A feast for five healthy men took place on alternate days, and this cost twenty drachmas. Ganymede said the healthy men were so chosen that they could absorb some of my bad humours and make my healing faster. He said their bodies would start succumbing to illness, which would make my fever go away.

A week after being on this schedule with Ganymede, I went to visit the oracle at Pylos, at the temple of Apollo. Since Asclepios is the son of Apollo, I felt that propitiating him directly might hasten my healing. This particular temple dedicated to Apollo had been built by a priest called Pythadorus, following a plague in Pylos a hundred years ago, which killed half its inhabitants. So the inscription said in the temple. The current priest was also called Pythadorus: he was the grandson of the original Pythadorus. Besides being the priest and performing the rituals, he was also a seer, though one who gave his words not on demand or after a sacrifice but only if he felt impelled by Apollo to do so. This, Ganymede told me. I was curious about Pythadorus and went to the precincts of the temple for four days consecutively, hoping that he would make some prophecy to aid me. For I was in a dilemma over how to proceed in my revenge against Polemon and Argus and where to go after my healing. If I went back to Olympia, it would be easy for the Macedonians to take their revenge.

So, every day I made my prayers and twice, I made the sacrifice of a goat. Pythadorus distributed portions of it according to the prescribed rituals, but never did he speak to me nor look at me with any interest. Since Ganymede had expressly forbidden me to talk to him – he said that in his knowledge Pythadorus had never made a prophecy about anybody who had talked to him first – I kept my silence.

But seeing how worried I was about Polemon and the lack of news from home, Pindar devised a plan to send one of Ganymede's servants to Olympia on horseback. His name was Zanylos and he was a Helot who had gained freedom from his Spartan master after taking good care of him at Ganymede's asclepeion. Pindar sent Zanylos to Olympia to meet Kelos, the physician Telos and my uncle Nicias. He was to reach Olympia and not reveal the purpose of his journey to anybody. If asked, he was to say that he was a carpenter and had come to buy timber from Olympia, of the kind not found in Messenia.

Pindar gave him twenty drachmas, one drachma for each day of travel to Olympia and back, and five drachmas for expenses. He also provided him with a letter from Ganymede to Kelos to serve as an introduction, so that Kelos would not think Zanylos to be a spy of Polemon.

After Zanylos left, I kept waiting for Asclepios and his daughters Panacea and Hygeia to come to me in my dreams. I gave up expecting Pythadorus to give any revelation but visited the temple every evening, as it was a good walk and Ganymede said that, in his opinion, the yellow bile stopped causing problems once the body made good exercise.

Then, on the full moon day, while the festival of Goddess Athena was being celebrated in Pylos, Pythadorus spoke to me.

It happened in the evening. In the morning, a procession had started from the city gates of Pylos and travelled two parasangs into the countryside. In front was a chariot carrying the image of the Goddess in marble, and following it were the basket carrier, the bread carrier, the carrier of the sacred fire and the water carrier. At the back of the chariot was the wicker basket with its secret contents, which only the designated priestess knew about. There were rumours, however, that the basket contained the skin of a goat which had two heads and six legs and whoever saw it even by accident would have to bear the wrath of the Goddess. It was only the consecrated virgins who could not only look at the skin but wrap it around themselves like a linen cloth, for on them the Goddess pronounced no anger, and it was these virgins who could be seen by mortal men and so be blessed by Athena herself.

After the image of the Goddess had been washed with sea water, the people in the procession made their offerings. And in each village they passed through, the headman made an offering on behalf of the whole village. In such a roundabout way the procession returned to the city gates of Pylos in the evening.

Then it was that the ephor came to the gates and admonished the Helots for not having informed the local Spartan garrison of their intention to make a procession of Goddess Athena. These Helots, who inhabited much of Messenia, were in fact Greeks but had been made slaves by the Spartans – to till their land and provide them with barley, wine, olive oil and swine. They had lost their independence about a hundred years ago to the Spartans and longed to become free. Though they, too, worshipped Apollo, who was the favourite God of the Spartans and who had a festival dedicated to him in the winter called the Carneian Festival, their hearts were with Goddess Athena. But the Spartans didn't like the Helots to worship Athena, as they felt it gave an opportunity to the Athenians to influence the Helots.

The Helots listened to the ephor with their heads bowed but said nothing and he soon left, after being provided with half the offerings collected by the procession. For the Spartans lived in military communes and the Helots had the task of providing them with supplies.

Ganymede, though neither Helot nor Spartan but an Elean, had been granted special dispensation by the ephor of Pylos to run his asclepeion for fifteen years, as there were many Spartans desirous of his way of treatment. The city of Pylos itself had been taken over by the Athenians for a short time in the Peloponnesian war, after some disgruntled Helots had allied with them, and so the Spartans were always watchful of them, specially since they were less in number to the people they had enslaved.

Being with the procession the whole day had tired me, so I went down to the Apollo temple, which was on the way to the asclepeion, and sat down on the parapet to gaze at the sea. It was then that Pythadorus came up to me and, without any preliminary greetings, said: 'There will soon come a sorrow which will make you seek revenge, but this is not the time to fight your enemies. I see you travelling east, and there you will gain strength.'

Saying this, he patted me on the back and went away, never to speak to me again. Even though he had talked about a sorrow and made me apprehensive, I was in great relief that he had spoken at last. I saw this as a good omen because I had started to imagine that he wasn't speaking to me only because he could see my death. I racked my brain for any sorrow that could come to me and decided it would be the defilement of my father Nicanor's grave, as that would give me even more cause for retaliation than I had now.

In the night of the evening that Pythadorus spoke to me, two girls came to me in a dream. They were simple pastoral girls with crowns on their heads and they were helping two old men, who were very sick, to walk to the temple of Apollo. I spoke of this dream to Pindar and he mentioned it to Ganymede, who came to me immediately, saying that I had seen Panacea and Hygeia and now my healing would be much faster. I was greatly pleased with this elucidation but was disappointed that Asclepios hadn't come in my dreams as Ganymede had originally said he would. Ganymede then said that it was only in the dreams and visions of men older than I was that Asclepios came himself. With younger people, it was usually his daughters. Thus soothing me, he prepared a big feast that day for five healthy men, which cost thirty drachmas instead of twenty. Wine was passed around and many beggars had the feast of their life. Late in the night, when all the healthy men were drunk and going home, two of them fell into a ditch and came back to Ganymede with a broken leg each.

I had gone to sleep by then, so it was in the morning that I got the news from Ganymede, who addressed me in this fashion: 'Though I do not rejoice at the misfortune of others, the breaking of the legs of two healthy men signals that your humours are getting balanced and shortly you can proceed to wherever you wish to go, fully cured.'

After hearing this, I felt much better in the body and gave thirty drachmas each to Brasidas and Connidas, the two men who had broken their legs. They were delighted at my generosity and wished me well for the future. Through Ganymede, I even contributed one hundred drachmas for the upkeep of the temple of Apollo at Pylos; I was impressed with Pythadorus, who appeared to be a seer without greed for the things that humans covet. I also conveyed through Ganymede my desire to be initiated into the worship of Apollo by Pythadorus himself, but he came back with a message from the seer that now was not the time to be initiated as much accomplishment lay ahead of me. When the time was right, he said, I would be initiated into the occult by someone much more powerful than himself. Being both disappointed and pleased with this answer, I didn't press the matter further and now waited only for Zanylos to come back with news from Olympia before deciding on the future.

From the next day, things moved speedily. Ganymede came with the news that four men had come into the town of Lepreum, which was between Olympia and Pylos, and made inquiries at a famous asclepeion there, run by a friend of his called Kronos, who was adept at blood-letting and the curing of his patients through anaemas. After staying for one day, they had revealed the real purpose of their visit. They said they were searching for the son of the charioteer Nicanor, who had fraudulently won the four-horse chariot race at the Games and who had stolen property that belonged to some others. They were willing to pay a sum of one hundred drachmas to anybody who came forward with information about him. After assuring themselves that the said person had not come for treatment to the asclepeion in Lepreum, they had left to search for him in other towns, armed with details about other famous physicians in the region, and even a list of asclepia. Kronos had warned Ganymede to be vigilant in case this son of Nicanor came to Pylos, for the men who were looking for him were dangerous and there was no need for him to get involved. It was his assessment that these men were soldiers, though not Spartans. Kronos, of course, had no knowledge that I was already with Ganymede.

There was regular business between Kronos and Ganymede. Patients whom Ganymede couldn't cure he sent to Kronos, and Kronos did likewise. Ganymede also sold some salts to Kronos, which had curative powers and were used in bathing. These salts Ganymede bought from a merchant sailor from Lesbos. This sailor, by the name of Phormio, sailed both the Ionian and Aegean seas, trading goods with a Phoenician crew. Phormio was due in the Pylos harbour with a consignment of salts for Ganymede within the next few days, and Ganymede suggested that I set sail with him to Lesbos or some other place to escape the Macedonians.

Finding the plan practicable, I decided to embark on the journey and return to Olympia once things had quietened down there. I told Ganymede to persuade Phormio to take me on as a sailor with pay, as it would not be wise to disclose my real identity to him in case he had dealings with the Macedonians. Since Pindar was unwilling to make the journey with me to Lesbos, being afraid of water, I decided to send him back to Olympia. I was worried that the Macedonians would defile my father's grave and I wanted him to organize a guard for three months to prevent such an occurrence.

So, after a tearful farewell, Pindar left with his wagon, promising to take care of my house and give all the news to my mother about my recovering health and my plans to sail to Lesbos. He was to mention to her the name of Pythadorus as the seer who had advised me on this course of action and tell her of the great respect that people of this region had for him because of his prophecies in the past. I thought she would rest easier if she knew this.

The next day, a series of incidents took place. It started with a basket arriving early in the morning for Ganymede. The basket had markings indicating that it came from Phormio. Ganymede opened it with great expectations as he had run out of salts, but when he opened it, he got a shock, for inside was Pindar's head, his eyes still open. It so frightened Ganymede that he passed water in his robe and started lamenting in fright and all the people in the asclepeion came to know of the matter. Even Brasidas and Connidas, with their broken legs, hobbled over to have a look at the basket.

Brasidas was the first to break the sorrowful news to me. Everybody started speculating that it was some secret cult of Demeter that indulged in human sacrifice which had caught hold of Pindar when he was on the road to Olympia. Coincidentally, the ephor himself was in the asclepeion when the pandemonium broke out, as he was seeking treatment for his wife, who was with child. He rushed to Ganymede and started making enquiries about the background of Pindar and about any enemies he might have made in Pylos. While they were still together, a letter arrived for Ganymede, asking him to bring Seleucus, son of Nicanor, in custody to the harbour and hand him over to a person called Polydamidas who, the letter claimed, was a magistrate from Olympia and was seeking the detention of Nicanor's son upon the authority of Themistocles, king of the Eleans.

Since the letter was sealed and had been delivered by a person on horseback to Ganymede's guards at the entrance of the asclepeion, it was presumed by the ephor that the delivery of Pindar's head in a basket and the coming of the letter were not events associated with each other. The ephor – I cannot recollect his name – then picked up Pindar's head and examined it in great detail and with no revulsion at all, as if he were used to such examinations. He said: 'It is not a Helot's blade that has made this head roll, for the edges are even in the cutting and it has taken only one blow. The eyes cannot be closed and the blood has gone cold.'

The ephor turned to me and started asking me questions, and since Ganymede hadn't tutored me with regard to interaction with an ephor or familiarized me with the fact that, being a foreigner, I had to report to the Pylos garrison upon arrival and give the reason as well as duration of my stay, I gave him the true story of how the Macedonians were following me to exact revenge.

To tell you the truth, I was in shock after seeing Pindar's head. Though I made a pretence of calm, it was more for the consumption of the ephor, for one thing I knew about the Spartans: they despised any form of weakness. So, even though Pindar's frightful murder had shaken me, my mourning was bereft of any tears, nor akin to the fearful lamentations of Ganymede. The ephor summoned troops from the garrison after hearing my account and took me in custody as well, even though Ganymede asserted that I was still with injury and had done nothing wrong.

The ephor brushed aside his protestations and said: 'Nicanor's son will be safer in custody with us than with you, Ganymede. We have no quarrel with the Macedonians at the moment, but if they commit murder in our territory, even though of people who are not Spartan, we shall deal with it appropriately.'

The ephor then took me to the Spartan garrison and sent some guards to the harbour to summon Phormio, for it was a mystery how Pindar's head had appeared in his basket of salts. Though Phormio was from

Lesbos and ran a ship with a Phoenician crew, he was welcome in Sparta because he brought supplies of Egyptian corn for the Spartans and traded it for olive oil. The guards were also to look for a person by the name of Polydamidas, who was a magistrate from Olympia.

Phormio was soon brought to the garrison and claimed to be clueless about how the head of a person he had never known could have appeared in his salt basket to Ganymede. He said that he had given the basket to a Helot called Arnos, son of Astyochus, who worked as a labourer in the harbour, and had told him to deliver the basket to Ganymede. It could be that the murderer opened the basket and put in Pindar's head with or without Arnos's knowledge.

The ephor then ordered for Arnos to be summoned. He was found with great difficulty, as he had gone off to sleep in a Spartan trireme anchored at the harbour. When the ephor showed him Pindar's head and asked him how it came to be in the basket that he had carried from Phormio to Ganymede, Arnos was deeply perturbed.

Arnos said: 'This same head belonged on the neck of the person who sat next to me in the wagon when I was journeying on the road to Ganymede's asclepeion. All I did was ask for a ride, as they were also going to the asclepeion.'

Arnos added that there had been four other people in the wagon and two others rode their horses alongside. Besides, he said, four horses were tied to the wagon and trotted on their own. Arnos further added that since he had two baskets with him, one to be delivered to Pythadorus, he had requested them to stop at the temple of Apollo for a few moments while he delivered the basket. When he came back, the person to whom the head belonged had disappeared.

Hearing this, the ephor surmised that the Macedonians, having recognized Pindar, had accosted him outside Pylos and thought it best to travel onwards in his wagon so they would attract less attention. When Arnos had gone to deliver the basket to Pythadorus, they had severed Pindar's head and placed it in the basket meant for Ganymede.

Thinking that half the mystery had been solved, the ephor sent a party of soldiers to look for a headless body in the vicinity of the temple of Apollo. He speculated that the assassins would not have continued on their journey with a headless body in the wagon.

By this time, the party that had remained at the harbour, looking for the magistrate Polydamidas, had also come back, saying that there was no person by that name at the harbour.

Desirous of bringing the perpetrators to account, I theorized to the ephor that the letter from Polydamidas was a trap to get Ganymede to bring me to the harbour. I suggested that Ganymede take me to the harbour in custody and a party from the Spartan garrison could be there dressed as Helots. If then this Polydamidas revealed himself, the Spartans could take him into custody and enquire further into the matter.

Thinking that the plan had some merit, the ephor agreed and summoned to the garrison Ganymede, who by now had recovered somewhat. Apprising him of what was required, he sent Ganymede and me to the harbour and forbade Phormio and Arnos to speak of the matter, even though he left them to go about their business. While waiting for Polydamidas to show up at a Helot's wine shop at the harbour, Ganymede discussed with Phormio the business of taking me on as a sailor, as I was keen to get away from the Macedonians, and now even the ephor, for the Spartans were unpredictable and could hold me guilty of drawing the attention of the Macedonians to their land when they had no quarrel with King Philip. When we had sat there for more than an hour without Polydamidas showing up and with Arnos himself taking the responsibility of twice going up and down the harbour of Pylos, looking for anybody that we could reasonably assume to be Polydamidas, we began to think we should drop the ruse for the night.

So Ganymede made over to where the Spartan soldiers were sitting, pretending to be Helots, and suggested that the exercise be repeated the next day but the soldiers, not having any orders from the ephor, refused to move from the place. The Spartans lived in fear of the ephor, for as a body they had the power to discipline even the king. An ephor was elected directly by the people for a period of one year and nobody who had been an ephor for one year could stand for election again. In this way, the Spartans avoided the danger of their rulers turning tyrants.

We sat down at the table again and had ordered another round of wine when Zanylos entered the shop and headed straight for Ganymede and me. Having been engrossed with matters relating to Pindar's murder the whole day, I had forgotten about him altogether.

'I am the Polydamidas that you are waiting here for,' Zanylos said, putting us all in great perplexity. 'But before I tell you how that happened, I have some bad news for you, Seleucus, son of Nicanor.'

He then turned to me and narrated his tale. Upon reaching Olympia, he had headed straight to Kelos and handed him Ganymede's letter. Kelos had then told him about the tragedy that had struck my mother.

He said that Polemon, having been given thirty days by Alexander to make good the loss of twenty talents, had failed to do so; Alexander had then extended the deadline by fifteen days but taken Polemon's wife Helena, daughter of Nicaretus, and their son Battus into custody, so that Polemon was not tempted to become a fugitive.

These actions of Alexander made Polemon desperate. It also made him believe that everybody was conspiring against him. As a result, Polemon became more suspicious than usual and even started keeping a watch on his servant Zanus, for he had become suspicious of the way Zanus had been listening in on his conversations.

This watch on his servant brought to his attention Zanus's frequent meetings with Kelos. Polemon then confronted Zanus with his guards and had him tortured till he confessed that he had been reporting on his affairs to Kelos. Enraged at this, he ordered his guards to take Zanus's son Zacynthus into illegal custody. He then had Zanus do his bidding, which was to get information from Kelos about my whereabouts and that of my mother. For very few people knew that she was just outside Olympia with her brother Nicias.

Kelos told Zanylos that Zanus had come to him one day and reported that Nicanor's house had been pillaged by Polemon's guards and he wanted to know where Nicanor's wife was, so he could go and tell her about it and help them post a guard at the house to prevent it from happening again. Trusting him, Kelos gave Zanus directions to reach my mother. Whereupon Polemon sent Zeferino with a few Macedonian guards to my uncle's place and they tortured my uncle in the presence of my mother and demanded to know where I was. My uncle, being a simple, God-fearing man, was unable to take the torture, and he lost consciousness, never to recover. My mother, seeking to relieve the distress of her brother, spoke the truth, but not knowing where I was, she could only tell them that I was in an asclepeion, recovering from my wounds.

They demanded to know which asclepeion I was in and, when she said she didn't know, they were left with the choice of either letting her go or torturing her for information she didn't have or putting her to the sword. They chose the last because she had been witness to the killing of her brother. When they informed her of their decision, she said that first she should be allowed to pray to her heart's content at the altar of Goddess Athena in her home. And they agreed to that and brought her to the house where I grew up and where, for many years, she had made a life with her husband Nicanor.

She locked the door behind her, after they had determined that there was no way for her to escape from the room. They waited patiently outside, having made preparations to bury her in the grounds of the house, fifty steps from the well. They heard her sing hymns to Athena and smelled the incense that she burnt. There was silence for a long time after this and, believing her to be in deep prayer, they didn't disturb her. But when the silence grew inordinately long, they discussed amongst themselves and one of the Macedonian guards opined that there might be a trapdoor that led beneath the floor which they had failed to notice. Zeferino, much agitated by this possibility, knocked violently on the door and, not getting any response, he ordered it to be broken. They found her bleeding on the floor, already dead. She had slit the veins on her wrist and not uttered a sound as the blood spread across the floor.

In this manner did my mother die, and a sorrow enveloped me for the rest of my life. As Zanylos narrated the story, I remembered Pythadorus's prophecy of a few days back that there would come a sorrow in my life which would make me seek revenge but that this was not the time to fight my enemies. He had said that he saw me travelling east, where I would gain in strength. I had imagined the coming sorrow to be the defilement of my father Nicanor's grave. The thought that it could be my mother's death and, before it, Pindar's, had never crossed my mind.

FOUR

After the death of my mother and uncle, Zanus was filled with remorse and he went and confided his perfidy to Kelos, who grasped the situation immediately and rebuked him. Kelos then reported the matter to the Elean king, Themistocles, who was enraged by the latest deeds of Polemon and Zeferino and ordered their immediate arrest. But the two had fled Olympia soon after and no one knew their current whereabouts. Some said they had gone back to Pella, and others that they had seen them at the coast, trying to escape the guards of both Alexander and Eleia.

But Kelos was not fooled. He surmised that they were searching all the asclepia that lay within twenty days of wagon travel from Olympia. He therefore told Zanylos to rush back to Pylos with as much haste as possible and warn me to leave the city. On his way back, Zanylos stopped overnight at a Helot's home in Messenia and heard from him that, a day earlier, a contingent of Macedonians had passed the same way and though they were dressed like Helots, they carried weapons hidden in their clothing. They were coming from Lepreum and were on their way to Pylos.

This particular Helot recognized the Macedonian dialect as he had recently travelled with a Spartan delegation to Athens and heard the Spartans negotiate over a few days with the Macedonians about the release of a Spartan priest who was in Macedonian custody. The priest had run into problems at the oracle of Delphi after making some disparaging remarks about King Philip, which included a prediction that he would die by a whore's dagger. Believing the priest to be in the pay of the Athenians, the Macedonians decided to teach him a lesson so that no such false statements would be made by any other religious figure at Delphi. Greeks from all over the Hellenic world arrived in Delphi to consult the oracle and King Philip was desirous of championing the cause of the Greeks.

After coming to know about the Macedonian soldiers, Zanylos increased his speed and travelled through the night, resting just enough to ensure that his horse did not turn lame or die of exhaustion. Two days before reaching Pylos, he learned that the Macedonians had crossed the place earlier in the day. Being just half a day behind them, he increased his pace even more and by the evening he came upon them at a small village called Asantes. From then on, he followed them at a distance, never letting them know that he was watching and never being so far behind that he could not observe their activities.

It was while following them in this manner, just half a day from Pylos, that he saw them come upon a wagon. He drew a little closer to see why they had stopped to chat with the wagon driver and realized that it was Pindar's wagon. Recognizing then the danger Pindar was in from the bloodthirsty Macedonians dressed as Helots, he ventured closer to them, looking for an opportunity to rescue Pindar from their grasp. He presumed rightly that Pindar had become their prisoner and was most likely being forced to turn around and lead the way to Ganymede's asclepeion so that they could take me into custody and exact their revenge.

Soon, they entered Pylos and it became easier for Zanylos to follow them. He observed that through their clothes the Macedonians pointed a sword at Pindar at all times. They had surrounded him so that Pindar could not attempt to run away. There were six of them and though Zanylos didn't recognize any of them, he assumed that the two men whom the others consulted frequently and who talked to Pindar the most were Polemon and Zeferino.

At Pylos, the Macedonians took refuge at the harbour in an Egyptian corn trireme, leaving their horses tied to a pole on the dock. Seeing that they would be resting for a while, Zanylos quickly made across to Ganymede's asclepeion, but he did not enter as he saw the bodyguards of the ephor standing outside. Zanylos, being a Helot, had been punished with flogging by the ephor two months ago for stealing a sword from a Spartan's house, a charge he had vehemently denied. But since the sword had been found in a ditch outside Zanylos's house, he had received the flogging along with a warning that he would be put to death in case of any future transgression.

Now, afraid of encountering the ephor and wanting to discuss matters unobtrusively with Ganymede and me, he returned to the harbour and searched for his Helot friend Zymindas, son of Ascopos, who knew how to write. Kelos had given Zanylos a papyrus with his seal so that

Ganymede could safely send a message back if required. But Zanylos used it to send a message to Ganymede instead, thinking that the impressive paper and seal would persuade Ganymede to immediately do its bidding. In such a manner was the letter devised: from a certain Polydamidas, who was a magistrate from Olympia and who was in Pylos at the directions of King Themistocles himself.

But after Zymindas wrote the letter and Zanylos had it dispatched by a boy, he noticed the Macedonian party emerge from the harbour and proceed by Pindar's wagon and on their horses towards Ganymede's asclepeion. He even saw Arnos get onto the wagon with a basket, which perplexed him at the time. When the wagon stopped near the temple of Apollo and Arnos got out with his basket, Zanylos approached the wagon on horseback and trotted straight to Pindar, who sat in the front, planning to somehow snatch him from the clutches of the Macedonians and escape to safety.

But as Zanylos rode up to Pindar, he recognized him and shouted, 'Help me, Zanylos.' The Macedonians, thus alerted, blocked off his route to Pindar and, being trained soldiers, they managed to strike him down from his horse. Zanylos, however, escaped from their clutches by running towards Pylos.

Though, initially, two of the Macedonians gave pursuit to Zanylos on horseback, they did not persevere. And that was the last time Zanylos saw Pindar. He came to know of what had befallen him late in the afternoon when the news spread throughout Pylos. Zanylos didn't even know where the Macedonians were any more. He was regretful that his intervention had not been successful and he was not able to inform us in time because of his fear of the ephor. The Macedonians, perhaps believing that Zanylos would come back with some assistance, had killed Pindar on the spot and put his head in Arnos's basket. They may have intended to enter the asclepeion, but were possibly halted in their tracks when they noted the presence of the Spartan ephor with his guards. So, it was because of the ephor's wife being in childbirth that I was saved that day. If they had not been there, the Macedonians would have entered the asclepeion and butchered me.

Zanylos became tearful as he ended his story and Ganymede consoled him. My own grief was slowly turning into rage against the Macedonians. Meanwhile, watching us in animated discussion, the Spartan soldiers grew suspicious and a certain Spiticos came to join us and asked what the matter was.

At this, Zanylos became very nervous and Spiticos became even more suspicious. He took him into custody in spite of our protestations that Zanylos had just come from Olympia with news of my mother's murder. And once the ephor came to know of Zanylos's involvement in the matter with respect to carrying out an errand of mine in Olympia, he ordered him to be brought into the Spartan garrison for questioning. Since I was already in custody, he ordered that my belongings be seized from Ganymede's asclepeion.

Thus, I found myself a prisoner of the Spartans the day I came to know of my mother being no more and on the day that my dear friend Pindar lost his life at the hands of the Macedonians. In such circumstances, and with my wound not yet healed, I took stock of the future. As the Spartans were taking me to the garrison, I took Ganymede aside and made him swear a blood oath with me that he would do certain things at my behest. Ganymede borrowed a dagger from a Helot and made a cut on his palm and I did the same; after the ritual of blood-letting and the mixing of our blood, I told him where I had hidden the one talent that I had with me in the asclepeion. I told him to hand over a thousand drachmas from that sum to the Spartans to keep them in a good frame of mind. I thought that if they didn't find anything in my belongings, they might get more suspicious and cause more problems. Then I instructed him to use another thousand drachmas to try and bribe the ephor into releasing me: to start with five hundred drachmas first and go up gradually, saying that it was *his* money he was spending and not mine. I also told him to give five hundred drachmas to Phormio and ask him if he would give me passage till Pireus. Pythadorus's words were fresh in my mind and I wanted to get to Attica first and thence to the east. I also asked Ganymede to ask Phormio whether he could set sail in the night itself, for I intended to escape from the custody of the Spartans that very night.

Of the remaining money, I told him to have two thousand drachmas sent to Pindar's father, the interpreter at the oracle of Zeus in Olympia, for the Macedonians would have robbed Pindar of the two thousand drachmas he carried in his wagon. I also told Ganymede to keep five hundred drachmas for himself. With the remaining sum, he was to meet me at the harbour when I sent word. I told him that whoever I sent with the message would tell him that Sarissa was the greatest horse. In this manner would Ganymede know that I had sent the messenger. I also told him to organize a search party to see if he could locate the Macedonians in the area and, if he did so, to inform me at the earliest.

In the night, Ganymede sent me a supply of powdered herbs to apply on my chest and also word that Phormio had accepted my request to take me as a passenger on his ship. Though he was ready to leave, he would wait for me to come, provided I pay his crew for the days of waiting at half their salary.

The ephor had detained both Zanylos and me in the barracks of the Spartan garrison. Zanylos told me that the barracks had been taken over by the Helots after the Theban general Epamonidas had defeated the Spartans in the battle at Mantinea. But twenty years ago, led by their ephors, the Spartans had regained many of their lost garrisons, the one at Pylos being the most important, as it gave them access to the harbour. They had done so by striking an alliance with the Perioikoi, who dwelled on the coast and along their borders with Argos and Arcadia. The Perioikoi and the Helots did not get on together, as both sought favours from the Spartans. But the Spartans feared the Helots more than the Perioikoi, as the latter spoke their dialect and had customs similar to their own.

I got no chance to escape the first night, as Spiticos lay next to me and he spent more time staring at me than sleeping. In the morning, the ephor sent a search party north of the temple of Apollo, with Spiticos leading the search for the Macedonians. Since that was where Zanylos had last seen them, the Spartans suspected that the Macedonians were receiving help from the Helots and had some other sinister design that was as yet unrevealed.

They were right in their suspicion as news came that a Spartan trireme at the harbour had been forcefully taken by the Macedonians at dawn; it had an all-Helot crew which was from near Argos and the Helots were more than willing to assist the Macedonians. Also, they had been promised a bonus over and above their salary, plus their freedom at the port of Nisea, from where they could proceed by land to Corinth and from there to Argos. All this the ephor learned from the captain of the trireme, who had been kept hostage at the harbour in his own ship by the Macedonians. They had also taken a Spartan by the name of Cannus as a hostage, as he knew best how to navigate the seas and also knew of places along the coastline where the ship could be harboured and where the Spartans kept provisions for their crews to replenish stocks while on the seas.

On hearing this, the ephor immediately readied another trireme and loaded it with provisions. Being apprehensive that he would be admonished by the Gerousia and the Spartan king, specially since he knew that the Macedonians were up to some mischief, he became even more harsh in his treatment of me. He shouted at me and said: 'Board our trireme as a slave rower on the lowest deck. It is because of you that our commune has lost a trireme. It is the first time that anybody has stolen a boat from our own harbour.'

The ephor then put Spiticos in charge of the trireme. We were to sail south from the Pylos harbour towards Methone, which was the direction the Macedonians had taken.

Even though Ganymede tried to intercede on my behalf with the ephor and offered him the bribe, the ephor was unmoved. He told Spiticos to pay me like any other rower and to make me a free man once the Macedonians were caught. Since I was the only one who could identify the perpetrators, there was no way he could let me go. For a bribe of one thousand drachmas, however, he granted me the right to carry my belongings and five hundred drachmas of my own, and the right to rest for seven days from the date of departure for my chest to heal fully. I told Ganymede to give the rest of the money to Phormio with instructions that he was to meet me at the port of Nisea four months from the date. I knew that Phormio had to go to Lesbos first, and could only come to Attica after that. If he didn't find me in Nisea, he was to seek out Pythagoras in Athens and give him the money for safekeeping till I managed to reach him. He was to deduct whatever this errand cost him from the sum of money entrusted to him.

With such plans for the future and with Spiticos's baleful glare upon me, I embarked onto the Spartan trireme. Spiticos was anxious to give chase to the Macedonians, as the Spartan Cannus, whom they had taken hostage, was his own brother, and he kept asking me the whole story of my dispute with the Macedonians and what had brought me to Pylos.

Spiticos divided the rowers in half after judging the strength of each one of us, so that the strokes fell on the water with equal force on both sides. Besides the rowers, the Spartan trireme carried sixteen soldiers on the deck – four archers, eight hoplites and four javelin throwers.

As a thalamite, I rowed at the bottom of the hold. Above me were the zygites, who sat on the hull's crossbeams, and right on top were the thranites, who guided the timing of the thalamites and the zygites, as they were the only people who could see the oars going into the water. Though the trireme could hold a hundred and seventy rowers, it carried only a hundred at the time that the ephor commissioned it, the rest having gone home on leave for five days. But since Spiticos had received information that the trireme captured by the Macedonians carried only eighty-five Helots as rowers, he was confident of catching up with them quickly if his crew started early and rowed hard.

Spiticos tolerated my presence on the deck, for the ephor had said that I could rest for seven days to get back my strength. During this time, I got friendly with a Helot by the name of Harmodius. He was a thranite and I spent a lot of time with him on the deck. Since Zanylos had also been ordered by the ephor to join the crew, he narrated to Harmodius my whole story and Harmodius, being a forty-year-old from Mount Ithome, the Helot stronghold, showed much sympathy. I also came to know from the other rowers Harmodius's own tale and the strange powers of prophecy he possessed, which made the captain of trireme he was on anuydeal with him with great care.

Lasimodus, who rowed sitting next to Harmodius, had been his companion for two years and he told us – for Harmodius rarely spoke, and when he did, it was in an accent difficult to understand – that during the battle at Mantinea, which the Spartans lost, Harmodius was ten years old. It was Harmodius's father Thasidomus who helped Epamonidas's army beat the Spartans by creating a desertion in the ranks of the Perioikoi. For his efforts, the Thebans made him their commander at Pylos. But five years later, the Spartans took back Pylos from the Periokoi and put to the sword the Periokoi officers who had been installed by Epamonidas. They hunted out the families of these officers and slaughtered them too. Harmodius, then fifteen years old, had watched in hiding from a tree as the Spartan Asidamus murdered his mother after violating her, and his two brothers and sister. They made his father watch as his family was butchered and, in the end, they put him to death as well.

Harmodius had at this point lost his mental capacities and, with no one to take care of him, had wandered around the Hellenes. Later, a Cretan took him on as a rower on his transport, and since then he had been a rower, for the sea calmed him, and his exertions as a rower for two decades had helped him forget the sorrow in his mind. It was while rowing that Harmodius began having visions. When the crew rested in the night, nobody slept close to Harmodius, for he spoke a strange tongue in his sleep. While some felt that the tongue had been in vogue during the time of Achilles, others felt that it was corrupted with Persian, as they recognized many Persian words and inferred that it was the court language used during the time of Cyrus the Great, who had invaded the Greek lands with his armies.

Lasimodus, however, persevered in sleeping next to Harmodius and had pieced his story together by listening to him talk in his sleep, and also from what Harmodius said to him whenever he did feel like talking. Lasimodus said that the blood had drained from Harmodius's face when Spiticos was appointed captain of the ship by the ephor and he had avoided looking at Spiticos's face. When Spiticos had desired to speak to Harmodius, having learned of his powers of prophecy, Harmodius behaved as if he were deaf and in this manner avoided engaging with Spiticos without giving offence. Lasimodus came to Harmodius's rescue by telling Spiticos that, after being bitten by a crab on the ear, Harmodius had developed faulty hearing, but when his ears were working, he would ask him for a prophecy on their hunt for the Macedonians.

On the morning of the second day, our vessel chanced upon a Spartan transport that was returning from Crete. It had gone there with a herald conveying a missive from the king of Sparta to the Cretan king, forbidding him to aid King Philip in his campaign against the Persians. The Spartans feared a Macedonian alliance with the Cretans, who had a good navy, as it could lessen their sphere of influence. The herald, Dominos, announced to Spiticos that he had been successful in his mission and the Cretan king had agreed that he would not befriend the Macedonians. The Cretans had more to fear from the Spartans than the Macedonians, as the latter were far away and without a navy, while the Cretans were dependent on the Spartans for olive oil and even had a colony of Spartans in their midst whom they didn't want to annoy by siding with the Macedonians.

The herald mentioned to Spiticos that he had seen a Spartan trireme at dawn and, though he had signalled to them, they hadn't responded. He had assumed that they were a coastal patrol from Pylos. But being made aware of the truth, he expressed his inability to help Spiticos in any manner, as he had to convey the tidings of Crete to Sparta. Besides, he said, there was soon to be war between the Greeks and the Macedonians. He had learned this from some Athenians in Crete, who were on a mission there to ask the Cretan people to join battle with them against King Philip. Dominos felt that he might be required by the Spartan king to travel to Athens and elsewhere with missives, and in expectation of this errand, he was hurrying to Pylos and couldn't help Spiticos in any way. However, he offered some provisions of corn and wine, which Spiticos didn't accept as he felt it would make his trireme heavier. He said he would rather replenish the ship with provisions at a depot along the coast.

Dominos then, in parting with Spiticos, addressed him formally thus: 'Farewell, Spiticos, son of Asidamus. May you catch up with the Macedonians and give them Spartan justice.' And as Dominos's voice rang on the deck, the mystery behind Harmodius's behaviour towards Spiticos became clear to Lasimodus and me. Fate had thus brought Spiticos, son of Asidamus, the butcher of Harmodius's family, to the ship where Harmodius was a rower!

By dusk that day, Spiticos was still to find the beachfront where provisions could be taken on board. Besides, his hoplites and archers were aggrieved with him, as he had turned them into rowers to increase the speed of the trireme. When night fell, Spiticos was forced to seek anchor and the men slept on the beach and had to eat into their emergency provisions. Outside of his hearing, they all cursed him for having refused Dominos's offer of wine and corn.

But Harmodius was silent. The next day, though my seven days of rest were not over, I rowed next to him and he looked at me a few times but didn't say anything. By afternoon, the hijacked trireme was sighted on the horizon and Spiticos had the rowers increase the speed of their rowing for one hour, hoping to gain on the Macedonians by dusk. But after an hour of fast rowing, they became slower than they had been earlier and the gains were nullified. As dusk was nearing, Spiticos pressed his archers and hoplites into work once again for one final burst, but being without experience, they spoiled the timing of the rowers around them and mixed up their oars, delaying things even further.

By nightfall, Spiticos had found a stocked Spartan beachhead and the men had a good feast. There was salted fish and ten legs of lamb that were portioned out amongst the men. Later, Spiticos made his way to where Harmodius was and asked him: 'Old man, I am worried for my brother Cannus, who has been taken hostage by the Macedonians. How many days more will it be before we catch them? The sailors on this boat are inexperienced and I don't know the position of any other depots, so we could also have problems with supplies.'

Though Harmodius was just forty years old, he already looked like an old man. This time, though, he didn't pretend to be deaf.

'Better for you to turn back, Spiticos,' he said, looking Spiticos straight in the eye. 'The third full moon from now, you will find them, but I see a lot of blood, and it's not Macedonian.'

Spiticos tried to ask him more questions, but this was all Harmodius would say, and as the men were getting curious, he had to go away to his tent. The men asked me what Harmodius had said and I lied to them, saying that Harmodius felt if we rowed fast over the next week, we would catch them.

The next week, the men rowed as hard as they could, but apart from the one sighting, there was no sign of the hijacked ship. The few experienced sailors could not locate the stocked beaches, so when, after hugging the coastline during the day, we came upon a small port, Spiticos decided to stock provisions for a whole week, even if it made the ship slower. If it had not been for Cannus, I felt he would have stopped chasing the Macedonians a long time back, specially after Harmodius's prophecy.

The port we stopped at was a fishing village by the name of Dramos, with a harbour big enough to accommodate just one trireme. Strangely, no one from the village came out to greet the trireme. It was only when a zygite by the name of Trachimedus, who had been to the village a year ago and knew some of its inhabitants, called out the name of the chief, Carmus, that some people emerged from their houses. It turned out that the Macedonians had been here two days ago and had stocked up their ship with provisions for many days. Upon being asked to pay for these, they had refused and Carmus had then blocked the way of their ship into the sea with a beam. This infuriated the Macedonians, who put Carmus and two others to the sword, and the rest of the villagers fled the harbour. This was why they had been reluctant to come out to greet our ship – they didn't know if we were friend or foe.

From their descriptions of the people on that trireme, I could identify Polemon and Zeferino. They also told us that the new chief of Dramos was the brother of the dead Carmus. His name was Harmos and he said that some of the Helots on the trireme were rebelling against the Macedonians. They had expected to be free men after helping the Macedonians escape from the Spartans but now it seemed to them that they had substituted one form of slavery for another. Harmos said that two of the Helots had tried to kill Polemon but had been intercepted by the guards, and now Polemon had the sailors locked below deck during the day. When they beached at night, he brought the rebellious men out in chains. The Helots were deeply aggrieved by this behaviour and were fearful that if the trireme was rammed by an opponent, they wouldn't have a chance of escape since the door of the deck was always kept locked.

Despite all this, the Macedonians were still ahead of us, and Harmos said that many Helots had whip marks on their hands and back from lashings given to them by the Macedonians. Spiticos was cheered to know about the trouble the Macedonians were having and he had the villagers load up the trireme with provisions and made a point of paying them what they asked for before loading.

But Harmos put a doubt in Spiticos's mind just as he was giving orders to cast anchor. He asked Spiticos how he was so sure that the Macedonians were ahead of him. Maybe they had taken shelter on the coastline. There were many places one could hide a ship – in fact, he said, he wouldn't be surprised if they were behind us!

Harmos then provided him with five sailors, who were relatives of the two whom the Macedonians had killed and who were willing to row for one whole month without pay as they were eager to avenge the death of their brothers. Spiticos was glad to have them, for, being fishermen, they had much knowledge of the coast and knew of places where the trireme could take shelter for the night.

From then on, Spiticos kept a watch on both sides of the deck and took Harmodius's prophecy to turn back to mean that the Macedonians were behind him. The third day after leaving the fishing village of Dramos, the lookout at the back spotted a trireme approaching. Spiticos had the bow turned around to meet the ship, but it turned out to be an Athenian trireme returning from Syracuse. It carried only a hundred rowers and, after exchanging pleasantries, the Athenians were soon on their way, without disclosing the nature of the business that had taken them all the way to Syracuse.

Soon, it was a fortnight since Dramos had been crossed and the volunteers had taken the boat to two fishing villages for more provisions. Spiticos was now getting despondent and the Helots were openly talking about the need to head back to Pylos, as the Macedonians were nowhere to be found. They reasoned that, with the Helots being rebellious, perhaps the Macedonians had discarded their ship and were proceeding over land. The Helots, having helped the Macedonians to get their freedom, would hardly return to Pylos; they would possibly have taken the ship to some island and sought refuge.

Soon afterwards, events took a turn for the worse. Two sailors started having visitations of the Gods. They started convulsing on the deck and saliva oozed from their mouths. They lost consciousness for close to a hundred breaths. This put all the rowers in great fear. Everybody started fearing the worst and Spiticos gave orders for the trireme to move even closer to the coast, so that in case of any trouble at sea, they could swim safely to land.

After we had crossed the harbour of Las, we came across a fast moving transport going to Pylos from the port of Argos. They were carrying foals from Thessaly and Egyptian linen that a trireme from Argos had seized in the open seas from an Egyptian transport. The captain of the Argos ship had not come across any Spartan trireme while sailing towards Pylos, and this put Spiticos in two minds about the location of the Macedonians.

Besides, Lasimodus had also overheard a conversation among the Spartans about how Spiticos had confessed that he had only two talents left, with which he would have to cater for the journey back to Pylos. It was not surprising then that Spiticos lost the motivation to continue. After being six weeks at sea, including one week at Las for some hull repairs, he made a speech and announced that the trireme would be turning back to Pylos. Every sailor who was on deck clapped.

We made it back to the fishing village of Dramos in twelve days, as the five volunteers had to be dropped off. There, more tragedy awaited us. As we approached the berth, everybody on deck saw a head fixed on top of a staff in the harbour and, as on our first visit, no one emerged to greet us. We saw that a few houses had been burnt down, and it was only when the volunteers got off the boat and started calling out to people that some emerged, amongst them Harmos.

This time, he had an even more tragic tale to tell. Two days after our trireme had left the village, the Macedonians had come back. Since Harmos thought that it was our ship returning, everybody had gathered on the harbour, only to be greeted by arrows and javelins from the trireme. The Macedonians killed five people in the harbour and took Harmos captive for two days, asking about our whereabouts. They had somehow come to know that Cannus, the Spartan they had taken captive at Pylos, was the brother of Spiticos, the captain of the trireme chasing them. After accusing him of deliberately sabotaging their ship, as the hull was taking water, they cut off Cannus's head and impaled it on a staff, so that when Spiticos came back, he would have a sight that would discourage him from pursuing them.

Spiticos calmly walked up to the head and took the staff down with his own hands. He then proceeded to bury the head of his brother at the top of the cliff overlooking the harbour. He dug a hole in the earth with his sword and bare hands. The Spartan guards followed him, but he didn't allow them to dig on his behalf. When the head had been buried, he turned to Hormos and asked: 'Will you help in the hull repairs to the trireme since the repair work at Las has not proved satisfactory?'

Harmos said he would.

Harmodius watched Spiticos intently, but displayed no emotion. Lasimodus watched Harmodius as if Cannus's death was his doing. And then a Spartan hoplite by the name of Zandimus accused me of bringing ill luck to many people, Spiticos included. Said Zandimus: 'Since you came to Pylos, you have caused the death of your own friend Pindar and also of many others unrelated to you. It is better you leave this boat and save us more ill fortune.'

Strangely, after hearing Zandimus speak thus, Harmodius spoke on my behalf. He said: 'He's a slave to the Spartans like the rest of us. He didn't ask you to chase the Macedonians. It's on the orders of the ephor that we have all spent time on the sea. He has rowed as hard as any of us and eaten the same food that all of us have eaten. So, Zandimus, your words are ill chosen.'

After hearing Harmodius rebuke Zandimus thus, everybody fell silent. The rowers had no quarrel with me and did not think like the Spartans. Spiticos did not give away his mind, but from his questioning of Harmos, it became clear that he thought the Macedonians were in hiding somewhere between Dramos and Pylos, as they had not been found on the way to Las. According to Harmos, the hull of the Macedonian trireme was leaking and was in need of repairs.

At this juncture, something regrettable happened, which put Harmodius in harm's way. Lasimodus told Zanylos, Ganymede's servant who was with the thalamites, about how Harmodius's mother and brothers had been put to death by Asidamus, father of Spiticos and the dead Cannus. And how the wheel had turned and Harmodius, though a rower, had seen Cannus's head on a stake. He also told Zanylos that he thought that Harmodius had arranged Cannus's death by pleading to Apollo in his prayers and that he had special powers bestowed on him by the Gods, who wanted to compensate for the ill luck he had suffered as a boy.

Zanylos, though warned by Lasimodus to keep the matter to himself, took another thalamite into confidence, and soon the tale spread and reached the ears of Zandimus, the Spartan hoplite who had earlier spoken against me. Zandimus conveyed the tale to Spiticos, and he summoned Harmodius to the deck and asked him whether he was the son of

Thasidomus, who had been a traitor to his homeland. Harmodius jutted his chin out and said: 'Yes, I am Thasidomus's son and proud of it. My father, far from being a traitor, liberated the Helots from the Spartans. Sparta is as much of the Perioikoi and the Helots as of the Spartans.'

Hearing him speak thus, a hush fell over the rowers. If such words had been spoken in Pylos by a Helot, the ephor would have ordered his death. But here they were at sea and Spiticos needed the rowers, and he knew that Harmodius was held in high regard by them. Any drastic action on his part against Harmodius would result in a rebellion and hinder him in his task.

Spiticos then asked Harmodius in front of everybody: 'Is it true, Harmodius, that you brought harm on my brother Cannus because he was the son of my father Asidamus, whom you accuse of killing your family in Pylos after the battle at Mantinea?'

Harmodius replied: 'Harm was done to your brother Cannus by the Macedonians and not by me, Spiticos, son of Asidamus. I did not pray for any harm to befall him, as I did not know of his existence and, even if I had known, he had caused me no harm. Your father Asidamus was a reptile in human form and I would have been happy to put him to the sword the way he did to my entire family. But he is dead now and I don't wish any harm on his sons because of the deeds of their father. But I don't grieve for your brother's death, nor will I grieve for yours.'

Having spoken thus, Harmodius went to his place amongst the rowers and Spiticos went into heated consultation with Zandimus, who seemed to be urging him to put Harmodius to the sword. Then Spiticos turned around and addressed Harmodius thus: 'The matter is not over, Harmodius. After we have sorted out the Macedonians, we shall deal with you.'

At this, Harmodius got up from his place and said: 'Better to deal with it now rather than later. If the Macedonians find you, you might go to your grave with unfinished business.'

Whereupon Zandimus leapt to where Harmodius was and hit him a blow on the head with the butt of his sword. Though it made Harmodius bleed, he did not lose his balance; he continued standing. 'You insolent son of a whore,' shouted Zandimus. 'Remember who you are speaking to if you want to live long.'

'I haven't wanted to live for twenty-five years. Do you think your sword scares me, Zandimus? I live in the world of Apollo and I see your death and I see Spiticos's, and they come before mine,' said Harmodius.

Spiticos turned red at these words. But his strength of character made him say: 'Whether it comes before or after your own, Harmodius, let it be known that it shall not meet a coward.'

There was a silence after these words of Spiticos, which was suddenly filled by Lasimodus beating the drums signalling the beats for the rowers. The trireme pulled away slowly. Harmodius rowed, and I rowed, and we all rowed like the matter was closed. Zandimus walked away and Spiticos avoided the eyes of the rowers. Lasimodus, by beating the drums at that moment, eased a situation that he had created in the first place.

Before our trireme left, Harmos volunteered to come on board and help in the search for the trireme bearing the Macedonians, for he was seeking vengeance. Spiticos gladly accepted his offer. All of the next week, with the help of Harmos, Spiticos sailed back towards Pylos, looking closely at every place where the Macedonians could hide a trireme on the coast.

The Helots rowed as best as they could. They were much concerned now about the welfare of Harmodius, specially after coming to know that he was the son of the famous Thasidomus. They let it be known to the Spartan guards that if Zandimus or Spiticos as much as moved towards Harmodius, there would be a rebellion, and since the Spartans didn't have the numbers to control the Helots, they let Harmodius be in peace.

On the third full moon, Spiticos met with his death as Harmodius had predicted. And so did Zandimus and the rest of the guards. It happened this way.

After crossing the town of Asine, we met with a group of fisherfolk who had lost their boat because of bad weather and were stranded on an island. They lacked the courage to swim to the main coast. Actually, Harmos spotted the fishermen when they waved and shouted for help. Once they were on board, they told Spiticos that a Spartan trireme had gone by two days earlier, but it had refused to help them. The description of the boat fitted the description of the ship the Macedonians had taken.

Greatly energized by this information, Spiticos had the sails spread and increased the speed of the rowers. He asked Harmos to take them to every inlet on the coast nearby, in case there was a hidden spot or a small island where the Macedonians could be hiding. By dusk, Harmos had led us to a Spartan beachhead and we all saw the silhouette of a trireme beached on it. Much excited, Spiticos crossed the beachhead and anchored just off the coast and out of sight. He then prepared his soldiers to land on the coast with the help of the inflated sheepskins that every trireme carried. He wanted volunteers from the Helots to increase his force to twenty, not knowing how many men he would have to face, but no Helot volunteered, even after Spiticos offered a sheepskin to each of them at the cost of his soldiers. Though I wanted to go and fight, Harmodius caught my ankles and forbade me, and so I kept quiet.

Spiticos and Zandimus entered into a long discussion then. They feared that the Helots would make off with the trireme once they had departed and they would be stranded. So they left four soldiers to keep watch on the ship and started swimming to the coast on sheepskins, with just ten men and a Helot by the name of Samcottus, whom they forced to go with them, for they needed somebody to swim across with the shields; the soldiers carried only their swords and spears. So this Samcottus swam back and forth to the shore three times, carrying shields; he was a strong swimmer who didn't fear the waters. Harmos, too, went with them. The Spartans, delighted by his decision, equipped him with arms, and Zandimus spoke under his breath about how fishermen were more trustworthy than Helots and possessed more masculinity.

Though I waited in the trireme and was in two minds, for I wanted my revenge, there was something about the manner in which Harmodius had urged me not to go that made me very nervous, specially when combined with his earlier statement that there would be blood and it wouldn't be Macedonian. I did not want to defy the Helots, as they were strongly behind Harmodius. If he had told them to fight, they would all have fought. Their refusal was motivated by their hatred of the Spartans rather than any fear of the Macedonians. Neither did they have any intention of escaping with the trireme as many Helots had families back in Pylos and the Spartans would do them great harm if they adopted such a strategy.

So all of us waited for Spiticos to sneak up on the Macedonians on the beach. The four Spartans who remained on the ship reasoned that once the Helots on the Macedonian ship came to know that the Spartans were attacking them, they would rebel against the Macedonians who had been treating them so badly. In this manner they discussed the operation quietly amongst themselves and waited for their companions to strike.

Since Harmos had guided our trireme to a point behind an outcrop, the scene of engagement could not be directly observed unless one swam to the mainland. Many of the Helots asked Harmodius whether they could do so, and though Harmodius was agreeable, the four Spartan guards were not in favour, as they felt it might alert the Macedonians.

But soon, a terrible ruckus started. War cries rose as well as a huge fire. We could hear the beating of drums and the clashing of shields and once, over the din, a war cry from Spiticos that everybody on board heard and was rattled by.

Then there was silence. The four Spartan guards were unnerved more by the silence than the noise before it and they stood at the edge of the trireme, waiting for news of their companions and the result of the battle. When the silence persisted, they gave permission to twenty Helots from our vessel to swim to the coast. Everybody desired to know the fate of Spiticos and his men and, finally, the Spartan guards also joined the Helots in swimming to the coast, each one gathering courage from the other.

After a while, those of us who remained on the vessel could see the Helot Samcottus join them on the beach in great agitation and everybody gathering around him, listening to what he had to say. After listening to him in full, some Helots swam back to tell the tale to those on the ship. From them we learned of the treachery of Harmos. It was an unbelievable tale. Harmos had led the Spartans into a trap!

After the Macedonians had visited their village Dramos the second time, they had, after killing some people, taken Harmos's young wife and son hostage along with five others, and they had instructed Harmos to lead Spiticos to this spot if he wanted to see them released. The Macedonians had learned from the transport from Argos that they had met with a Spartan trireme near Las and it had a captain called Spiticos, who had made the decision to turn back to Pylos, as they had been unable to locate the ship of the Macedonians. The Argos transport hadn't known of the matter between the Macedonians and the Spartans.

After knowing of this, the Macedonians had hatched their plan to lead the Spartan trireme to a particular spot and they had used Hormos for that purpose, as the Spartans would not suspect him. They had instructed the villagers to act in a particular way when the Spartans returned and Harmos had even planted the fishermen on the island who had claimed that a trireme had gone by two days earlier.

With these acts, Harmos had managed to lure Spiticos to the spot, and his joining of battle with them was because he thought he had nothing to fear from the Macedonians. The Macedonians had been very concerned about the strength of the force which Spiticos would be able to muster, not knowing whether the Helots on the ship would join him in battle against them. They had instructed Harmos, therefore, to approach their trireme in a certain manner if the Helots were with the Spartans in battle, and another way if they were without them.

Harmos had led the Spartans as instructed. And he had led them to their death. Samcottus, who had pieced together the story from what he saw and from what he heard from the Helots on the other ship, was distraught at the manner of the death of Spiticos.

Said he, weeping: 'The manner of his death was not worthy of a warrior like him. The Macedonians had surrounded the Spartans with the help of the Helots on their ship. They had spread stories that if they didn't help the Macedonians, and they lost, the Helots would be slaughtered by the Spartans and their families back home would also not be spared. Because of this, the Helots gave support to the Macedonians.'

According to Samcottus, the Macedonians had been particularly severe on Spiticos. After overpowering him, they had torn his limbs apart. Zandimus had been impaled upon two spears against the side of the trireme, and it took him some time to die: they smothered his cries of pain by sticking the handle of a sword into his mouth. The rest of the Spartans had met a similar fate. Even in their last living moments, they did not realize the treachery of Harmos.

The Macedonians, after securing their victory, sent Helots from their ship to negotiate with the Helots on ours. They came with a proposal to combine both triremes and sail to Pireus in Attica, and so gain their freedom and lead a new life.

The four Spartan guards who had gone to the coast to learn about their companions had sought to escape back to the trireme after hearing Samcottus's story, but they had been taken prisoners by the Helots from the other ship and taken to the Macedonians.

After hearing the story of Samcottus as told by the Helots who swam back from the coast, the Helots on our ship broke into two camps. The younger men without families in Pylos were agreeable to the Macedonian proposal to sail to Pireus but the older ones with families were opposed to it.

I was stricken with horror at this turn of events and stayed close to Harmodius, desirous of his guidance. Zanylos and Lasimodus too stayed with us and looked to Harmodius for what he had to say. If the Helots combined together, I feared they would hand me over to the Macedonians, and Zanylos feared the same. Gradually, all the older Helots, numbering forty, gathered around Harmodius and asked what they ought to do.

Before he could answer, the Helots from the other ship began swimming to ours and these was concern that they were coming to seize the ship at the behest of the Macedonians. Harmodius gave instructions – as everybody including the younger Helots now considered him to be their leader – that nobody should be allowed to board our trireme. Some oars were brought on deck and when the other Helots reached the side of the ship, they were warned and pushed back with the oars. Of the twenty Helots who had swum to the coast from our ship, only five returned with Samcottus and they were allowed on board.

The rest of the Helots stayed on the shore and shouted at the Helots on our ship to join them. Samcottus opined that it would be foolhardy to trust the Macedonians, as they had even put to the sword the four Spartans they had captured, and he feared they had plans to sell the triremes after they reached a neutral port like Pireus. They were unlikely to be concerned about what happened to the Helots. Anyhow, the Helots could go wherever they wanted to, without the aid of the Macedonians, now that they had a trireme under their command.

All the Helots approved of this idea. Lasimodus had already taken possession of the two talents left behind by Spiticos. And so it was decided by Harmodius to lift anchor immediately and set sail before the Macedonians got wind of the decision and tried to thwart us.

Harmodius then shouted to the Helots on the shore, 'Come now, all of you who are on the shore, for we intend to depart. If you don't, you will be left here on the beach at the mercy of the Macedonians.'

But none of them swam over. By now, the Macedonians had joined the group on the beach. I could even see Polemon and Zeferino. Polemon shouted across from the beach: 'Helots, we have no quarrel with you. Only against Seleucus, son of Nicanor. If you hand him over to us, all of you can depart in peace. If not, we will chase you down and slaughter all of you. We have more rowers than you.'

Listening to them, I was in a rage, but had to calm myself by touching the charm around my neck that my mother had given me at our last meeting.

Harmodius then took it upon himself to shout back to the Macedonians and Helots on the beach as the men weighed anchor, and he said: 'You killed Seleucus's father Nicanor, and his mother and his friend Pindar out of spite. Today, helped by the treachery of Harmos, you killed the Spartans. And how did you reward Harmos, who helped you in your vile victory? For they tell me that having no more use for him, you killed him too, and if you have not, it will be better to produce the face of thc villain for us to see closely, so we might all be better prepared in the future for men like him. Though we were no friends of the Spartans, Spiticos was a brave man. And defiling corpses, even of enemies, is behaviour not worthy of men. I call upon you to free all the Helots you hold by force and to give up your bloodthirsty ways, for they are against the laws of a people whose Gods are Zeus, Apollo and Athena, and even Dionysus, whom you respect so much. Would he be pleased at the manner of your victory or at the defilement you have caused to people already dead?'

Harmodius spoke a great deal more, but the above is what I remember.

Then Harmodius ordered Lasimodus to start the beating of the drums and the trireme moved towards Las, in the direction opposite to Pylos. The Macedonians too started readying their trireme, but we were a good five stadia ahead of them before they could muster off the beachfront, and by then we were ghosts, in as much as ghosts can be, on a full-moon night with clouds.

The clouds became thick soon and though sailors never row at night out of fear of hitting a rock, Harmodius decided to do so now as everybody was desirous of getting as far away from the Macedonians as possible. So Lasimodus kept the drums beating till early in the morning and Harmodius posted four watchers each on the stern and the bow. He wanted to keep an eye on what the Macedonians were up to, so as not to be taken by surprise.

Samcottus then told us that a Helot from the Macedonian ship had informed him that Polemon intended to sell the Spartan trireme in Pireus. His objective was to capture our trireme also, so that he could sell both and get a sum of fifty talents. And with that sum he intended to pay off his debt and free his son, who was being held hostage by Prince Alexander. Out of the fifty talents, he had promised ten talents to the Helots, to be divided amongst them, and that was what had quelled the brewing rebellion. Even the Helots who had been against him earlier had come over to his side.

After the early hours of the night, the trireme with the Macedonians could no longer be seen, and Samcottus believed they had berthed for the night. At midnight, Harmodius gave a short break to the rowers and put to vote the plan he had in mind, which was to reach Nisea, for it was a big port, where they could sell the trireme and divide the proceeds equally amongst everyone. Once the plan was disclosed, everyone voted for it. The rowers who had families back in Pylos thought they could take a transport back there from Nisea and those who were bachelors felt they could use the money to make a fresh start as free men in Attica.

Harmodius took stock of all the supplies and discovered there were rations enough for two days, which meant that the trireme would have to find supplies soon. While some Helots suggested stopping again at Hormos's village, the majority rejected the proposition, feeling that the Macedonians would be sure to check the village first and might have left secret instructions with some of the fishermen.

A little before dawn, however, disaster struck. Half the rowers were asleep and the other half were rowing very slowly. Early morning is the time when sleep is at its most dominant in the human mind – so I have observed. All the four watchers posted by Harmodius at the stern to keep a watch on the Macedonians had fallen asleep and by the time one of them woke up and shouted a warning, the Macedonian trireme was only three stadia away and moving with the intent to ram our ship.

Harmodius immediately gave orders for the bow to be turned around, as there was no way we could have out-rowed Polemon's stolen ship. Not only did they have more rowers, they had also built up a lot of momentum. Thus, Harmodius, who had rowed in Athenian triremes and was the most experienced sailor amongst us, chose to present the strongest part of his trireme for the blow and, in fact, signalled Lasimodus to increase the beat of the drums, so the rowers would row faster. Though they wouldn't be able to build up as much speed as the Macedonians, the defensive manoeuvre would cause the least damage to the trireme and would make it difficult for the Macedonians to board our craft with arms.

Harmodius based his tactic on the knowledge that our trireme had a stronger prow with more supporting beams than Polemon's: he knew this since he had sailed in it earlier. He felt the stoutness of the prow would smash the bow of the other trireme, which was differently built. The shock of the impact would travel equally in all directions in the trireme we were in but would make a hole in the bow of the other trireme below sea level. Harmodius then ordered for all the deck doors to be opened and fastened in such a way that they couldn't lock and cause the rowers beneath to be trapped. And he placed five of his strongest men at the bow, with metal pikes to deter any boarding party. To protect them from javelins thrown from the Macedonian trireme, he equipped them with the armour that Spiticos's party had left behind.

But, there not being many arms on board our trireme, we knew that if the plan failed, the two triremes would float broadside of each other and the Macedonians would then use grapple hooks to tie the triremes together. They would have their Helots throw javelins at our rowers, and then the soldiers would board and slaughter everybody on the deck and lock the deck doors so that none of the rowers below could escape.

The thalamites at the bottom were the most afraid. Those on the deck, once they saw things going wrong, could jump into the sea and swim to the shore, but it took much more courage to row at the bottom, not knowing what was happening above and trusting the instructions from the person giving the beat, in this case Lasimodus.

As the two triremes converged, we let out a war cry which must have sent a shiver through the Helots on the other trireme. The bows crashed into each other. The front portions of the two triremes rose up in the sea and then fell back in the water. Though I had been standing next to Harmodius, holding the rails, the crash sent me sliding aft. Harmodius had taken me off the oars, needing somebody to carry out his instructions on the deck. But I suspect it was because he knew which way the battle would swing and he wanted me to have a chance to escape. For, even if the Macedonians pardoned the rest of the Helots, they would put me to the sword in no time.

For a long time, the two bows locked together like two sea wrestlers. The drum crier in the other trireme kept issuing instructions to the rowers to fold their trireme broadside. Javelins came flying through to our deck, striking three of our Helots, but the bows were interlocked and the triremes rotated, locked in embrace, till they turned a hundred and eighty degrees and their bow came to be where our bow used to be. While earlier the morning sun was behind us, now it was in front. We knew that if we allowed their trireme broadside, we had no hope of survival. Our only chance lay in their trireme catching water in the hull below the sea line and their boat sinking before they got an opportunity to board our vessel, in which case there would be no chance for us, as our Helots were not armed, nor were they trained soldiers.

But as luck would have it, though we had crushed their hull, the damage was above the water line. The decoration on their bow, however, pierced us below the level of the sea and we started taking water. As we became heavier and sank a little, it freed the two bows, and though we moved between them and the coast and shaved off their bank of oars on one side, it gave them the opportunity to throw grapple hooks and lines with which they fastened our trireme broadside to theirs.

Then it was that Harmodius shouted: 'Abandon ship, abandon ship. Swim to the shore as quickly as you can.' The thalamites were waiting for this call. They rushed to the deck and jumped into the sea to swim to the shore.

Harmodius, Lasimodus, Zanylos and I did the same. I could see Polemon and Zeferino standing on the deck of their trireme, issuing orders to the Helots. Swimming to the shore was dangerous, as the Macedonians and some of the Helots whom they had trained started raining bow-shots on us in the water and throwing javelins at those who were slow. Many of our oarsmen were killed in this manner and barely twenty made it to the shore. Some preferred to stay on the trireme to take their chances with the Macedonians: they believed that no harm would come to them as the Macedonians would need help in repairing their vessel.

We watched the Macedonians from the shore to see whether they were inclined to give pursuit. But they were putting all their hands to salvaging the two triremes and had no heart to give chase, as they didn't trust the Helots not to come together and leave without them.

In this manner did my first adventure at sea end, with Harmodius, Zanylos, Lasimodus and myself together on the beach, watching the Macedonians plug the hole in our trireme and tow it away towards Las. Lasimodus had been able to swim to the shore with only one bagful of drachmas of Spiticos's money and I had lost all of mine.

We were still in Spartan territory and, strangely, Harmodius's prophecy regarding the Spartans played in my ears. I remembered that Harmodius had advised Spiticos to turn back from chasing the Macedonians and he had predicted that Spiticos would find them on the third full moon from then, which he did, and that a lot of blood would be shed and it wouldn't be Macedonian.

To Zandimus he had also said, and the words rang in my ears: 'I live in the world of Apollo and I see your death and I see Spiticos's, and they come before mine.'

FIVE

We lay exhausted on the beach for a long time and tended to the injuries of some of the Helots. We were not worried about the Macedonians coming to shore, as they couldn't have swum with their armour, and without it they didn't stand a chance against us. Polemon stood and watched us from the deck of his trireme, particularly when we talked to a Helot who had escaped from his ship.

His name was Zicos and he said that Polemon was worried about the reduced price the triremes would fetch after the damage to both. Steering a damaged trireme and towing another, Polemon had his task cut out. Zicos also told us that the Macedonians had made slaves of the Helots on our ship and put them to the task of repairs, which information relieved Harmodius and the rest of us; at least they had not been killed.

The Helots with the Macedonians had made it clear to their new masters that they didn't want the proceeds from the sales due to them to be shared by the Helots from our trireme and the Macedonians had agreed, as it was none of their business. But Zicos had objected, as he didn't want the Helots to be divided into two camps since they had a lot more in common with each other than with the Macedonians.

Zicos, therefore, urged the Helots with the Macedonians to rebel against their new masters, but Polemon had come to know of it. Before they could capture him, however, he had jumped into the sea and swum ashore.

Thus the Macedonians cleverly used the rivalry within the Helots to their advantage.

By late afternoon, the Macedonians had left with both triremes and we watched them all the way to the horizon for fear that they might be laying another trap for us, but when they were gone, Harmodius, who had been quiet for long, spoke. He said: 'I had a dream in the afternoon. I have to go to where Spiticos and Zandimus lie and give them a proper burial. If any of you wants to come with me, you are welcome. Let me not take you against your wishes. For we are all free men now, and wherever we wish to go, we shall. Lasimodus will divide the money he managed to come ashore with equally amongst us all, and those of you who wish to go to Pylos, can go to Las and take a transport back or proceed by way of land to Mount Ithome and thence to Pylos. There, you shall tell the truth to the ephor about the death of the Spartans, so that no suspicion falls on the Helots on our ship. After I have managed a proper burial for the Spartans, I have it in mind to proceed to the temple of Apollo in Sparta and there wait for a pronouncement from the Gods. Those of you who wish to come with me may do so. I will start at dawn.'

Zanylos, Lasimodus and I went with Harmodius. The rest said that they didn't care what happened to the bodies of Spiticos and the other guards: they were Spartans and deserved what was coming to them. They also expressed surprise that Harmodius wanted to bury Spiticos in spite of his father Asidamus having been responsible for the murder of his father. After saying this, they went to Las to look for a ride on a transport back to Pylos. Zicos didn't come with us either. He said that once, he had committed an offence by beating up two Spartans for stealing wine from his brother's shop in Sparta and they had turned him into an offender; his name was in the black book and they would throw him into prison if he was caught there. But he gave us directions to reach his brother's shop from the city square and told us to take tidings about him. He was sure that for the duration of our stay, his brother Cnidus would take good care of us.

It took us two and a half days of fast walking to reach the site where Spiticos and his troops had met their end and the crows were upon them. We counted eighteen bodies. The four others being Hormos, his wife, his infant son and one other from their village. Hormos's wife seemed to have been ravaged before her death.

We dug their graves with some tent pikes that the Macedonians had left behind on their camp site and some implements that we had bought from a fishing village on our way. No one spoke during the labours, as we had our faces covered due to the stench. But after each burial, Harmodius would say a prayer and we would repeat it.

Towards the end, he sank into a pensive mood and ruminated.

Said Harmodius: 'The end of a traitor is always bad. Hormos, of course, betrayed not for money but out of compulsion to save his wife and infant child and therefore deserves our sympathy, but the lust for blood in the Macedonians made them kill a person who had helped them. Their fate will be worse than the fate of those they managed to kill by using trickery. My entire life I thirsted for revenge, but Asidamus, father of Spiticos, died when I was in my youth and he died a natural death. I never got to know the name of his children, but his murderous acts have played on my mind every day since then and given me much sorrow. It was after I met Augusta, the priest in the Apollo temple in Sparta, that I got direction in my life and became a wandering sailor, and it brought me peace, even though others thought I was mad because of my talking while asleep and the many visions that visited me, which in my youth I never could interpret accurately.

'Augusta told me that the pain in my life at so young an age had made me dear to Apollo and because of the strength of my will and my prayers to him, he had granted me the gift of visions, so I could guide those who needed guidance to be on the right path. For the last two years, I had learned to forgive even Asidamus and this gave me great peace, but that day, when Dominos the herald took Asidamus's name, my body shuddered and revenge came back in me and I had to fight hard not to pray against Spiticos. For I have noticed that when I pray with all my heart, things happen in the manner that I desire. But since I didn't wish him any ill luck, I didn't pray in that manner. But after Spiticos's death, I have feared that in my sleep, unknown to me, I have wished him ill, which is why he had such a horrible death. That is why I am here, to atone, because if I did wish him ill, I have to pray for his forgiveness, and in giving him and his troops a proper burial, I hope this objective of mine has been achieved.'

We all heard his words quietly and, after it was all done, we washed ourselves in the sea and proceeded to Usa, the nearest village in those parts. We reached there at midnight, causing a big commotion. Harmodius and I had to quell the villagers' apprehensions that we were brigands out to steal from them. They gave us shelter for the night at the village school and brought food in the morning for our consumption – bread and salted fish and barley. As we ate ravenously, we learned that six wagons from a nearby village were on their way to Sparta with their annual olive oil produce, as the prices they got at Sparta were better than at Las or even Pylos, and they needed guards to take them safely.

Hearing this, Harmodius offered all of us as guards for the wagons, and this message was conveyed to the next village. They were not too convinced, as we didn't look like soldiers and had no arms. Then Harmodius offered to be guards at no salary at all, for riding on a wagon would be faster than walking, and less tiring, and they acceded to this proposal and agreed to feed us on the way.

It took fifteen days on the wagon to reach Sparta, and we went straight to the wine shop of Zicos's brother, Cnidus. He stayed alone in his house, which was behind his shop. The ephors had given him a licence to run a wine shop, provided he supplied wine to their commune at a low price; to other people, he could charge the prevailing market rate. He sold wine by the quart to households and even sold it by the cup in his shop. He bought his wine from the provinces, where he struck a good deal on account of the large quantities that he bought.

Cnidus arranged for Harmodius to go to the temple of Apollo the next day with his servant Trilomachus, who was a Helot from Argos and had been in Cnidus's service for only two months. Any Helot coming to Sparta from the provinces had to register at the Spartan bureau of Helots. This practice had started five years ago. The Spartans were fearful of the Helots since they ruled over them with an iron hand and indulged in purges on the mere suspicion of rebellion. Upon registration, the Spartans provided them with a sealed papyrus that they were supposed to carry on their person for the duration of their stay. The seal differed depending on whether they sought employment or temporary residence.

Thus, if a Spartan patrol became suspicious of a particular Helot, they would demand to see his papyrus, and if he didn't have any, they would take him in for questioning and impose a fine or a period of employment without money as punishment. In this manner did their city function, as at any given point of time there were ten thousand Helots in the city of Sparta alone and some soldiers took a daily bribe of a few ogols to ignore the illegal stay of certain Helots. All this was explained to us in detail by Trilomachus, who had applied for a papyrus for employment and had to pay twenty drachmas as a bribe to get it.

Not having known this method of rule in Sparta, and Zicos not having mentioned it to us, we were in a dilemma whether to report our stay to the authorities or not. We were sure that a report on the incident with the Macedonians would have been conveyed to Sparta by the ephor in Pylos, and if any detailed questioning took place about how we came to be in Sparta and we spoke the truth, they would surely take us in for further questioning. And it would be assumed that the Helots had taken the side of the Macedonians in a rebellion which caused the death of Spiticos and his men. It was a natural assumption, and likely enough, because the Macedonian contingent was small in size and, if it hadn't been for the Perioikoi on their boat who switched sides, they wouldn't have been able to decimate the Spartans on our trireme.

Keeping in mind all this, Cnidus, to whom we confided our predicament, advised us not to seek the papyrus and to go about our business in groups of not more than three, one of those three being Trilomachus, or Cnidus himself, as both had the relevant papers. Cnidus added: 'If any Spartan patrol or checkpost questions you and asks for papers, you must claim that you were ignorant of such a formality, but now that you have been told of the procedure, you will do the needful immediately. To the authorities you are to speak the falsehood that you are Helots from Argos and have come to visit the temple of Apollo for religious purification.'

Cnidus, who had been to Argos many times, described the city for us so that we could withstand questioning about it.

Harmodius had been silent throughout and I wasn't sure if he was listening to our discussion. But when it was revealed to Cnidus that Harmodius had a special gift of foretelling and we made him aware of his recent proclamations about the Spartans and how they had come true, Cnidus started paying more attention to Harmodius than he had hitherto, and started plying him with questions regarding his own business and whether he should stock wine from the province of Pylos or consider buying from Messenia.

With such frivolous questions he started annoying Harmodius, but since he was our host, Harmodius tolerated him, though I could feel that he was getting fed up. Then Lasimodus decided to play a prank on Cnidus. This we came to know later, after the prank had been played, which eventually exposed us all to danger.

He took Cnidus aside and told him that after walking to the temple of Apollo barefoot and making four rounds of it, he was to go to the river and bathe. After thus cleaning himself, he was to go back to the temple of Apollo and pray the whole afternoon that he might get guidance on his business from the God himself. After he maintained this routine for three days, he was to sleep to his heart's content, and whatever thought he woke up with he had to come to Harmodius and tell him about it, and then he would receive the truth from him.

With this stratagem he was able to get Cnidus out of the way and spare Harmodius. And also he was able to get access to Cnidus's wine shop, where he drank many glasses of costly wine, the caskets of which Trilomachus pointed out to him.

Of course, all this came to light later.

Harmodius was eager to find out if Augusta was still alive, for it was fifteen years since he had last seen him, so Trilomachus escorted both him and me to the temple. Though Zanylos too wanted to come, we kept in mind Cnidus's warning not to travel in large groups, as it would attract the attention of the Spartan patrols.

Harmodius and I bathed in the river before proceeding to the Apollo temple. Upon reaching the outer sanctorum of Apollo, he started chanting the Apollo incantations and, so musical was his cadence that a crowd gathered around him, enchanted by the manner of his devotion. Then something miraculous happened. The old man Augusta himself appeared. Now much withered by age and his back a little bent, he headed straight for Harmodius with an expression of delight and Harmodius, upon noticing him, shouted with joy and hugged him.

Said Augusta with delight: 'My friend, my son, what a surprise. You bring me great joy by being here.'

Augusta then took us to the inner sanctorum, where many sacrifices were taking place and where very few people were allowed. That day, they were sacrificing ten rams to Apollo and the priests were busy appropriating the meat once it had been offered to the deity; they were less greedy about having the meat than the priests at the oracle in Pylos. Augusta got some meat for us from the sacrifice, as it was considered auspicious, and then he took us to his house and inquired in detail about Harmodius's well-being.

Harmodius then sent Trilomachus to get some wine from the shop to toast his friend, but I suspect the real reason was that he wanted him out of the way. To Augusta he narrated his story of the last fifteen years, and specifically of the last few months since the Spartans began chasing the trireme the Macedonians had stolen from them.

Augusta listened quietly, interrupting only when he wanted to clarify a point. Then he looked at me and asked to examine my hands. And he kept nodding his head at intervals, as if my palms revealed to him deep secrets about me.

Harmodius told Augusta: 'For many years, I have had to sing Apollo's hymn in my head, for he would come to me in my dreams with his bow stretched and arrows about to fly. And it was only after I sang the paean that his rage would leave him and he would unstretch his bow. It was you, Augusta, who taught me the hymn many years ago.

'On the night that the paean failed to calm him and he clanged his arrows through the air, something bad would happen. For instance, on the night before Spiticos died at the hands of the Macedonians, Apollo came to me again in my sleep and I sang the paean for him, but he still twanged his bow and the next day all the Spartans died. On that occasion, the lion behind him roared when he fired his arrow and there were five stags behind the lion. Feeling guilty about Spiticos's death, for I fear that in my sleep I may have prayed for revenge, I went to afford the Spartans a proper burial, and once we reached the spot, we found eagles and crows eating their flesh. That night, Apollo appeared to me again in my dreams, and this time he didn't come with his bow and quivers but with his phorminx, on which he played a song whose words I couldn't recognize, but which was the most melodious I have ever heard. I took it as an omen that he was pleased with the fact that the Spartans had been afforded a proper burial.

'But Apollo comes to me more often with his bow and quivers and his lion, and when he roars, he gives me a fright beyond what any human has ever given me. You know, Augusta, that I am cursed with these visions. They come to me when I don't seek them, and when I seek them, they desert me. For many days I have striven to get guidance from Apollo about what I should do with the rest of my life, but the visions he sends me give me answers I cannot read, or visions that are so dark that nothing is discernible.

'Even though you stay amongst the Spartans in Sparta and I have nothing against them now, I feel I can open my heart to you as you are originally from Delphi. Kindly guide me in the right direction, for I feel that my life is about to end and the fear of death has gone out of me. I have seen a vision of being in a battle on the side of the Thebans. And last night, Apollo came to me again with his lion and stags and this time the lion roared, looking at me as though warning me, and Apollo smiled, and then I saw a scene of battle: I was lying on the ground and Nicanor's son was looking over me. I think the lion was warning me of some imminent danger, I know not what, and Apollo was telling me of the consequences if I chose to battle alongside the Thebans.'

Hearing these words, Augusta patted his back. Then he said: 'Seven is the number of Apollo, so it's not surprising that he comes to you with five stags and a lion. When Apollo entered Olympus with his ominous bow, all the Gods jumped to their feet in fear. It was only Leto, the mother of Apollo, who remained sitting, and she basked in the glory of her mighty son. She alone had the courage to take away the weapons from Apollo and show him to his seat. So I would advise you to pray to his mother Leto, for only she can take away his weapons and calm him more than even his paean can. When Apollo plays the lyre, he is the giver of radiance and he can heal the unhealable. There are many priests, Harmodius, who go through their whole life without Apollo appearing to them in their dream, but he trusts you and makes you his favourite for revealing what he has in mind. I fear that the battle you mention is about to take place between the Greek allies and the Macedonians. In fact, the ephors are to meet me today for advice on whether to aid the Greek allies against the Macedonians led by King Philip. And two heralds have come from Athens and they are to address the ephors, the Gerousia and the two Spartan kings together the day after tomorrow, to make their case for Spartan assistance. But Harmodius, I am glad to see you, and I welcome Seleucus, son of Nicanor. I invite both of you and your other companions to come and stay at my house. My wife still remembers you very fondly as Apollo's most favourite Helot.'

So insistent was Augusta that Harmodius, Zanylos and I moved to his house the same day. Lasimodus moved the next day with great reluctance, and only after Trilomachus provided him with a small casket of wine that he kept in the quarters assigned to him. Since Lasimodus had been doing several months of rowing, Harmodius smiled at him indulgently. Also, though I didn't know it then, Harmodius and Lasimodus were lovers. I was too young at this time to understand the subtle gestures between people.

The suddenness with which events had overtaken us in the past few months had taken their toll on me. Sorrow and the thought of revenge alternated within me with great rapidity and, more than that, the urge to become powerful, so as to be able to take my destiny in my own hands. Such were my youthful emotions. For only youth can think that fate is the handmaiden of the powerful. Seeing me in this pensive mood, Augusta asked the next day what troubled me. And I told him my life story from the time that my father had been murdered by Argus.

Augusta smiled at me in the way people with wisdom smile at youth. He said: 'I have seen your hands, Nicanor's son, and you shall be king one day; I read signs which tell me that. But before that, there lie many twists and turns and much agony. You have a peculiar destiny and nothing shall come to you on a platter. But your struggles shall be rewarded and, in time, all your desires will be fulfilled. Beyond this, I cannot say much. I have seen hands similar to yours, and they belonged to the Theban general Epamonidas. After his first success in battle against the Spartans, he was desirous of knowing whether his victory was a fluke or if it would be repeated, for he and the others were surprised at the manner of the Spartan collapse, having supposed that they would offer much tougher resistance. Since I had been taken prisoner at the first battle and the report reached him that I could read the future by seeing a person's hands, he showed me his. I told him then that he would win all the battles against the Spartans, and he did. And though every human has a destiny which is his own, many men have common characteristics.'

'I am unable to decide whether I should go back to Olympia and travel east later, as Pythadorus, the priest of the Apollo temple at Pylos indicated I should. There is great confusion in my mind, and I look upon Harmodius now to give me guidance,' I told Augusta.

'Harmodius is capable of guiding you much better than I am, for he is blessed by Apollo himself, but I feel you will soon be taking your own decisions, and that is the way it should be,' said Augusta.

That same evening, he organized a dinner in Harmodius's honour. He invited priests from the temple of Apollo and Harmodius regaled them with tales of his travels. He compared Apollo's temple in Sparta with those found elsewhere in the Hellenic world and in Ionia, for he had travelled a lot, and he concluded that the one in Sparta was more magnificent and more powerful than the others. Everybody, including Augusta, was happy when he said this and though the thought crossed my mind that he was saying it to please his host and his host's friends, the nature of his love for Apollo made me conclude that, for him, this was the way it was, and if he had found the Apollo temple at Thebes to be more magnificent and powerful, he would have said so, even at the cost of annoying his guests.

In fact, the feast became memorable towards the end when Harmodius began to sing the paean to Apollo after dinner and Augusta accompanied him on the lyre. But after two songs, which mesmerized everybody, Harmodius suddenly stopped singing and started muttering and saying things to a being he alone could see. This made the others very uneasy and those seeing him for the first time came to the conclusion that he was not of a healthy mind and suffered from a sickness of some sort. Augusta started leading his other guests away, so that no one would disturb Harmodius in his reverie. He remained thus until two hours beyond midnight. And even Augusta retired to his room to rest, leaving

Harmodius in the care of Lasimodus, who insisted that he had seen many an occasion like this and knew exactly how to deal with Harmodius. So Lasimodus sat with the casket of wine which he had brought from Cnidus's house and drank it down while Harmodius talked with invisible beings.

The day after the feast, Augusta took us in the afternoon to where the Spartan assembly was, to hear the two heralds from Athens. But before we left, Cnidus landed up at Augusta's house and went straight to Harmodius and in my presence addressed him thus: 'I have walked around the Apollo temple as you said, for three days, and the first thought that came to me after I finished all the rituals is that if Petra, the wife of the Spartan Masicus, does not run away with me, my life is doomed. It is to win her that I want to make money in my wine business, for she once promised me that she would leave Masicus if I became rich enough. It is with this in mind that I asked you where to buy wine from, for I wanted to know which wine people would like the most. But you wanted to know the first thought in my mind after the rituals, and it is this, that I want to marry Petra. So please tell me, Harmodius, whether my prayers will be heeded by Apollo and whether my desire will be fulfilled, for it burns me every living hour of every living day.'

Since neither Harmodius nor I knew anything about the matter, we were perplexed, and seeing us bewildered thus, Cnidus spoke further. By this time, Augusta and Lasimodus had joined us and Cnidus, unmindful of the company, added: 'I know that it is against the rules to covet somebody else's wife, but Masicus, husband of Petra, ill treats her and bruises her with his beatings, and I can hear her cry all night. She is from a village near Las and not sophisticated like the women of Sparta and so, she endures a lot of humiliation. I met her when she came to purchase wine from my shop. I propose to become rich and run away with her because I know that for her to leave Masicus and marry a Helot would mean death for both of us. So tell me, Harmodius, now that I have fulfilled your conditions, will you talk to Apollo on my behalf as Lasimodus tells me you do every day?'

At this point, everyone looked at Lasimodus accusingly and Lasimodus burst out laughing. So did the rest of us, and even Harmodius smiled. Harmodius then spoke to Cnidus, who had begun to look uncomfortable: 'The ritual you have just described is the walking prayer of Apollo, and it's a ritual for women, not men. I never advised you to follow this ritual. It is the ritual meant for women who are finding it hard to conceive, and they are supposed to do it with their husband; the fruits of the husband performing it will go to the wife. Since you have no wife, Cnidus, and you did it with this woman Petra in mind, I would not be surprised if she becomes soon with child. Though, of course, it will not be yours, for it will have been sired by the loins of Masicus. I know of a case in Messenia, where a man performed the ritual in error and the result was to get the wife of a friend of his, whom he coveted, pregnant.'

Cnidus turned red and looked at Lasimodus with great anger and shouted obscenities at him. It was with some difficulty that Zanylos and I separated him from Lasimodus, and not before he had landed a few blows to his face. He then left Augusta's house with great resentment and shouted that he would have his revenge, and he didn't spare Harmodius, Zanylos or me in his invectives, accusing us of having instigated Lasimodus into misleading him in spite of his having been such a good host to all of us. Harmodius requested Augusta to go after Cnidus and calm him down and bring him back, so he could rebuke Lasimodus in his presence and ask him to apologize, but Cnidus rebuffed Augusta and told the old man to return before he ground him to dust. This then was the start to the afternoon when Augusta took us to visit the grounds where the Spartan assembly was in progress.

The two kings, all the ephors and the Gerousia were sitting together to deliberate on important matters. No Helots were allowed to participate in the assembly. But since it was being held in the open grounds behind the Apollo temple, the Helots could see and hear all that was going on, and many of them were performing their duties as servants on the grounds.

In fact, though the Helots couldn't participate in the deliberations, two representatives each of the Perioikoi and the Neodamodeis could sit as observers and, if any of the two kings asked them a query, they were supposed to answer. Augusta explained this was done so that any decision with respect to the Perioikoi and the Neodamodeis could be implemented immediately by them. Augusta himself was there with other priests from the Apollo temple, as the assembly could only open after they had purified the grounds and made sacrifice to Apollo of a bull. This was done to bring Apollo's wisdom into the deliberations of men.

Zanylos and I were apprehensive of being amidst the Spartans so openly because we had no legal documents, but because it was Augusta himself who had accompanied us, the Spartan guards looked at us without hostility. As for Harmodius, he watched everything like a child, without any fear on his face.

The Spartans would allow only one Athenian herald to speak in the assembly and left it to them to decide amongst themselves who would. The taller herald by the name of Anos spoke thus: 'I have been waiting for ten days to get a chance to speak in this great gathering. The people of Athens have sent me to solicit your aid in the battle that we are headed for against the Macedonians. After defeating the Illyrians, Philip of Macedonia conquered Amphipolis in Thrace, a colony of hard-working Athenians, and gained possession of the gold mines of Mount Pangaeus to finance his illegal aggressions. Then he captured Potidea in Chalcidice, Pydna on the Gulf of the Thermaic and the Thracian town of Crenides, where he inflicted a massacre such as the town had never known before. Next, he took Methone, but failed to take the pass at Thermopylae two years later, as it was guarded by the Athenians very strongly. Subsequently, Philip annexed the Olynthus and the Chalcidice and made war with the Phocis over Delphi. By subterfuge and by weight of his conquests, he was given a seat in the Delphic council. I have mentioned to you his various aggressions so you can judge for yourselves the menace this barbarian is becoming to the Greek way of life. He now seeks to acquire the Dardenneles and in all probability we will be proceeding to war against him along with the Thebans. If the forces of Sparta too joined hands with us, we could defeat Philip and make sure that he doesn't become a bigger threat to Greece than he already is.'

After hearing him out patiently, the Spartan king Zetomandus, son of Spitamadus and the elder of the two kings, addressed the herald thus: 'You seek our help alongside the Thebans – who caused us so much destruction – against people who have never troubled us. Even if Philip is a tyrant, he is not imposing his tyranny on us. Where was Demosthenes, your famous orator who makes a living critiquing Philip, when Epamonidas was burdening us with his aggression without any provocation from our side? Your great orators Timos and Aeschylus too were nowhere to be seen. Was our cause not worthy enough then? Later, Athens did send some troops, but it was not out of love for us but out of resentment at the growing power of Thebes and Epamonidas. Now you ask us to support Thebes. The same Thebes which, at the end of the Peloponnesian wars, demanded that Athens be razed to the ground and its inhabitants sold into slavery. Was it not we Spartans who resisted these demands of the Thebans and spared the city any calamity at the hand of Thebes? But it is the nature of man that he forgets what has happened in the past, for he seeks not wisdom from his past actions but immediate benefit from acts in the present.'

After addressing the Athenian heralds thus, Zetomandus bade them to wait at the temple of Apollo, as precise answers would be given to them by the ephors who wanted to discuss the matter further in the Gerousia with other members. Just as I thought that the proceedings were going to be over soon, in walked the ephor from Pylos, and I all but fell from my vantage point. After drawing the assembly to order, he conveyed to them the entire incident concerning the Macedonians and how they had chased a certain Seleucus, son of Nicanor, to Pylos. This was the same Nicanor's son, he said, who had won the chariot race at Olympia. The ephor went on to detail how the Macedonians had escaped with a Spartan trireme and how he had sent Spiticos and his team to hunt them down. But now he had graver matters to narrate and he made way for the port commander of Las to report certain facts. His name was Astyochus and I had seen him briefly from a distance, when Spiticos had docked the trireme at Las for hull repairs.

Astyochus, the Spartan harbour commander from Las, said: 'King Zetomandus, King Dandymede, all the ephors and members of the Gerousia, I came to Sparta but two hours ago at full speed from Las. I have terrible tidings. The same Macedonians that the ephor from Pylos just talked about came to the port of Las towing Spiticos's trireme. They had taken off their Macedonian attire and adopted the attire of the rowers. A Helot by the name of Cimon told us how the Macedonians had put to death Spiticos and his men at a spot which was three days' sailing from Las. Cimon and the other Helots had somehow escaped from their clutches and made off with the two triremes while the Macedonians were engaged in fighting with Spiticos's men. Cimon knew the spot where the Macedonians were boxed in; they were waiting there for any merchant ship or transport to pass so they could take a ride to Syracuse, and they had plenty of money to offer.

'Cimon then proposed to take Trachomus, the military commander of Las, and his contingent of twenty troops to the spot where the Macedonians were, to bring them to Las and try them for murder. He feared that any further delay in getting to the spot would result in the Macedonians escaping. Since Trachomus was in any case awaiting the arrival of a Spartan trireme from Argos to take him to Pylos, as he had to deliver a sum of forty talents to the ephor, he decided to use Cimon's trireme to get there instead. He thought that he could proceed with the Macedonians to Pylos, where they could be tried and the full extent of their crime ascertained.

'Thus Trachomus and twenty other hoplites boarded Cimon's trireme with forty talents, after two days had been spent in hull repairs. I myself was at the harbour to see them off and Cimon swore to take them straight to the murderous Macedonians. But one day later, a fishing vessel came to Las with Trachomus's body, and those of two other soldiers – an archer and a javelin thrower. The bodies had been found floating in the sea, devoid of any armour but one of the fishermen had recognized Trachomus as the Spartan commander from Las, as he had come to Las often to fetch corn for his village in return for fish. We were greatly puzzled by this development and became anxious for everybody else, when a soldier from Trachomus's party managed to reach us in a fast-moving fishing boat. He reported this most extraordinary tale: the Macedonians were all the time in Cimon's trireme itself! Even while he was at Las!

'The soldier said that they took to sea from Las, and when they berthed in the night, Cimon took ten soldiers away from Trachomus's party, with the excuse of assisting in rolling the trireme onto the beach, so the hull could be dried and the ship could move faster the next day. The rest of the soldiers rested with Trachomus at a little distance out of sight of the trireme, and this soldier who escaped was one of that party. According to him, the Macedonians and their Helot collaborators first murdered the party of ten that was assisting Cimon in pulling the trireme onto the beach; since they had laid down their arms, it was easy to attack them. And after dealing with them, Cimon proceeded to deal with the rest of the Spartans, along with the Macedonians, but this time one of the soldiers had some doubt over the approach of the party and raised an alarm and a brief but intense struggle ensued. Our soldiers were hampered by the fact that their arms were at some distance and not all of them could reach them, but those who did managed to kill quite a few of the Helots before they were killed. Only one managed to escape by jumping from a cliff into the sea and swimming three leagues to the coast, from where he walked to a fishing village and then took their fastest boat to Las. It was from this soldier named Bonitos that we received all the information. And I have brought Bonitos with me here to Sparta, for aid from the physician Lespos, son of Organtes, as he is injured in his leg.'

After Astyochus spoke, there was a great commotion in the assembly and one of the ephors had to call for order. King Zetomandus then asked Astyochus where he thought the Macedonians were and whether they could send a fleet of Spartan triremes to chase after them. But Astyochus replied that since nearly a week had passed since the time of the incident, he had no way of knowing where the Macedonians were headed, though he suspected they might choose Syracuse, as they would know that the Spartans would alert every port from Pylos to Nisea and so their best interests might be served in going in the opposite direction, either to Rhegium or Syracuse, and thence over land to Macedonia. Astyochus added that he himself had sent fast moving boats to various ports to make enquiries about the Macedonians.

At this point, Harmodius's voice rang out from the edge of the Gerousia, where he had been standing behind the priests, hearing all that was going on. My heart missed many beats at hearing his voice so loud, here at the Spartan assembly, where our mere presence, if known to the ephor, would be enough to earn for us our deaths.

But this is what Harmodius said: 'The Macedonians are at the port of Rhegium to sell the triremes and proceed back to Macedonia.'

At this, all eyes turned to him and, observing that he was a Helot, the guards came immediately to take him away as no Helot could speak in the assembly except if he were ordered to by the king. I could see that Augusta's face had turned ashen, for it was he who had brought us here.

King Zetomandus, however, intervened and asked for Harmodius to be brought forward. The ephor from Pylos gasped when he saw him. I saw that Dominos the herald was present and he gasped in surprise as well.

King Zetomandus addressed Harmodius directly after he was brought forward: 'How dare you speak in this assembly, Helot?'

Before Harmodius could answer, the ephor from Pylos walked into the well of the Gerousia and addressed everybody thus: 'This is the Helot who was on board the trireme which was under the command of Spiticos and which Cimon towed to Las. He was, therefore, in conspiracy with the Macedonians to kill Spiticos.'

Dominos the herald also stepped forward and identified Harmodius as a rower he had seen on the deck of Spiticos's trireme when he had encountered it on his way back to Pylos from Crete.

'I told you, O king, what I just saw in my mind and, seeing that all of you were seized by the matter, I decided to inform you where they were,' explained Harmodius simply.

At this point, I saw Cnidus come and inform the guards of the presence of Lasimodus and myself and they came and surrounded us. Hearing the commotion, the ephor from Pylos looked my way and recognized me immediately. He got up and shouted in excitement: 'And there's Seleucus, son of Nicanor. He's the charioteer who won the quadregi at Olympia this year! It looks like a conspiracy, King Zetomandus. We must get to the bottom of this.'

And then everybody looked at me and Dominos identified Lasimodus as well. In the commotion, the only good thing was that Zanylos slipped away quietly, as Cnidus hadn't pointed him out to the guards. But I could see that Augusta was trembling.

Harmodius was calm and, though I was furious at him for bringing this upon us, I realized that if he hadn't, Cnidus would have, and that would have been worse. I took it upon myself to address the assembly. I said: 'Yes, I am Seleucus, son of Nicanor, as the ephor says. And we escaped the Macedonians the day they killed Spiticos and his men, about two days from Las. The Macedonians then chased us on their trireme and caught up with us at dawn and rammed us, and we jumped from our trireme and swam to the shore, where they didn't pursue us. The name of this Helot who just addressed you is Harmodius. He was the one who took us back to the spot where Spiticos and his men lay, to bury them in a proper manner with prayers and ritual. It was Harmodius's desire to visit the temple of Apollo in Sparta, where he had been many years ago, and thus we happen to be here. Excuse him, O king, if Harmodius sounds a little strange, but it's true that he's blessed by Apollo and sees things which other men don't.'

Everybody looked at Harmodius in a new light.

The ephor from Pylos, though, wasn't moved by what I had said. He spoke with great venom against me. 'Since he arrived at Pylos, my king, we have been struck with great misfortune. The Macedonians came chasing him and committed a foul murder. Then they incited the Helots to revolt and stole a trireme from the harbour, and now Astyochus has told us what further harm they have caused to Sparta. They have murdered our people and stolen our triremes and our money. That these men are in Sparta means that they have come with some evil intention and are colluding with the Macedonians to hatch some evil enterprise. We should keep in mind that the Greeks will soon be at war with Macedonia – I suspect they are here as spies of the Macedonians to commit evil.'

Harmodius interrupted the ephor and said: 'The crimes of the Macedonians are not the fault of Nicanor's son. He himself has suffered much at their hands, including the death of his parents and his friend Pindar. If we were spies of the Macedonians, we wouldn't have suffered at their hands.'

King Zetomandus then addressed Harmodius, Lasimodus and me: 'Tell us the real reason why you happen to be in Sparta. It's foolish of the three of you to have come here after having revolted against Spiticos and delivered him and his men to the Macedonians. You face death here. Explain yourselves.'

I answered on everybody's behalf: 'It wasn't we who revolted against Spiticos and his men, great king. We escaped from the Macedonians after the death of Spiticos, who had been led there by the treachery of the chief of a fishing village – his name was Harmos. We have just heard from Astyochus that some Helots led by a man called Cimon interacted with the Spartans at Las, but about that we know nothing. If we had revolted, we wouldn't have been so foolish as to have come here and Harmodius would not have spoken without being called upon to do so.'

Though the two kings were silent upon hearing this, the ephors weren't. They had been conversing privately with Cnidus and, after I had finished, an ephor by the name of Gamyetus, son of Noseimodon, got up to speak. Said Gamyetus: 'Noble kings, these two Helots, Harmodius and Lasimodus, and another by the name of Zanylos, have been staying at the place of Cnidus, the wine seller. They had been referred there by Zicos, the brother of Cnidus, who was one of the Helots who escaped from the trireme the Macedonians stole from Pylos. Cnidus tells us that he overheard Nicanor's son and Harmodius talk about some spying matter for the Macedonians and also a plan for desecrating the temple of Apollo in Sparta, so that the Gods would be against the king and the city. They were to do this on behalf of the Macedonians, as one of the uncles of Nicanor's son is still in the custody of the Macedonians, and the story that the Macedonians are hunting for Nicanor's son is all a lie, as they are acting in complicity. And most important of all, this Harmodius, Cnidus tells me, is the son of Thasidomus, who turned traitor with the Theban Epamonidas at the battle of Manitea. And Cnidus tells me that they have been staying at the house of the priest Augusta and they had a banquet a few nights ago, where they managed to corrupt some of the priests to plan this desecration.'

Such lies did Cnidus feed the ephors because of the trick Lasimodus had played on him.

At the mention of Thasidomus's name, however, the entire assembly sat up. And when Augusta's name was mentioned in the end, pandemonium broke out in all quarters, for Augusta was a friend of almost everybody in the assembly. But his name having been spoken, Augusta came forward to defend himself and, to his credit, he started by defending Harmodius.

Said Augusta: 'Yes, Harmodius is Thasidomus's son, and I am honoured to know him, as any man would be who fears the Gods. That Harmodius is Thasidomus's son is a fact and it is something that neither Harmodius nor any of us can do anything about. However, when I first met Harmodius many years ago in Sparta, I spotted within him a love for Apollo that was rare. It's a love that has now become huge like a mountain and great harm will come to us if we listen to that liar called Cnidus and harm Harmodius or his friends, as a devotee of Apollo is not to be trifled with. As to Harmodius seeking to corrupt the priests of the Apollo temple to plan some defilement that would bring Apollo's rage on us, I draw your attention to the magnificent character of the priests of our temple. There is Polyarctes, son of Asthon, who has been our leader and chief priest and almost like a father to all of us for thirty-five years now. He is the same Polyarctes who conducted sacrifices for the welfare of Sparta from his own rations when all our resources had gone to subdue the revolt of the Helots and we had none to spare for the temple. Then there is Orionos, son of Nabicides, whose predictions are next only to the oracle at Delphi. Did he not warn us to be on guard against Thebes and beware of a general who would introduce tactics in war that we could not counter? Didn't the Theban Epamonidas come on the scene and fight a war with a phalanx that we were not used to fighting and so caused us to suffer disastrous consequences? And how can I forget Masticion, son of Buticos, who, after studying the entrails of a sacrificed bull, predicted that if the Spartans became overconfident of winning any battle, they would lose it. And within ten days, didn't we lose the battle at Manitea, after boasting that we would win it by noon?

'These are the men that Cnidus claims Harmodius seeks to corrupt. Men who have served Sparta with all their heart and who have sacrificed their personal comfort so that Sparta could flourish. These were the men who came to my house for a meal, where Harmodius sang a paean to Apollo so melodiously that it was as if the walls of my house themselves were dancing with joy. I didn't know it was against the law in Sparta to invite someone to a meal or sing a song to Apollo in one's house. This is what happened, and may Apollo strike me down right now if what I have spoken is false. As to Nicanor's son, I have myself examined his hands, and in front of everybody I predict this, so that those who remember may know that it was Augusta who first pronounced it: this boy will be the cause of the downfall of the Macedonians in more ways than one, and since we don't want Macedonia to hold sway over Greece, Seleucus, son of Nicanor, will be an important ally to have.'

With these words Augusta managed to draw some of the venom away from Harmodius. As to his prediction about me, I thought he was saying these words to please the Spartans so that they didn't become too harsh with me. Then something unexpected happened. Clonus, son of Elonas from Sparta, stood up in the Gerousia to speak. I had not recognized him in the assembly and he had not drawn attention to himself even when I had addressed King Zetomandus. This was the same Clonus who had raced against me in Olympia and had come in after Argus; he had fallen back in the race because he had scooped up a boy from the tracks. He was also one of the drivers I had gone to ask for blessings the night before the race. And I must say I was mighty pleased to hear him speak.

Said Clonus: 'I raced in the same chariot race as Nicanor's son, and it was Argus the Macedonian who conspired with Polemon and others in the Macedonian camp to murder Nicanor, who was to race against us, even though Nicanor himself was a Macedonian and so too is Seleucus. It is true that the Macedonians gambled in the race and lost money and blamed the fact on Seleucus, and now I hear they caused the death of his mother and uncle and later even his friend Pindar, whom I also knew. So there is no substance in the ephor Gamyetus's suggestion that the Macedonians are colluding with Nicanor's son. I know for a fact that it's not true, having witnessed events with my own eyes in Olympia during the Games.'

After Clonus spoke thus, he came down to embrace me, and then King Zetomandus ordered the guards to take Harmodius, Lasimodus and myself into custody, so that matters could be ascertained further. The four ephors led by Gamyetus huddled together to confabulate and the two kings discussed matters amongst themselves, as did the members of the Gerousia. Then Thucydides, son of Asthamon and the oldest man in the Gerousia, stood up to speak and such was his reputation and the respect he commanded that the Gerousia instantly went quiet.

Said Thucydides, son of Asthamon: 'My mind is still preoccupied with the request from the people of Athens for our help in the war they fear is about to break out with the Macedonians and which they feel will be a decisive one. I do not wish the debate on the fate of Harmodius or Nicanor's son to occupy more of our time than it deserves. In fact, if anything, we can join both the events to our advantage. The ephors have informed me that there are a hundred Helots in custody, against whom charges are to be pressed for rebellion, and we know that they will all be put to death. Our laws don't forgive rebellion of any kind and these hundred Helots had rebelled against the garrison at Argos for wages. Since we live in constant vigilance against the Helots, as their numbers are more than ours and they resent our superiority, we have no choice but to deal with them in a manner that puts them in fear of us. But I suggest, after great thought, that we send these hundred Helots and these three people here, Harmodius, Seleucus and this third man whose name I do not know, to fight alongside the Athenians against the Macedonians, for that would serve many purposes with one act. We would not be shedding Spartan blood, we would take care of this peculiar situation with Harmodius and Seleucus, as we cannot really take them to task for the harm that their Macedonian pursuers have caused us, and we will also have come to the aid of the Athenians, even though with a small force. If the Athenians win, they can't say that we didn't help them, and if our contingent loses, we are not going to be mourning their loss.'

After making this speech, Thucydides, son of Asthamon, sat down, and it seemed his words had had an effect on the Gerousia. King Zetomandus was quiet for a while, but he spoke soon: 'I respect your opinion, Thucydides. We should not forget that Athens helped us when we were at war with the Thebans. When the rogue Epamonidas invaded Laconia with fifty thousand men from Arcadia, Argos and Eleia, it was with great difficulty that we prevented his forces from entering our beloved city. And, later, it was the arrival of Ephicrates's army from Athens to Arcadia that made Epamonidas rush back and leave our territory. The Athenians helped us at Mount Onean and Kenchreae too, to prevent the Thebans from entering the Peloponnese the following year. But now the Thebans and Athenians have joined hands against the

Macedonians, and if it had been the Thebans in trouble, alone against the Macedonians, we would have enjoyed their plight, but seeing that the Athenians are equally troubled, we should feel moved to help them the way they helped us in the past. But our own position against the Helots doesn't allow us to send our army to war against the Macedonians, for it might incite some of our Helots to make use of the opportunity to revolt, so I am quite content to do what Thucydides suggests, which is to send the imprisoned Helots in aid of the Athenians. For, in reality, we would like the Thebans to be crushed by the Macedonians, as that would be just revenge for the manner in which they ravaged our land and broke it up.'

Accordingly, it was conveyed to the Athenian heralds that the Spartans would send a force of about a hundred to help the Athenians in their coming war against the Macedonians. Harmodius, Lasimodus and I were sent to custody with the hundred Helots and marching orders were issued by King Zetomandus, to be complied with within three days. Zetomandus appointed Zumidos, son of Mestos, as our leader and the Helots were pleased indeed at this development, for it was conveyed to them that if they won the war on the side of the Athenians, they could consider themselves free. As a precaution, it was ordered that a relative of each of the hundred Helots be held captive till the war ended, so that they wouldn't consider escaping before or during the war.

Within me, however, there were conflicting emotions. If you remember, I had instructed Ganymede at Pylos to tell Phormio, the Phoenician sailor, to meet me at the port of Nisea after four months, with my money. If I wasn't there, he was to hand over the drachmas to Pythagoras at Athens. I was in half a mind to leave Harmodius and proceed to Nisea and collect the money, then proceed onward to the east as Pythadorus had said I should. Through my travels, I would have discovered the whereabouts of Polemon, Argus, Zeferino and the rest of their accomplices and taken suitable revenge. But having come to Sparta, events had got out of hand and now I found myself headed to Chaeronea to fight the Macedonians, which was also good, except that I didn't know if I was prepared for war. Though my father Nicanor had taught me how to fight with a sword and a spear, I had never been in a battle and never fought in a phalanx. But I was far from fearful and relished the prospect of battle with the Macedonians, my only concern being that I didn't want to die till I had had my revenge.

Zumidos, son of Mestos, whom Zetomandus had appointed commander of the Helot contingent, was a soldier who had fought many years back against Epamonidas in the army of King Agesilaos of Sparta. He now told the Helots about the Theban band of three hundred, the Sacred Band as they were called, which was made up of couples. It had been founded by the commander Gorgidas, who scattered the couples through the army, but later, Pelopidas, a friend of Epamonidas, welded them to fight as one unit and turned them into devils on the battlefield; he used them to break the enemy where they were the strongest.

Pelopidas and Epamonidas themselves fought in the Sacred Band against the Spartans at Tegyra and defeated an army that was three times the size of theirs. Later, at Leuctra, they routed the Spartans and ended the Spartan hegemony over the Thebans.

After Zumidos told this story, which most of the Helots knew already, Harmodius commented thus: 'It was love for each other that made the Sacred Band fight so valiantly. Lovers don't want to fall in the estimation of their partners, hence they fight nobly and get courage from each other.'

After hearing Harmodius, another Helot, Scion, commented: 'I would prefer my wife as a lover. I wonder when they will allow women on the battlefield, though.'

Everybody laughed, listening to Scion. Harmodius replied that they would allow women on the battlefield when Scion could fly, and Scion said that he had flown many times in his dreams. To which Harmodius said that he could then fight alongside his wife in his dreams, and everybody laughed again.

By now, my resolve to participate in the war against the Macedonians had melted, mainly because I didn't want to die before exacting revenge, and I was not sure whether I would meet Polemon, Argus, Zeferino and the other murderers I sought on the battlefield at Chaeronea. So I started thinking of escaping from the Spartans. I had also grown aloof from Harmodius and had started thinking that our present predicament was due to his conduct. I was in this frame of mind when Zanylos came to meet me in the place where all the Helots were kept grouped together, in the open. It was good that he had escaped. Accompanying him was Trilomachus, who claimed to be fed up with the behaviour of Cnidus, his master, and wanted to help us in any way he could and join our group in whatever endeavour we chose in the future. I told Zanylos to prepare for my escape, as I had already developed a plan after hearing Scion talk in private.

Scion and the other Helots, it appeared, wanted to be with the prostitutes at Zeros, a locality in Sparta, which was next to the river and within the city defences. That was when a plan developed in my head that if I could, through a stratagem, go with the men to Zeros, I could escape over the river by boat and in this way cross the Spartan city defences – I had been told that they did not mount patrols on the river. After having left the city far behind, I could proceed to Nisea and try and locate Pythagoras and see if Phormio had been true to his word.

So, I encouraged Scion to make his desire public about wanting to be with a woman before going to battle with the Macedonians. He said that the men were upset that they hadn't slept with a woman for close to six months. I persuaded Scion to make his entreaty to the Spartan soldiers first, and they led him to Zumidos. He then entreated Zumidos to talk to the Spartan ephors, so they would allow those men who wanted to be with women to go to Zeros.

Zumidos went with the proposal to Thucydides. He knew that if he spoke to the ephors directly, they would reject the request, but if Thucydides spoke, they would give their consent. And that's what happened. The ephors agreed that on the last night that the Helots would spend in Sparta before the march to Attica and Chaeronea, those men who didn't have lovers and wanted to visit the quarters of the Helots could go accompanied by Spartan guards and find any women willing to be with them. Fifteen men went in the night with the guards, and I was amongst them.

Harmodius gave me all the drachmas that he had, to do whatever I could to make the men happy. Augusta, who had come to meet Harmodius, had brought with him a gift of two hundred drachmas for the Helots. Harmodius gave me fifty more drachmas out of this amount and kept the rest for expenses during the march to the battlefield.

To be truthful, I had never been with a woman until then. In the Helot quarters of Sparta at Zeros, there were many women who had lost their husbands to purges by the Spartans and there were many others who had not been married at all, as there were fewer Helot men than there were women. The price of a woman for one night was seven days of wages for a man or seven drachmas. Since there were fifteen of us, it would cost us hundred and five drachmas for fifteen women. We were short by twenty-five drachmas. Besides, Scion and Zesticos wanted a beautiful woman called Larcinus, who demanded ten drachmas from one man for the night and wouldn't come down from that price. But the rest of the women took ten drachmas for two men, and in this way we managed to provide every man with a woman, though the ones who went second had to wait for their turn.

It was in this place, then, that I first went with a woman. Her name was Eudora. She was ten years older than me and came to know very quickly that it was my first time. She was more angry than caring when she realized this, for a reason I was never able to fathom. She made a big fuss when I finished quickly, and asked me to leave. I would not, however, as I had negotiated to stay for the whole night. But she argued that it was only for as long as I took to finish my task. She said that if I wanted to do it again, it would cost the same amount of money all over again. I was very angry at this and argued for a long time, at which she said that since I was wasting her time by arguing, she would charge me one drachma for that too. I refused to pay, but then suddenly, a man appeared from the room next to hers. He was one of the tallest men I had ever seen.

'What is the problem?' the giant snarled.

I was at a loss at this sudden development, as Eudora had told me that she was unmarried. But it turned out that the man was her husband and he allowed his wife to work at night to increase his earnings!

As all the other Helots were busy with their business and even the Spartan guards had found some women, I could call on no one for assistance. I had to pay the sum she asked for, as I did not want to create an embarrassing situation for myself.

When I emerged from Eudora's home with her husband scowling at me, I found Zanylos and Trilomachus waiting for me outside. I decided to teach Eudora's husband a lesson.

'I desire that you, my friend Zanylos, and you, Trilomachus, should avail of Eudora's services. I think we have a long journey ahead and being with a woman will help us suffer our hardships better,' I said.

Zanylos was much embarrassed by my offer, though when I insisted, he agreed, and Trilomachus was only too happy to accept. Zanylos took me aside to inform me that Trilomachus had stolen two talents from Cnidus's house since he knew where Cnidus hid his treasure and Zanylos had agreed with the plan because Cnidus had lied in front of the Gerousia and got us all into trouble.

The stolen talents had been strapped under provisions on Cnidus's two horses and had been left under guard with a boatman, who had been told that a merchant from Crete wanted to take his goods to the coast and on such a pretext they had hired his services. Trilomachus said that the boatman's name was Masicus and he was a Spartan. He was the same Masicus whose wife Petra was being courted by Cnidus. Hearing this, I was much agitated because I didn't want to involve any Spartan in my escape. But Trilomachus said that Masicus was a fool's fool and wouldn't guess anything. All I had to do was dress like a Helot and not speak in front of him.

In spite of these exhortations, I wasn't too convinced and felt that Trilomachus had made a wrong decision to involve someone like Masicus. But he said that only Spartans could ply boats on the river in the night: they were so fearful of a possible Helot uprising that they had taken away their right to do so. This being the case, and with Trilomachus knowing no other Spartan who owned a boat, there wasn't much he could do in the matter.

Zanylos also informed me that this Masicus was in size and shape a match for Eudora's husband and had been promised three hundred drachmas for the journey. Whereupon a plan developed in my head and, after I had struck a deal for both Zanylos and Trilomachus with Eudora, I proceeded to load the boat alongside Trilomachus while Zanylos was with Eudora.

Masicus turned out to be quite a character. Perhaps even taller than Eudora's husband, he slept on his boat cross-legged, and upon hearing me approach, he got up like a lamb and greeted me with more spontaneity than Spartans are known for.

After setting him to the task of loading the boat with the goods from Cnidus's two horses, I had Trilomachus tell Masicus that he would have to collect half of his three hundred drachmas from a woman in Zeros who was known as Eudora; he would have to go there in an hour's time, as soon as Trilomachus came back with Zanylos.

Trilomachus, on the other hand, was to tell Eudora that she would have to satisfy another customer by the name of Masicus, who was a giant, and she could then collect fifty drachmas from him. When Trilomachus and Zanylos came back together, both having had their time with Eudora, they sent Masicus on his way to collect his advance. We told him that he would have to treat the woman Eudora very gently since she was a friend and liked giants very much. However, we warned him that her husband was a giant like him and prone to lies, and if he started misbehaving with him, he was to break his leg and come back as fast as he could – we would be waiting for him. Masicus nodded with great enthusiasm and was much intrigued by Eudora even before he met her. And as soon as he left, we made off with his boat, laughing heartily.

Later, I learned that Masicus had been taken in by Eudora, and when she demanded her fifty drachmas, Masicus, who had none at all, was flabbergasted and demanded his three hundred drachmas, at which time Eudora's husband butted into the room. Since Masicus had already been warned about him, he instantly set upon the man and a terrific fight ensued, as both were evenly matched. The ruckus woke up all the Helots who were having a good time in Zeros and brought the Spartan guards to the scene.

It took five men to break up the scramble between Masicus and Eudora's husband; Masicus emerged with a broken jaw and Eudora's husband's nose was broken in two places. The Spartan guards arrested Masicus on the spot, even though he was a Spartan, as it was assumed that he had wanted to have Eudora without any price. All the other prostitutes came out in support of Eudora and started berating Masicus and throwing small stones at him. Zumidos then gave orders for everybody to leave the scene without a roll call and, as a result, the Spartans came to know of my disappearance only in the morning, by which time we were many plethrons away from Sparta.

However, once the roll call was taken and my disappearance noted, Zumidos set up an enquiry to get to the bottom of my escape and Scion was held the culprit, as it was he who had come up with the idea of the trip to the prostitutes. But since it was felt that no good would be achieved by reducing the fighting force, he was given only fifteen lashes as punishment and was allowed to remain in the force that was to join the Thebans and Athenians at Chaeronea.

But a stranger fate awaited Masicus. After he was arrested for improper fornication, his wife Petra turned against him and Cnidus ran away with her to Boetia, repenting for having misbehaved with Harmodius, Zanylos and me, for now he believed that it was his worship of Apollo in the manner suggested by Lasidomus that had finally appeased the Gods and got him Petra. Frankly, I am not fully convinced that it was not Harmodius who, in some way, influenced this outcome, for Cnidus performed the rituals suggested in good faith, and perhaps for the Gods it is the depth of feeling that counts rather than the procedure that priests follow for sacrifice. As for poor Masicus, though I never felt any repentance for having played the prank on him that eventually lost him Petra, I did have an opportunity many years later to make amends to him. To that story we shall come in due course.

After we had travelled a considerable distance by boat, we took to shore, as Trilomachus warned us of rapids ahead. By this time, I had also started questioning the presence of Trilomachus. Because of the easy manner in which he had become disloyal to his master, the doubt arose in my mind that at the first opportunity he would do to me what he had done to Cnidus. Such being my feeling, I decided to part ways with him through a ruse. I told him that Harmodius had warned me that if I escaped, I should be sure and not travel with more than two people, for if we were three, we would get caught by the Spartans.

On hearing this, Trilomachus became scared and asked what was to be done. Since I had no desire to use his stolen money, I told him that he could go and buy four horses. Two of these he was to take for his own use and the remaining two horses he was to hand over to Zanylos and me, as we had plans to get to Attica.

Trilomachus then asked where he was to join us. Not willing to annoy him with the truth, I said: 'You are to meet us within fifteen days at the temple of Athena in Athens. You are to travel in a manner that does not attract any attention, for there are many robbers and dangers on the way. It will be better for you to use unused roads and avoid the main pathways. If you don't find us at the temple of Athena, you are to presume that we have been captured by the Spartans and proceed independently from there on.'

Within half a day, Trilomachus and Zanylos went and bought four horses; luckily, there were some Helot settlements nearby. The Helots did not ask many questions, but they charged twice the normal rate and the horses were not the best, but they were healthy and without disease and served our purpose.

And so Zanylos and I parted ways with Trilomachus. After we had gone some distance, Zanylos confided in me that he was happy that Trilomachus was no longer with us, for he did not trust the man, and he asked me when it was that Harmodius had given his advice about the escape. Upon coming to know that Harmodius had given no such advice and that it was only a ruse of mine to get rid of Trilomachus, he was even happier and said he could trust my judgment henceforth.

It took us ten days to reach Nisea. We avoided the city of Tegea, as the Spartans could have sent soldiers there to look for me. Through back ways, we reached Corinth and, without stopping, crossed the Isthmus on our way to the port of Nisea, where Phormio was to meet me. But, though I waited at the harbour for two days and visted all the taverns, there was no news of him. I even checked at the temple of Apollo in Nisea and the port magistrate's office whether a person by the name of Phormio had left a message for anybody, but drew no response. So, assuming that he had come and gone, I left for Athens with Zanylos.

Athens was abuzz with orators who were making speeches against King Philip of Macedonia. Chief amongst them was Demosthenes. The city was preparing for war and there was a flurry of activity. People coming to the city were being checked for hidden weapons and being interrogated to determine if they were Macedonian spies.

Since neither Zanylos nor I had come to Athens before, and had heard so much about it as the centre of the Greek world, we absorbed everything like children. We took lodgings in a tavern and enquired about the whereabouts of the famous temple of Athena, but we were told that there were three. When we asked which was the main one, the people said each had its own followers, who considered theirs the main temple. So I asked which was the biggest and the oldest, and they pointed out one near the Parthenon and said it was the biggest, but another temple outside the city was the oldest. Presuming that Trilomachus would come to the biggest temple, thinking it was the main one, I enquired about the name of the chief priest there. It was Calliphus, son of Aristomus, and he was from Crete. I learned that he was the chief organizer of the debates against King Philip. He would gather an audience of the worshippers of Athena, who would come at his bidding, and to this ready audience Demosthenes and others would speak. Slowly, more and more people would join the gathering and it would become a huge crowd.

It took me half a day to locate Calliphus. I found him finally at a magistrate's office, where he was involved in legal hostilities with an aristocrat called Timines, son of Claus, who had made a portion of the temple's land in the countryside his own and refused to part with it, claiming falsely that it was land his father had bestowed upon the temple temporarily. This much I gleaned from the proceedings at the magistrate's office.

Calliphus was in tears when he came out. I knew not whether to approach him in such a state, but he came on his own to me and asked what I was waiting for. I told him my business and requested him to keep the horses in the temple stable till a certain Trilomachus came by and identified himself. I also told him that if the person didn't turn up, he could keep the two horses as a gift.

Calliphus then asked me about my antecedents. And when I gave him a summary of what I had been through in the last five months, beginning with the death of my father and the escape from the Spartans, he looked at me with great interest and invited me to his house in the evening to meet the great orator Demosthenes and tell him my story. I accepted his invitation, as I was eager to meet Demosthenes, whose fame had travelled all through Hellas.

For the remainder of the day, I searched for Pythagoras. Though people knew about him, I could find none who knew the location of his dwelling. Then I learned that Caric, son of Tempos, had been appointed one of the Athenian generals to lead the fight against the Macedonians. Thinking that Pythagoras might be one of his officers, as he was well versed in military matters, I sent Zanylos to make enquiries, and sure enough, Pythagoras had been put in charge of the javelin throwers. Zanylos, after enquiring about the whereabouts of his house, took me there in the evening, and Pythagorus was delighted to see me.

Said Pythogoras: 'Your friend Phormio came to see me two weeks ago and left a sum of one thousand drachmas to be given to you when you came to Athens. I came to know from him of the events that happened after you left Olympia. He told me that you were in the custody of the ephor at Pylos. I was sorry to hear about the murder of your uncle and mother and also Pindar at the hands of the Macedonians and I was worried about you. But you must forgive me for not having come to your rescue, as we are in the midst of preparing for war ourselves. And I must also tell you that your friend Phormio himself came to much grief and is currently in custody in Athens.'

This came as a big surprise to me. Pythagoras then told me the whole story.

Said Pythogoras: 'When Phormio left Pylos for Lesbos, he stopped at Argos to deliver some goods. There he learned that a Phoenician pirate by the name of Ahinadab had waylaid ten Persian ships carrying supplies of arms and other materials as well as a treasury of two hundred talents for the island of Thamos, which was at war with the Macedonians and was being aided by Persian, Byzantine and Athenians soldiers. Thamos is just five days rowing from the city of Amphipolis in Macedonia and Philip had declared war on it for its failure to pay its annual tribute for the past two years; it was a sum that he needed to prepare for his Persian campaign. He then sent a few vessels to Thamos to intimidate them. The king of Thamos, Dorkis, somehow managed to repel the forces, aided by bad weather. However, expecting a larger force to be sent to subdue him, he sent a herald to the king of Persia to ask for aid; he was provided with the same expeditiously. It was these vessels carrying the aid to Thamos that had been intercepted by the pirate Ahinadab.

'Since Phormio was good friends with Ahinadab, both belonging to the same village in Phoenicia, he changed course to meet Ahinadab, who he learned was resting on an island in the Aegean Sea. He made there with haste as he saw in this act of piracy some opportunity for himself. Meeting Ahinadab on the island which was known to Phoenicians as the home of Ahirom, Phormio struck a pact with him to sell the captured arms and ships to a city in Euboea, where a Macedonian garrison was engaged in organizing purchases for King Philip's many wars, specially the coming one in Chaeronea.

'The Macedonian garrison at Euboea was new and under siege from the citizens of the island. They were much in need of armaments for themselves, as well as for Philip's main army, which was building up in Elateia and would soon move to Chaeronea. The ten ships had enough arms to equip five thousand soldiers. In the meantime, the Persian governor in Lydia by the name of Spithridates, who had organized the shipment on behalf of the Persian king, was aghast that the ships had been taken by pirates. He had the sailors who managed to escape flogged and then sent back to negotiate with Ahinadab terms of purchase of their own ships!

'Not wanting the consignment to reach the Macedonians at any cost, for they knew of the ambitions of King Philip to make war on Persia and because a Macedonian ascendancy in Hellas would be detrimental to Persian interests, Spithridates offered to buy back the arms from Phormio at two times the market rate. When the Macedonians came to know of this, they offered to equal the price the Persians were willing to pay, so that they could have quick possession of the arms, as the Persians had made them to the specifications of the Greek hoplites and the Macedonians intended to pass them on to their partners-in-arms, the Thessalians, who were facing a shortage. In so doing, the Macedonians were also ensuring that the Persians didn't get repossession of the arms, as they would then send them on to the island of Thamos, against whom the Macedonians were intending to send another expedition.

'So Phormio passed on the arms to the Macedonians, as the Persians had asked for two weeks' credit while the Macedonians were paying on the spot. After splitting the proceeds of the Macedonain payment in half with Ahinadab, Phormio proceeded to Lesbos, where his original business lay, and later returned to Nisea to find me and honour his word to you.'

'Phormio is a friend of Ganymede. And it was Kelos who sent me to Ganymede to recover in his asclepeion. I am happy that Phormio turned out to be so adventurous,' I said.

'Well, the tale begins to sour here. When Phormio reached Athens, he found me and delivered the one thousand drachmas meant for you. He also gave me the news of all your troubles. But he was arrested the same day by an Athenian magistrate for being a Macedonian spy! It happened thus: a contingent of Persian emissaries had come to Athens to meet Demosthenes, for he had asked for help from the Persian king in the coming battle against the Macedonians at Chaeronea. One among that group was a sailor from the vessel which had been snatched by the pirate Ahinadab and he had also subsequently been part of the party that had negotiated unsuccessfully with Phormio. Recognizing Phormio near the temple of Athena, this Persian narrated the entire story to Demosthenes, who promptly moved the law courts and prevailed upon a magistrate to arrest Phormio at the behest of the Persians.

'The Persians wanted to take Phormio into custody and sail back with him to Lydia and produce him before their governor Spithridates, so that he could make an example of him that would deter the pirates from ever touching a Persian ship. Since there are no laws that deal with handing over a foreign citizen on Athenian soil to another country, Phormio moved the matter legally through a friend of his, who happens to be the aristocrat Timines, son of Claus. Timines is a lawyer of great eminence and through his power of oratory he has held sway over the council. And there the matter rests.'

Some part of this story Phormio himself had told Pythagoras and some of it he had got from others. I felt sorry that it was because of his rendezvous with me that Phormio had ended up in this plight.

'I will need some help in the matter then, Pythogoras. I would like to go and meet Phormio wherever he is in custody,' I said to Pythagoras.

'That is easily done. I will write an introductory letter for you to the jailor Aumides, who is a friend of mine, and you shall be able to meet Phormio,' said Pythagoras.

I immediately set about gaining access to Phormio, and he was overcome to see me, having imagined on many occasions that the Spartans must have put me to death.

He had much more to add to what Pythagoras knew. I first assured him that Pythagoras had handed me the money. He was relieved, but added in a whisper that my share was twenty talents and it was in a safe place. He had not wanted to hand it all over to Pythagoras as he was not sure whether I lived or had died. After I expressed my ignorance about the 'share' he mentioned, Phormio explained further.

Said Phormio: 'To seal the deal with my friend Ahinadab the pirate, I had to offer him some advance, and I therefore used all the money that you had given me for the purpose and some of my own as well. Having made a handsome deal with the Macedonians, I intended to pass on the benefit to you as well. From the total of sixty talents that I made, I calculated your share to be twenty talents, after giving Ahinadab a fifty per cent share. All this I have stowed in one of his ships on an island which only I know of. I have but to send word through one of my sailors and the money will arrive within seven days. This island is close to the Pireus harbour, and even the Athenians know little of it. Those that do know, don't venture there, as they have been warned by their forefathers that it is a place of strange and untoward happenings.'

Phormio said that Ahinadab had seized fifteen ships in all. Five were still in Phormio's possession on that same island and were full of arms. He had hidden them carefully in a cave and only his trusted sailors knew where they were. He wanted to know if I could use this information to somehow to get him out of his current predicament. Even though he had an escape plan ready, he did not want to attempt it for fear that he might get caught and the Athenians would then hand him over to the Persians; this move, at the moment, was being deftly opposed by Timines with his legal wranglings.

I told him that I had been invited by Calliphus, the chief priest of the Athena temple, to meet Demosthenes that night. If Phormio agreed, I could mention that there were five ships full of arms that could be delivered to aid the allies against the Macedonians, and they would be foolish not to make use of these. In return, they should release him. Phormio weighed this proposal and then asked whether I could put it to the Athenians without involving him, as that way they would not have a reason to torture him. I told him that if I put as condition his release from prison, they would understand there was a link, so I would have to do it in a manner that suspicion did not immediately fall on him. Phormio was relieved, but he was also worried they would find out that I had met him in prison. Fortunately, Pythagoras's letter didn't mention me by name, it had simply said to the jailor Aumides that the bearer of the letter be allowed to meet Phormio.

Thus, with a mission to save Phormio, I reached the priest Calliphus's house in the night. There was already a gathering and Demosthenes was arguing with Timos whether they should accept the hundred-odd contingent from Sparta, considering that they were all Helots and the Spartans were not disposed to sending their main body of troops. This was the same Timos whom the Macedonians had promised to bribe in Olympia during the Games. Of course, only I knew this and I felt I could utilize this piece of information now for the release of Phormio.

Seeing me, Calliphus promptly jumped up and spread the word that I was the person who had escaped from the Spartans and the great Augusta had made a prophecy in the Spartan Gerousia that I would some day be a big thorn in the side of the Macedonians. The Athenians had apparently met Augusta on many an occasion at Delphi and had a high opinion of him, more so perhaps because he was not a Spartan by birth and spoke his mind without fear of consequences. Both Demosthenes and Timos greeted me personally, as they were part of the Athenian delegation to the Games at Olympia and had witnessed my exploits in the chariot race.

Calliphus then narrated, for the benefit of many others, how the Macedonians had killed my father, a Macedonian himself, and how I had avenged his death by winning the chariot race at Olympia. This fact put me in great honour amongst the persons there, and though Demosthenes didn't address me, he looked at me with interest, as if wondering what use I could be put to.

They were all curious about what had brought me to Athens. I said that having heard of the coming battle at Chaeronea with the Macedonians, I had come to help in any way I could, and that pleased them.

Demosthenes then asked me if I did not feel strange supporting an effort against the Macedonians when my father had been a Macedonian himself.

I replied: 'I was born in Eleia and consider myself an Olympian, having grown up in that city, and though I can also speak in a Macedonian accent, I hate the Macedonians, as they murdered my parents, my uncle Nicias and my best friend Pindar and commited other crimes to which I was witness. A desire for revenge burns in my heart;

it will not be assuaged till I have avenged all their deaths.' Demosthenes was reassured by my answer, for he could sense it was true.

The Athenians soon forgot about me, however, and became busy talking among themselves. Demosthenes was debating whether it would be appropriate for him to take to arms in Chaeronea, as he was getting old. Timos was insisting that he should go, as he was the one responsible for the alliance between the Athenians and the Thebans and the Thebans would lose confidence if he did not. Calliphus, on the other hand, was insistent that Demosthenes stay in Athens and put all his energies into organizing more allies, arms and equipment, at which he was good.

Then there was Hypereides, who expressed the apprehension that using festival money for the purposes of war may not be supported by the people in the long run, as they had grown used to the festivities and looked forward to them every year. Apparently, Demosthenes, with the aid of Lycargus, who was the controller of the festival fund, had appropriated a major portion of it, to be used by the army and the navy. The need for funds had arisen because of King Philip's recent actions, wherein Cottyphus, a Thessalian general appointed by the Amphictyonic council to pursue war against Amphissa, had abdicated responsibility because the Amphictyonic states were sending neither men nor material to aid the war against Amphissa, which had violated the holy plains of Cirrha by cultivating grain there. The council had appointed Philip as the general and he, instead of moving against Amphissa, had sent his armies to Elateia and fortified the city. This act of Philip had raised the fears of both Athens and Thebes and prompted the Athenians led by Demosthenes to make an alliance with the Thebans. And it was his successful diplomacy which had led to his being conferred the golden crown after a proposal for the same was moved by Demomeles and Hypereides.

As everybody got drunk on wine at Calliphus's place, Timos asked Demosthenes whether he preferred this golden crown which had been conferred upon him at the festival of Dionysia, or the one which had been given to him two years before that, at the Great Dionysia, for his efforts in Byzantium, when he organized a league against Philip consisting of Corcyra, Megara, Corinth and Acarnania, which formed under the leadership of Callias of Chalcis. Demosthenes, after much silent deliberation, said that the first time one gets the crown is always special, so he would have to give his vote for the crown he received at the Great Dionysia.

Timos, however, maintained that, in his judgment, this year's golden crown was more important. For, if Demosthenes had not managed an alliance with the Thebans, Philip would surely have been eyeing Athens itself as a prize. Calliphus then remarked that if Philip wasn't defeated in the battle of Chaeronea, this might well happen. Everybody fell silent at this remark, for it was not an eventuality they wished to consider.

Timos broke the silence by saying that he had to leave early in the morning for the Pireus harbour and so wished to take leave of Calliphus. Even though everyone insisted that he stay, he left the premises, and I slipped out unseen behind him. I caught up with him a few plethrons from Calliphus's home and addressed him thus: 'It was a great honour to have made your acquaintance today. The people of Hellas need someone like you to lead them in the right direction, for tyranny by the name of Philip looms large.'

He was much flattered by my words and held my hands and said: 'Son of Nicanor, any help I can render you I would be happy to discharge, as your victory at Olympia was great indeed.'

I said: 'I once overheard Polemon, the Macedonian, talk about you when he was helping Argus to practise with my father. He had many good things to say about your prowess in oration, and how he enjoyed meeting you. Even his servant Zanus admired your talents and told me he had never met anyone who could use words so powerfully, not even the great Demosthenes.'

Upon hearing the names of Polemon and Zanus, the face of Timos went white, for he knew that I knew of the transaction that was supposed to have taken place between him and Polemon, even though I had not mentioned it. He looked away and walked quickly into the night.

The encounter with Timos gave me confidence, for though I had suffered much until then and faced danger, the fact that I could approach and deal with aristocrats such as Timos on my own gave me a sense of added strength. If I could do it with Timos, I thought, I could do it with others.

But it was also dangerous, and perhaps that was the reason I enjoyed it. For an accusation against Timos for having considered a bribe from the Macedonians would be detrimental to his standing: at present, he was next only to Lycargus and the deputy controller of the festival funds. An accusation would start an inquiry and, depending upon which quarters the accusation came from, he would have to sit out of office for the duration of the inquiry.

I went back then and managed to get Demosthenes alone with Calliphus. I offered him the sum of two talents for the war fund, which he was managing from private sources. He was much moved and surprised by the offer and asked how I could afford such a sum. Without answering his question, I asked whether they were in need of arms and ships, as I knew of a Helot fishing village near Argos that had recently seized many Persian ships bearing arms and was looking for buyers. They could be got at a very low price, or perhaps nothing at all, if we were able to convince them of the importance of defeating the Macedonians.

Demosthenes was at once interested and wanted to know how soon a message could be sent to them to negotiate the matter. I told him that since one of the Helot pirates was in town and looking to see if he could get the Athenians interested in the ships, no time would be lost. I said that I had met him recently at Argos and struck up a friendship, and the Helot was very surprised to see me in the market square, having come today himself, and it was a most amazing coincidence. Demsothenes asked to be taken to the person immediately, as he felt it was a miraculous intervention from heaven. Since the Athenians had been charged to equip the allies, they were looking for ironsmiths to make arms and protective gear as quickly as possible, as they were running against time.

'I am supposed to meet the Helot in the morning tomorrow. You are more than welcome to accompany me, Demosthenes, provided you promise that no harm will come to him,' I said.

Demosthenes agreed to the condition and so, the next day, I prepared Zanylos for the encounter. Since Zanylos was a Helot, there was no need for him to pretend to be one. He priced his cargo at twenty talents, after describing all the goods therein, and asserted that the whole contraband was worth more than a hundred talents. It was only because he hated the Macedonians, for having killed his brothers, that he was willing to settle for such a low price.

Demosthenes replied that even twenty talents was too much for the festival fund to organize, as the war effort was eating up funds in all directions. But he said he would get back to Zanylos after talking to Lycargus, and after ascertaining that it would take seven days for the ships to be in port from the time that terms were decided, he left, directing me to meet him at Calliphus's house in the afternoon.

When we met again in the afternoon, Demosthenes told me that Lycargus had sanctioned only fifteen talents for the purchase and wondered whether Zanylos would agree to that price. I told him that

I could go back to Zanylos and find out. With this excuse, I returned within half an hour and told him that Zanylos had agreed to seventeen talents, but in return for having reduced the price by three talents, he wanted the release of a prisoner now in custody of the Athenians.

Demsothenes readily agreed to the proposal, but said that no advance would be paid as the condition of the goods was not known. I said then that Zanylos wouldn't agree to such a condition, as he feared that once he reached the Pireus harbour with the ships, they would be seized and he would get no money at all. Demosthenes, however, insisted this would not be the case, and so I took leave of him once more as if to go and consult with Zanylos. Returning after half an hour, I told him that Zanylos was willing to accept the condition if the prisoner was released in time for him to travel in his boat, for he was the most knowledgeable about the seas and would help in getting the ships to port as quickly as possible.

Demosthenes appeared pleased at this development and gave his word. He then asked who the prisoner was and I told him with a straight face that he was a Phoenician by the name of Phormio, who had been taken into custody by the Athenians at the behest of the Persians. I said that the Phoenician was a friend of the Helots in Zanylos's village, having done much trade with them at Argos.

Demosthenes was indeed surprised at this development, not having anticipated it. By this time, Calliphus, in whose house this conversation was taking place, returned and, seeing Demosthenes in a deliberative mood, asked him what the matter was. Demosthenes explained to Calliphus the problem that he did not want to annoy the Persians by releasing the Phoenician Phormio as he sought their support against the Macedonians. Calliphus gave him an easy solution to the problem.

'That is simple. All you have to do is fake Phormio's escape from the prison, and that way the blame will not fall on us Athenians,' advised Calliphus.

Demsothenes's face lit up at this scheme, and he sent for Timos to implement it. For, not only was Timos the deputy controller of the festival fund, he was also the deputy controller of the fortifications in Athens, and in that capacity, which the assembly had given him, he exercised control over the jailor Aumides. To him then Demosthenes gave the task of faking the escape of Phormio and, though I had a feeling that Timos suspected there was more to the story, he chose to keep his counsel rather than air his doubts to Demosthenes. My conversation with him the night before had made him fearful of me.

After Phormio learned through Zanylos what had transpired, he was relieved and waited for his fake escape to take place. He also organized with his men, who were in Athens planning his real escape, that if things went wrong, they should sail to the island where the ships were harboured and bring them to the Pireus harbour. I told him that I had secured his release in lieu of the five ships full of arms that he had said his men had custody of. Thereafter, I told Zanylos not to leave the tavern he was in, for fear that he might be seen by Demosthenes and our ruse would be exposed.

SIX

Phormio kept his word. He got the five ships into the harbour at Pireus within seven days. They sailed in the night, taking great risks, and cooked on board. However, it was still too late, as news had come that Philip had moved from lateia and was on his way to Chaeronea and there was a fear that, if he was not checked soon, he might head straight for Athens. Therefore, all the fighting men had left for Chaeronea and the ships stayed at the harbour, waiting to be unloaded.

In Athens, I had thought a great deal about whether to join the Greeks against the Macedonians or not. It was not my urge for revenge which was faltering but my fear that I might die before I achieved it. In war, anything can happen. Though I had left Sparta with the intention not to fight at Chaeronea, it was Pythagoras and Demosthenes who influenced me to proceed to the battlefield. And while it was partly my concern for Harmodius that drew me back, what Pythagoras said also made sense to me.

Pythagoras said: 'If you do not fight at Chaeronea, there will be people who say that Nicanor's son escaped from Sparta because he was scared of fighting the Macedonians, even though they murdered his father. But I know that you are no coward. You are the son of Nicanor, and he was a lion amongst men.'

Demosthenes, on the other hand, insisted that it was the duty of every right-thinking Greek to oppose the Macedonians, who were barbarians and didn't respect the voice of the people, and the masses always suffered when despots came to rule. He also said that he would assign ten men to me, and if I saw Polemon or Zeferino or Argus on the battlefield, I should leap forward and exact my revenge.

That made sense, though I knew that there would be thousands of men on the battlefield and my inexperience would work against me. But I accepted his offer and General Lysicles, son of Tempos, introduced me to the ten men on the wagon trail, only two of whom were full-time soldiers. Their names were Agos and Dorian.

Agos, son of Lemnos, was from Ionia and had come as a bodyguard to Minos, who was the chief of a delegation which had come to Athens demanding help against the Macedonian general Parmenio, who had established a bridgehead in Asia at the behest of King Philip. The Macedonians had plundered their land for grain and taken many of their women. Coming to know that Athens itself was in danger from Philip, Minos offered twenty of his fighting men to Demosthenes, and Lysicles promptly drafted them, preferring to distribute them all over the fighting ranks according to their skills.

Dorian was a Helot who had escaped from Sparta and, though he had settled in Boetia, he wanted to fight alongside the Athenians rather than the Thebans. He had some issues with the Thebans, having been promised and then refused a tract of land by the local assembly.

The day before the big battle, Agos and Dorian brought news that they had heard Tymos, the lover of Tepidas, say that Tepidas was worried because the Sacred Band was not at its full strength. Tepidas himself was the leader of the Sacred Band. They needed fifty-six more men to reach the figure of three hundred, and it had never happened that the Sacred Band had gone to war with less than three hundred men. Tepidas saw it as a bad omen and was looking desperately to fill the positions.

Earlier in the day, Zumidos had arrived with the Helots and everybody was surprised to see me there with the Athenians. Since I was now outside Spartan territory, Zumidos had no authority over me. Harmodius and Lasimodus were surprised and pleased to see me, and so was Scion, even though Zumidos had had him publicly whipped for having suggested the Helot trip to the prostitute quarter in Zeros, from where I had made good my escape.

Zumidos, though he was allied with the Thebans and Athenians, took me aside. He said: 'You, son of Nicanor, had better not come in front of me in the battlefield, or I will treat you the way I would treat a Macedonian. I will butcher you. You made me look like a fool with your escape from Zeros.'

Not willing to be cowed down by him, I looked him straight in the eye and said: 'It will be a pleasure to meet you on the battlefield, Zumidos, as the Spartans have troubled me enough, and needlessly. By spilling your blood at Chaeronea, I will give them back some of the troubles they have given me.'

Zumidos was surprised by my answer, though I wouldn't say that he was offended. He just smiled at me and walked away muttering: 'Hear, hear.'

Lasimodus, who had heard the exchange, was amused. He thumped my back and said that I was becoming a man. And he went and told the tale to everybody, and the Helots said they would have to keep me away from Zumidos because he was a great swordsman, and I said that I was not worried, for I was Nicanor's son.

The Greek forces at Chaeronea had to assemble quickly because the mercenaries they had posted in the mountain passes to check Philip's advance had been overrun at Amphissa. Also, they wanted to occupy the space between the Acropolis and the river when they faced Philip, for that would protect them from two sides. Harmodius, however, felt that was a bad spot as the statue of Athena in the temple at Chaeronea would then face away from the Athenians. Lasimodus took me aside and told me that Harmodius had had a dream that he would find me at Chaeronea and he had told Zumidos this two days back. Zumidos had then disparaged him, saying he had no time to listen to the dreams of men, and if he did see Nicanor's son, it would be because he was destined to die by his sword. But now, having seen the prophecy come true, he was intrigued, and called Harmodius to his tent and asked him what outcome he saw of the battle tomorrow. And Harmodius said: 'We have to occupy the ground opposite to the one we are now on, as then Athena's eyes will be on us. If we do not, the battle will be lost.'

The Greek alliance at Chaeronea consisted of soldiers from Megara, Leucas, Corcyra, Athens, Thebes and Corinth. Besides soldiers from these provinces, it also comprised five thousand mercenaries. Since the Spartans had not come themselves but had sent a force of Helots, the Athenians had assigned them to fight alongside the mercenaries. They were to hold the Greek frontlines on the left, with the Thebans holding the right, led by the Sacred Band. Zumidos was not too happy to be placed next to the mercenaries, but General Lysicles gave him no option. Vexed at this treatment, Zumidos didn't bring up the subject of the grounds the Greeks were occupying.

But when I told Harmodius about the desperation of Tepidas to bring the Sacred Band up to three hundred, his eyes lit up and he went to see him with his proposal to include fifty-six Helots in the Band, as they were all warriors and lovers. Though Tepidas was dismissive of him initially, Harmodius won him over with his charm and Tepidas, without taking the other Theban generals into confidence, gave instructions to his men to welcome the Helots with open arms. Since quite a few of them had fought the Spartans together and remembered each other, there was no acrimony over Tepidas's decision. In this strange way did Tepidas fulfil his lack of numbers and Harmodius give some of the Helots a higher purpose for the battle the next day. And though Zumidos's party got reduced by fifty-six men, he did not protest, as after Harmodius's gloomy prediction, he had withdrawn into a shell and was preparing for a glorious death, so said Lasimodus.

On the morning of the battle, a dispute emerged amongst the Athenians and the Thebans. The Athenians wanted to offer sacrifice to Athena and the Thebans to Ares, the God of war. The Thebans maintained that their ancestor Kadmos had propitiated Ares after slaying his dragon son and married Harmonia, the daughter of Aphrodite and Ares, and so established a stable rule in the city of Thebes, which he had founded. Since then, the Thebans had always propitiated Ares before the start of a battle.

Demosthenes maintained in private that Athena was more powerful and had always triumphed over Ares. Said he: 'In the battle of the Gods, Ares's spear sailed harmlessly past Athena, but the stone which Athena aimed at Ares hit him in the neck and brought him down. Another account says that she guided the spear of Diomedes to pierce Ares in the belly and make him bleed like a man. Even in the Trojan war, Ares was on the losing side and it was Athena who guided the Greeks to victory. When Ares's son was killed and he himself rushed to battle, it was Athena who took away his spear, shield and helmet and denied him that opportunity. Should we then sacrifice to Ares or Athena in this great battle which will decide the future of our world?'

In this manner did Demosthenes convince the Athenian generals Lysicles and Chares to not bow down to the Theban demand. But Tepidas from the Sacred Band would not bend to the will of the Athenians either and so, as a compromise, it was decided that both Gods would be propitiated. The Athenians would sacrifice ten rams on their side of the field and the Thebans would conduct their rituals to appease Ares on their side. In this manner did they resolve the issue.

Harmodius, who stood and watched the rituals, said: 'By trying to appease both Athena and Ares, the Athenians and Thebans have been able to please neither. In fact, they have made things worse for themselves, as these two Gods are not to be worshipped together; they would then work at cross purposes.'

The day before the battle, I had also come to know that there was a certain Polemon in the ranks of Philip's army. It came about thus: Dorian had met an Euboean scout who had been with the mercenaries guarding the mountain passes at Amphissa. When the passes were run over by the Macedonians, this Euboean scout had been captured along with twenty others. The Macedonians had managed to corrupt five of the captured mercenaries and sent them back to Thebes and Athens to learn about the Greek preparations for the coming battle, and while four of them had been loyal to Macedonian money, Brunic, this Euboean scout, had gone straight to Tepidas, the leader of the Sacred Band, and revealed all to him. Tepidas had taken him to the generals, Lysicles and Chares.

It was this Brunic whom Dorian made friends with by supplying him with greaves for his legs, as personal armour was in short supply and not all soldiers were protected in the manner that they should have been. And it was he who informed Dorian, when asked whether he had heard of a Polemon or Argus or Zeferino in the ranks of the Macedonains, that he had seen and heard a senior Macedonian officer being addressed as Polemon, and the description matched that of the Polemon I knew. After getting this information from Brunic, I was euphoric and prayed to my mother that I might avenge her death.

Once the armies came face to face in battle and the soldiers in the Macedonian phalanx beat their shields with their sword handles, the gloom that had prevailed earlier was forgotten. The Sacred Band snarled like lions and the bugles sounded on both sides. I was with the remaining Helots and my detachment of ten men was in the centre of the Greek lines bordering the Sacred Band. Even before the armies marched to meet each other, I knew that it would be a hard day: you could tell from the Macedonian discipline and the shoddiness of the Greeks. The Macedonian phalanx made some rapid exercises and changed shapes from a square to a rectangle and then separated into two and rejoined again, all in very short time. This caused much silent amazement in the frontlines, though those at the back could not see as clearly, which was for the better. For to see such discipline in the enemy would have reduced their morale further.

The Macedonian right advanced at a slant towards the Greek centre. The first engagement was between the mercenaries before the Athenians and the Thracian peltfasts. Behind the peltfasts were the Macedonian hypaspists and the Macedonain phalanx which was eight men deep. So was the Greek left flank, except for the Thebans, who were twenty-five men deep.

In the first skirmish, the mercenaries pushed the hypaspists back, and then I saw Zumidos lead a charge with ten of the Helots straight into the heart of the Macedonian peltfasts. So furious was their charge that the Macedonians took them to be mad people and withdrew a little. I saw Zumidos kill ten people, and this was even before the entire Greek centre had engaged with the Macedonians. So quick were the movements of his body and hands that he was knifing through the Macedonians; the danger was that he was getting too far into their lines. So the entire Helot contingent broke line to assist Zumidos, and then the other mercenaries followed and they created an infantry wedge into the Macedonian phalanx. Seeing how deep they had proceeded into the Macedonian line, the Athenians too broke ranks and poured into the wedge.

Even Demosthenes urged the men to follow into the wedge. The generals Lysicles and Chares stared stupefied because they had left instructions with all the line commanders not to break line under any circumstances. Their strategy had been to fight initially with locked shields and let the Macedonians come to them instead of the other way around. But within minutes of the two armies coming together, the Spartan Zumidos had wrecked the plan of the generals.

I don't think Zumidos did what he did with any purpose of sabotaging the Greeks. From what Lasimodus had told me, he had prepared for death the whole night and wanted to be glorious in battle. But in battle, individual acts of bravery mean little unless they fall within the overall plan of the commanders.

Because the Greeks rushed forward to pour into the wedge, they moved ahead of the Theban line and a gap of nearly half a plethron emerged between the Athenian and Theban lines. I was right in between them for a while and didn't know whether to move forward or stay with the Thebans. Soon, I couldn't have moved forward even if I wanted to, for the heavy cavalry of the Macedonians thundered into the gap and cut the Thebans off. It was led by Alexander himself. Some of the men had tied black cloth over the eyes of their horses and bells around their legs. The cavalry charge produced a sound like thunder and the ground shook as the horses approached. For many men, it was their first time in front of a cavalry charge and they were fearful. The Greeks, having no cavalry, couldn't face the Macedonians head on. With the heavy cavalry surrounding the Sacred Band on their left and the Macedonian light cavalry charging on their right, they were soon encircled.

So the Thebans met with disaster because the Athenians broke their lines. The Athenians too came to grief because, after Zumidos surprised them with his band of Helots, Scion amongst them, the Macedonians reeled back thinking they were dealing with mad people. The Macedonian commanders, however, quickly rejudged the situation and pretended to withdraw. This coaxed the Athenians further into the wedge of their own making, the men thinking that just a little more had to be done to break through the Macedonian lines. But those were just the hypaspists; the Macedonian phalanx had not even engaged with the Athenians yet. It was the Corinthian unit, in fact, which first came in contact with the Macedonian phalanx at the same time as Alexander headed for the gap with his heavy cavalry. Once the gap was created by the Greeks, the battle was over, for the Macedonians were a professional army and the Athenian side of the Greek forces was composed of part-time soldiers who did not drill together.

I killed my first Macedonian that day at Chaeronea and went on to kill five more. I had a Theban spear in my hand, which is not as long as the Macedonian pike but just a little shorter, and I ran it through their horses first. When they went down, Agos and Dorian pounced on the men with their swords and gave them no chance to recover. I then ran my spear through their chest. But the Macedonians were surrounding us now and the Sacred Band was getting hit by javelins from the light cavalry. Though they fought as one unit, one half was facing the Macedonian heavy cavalry and the other half the light cavalry. In this manner the Thebans were pegged down and because the two cavalries had encircled the Theban Band and were concentrating on them, the rest of the Athenians, who were still at the back of the lines, took the opportunity to escape the battlefield. Demosthenes was one of them.

A segment of the heavy cavalry then headed straight for us and surrounded Agos, Dorian and me. The rest of the men assigned to me by Demosthenes were nowhere to be found, some having been wounded and some taking the opportunity of the rout to run to safety. Seeing us thus surrounded, Harmodius, along with the rest of the Helots in the Sacred Band, broke away to help us. I suspect it was something that Harmodius had told Lasimodus would happen because, on the morning of the battle, Lasimodus had told me: 'Harmodius doesn't want you to stray far from the Sacred Band. He wants you to fight within sight of him.'

Lasimodus gave no reason for this advice from Harmodius despite my asking. I had to pick a fight with Cratinus, the stooge of Demosthenes, who wanted my ten men and me to be stationed alongside Demosthenes. The orator had been getting nervous and wanted to create a tier of men for his own protection. But such was the Greek lack of discipline that nobody questioned me as I moved to be next to the Sacred Band, disobeying the order from Cratinus.

Demosthenes, I came to know later, turned out to be a rather timid soldier, unlike his manner with words. He was one of the first to turn and run after the Macedonian phalanx started advancing and Alexander encircled the Sacred Band with his cavalry. And when he started running, a bush caught his vest and he turned around with great fear, thinking it was a Macedonian soldier who had caught him, and started begging for his life, asking how much ransom the soldier desired! Upon seeing it was just a bush, he was deeply embarrassed and forbade Cratinus, who ran with him, to talk about the episode. But once they were back in Athens, Cratinus told this story to everybody. Some said he was paid by Demosthenes's rival Aeschines to speak about it and add words and actions that were not true, only to humiliate Demosthenes further.

By the time the Helots came to my rescue, led by Harmodius, Tepidas had already fallen next to his lover Tymos and the Band was getting smaller. Even the supporting Theban infantry around the Band was getting slaughtered by the Macedonians, although some managed to escape. Then the battle started between the Helots and the Macedonians. There were just ten Helots now – the rest had died – and the light cavalry continued to hurl javelins at us, which we did our best to ward off with our shields.

At one point, Agos lost his pike and Dorian threw him his. This gave two Macedonian horsemen the opportunity to hit him from behind, but Dorian jumped up behind one of them and used his dagger to slit his throat, then took possession of his horse. This prompted the other Macedonian horsemen to give him chase and thus lessen the number of horsemen we had to deal with. But there were still too many of them, and those who went after Dorian were replaced by others. Those who had chased the fleeing Athenians also came back to where some fight was still left, which was next to the Sacred Band.

I did not see the death of Harmodius or Lasimodus, but I was told later by Agos that it had been glorious and the two together had frustrated the Macedonians for longer than any two men should have.

But when Harmodius killed Busemon, the flagbearer of the Macedonian heavy cavalry, they were all so outraged that they got down from their horses and proceeded to give Harmodius and Lasimodus a quick death before impaling them on their spears. I did not see any of this because I had been knocked over by a horse and had lost consciousness. When I came around, I was lying amidst a heap of bodies, with Agos tending to me.

Part Two

SEVEN

It was in this manner that I ended up as a prisoner of the Macedonians, along with Agos and Dorian. Even though Dorian had managed to escape on horseback, he came back to tend to me, and after the battle, the three of us became inseparable. I came to know later that, the night before, Harmodius had singled out Dorian and Agos amongst the men assigned to protect me and asked Lasimodus to bring both to him so he could have a word with them.

Agos said to me: 'He held our hands and told us about our past. He told us things nobody could have known but us. We felt as if he was transferring some of his life force into us. Dorian felt as though he was dying and I felt as if I would soon become unconscious. Then it all suddenly stopped. He told us that our well-being and future lay with you. He said that we were to always protect you from harm. In doing so, we would take care of all our desires. Both Dorian and I had intended to run away from the battle yesterday, but after we met Harmodius, our reasoning changed. We will therefore be by your side for as long as you want us to be.'

In this way did Harmodius reach out to me even beyond his death.

The Macedonians had butchered the entire Sacred Band and taken more than two thousand Athenians as prisoners. Philip came to inspect the wounded on the battlefield and was much moved to see the bodies of the Sacred Band, even though they were Thebans. He had the bodies counted in front of his eyes and was intrigued when the number was less than three hundred. Somebody pointed out that a group of them had left the main body to fight separately and Philip wanted to get to the bottom of this mystery, for during his imprisonment at Thebes, and later, he had never known of the soldiers in the Band separating to fight elsewhere.

Then, one of the Thebans who had been captured told him that amongst the Sacred Band were a few Helots from Sparta; Tepidas had recruited them just the day before the battle. It was they who had broken off to protect a person known as the son of Nicanor. The

Theban further told him that a person by the name of Harmodius had told Tepidas the night before that he would have to protect the boy, as Zeus himself had told him to do so in his dreams. Tepidas, thinking that the battle would go in favour of the Greeks, had given him permission, specially after Harmodius told him that this Nicanor's son would be a thorn in the flesh of the Macedonians for a long time to come. Tepidas believed Harmodius implicitly, as he had come to know of his powers as a soothsayer. Harmodius had apparently told Tepidas of all that had happened to him over the years and there were a lot of facts which nobody but Tepidas himself could have known. All this had confirmed to him the powers of Harmodius, so when he asked for the indulgence to protect the son of Nicanor, Tepidas had not objected, even though it went against the military discipline of the Sacred Band.

Philip heard this story with great incredulity and ordered Amyntas, son of Pausanias, to get to the bottom of it. Amyntas went to the prisoners to ask who this Nicanor's son was and resorted to bribes and beatings to get the information, but since nobody knew about me, he achieved no success. Agos tore a piece from his tunic and bandaged my face to make it impossible for anyone to recognize me and Dorian cut his hand for blood and wiped it over the bandage. It had rained after the battle and everybody was plastered with mud, so it was difficult to distinguish between people.

Amyntas, not wanting to disappoint Philip, hunted out a Theban who was willing to say that he had seen Nicanor's son die at the hands of the cavalry. Philip then ordered Amyntas to take the prisoner to the battlefield and identify Nicanor's son, and he looked for an hour, but could not find him. Whereupon Amyntas reported back to Philip that many bodies were disfigured beyond recognition and some had been buried, and it was likely that Nicanor's son too was amongst them.

Nobody thought of looking for Nicanor's son among the prisoners till Prince Alexander came around and asked the reason for the commotion. When it was explained to him, he wanted the Theban to have a look at all the prisoners in their custody to see whether Nicanor's son was alive, so Panormus – that was his name – was escorted from prisoner to prisoner. In this manner did he come in front of me too, but he did not pause in his stride nor give me a second look. After all the prisoners had been seen, he reported that Nicanor's son was not to be found amongst them.

Of course, Panormus was a stooge put up by Amyntas to please Philip, but Alexander wanted to meet the Theban who had originally told the story to Philip. His name was Flavius and he said that he had never seen Nicanor's son himself, he had only heard him talked about by Harmodius. And so Alexander ordered for Harmodius's body to be located amongst the corpses.

Flavius took Amyntas to the corpse of Harmodius and the soldiers brought it in front of Alexander. The prince then confirmed with Flavius once again that this was the Harmodius he was talking about, and he said yes. Then one Cleon from the Macedonian heavy cavalry got up and said that this Harmodius was the same person who had killed Busemon, the flagbearer of the Macedonian heavy cavalry.

Everybody looked at Harmodius's corpse with renewed interest, as Busemon was a great hero amongst the Macedonians and known for his toughness in battle. For Harmodius to have got the measure of Busemon was a cause for great awe.

'Tell me, what else do you know about Harmodius and what else did he say about Nicanor's son?' asked Alexander of Flavius.

So Flavius repeated to Alexander what he had told Philip. Then he added: 'Harmodius was a great worshipper of Zeus and he used to have visions. The Spartans, however, had him arrested and sentenced in a matter related to the hijacking of some Spartan triremes by Macedonian troops. This, his friend Lasimodus told me. The Macedonians had come to Pylos looking for the son of Nicanor, who had caused a Macedonian by the name of Polemon much grief in money matters. This Polemon had harmed Nicanor and murdered his wife and other people related to Seleucus. Lasimodus told me that Seleucus intended to kill all the Macedonians who had caused him and his family so much grief. Beyond this, I know nothing of the matter, for when I asked Lasimodus to point out Nicanor's son, he refused to humour me. As to the truth of what he said, I have no idea. You would be a much better judge than me. I only repeat what Lasimodus told me the day before the battle. As far as I know, it could all be lies and Lasimodus could have been spinning a yarn as all Helots are prone to do.'

But Alexander listened intently and then asked his companion Hepasthion to call Polemon. Before Polemon could be summoned, however, a Macedonian by the name of Aristos, who was standing nearby, kicked the corpse of Harmodius, thinking that he would gain favour by this deed from Alexander. Since all this was happening outside the stockade of the prisoners, the Thebans and the Athenians alike shouted at Aristos. Alexander, once he came to know what had happened, having missed seeing the deed, admonished Aristos and ordered ten lashings for him, saying: 'The defilement of a corpse is no mark of bravery, Aristos.'

The prisoners were greatly pleased by Alexander's decision and hailed him. But I personally think that he punished Aristos because he expected the action to receive such a response. If it had not taken place in his presence, he would not have done anything about it and might have even been pleased, for Busemon had been a cavalry officer much respected by the Macedonians.

By the time Polemon came up to the prisoners' stockade, Alexander had already left for his tents and Polemon was escorted there. He walked so close to where we prisoners were chained that I could have touched his robe if I wanted to. But since my face was heavily bandaged, Polemon failed to spot me.

The next time I had a good look at Polemon was when Alexander and Antipater marched all two thousand Athenian prisoners to Athens from Chaeronea, along with the ashes of the cremated Athenians. This happened after two weeks. Philip had sent Demades, who had been taken prisoner at Chaeronea, to the Athenian assembly with a message of peace, and the assembly had responded by sending Demades, Aeschines and Phocion back to Philip with a request to him to release all prisoners. Philip surprisingly acceded to the request; everybody had expected him to take his armies into Attica and ravage Athens for having made battle with him in alliance with Thebes. Alexander went, instead, with terms of peace, whereby Athens lost all her cities on the Hellespont and the Chersonese, but retained Salamis, Delos and Samos and also gained Oropus from Thebes. Philip then placed a Macedonian garrison at Thebes and put his friends who had been exiled from Thebes in charge. He also constituted a council of three hundred to manage the affairs of the state and granted independence to Plataeae and Orchomenus.

Since the terms of peace had been made public even before the Athenians were offered them officially, they were the subject of discussion among the prisoners on the march back to Athens. Some said that Philip was not to be trusted and recalled the time when he had seized Amphipolis, which had the largest gold mines in Greece; when the Athenians objected, he offered them the important port of Pydna in exchange for Amphipolis. But when the Athenians evacuated Pydna, he occupied the port without relinquishing Amphipolis!

But Alexander was just a prince and was travelling with a contingent of only three thousand soldiers, the majority of whom were employed in guarding the prisoners on the march. Though news had leaked that Philip had agreed to the release of the prisoners, he wanted to extract the maximum price from Athens and seek its unconditional support for the campaign that he sought to launch against Persia. And so, while the Macedonian army squatted on the outskirts of Athens, Alexander and Antipater went into the city with just a personal bodyguard to negotiate terms with the assembly, and they stayed in Athens for a month to make alliances with aristocrats and other important people. Alexander also sought out his tutor Aristotle, who lived in Athens, and told him not to worry about any Macedonian aggression.

But the Athenians were throughout in great fear of the Macedonians. There were rumours that the Macedonian terms of peace were a secret ploy to give Philip time to move his army in triremes to the harbour in Pireus and thereby take possession of Athens in a surprise attack and plunder it to his satisfaction.

So full of fear were many citizens of the assembly that they commissioned Demosthenes himself to superintend the repair of the fortifications around the city. Through a private collection of money, they urgently secured a supply of corn from the Black Sea, so that in the event that the rumours were true and the Macedonians laid seige, there would be enough food available for at least four months. A committee led by Lycargus, Demosthenes and Hypereides saw to the financing of the defences and, since people were so fearful, the council even authorized the committee to use festival funds for purposes of defence if the need arose.

It was during this period that Phormio's five ships full of arms proved to be a blessing. The Athenians who had escaped from Chaeronea had shed their arms in order to be able to run faster and so avoid the Macedonians, who ran with their armour strapped to their bodies. Having returned without arms, they were relieved to find the ships waiting to be unloaded at the harbour in Pireus, and Demosthenes was so pleased with Phormio that he admitted him as a guest to his house. The arms were distributed by the men of Timos, who was the deputy controller of the fortifications.

On the march back to Athens from Chaeronea, several incidents of significance occurred. The prisoners moved without chains and were allowed to mingle with one another and the guards were not too strict about checking their movements either. No one was thinking of escape because they knew that Philip had ordered their release after terms were agreed upon, whereas if they were caught while escaping, it would invite harsh measures from the Macedonians. Everybody was willing to endure a few more days of imprisonment.

It was during this time that I planned with Agos and Dorian to find out the identities of the other Macedonians who had accompanied Polemon and Zeferino to Pylos. Though Zanylos had seen six of them, there could have been more.

So I devised a scheme whereby I identified a youth who could pass off for me. He was of my age, and had injured his face in many places; his mouth was swollen and he could not speak clearly. It took Agos, Dorian and me four days to identify the man from amongst the prisoners. After this, Agos promised two hundred drachma to a bold Athenian by the name of Alcibiades if he would perform a series of tasks well. He was to go to Polemon and tell him that he had information that Seleucus, son of Nicanor, was amongst the prisoners and ask for a hundred drachmas to lead him to the right person. After Polemon fulfilled his demand, he was to lead him to the youth we had identified. This youth had no friends and he was in no state to tell anybody where he was from or what his name was, unless of course he knew how to read or write, which appeared doubtful.

Alcibiades was to tell Polemon that the youth had talked in his sleep about how he was planning to kill Polemon and that he had hired assassins for the job. In this manner, Alcibiades was to say, he had come to know of his identity. Alcibiades was also to watch which other Macedonians Polemon discussed this matter with and he was to engage in conversation with them too and find out whether they had also pursued Nicanor's son in Pylos. That way, I would know for sure whether they had been part of the murderous Macedonian party.

Alcibiades did a good job. He approached Polemon in his tent at night and, though initially the guards stopped him from entering, he insisted that what he had to say was only for Polemon's ears and so, after checking him for weapons, they let him into Polemon's presence. He then whispered to Polemon that Nicanor's son was alive and had hired assassins to kill him. Polemon was to be very careful over the next two weeks, he said, as the assassins had already been paid money and they were Ionian mercenaries who had taken an oath to murder him before the next full moon.

Polemon turned white when Alcibiades revealed this to him. He promptly summoned four people. They were Menechus, son of Caunus;

Clearchus, son of Maximus; Leon; and Alcidas. They were all from Pella in Macedonia. After Polemon had brought them abreast with Alcibiades's revelations, he ordered Leon to accompany Alcibiades so that he could have Nicanor's son identified and then have him watched for a day to identify the people he interacted with before taking him into custody.

So Leon kept watch over the youth whom no one talked to for a whole day and reported back to Polemon that Nicanor's son was sick and heavily bandaged because of many injuries and talked to nobody. That evening, Alcibiades got Leon intoxicated with wine and spoke to him of many things, including life in Sparta. Leon told him that he didn't find Sparta attractive at all and neither did Menechus, Clearchus or Alcidas, who had comprised the travelling party of Polemon along with Zeferino and Argus. In this way did Alcibiades discover for me the names of the men I sought.

The youth was picked up two days later for interrogation and such was the excellence of our choice that even Polemon, who had seen me earlier, could not say for sure whether he was Nicanor's son or not. Alcibiades was present while the youth was being questioned and he reported that the youth stuttered and stammered, so Polemon was sometimes sure that he was Nicanor's son and sometimes he had doubts and thought that he was just a deranged Athenian who had heard Alexander in conversation next to the stockade and was imagining things in his dreams.

Polemon refused to pay Alcibiades the remaining hundred drachmas due to him till such time as it was resolved that the youth was Seleucus, son of Nicanor. And so the questioning of the youth went on until we were a day's march from Athens. At this time, a certain Euboean by the name of Lamachus, who had been in fever and had lain in the wagons for the sick, emerged and said that the youth was his brother Gongylus. He even produced witnesses and Polemon, being convinced, released the youth to Lamachus's custody.

After Gongylus was released, Polemon started hunting for Alcibiades, but by that time the prisoners had already been released, as Alexander, even before placing the Macedonian terms of peace to the Athenian assembly, had decided to free them from bondage. This decision gained him much popularity in Athens and quashed rumours about a Macedonian invasion, though some people were still sceptical and went to Lycargus with a plan to hold Alexander and Antipater hostage. Sensibly, Lycargus rejected the plan outright and put these men in temporary confinement for the time Alexander was there, so they didn't attempt anything foolish.

It is my assessment that Polemon realized after he couldn't find Alcibiades that he was the victim of some mischief and, wanting to get to the bottom of it, he made a request to the Athenian committee through Antipater that Alcibiades be produced with regard to a personal matter. Earlier, while negotiating the terms for peace, the Macedonians had asked for thirty Athenians to be handed over to them for trial, and now the committee headed by Lycargus dealt with Polemon's request in the same way they had dealt with the request for the other names: they said that the person had absconded and couldn't be found! Which was not true, as most of the men the Macedonians had asked for were in Athens itself and Demosthenes, who was number onc on the list, was holding meetings at his house, denouncing the terms of peace. But such was his popular appeal that neither Lycargus nor the Macedonians could do anything about it. Though the Macedonians moved the Athenian courts as Greek citizens and demanded that Demosthenes be tried for his offences in inciting people against King Philip, the courts never ruled in their favour.

King Philip of Macedonia, however, was enraged by the story of Nicanor's son and the fact that the Spartans had sent a contingent of condemned Helots to fight against his forces. To teach the Spartans a lesson, he stationed a Macedonian garrison at Corinth and also ravaged Laconia. The new ephors deposed King Zetomandus and put in his place King Aegis, who had to temporarily consent to having a Macedonian garrison outside the city of Sparta. After thus subduing the Peloponnese, Philip returned to Macedonia and prepared for war with Persia.

EIGHT

During the stay of Alexander and Antipater in Athens, many dramatic events took place. After Alexander turned over the urns containing the ashes of dead Athenians from the battle of Chaeronea, a date was set by the assembly for a memorial service and Demosthenes was given the honour of speaking at the ceremony. At this, Antipater remonstrated to Lycargus, but he expressed his helplessness in the matter, as the people would gather in throngs and start chanting Demosthenes's name, and if he wasn't given permission to speak, rioting would break out. But to appease Antipater, he rounded up five of the thirty people whom the Macedonians had demanded and handed them over to him. Out of those five, two were Euoboeans and the remaining three were men who had hurled insults at Antipater when he had come with terms for negotiation to Athens ten years ago.

Once Alexander came to know that none of the five had participated in the battle at Chaeronea and two of the three had a physical disability, he ordered their release and thus gained a little more popularity. Lycargus was castigated for having acceded to the wishes of the Macedonians, but I think he had anticipated their release and handed over the five on the list knowing that this would be the outcome. In this respect, he was a clever politician.

With Phormio's ships proving to be so helpful, Lycargus, at Demosthenes's insistence, released fifteen talents from the treasury to me as originally agreed. And Phormio told me where he had stored the twenty talents which were my share of the transaction he had had with the Macedonians and offered to have them delivered to me in Athens. In this manner did I come to possess thirty-five talents, riches far beyond my wildest dreams.

It came about that on the fifth day of their stay in Athens, Antipater himself asked Lycargus if he knew anything about Seleucus, son of Nicanor. Lycargus, not having been briefed properly by Demosthenes, joked that it was arms organized by Nicanor's son that would have greeted the Macedonians had they decided to plunder Athens. Antipater heard all that Lycargus had to say very quietly and proceeded to report it all to Alexander. The report infuriated Alexander so much that he gave secret orders to his companions to hunt out Seleucus and produce him in his presence, dead or alive, before he left Athens.

This information was conveyed to me by the priest Calliphus, whose servant had been temporarily loaned to the Macedonian entourage to facilitate their stay. Alexander and Antipater, it seemed, were housed in two adjoining properties of the Athenian aristocrat Mios, son of Phicias, who was a landowner of repute and belonged to an old aristocratic family of Athens. And it so happened that Calliphus's servant Erineus had been loaned to Mios.

Erineus told Calliphus, who told me, that Alexander was in the habit of performing daily obeisance to the Gods and Goddesses of the city he was in, besides the Gods that he worshipped. Calliphus had trained Erineus in all such matters, and so he was attached to Aristander of Tellimus, who was a soothsayer of great repute and had been with both Philip and Alexander for a long time. According to Erineus, Alexander had made his 'dead or alive' comment with respect to me in the midst of his morning ceremony to Athena.

After getting Calliphus's warning, I went into hiding and communicated with the world only through Zanylos, Agos and Dorian. Though all three were older than I was, they looked to me as their master: such is the affinity that develops when men have faced danger together. In the case of Agos and Dorian, there was also the matter of the promise they had made to Harmodius.

After Chaeronea, I had decided to grow a beard and always had my chest covered so that my wounds could not be seen, though Polemon and Argus were the only Macedonians who would recognize me, Alexander having seen me too briefly in Olympus to remember my face. Once I had grown my hair long and sported a heavy beard, even the few men who knew me by face failed to identify me. I received proof that my new appearance was effective when I walked past Demosthenes at the temple of Athena. Though he looked at me, he failed to recognize me.

Erineus had also informed Calliphus about the whereabouts of Polemon, my chief tormentor. He was staying at the house of Ainis, an aristocrat from the town of Nisea, who had several properties in Athens. Polemon and his murderous comrades Leon, Menechus, Clearchus and Alcidas had been apportioned different quarters of the city to search for me. Erineus got this information from Menelus, one of the wagon drivers of Antipater, who brought in provisions for the morning ceremonies. Menelus got the information from Leon, who had asked him where the best prostitutes could be found in Athens and asked him to arrange a few for himself and his friends. Though he was supposed to be looking for me at the port at Pireus, Leon spent most of his time in a room above a tavern, where he entertained girls whom Menelus procured for him from the prostitute quarters.

Polemon, meanwhile, moved around with bodyguards, believing that Seleucus had sent assassins to kill him; he now believed that Alcibiades was one of them. Alcibiades himself, after receiving the two hundred drachmas from us for his help, was eager for more work and so, at my behest, Agos set him to the task of identifying where the prettiest courtesans could be procured in Athens. For a plan was forming in my mind.

Alcibiades duly came and informed us that there were two sisters, Athele and Carmene, who had been widowed two years ago. They had been married to two brothers who had drowned at sea. Subsequently, they had taken to entertaining aristocrats to make a living and they had a reputation for being very beautiful, though Alcibiades himself hadn't seen them.

I had already put Zanylos on the job of corrupting the wagon driver Menelus without the knowledge of Erineus, for I wanted my plans to be kept secret. And this was what Zanylos reported: 'Menelus owes five hundred drachmas to Phisias, a moneylender in Athens. He has already been beaten up twice by Phisias's men for not paying the usury on time.'

When I heard this, I instructed Zanylos to buy up Menelus's debt from Phisias for four hundred drachmas. Since Phisias was not sure whether Menelus would ever have the money to repay him, he was happy to get at least a major part of it back. Then Zanylos confronted him along with Dorian.

Menelus was in his wagon, going to Pireus with two girls for Leon, when Zanylos spoke to him. He was surprised and troubled, specially when Zanylos talked about impounding his wagon, which he was within his rights to do since it had been committed by Menelus as insurance for his debt. Zanylos also accused Menelus of wasting his time with whores instead of working to pay off his debt. But Menelus pleaded that the women were not for him and he was just making a paltry sum by taking them to a Macedonian named Leon.

Zanylos then made the condition that Dorian would henceforth remain with Menelus as his assistant, accompanying him everywhere, and in this manner ensure that the debt was repaid as quickly as possible. Menelus, having no other option, had to agree. And this is how Dorian made friends with the women Menelus was taking to Leon and came to know that after Leon had recommended Menelus to his companions, Alcidas and Clearchus, they too were expecting him to bring women for them.

At this time, Menelus, not suspecting anything, suggested to Dorian that since he couldn't be in two places at one time, Dorian could take the wagon with the girls to Alcidas and Clearchus while he would take some other girls to Leon. In this way, their time would be well divided and more earnings would accrue. Dorian readily agreed to the proposal as it fit in with my instructions to him.

It was by this strategy that access to the men was obtained. And so Dorian took the whores to Alcidas and Clearchus, who happened to be at Ainis's place, where Polemon also resided. They had been given rooms in the outhouse and that was where Dorian took the two women.

Alcidas and Clearchus weren't too happy with the women, claiming that they were dirty and not deserving of men of their rank. They instructed Dorian to bring them prettier women the following afternoon. By then, Alcibiades had established contact with Athele and Carmene, the two courtesans residing outside Athens, and transacted with them a sum of hundred drachmas each for entertaining the Macedonians for the afternoon.

The killing of Alcidas and Clearchus was elaborately planned by us for the next day. First, Dorian would go to them in the morning and inform them that the women, being from good families, were fearful of being recognized as they approached the house of Ainis, whom they happened to know, and so desired that no guards be around or even servants of Ainis, or their shame would be revealed. Though they might have protection while the Macedonians were around, they would be ridiculed once Alexander left Athens.

Hearing this, Alcidas and Clearchus ordered their entire retinue to go to the port of Pireus and assist Leon in hunting for Nicanor's son while they remained at the outhouse. The guards at the gate were ordered to go to the main house and remain there for three hours, as Clearchus and Alcidas would be entertaining some important Greek spies who worked for Polemon and whose identities had to be protected.

In this manner did the Macedonians expose themselves to danger. As Dorian approached Ainis's residence with Carmene and Athele in Menelus's wagon, the guards left their position and went to the main house where Polemon was. This allowed Zanylos, Agos and myself to climb the wall around the outhouse undetected and hide in the bushes, awaiting a signal from Dorian, who was to wait outside the outhouse as the Macedonians went about their business with Athele and Carmene.

Athele was a beautiful woman and young. Carmene was her elder sister and pretty too, though a little plump. After twenty minutes, Clearchus and Alcidas emerged from the outhouse, arguing about which woman would go with whom, for they both desired Athele. They decided to draw lots and Alcidas called correctly, so he went with Athele. While they argued thus, their backs were to us and we could have easily killed both of them, except for something unexpected that happened: Antipater came to visit Ainis with his entourage of soldiers.

They entered the main gate and headed for the courtyard in the main house. Hearing the commotion, Alcidas and Clearchus came half undressed out of their rooms and, at the same time, a dog started barking at us where we stood in the bushes. The dog's barking attracted the attention of Antipater's guards and they started in the direction of the outhouse. This put Alcidas and Clearchus in great panic and they asked Dorian, who stood silently in a corner, to quieten the dog. Dorian kicked the animal with such force that it yelped and scampered away in the direction of the main house. Then Dorian yelled to the guards that the dog was mad and they had better be careful, on hearing which the guards hastily withdrew to the gate.

By this time, Alcidas and Clearchus were in great palpitation, as Antipater was a very strict disciplinarian, and if women were discovered in their dwellings, he might well determine a punishment for both of them and Polemon too. So Clearchus said to Dorian: 'Depart now with the women as quickly as you can. Bring the wagon to the door so Antipater's guards are not able to see them. We will pay you a sum of fifty drachmas if you do this quickly.'

Alcidas and Clearchus left then, to go up to Ainis's house, and Dorian left with the women in the wagon. The guards didn't bother him. But before Agos, Zanylos and I could jump the wall and leave too, Antipater, Ainis and Polemon emerged from the house and started walking around the grounds. The bushes we were in lay in their path, so we had to swiftly climb to the roof of the outhouse.

As fate would have it, the three of them walked to the walls of the outhouse and stood there talking, and we listened to every word they said.

Antipater was seeking to use Ainis as his intermediary with Lycargus. He told Ainis: 'Since we did not ask for any ransom for the release of the prisoners, we expect to use the Athenian triremes to transport our body of advance troops to Asia. Please make this clear to Lycargus. Philip expects this much. Also, we will need the best Athenian sailors to bring supplies to us to maintain our garrison. I say the best because the Persian navy is strong and they have many allies on the Ionian coast; the Phoenicians are also with them. The only people not with anybody are the pirates.'

Ainis assured him that he would get Lycargus to agree to the proposal, specially as it was a business proposition and the Macedonians would be paying the sailors directly. He added: 'There are also many wealthy people in Attica who own transports, we could utilize their services too for Philip's campaign.'

'It should be the campaign of all the Greeks and not Philip alone, Ainis,' said Antipater. And Ainis replied: 'That is true.' And Polemon remained silent as he was too junior to speak in the presence of Antipater unless he was asked something.

Then Antipater turned to Polemon and ordered him to find out how many private triremes he could organize from the Pireus harbour to go to the Ionian coast and in how many days and also what wages he would have to pay the sailors and what the fee would be for the owners of the boats. Then, surprisingly, he went on to ask him about the matter with Seleucus, even as I lay twelve hands away!

Polemon replied: 'He has sent assassins for me and Alexander and we have sent search parties throughout Athens, but the Athenians are not helping us in the matter.'

'Well, if he has sent assassins, you are lucky, for they will be caught and you will be closer to finding out where he is. Ainis, I would like you to also bring up this matter of Nicanor's son with Lycargus. We would like all cooperation from you, for we have acted in good faith. Even though we defeated Athens on the battlefield, we still treat you like an independent ally,' said Antipater.

'King Philip wants us to establish a bridgehead on the Ionian coast, to prepare for the Macedonian army next year. Tell Lycargus that I want all possible help to be extended to that effort, which will be headed by Parmenion,' Antipater continued. 'Also, convey the message to

Demosthenes that we would not like him to publicly oppose the dream of Philip to conquer Persia. If he does, we will find him and lynch him, whatever the price.' With this threat, Antipater dismissed Ainis, saying that he had some private matter to discuss with Polemon.

He then addressed Polemon. 'How do your talks with Timos proceed?'

'Timos has agreed to invite all the Athenian aristocrats to dinner tonight to meet Alexander. He will also invite you in order to thank you for bringing back the ashes of the Athenian dead. And he will invite Demosthenes also. He has agreed to a sum of thirty talents to poison Demosthenes and Charimedus at the dinner – this Charimedus, I am told, has sworn to devote his life to resisting King Philip.

'The plan is that Timos will mildly poison several Macedonians to make it look like an Athenian plot against them, instead of the other way round. He has told us to bring our own poison so that we may become dizzy and nauseous, and that will make everybody think it was a plot to destroy the peace between the Macedonians and the Athenians. That way, suspicion will not fall on Timos. He also wants to know if there is any Macedonian we can actually poison so that Demosthenes's death will be deemed an accident,' said Polemon.

Antipater remained silent for a long time after hearing Polemon and then he asked: 'How much do you trust Timos?'

'As much as you can trust any Athenian. But we pay Timos after the deed is done. He takes only a ten-talent advance, which he has promised to return if Demsothenes survives,' said Polemon. 'We have nothing to lose.'

'The people of Athens adore Demosthenes, so we have to make it look like an accident or we will have a rebellion in Athens, which is not what Philip wants. It would only take away attention from the conquest of Persia,' said Antipater.

'The dog will die,' declared Polemon. 'And to make it all appear entirely above board, we will kill a few of our Platean prisoners too, after dressing them as Macedonians.'

NINE

We had to stay on the roof for another hour before Antipater left Ainis's house along with his guards. In the evening, I met Demosthenes and asked him if he had received a dinner invitation from Timos; he said yes. I told him immediately not to go to Timos's place the next day, as there was a conspiracy to poison him. He was tremendously agitated and wanted to know where I had learned my facts. I said I would tell him everything, but first I needed a favour.

I then requested him to appoint Phormio as the principal contractor who would supply the Macedonians with any triremes they might require to transport troops and supplies to Asia. This he readily agreed to, as the Macedonians had not made a formal request for these until then and Demosthenes didn't think they would, so he conceded a favour which he thought was worthless.

It was then that I told him the whole story of how I came to be on the roof of Ainis's outhouse. After hearing my account of the conversation between Antipater, Ainis and Polemon, Demosthenes cursed Timos and wanted to know if Ainis was in the conspiracy as well. I told him he was not, as Antipater had spoken to Polemon about Timos only after dispatching Ainis to talk to Lycargus about the triremes. I also told him how Antipater had wanted Lycargus to aid in the search for Nicanor's son and how he had been told to warn Demosthenes not to say anything publicly against Philip's plan to invade Persia.

Demosthenes was fuming as he listened. Then I gave him an idea.

'You must accept the invitation for dinner at Timos's place and pretend to eat and drink. That way, you will come out alive while the Plateans and some others who the Macedonians also intend to poison, to make it look like a conspiracy against them, will die. And you will come out as the hero for having outfoxed the Macedonians, since they will end up killing and making their own people sick while you will be declared poison-proof,' I said.

Demosthenes was taken with the plan and decided to do exactly as I had suggested. He even had Timos invite a bevy of beautiful women as was his wont, so that the Macedonains would be distracted and would not observe him too closely. Demosthenes hated Timos now for being a traitor, and he did not confide in Lycargus either, for he wanted to be sure that he was not involved in the conspiracy.

The next day, while Timos played host, Zanylos, Agos and I cut off the head of the murderer Leon. It happened this way: Menelus, having been told by Leon to bring a new set of girls, was proceeding to the tavern where he was when, in accordance with the plan, Dorian suggested to him that he should collect the full payment due to him from Alcidas and Clearchus – though they had paid money for them to leave quickly, they hadn't actually paid for the women. It was not the fault of the women, surely, that they had to leave early. Menelus, convinced that this was a good argument, proceeded to Ainis's house, leaving Dorian to take the two women to Leon.

It did not take Dorian long to convince Leon that he was Menelus's assistant and had been sent by him. He told them that Menelus had gone to meet his friends Alcidas and Clearchus, to see if they needed anything. Leon was drunk by then, though the liquor wore off by the time he finished with the women, who were loud and noisy. In fact, the tavern keeper had to come up to Leon's room to warn them to be silent, as they were disturbing the wine drinkers downstairs. But Leon was disrespectful and pushed him down the stairs and started shouting even more loudly, and the tavern owner by the name of Gelon was too afraid to accost the Macedonian. We watched everything while sipping wine in the hall downstairs.

When all of Gelon's customers had left and the whores in Leon's room had departed, he prepared to shut his tavern for the night. But before he did that, Zanylos, Agos and I climbed the stairs to Leon's room. The door being ajar, we entered quickly. While Zanylos clamped his palms over Leon's face, Agos and I tied his hands and legs with rope and overpowered him. Then we lit a lamp so he could observe our faces.

When I introduced myself as Seleucus, son of Nicanor, the blood left Leon's face and he started making strange, choking noises, even though Zanylos had stuffed his mouth with linen. Agos placed the tip of his sword on Leon's throat and Zanylos asked him: 'Who killed Nicanor's wife Stella? Did you, or did Clearchus?'

I took out the linen from Leon's mouth, so he might be better able to speak. But all he said was: 'I don't know anything about it.' Agos then took the linen from my hands and stuffed it back into Leon's mouth and Zanylos in one swift movement chopped off the little finger on Leon's left hand and the blood ran on the floor.

His howls were absorbed by the linen and the sweat came pouring off his face and his legs thrashed about, but the ropes binding him were taut and Zanylos was sitting on top of him. Leon motioned that he wanted to say something, and so Agos took out the linen from his mouth. He started frothing then and shouting for help, so Zanylos cut off his left ear and Agos stuffed the linen back in his mouth. There was blood everywhere. When the flow from his ear ebbed a little, Agos motioned for him to be silent, and when he nodded, he took out the linen once again from his mouth.

Leon gasped for breath and said to me: 'Your mother took her own life. We didn't expect her to. We were following the orders of Zeferino.'

'Liar,' I shouted and hit him with the back of my hand. 'Speak the truth, for your end draws near. You first killed my uncle and then told my mother that she would have to die too, as she had witnessed the murder. And then she entered the altar room to pray to Athena. Who killed my uncle? Was it you, Leon?'

Leon was surprised that I knew so much. 'Not I. It was Clearchus who killed your uncle. He did it at Zeferino's behest, and Zeferino himself was following Polemon's orders. Therefore he killed him.'

'And did you do anything to protect an old man who had not harmed you?' I asked him. Leon remained silent.

'And Pindar? Who killed Pindar at Pylos?' I asked.

'Alcidas and Clearchus killed him. Not I,' said Leon, as Zanylos cleaned his knife on Leon's tunic.

'And Spiticos, the Spartan?' I asked.

'All of us killed him. If we hadn't killed him, he would have killed us,' said Leon.

Though Spiticos was not my blood, strangely I felt that I was avenging his death as well. And then I did not want to question Leon any more, as I felt the danger of becoming weak and letting him live, and to let Leon live after he had seen our faces would be risky. So I told him to say his prayers and Zanylos cut the ropes that tied his hands and legs. Leon threw himself on his knees and sobbed for life, but that was a feint. Suddenly, he charged at me full tilt and, soon, we were grappling for life till I got my right arm around his neck and squeezed. He thrashed about, but I did not let go. I squeezed tighter and he thrashed about even more. But after many minutes of struggle, life slowly ebbed out of him. I was helped in my efforts by Zanylos, who grabbed his hands and held them tightly.

And then Zanylos severed Leon's head from his torso and put it in a box. Next morning, Dorian gave the box to Menelus and said it had been given by Leon to be delivered urgently to the Macedonian, Polemon, who was staying at Ainis's house.

Ainis later conveyed to Demosthenes what had happened that morning, when the wagon driver Menelus delivered a package to Polemon at Ainis's house. Antipater was there too, as Ainis had invited him over to tell him what Lycargus had said regarding the Macedonian need for triremes. Lycargus, it appeared, had agreed to all the Macedonian requests and had even agreed to prevail upon Demosthenes to be silent regarding Philip's Asian ambitions.

As for the dinner the previous night at Timos's place, Lycargus denied that there was an Athenian conspiracy to poison the Macedonians and he cited the fact that four Athenians were among those dead; besides, half a dozen or more were sick and recovering at an asclepeion. He further declared that not only would Athens provide thirty transport triremes to transfer the advance units under Parmenion's command to Asia, but they would also appoint a contractor who would source ships from other allies if more were needed and who, being an expert in naval matters, would facilitate any other Macedonian needs in this regard.

As for the suspected poisoning at Timos's place the previous night, Lycargus sent his assurance that he had summoned the topmost physicians in Athens and they were inspecting all the sick patients and those that were dead to ascertain whether the poison had developed naturally in the food consumed or it was an artificial addition. If the physicians declared it to be the latter, an inquiry would be ordered to get to the bottom of it.

As Ainis was finishing his briefing, Menelus arrived with the box and Polemon ordered Alcidas to open it. Alcidas and Polemon uttered a shriek when they saw the contents and the package fell from Alcidas's hands. The head of Leon rolled to where Antipater sat with Ainis, and Ainis got up from his chair and ran from the sight, petrified, though his tunic caught on the chair and he ran half naked. Antipater, though, calmly picked up Leon's head by the hair and put it on the table and asked Polemon whether he recognized the man whose head it was.

'The head is of Leon, a soldier in my unit. And I know the perpetrator. It's Seleucus, son of Nicanor,' shouted Polemon. 'He has hired assassins to kill us all.'

Antipater continued chewing his olives, unmindful of the head of Leon, and observing his composure, Ainis came back. Antipater then addressed Polemon and Ainis.

'News of this incident will not spread outside of the people who are here today. For it would make everyone angrier and divert attention from Philip's objective of conquering Persia. As for you, Ainis, tell Lycargus that if Nicanor's son is not caught by the end of the week, the Macedonians will take back the territory of Orupus from Athens and give it to Thebes,' he said.

With this threat, Antipater had left Ainis's residence. All this Demosthenes told me, having heard it in detail from Ainis. He also recounted how the Macedonians had looked at him during the dinner party at Timos's place, expecting him to fall on the couch at any moment, and how even the impassive face of Antipater started crumbling when the Plateans dressed as Macedonian officers fell due to poisoning and even some of the Athenians, but Demosthenes kept sitting there like a rock, unaffected by all the poison. Timos's face fell the most as he kept pouring the contaminated wine and the orator kept smiling and drinking more of it. Of course, by sleight of hand, he had poured the poisoned wine on the ground, even as he gave the impression of drinking it.

Towards the end of the evening, confusion reigned and everybody was alarmed, seeing that they had all consumed the same wine. People started seeing ghosts and spreading rumours that it was a Persian conspiracy to poison the Greeks before the advance scouts from Macedonia could reach Asia. Timos was devastated as the Macedonians privately accused him of playing a double role. The Athenians, on the other hand, not only suspected that he had been bribed by the Macedonians, but they also accused him of plotting to embezzle the festival funds. Thus, Timos lost out with both the Macedonians and the Athenians and came to grief. Shortly thereafter, he was removed from all his official positions in Athens.

Two days after Demosthenes escaped unscathed from the dinner at Timos's place, he called me to his estate and made me a proposal. When I reached there, I met my friend the charioteer Clonus, who had intervened on my behalf in the Spartan Gerousia. He had been elected as one of the ephors in Sparta after the last batch of ephors had finished their terms and was on a secret visit to Athens as an emissary of Aegis, the new king of Sparta. He had come with Aegis's proposal for Sparta and Athens to join together to sabotage the Macedonian invasion of Persia, as he felt that defeat for King Philip there would lift the Macedonian yoke from the Greek states. The Persian king Artaxerxes had already been in touch with King Aegis and Demosthenes to develop secret plans to halt the Macedonians and bring grief to them. He had asked for mercenaries to be sent to reinforce the central Persian army and the armies of their governors in the different provinces of Asia. But since the Corinthian treaty with Philip forbade any action against the Macedonians by any Greek state, the Greeks were in a bind.

'We will supply the Persians with Greek mercenaries. No state can help Persia, but we can always take the stand that the Greek states are not responsible for the conduct of private individuals,' said Demosthenes.

In this manner were plans being made to thwart the ambitions of the Macedonians. Demosthenes then laid his proposal to me in front of Clonus. He said that he wanted to appoint me as a secret emissary of the Athenians and the Spartans to the Persians. He also wanted me to organize all the Greek mercenaries in the region into a force against the Macedonians. This is what he said: 'We want you to organize the mercenaries against the advance party of Parmenion in Asia. The Persian herald from Lydia is here and he wants to recruit Greek mercenaries, as he feels the Persian soldiers will not be capable against the Macedonians and their allies. All previous emissaries we sent to work against the Macedonians were corrupted by them, for they didn't hate them enough. But with you I feel, even though your father was a Macedonian, the hatred which you possess against them for the murder of your family and friends is a shield against corruption, and it generates confidence in us that your actions will be in accordance with our instructions and wishes. From what I can see, you have a lust for adventure and you are mature beyond your years, and that has happened because of the tragedy that has engulfed you. You have proven yourself loyal to your friends: if you hadn't warned me, I would have died at Timos's house. For that I am grateful to you, but it's not my gratitude that is pushing me to make this offer, for if I based my judgement on that alone, I would not be serving Greece well. Though Clonus had Pythagoras in mind as an emissary, I convinced him by force of argument that you were better, and it wasn't your hatred that won the day for you but your bravery in battle, your plotting to seek revenge, your aptitude for business, your daring, which you have proved in your escape from Sparta, and your ability to make friends who are loyal to you. These are some of the traits needed in a good emissary.

'You will have to take decisions on your own, and if you have no inner mettle, it will be a lost cause for the Greeks. You are young and will therefore make mistakes, but the advantage is that you aren't so old that your experience will weigh you down with fear, as would have been the case with Pythogoras. Besides, he is a much recognized figure, as he has won the four-horse chariot race in Olympia many times. You have won it just once and not many people recognize you, which will be to your advantage. Though the Macedonians look for you, they know not how you look, and this is a fact you can put to great use. Another advantage is that you can speak the Macedonian tongue and pass off as one of them and thus infiltrate their ranks. All these qualities I see, and I have been told there are some predictions as well. Clonus told me that Augusta, the respected priest at the Apollo temple in Sparta, has prophesied that you will be a thorn in the side of the Macedonians. I have heard many good things about him and, seeing your qualities, I think the old man is right. Clonus also told me that there were similar predictions by a Helot called Harmodius, who died at Chaeronea.'

After Demosthenes finished, Clonus spoke briefly. Said he: 'I agree with all that Demosthenes has said and, after hearing him speak, I am convinced there is no better candidate to oversee what we desire to do.'

'The predictions are best known to those close to the Gods. I will travel to the east as you desire and do what you want, as it is something after my own heart. However, as you know, I seek revenge, and if Polemon and his aides don't travel to the east, I will first have to go where they are to finish my business with them, for my heart won't allow me to do anything else. But if they go to Asia, which they might, then I shall proceed as you desire and try to do what you want to the best of my ability,' I said.

'Then we shall make sure that they do follow you there,' said Demosthenes.

He then issued me letters of introduction to Spithridates, the Persian governor of Lydia, describing me in detail and mentioning that I would be the chief contractor for hiring mercenaries. Clonus also gave me a letter of introduction with the seal of King Aegis of

Sparta, which described me as the chief Greek emissary recognized by both Athens and Sparta. They fixed an annual remuneration of twenty talents for me, to spy on the Macedonians and maintain relations with the Persians, such that help could be obtained from them against King Philip. Both Demosthenes and Clonus also swore me to secrecy about our relationship, as it violated the league of Corinth, which Philip had established in Greece and which was a body to maintain Macedonian domination over Greece, even as Macedonia embarked on war against Persia.

After Menelus had delivered the head of Leon to Polemon and Antipater had forbidden everybody to speak about it, the Macedonians took Menelus into custody and showed him Leon's head and asked him how it happened to be in the box that he had delivered.

Menelus fainted when he saw Leon's head and a fever arose in him out of fear.

When he recovered, he said: 'A certain Demetrius took over my debt of five hundred drachmas from the moneylender Phisias. He then appointed an assistant by the name of Flavius to monitor my business. It was this Flavius who gave me the box to carry to Ainis's house; I knew nothing of what was inside. If I had known, I would have caught Flavius and taken him to the officials to explain the matter.'

Zanylos, when he confronted Menelus that first time, had called himself Demetrius and Dorian had used the name Flavius. Now the Macedonians asked Menelus to take them to the tavern where Leon had stayed and Menelus took them there. Gelon, the owner of the tavern, was surprised when the Macedonians demanded to examine the room and horrified to discover in it the body of the dead man. Thinking that the Macedonians suspected him of the murder, he ran away, leaving his wife to run the tavern. Thus was discovered Leon's body; they buried it the same day after attaching the head.

After the incident of Leon's head, the Macedonians announced a reward of ten talents for any person who helped them capture Seleucus, son of Nicanor, alive. Announcements to this effect were made in the city. It was pronounced that Seleucus was wanted for his role in murdering an Athenian – which was a lie – and for violating the terms of peace as sealed between the Greeks and the Macedonians. Demosthenes advised me to be cautious and always be with my people, Zanylos, Agos and Dorian, as it would give me a chance to escape in case the Macedonians surrounded me.

Phormio had left Athens for a while to visit the port of Nisea, and now he came back with a report of how many triremes he could organize for the Macedonians to sail to Asia. I had earlier briefed him on his appointment as chief contractor and he was grateful and saw it as a business that the two of us could partner in. For me, it was a way of keeping an eye on the Macedonians.

There is one other thing that I must mention here, for it was soon to become a big part of my life. As I had stood that day, in hiding outside Ainis's outhouse, watching the two women, I had become enamoured of Athele, the younger of the two sisters. After getting all details about them, I had approached their house directly and proposed to Carmene that she let her younger sister be with me for a few days at their house itself.

Though both sisters offered their services to the aristocrats, it was Carmene who negotiated for both. Thus it was that I started staying at their place and, being embarrassed by my actions, I was not willing even for my men to know about it. I was shy and believed that such knowledge would create indiscipline in them. By now, Zanylos, Agos and Dorian were in my pay and Phormio and I were partners. I communicated with them every morning by reaching a pre-decided place and receiving all communications regarding events that concerned us. After giving the necessary instructions, I would return to the arms of Athele.

I was younger than Athele. I had told her my name was Demetrius and given her enough drachmas so she stopped working with her sister while I was there. Now she prepared food for me and bathed me and initiated me into the art of passion and became fond enough of me to be jealous if Carmene talked to me or showed me any kind of attention.

At our meetings in the morning, I often took Zanylos aside and instructed him to buy the finest jewellery. He would get necklaces and bracelets and rings for me the next day, and these I would present to Athele to earn her devotion. Things went on in this way for nearly two weeks, till the time that Alexander's deadline for getting Nicanor's son expired.

It was Polemon who took the story of Leon's head to Alexander, and it infuriated the young prince. He upbraided Antipater for not bringing it to his notice earlier. He then sent a messenger to Philip, detailing what had happened and asking Philip whether the terms of peace could be broken, as he considered the beheading of Leon a deliberate insult and one which, if ignored, could encourage the Athenians to become more brazen in the future. He also asked that even if all the terms of peace could not be broken, if Orpus could be taken back from the Athenians and given to Thebes to teach them a lesson, as Antipater suggested.

Erineus, as before, kept us informed of all these developments. Zanylos had corrupted him to the extent that he now reported all matters related to the house of Mios directly to Zanylos, instead of reporting them to Calliphus, from whom he got no reward in exchange.

According to Erineus, he had overheard Antipater giving instructions to his chief of staff, Paucinias, to ensure that the two messengers that Alexander had sent to Philip did not reach the Macedonian king. It was my assessment that Antipater wanted to send King Philip to Asia as soon as possible, for this would make his own standing more powerful in Macedonia and Greece and might even provide him with an opportunity to plan a rebellion. If the messengers reached Philip with the tale of Seleucus, Philip might break the terms with the Athenians and discord would affect the region, to the extent that Philip might postpone his decision to go abroad.

Antipater had made the decision to put out a reward of ten talents on Seleucus, and Paucinias had seen to it that pronouncements to this effect were made throughout Athens. But, by now, my beard and hair had grown long enough to change my appearance totally, and I moved around on horseback, introducing myself as Demetrius, a trader from Nisea, who came to Athens frequently on business. It was an identity that I did not disclose even to Clonus or Demosthenes.

It was during the time that I stayed in Athele's home that the idea came to me to send a fake Persian herald to Prince Alexander. The fake herald was to make the claim that he came from the court of the Persian king Artaxerxes with the message that Seleucus, son of Nicanor, had sought refuge in Persia from Macedonian atrocities. He was to add that with the Persian king having given asylum to Nicanor's son, anybody seeking to harm him would have to face the king's ire. Finally, he had to say that if the Macedonians had the courage to seek out Seleucus in Lydia, they were welcome to do so, but only if they valued their life cheaply.

Not seeking anybody's advice on this plan, I waited for Phormio to return from Nisea and met him at a pre-designated spot. From there I took him to Athele's place and asked for details of his trip. Phormio being a partner, I felt I could take him to Athele's place. I requested him to transport the money he owed me to his brother Zamos, who was based in Larisa on the Asian coast. I told him to seal the money in wooden barrels of olive oil and also take in a lot of corn and wine, so that if the ship was searched, the talents would remain undetected.

I further instructed him that the men he used to conceal the money should be different from the sailors on the transport. In this way, the sailors wouldn't know of the contents and wouldn't be tempted to steal the talents. And those who had concealed the talents wouldn't know where they were to be dispatched. I also made a pact with Phormio that he was to release a message to his staff and sailors that if something happened to him, they should consider me their master. I told him that if the Macedonians succeeded in harming me or if any accident were to happen to me, he was to divide my share of the business in many ways. Most of it would go to the temple of Zeus in Olympia, the Apollo temple at Pylos and to those in my employ. Phormio was to keep a portion of it to employ assassins to kill Polemon and his friends who had brought death to my family and friend. With these understandings sealed between us – Phormio provided me with his seal, which would identify me to his brother Zamos – I felt more at ease.

I then moved to the execution of the plan that had sprouted in my head during my stay with Athele. I told Phormio to identify a Persian who could be dressed as a herald and who would convey a sealed message to Alexander, which would resemble an official Persian communication. Phormio, impressed by my plan, resolved to find such a person from amongst the Persian sailors in his employ.

After Phormio put in motion my instructions regarding the moving of my money to Zamos, he identified a dependable sailor. He organized a suitable Median outfit for him, gave him two years' wages in advance to buttress his courage for such an endeavour and then sent him to one of the islands, from where he was made to hire a Phoenician trireme and sail to the harbour at Pireus as a Persian herald. The crew were told to depart as soon as they deposited him at the harbour for fear that some authority might question them and discover the truth.

This fake herald then assumed the Persian name of Masitus and approached the Athenians, who took him to the Macedonians. He declared there that he had a sealed letter from the Persian king, with instructions to hand it over to King Philip himself or his son Prince Alexander. The Macedonians then conveyed him to Alexander and, despite the herald saying that the letter was only for Alexander's eyes, the prince had it translated and read out loud at the aristocrat Mios's house in the presence of all the Macedonian officers, including Antipater.

Masitus, not having been told of the contents of the letter or of the gravity of his act, became nervous as the letter was read out. But he remained loyal to Phormio and, even when the Macedonians heaped insults on him, he remained umoved. Reports of these events, Zanylos got from Erineus later.

Alexander then addressed Masitus thus: 'Since the Persian king thinks that if we come to Persia, we value our lives cheaply, let me tell you to convey to him, for we will not grace his insolence with a written communication, that when we do come to Persia, it is the Persians who will die like flies. If your king values the lives of men more than flies, he should pray to his Gods that the Macedonians may not cross the Hellespont into Asia. As for Seleucus, son of Nicanor, tell your king that he's welcome to give asylum to rats like him, for the more rats he collects, the more holes will there be in his royal dress, and the sooner he will trip on his gown.'

All the Macedonian officers cheered Alexander's words. After having spoken thus, Alexander dismissed the herald, but forbade any harm to come to him. But before Masitus could leave, Buserne, a Persian exile attached to the office of Alexander, who had been summoned to translate aloud the letter of the Persian king, expressed his desire to question the herald further and, permission being granted, he asked Masitus in Persian where the king was now based and how much time it took him to complete the journey and what route did he take from Persia to Athens. Masistus had been briefed properly by Phormio on these matters, anticipating such questioning, and he gave the answers that Phormio had tutored him with. But even Phormio wasn't too well versed in matters regarding the Persian court and he knew not that Persian heralds on a mission for the king carried a dagger on which prayers to their God, Ahura Mazda, were inscribed. It was supposed to be a mark of identification. They were also supposed to give the names of the nobles who held various offices in the king's court and carry a tattoo of the sun on their back, which also had the name of their father and his father and so on till the fourth generation inscribed on it. For, in Persia, as in Egypt, the profession of heralds was hereditary and there were many families who had performed this task for the king for many generations.

Once Buserne's questions started getting more and more complicated, Masitus answered him with silence, for to have answered any of those questions would have revealed his ignorance. Buserne then addressed Alexander in Greek. Said he: 'Prince Alexander, I find the answers of the herald unsatisfactory. It could be because he has just been initiated into the profession, and there is a hierarchy even amongst heralds, or he has been purposely briefed to be silent on certain issues.'

Alexander, thinking that the Persian king had not considered King Philip or himself to be of sufficiently high rank to send a top-ranked herald, cursed the Persians some more and said that he would break their insolence one day.

Alexander then ordered Masitus from his sight, but Antipater, seeing that Buserne had a point, summoned Masitus to his presence and questioned him further and arrived at the conclusion that he could be a spy. Antipater particularly questioned Masitus on how he could have arrived so soon from Sardis, where he said the Persian king was, as the journey took a minimum of twenty days. Besides, he said, Nicanor's son had just a few days back murdered a Macedonian by the name of Leon and so could not have reached Sardis so soon. Masitus then told Antipater that he did not know who Nicanor's son was or when he got to Persia, his only job was to bring the sealed letter to Athens.

Antipater and his chief of staff Paucinias then confabulated, after ordering Masitus to wait outside. Antipater instructed Polemon to get his men Alcidas and Clearchus to trail Masitus in Athens and see if he met someone else, for if he was a spy and in league with the Athenians, it would be revealed by his conduct. Antipater felt that it could be the Athenians who had helped Nicanor's son escape to Persia and Leon's murder could have been committed by the Athenians to make the Macedonians leave their city as quickly as possible.

At the same time as I had Phormio send Masitus to Alexander as a herald of the Persian king, I also had Zanylos spread several rumours in Athens through its taverns and temples. I learned this strategy from Demosthenes, who, in speaking to Clonus, had remarked that no society exists without rumours and a good politician learns to manipulate them, for it is better to have your own rumour circulating than somebody else's rumour. This, he had said, was true of both a democracy and a tyranny. Realizing the truth of this statement, I spread three rumours through Athens. One, that Seleucus, son of Nicanor, had hired forty assassins and promised to pay them a talent each to get the heads of the Macedonians Polemon, Alcidas and Clearchus, and that some of the assassins had come all the way from Egypt, equipped with poison darts that put a person to painful death in the time it took him to make ten blinks of the eye.

The second rumour I spread was that the Macedonian request to let their troops pass through Athens on their way to the Pireus harbour, to board transport ships for Asia, was a ploy – that they intended to ravage Athens once they were inside and, Lycargus, keeping in mind this eventuality, had lined up two thousand fully armed Athenians. They would hide in houses along the route the Macedonians would take and leap on them at an opportune moment.

The last rumour I spread was about how the Athenians had summoned some Libyan divinators, who had arrived with ash of elephant dung. The dung, when mixed with corn and fed to horses, made the animals bite their owners and shake them off their backs. The story went that the Athenians were waiting for an opportune time to feed the Macedonian cavalry horses with this ash.

Such was the power of these rumours that the Macedonians grew apprehensive, and while earlier they had thought nothing of moving around independently, they now went about in groups to allow themselves better protection. The day Masitus delivered the letter to Alexander, even Lycargus came to meet him and Alexander had him waiting for one hour before he gave him audience. Lycargus assured Alexander and Antipater that there was no truth in the rumours and they were perhaps being spread by the Spartans or the Persians to drive a wedge between the Greeks and the Macedonians; he said they wouldn't succeed. Both Alexander and Antipater were cold to him, and Lycargus then offered to have Athenian guards accompany the Macedonians everywhere they went in Athens. These guards would belong to the unit of the jailor Aumides, who had earlier helped in the fake escape of Phormio.

Antipater accepted the offer, as he was desirous of avoiding any incident that could upset the peace established by the league of Corinth. And it was this decision of his that perhaps saved my life. For two groups of soldiers landed up at the door of Athele and Carmene while I was there the day that Masitus made his appearance in front of Alexander. It happened thus.

While Alcidas and Clearchus followed Masitus, some of jailor Aumides's soldiers followed Alcidas and Clearchus, unknown to them, as Lycargus had issued clear instructions that the Macedonians were to be protected at all costs, and even if some Macedonians refused protection, they were still to be followed at a distance, unknown to them, to keep a watch on things.

Masitus, not having been properly briefed by Phormio, was careless on his journey back. He was supposed to head straight to the port at Pireus and board a transport Phormio had arranged for him. Once on the open seas, the trireme would head for Salamis, where Masitus would join Phormio's crew. Though Masitus had been forbidden by Phormio to talk to him at the port, as he was there only to observe if everything went smoothly, Masitus headed straight to him and talked and laughed with him. Phormio tried to be distant and behaved like he was talking to a stranger; nevertheless, the Macedonians got suspicious. One of them also recognized Phormio as the sailor from whom the Macedonians had brought triremes full of arms, which had been stolen from the Persians. Thus, though they had instructions from Polemon to follow Masitus, once he departed from the harbour in a transport, they followed Phormio, as they had become suspicious of him. They were intrigued as to why Masitus had talked to Phormio and, more importantly, how he knew him at all. Since Antipater had openly said that the Persian herald could be part of an Athenian conspiracy, they felt it was necessary to get to the bottom of the matter.

Phormio, not observing that men were following him, headed straight to the residence of Athele and Carmene to brief me about how the matter between Masitus and Alexander had proceeded. It was while we were talking and having a laugh together that Athele pointed out that soldiers had surrounded the house. Since the soldiers had come some time after Phormio's arrival, I deduced that they had followed him. As he cursed under his breath, a voice rang out asking for the master of the house to reveal himself.

I asked Athele to go outside immediately and talk to the soldiers and find out why they were there and, more importantly, to ascertain if they were Athenians or Macedonians. This is how the conversation went between them.

'Why are you disturbing the peace here?' asked Athele. Carmene was not in the house then. 'If you want a drink, there's a well at the corner there, with a bucket and a rope.'

'Lady, we would like to drink more than your water,' a voice said, not the same as the first.

'Mind your manners, soldier, and state your business. I can see you are not from these parts but are barbarians from Pella, who roam around like Greeks though you are not,' said Athele.

'Mind your tongue, for we might start acting like barbarians if you call us so,' said the first voice. I managed to see the person who spoke thus, through the window at Athele's house: he was dressed in a Macedonian tunic.

There were four Macedonians near the house and two further away, who couldn't see or hear what was going on. The four Macedonians edged towards Athele and she warned them not to come any closer or she would let loose her dogs on them. Athele had two ferocious dogs, who looked more like jackals and who obeyed her with great fervour. She whistled for them and they came and stood beside her without barking. The Macedonians stepped back.

'We want to talk to the man who just entered your house, for we saw him talking to Masitus, the Persian herald, and we want to know what his business was with him,' said the Macedonian who had spoken first. 'And lady, please control your dogs, for we could harm them in fear.'

'More likely, they will harm you. Why, the man you speak of is my husband. Is there a law in Athens that denies a man the right to talk to a Persian?' asked Athele. 'And why should I have to answer the questions of a barbarian? Philip rules us not here.'

Without waiting for guidance from me, Phormio stepped out of the house.

'I am here. What question do you have for me, soldier, and by what authority?' he asked.

'Why were you talking to the Persian herald at the port?' asked the second Macedonian.

'He rented a boat from me to go back to Asia. He was a herald from the Persian king,' explained Phormio.

'But why did you speak so long?' asked the second Macedonian.

'We were negotiating a price. He wanted to be dropped to the port of Cym and not Mindos, where he came from in Asia. Since he is a herald, I told him he could afford a better rate; it wasn't his money, after all,' said Phormio.

'Is that all?' asked the first Macedonian.

'Well, he also asked for the best captain to take him the safest and fastest way and I said he could have what he wanted, provided he paid for extra rowers. And we haggled over the price of extra rowers,' said Phormio.

There was silence after this, and then the Athenians who had been keeping watch on the six Macedonians approached Athele's house and asked what the matter was. Their leader identified himself as Cleomenes. Phormio told Cleomenes that the soldiers were pestering his wife with questions and had evidently followed him home from the port, and he didn't know why they had been spying on him.

'You are not Greek, you are a Phoenician. How are you married to a Greek?' asked the first Macedonian.

Athele made a vulgar gesture at the Macedonians and hugged Phormio and said, 'If you were as handsome as my man here, I could have considered you, but all of you have faces like the horses you ride.'

'Hold your tongue, woman,' said Cleomenes, the Athenian soldier from the jailor Aumides's unit.

'Well, if you were real Greeks, you would have known that the Phoenicians claim descent from Aphrodite and are the best lovers in the whole world. But since you are barbarians, you wouldn't know such things,' said Athele, still hugging a blushing Phormio.

Athele's light talk changed the mood of the Macedonians. They called over their two companions who were resting under a tree some distance away.

'Well, if you try me in bed, you will give up this Phoenician altogether,' said the first Macedonian to much laughter amongst his comrades.

'Hear, hear,' said Athele and Phormio blushed again and made as if to take his wife inside the house.

But before he could do so, the two Macedonians who had been resting under the tree came up and they saw Athele and she saw them and was startled, for they were Alcidas and Clearchus.

Alcidas and Clearchus were surprised as well. They climbed down from their horses and came up to Athele.

'Is this your house, Athele?' asked Alcidas.

'The Phoenician claims to be her husband; it was he who was talking to the herald at the port,' said the first Macedonian.

Athele then took Alcidas aside for a moment and talked to him and as she brought him closer to the house, I could hear what she said.

'Please don't tell Phormio that we met you at Ainis's house. It will make him very jealous and he will leave me,' said Athele. Then loudly, she explained to Phormio in front of the others, 'I met these two soldiers at the marketplace. Their horses started whining when they saw my mare and wanted to smell her. And my mare got scared and started running away with the cart. They galloped and stopped her, saving me and Carmene from falling.'

Athele was a very clever woman. Alcidas and Clearchus were clearly made to believe by her that Phormio was her husband, and she thus converted a serious situation into a comical one. Though Athele knew me as Demetrius, it was the first time she had met Phormio. I had introduced him to her as a friend with whom I did business and had instructed Phormio to call me by the name of Demetrius. But I had warned her that the Macedonians were looking for me as I had killed many of them at the battle of Chaeronea and had fled with their treasure. This I had done to impress her and she believed it, though Carmene did not. So now Athele was acting to protect me from the Macedonians, and though Phormio did not know her history, he knew that I trusted her and so he was willing to accept whatever role he was given by her.

As I listened to Athele speak, an opportunity presented itself to me: to put to death Alcidas and Clearchus. I hadn't planned for it, but both had just walked to the door behind which I stood.

TEN

As I stood there quietly, watching and listening, there was a sudden noise on the roof and the sound of something falling through. Thinking that one of the Macedonians had managed to get on to the roof, I ran to Carmene's room, from where the noise had come. My sword was drawn and I was ready to pounce on the intruder, but I was surprised to see Zanylos standing there with a bow in his hand. I was never so happy to see another man in all my life.

Zanylos had seen the Macedonians follow Phormio and the Athenians follow the Macedonians. So he decided to follow too, realizing that the Phoenician could be in some danger. Seeing Athele outside the house with Phormio, he reasoned that he must have come to meet me here. As I had been using Zanylos to fetch presents like necklaces and rings, he even guessed that I had bought them for Athele. And since he recognized Alcidas and Clearchus in the Macedonian party even before I came to know they were there, he knew how dangerous the situation was and so he reached the roof of the residence by climbing the neighbour's house. But while he was climbing the neighbour's house, some armed men had seized him. They turned out to be Theban exiles who were wanted by the Macedonians. They had spoken against King Philip and were in opposition to the stooges whom the Macedonians had planted in Thebes to rule them.

The neighbouring house was a stronghold of the exiles and the Thebans always posted a guard on the roof. It was this guard who had spotted the Macedonians outside Athele and Carmene's house. Subsequently, he had raised an alarm thinking the Macedonians had come for them. But when Zanylos explained the situation, the Thebans lent him a bow and arrows and promised to help if there was a fight. All this Zanylos told me even as he was catching his breath.

Outside, the conversation went on between Athele and the Macedonians. Both Zanylos and I listened intently.

'Where is Carmene?' asked Clearchus.

'She has gone to the market to fetch some provisions,' said Athele. She then asked Phormio to go inside and fetch wine for the soldiers. Phormio quickly did so, as he was running out of ideas, and seeing an armed Zanylos, he too was pleased. He had been worrying that there weren't enough arms to sustain a confrontation if the Macedonians decided to come inside the house.

'I think they will go away. They are not suspicious,' said Phormio.

I said: 'You have to go back with the wine and invite Clearchus and Alcidas into the house. Take Athele aside and ask her to do this, saying that since Clearchus and Alcidas have come to her house, they should not leave without having a meal and meeting Carmene as well. They will probably send the rest of the Macedonians away, once they are invited to stay. And remember, you have to bring them to the house one at a time. That way, we will be able to deal with them singly, instead of together.'

Athele did as she was told. She had Phormio take a pitcher of wine and glasses for all the Macedonian and Athenian soldiers, and then took Alcidas and Clearchus aside and, planting a kiss on each while Phormio was busy pouring wine, she invited them to come inside once the soldiers were on their way. She even told them that once inside, she would send Phormio out on an errand and they would have some time with her. Alcidas and Clearchus, thinking that the Gods were being gracious to them that day, sent the Macedonian soldiers back to the temporary barracks they had constructed next to the house of Mios, where Antipater and Alexander were staying. The Athenian Cleomenes too left with his unit, seeing that the matter had been amicably sorted.

Alcidas was the first to enter the house. Clearchus was taken by Phormio to the well on the property, to help draw some water. When Alcidas entered the house with Athele, both Zanylos and I pounced on him. Zanylos wrapped him in a bear hug while I clamped my hands over his mouth and put a dagger at his throat. Zanylos then stuffed his mouth with linen the way he had with Leon.

Athele was shocked at the treatment that we meted out to Alcidas, and so I told her to go to Carmene's room. Then, because Alcidas was struggling vigorously, Zanylos cut off his ear.

Zanylos said: 'There is no rope here, Seleucus, to tie him up. It would be better to kill him before Clearchus comes in, as we don't have sufficient resources to deal with both at the same time.'

I nodded my head in agreement and Alcidas turned white.

'Alcidas, I am Seleucus, son of Nicanor. I identify myself to you so that you know why I am about to execute you. I am going to kill you now for your crimes against my family and my friend Pindar. It would not serve my purpose if you died without knowing this,' I said.

Alcidas's eyes widened with horror when I revealed my identity to him. But that was the last thing he did, for I slit his throat. The blood gushed from his neck and he thrashed about as Zanylos held him. There was barely time to push his body aside before Phormio ushered in Clearchus.

When Zanylos gripped Clearchus in a bear hug, they both slipped on Alcidas's blood and fell on the floor. Phormio fell on top of them and, in the fall, Clearchus broke his arm. He started howling in pain as Zanylos pulled his broken arm to his back and then planted his knee on top of it. Clearchus lost consciousness from the pain.

Hearing Clearchus's howls, Athele came running downstairs from Carmene's room. She became hysterical when she saw the blood on the floor, and Alcidas's body. I tried to calm her down and explain to her that these men were murderers who had killed many people. But she became angry with me for having killed Alcidas in her house. I told her that I had no choice and had not planned it this way and that the Gods themselves had brought him to where I was.

When sometime later, Clearchus came to consciousness, Athele begged me to be merciful to him. But I sent her to the other room with Phormio. I then identified myself to Clearchus as Seleucus, son of Nicanor. The identification brought no fear to Clearchus's eyes, even though he could see his friend Alcidas lying dead on the floor in his own blood.

'Before you die, would you like to tell us where Argus, Zeferino and Menechus are?' I asked Clearchus.

Clearchus spat on the floor with disdain. Zanylos twisted his broken arm and he shouted in pain.

'Your mother died like a dog and so will you one day,' said Clearchus.

'That might well be, but at this moment you are the one dying like a dog before me,' I answered calmly. 'You can say your prayers and tell me how you wish to die. Do you want your throat cut, or this sword through your heart?'

Clearchus remained stubbornly silent. Then he said, 'I know where Alexander keeps his treasure. Philip has given him three hundred talents to finance the setting up of the advance guard in Asia. I will tell you where he keeps the money if you spare my life.'

'Do we look like thieves to you, Clearchus?' I asked him. 'But if you tell us where it is, I promise you a swift and painless death. Otherwise, Zanylos here is going to cut off your testicles first and feed them to you. You know how painful that can be.'

For the first time, a flicker of fear crossed Clearchus's face.

'I will tell you where he keeps the treasure if you let me live,' he repeated.

'I don't have time for this, Clearchus,' I said and signalled to Zanylos. 'You choose a painful death.'

Zanylos cut Clearchus's left ear and the blood poured forth. Clearchus started shouting again and Zanylos stuffed linen in his mouth. Athele sobbed in the other room and Phormio closed the door between the two rooms.

'Last chance, Clearchus. You want more pain, or do you want a painless end?' I asked. I motioned to Zanylos again, but Clearchus indicated that he wanted to speak. Zanylos took the linen out of his mouth.

'The treasury is at Mios's house under the control of Antipater. The money is in an iron safe and the key is with Paucinias, his chief of staff. Now let me die in peace, you dog,' said Clearchus.

'No. I will let you go, Clearchus, and give you a chance. The chance you never gave my mother or Pindar. I will let you go. I want you to have nightmares for the rest of your life that I could catch you again. I want you to suffer not one but hundreds of deaths,' I told him.

Saying this, I released him in his bloody tunic and he went holding his bloody ear with his unbroken arm.

Zanylos was surprised by my decision.

'I let him go as you wanted, Athele,' I said, even as Phormio consoled her. I then instructed her to pack whatever she wanted of her personal effects and leave immediately with Zanylos for his hideout, for if she stayed here, the Macedonians would surely do her harm.

'Go, Athele, go. I didn't plan this, but now that it has happened, I have to take responsibility for your safety. And let me tell you now that I am not Demetrius, as you think, but Seleucus, son of Nicanor. I withheld my real identity from you for your own safety,' I told her.

Before we left, Phormio, Zanylos and I had a discussion on what to do with Alcidas's body. If we let it remain there, Carmene, when she returned, would get the fright of her life. So we decided to take his corpse and hang it from a tree far from the house, using the rope from the well. The Thebans, who had been keeping a watch on proceedings, came from the house next door and helped us to haul up the body. Their leader was a man called Boridas, son of Ariphron.

After introducing himself, Boridas and his men clasped hands with Zanylos, Phormio and me. Boridas said that if we needed any help, he could supply twenty men to us, all of them Theban exiles who had vowed revenge against the Macedonians on behalf of their relatives who had died at Chaeronea, some of them in the Sacred Band. When they learned that I had fought alongside the Sacred Band, they were much impressed and desirous of friendship. But they disappeared soon after helping us with Alcidas's body. They didn't want the Athenians to know that they had helped us, for they were dependent on their hospitality. Before leaving the place, I wrote on Alcidas's tunic with his own blood: 'The assassins in the employ of Seleucus, son of Nicanor, have struck'.

That evening, I went to Pythagoras's place. I had not met him after the battle at Chaeronea. Though he had been taken a prisoner as well, I had avoided contact with him for fear that the Macedonians might then stumble on my real identity. But now I needed his help in recruiting Greek mercenaries to fight the Macedonians in Persia.

I had already instructed Phormio to prepare a transport for the coastal town of Larisa in Asia, where his brother Zamos was posted, and to keep the crew ready for sailing. He was to tell anybody who asked that the ship was bound for the island of Megara, to get a supply of cattle. Even the sailors were to be told this; once on the high seas, the vessel's course would be changed.

Pythagoras was elated to see me alive.

'Seleucus, I have been hearing rumours about you. I was not sure, though, whether you had survived Chaeronea. I thought it could also be that somebody had usurped your identity for their own purposes. Since I didn't know who your friends were, I made no enquiries and instead offered prayers for you at the temple of Athena,' said Pythagoras.

I was much moved by this gesture of his and requested him to help me in my new venture to fight the Macedonians in Persia through mercenaries, for the Corinthian treaty said nothing about Greek individuals and only concerned itself with Greek states.

'I have established contact with a few Persian governors and contracted with them to supply mercenaries for their satrapies, as also for the Persian king. They want the mercenaries to be recruited before King Philip's army moves to Asia next year. As an advance for your services in identifying and recruiting the mercenaries, I can offer you a sum of one hundred and fifty minae,' I said.

Pythagoras was very pleased with the offer and agreed to start on the job straightaway. I told him that a person by the name of Phormio or Agos would be in touch with him to explain other modalities.

That night, I asked Zanylos to meet Erineus to glean the latest developments in the Macedonian camp. Zanylos came to me with the information that after Clearchus had been delivered unconscious to Ainis's house by some traders who had found him in a ditch and doctors had been summoned by Polemon to treat him, there was consternation in the Macedonian camp. The soldiers who had been with Clearchus were asked what had happened and they said that after they had trailed the Phoenician, whom the Persian herald Masitus spoke with at the port, to his home, Clearchus and Alcidas had ordered them back while they themselves were invited inside by the Phoenician.

While everybody waited for Clearchus to regain consciousness, the Macedonian soldiers were sent on a scouting mission to the Phoenician's home to look for Alcidas and to ascertain more facts. There they discovered his body hanging from the tree and brought it back to Mios's house for funeral arrangements. Surprisingly, the body was found without the head and was recognized only by certain marks on the torso. This was baffling, for we had left Alcidas's body intact.

Erineus further informed Zanylos that after they read what was written on Alcidas's tunic – about the assassins recruited by Nicanor's son being responsible for the outrage – they immediately informed Alexander about the incident. The prince flew into a rage and wanted to order the body of Macedonian troops stationed six parasangs outside Athens to come into the city and hunt out the perpetrators of the crime, but Antipater politely informed him that this would require the permission of King Philip. Besides, Antipater brought to his notice that Philip hadn't responded yet to the message that Alexander had sent through a herald – whose murder Antipater himself had organized – some days ago.

Since the troops were under Antipater and not Alexander, there was nothing the prince could do about it. While this conversation took place, Alexander was sitting with his tutor Aristotle, who diffused his anger by suggesting that it could be the handiwork of people in the pay of the Persians, who desired nothing more than for the Macedonians to be involved in continuous warfare with the Greeks, as that would save them the wrath of Philip's sword when he took to Asia.

All this Erineus overheard himself or was told to him by other servants in Mios's household who overheard the talk. Erineus also added that a mysterious ceremony was about to be conducted at the house of Mios at the behest of Antipater. He said that Antipater had specially summoned an Egyptian priest to perform the rituals and had chosen Erineus himself to assist in the preparations. Erineus added that he would come to know the purpose of the ceremony the following day. He told Zanylos that the provisions for the ceremony had been summoned from as far as Thessaly and, by evening the following day or even before that, ten carts were expected to arrive, carrying various items, including 50 kg of horse dung collected only from black stallions.

Erineus reported that while he was assisting in the preparations for the ceremony, for which a sacrificial altar was being constructed, a man and a woman had arrived at the gate and insisted on meeting Antipater. When the guards asked them what their business was, they refused to state it, saying that it was only for the ears of Antipater or Paucinias.

The guards were about to chase them away when Paucinias, Antipater's chief of staff, arrived at the gate with his bodyguards, and seeing the man and the woman, asked the guards what the matter was. Upon being told that they insisted on talking only to Antipater or himself, he summoned the two of them to a chamber. It was the same chamber where Erineus was busy applying dung on the floor as instructed by the Egyptian priest. And it was here that the woman told Paucinias that they had come to seek the award of ten talents, for they had information that could lead to the capture of Seleucus. The woman added that Seleucus, son of Nicanor, was enamoured of her sister and had stayed at their house many a night. The man who accompanied her corroborated the story and told Paucinias that it was he who had identified Nicanor's son, as he had met him at the battle of Chaeronea, and if it hadn't been for him, the women would have continued to think of him as Demetrius, the name under which he was operating.

According to Erineus, no emotion crossed Paucinias's face upon hearing their story. This could have been due to the fact that since the ten-talent reward had been announced, many dozens of people had come with tales about Nicanor's son and, upon investigation, each one of them had been proven to be false. So Paucinias did not give their story too much importance, and though the woman – whose name Erineus failed to hear – implored him to send troops with them back to her house so that they could lie in wait for Nicanor's son, Paucinias said that there were no spare troops that day and that they should come again next morning, by which time he would determine what could be done. Saying this, he dismissed the two and they left very forlorn since their story had not been given the importance it deserved.

When Zanylos heard this account from Erineus, he was disturbed, for he deduced that the man and woman were Alcibiades and Carmene. Alcibiades had not been in contact with Agos, Dorian or Zanylos for the last few days.

'All of you will have to change your dwellings. Alcibiades knows where all three of you live,' I said. 'Zanylos, you are to accompany Athele to a new dwelling, which only you should know about. And it might be time for you, Phormio, to proceed to the port to get a ship ready to depart for Asia whenever required.'

Obviously, Paucinias had not been overly excited about what Carmene and Alcibiades had told him because he had not yet drawn a connection between them and the severed body of Alcidas or the injured Clearchus. While Zanylos went to change his dwelling, I sent Agos to Erineus to reconfirm all that had been said by him to Zanylos, for after the treachery of Alcibiades, I was suspicious of everybody and wanted to take extra precautions.

Erineus had erroneously assumed that Demosthenes was the master of Zanylos and Agos and had been more than pleased to be helping Demosthenes as he had a high opinion of him. He was also looking for a new and wealthy master after the Macedonians left, as he wanted to leave the employ of Calliphus. This made him more eager to help us. Zanylos and Agos were particular not to mention that it was Nicanor's son who sought the information, as that would have scared Erineus.

When Agos went to him at night, Erineus confirmed everything he had said to Zanylos. He said that the guards were drunk in the night, as they did not think anybody would dare harm them where they stayed. Also, though he had not seen the treasury himself, he knew where Paucinias went each time money had to be paid for goods. He said that Paucinias went to Mios's study, where the treasurer, a man by the name of Piros, would hand over the amount needed from an iron safe kept there. Erineus said that the room also contained Mios's collection of ancient parchments and medical instruments, for Mios was studying medicine. He added that money had been sent under guard to Antipater from the Macedonian garrison at Thebes – rumour had it that they had robbed the temple fund of the city and sent the loot to Antipater.

'I think we should loot the Macedonian treasury, as it is wealth that has been looted from Thebes. What Clearchus said about the treasury is true. It will be a proper rebuttal to Philip and Alexander for their treacheries,' suggested Agos to me.

Though the idea had originally been planted in my head by Clearchus, when he had suggested it to save his own life, I hadn't given it much thought. But after Agos mentioned it, I decided to go about looting their treasury in a systematic manner.

In the morning, Zanylos, Agos, Dorian and I approached the Theban exiles, whom we suspected of severing Alcidas's head. I went with all my team so their leader Boridas, son of Ariphron, would not think in terms of capturing me for a reward from the Macedonians. Boridas did not hide the fact that his men had cut the head off Alcidas's corpse, as they wanted to scare the Macedonians into leaving Athens quickly. He said that the longer the Macedonians stayed in Athens, the more arrogant they became, as if they owned the place. He had already embalmed Alcidas's head, he told us, and wanted to send it in a parcel to Alexander.

Boridas said that in his travels to Libya and Egypt, as a sailor, he had come in touch with Egyptian doctors who embalmed bodies, and he had learned the procedure. He had already emptied Alcidas's brain from his head by means of inserting a hook through his nose and making another hole at the base of his skull. He continued: 'After using a scapula to scoop out all the brains from his head, I inserted nator and some sawdust inside to dehydrate it. Then I inserted nator and sawdust and earth under the scalp and then put the head to bake in a hole under the earth. After that, I anointed the head with oils and perfume to take away the evil odours and painted it with stripes to make Alcidas scarier than he was when he lived. Now, I intend to send his head to Alexander as a gift.'

'Boridas, I have a better use for Alcidas's head, one which will earn you more drachmas and talents than ever before in your life,' I told Boridas.

He listened eagerly to me. I told him that I had information about where the Macedonian treasury was and had a plan to capture it. He liked the idea, but thought it dangerous. There is risk in all ideas that provide gain, I said to him. I told him that he would have to intercept the ten wagons coming with provisions for a sacrificial ceremony all the way from Thessaly. Since they were only carrying items for a ceremony and would therefore be without guards, it would be easy for his men to detain all the wagon drivers in the woods with just a small detail of men.

I added: 'Then some of you will take their clothes and dress like Thessalians and drive the wagons straight to the house of Mios, where Antipater and his Egyptian priest await the goods. There, you will have to wait till I arrive with my men. Together, we will overpower or fool the guards and load the Macedonian treasury on the wagons and depart from there. I assure you that I have a spy in the Macedonian camp who provides me with relevant information so we can always plan for our safety.'

'How many Macedonian guards will there be for us to take care of?' asked Boridas.

'I plan to create a diversion which will take most of the soldiers and guards away from the place, and for that I will have to use the head of Alcidas,' I said.

It was my intention to have Agos approach the traitor Alcibiades with the ear that I had cut off Alcidas's head. Zanylos had for some reason preserved it in wine and it could be identified as that of Alcidas's, as there was a metal piercing in the lobe, on which his name was inscribed. All of his friends would remember it.

Alcibiades had no knowledge that we knew of his treachery and I intended to make use of this fact. I told Agos to go to him and tell him to have the ear delivered in a parcel to Antipater's guards and leave the place immediately, for he would be seized if they opened the packet in his presence. The parcel would contain a papyrus note along with the ear, which would declare death to King Philip unless he gave independence to the Greek allies. Then Agos was to show Alcibiades the head of Alcidas, with its one ear, and tell him that he was taking it to a certain place to preserve it better and that Alcibiades was to come at a certain time in the evening behind the Athena temple at the Parthenon. There, Nicanor's son himself would hand him Alcidas's head to be placed on a stake in front of Mios's house. Alcibiades was to do this when the attention of the guards was elsewhere. Agos was also to promise Alcibiades a decent sum for his efforts.

Of course, knowing that Alcibiades had already become treacherous, I was sure that he would run immediately to Paucinias and show him Alcidas's ear and Nicanor's warning to Philip on the parchment. He would then tell Paucinias that Seleucus himself planned to hand over to him the head of Alcidas, to be planted on a stake in front of the

Macedonian camp. And then Alcibiades would claim his reward money before he told Paucinias where Nicanor's son would come to hand over the head of Alcidas to him. Paucinias might pay some advance to him and depart with his men to hide near the temple of Athena so they could pounce on Nicanor's son the moment he gave the parcel containing Alcidas' head to Alcibiades. In this way, I would be getting the soldiers out of Mios's house and nearly two parasangs away and gain enough time to load the wagons with the Macedonian treasure.

All this I explained to Boridas and he was well satisfied with the plan. He even identified two of his men who had spent time in Thessaly to lead the entire exercise of capturing the wagons. For he knew that the Macedonians, used as they were to dealing with Thessalians, would take it amiss if the leaders spoke in a non-Thessalian tongue.

I advised Boridas to instruct the rest of his men not to speak at all, even if addressed. This included Boridas himself, as he had a pronounced Theban accent. And if some of them did have to speak in the presence of the Macedonians, then the leader of the group, the one who spoke with a Thessalian accent, would claim that his was a trading enterprise with lot of dealings with Thebes, which was why he employed Thebans. Besides this, I instructed Boridas to talk in detail with the leader of the Thessalian wagon trail to ascertain the exact nature of the goods and the amount due from the Macedonians for these. For, all of this would have to be presented accurately and without any cause for suspicion to the Macedonians.

As for the meeting that I was supposed to have with Alcibiades, I chose a fool by the name of Himerius, son of Macrobius, who frequented the Athena temple, someone of my age, who was known to rant and rave like a madman at all present. I intended Agos to hand him the parcel containing Alcidas's head and, after getting him drunk, instruct him to hand over the parcel to a person who identified himself as Alcibiades, behind the Athena temple. Himerius was to wear a tunic in the ochre colour, which would distinguish him from the crowd, but he would sit with his head covered and his back towards the entrance so that Alcibiades would not know who he was till he turned around. The Macedonian soldiers with Paucinias, who I assumed would be trailing Alcibiades, would then pounce on Himerius and declare that they had caught Nicanor's son. And when there were denials from Himerius, the parcel would be opened in the presence of all and a scandal would ensue.

This would keep the Macedonian soldiers preoccupied for a long time, away from Mios's house, which was my main purpose.

In order that there were no misunderstandings later, I spelled out to Boridas what his share of the loot would be.

'Your share and that of your men will be one-third of the total talents found after fifty talents have been deducted for the Apollo temple at Thebes, from where part of the money was reportedly seized by the Macedonians. I will also provide you with an advance of one talent for any expenses that you might incur while you are on the road searching for the ten Thessalian wagons. But you will have to make haste now and intercept the wagons as far from Athens as possible so that nobody reports the waylaying to the authorities,' I told Boridas.

Boridas had no problem with his share being just one-third, as I had made a consideration for the Gods and planned the whole event. We made a prayer in front of an image of Goddess Athena and I bade him and his men the best of luck for the task ahead. As a parting instruction, I told Boridas that if there was a change in plan, it would be conveyed to him only by Zanylos, Agos, Dorian, Phormio or me. He was to believe none other, and once they had intercepted the wagons from Thessaly, Boridas was to send one of his men on horseback with a message to me, intimating their approximate time of arrival at Mios's house.

Boridas soon left with his men, after handing over Alcidas's head to us. Agos then went to the dwelling of Alcibiades, as if everything was normal. Alcibiades did not invite Agos inside and Agos knew it was because Carmene was there and Alcibiades did not want him to know that she was. Agos then handed him the packet containing Alcidas's ear and Alcibiades was frightened when he received it, for he had not known that Alcidas was dead. Agos then proceeded to tell him what he was supposed to do with the packet containing Alcidas's ear and the parchment asking for Philip to give independence to the Greeks or face death. He was to have it delivered to Paucinias through a beggar, madman or poet, for such people, Agos advised him, were amenable to errands such as this.

Though he was fearful, Alcibiades agreed to do the needful and Agos gave him a hundred drachmas for the task, which he greedily pocketed. When Alcibiades asked Agos what he carried in the larger packet under his arm, Agos showed him Alcidas's head and Alcibiades was consumed with great fear. Agos told him that he was going to have the head painted some more and that the brains had already been eviscerated and nator had been used to dehydrate the head. He then told Alcibiades that Seleucus, son of Nicanor, would himself hand over Alcidas's head to him at the time when the priests conducted worship to the Goddess Athena at the temple near the Parthenon, at night.

'Seleucus will deliver Alcidas's head to you personally and you will then have to take it and put it up on a stake in front of the house of Mios, undetected by the Macedonian guards. If the task is done satisfactorily, Seleucus will pay you another five hundred drachmas,' Agos told Alcibiades.

Alcibiades listened and agreed to Agos's proposal, but not with the joy he would have shown if he had not been corrupted by his greed and that of Athele's sister Carmene. Departing from Alcibiades's place, Agos went on to locate Himerius so that he could start plying him with salted fish and wine for his role in the evening. Dorian was to keep a watch on Alcibiades's movements to see whether he proceeded to Mios's house to meet Paucinias. Zanylos had already alerted Erineus in Mios's household and told him to keep an eye out for the man and woman who had met Paucinias the previous day about the matter of Nicanor's son, as they were likely to come again.

Erineus, who had been deputed for the duration of the ceremony, was well placed to observe everything that went on, as he had been made the overseer of all that the Egyptian priest wanted done for the ceremony. This involved travelling all over Mios's property, except Antipater's private quarters. Erineus also left instructions with the Macedonian guards to inform him immediately when there was a message for him regarding his wife, as she was very sick and he was concerned about her health. With this strategy he managed to assuage the suspicion of the guards and could meet Zanylos or Agos or Dorian without anyone questioning the purpose of these meetings.

Dorian watched Alcibiades and Carmene leave their dwelling and, following them at a safe distance, he observed that they proceeded to Carmene and Athele's house, where Alcidas had died at my hands. Until this point, they did not know about the incident with Alcidas and Clearchus. But once they reached the house, they were at once seized by the Macedonians who kept watch on the house, hoping that Phormio or Athele would return, for they assumed that they were the murderers of Alcidas and the tormentors of Clearchus.

Therefore, when Alcibiades returned there with Carmene, the Macedonians confused her for Athele. Even though Carmene was older and a little plump, her features were very similar to Athele's. The Macedonians also recognized Alcibiades as one of the Greeks who had been captured at Chaeronea, one of those whom Polemon had been looking for in connection with Nicanor's son. So, thinking they had caught the people who were involved in Alcidas's killing, they promptly took them to Mios's house to meet Paucinias. That was where Alcibiades and Carmene would have headed in any case, later in the day, on the errand of delivering Alcidas's ear. Dorian followed everybody quietly, which was easy because by then a crowd of Greek neighbours had gathered, seeing Carmene being taken away by the Macedonians. They protested that the Macedonians had no authority in Athens and some even followed them all the way to Mios's house and demanded that Carmene be released.

Carmene and Alcibiades, on the other hand, were most fearful about being accused of something they had no knowledge of. Carmene started wailing for her sister Athele when she was asked by the Macedonians to explain the reason for the dried blood on the floor of her house. She started accusing them of murdering her sister in her own house and claimed that she did not know anybody by the name of Alcidas. When the Macedonians sought to examine the packet in Alcibiades's hands, he clutched it firmly to his chest, saying it was meant only for Paucinias or Antipater to see, and that he was on his way to see them and had only made a detour to drop Carmene off at her house. He insisted that he and Carmene had both seen Paucinias yesterday and that he had called them for an audience today. If anything happened at Carmene's house yesterday, they were not privy to it, as they had not been present there. These were the explanations that Alcibiades gave the Macedonians, but they disbelieved whatever he said.

Dorian and Zanylos then waited for Erineus to come out and tell them what had transpired in Mios's house. They waited at a little distance, not wanting Alcibiades to point them out to the Macedonians. Erineus took a long time to come out on this occasion, but he reported all that had happened in great detail. Since by this time Paucinias had come to know of Alcidas's death, a fact he hadn't known the day before when Alcibiades and Carmene had first met him, he had looked at the two with great interest and was partial to them in his hearing, even though his men pointed to them as the main culprits behind Alcidas's death.

But Paucinias said: 'They wouldn't have come to me if they had committed the murder. That fact alone exonerates them to a great degree.'

The men told him then about how Polemon had been looking for Alcibiades, for he was the one who had come up with the story of having located Seleucus on the way from Chaeronea to Athens. But the person he had led them to turned out to be a certain Gongylus from Euobea and not Nicanor's son. Therefore they accused Alcibiades of disappearing with the advance that Polemon had given him and of being in league with Seleucus, son of Nicanor.

At this point, Paucinias sent for Polemon to confirm the story and to identify Alcibiades. Seeing that his game would be up if Polemon arrived before he gave any explanation, Alcibiades stepped forward to confess.

'I admit to being the same person who approached Polemon. I did it because Nicanor's son saved my life in the battle of Chaeronea and I could not refuse the favour he asked. But then, becoming aware of the terror he had spread and the fact that he had recruited assassins to kill Alexander and Antipater, I decided to bring him to justice so that the amity between the Greeks and the Macedonians did not rupture. It is with this objective that I tried to meet the great Antipater himself to offer information that would have led to the arrest of Nicanor's son. But I met you, Paucinias, instead. It was while I was coming to meet you again today that I was seized. I was given a packet this morning by Nicanor's son himself, to be delivered to Antipater or you. I now hand over the same packet to you for inspection,' said Alcibiades with great histrionics.

Paucinias then opened the packet in front of everybody and out fell Alcidas's ear and the message from Nicanor's son.

When Alcidas's friends identified the ear as none other than Alcidas's, Paucinias's temper rose several notches and he cursed Seleucus, son of Nicanor. He then threatened Alcibiades and Carmene with execution unless they told him whatever they knew about Seleucus.

Hearing this threat, Carmene grew agitated and started blaming Alcibiades for having misled her. She slapped him and put her nails to his face before the guards could separate the two. She wailed that she knew nothing about Seleucus, son of Nicanor, till Alcibiades came to her one day and claimed that Demetrius, whom her sister was seeing and who stayed at her house, was in truth known as Seleucus. He told her that if they reported the matter to the Macedonians, there was a reward of ten talents to be had from them. It was with this motive alone that she had agreed to help Alcibiades, and also because she didn't like the influence of Demetrius on her sister. She said that she knew nothing more about Alcibiades or his meeting with any Polemon. She started sobbing uncontrollably after this and, there being no other women there, nobody knew how to react till Paucinias started questioning Alcibiades further and everybody's attention shifted away from Carmene.

Alcibiades claimed that what he had said so far was the truth and he could give further information that would help the Macedonians capture Nicanor's son that evening itself and end their suspicion of him. After he helped them capture Seleucus, he speculated, the Macedonians would come to believe that he was a man of honour and treat him with some respect.

'But I will give you this information only if I receive the reward of ten talents declared by you. As for Carmene, she is just a whore and there would have been no better person to tell you this than the soldiers Clearchus and Alcidas. Unfortunately, one of them is dead,' said Alcibiades. Saying this, he spat at Carmene and she leapt up again at him and clawed his face.

Ignoring his comment about Clearchus and Alcidas, Paucinias asked him what information he had that would help capture Nicanor's son. Alcibiades said that Nicanor's son had asked to meet him in the evening at a certain place to hand over the head of Alcidas, to be put on a stake in front of Mios's house so that the Macedonians would be terrorized. He assured them that he had himself seen Alcidas's head that morning; one of Seleucus's men by the name of Agos had shown it to him.

'And where is it that you are supposed to meet Nicanor's son in the evening?' Paucinias asked Alcibiades.

'I want my reward before I tell you that, for once you catch him, what is the guarantee that you will keep your word?' asked a greedy Alcibiades.

At that, a Macedonian soldier hit Alcibiades with the flat of his sword and told him to beware in whose presence he spoke, but Paucinias signalled to him to desist.

'I will give you one talent as advance and the rest after Seleucus is caught. But if it be that you are making a fool of us, you will pay with your life,' said Paucinias to Alcibiades.

He then ordered Piros, the person under whose guard the treasury was, to give Alcibiades the sum of one talent. Piros, needing help to count such a big sum, looked about for a servant. Spotting Erineus, he took him to Mios's study. There the two of them counted the drachmas into two bags, which they deposited on the floor in front of Paucinias.

Paucinias himself handed over the drachmas to Alcibiades and told his men to organize a cart to help him take the money home. He then addressed Alcibiades again. Said Paucinias: 'My men will help you take the drachmas home. The rest will be made available to you after Nicanor's son is in our grasp. My men will bring you back after you deposit the money in your home and secure it to your satisfaction, but you must tell us now all that you know, so that we might plan better for the evening. Nicanor's son cannot be allowed to escape.'

'My lord, Seleucus intends to meet me this evening at the Parthenon, behind the temple of Athena, at the time when the priests begin their evening prayers to the Goddess. He will be wearing an ochre tunic so as to distinguish himself from the crowd of revellers that inhabit the place. The moment he hands over the package containing the head of Alcidas, your men can seize him,' said Alcibiades.

'It shall be the way you say,' said Paucinias and ordered his men to be at the Parthenon square in the late afternoon. 'You shall go as common people and not be dressed as soldiers and you will have weapons that you can hide under your tunics. Once there, you will spread yourselves in groups all over the Parthenon so that if a person seeks to escape, it will not be possible. Cover all the points leading out of the Parthenon and mingle with the Athenians as devotees of Athena, but do not reveal your purpose to anybody. Nor will you speak unless spoken to, so that your accent might not give you away. For, seeing so many Macedonians in the square, the Athenians might get fearful, thinking a conspiracy of some sort is afoot. I will be there myself and you will wait for my signal before moving on Nicanor's son.'

At this point, Carmene started wailing again and said that half the money should come to her, as they had come together and it was unfair of Paucinias to give the reward to Alcibiades alone when it was her sister that Nicanor's son was enamoured of. This brought a laugh from all the Macedonians and one of them said that there were never any rewards for whores. This made Carmene mad and she rushed and scratched the face of the man who spoke thus and it took many hands to separate the two. Finally, Paucinias indicated for her to be detained till Seleucus had been caught in the evening, so that she wasn't able to warn anybody about their plan.

All this Erineus told Zanylos and Dorian before going back to help the Egyptian priest in his preparations for Antipater's mysterious religious ceremony.

ELEVEN

Boridas's messenger reached me in the afternoon of that day. He told me that the Thebans had captured the wagons of the Thessalians and, after rounding up the men and telling them to strip naked, they had worn their tunics and cloaks and were on their way to Mios's house, after leaving a detachment to guard them in the woods till such time that a message arrived to release them.

The messenger also added that Boridas had made the effort to be properly briefed by their leader regarding the many goods they were bringing for the Macedonians and wanted particularly for me to know that he thought that Antipater was conducting the secret ceremony of Dionysus, which was known only to the Egyptians and Phoenicians. Boridas, the messenger added, because of his travels in Egypt as a sailor, had been witness to a few such ceremonies and it involved the sacrifice of children and men to appease Dionysus and obtain certain favours. Boridas had reached this conclusion because amidst the goods that the Thessalians were bringing were cakes made by mixing the blood of sheep with corn, the collected menstrual blood of many women in a jar, the heads of leaders of men of the northern tribes who had been captured and killed by the Macedonians and heaps of cow dung.

According to Boridas, it was exactly these ingredients and a few others which had been used in the ceremonies he had witnessed. The men who were about to be killed for sacrificial purposes were coated with cow dung, fed the cakes and made to look at the heads of the dead men. When they were much in fear, they were cut in the stomach by the sword in a way that caused great pain and took them a while to die. The priest not only appeased the God by such cruelty, but also divined the future from the paroxysm of the dying man. The children were similarly dealt with, except that they were thrown into pits of fire and the future divined by their cries as they died in pain.

After coming to know this, I asked Zanylos to go back to Erineus at Mios's house and determine whether there were any children there, who had been brought by the Egyptian priest, and also any other prisoners of war from the battle at Chaeronea, being kept secretly by the Macedonians for the purpose of sacrifice. For, in the Greek world, human sacrifice was looked down upon and those who indulged in it were ostracized and penalized.

But it was not possible for Zanylos to meet Erineus on this occasion. The guards said that he was busy and Zanylos didn't press further. But on the way back, while scouting around Alcibiades's dwelling, he discovered that after the Macedonians had let Alcibiades keep the one talent at his house and were escorting him back to Mios's place, a party of them had doubled back to Alcibiades's dwelling. There they broke open the door and repossessed the money, unknown to Alcibiades. This then was the scheming nature of Paucinias, for it couldn't have happened without his orders.

Zanylos also discovered that the Macedonians had sent a party to Athele's house and they were there with the dogs of Athele and some other hunting dogs that they had borrowed from an aristocrat. The minders of these dogs were putting certain clothes to the nose of the dogs, hoping that they could follow the scent. This alarmed Zanylos and he immediately rushed to tell me about it.

The news alarmed me as well. I told him to tell Athele to take a bath with olive oil and then sprinkle perfume on her body in a great quantity, so the dogs would not catch her scent. I then left immediately for Pythagoras's place to request him to keep Athele in his house for a short period of time, as the Macedonians sought to capture her and cause her harm. Pythagoras consulted his wife on the matter and, after her consent, he agreed to my request. I then escorted Athele, after she had taken a bath, to his house on a bed of hay, in a wagon that Zanylos had rented from the market square.

I had heard my father Nicanor say once that olive oil and hay put the dogs off their scent and I didn't want these dogs to reach Athele's new dwelling, even if they managed to trace her scent to where Zanylos had kept her for the last few days.

After these precautions, I waited till Dorian told me that Paucinias had moved with Alcibiades and all his soldiers, except for the guards at the gate, to the Parthenon. It was a favour from the Gods that the Thessalian wagon train with Boridas and his men reached Mios's house after Paucinias had left, and so there was no questioning of his men, even though Boridas had prepared them well. The guards, having been told to expect them, were not the least bit suspicious of Boridas and his men and welcomed them and helped them unload their goods under the directions of the Egyptian priest. All this Dorian observed standing at a safe distance from Mios's house.

It was then that I moved with Zanylos, Dorian and Phormio to Mios's house with a wagon full of cow dung. We were dressed as Athenian peasants and the guards, thinking that we were part of the Thessalian wagon trail who hadn't managed to keep pace with the rest, allowed us inside.

Once inside, I went up to Boridas and his men – they were happy to see me, as they were at a loss as to how to proceed further. Boridas took me aside and told me what he had discovered. He was certain now that the religious ceremony was the secret sacrifice to Dionysus. After a walk around Mios's house, he had ascertained that Antipater was in an inner chamber with the Egyptian priest. The priest also had two Phoenician assistants, who had just arrived and were chanting certain texts and playing the harp under instructions from the Egyptian. Boridas cautioned me that there were three guards within the chamber, who were guarding Antipater.

Boridas also said that he had discovered three men with their legs and hands tied together, lying like sacks at the back of the outhouse. All their hair had been shaved off and their bodies had been painted with purple dye and strange symbols had been painted on their backs. Their mouths were stuffed with linen and they looked at everybody with terror in their eyes. There were three children too, six or seven years old, two boys and a girl, and their hair had been shaved and bodies painted like the men's, though they had not been tied up. They were in a room adjacent to Antipater's private chamber.

'I once saw a sacrifice to Dionysus exactly like this in Egypt. And a little while earlier, I even heard the Egyptian priest read out the objectives of the sacrifice to the image of Dionysus. Though I couldn't understand all of what he said, I heard enough to make out that the sacrifice was to make Antipater the lord of Macedonia and, though that was the main objective, there were a series of favours being asked as well by him of Dionysus, and one of them was to send both King Philip and Alexander to Persia, so that Antipater can rule as the regent in Macedonia and all the Greek territories,' finished Boridas.

Paucinias having left with close to twenty Macedonian soldiers for the Parthenon, there were just six guards left with Antipater, three at the gate and three within the chamber, where the chanting was in progress. These included Piros, under whose supervision the treasury was. Counting the ten men with Boridas, we were fifteen, but Alexander's camp was just half a stade away and it had close to a hundred soldiers. Hence, I was wary of using any force unless necessary. It would take just one guard to run across to Alexander's camp and alert them, and then we would be surrounded by Macedonian soldiers and all would be lost.

I made Boridas draw the wagons up close to the entrance of Mios's house, which was where my men would be loading the wagons with the Macedonian treasury. The wagons were parked in such a way that the young guards at the gate would not be able to see what was being loaded. And as the Egyptian priest was constantly dependent on Erineus for conveying instructions to the guards, they never questioned anything he ordered them to do, assuming that the instructions came straight from Antipater or the priest.

When the wagons were loaded with the talents that were kept in wooden boxes in the safe in Mios's study, Boridas's men covered them with a little cow dung, as there was plenty of it. The men were careful not to make any noise that could be heard by Piros in Antipater's chamber. But in between, one of the young guards at the gate came to ask Erineus what was to be done with a wagon load of flowers that had been delivered by an Athenian trader who was asking for his payment. Erineus asked how much it was and he said that the trader was asking for fifty drachmas. Zanylos gave Erineus fifty drachmas for the guard to pass on to the trader, as we didn't want Piros coming out from Antipater's chamber and getting a hint of what was going on.

But after paying off the trader, the guard returned and observed that the wagons were being loaded with talents and asked if Piros knew about it.

'It's Piros who told us to do it. The treasury is being shifted and Piros wants to use our wagons for this purpose before we leave for Thessaly,' I told him.

'But why are you covering the boxes with cow dung?' asked the guard.

'Because that way the ants won't eat the money,' I replied because I could think of nothing else to say. 'In Athens, there is a species of ants that can digest metal by spitting a special saliva from their mouth. Some of the ants here grow as big as fingers.'

The young guard was astounded by this information. He went and told the other two guards what was happening and they too came to see how the boxes were being covered with cow dung to save them from the Athenian ants!

One of the guards was a little older than the others and he asked, 'Can you show us one of these ants from whom you protect the drachmas?'

And Boridas, Zanylos and Dorian, who were listening to my conversation with the guards, took them aside, into a room that was furthest from Antipater's chamber, and asked them to leave their arms outside the door as the ants could smell metal and would be on their arms in no time at all and start biting them as well. Hearing this, they deposited their swords and staffs at the door and then Boridas, Zanylos and Dorian took each one of them alone inside the room, for the ants wouldn't come out into a crowd of people. In this way, they overpowered each one separately and tied them with rope once they were inside the room and stuffed their mouth with linen so that they couldn't make any noise.

This is how we made fools of the three Macedonian guards at the gate: by promising to show them ants the size of human fingers, which could eat metal. It sounds unbelievable, but that's what happened and it's one of those memories which still makes me smile.

After the wagons had been loaded and were ready to leave, I told Boridas to take with him the three men and three children who had been seized for sacrifice and in this way save their lives. So the ropes that tied their hands and legs were cut and the men were loaded onto the wagons. They were happy that they had been rescued from the pain of many days, and once they were told of the death that had awaited them, they were doubly grateful and vowed their lives to me.

Dorian and Zanylos quietly brought the children over to the wagons and they entered playfully, happy to be going on a journey. One of Boridas's men then discovered Carmene, who had been tied to a post in one of the rooms in the outhouse. Carmene was surprised to see me, and when I confronted her with the treachery that she had intended, she started crying and was deeply penitent and vowed lifelong allegiance to me if I rescued her from the Macedonians. Considering that she was Athele's sister, I consented to assist her if she took a vow of loyalty to me in the presence of Zanylos, Dorian and Boridas. After she did that, I told her to join the men and the children in the wagons.

Thereafter, I dispatched all the wagons under Phormio's command and told him to go straight to the port and load the Macedonian treasurey in the trireme that was waiting to take us to Larisa. He was to give one-third of the boxes, for the money was divided equally amongst all the boxes, to Boridas's men to take wherever they wished. The fifty talents due to the temple of Apollo in Thebes were also to be given to Boridas and his men to be delivered there. I told Phormio to explain to them that if news came to us that they had kept those fifty talents for themselves, we would hunt them down and there was no place where they could escape from us.

Phormio had already stationed fifteen of his crew not far from Mios's home and they would join the wagons as an additional guard. This was a precaution I took to protect us from any double-crossing that Boridas and his men might have in mind. I also asked Boridas to be at my side at Mios's place, for not only did I need him to understand what was going on in the sacrificial chamber, but also it was a strategy to keep him and his men apart so that, even if his men were contemplating any treachery, they would be without their leader. But, to be fair to them, the Thebans did not suggest by their deeds that they harboured any such thoughts.

Once the wagons had departed, only Zanylos, Dorian, Boridas and I remained at Mios's place. I had the three Macedonian guards taken to the outhouse and had their clothes taken off, all their hair shaved and their bodies painted purple in the manner of the three male prisoners whom we had just rescued. Zanylos then wrote on them the same signs that he had seen on the others. All this was possible as the colours were still there in drums behind the outhouse. Then we tied them in the same way that the men had been tied. Since they were the same age and build as the captives, it would be difficult for even the Egyptian priest to notice the difference unless he looked very closely or removed the linen from their mouth and allowed them to speak.

Then we all observed through a small window set in the wall, which had been left half open for the smoke to escape, all that went on during the Dionysian sacrifice. We could hear the priest talking to Antipater in a strange dialect. Boridas said that the priest was offering Antipater two choices. One, by which they would proceed as earlier, and two, if he would get Prince Alexander to participate in the rituals. The prince, not knowing the established objective of the sacrifice, could be lied to and told that it was for the well-being of King Philip. According to the priest, if Alexander participated at this stage, it would damage him beyond measure and make Antipater the virtual king. If Antipater could persuade Alexander to sacrifice the three Athenians and the children with his own sword, then the Macedonians would rule over them for many years to come, but it wouldn't be Alexander or Philip but Antipater himself who would rule, for the fruits of the sacrifice would go to the one who had called the priest and only tragedy would visit the person who made the sacrifice. This, the priest said, was the nature of the secret Dionysian sacrifice which few knew about.

At this point, Boridas insisted that we leave, for if Alexander came to the premises, we would all be discovered. But I signalled to everybody to wait. I did not want Antipater's sacrifice to succeed. Erineus came out just then on an errand and I instructed him to inform Antipater that Paucinias had taken all the guards, even those guarding the gate, to capture Nicanor's son at the Parthenon and the Thessalian chief had sent back his wagons and was now demanding payment for the goods brought from Thessaly.

On hearing this, Antipater consulted the priest, who instructed him to give one gold talent to the Thessalian chief, as it was necessary that everybody who brought material for the sacrifice should go away happy. All this he said in Greek, so all of us understood. Antipater then instructed Piros to give a gold talent to the Thessalian chief from the money kept for this purpose within the sacrificial chambers. Piros came out and met Boridas and handed over the one talent in gold, which came in just one leather bag, and Boridas kept it happily, though I instructed him later to pass on the amount to the Thessalians we had held captive outside Attica, for it was money due to them. They were simple peasants and I intended no loss to come to them because of us.

Piros then went back inside and the priest told Antipater to get the three men marked for sacrifice inside the sacrificial chamber. Antipater sent Piros and the two other guards to bring the three men from the outhouse and, though the guards saw us standing outside, they presumed we were the Thessalians who had just been paid by Antipater. I instructed Boridas to give the guards hundred drachmas each and the same to Piros too, as thanks for having brought the payment so promptly. This act pleased the two guards and Piros. They then asked Zanylos and Boridas to help carry the three men to the door of Antipater's chamber, from where the two assistants of the priests took them, one by one, to the spot next to the sacrificial altar. All this while, the men squirmed and made noises in their throats, but Piros and the two guards didn't recognize them for who they actually were, so extensively had we worked on their appearance.

The Egyptian priest then had the men placed in front of the altar to Dionysus and had all the fires extinguished, except for the one that illuminated Dionysus himself. The chamber fell into complete darkness and the Egyptian priest said to Antipater in Egyptian that he would resume chanting now to awaken Dionysus, so that he could witness the sacrifices with his own eyes and be pleased. If Antipater wished to involve Alexander, he had to do so now or have one of his guards kill the men, but the priest warned that whoever killed the three men would meet with a terrible fate. All this Boridas interpreted for us.

Antipater then left with Piros for Alexander's camp, leaving the two guards watching over the Egyptian priest and his two assistants and the three trussed-up Macedonian guards at Dionysus's feet, whose identities remained unrevealed.

Boridas, Zanylos and Dorian now entreated me to leave, as our purpose of depriving the Macedonians of their treasury had been achieved. But I was too engrossed in the ceremony and wanted to watch for as long as I could. So I granted them permission to leave on foot. Before they left, they were to unhitch the horse from the wagon we had left and tie it behind the outhouse, so that even if I had to leave in haste, I could simply run to the horse and race out of Mios's estate through a gap in the wall at the back. Boridas and Dorian left immediately, but Zanylos would not leave my side as he was more concerned for my safety.

After some time we saw Antipater return with Alexander on horseback. Alexander was accompanied by ten guards. While Antipater and Alexander went straight to the sacrificial chamber, the guards didn't enter the compound, preferring to stay outside.

The Egyptian priest hadn't finished his chanting. Though you couldn't understand the meaning of the words, they flowed, melodious and mesmerizing. Alexander and Antipater sat quietly through the chanting till the priest finished and opened his eyes. Seeing Alexander, he bowed towards him and, addressing him in Greek, said: 'O prince, we do this sacrifice for you to attain glory in the war in Persia and for the Greeks to always be subordinate to Macedonia and for you to have riches beyond your wildest dreams. Lord Antipater has specially called me all the way from Memphis in Egypt to conduct the secret sacrifice to Dionysus and it will reap you all these rewards, for I see that Dionysus is pleased with all that we have done so far. The chanting has awakened him and now we wait for your sword to bleed the three chosen Athenians who were captured by your army at Chaeronea and for whom it should be an honour to die at the feet of Dionysus by the blade of your sword. Complete the sacrifice, great prince, and glory will be yours!'

Thus the Egyptian priest proclaimed and Alexander, who was partial to Dionysus, listened gravely and replied thus: 'I seek no glory apart from what I earn myself and I seek no riches apart from what will come naturally. However, I seek a healthy life for my father King Philip and I seek to put Demosthenes at a disadvantage in the Athenian courts, where justice is hard to come by against somebody who goes against the Corinthian treaty and who preaches treason against us and desires us to fail against the Persians. I also seek to capture Seleucus, son of Nicanor, a person so elusive that very few of my men know what he looks like. I seek to know whether he has escaped to Persia and is under the protection of Artaxerxes or remains in Athens. These things I seek to be added as further requests to Dionysus in this sacrifice.'

'I will do that,' said the priest and returned to chanting for five minutes. Then he beckoned to Alexander to stand up. The priest's assistants picked up one of the men to be sacrificed and they untied his legs and held him tightly by his arms. Alexander then took out his sword and the priest told him to make a small, slanting cut on the man's belly. When he had done that, the priest got up and put his fingers on the man's belly and started reading the blood for signs that only he could understand. Then he marked a particular spot on the belly and gestured to Alexander to make a thrust there with his sword. As the eyes of the man widened in fear, Alexander thrust the sword into his belly until the tip of the sword penetrated his back and got stuck in the wall beyond. Then Alexander pulled the sword out and the blood flowed like a river. The priest took the linen out from the man's mouth and put his hand in the hole that the sword had made and started looking for signs. The man gasped and said as he died, 'Prince, I am Dradocotus, son of Minyus. I am your page.'

The life left Dradocotus, but his words were loud enough to be heard above the chanting of the Egyptian priest. Alexander turned pale and the blood left Antipater's face too. The two guards and Piros stared at each other, frozen in their places. Erineus too stood transfixed, for I think everybody realized that the dead man had spoken the truth.

It was then that Zanylos and I moved in. Zanylos thrust at the two guards with powerful strokes and they died without being able to pull out their swords. My own sword was at Alexander's throat in no time at all. I kicked Antipater to the ground as he tried to get up and halt us. The Egyptian priest howled in terror and huddled together with his two assistants and Piros, having no sword on him, had his eyes on Zanylos and circled him, but Zanylos covered the door, knowing that if anybody got out and alerted the guards outside, it would be the end for us. And I addressed Alexander thus, without removing the cloth from my face: 'The Macedonian prince lies at the mercy of Seleucus, son of Nicanor. The same Seleucus whom you sought to capture through the aid of Dionysus. Well, Dionysus granted you your wish sooner than you expected and here I am, Prince, with my sword at your throat. Do you have anything to say?'

'What do you want, you imbecile?' said Antipater. 'How dare you interrupt this ceremony? Don't you know who you address thus?'

Alexander's eyes showed no fear though, and I took the precaution to kick his sword away from him. Without looking at Antipater, I replied, 'I address Prince Alexander, son of King Philip, and not you, old fool, who is having his own men killed for personal gain. Believe not this man, Prince, for he enlisted this priest to perform the ceremony to bring harm to you, desiring that the crown of Macedonia be his own.'

'Liar,' shouted Antipater. 'I will have your tongue pulled out for such lies. Your sword scares me not.'

'You can pull my tongue out if you can reach it, old man,' I told him without looking at him. My eyes were fixed on Alexander, who watched me without any emotion or fear in his eyes. Addressing Alexander, I said: 'I ache to settle scores with Polemon, Argus, Zeferino and Menechus, murderers of my parents and my friend Pindar. I have no quarrel with you, Prince of Macedonia, for I grew up a Macedonian, though based in Olympia. But the actions of your men have made me turn away from my own country and now I seek to be an obstacle to you and Macedonia. Be not in fear that I seek to take your life. But remember for the rest of your life that you owe your life to Seleucus, son of Nicanor.' Then I showed him the ring I wore, which I had bought from a jeweller in Athens – he had told me that it once graced the finger of the Spartan king Leonidas, who had led the three hundred at Thermopylae against Cyrus. I added: 'And remember, Prince, to return the favour if somebody shows you this ring of the Spartan king Leonidas.'

The story was that Leonidas had given the ring to a man to take to his wife when he knew he would die fighting the Persians. The man had gone and sold the ring in the market, but it had landed in the aristocratic family of the Kelambothros in Athens and they had preserved the ring with great care and respect till it was robbed and over time had made its way to a jeweller whose sons had died at Chaeronea and who was fallen on hard times. The jeweller had sold me the ring for two talents.

It had an eagle minted on it on a drachma coin and the name Leonidas engraved at the bottom.

After the brief exchange, Zanylos and I left the sacrificial chamber in haste. We bolted the door and barred it with a javelin from the many hanging as ornamentation on the walls of Mios's house and then ran to the outhouse, crouching behind bushes to avoid being seen by Alexander's guards at the gate. We mounted the horse waiting there and galloped through Mios's estate. But even as we moved in haste, we could hear the breaking down of the door of the sacrificial chamber behind us and shouts from Alexander himself to stop us. When we were one and a half plethrons beyond the wall of Mios's estate, javelins flew past us, and a few arrows. A turn awaited us just half a plethron away and then Alexander's guards would no longer have been able to see us. Just then, an arrow hit the rump of our horse and he neighed and rose. Zanylos had to pluck it out of his rump to calm him down. But before we could turn the corner, there was another thud and Zanylos's body shuddered and he gurgled, 'Alexander got me...' and his hands grew weak around my waist. As I galloped away, I turned around to see that a javelin had gone through Zanylo's chest and he was vomiting blood on my tunic. When I stopped some ten minutes later, it was a dead Zanylos that I lowered to the ground.

TWELVE

The javelin had hit Zanylos from a distance of two and a half plethrons. It had been thrown by Alexander himself. I came to know this later from Demosthenes, who was informed by Erineus that very day. Erineus had stood unobtrusively in a corner while I spoke to Alexander in the sacrificial chamber. After Zanylos and I left, Erineus helped the prince break open the door with Piros. He then watched as the guards rushed behind Alexander to the estate wall and Alexander himself hurled three javelins in our direction; the last one hit Zanylos. Erineus heard cries from within the sacrificial chamber and, when he came back, he saw that the Egyptian priest and his two assistants had been killed by Antipater with his sword. When Alexander came back and asked what had happened to them, Antipater replied that the priest had confessed to his involvement with Seleucus, son of Nicanor, and so he had killed them on the spot. In this manner did Antipater get rid of all those who could have revealed to Alexander his real motives in performing the secret sacrifice of Dionysus.

Alexander then went to the two Macedonian guards lying tied up next to the dead page Dradocotus, and while he and the others were busy untying the two men and determining their identity, Erineus slipped out unnoticed for the house of Demosthenes, for he was terrified and desirous of protection. There he told the orator the entire story. Demosthenes was amazed and immediately swore him to secrecy. He then sent him to an estate in Attica far away from Athens, with instructions to remain there till after the Macedonians had left Athens, for he wanted no blame for the episode to attach to him. If the Macedonians saw him with Erineus, they might assume his involvement.

In the night, Zanylos's body was retrieved by Agos and Dorian from where I had hidden it amidst the bushes. We buried him with proper rituals performed by the priest Calliphus. Thus ended the life of the Helot Zanylos, whom I had met at Pylos and who had stayed with me through thick and thin. I resolved then that if I ever had a son, I would name him Zanylos in honour of his memory. If he hadn't been sitting behind me, the javelin would have killed me that day.

After the rituals were over, Agos told me the story of Himerius at the Parthenon. After satiating him with wine, olives and dried fish, Agos had taken him to a secluded place near the Athena temple and made him wear the ochre tunic he had brought. Then he slung the leather bag containing Alcidas's head over Himerius's shoulder and put a jug of wine in his hands. Himerius was too drunk to understand what Agos was doing with him. Finally, Agos took a razor and shaved Himerius's head so that even Alcibiades would be in doubt whether it was actually Nicanor's son or not. All these things done, he walked Himerius to a spot in between the temple of Athena Nike and the Parthenon. There he sat him down with his back towards the entrance so that Alcibiades would not have much time to deliberate his appearance.

Agos continued: 'I also took the precaution of placing four Athenians at different points of the Acropolis. One on the southern slope near the sanctuaries of Dionysos Eleuthereus and Asclepios. One on the south-west slope near the temples of Ge Kourotrophos and Demeter Chloe. One on the north-west slope where the cults of Zeus, Apollo and Pan are. And the last one I posted overlooking the theatre of Dionysus. I gave instructions to each one of them to keep a watch on the slopes and the pathways leading to them so that they could warn me whenever a group of men more than four in number came up the slopes. I didn't want to be surprised by the Macedonians. And there were already a lot of people there as the swearing-in ceremony of some archons was going in the cave of the Acropolis.

'Soon the man I had placed above the theatre of Dionysus came running to me and said that thirty or forty men were walking up the slopes towards the Propylaia, the entrance gate to the Acropolis. On hearing this, I attached myself to a large group of people to remain unseen. The group comprised couples who were resting at the Parthenon after having dedicated plaques at the open air temple of the Nymphe to better protect their marriages. The men who had been spotted by the Athenian were indeed Macedonian, as I recognized some of them from having seen them at Antipater's dwelling. They were not in their military apparel though.

'I left him there amongst the other drunkards and revellers after providing him with a bag containing more leather bags of wine. I told him that a certain Alcibiades would come and talk to him shortly, and if he handed him the leather bag on his shoulder, he would give him more wine. Hearing this, Himerius was very pleased,' said Agos.

And so Agos watched over Himerius till he noticed Alcibiades approach with Paucinias and his men. Then he left. Alcibiades, seeing the ochre tunic of Himerius, walked towards him and they soon got talking. Agos noticed Himerius hand over to Alcibiades the bag containing Alcidas's head. Thereafter, a fight started between Himerius and Alcibiades, as Himerius started demanding wine from him, and seeing that Alcibiades was not offering any, he wanted the bag back from him.

It was at this moment that Paucinias and his men pounced on Himerius and it took many Macedonian soldiers to pin him to the ground, for not only was Himerius strong but he was also excitable when drunk, like most men. Observing the fracas, a crowd gathered and nobody asked Alcibiades's views on whether it was indeed Seleucus, son of Nicanor, who had been caught. Paucinias took the bag from Alcibiades and examined the contents, then took the head out to show to his countrymen. This convinced them that Himerius was indeed Nicanor's son and they started dragging him across to their waiting carts. But by then a big crowd of Athenians had gathered and they objected to the way Himerius was being treated. Paucinias showed them Alcidas's head and said that the person was Seleucus, son of Nicanor, and they were taking him into custody on charges of murder.

By this time, the name of Seleucus had acquired a certain aura in Athens. So, once the news spread that Nicanor's son had been caught at the Parthenon by the Macedonians, all manner of people started flocking there and, soon, the Macedonians were outnumbered by almost two hundred people. News even reached the jailor Aumides and he came with his soldiers to restore peace. Scuffles had broken out by now between the Macedonians and those Athenians who had adopted Nicanor's son as a local hero.

Once the crowd grew bigger, Agos entered it and started inciting the Athenians to even more violence and Aumides had his hands full, controlling the mob. After he and his men had brought some semblance of order, Aumides himself talked to Paucinias to determine what the matter was, and Paucinias explained how Alcibiades had led them to Nicanor's son, from whom the head of a Macedonian soldier by the name of Alcidas had been recovered and that the Macedonians intended to put Nicanor's son on trial for murder. As soon as the mob heard that

Alcibiades, an Athenian, had led the Macedonians to Nicanor's son, cries rang out denouncing him as a traitor and many men who did not know who he was asked that he be identified so they could vent their anger on him. Aumides, to protect Alcibiades, took him into custody. Then he explained to Paucinias that only Athenian law was applicable on Athenian soil and Nicanor's son could not be tried by the Macedonians here. He intended therefore to take him into his own custody and the Macedonians could provide all the evidence before the Athenian court where he would be tried.

Saying this, Aumides firmly extracted Himerius from the clutches of Paucinias. But when Himerius turned around, Aumides immediately recognized him as the son of Macrobius, whom he had arrested many times for vagrancy in the temple premises of Athena. His surprise was such that Aumides shouted out, 'But this is Himerius the drunk, son of Macrobius, and not the person you call Seleucus, son of Nicanor!'

When the crowd heard this, they fell silent and then they started laughing at the predicament of the Macedonians. There were many within the crowd who recognized Himerius and they came forward now to see if it was indeed him. Himerius's face was made visible to all and those that recognized him confirmed that it was indeed Himerius, son of Macrobius.

Now a huge sigh of relief went up that Seleucus had not been caught.

'Alcibiades, to claim the reward from the Macedonians, gave them Himerius as Nicanor's son!' shouted a voice and Alcibiades soon started to be seen by the mob as a shrewd person who had hoodwinked the Macedonians.

'Alcibiades got ten talents for it!' shouted another voice, and Agos said this increased the status of Alcibiades from villain to hero in no time at all.

Paucinias then asked Aumides how Himerius had come to have in his possession the head of the Macedonian soldier Alcidas. When Aumides asked Himerius this, he looked at him with perplexed eyes and vomited on Aumides's tunic. He had drunk too much wine and the commotion and jostling had made him nauseous.

This caused great amusement to the many people around and even Paucinias smiled. Agos said it was at this point that Paucinias was convinced that Himerius was not Nicanor's son and that they had been deceived by Alcibiades. So Paucinias left the Parthenon with his soldiers to go back to Mios's house, with a guarantee from Aumides that Himerius would remain in his custody and Paucinias would be allowed to interrogate him the next day, when he came to his senses.

After listening to this story, I went to pay a farewell visit to Demosthenes and to apprise him of all that had happened, but Erineus had already done that. All that remained was to tell him about the events at the Parthenon, and he was delighted by the outcome. He even sent for Clonus and we all debated if the Macedonians would stick to their plan of sending an expeditionary force to Persia and I opined that they would because it was King Philip's lifelong ambition to do so. I maintained that for them to withdraw now, after declaring their intent in the Corinthian league, would be a great loss of face. Clonus and Demosthenes thought the same. But I added with a smile that, with their treasury having been depleted by us, it might take them some time to raise the funds.

Clonus and Demosthenes then mentioned that they would be unable to provide me the annual sum they had promised me for my expenses as King Aegis had not been able to send his part of the funds for me and Demosthenes himself had not been able to convince Lycargus to release some secret funds from the office of the festivals, from which Demosthenes had intended to pay me.

Said Demosthenes: 'In view of this development, if you decide to reject our appointment of you as our secret emissary, we will understand and not force the issue.'

'The responsibility that you have offered me is close to my heart and so I will take it even if you cannot support my endeavours with wealth. I offer my services for free to both Athens and Sparta. But in return, I want letters from you, addressed to all the Ionian city assemblies, the Persian governors and the Persian king himself, so that my task in Asia as an emissary is facilitated by official support. I also want my men to be the sole contractors for supplying material to the Macedonians, and I will need your help and direction in identifying mercenaries in all of Greece to fight the Macedonians in Persia,' I said to Clonus and Demosthenes.

They were both greatly relieved to hear this. All my conditions they readily agreed to, and this is how we parted. But recollecting these events after so many years, I have come to the conclusion that Demosthenes and Clonus did have the talents to give me, they simply kept it for themselves once they learned that I had looted the Macedonian treasury. But I bear them no grudges.

When I arrived at the dock, the three men whom we had rescued from Mios's house were waiting for me. Their names were Tyros, Menicus and Otanes. They were Athenians and desirous of joining me in my voyage to Asia.

Tyros, speaking for himself, Menicus and Otanes, said: 'Since we owe our lives to you, we will dedicate the remainder of the time we live to your service, or till such time that we have repaid our debt by saving your life.'

'There is no need for you to think along those lines. You have my permission to go wherever you wish as free men,' I insisted.

'But we insist on following you wherever you go,' said Tyros, Otanes and Menicus together.

'My task in Asia will be dangerous and great harm could come to you all from the adventures that might be forced on us,' I said.

'We look forward to the adventures that will be. We don't need any pay either,' said Tyros.

With these answers they gained my confidence and were then assigned to duties on the vessel.

Carmene was also waiting to meet me to enquire about her sister Athele, for nobody had any information about where she was and she was getting very anxious. She was equally desirous of mending bridges with Athele, for she regretted hugely her betrayal of me in partnership with Alcibiades, who had since been arrested by Aumides. I gave Carmene the task of taking care of the three children we had found at Mios's place, who had also been slated for sacrifice, and told her to be a mother to them till such time that their parents could be located. She was pleased to be given this task, specially since I made all arrangements for her stay and provided her with money for expenses. I was apprehensive of sending her back to her house, for I feared the Macedonians would kidnap her and ask ransom from me because of my relationship with Athele. So I forbade her to visit her house and then bade her goodbye.

I had fixed the afternoon of the next day as the time for sailing, as I wished to visit Athele at Pythagoras's place before departing. I had placed lookouts along the port to spot any suspicious movements and had a fighting crew waiting in a tavern at the port to gain us some time in case a Macedonian party came to thwart us.

But bad news came in the morning.

It so happened that a Thessallian had escaped from the custody of Boridas's men in the woods, where they had been holding the wagon drivers. He had alerted the nearest Macedonian garrison and they had summoned troops and surrounded the woods and moved on Boridas's men silently, dressed as local Athenian peasants. Then, in a sudden manoeuvre, they had surrounded Boridas's men. After an initial fight, everyone had surrendered. Luckily, one of them had escaped later to bring the news to Boridas.

With the Macedonians now privy to how they had been duped at Mios's house – several of Boridas's men had confessed under beatings – they looked with great energy for Boridas and the rest of his men to teach them a lesson. But Boridas had gone into hiding with his share of the treasury.

I had earlier intended to send Athele to Thebes with Boridas's men, for I felt that she would be safer there than in Athens, where there were many Macedonian stooges. But now, I decided to let her remain at Pythagoras's house. Of course, I first visited him and obtained his consent. To his credit, he was more than happy to agree. He also conveyed to me the information that an Athenian sailor had seen fifty Macedonians leave in a trireme for Abydos in Asia the previous day, amongst them Polemon and Argus. The sailor, who had been at the Games at Olympia, had recognized Argus the charioteer in the port and Argus had introduced him to Polemon. The Macedonians were in a great hurry, as they were under instructions to quickly establish control over the city of Abydos. The city was important because the Macedonians planned to cross over into Asia through the Hellespont and Abydos was the first city near that point and, hence, important for them to hold if King Philip's dreams of conquering Persia were to succeed.

Pythagoras's information quickened my own sense of urgency. I assessed that if I could gather a mercenary force quickly, I could try and create a setback to the Macedonians at Abydos. With this objective, I sent a message to Phormio to prepare to sail by afternoon. What also prompted my haste was the news that Polemon and Argus had already departed for Abydos. The prophecy of the priest from Pylos preyed on my mind. He had said that it was in the east that I would gain in strength.

I apprised Athele privately of the conduct of her sister Carmene. She was very upset and believed it was due to the jealousy she had felt when I bestowed Athele with costly gifts. I agreed to the reasoning, but felt that Alcibiades was more to blame. I gave Athele a talent of silver for her personal needs and told her to get in touch with Phormio if she needed any help or if she felt in any danger. She wanted to travel with me to Asia, but I told her that it would be too dangerous for her. It was better that I went first and saw the land for what it was. Besides, I was going to war with the Macedonians. I promised to tell Phormio to bring her to me if events proved congenial and a safe passage could be had, but I doubted that would be the case.

Then, with reluctance, I told her of the manner of Zanylos's death and she grieved for him, sensing my grief. Sleep had left me the previous night and I grieved for him more than I had grieved the death of Harmodius. For now, I travelled to Asia without any of my old companions and with no one to watch my back, except friends I had made only a few full moons ago.

Part Three

THIRTEEN

I know not how long I have to live. My circumstances, even as I write this account, are perilous. I sometimes fear that I might die before I finish the story of my life, for it takes time to recollect and present matters the way they were – or the way I now think they were. For, in writing this, I have discovered that memory is not infallible and there are occasions when even one incident can be remembered in different ways by the human mind; two persons would most certainly remember it differently. Many people I write about have died, and the location of many who may not have is unknown to me. Even as I remember and write about men such as Harmodius and Zanylos, tears come to my eyes and I grieve that they are no longer in this world. Alas, death is the most certain human condition and we are all as lamps burning in the wind.

In the course of these writings, I have stuck to the facts without any embellishment. For glory does not matter to me any more. Peace of mind has become the single most important thing. That is what life has taught me. From peace stem other important qualities like love. Or maybe love comes first and peace later. I have come to realize that what lies ahead of us and what we have already been through are finite when we compare them to what lies within us. This, a seer taught me. After suffering many wars, I have also realized that there is nothing like a good war and one should never speak against peace, even if it is poorly managed. I have been fortunate to have been guided by many wise men and, though there may be limitations to what a man can do and we may give it names like fate, what I have learned after great hardship is that the worth of a man lies not in his attainments but in what he aspires to attain.

When I look back at my youthful aspirations, I find myself of no significance, though some men covet my adventures and the wealth these brought me; the wise among them look for wisdom in my failures. Then again, I have learned that nothing is insignificant and success is often the sum of many failures. Even the pursuit of wealth and hatred requires the development of certain qualities, and a man claiming goodness might be lazy and in many respects devoid of the steadfastness of purpose that inhabits people we call evil.

But I have no time now to ponder the human predicament, for I have an account to complete. If any time remains, I shall impart in it the wisdom that has been imparted to me by people far superior to me. But I also think that every true story, even one told in plain facts, contains something in it for the discerning. For when one learns of the choices that people made in the circumstances they were placed in, one learns that chance has little role to play in destiny.

This is how I always argued with the Indian holy men whom I shall talk about later. It is not within my power to throw light on whether there is a fate that comes to us separate from what we do, or if the future is what we build through our actions and nothing else, or whether the truth lies somewhere in between, so I shall not speculate upon it. I shall stick to the main story of my life, for if I start dictating to Agos the story of my adventures on the voyage to Larisa in Asia and the four months after that, it would occupy a great deal of time and material, and though I am tempted to tell the story, I fear that the danger that surrounds me may soon claim my life. So I will, for the present, take you straight to the siege of Abydos and continue from there, and if I am still safe, I shall return and write a separate account of those four months after I left the port of Pireus in Attica for Larisa, very near Abydos. For those days were significant and I met a number of people whom the great Herodotus himself had encountered or heard about during the course of his travels, and whom he wrote about in his histories of the known world.

In Abydos, the Macedonians had taken command through subterfuge. Polemon had been promoted as chief officer of the siege; I think it was because the Macedonians wanted to use him as bait for me – they were cunning animals. The city had until then been under the Macedonian general Parmenio, but he had left for an unknown destination, leaving Polemon in charge.

Meanwhile, at Larisa, Zamos, the brother of Phormio, had assembled a mercenary force of a thousand Greeks from Sparta, Athens, Thebes, Cyprus, Crete and even Ionia. Since the treaty of Corinth forbade the Greek states from having armies beyond five thousand men, the soldiers from those lands sought employment elsewhere. Pythagoras and Phormio recruited several on the mainland and shipped them to Larisa, where Zamos employed them through his men, for I had instructed him never to appear before them himself. If word got to the Macedonians through a spy that Zamos was Phormio's brother, it would be the end of Phormio in Athens.

At one time, when I was tired and seeking answers after my escape from the Amazonian women – which is part of the story that I am not narrating at the moment – Zamos had taken me to a seer in Larisa, who was not a priest at a temple but a simple shepherd. According to Zamos, visitations came to the priest from his ancestors. His method was to lie next to the graves of his forefathers whenever he had a problem that needed to be solved and, in the night, dreams would come to him, which would indicate answers to his questions. In this manner he satisfied the queries of many people who came to him with their problems. His name was Mistros and he was a Persian who could speak Greek. He made no distinction amongst those who came to him for answers to various problems, and in many cases, he forbade people to ask any questions at all, for he could divine what they wanted to ask just by holding their hands in his own for a short time and going into prayer.

Mistros forbade me to speak as well and, though I didn't go to him with any particular question in mind, his instructions were mysterious and puzzling. He said, after he had made me fast the whole day as a mark of respect towards his ancestors, 'The monster is your friend, use it and victory shall be yours. Beware of treachery by a friend, for if you are not careful you will be roasted alive. A woman shall come into your life now. Embrace her, for she is good for you.'

Saying these things, Mistros kept quiet and, though I asked him several questions to try and throw some light on what he had said, he told me that he only said what his ancestors told him to say, and even if he wished to say more, he couldn't, as a force held his tongue down. I did not insist thereafter, but kept wondering about the monster that Mistros spoke of, for it was only sailors who talked about monsters in the sea. And how was I to be able to use such a monster? I also started wondering which friend of mine would turn treacherous. Would it be Agos, Dorian, Zamos, Phormio, Pythagoras, Demosthenes, Clonus, or somebody else? Such questions started troubling me in the night, but then I would start dreaming about the woman who was supposed to come into my life and wondering what she would be like. So I started imagining different shapes and sizes of women!

The mercenaries that Zamos had assembled were now longing for action. In my absence, Pythagoras had arranged for them to be trained in battle by sending over two veteran soldiers, Miletus, son of Megakles, and Hesiod, son of Strabo. While Miletus was from Athens, Hesiod was from Thebes and had previously trained with the Sacred Band, though he hadn't joined them. These two soldiers had brought discipline to the force and even recruited mercenary archers from Crete, who had agreed to join at a pay of two drachmas a day, whereas the others were content with just one drachma. But Miletus felt that good archers were hard to come by and these Cretan mercenaries had been in contact with the Scythians when the Persians had taken them on a campaign and had learned much about bows and how to use them, for the Scythians were the best archers and their bows the most powerful in the whole world.

The Cretan archers numbered fifty and were led by Boriphon, who could nail a bird flying in the sky with his arrow, such was the power of his bow and stretching arm and the accuracy of his eye. Boriphon had been recruited at five drachmas a day and Miletus was being paid seven drachmas a day for training and leading the mercenaries. It cost me nearly a talent a day to maintain the thousand mercenaries. But I could do it because of the wealth that I had come by soon after leaving the harbour at Pireus. But of that I shall tell you later.

I began now to approach the neighbouring satraps with the letters of introduction that Demosthenes and Clonus had provided, in order that they might help in laying siege against the Macedonians at Abydos. Accompanied by Agos, Dorian and also Tyros, Menicus and Otanes, I made my way to meet Mazus, Governor of Mysia. He was at that time camping in the city of Dardonos to hunt down some robbers who had fled with valuables from his court.

After the Governor's bodyguards had given chase, one of the robbers had been caught and, upon being produced before Mazus, had informed him that the others were headed to Abydos to seek refuge with the Macedonians.

Mazus did not know until I told him that the Macedonians had taken possession of the town, believing instead that it was still governed by Phicias, son of Sistos, who had established a colony there twenty years ago and had been given the city to govern by Mazus's father Asmetus, whose life Phicias had saved by slaying a bear that had got Asmetus in its clutches.

Mazus asked his treasury officer whether Phicias had been paying his annual taxes and the officer confirmed that Phicias had deposited twenty-five talents of silver, forty horses and two thousand sheep two months ago and there were no taxes due for another six months. On being told this, Mazus accused me of misleading him.

'It is unbecoming of an emissary, no matter how highly recommended, to speak false before those whose favours he seeks. Is this what the great Demosthenes has instructed you to do?' Mazus asked me.

'Sire, I have no intention of feeding you with lies. For you have the power to confirm the truth yourself. But if what I say is proved wrong and your scouts report to the contrary, you can punish me in any way you want, for I will have been proved a liar. I am not privy to the arrangement between Phicias, son of Sistos, and the Macedonians, if there is any, but it might also be that Phicias is a prisoner of the Macedonians and does what they force him to do. If he had not paid his annual tribute in time, your lordship would have been alerted to the fact and asked for an explanation, but the fact that he did may just demonstrate that the Macedonians are cleverer than one might expect. Their purpose is to survey the region and scout all the satrapies and gauge the strength of their fighting abilities, since King Philip intends to avenge the hardships suffered by the Greeks during the invasion of their lands by the great Persian kings,' I said.

My arguments impressed Mazus and he instructed his officers to find out the truth. He requested me to accept his hospitality till such time that his officers returned with reports from Abydos. Accepting their hospitality, I stayed on with my men in a camp designated by Mazus, and that was where I met Mazus's wife Luminas. She was twenty-five years old and had all the freedoms of royalty. Since I was a special guest of Mazus, part of her duties lay in making my stay as comfortable as possible. We stayed in tents, not in proper habiliments, but even then the luxury was unimaginable. There were rugs into which your foot sank as you walked, all kind of fruits lay on the tables – many of which I hadn't seen or tasted before – and the tents had windows through which the air could flow in to cool the inside.

Since I had been assigned one whole tent to myself and my men given another, I requested for a tutor to teach me Persian so I could spend my time fruitfully. When Mazus came to know of this request, he was very happy and ordered his wife to help me learn the Persian alphabet. Being away from their city, they had no learned tutors and his men were not proficient enough to be able to teach another the language they themselves spoke. The majority of them, though able to speak Persian, had not been taught to read or write. Mazus's wife Luminas was a poetess and was even familiar with Homer's *Iliad*, having learned Greek at her father's house in Sardis. Her father Irdabamana was a nobleman whose sister had been the wife of a former Persian king who had died young of illness. Luminas, being the only daughter of Irdabamana, owned several estates in Persia and even a village next to the river Scamender in Mysia. All this she told me herself.

Luminas was a beautiful woman. At the outset, I must remark that Persian women appeared to live more independently than their Greek counterparts. This came as a surprise to me, as the stories I had been told about them in Olympia and Athens had led me to believe that the noblemen kept their women in seclusion in the palaces and had eunuchs guard them, as they were afraid for their celibacy when not with them. But Luminas as well as Mazus's concubines had no eunuchs to guard them and roamed freely amongst the men. Mazus apparently had confidence in his women or didn't care much if they had intercourse with others. Or so I thought.

Luminas was the one who started making flirtatious advances first, by patting me on my thighs as I wrote the Persian alphabet under her supervision, and then by standing behind me and twirling my hair as she watched me write. She did this even as her attendant cooled us with a fan made of papyrus leaves glued together and painted in the colours of the sun. I froze with fright when she first did it and looked at the attendant, but she stared impassively back.

It was on the seventh day that Luminas undressed herself and bade me come to bed. I was less frightened than when she first gave indications of interest and my own sentiments subdued my fears as both of us gave in to passion, even as Luminas's attendant fanned us without any emotion on her face. When it was all done, Luminas and her attendant left as if nothing had happened and came back the next day and behaved as if nothing had changed. I was even more surprised when, this time, the attendant joined in our passion at Luminas's order. She helped Luminas undress and then undressed herself. Without her tunic, she was even more beautiful and shapely than Luminas. When I started giving her preference in my passion, Luminas appeared unmoved by any feeling of jealousy.

In this manner did two weeks pass. To be honest, I did not remember the words of Mistros the shepherd who had predicted that a woman would come into my life till the men of Mazus came back from Abydos and I was confronted with the reality of my situation. Mazus's men reported to him that they were able to approach Abydos without any resistance. In fact, they added, they had behaved in the manner they usually did and sent a message to Phicias's office of their imminent arrival. They were greeted by his men and taken to lodgings inside the town, and though they saw several Macedonians, they felt they were traders of some sort who had come there to fetch a supply of corn as their own crop had failed because of pestilence.

When Mazus enquired about military matters, they reported that the fortifications were bigger and the moat around the fortifications had been widened and filled with water. Phicias's men had explained that they had erected the fortifications ten years ago and, having neglected them too long, they now felt it was time to strengthen them. This year, the crop had been good and the tax collection allowed them to spend some money on defence, for when the need arose to defend themselves from an enemy, they shouldn't be found wanting.

Mazus then asked his men whether they had had an audience with Phicias himself. The men replied that they had, and though none of them had met Phicias earlier and couldn't therefore say if it was the same Phicias Mazus himself knew, yet during their stay at Abydos, none of the men had heard anybody claim that the Phicias who met them was a fake Phicias.

I myself was astounded by this report. Mazus looked at me very sternly and said: 'Now that you have been proven false, what punishment do you think you deserve?'

This is how I replied: 'Sire, I am astounded by what your men have reported to you. They have apparently not seen what my men have. Whether the Macedonians have occupied Abydos with the consent of Phicias or without, I don't know. What I do know, I will tell you. They have laid ropes protecting the harbour that are as thick as a human thigh and stretch more than a mile, and in this way they protect themselves from any naval attack. As a second tier of defence, they have dug sharp pikes in the water that lie unseen from above. If an enemy trireme were to approach the harbour, the pikes would damage the hull and the ship would take in water and then it would hit the ropes and get entangled. The Macedonians have also placed triremes in the harbour with their bows facing outward so as to be able to flee Abydos quickly, if they so desire.

'They protect the port so that their supply line would remain unhindered even if the city were besieged from three sides. Besides, they have stocked the town with two years' supply of corn and dug many wells so that the city will never be short of water during a siege. If your men had looked carefully, they would have noticed that the city walls have been widened and ramparts built all along the walls for catapult machines to be placed, which can fire arrows at great speed and to great distances. These are some of the things that cities do when they are preparing for war. I would like you to ask your men whether they saw any of these things and questioned Phicias about them.'

Mazus pondered over what I had said and then asked his men whether they had noticed any of the things I spoke about. His men said confidently that they had not; being soldiers, they would have noticed and sought explanations for such military measures from the men of Phicias.

To be honest, this report of Mazus's men put me in grave doubt about the report I had received from Miletus, the leader of my mercenaries, as well as from Boriphon, the Cretan archer, and Agos and Dorian who had gone on a scouting mission and had managed to enter Abydos disguised as corn merchants and shepherds. I remembered the prediction of Mistros about treachery by a friend and wondered if Mistros had meant friends and whether Miletus, Boriphon, Agos and Dorian had come together to mislead me for their own gain.

Mazus then spoke some very harsh words to me and had me arrested. Said he: 'I gave you a chance to prove yourself, but my men have proved you wrong. Phicias saved my father Asmetus from a bear with his own hands, at great risk to himself; the scar on his face testifies to his courage. Since then, he has received annual gifts from us befitting a king, and he has sent gifts in return. I do not for a moment believe that he has turned traitor to his friends, even though he's from Ionia and settled at Abydos. Tell me what punishment you deserve for speaking such lies.'

'Sire, I can think of one remedy which would conclusively prove to you the truth of what I say. I think your lordship should make an unannounced trip to Abydos and judge with your own eyes. If you are convinced that the Macedonians are there just to buy corn because their own crop has been lost to pestilence and that the military preparations in Abydos are only a matter of improving the defences of the city, you can come back and have me beheaded and put my head on a stake for all Persians to spit upon. But until your lordship sees everything with his own eyes, I would request that he withhold his judgment,' I said.

Even as I spoke, I was thinking of ways to make my escape when Mazus was away, for I was now no longer sure what was true and what was not.

Before Mazus could pronounce his intention, one of the men he had sent to scout in Abydos got up. He said that the Phicias they had met had no scar on his face and if what Mazus said was true – that he had acquired one while saving the life of Asmetus – then surely there was something wrong, or a miracle had made the scar go away. Mazus then enquired of the other men whether they too stood by this observation. While one of them said that he had been too far away to notice properly, the other man said that Phicias had talked to them with his back towards them and he could see only one side of his face and that side had no scar. I think, apart from the man who spoke first, they were afraid to give any definite answers.

When his men spoke thus without any provocation from me, Mazus deliberated that he found merit in the idea suggested by me, specially as the thieves who had robbed him had gone to Abydos. One of the things the robbers had got away with was a ring that had been in his family for six generations and had been given to his ancestor by Darius the Great himself. It had since brought luck to his family and Mazus wanted it back at any cost. He therefore decided to make for Abydos on a surprise visit and meet Phicias to determine the exact nature of things.

Soon thereafter, Mazus set out for Abydos with his entire entourage and the soldiers he had been travelling with.

'Seleucus, you too will come along with us. But I warn you that if things are not as you say, I will have you executed on the spot, even though you are an emissary from Athens. But if they are indeed as you say, I will not only release you, but also reward you for bringing the truth to my notice,' said Mazus.

'I will accept whatever punishment your lordship heaps on me if I am found false,' I reiterated.

We travelled all day and, in the evening, when Mazus would announce a halt to the march, Luminas would come to me with her attendant. The bodyguards of Luminas were from her father's house and did not owe their pay to Mazus, which made them more loyal to her than to her husband. As long as they guarded the tent in which Luminas met me, there was nothing for her to worry about. I was learning more about passion from Luminas than Persian. But by now, largely from my wanderings during the four months since I left Attica, I could understand a bit of the Persian tongue, though I couldn't speak it fluently.

Luminas was worried about what Mazus would find in Abydos. If all was peaceful, she feared for my life. I was myself in two minds, whether to escape from Mazus's camp before we reached Abydos, as my men entreated me to do, or to reach Abydos and let Mazus make his enquiries before doing so. Though my mind told me to escape, I kept prolonging the decision because of my passion for Luminas. Soon Mazus was camped within two parasangs of Abydos, and though Agos and Dorian reassured me that the Macedonians had indeed taken over Abydos and that Mazus's men had probably been fooled by Polemon, I still took the precaution of sending a message to Zamos to instruct Miletus to march with all our mercenaries to within a parasang of Mazus's camp, so that if he procured information that the situation in the town was normal and decided that I had to be punished, the mercenaries could intervene and rescue me.

I must also admit that I was conscious that I had steered Mazus into a trap, for if Abydos had been taken over by the Macedonians, as my men informed me, there was little chance of him coming out alive from there, specially as he couldn't march on the city with his main force, which consisted of ten thousand men and which was near Parium, a city that lay thirty parasangs away from Abydos and to its north. They were slated to join him five days later, at Abydos.

After having a meeting with his officers, Mazus decided not to wait for his force to reach but to proceed to Abydos promptly, with just his entourage, in the manner that he had done two years ago, so that Phicias thought everything was normal. Accordingly, the next morning, Mazus sent a message to Phicias that since his travels were taking him to Parium, he had decided to halt in Abydos for a few days with his men to rest and enquire about matters in the state before proceeding further. And then, without waiting for a reply to this message, he proceeded towards Abydos along with his wives and concubines. Even though I entreated Luminas to find an excuse to not go with Mazus, she insisted that such was his wish and she didn't wish to defy it.

So, leaving just a portion of his camp to guard me, Mazus proceeded with everybody else to Abydos. He was met at the gate by functionaries of Phicias, who welcomed him and everybody with him into the city. Mazus was used to Phicias welcoming him at the gate, but he was told that Phicias was sick and unable to walk, and shortly his men would bear him on a stretcher and bring him to have an audience with Mazus. Pleased at this explanation, Mazus went to the quarters assigned to him, which were near the city's docks and contained the biggest house in Abydos. He took his four wives, Luminas among them, and his concubines to stay with him. He even sent a messenger back through the gates to the remainder of his forces to say that all was well and he intended to stay there for three days and make enquiries before leaving.

I was alarmed and perplexed at this turn of events, for I had imagined that Polemon would refuse entry to Mazus, knowing that he wouldn't be able to deceive the Persian satrap. It even raised doubts in the minds of Agos and Dorian and they sent Tyros once again to Abydos, dressed as a merchant, to get to the truth of the matter and to determine if, unknown to us, the Macedonians had indeed left the city.

Menicus and Otanes accompanied Tyros to the gates of Abydos. They came back to report to Agos that he had got into the city with his cart full of corn and had been given a permit to stay for three days to conclude his transactions and thereafter he had to leave. Such a condition had not been imposed on the five of them when they had spied on the fortifications of Abydos the last time they were there.

After three days, when Mazus was supposed to have returned from Abydos and there was no sign of him, his men, numbering fifty, grew alarmed and worried about his safety. They sent a messenger to Abydos to determine if all was well. Although the messenger was admitted to the city, he didn't come out at the appointed time and the armed party came back in the evening with no news at all. The next day the party went again and this time two soldiers were admitted readily by the guards at Abydos, and though their instructions were to come back within the hour, after determining that all was well with Mazus, they too never returned. The remaining soldiers waited till nightfall and then returned empty-handed to the camp once again. Now their leader determined to send a fast messenger to the forces of Mazus to make their way promptly to Abydos, as something suspicious was going on and he wanted the commander of Mazus's forces, a general by the name of Megabos, to determine the future course of action.

On the sixth day, Megabos arrived with his forces and camped two parasangs from Abydos. Mazus's soldiers then narrated to him all the events that had led him to enter the city walls of Abydos and what had happened thereafter, right up to the present moment. Megabos, greatly perturbed by this news, decided to send an army herald to Abydos, for he reasoned that there was a tradition of never harming heralds and hoped that once the herald returned, the true picture would emerge.

And so two thousand of his troops waited within nine stadia of Abydos in full sight of the city as their herald announced at the gates that he was there to seek out his master Mazus and so be allowed inside the gates to meet him.

An officer emerged from behind the gate, in Persian dress. He said: 'You are welcome, herald, to enter Abydos whenever you want, but the truth is that Mazus left Abydos in the night with his entourage. We know not where he was headed, but some soldiers in his employ said that he was headed for Sardis to meet his mother who was sick.'

Not expecting such an answer, the herald hastily returned and informed Megabos.

'Did you post men all around Abydos to keep a watch on who came in and who left the city?' Megabos asked his senior officers.

Sheepishly, they said that they hadn't and Megabos was livid with them for such a grave lapse, for now they couldn't determine if the news was true or not. Megabos was in a dilemma. If Mazus was a prisoner inside, he could move against Abydos only at the risk of harming his lord. And if Mazus had indeed left Abydos for some other place, he had to seek Mazus's permission before he launched an attack on a Persian city.

Therefore he decided to send four heralds who had been to Abydos before and knew the city well and who also had friends within its walls. These four were to come back within the day with reports about the goings-on in the city. Megabos decided that if they didn't return by evening with news that all was well, he would have to proceed against Abydos with his army. The four heralds then presented themselves at the gates of Abydos and were granted a very cordial entry. They left their horses at the gates and proceeded inside on foot.

Megabos waited with two thousand troops outside the city. In the afternoon, the four heralds came back to Megabos and one reported: 'Sire, the men of Phicias took us wherever we desired within the city and we saw no sign of Lord Mazus or his entourage or the soldiers who accompanied him. Even the quarters where he stayed were empty and the cooks there said that the satrap had left two nights ago in great haste, as news had come to him that his mother was sick at Sardis and he wished to get to her before she died. Therefore he had no time to even pack all his belongings and, sure enough, the master's tents were in the grounds outside and even his favourite rugs which he used while in prayer. The big chest he used for his clothes was inside the house and the officers of Phicias asked if we intended to take all the belongings of Lord Mazus back with us or let them remain there in anticipation of his next visit. When we asked the officers about the fortifications, they gave the answer they had given earlier. When we asked for a meeting with Phicias, we were told that he was very sick and not in a position to grant an audience, but when we insisted, we were taken to his quarters. He was lying on his bed and he spoke to us in a very hoarse voice from behind a transparent curtain, and it appeared from his answers that he was not in a lucid frame of mind.

'From where we were standing, we couldn't make out any scars on his face or, for that matter, any part of his face, for there were attendants and doctors serving him and we were standing behind a curtain. But the officers of Phicias asked us to convey a message to you, sir, that they were perplexed as to why the army of Megabos stood watch over them and told us to convey to you, sir, that they are very fearful of this fact and want to know what wrongful acts they have committed or are being suspected of, that Megabos should stand looking so sternly at them. Later, when we went looking for our friends in the marketplace, we were told that Phicias had sent thirty merchants, including the friends we sought, on an errand to Lydia to exchange the excess corn they had for marble, for he intended to build a temple to Athena with the best marble available in the world, so that the Gods would cure him of his sickness as soon as possible.'

This being the report of the heralds, Megabos was at a loss regarding how to proceed and so he dispatched messengers on the quick to Sardis, reasoning that they might be able to catch up with Mazus if indeed he was on his way there to meet his mother. He instructed the messengers to proceed to where Mazus's mother was if they failed to encounter him. But he told them not to convey details of any of the events that had happened to anybody else, for he was not sure how to report the matter to the Persian king and wanted to ascertain the truth before taking that step.

Megabos then summoned me to his tent for the first time and enquired how I had come by the information of the Macedonians taking over Abydos. I told him that I had sent my men into the city disguised as corn merchants. They had visited all parts of the city and seen everything with their own eyes and then reported back to me.

Megabos was impressed. 'What would you do if you were in my position?' he asked me.

'I don't have your experience or the knowledge of these parts, but I would march on Abydos with three thousand of my troops and take over the city. And if I faced any resistance, I could be sure that the city was being held by people other than Persians. Then I would lay siege to the city and report the matter to the Persian king, since Mazus would be nowhere to be found and in all probability would be a hostage of Phicias. I have already sent one of my men called Tyros within Abydos to ascertain the truth, but he hasn't come back yet and my men are worried for his safety,' I replied to Megabos.

Megabos pondered over my suggestion and decided that, in these circumstances, it was the best he could do. He determined that if his messengers returned from Sardis with no conclusive news of Mazus, he would move his army against Abydos. He conveyed this information to his officers and they began preparations.

The messengers returned from Sardis after a week. They had travelled on the royal road where fresh horses were stationed every ten parasangs for them and, travelling day and night, they came back with the news that Mazus's mother was in full health and tending to her estate and Mazus was not found there or on the road to Sardis.

Megabos then decided to move his army against Abydos. First, he sent a message that Mazus had ordered him to take over Abydos and that Phicias had been summoned by the Persian king, for he desired him to take over the campaign against the Bactrians, who had ransacked many Persian villages in the eastern provinces. Then, instead of proceeding cautiously, he summoned three thousand troops and, placing himself at their head, marched pompously to the gates of Abydos, expecting that Phicias would be in panic once he saw his troops approaching and would allow them entry into the city without any resistance.

But when he reached within three plethrons of the walls, the drawbridge over the moat was withdrawn and a herald shouted to Megabos to make his intentions clear.

Shocked by this behaviour, Megabos strode up to the edge of the moat and said rather theatrically: 'I order you to lower the drawbridge. I come here on the authority of the Persian king to seize the city.'

The herald replied: 'Sire, the drawbridge has developed a mechanical problem and Phicias is requesting you to send some engineers over the moat on ladders, so that they can come and fix the pulley themselves. After fixing it, they can lower the drawbridge and you can bring your troops across as Phicias has no objection to the troops entering the city.'

It was the fate of Megabos to believe the herald, even though his engineers warned him that it was a trap and refused to cross over on ladders to an unknown fate. But Megabos ordered them to do so and ten of his engineers crossed the moat and climbed the walls of Abydos, and then Megabos waited for them to fix the drawbridge. After some time, he shouted again to the guards at the gate to lower the drawbridge and the herald came on the ramparts once again and said that the problem was beyond the engineers, as the pulley had broken and it would take ten days for them to construct a new pulley.

Megabos then thundered for ladders to be laid across the moat so that he and his soldiers could climb the fortifications into the city, as they didn't have ten days to wait for a new pulley to be built. The men at the gate promptly obliged and set down twenty ladders. Megabos ordered his troops to proceed across the moat. When his officers advised him against this move, he berated them and got down from his horse and stepped on a ladder himself and, seeing him do so, his officers were shamed and proceeded behind him and so did the soldiers.

In this manner did they proceed to their deaths, for after fifty of them had climbed over the wall, including Megabos and his officers, cries and shouts could be heard across the moat and also the sound of swords clashing. The men who were at the top of the wall shouted for their comrades across the moat to come quickly and join the battle as Phicias's men had surrounded them and were slaughtering them. Hearing this, there was a great rush to get across quickly. Then the mechanical catapults on the ramparts, which were hidden from the human eye, started raining arrows on the soldiers who were climbing up the ladders and killed them all, to a man. The main body of troops which waited across the moat also came under fire from archers within Abydos, causing them to withdraw to a safe distance.

Now Megabos's army, bereft of its officers and chief engineers, was thoroughly confused. Within the city itself, there was a deathly calm. Even the soldiers who had been sitting on top of the walls, shouting for help from the main army across the moat, were slumped on the walls with arrows sticking out of their bodies. And even as Mazus's army watched helplessly from beyond the moat, the heads of Megabos and his officers were hung from the gates and a Macedonian officer made his appearance on top of the gate, after the beating of drums, to announce thus: 'Look, ye all. This will be the fate of any Persian soldier who dares to cross the moat at Abydos. Take a message to your lords that King

Philip is coming and it will augur well for the Persians to vacate these lands if they want to keep their heads on their shoulders. Look at the head of Megabos and be afraid, and rejoice that your own head has been spared.'

Thus spoke the herald in Greek, and there not being many Persians who understood Greek, it was Agos, Dorian, Menicus and Otanes who translated his words. The soldiers were in a helpless rage and lusted for revenge. But it was too late now. I could only think that if it hadn't been for the foolishness of Megabos, the lives of hundreds would have been spared.

FOURTEEN

Tyros returned that night of the massacre. He recounted for us the day's happenings: 'Polemon had his men put a dagger to the throats of all the engineers as they climbed over the wall and had them led away and slaughtered. Then the Macedonians pounced on Megabos and his men, when they came across, and cut off their heads without suffering a single casualty on their side.'

Earlier, when the four heralds of Megabos had come visiting, Polemon had quarantined all the Macedonian soldiers in a separate quarter so the heralds didn't get to see them and he let the local Persians take the heralds around. These Persians were eager to please Polemon, as he had imprisoned their wives, daughters and sons. In this manner did he fool the heralds of Mazus and Megabos. The person who had been presented as Phicias was an impostor and had been forced to pretend, as his family too had been taken captive when the Macedonians had initially deposed Phicias and taken over the city. The real Phicias had been beheaded by Polemon himself, as the locals venerated him and Polemon wanted to deny them a rallying point.

As for Mazus and his entourage, Tyros said that they were captive in that part of the city which was near the docks. Polemon and his men had never thought Mazus would be so foolish as to come into Abydos to meet Phicias, but seeing that he had, they had decided to play along and make a fool of his general Megabos too. In this brutal manner did the Macedonians show their true colours to the Persians. Tyros added that, for the moment, Polemon and his officers had caused no harm to Mazus and his wives, though they had distributed his concubines amongst the officers, Polemon himself taking two. Tyros had heard from some Macedonians that Polemon was keeping them hostage and intended to bargain for their release at an appropriate time.

All this information Tyros got from Macedonian soldiers and some Persians who spoke Greek, who, though aristocrats themselves, had been forced to vacate their houses and live like beggars. All the Persian soldiers in Abydos had been massacred and the civilians lived in terror, expecting that they too would meet the same fate unless they were able to escape. But the Macedonians did not wish to release them, for they needed free labour to defend the fortifications and also feared that, knowing the city well, they would reveal its secrets to an assaulting Persian army.

The Macedonian officers who managed the food supply had grown to trust Tyros as he was a Greek. Expecting the Persians to lay siege, they had told him to get as much grain into the city as he could through the secret tunnels. Tyros claimed that the Macedonians had obtained provisions to last many months and sought to add to them in case the siege went on for a long period of time, before the armies of King Philip could reach Persia. They expected the main Macedonian army to defeat the Persians easily, as they weren't impressed with Persian discipline at all and didn't count them as worthy opponents.

Seeing the way Megabos had behaved, I didn't have much faith in the Persian army either. The surviving officers of the army had sent word to the Persian king about the disaster and awaited further orders. Seeing that my warning had come true, they sought my opinion on military matters and I promised to help them, provided they released me, as Mazus had promised.

After ascertaining from Mazus's remaining household staff that this was indeed the truth, they released me and I proceeded to plan with my men how to rescue Luminas from inside Abydos. I wanted to accomplish the task without delay. According to Tyros, she was still alive and I didn't want Polemon to change his mind about Mazus and his wives. I also feared that the next Persian commander who would come to oversee the situation might be as incompetent as Mazus and Megabos. I intended to execute my rescue of Luminas before he arrived and before the Persians could recover from their losses and their confusion.

It was at this time that Boridas arrived from Attica. If you remember, he was the Theban who had helped us to loot the Macedonian treasury. He had got in touch with my partner Phormio in Athens, who had sent him across the seas to Miletus, the commander of my mercenaries. Boridas intended to serve with us, as the Macedonians had located all his men and killed them and he alone had survived their plots. He said that when he and his men had reached the Apollo temple at Thebes and offered fifty talents as I had instructed them to do, the Macedonians had got wind of it through the priest. Wanting to see for themselves who had brought such a large amount as a temple offering, they had managed to take some of his men into custody and got the truth out of them, unknown to Boridas. Then they lay in wait for Boridas, as he was supposed to consecrate the fifty talents in a ceremony so that he, his family, his men and their families could benefit the most from this act of goodness. When he came at night to the temple with his party, the Macedonians had surprised them and taken them all into custody.

Boridas had managed to flee only with great ingenuity, but he had not been able to save his wife or any of the others, and he did not know how they had been dealt with by the Macedonians.

Boridas ended his account thus: 'It had become impossible for me to stay on in Thebes or Attica, as the Macedonians had sent search parties all over the place, leaving me with no option but to come to Asia if I valued my life.'

This was Boridas's story and I expressed my sorrow at the turn of events with regard to his family and friends. At the same time, I welcomed an extra pair of trusted hands and decided to use him as well in my plan to extricate Luminas from within Abydos.

The Macedonian officers managing the food supply within Abydos had instructed Tyros to bring grain from Larisa, five nights after he met with them, and to signal with fire so that the triremes guarding the port would recognize him and guide him in, avoiding the ropes and pikes that were meant to damage enemy ships. Tyros felt they were fearful that the food supply within Abydos, a major part of which had caught fire, was not enough and they were eager to replenish it before the Persians put a stockade on the seas and around the city itself. They had promised Tyros three times the price of the corn that he brought and promised to pay him on the spot.

Melitus, the commander of my mercenaries, then sent one hundred troops back to Larisa along with Tyros and told them to load a transport ship with as much corn as could be procured. They were to do this within a day and then proceed to the port of Dardonos, which was halfway between Larisa and Abydos. There they were to halt and await further orders from Miletus.

There was a difference of opinion between Miletus and me as to the best way to mount a rescue plan for Mazus. Miletus was unable to understand why I had to mount a rescue at all. I couldn't explain to him that my focus was Luminas and not Mazus. He would certainly not support the idea of endangering Greek men to rescue a Persian woman who was not even my wife.

'We have to garner Persian goodwill in the region by attempting such an act. If we succeed, we will make Persia beholden to us. We would then be better placed to fight the Macedonians,' I argued with Miletus.

This brought him around to my plan.

Miletus then devised a plan and came to me for approval. Having questioned Tyros at length before he departed for Larisa, Miletus had ascertained the exact location of Mazus and his entourage. He now drew a map on the sand and explained to me the various quarters within Abydos. He said: 'We will have to take the help of the Persians for the plan to succeed. On the night that Tyros is to approach the docks, the Persians will have to start an aggression on the opposite side of the city to draw the Macedonian soldiers away from the docks.'

This manoeuvre would make the Macedonians less attentive to Tyros and his ship. Miletus intended that ten soldiers be amongst the sailors on board and they would slip into the sea, then climb the docks and proceed to the place where Mazus was. Since it would be difficult to rescue Mazus and all his entourage, Miletus suggested that we could look at rescuing Mazus only, or just one or two others apart from him, and leave the rest to their own devices. To get all of them to the dock and aboard the transport without detection would not be possible.

Miletus had identified a place at the dock which had a tunnel that led into the city, which the Macedonians were ignorant of. It had apparently been built to connect an aristocrat's house to the dock for escape during any surprise attack. Agos had given this information to Miletus, having heard it from one of the Persians he was friendly with and to whom he had revealed his real identity. The Persian intended to use the tunnel along with a few close friends to try and escape if the Macedonians found no further use for the civilian population and planned to kill them to save on food. Though he could have escaped by himself, he felt it was his duty to stay and help the older Persians who were being ill-treated by the Macedonians because they consumed food but were not useful for any military labour.

The Persian had converted the house into a place of worship and the Macedonians, being fearful of the Gods, had left the place alone, believing that since they were involved in a battle with the Persians, it was better to leave their Gods in peace and not have them help the

Persians too much. Agos, thinking that the tunnel could be used by us to fight the Macedonians sometime in the future, had left fifty drachmas with the Persian whose name was Alabanda, and this foresight would stand us in good stead now.

Alabanda had also guided Agos to the location of four secret tunnels within Abydos. According to him, these led out beyond the moat, opening in the shrubbery two stadia from the city, at a place that was camouflaged by big mounds of earth. Trees had been planted there to make it difficult to spot any movement by people exiting the tunnel. Alabanda had pointed to two tunnels, which the Macedonians knew about and guarded with their soldiers. They intended to use these to augment their food and water supply if the siege lasted for a long time. They had even made preparations to seal the tunnels with rocks if they suspected that the enemy had come to know about them and was using them to infiltrate into Abydos.

But the Macedonians didn't know about the two other tunnels and these Alabanda pointed out to Agos. One of them started from beneath the Macedonian barracks, which were previously barracks for the Persian soldiers, and the entrance for it lay in the baths next to the barracks. The other started from the small graveyard within the city, from the inside of a tomb, and it came out in the big graveyard outside the city, which was used by the common Persians to bury their dead. The Medes and some Scythians, who also lived in Abydos, had a separate burial place next to the Persians, where they burned their dead or left them for the animals.

To safeguard this tunnel from the Macedonians, Alabanda had killed the Mede who tended to the graves, as he couldn't be trusted. He was prone to heavy drinking and was known to divulge secrets once inebriated. Alabanda then spread the rumour that there was an ancient curse by an Assyrian God on anybody who roamed the tombstones if their ancestors did not lie there. The curse would make them lose a leg in battle. All the one-legged Persians in Abydos had once entered the ancient graveyard within the city, though their ancestors lay buried outside in the common graveyard, and thus had been affected by the curse. After hearing this story, no Macedonian ventured near the aristocrats' graveyard for fear of becoming lame. In this way, Alabanda protected its secret from the Macedonians so he could use the tunnel at an appropriate time.

Alabanda told Agos that it was Phicias's misfortune that a traitor had informed on him when he was about to use one of the tunnels to escape the city after the Macedonians took over the barracks and slaughtered all the soldiers. The bigger misfortune, according to Alabanda, was the discovery of the particular tunnel that Phicias was using, as it was the biggest one leading out of Abydos and could accommodate three soldiers walking abreast. It was brick lined and without the usual problem of water seepage. Alabanda knew of the tunnels from his father who had been the chief engineer of Abydos before Phicias had become its governor. He had no good words to say for Phicias, for Phicias had ignored his warnings about the Macedonians when they had first come to Abydos.

But, said Alabanda, Phicias had been plied with gifts by a Macedonian called Polemon and his greed had led to his downfall. Among the gifts that Polemon had brought for him was a black mare from Thessaly.

Miletus, Agos and I then planned that while Tyros guided the corn-laden transport to the port as the Macedonians dictated, ten men led by Agos and myself would slip out of the transport into the water and swim to the tunnel that opened at the house of Alabanda. With Alabanda's help, for which we would offer him two talents, we would go to the place where Mazus was being held captive with his wives. There we would break up the whole party into two groups. One group, which would comprise good swimmers, was to return the same way to the ship, and the other group would use the tunnel whose entrance lay in the graveyard and emerge on the other side of the moat.

Miletus had asked the Persians discreetly whether Mazus could swim and he was told that Mazus was terrified of water and would not even step on a boat! There were also some amongst the mercenaries who would not get into a tunnel as it made them fearful for want of air.

Thus, out of necessity, we had to plan on breaking up the rescue party into two. One party would lead Mazus through the tunnel and the other would exit through the dock. Miletus felt that breaking up the party into two groups would be advantageous because a single party of many men travelling around Abydos at curfew time might attract the attention of the Macedonians.

'We will be dividing the two talents meant for Alabanda so that the load on each of us is manageable. We will also each carry a Macedonian soldier's uniform in a waterproof sheepskin bag. The only weapons concealed upon our bodies will be daggers. If we need any others, we will have to snatch them from the Macedonians or see if Alabanda can provide us with some,' I said, briefing the rescue party I would be with.

The ten of us getting into Abydos through the docks would have to wear Macedonian army uniforms once we reached Alabanda's house through the tunnels.

This being the plan, Miletus and I approached the Persians to provide us with a diversion around the time that we approached the docks of Abydos with the transport. The reason, as I said earlier, for not wanting to delay the rescue of Mazus was that the Persians were still in confusion and a new general or satrap might not like our plan to rescue Mazus, even though he was a Persian, as then Mazus would continue being satrap, whereas with him out of the way, they would become more powerful than before. Already, a Persian lord by the name of Mritphakes was on his way to the Persian camp outside Abydos to take stock of the situation. He was the brother of the Persian satrap in Lydia.

Officers in Mazus's army felt that Mritphakes would be appointed as the new satrap of Mysia, for not only was he the brother of the Lydian governor, but also a nephew of the wife of the Persian king Artaxerxes.

But they were not happy at this development, as Mritphakes had once come to Mysia and acted very boorishly and snapped at the officers escorting him around on the business of inspecting the tribute collection. The Persian king occasionally sent these noblemen who were considered officers of the realm to report on the way the satraps were conducting business, and while some of them were honest, some saw it as an opportunity for advancement and sought bribes from the satrap in return for not sending an adverse report to the king. Mritphakes had in this fashion taken ten talents from Mazus and then had proceeded to send an adverse report to the king. It had taken all of Mazus's ingenuity and several gifts not to fall out of favour with Artaxerxes.

Therefore, the remaining Persian army officers who had been with Megabos were unhappy that Mritphakes was coming to take stock of the situation, for it was these same officers whom Mazus had used later to take back the ten talents from Mritphakes when he was still on his way to Lydia. They had done it at sword point and were now worried about their fate, for Mritphakes would surely replace them with his own men and make things difficult for them. This group of officers was led by Gophoredes, who was particularly keen on rescuing Mazus. For it was Gophoredes who had put a sword to Mritphakes's throat and, after he had ordered for the money to be released, he had cut open his trousers with his sword and insulted Mritphakes in front of his wives.

Since Megabos's army was right now without a leader, it was this group of officers who commanded it jointly until Mritphakes joined them. I convinced them to launch an operation against Abydos in the night. I explained what they had to do in detail: 'You are to use your contingent of archers to fire flaming arrows beyond the walls of Abydos and try and set on fire any combustible object within the city which your arrows can reach. You are also to set up ladders and try and climb the walls with as few casualties as possible, using the cover of darkness. This must happen in an area other than where the archers will be firing their arrows. With these manoeuvres I hope to draw the bulk of the Macedonian soldiers away from the dock. While some of them will be involved in trying to put out fires caused by the arrows, the others, for fear of an imminent assault by the Persians from the eastern quarter, will be deployed on the ramparts to thwart them.'

The Persian officers gave their assent to my plan.

This diversion I planned to create once the transport carrying us entered the port and before it docked, so coinciding the two events was most important. If the Persian hostilities started before our ship made it past the Macedonian defences at the port, they would most likely deny it entry out of fear, but once we had made it past those defences, there was nothing they could do except allow us to dock.

Gophoredes, understanding the importance of beginning hostilities at exactly the right moment, posted a picket of men at a point on the coast from where they could observe the approach of the transport to the harbour. When it crossed the Macedonian defences, the picket was to start a fire, which could be seen by the main Persian army. The archers, having already taken positions under cover of darkness, would set the cloth around the arrowheads on fire, using molten wax and oil, and start firing into the city. The Persian infantry would in turn protect the archers by standing in front of them with their shields and taking cover behind trees or any wooden structures they could arrange as protection. For the archers would be well within range of the Macedonian catapults on the walls.

To make it easier for the Persian picket on the coast to spot our transport on the high seas, Miletus explained to them the route we would take and the number of lanterns we would keep alight on the deck for them to be able to identify us without error. Miletus even posted some of our own men in the picket to make sure everything went smoothly and Boridas was appointed by me to head the men who would be stationed near the end of the tunnel to protect the party that emerged with Mazus. Boridas wanted to be in the rescue party that went in with Tyros, but seeing that he had a strong Theban accent and was tired after a long sea voyage, I initially rejected his offer. But when two of our raiding party fell ill, I decided to let Boridas fill in for one of them, as I needed another trusted hand in the middle, apart from Agos.

Miletus would also be in the transport, disguised as a sailor, along with twenty other soldiers who would be similarly disguised. And though they wouldn't be coming off the ship, they would protect us if our plan was discovered on the way out or the Macedonians decided to stop our ship from getting away by launching a boarding party. Miletus and his men would also try and set on fire the Macedonian triremes in the port while we were leaving the harbour. All our weapons, though, would be concealed under the floorboards of the lower deck. The Macedonians could not be allowed to see any weapons while the corn was being offloaded, except for those carried by the four or five guards on the upper deck, which was the norm on such ships.

With all this planning done, we sailed into the port of Dardonos and proceeded towards Abydos forthwith. As we neared Abydos, the lanterns were lit for the Persians on the coast to spot us, and when we signalled to the Macedonians, they sent a pilot craft to meet us that guided us through in a manner such that we avoided the ropes and pikes. After we had cleared the obstacles, we blotted out the lanterns and, when we were a plethron from the docks, ten of us slipped naked into the sea with bags slung over our shoulders and swam towards the portion of the dock where the tunnel started from under the jetty. We swam underwater and emerged under the wooden boards of the jetty. We could see the Macedonian soldiers pacing above us.

By this time, the Persians had started hostilities as planned and we could see arrows lighting up the sky on the western side of the city. The Macedonians were shouting for all hands to gather there and the commotion allowed us time to dry ourselves and put on the Macedonian uniforms, minus the armour. Then Agos removed the grille at the mouth of the tunnel and led us through till we reached an incline where two paths emerged. Not having taken the tunnel earlier, we were all in a quandary. Agos decided to choose the path on the right as that appeared to be the direction we had to travel in. After walking on that course for two hundred paces, we reached the end of the tunnel. A trapdoor lay above with a rope ladder hanging down from it. Agos climbed up and banged on the door while the rest of us stood at the foot of the ladder, holding aloft the lanterns for Agos to see where he was going. There were many lizards and rats in the tunnel and they ran between our legs, causing some of the mercenaries to panic, but order was maintained.

Agos knocked on the door for a long time and we grew despondent at the lack of response. The men were getting fearful, being in a closed space, and started imagining things.

Boridas said: 'If somebody closes the opening from where we entered the tunnel, we could all be buried alive.'

I was angry with him for speaking thus and inducing panic in the others. His behaviour was the opposite of what I had imagined when I agreed to include him in the rescue party. Fear is contagious in a warring party, and so is courage. Boridas was increasing the fear in all the men. At one point, the lanterns went out because of a draught that travelled through the tunnel and this added to the panic, for now we couldn't see even each other's faces in the dark.

Boridas then addressed me and said: 'I want to speak to you in private.'

'What is it about?' I asked him.

'I will not speak in front of everybody,' he said.

'Wait till the trapdoor opens,' I replied.

'It might never open, and if we don't return the way we came, we might all get trapped in the tunnel forever,' he said sarcastically.

I swore at him in the dark, and though the other men muttered among themselves, they kept their peace. All of a sudden, we heard a voice that did not belong to any of my men and it created such a fright amongst them that one of them dug their nails into my arms.

The voice through the trapdoor asked us to identify ourselves. Agos said that he came in peace and was a friend of Alabanda and he gave his name. By this time, some of the men had got the lanterns working again and a semblance of calm descended because we could see each other. Then the voice asked how many of us there were and Agos said he had just four people with him, so as to not scare the person on the other side. We heard a lot of noise, then the door opened upwards and a face looked down. Agos quickly climbed up without waiting for an invitation and so did the others. I went up last, not wanting to give the impression that I was scared of being down in the tunnel.

It was Alabanda himself who had opened the trapdoor. He was surprised when he heard Agos's voice, for Alabanda had never expected him to emerge from there, since he thought that the tunnel was only to descend into and escape. With all the commotion that was taking place on Abydos's eastern quarters and now western as well, he had been getting apprehensive. Not knowing what the commotion was about, he had come into the room, intending to remove the objects above the trapdoor so that he and any others could hide in the tunnel if the need arose.

Alabanda wanted to know if a Persian attack was imminent and whether more men would be coming through the tunnel to fight the Macedonians. Without answering his question, I told him that we had brought him two talents as a gift because Agos had told us how good a man he was. After collecting the drachmas that each one of us had been carrying for Alabanda, I dropped the bundles at his feet and asked him whether he could take us to where Mazus and his wives were, for we intended to rescue them that night from the clutches of the Macedonians.

In this manner did we induce Alabanda to help us. I told him that the Persian attacks were a diversionary tactic to take the Macedonians away from the port and instil confusion and fear in the city so it would make our task easier. All the mercenaries were surprised that this was the case, specially Boridas, as Agos and I hadn't revealed the larger plan to them. Everybody, except Boridas, was happy at the revelation, for they felt now that their activity was being supported by a larger force outside the city.

Seeing Boridas the way he was, I took him aside

'What bothers you, Boridas? Speak without fear,' I said to him.

'Being in the tunnel, I felt that I would be entombed there forever. And I knew a great urge to tell you something: Athele is with child. I felt that you should know this before any misfortune befell us,' said Boridas.

This was his explanation, and I must say that I was surprised, though I forgave him his strange behaviour for bringing me this happy bit of news. But I also urged him to concentrate on the rescue.

After this, however, he revealed what was really bothering him.

'I didn't like the way Tyros was talking to the Macedonians at the dock. Since I was the last to get into the tunnel, I heard snatches of their conversation. Tyros told them about our rescue party and then pointed in the direction of the tunnel we were getting into. This is what has been bothering me. I fear that Tyros may have turned traitor after being bribed by Polemon when he visited Abydos as a corn merchant to spy on the city,' said Boridas.

I was much alarmed by what Boridas said and consulted with Agos about the course to adopt if he were right in his assessment. Agos asked the other mercenaries if they had seen or heard what Boridas had. But the rest claimed ignorance, though Memphios, son of Benitos, claimed that he had always known that something was wrong from the way in which Tyros walked. He said traitors usually rested on their left leg while standing. I didn't give any importance to what Memphios said because he was easily swayed and his observations were usually foolish. While I was still deciding what to do, Boridas volunteered to go back to the docks and observe Tyros closely to see if the Macedonians were plotting something with him and whether they had boarded the ship and arrested Miletus and the other soldiers. For if that was the case, then we would all have to escape through the tunnel in the cemetery.

Thinking this to be a good idea, I told Boridas to proceed back to the docks through the tunnel, as that was the way I intended to return to the docks. I told him to come back through the tunnel and wait for us at Alabanda's place if everything was normal and the ship hadn't been taken over by the Macedonians. But if it had, and the Macedonians were inspecting the tunnel, he was to destroy the ladder leading up to the trapdoor and keep some heavy objects on top of it so the Macedonians could never come out at Alabanda's place and would remain ignorant of where the tunnel led. I said all this to Boridas in the absence of Alabanda so that he wouldn't get scared and stop helping us.

Boridas, who had expected to go to the docks through the city, was nervous when I told him to proceed through the tunnel, but he kept quiet and stepped up to the trapdoor, and Agos lit a lamp for him and the others helped him climb down.

After the departure of Boridas, Agos explained to Alabanda how we wished to utilize the tunnel from the graveyard to help Mazus escape, since he was afraid of water. Then he took Alabanda to the roof of the building to survey what was happening and they noticed the Macedonians forcing the locals to the eastern quarters to help put the fires out.

The bulk of the Macedonians, however, were moving to the west to repel the Persian attack. Alabanda pointed out to Agos the quarters that Mazus was in and, after ascertaining the way there, all of us trooped out behind Alabanda with barrels of water on our heads. If the Macedonian soldiers came upon us, they wouldn't question us since the eastern quarters where Mazus was being held captive was afire and every non-Macedonian was rushing there to put the fire out under Macedonian supervision. Even the soldiers were carrying water in whatever container they could find.

FIFTEEN

When we found Mazus, he was fighting to stay alive. The fires had engulfed half his residence and just two Macedonian guards were struggling to put them out. Agos took charge of the rescue operations while I pretended to be a Macedonian officer sent by Polemon to take Mazus to a safe location. The Persians had stopped firing arrows and were concentrating on the western quarters, but there was total chaos in the eastern quarters because of the fires.

Mazus had by now stepped out of his residence along with his wives, Luminas amongst them. I went up to Luminas as Agos and the mercenaries flung water from the barrels they were carrying onto the burning house. At first, Luminas didn't recognize me, but when she did, she was both shocked and relieved. I told her that I had come to rescue her and Mazus and asked her whether there was anybody else in her retinue she wanted rescued. She took the names of the two attendants she had, one of whom used to accompany her to my tent, and so I told her to gather them at one spot. Then I spoke to Mazus, who was also very surprised to see me and started blaming his fate on the fact that he hadn't listened to my warnings. But I told him to have courage as I had taken great risks to come and rescue him. He was pleased to hear this, but wondered how it could be achieved since the Macedonians were all over the place.

'You have the option, sire, to proceed with my man Agos through a secret tunnel which will take you outside Abydos or of travelling with me to the docks and swimming to our ship where there are mercenaries in my pay who will row you to Dardanos,' I said to Mazus.

'I would prefer to proceed through the tunnel,' said Mazus.

It was how I had expected him to react. I told him that it would be safer to divide his party into two and asked him whether there were some others that he wanted rescued as well, as we couldn't rescue everybody. Mazus took the names of three of his wives and said that he wouldn't leave without them as they had all borne him children. I was surprised that he didn't mention Luminas's name. And when I asked him about Luminas, he said that she too could come if there was an option to rescue more.

So I sent him and three of his wives with Agos and four of the men, along with Alabanda, to be escorted to the graveyard where the tunnel was. The other party comprised Luminas, her two attendants, four of my men and myself. I moved with my party towards Alabanda's place, intending to meet Boridas and, if all was well, to take the tunnel to the dock and then swim to the ship in the darkness. Mercifully, Luminas and her two attendants knew how to swim. The rest of Mazus's entourage he left behind adroitly by deceiving them with a lie.

'The Macedonians have decided to execute my wives and me and those attendants closest to us. They intend to do so on the city walls, in sight of the Persian army, as a retaliation to the Persian attack. If any of you want to die with us, you are welcome to accompany us,' Mazus told them.

The old man was as sly as a fox. After hearing him speak thus, the remainder of his entourage promptly scattered, for they did not want to be executed along with Mazus and his wives. In this manner did Mazus get rid of them!

As we approached Alabanda's place, a big unit of Macedonian troops appeared. I had sent Memphios ahead to be on the lookout for them so that we were not taken by surprise, and now he came back in much panic and said that Boridas was at the head of thirty-odd Macedonian troops and they were making their way towards the quarters from where we had just rescued Mazus and his wives! I asked Memphios whether he meant that Boridas was a captive of the Macedonians.

'The way Boridas was walking, it looked like he was their leader. Also, when for a moment all of them stopped to converse amongst themselves, I noticed that Boridas put his weight on his left foot, and that surely means that he is a traitor,' said Memphios.

I told Memphios to shut up, and after telling the rest of my group to hide behind a house, I climbed its roof and saw Boridas standing amidst a big group of Macedonian soldiers. They were in front of the burning house of Mazus and were interrogating Mazus's remaining attendants and also the two Macedonian soldiers who had been guarding him, and whom I had informed that Mazus and his wives had been summoned by Polemon.

After seeing this, I too was shocked, for I could not have imagined that Boridas would turn out to be a traitor! Though I was too preoccupied to analyze his behaviour then, it was obvious to me later on that he had always intended to create fear in us and then make an excuse to leave our party and inform the Macedonians about our presence. I didn't know now whether to believe his news that Athele was with my child.

At that point, I became truly worried about our escape. I told everyone to hurry, and when we reached outside Alabanda's place, I told Memphios to go and check if the Macedonians had placed a sentry there, for Boridas could have told them about the tunnel or would soon – or maybe he had told them about it, but with their soldiers being preoccupied, they had all gone to catch me at Mazus's place, knowing that I was headed there. Memphios came back and told me that Alabanda's place was empty and the entrance to the tunnel was as we had left it.

But I was scared to take my party through the tunnel, for if the Macedonians knew we were in there, they could seal it off and we would be able to do nothing. And if we took the main path over the roads within Abydos to the docks, we risked passing many Macedonian units and they could question us.

Besides, I didn't know whether Miletus and the other mercenaries on the ship had also been betrayed by Boridas. So I decided to send Memphios to the docks and urged him to go as fast as he could – while we waited in an orchard – to find out if the Macedonians were behaving suspiciously with our crew. Memphios went like the wind and returned in no time at all and said that he could see that the unloading of the corn was over and Tyros was at the dock with Miletus, making preparations for departure. Memphios also added that this time, Tyros's weight was on his right foot and therefore he was wrong to have called him a traitor. I thought Memphios was an idiot, but the best thing about idiots is that they are not easily scared. That has been my experience.

I then decided to take my group to the docks along the normal path and not through the tunnel, and that decision saved our lives. The Persians had made a great success of their aggression on the western part of Abydos and a team of fifty soldiers had defied the order of Gophoredes and climbed the ramparts at Abydos because half the attention of the Macedonians was in putting the fires out in the eastern quarter since that was where their food grain was stored and they were fearful that the fire would destroy it. When they had successfully scaled the ramparts, a dozen-odd Persians jumped inside and that created panic among the Macedonians, for they feared a much larger force was inside the walls than in reality. So, to push back the Persians, all the Macedonians rushed to the western quarters, even forgetting about the fires. This made the roads ideal for us to travel out of Abydos.

Tyros was surprised to see us coming straight to the docks over land, instead of swimming to the ship as we had originally planned. He was in the process of accepting money for the corn from two Macedonians. They were paying him only half of what they had promised and Tyros was arguing with them. The Macedonians then asked who I was, for they didn't recognize me as an officer.

'I am Demetrius and I've been sent here on an urgent errand by Polemon. I need to get these soldiers and other people with me quickly to Dardanos, as we have to ask for help from certain friends there for corn and other necessities that the fire today has destroyed. Is there any ship available by which we can proceed to Dardanos immediately?' I asked them.

Since I spoke in the Macedonian accent, I gave them no reason to disbelieve me. The soldier in charge of the docks addressed me then.

'There is nothing here, except for this transport commanded by Tyros. His ship isn't Macedonian. But none of our vessels are in any state of readiness to sail as all the sailors have been summoned to battle the Persians soldiers within Abydos,' said the soldier.

I turned to Tyros and winked at him slyly.

'How much will you take then, Tyros, to ferry the eight of us to Dardanos?'

'I will take you all free of cost as I am going there myself. I intend to travel through the night and reach there in the morning,' answered Tyros.

I then ordered the two Macedonians to summon the pilot boat so that we could climb into it and board Tyros's transport, for the ship wasn't alongside the docks. They rushed to hail the pilot of the boat and, once he came alongside with his crew, all of my party climbed into it, along with Tyros, and we rowed as fast as we could to our ship, where Miletus waited for us. The moment we were on board, he gave orders for the ship to leave and the pilot boat rowed in front of us to guide us through the port's defences of pikes and ropes, but since Miletus and the sailors knew the safe way already (having been guided in by the pilot boat), they took out their bows and arrows from the lower deck and lit the arrows. They started raining the flaming arrows on the six Macedonian triremes that were within range and they alighted on their decks and hit the sides, causing the triremes to catch fire. The two Macedonians who were on the docks stared aghast at our actions.

In this way we destroyed the triremes that could have given chase to our vessel. Since the sailors were all away in the city, there was nobody to try and put out the fires and, in a short time, the flames reached the ships' masts and all of us could see Macedonian soldiers rushing to the docks and gesticulating at our vessel.

The crew of the pilot ship, seeing what we were up to, tried to stop us on our way out, but our ship was too heavy for them and our rowers rammed our bow into them from behind, causing their boat to capsize and their crew to jump into the water. In this manner did I escape with Luminas beside me. Miletus hugged me, for he confessed that he had not hoped to see me alive again. But now that I had made it, he said that he was sure the Goddess Athena watched over me and that I was destined to do great things. For in his entire life – and Miletus had seen many wars – he had never seen an escape so daring.

SIXTEEN

I told Miletus about the treachery of Boridas and how we had narrowly escaped the consequences of having a traitor in our midst. I also instructed the crew to take us to some point on the coast much before Dardanos so that we could reach Gophoredes and his men sometime in the night itself, rather than the following morning, because I was anxious to know the fate of Agos and Mazus. So Miletus directed the trireme to the nearest beach where we could all disembark and proceed to where the Persians had camped outside Abydos.

Luminas clung to me all the while. Miletus had wine served to all the sailors and soldiers. We did all this in the dark, for Miletus had ordered the lamps to be snuffed out as he didn't want the Macedonians to chase us down in the night. When we reached the camp, it was past midnight. Agos was already there and he had a fantastic tale to tell us.

After Agos and my men left with Mazus and his three wives and were taken by Alabanda to the cemetery, Agos posted himself on a treetop while Alabanda and the men dug earth out of a grave to get to the entrance of the tunnel. Alabanda had covered the entrance with earth after he had killed the Mede who looked after the cemetery, so that the Macedonians would not stumble on it even by accident.

Posted atop the tree, Agos noticed Boridas leading the Macedonians towards the house from where Mazus had been rescued. Surprised by this and concerned that Boridas might lead the Macedonians straight to where I was, he gave instructions to Alabanda to take Mazus and his wives through the tunnel to the other side while he himself, along with one of the mercenaries, followed the Macedonians at a safe distance, so that in the event the Macedonians took us captive, they could try and rescue us.

Agos also observed from a distance that Memphios, having noticed the treachery of Boridas, had warned me and knew therefore that I would take appropriate measures to avoid the Macedonians. When

Boridas and the Macedonians reached the place where Mazus and his wives had been staying, they were surprised to find that Mazus had already fled with his wives. They ran immediately towards Alabanda's place, where the tunnel was. Anticipating this, Agos moved swiftly towards the dock where the tunnel emerged and, swimming under the jetty with the mercenary, reached the end of the tunnel and blocked it by locking the wire mesh and putting rocks on it so that no one would be able to exit the tunnel. Agos was sure that we were not inside the tunnel, for he had seen the pilot ship help us board the ship. Having done this, Agos went right back to see whether the Macedonians had entered the tunnel with Boridas at Alabanda's place, thinking that we had taken the route of the tunnel as planned.

'What then?' I asked eagerly.

'I observed them from a window and noticed that they were busy counting the drachmas that we had brought for Alabanda. Boridas was arguing for a larger share, for he was the one who had revealed all to them. The leader of the Macedonian unit, however, examined the trapdoor and ordered lamps to be found and lit and then he forbade anybody to touch the money as first Seleucus, and Mazus himself, had to be apprehended or Polemon would have all of them whipped to death. This brought upon them a sense of urgency. After the lamps were found and lit, the leader of the unit left two sentries at Alabanda's place to guard the entrance of the tunnel while he, along with Boridas and the others, descended into it.

'After they had all disappeared into the tunnel, I entered the house with my companion and killed the two sentries. It was an easy thing to do, for they were busy hiding some of the drachmas in their personal belongings and some they were hiding by digging a hole in the ground so that when the money was divided they would not only get their share, but also the share they had stolen. So preoccupied were they in hiding this money that they didn't observe the two of us creep up on them. We slit their throats quickly and I then shut the trapdoor of the tunnel and placed heavy pieces of furniture on it to make sure that it could not be opened from below. In this manner I trapped Boridas and the other Macedonians inside the tunnel. I then disposed of the two corpses in the grounds outside, so that if new Macedonian units came looking for their comrades, they would not chance upon them at Alabanda's place.

'After these exertions, I hid the money we had brought for Alabanda in a particular grave, so that it would be available to him when he returned to Abydos. After that, I came back to the tunnel from which Mazus had escaped earlier and made good my own escape,' finished Agos.

Agos's adventure had been greater than that of our party. Miletus thumped his back and even Memphios was happy that the traitor Boridas had met with a fate that he deserved.

Mazus was very grateful to me for having rescued him and he offered me a hundred talents for saving his life, which I refused. This refusal made him even more obliged to me and he himself offered to send me to meet the Persian king with letters of introduction detailing how I had rescued him from Abydos at great risk to myself. He even ordered Luminas to accompany me, so that she could obtain an audience with the king immediately and also help me with my Persian along the way.

Gophoredes and the other officers were also happy with the rescue of Mazus, even though they had lost two hundred of their men in the effort. The Macedonians had killed all the overzealous Persians who had climbed down the ramparts into Abydos and they had brought the catapults which were in the eastern sector to the western sector to attack the aggressors on the walls. They managed to kill many of them before Gophoredes gave the order to withdraw. But it was the Persian attack on the city that had made the rescue a success because it drew the Macedonian soldiers away from the dock.

The next day, when the Persian lord Mritphakes arrived outside Abydos to take stock of the situation, he was surprised to learn that Mazus had been rescued and there was nothing left for him to do. Another person to arrive that day was a messenger from Athens, sent by Phormio. He carried messages from Phormio and a sealed note from Demosthenes for me.

Phormio's message had arrived a day late, for it warned me about Boridas. Phormio had found out that the Macedonians had arrested Boridas and all his men and their relatives at the Apollo temple in Thebes. Having taken entire families hostage, they had proposed to Boridas that he travel to Asia and meet Seleucus, son of Nicanor, and deliver him by stealth to Polemon, who was the chief Macedonian functionary in Abydos. They promised to release everybody after Boridas had done this, and it was Boridas's luck as well as misfortune that I planned Mazus's escape around the time he arrived, for though it gave him an opportunity to deliver me to Polemon, it also brought about his own death in the tunnel. Alabanda informed me that there was no way out of the tunnel, and even the path to the left which we hadn't taken, was a dead end. He calculated that the lamps which the Macedonian had carried with them would have run out of oil in a few hours, and after that there was nothing much the men would have been able to do except wait for their deaths, for they would have exhausted their energies in trying to push the trapdoor and the rocks and would have failed. Once the lamps ran out of oil, the darkness would have brought such deep despondency that the men would have fought amongst themselves and cursed Boridas for their fate.

Boridas's treachery reminded me of the prophecy of Mistros. Two of his predictions had come to pass. I had met Luminas and Boridas had turned out to be a traitor. Just one prediction of his remained, which was for me to embrace the monster.

Miraculously, when I opened the letter from Demosthenes, it said that he had received information from Cretan sources that the Macedonians had taken delivery of a transport trireme from the Phoenicians, which was two and a half plethrons in length and half a plethron wide and, though it moved very slowly, it was carrying a monster from the island of Rhodes to Abydos. It would halt at the city of Methymyna on the island of Lesbos before proceeding to Abydos. Demosthenes said that his source was a Cretan who had heard from one of the builders of the trireme in Crete that the cargo hold of the ship was three times the size of a normal trireme and that no ship of that size had ever been built. Even the Cretans who built it were initially not sure whether it would float or sink.

The monster which this ship carried was fifteen times the size of a man of six cubits; the Macedonians intended to use it to fight the Persians at Abydos. This monster, when unchained and let loose on the enemy, could kill them by the thousands, and only the Macedonians could control it. Though the Cretans had not seen the monster, they had heard the Macedonians talk about it. Only a few Macedonians had seen it, but those who had not spoke of it as Ares himself, and it was agreed amongst them that whoever controlled the monster would win any war amongst humans.

Demosthenes was concerned by the news and wished me to find out what this monster was and capture it from the Macedonians, so that Philip and Alexander could not become invincible. Demosthenes urged that I journey to Lesbos with my mercenaries since the trireme carrying the monster was scheduled to arrive there a month from now. He added that the Macedonian general Parmenio was himself leading the forces which were guarding the monster from the pirates and the

Persians. Parmenio was earlier commanding the Macedonian operations in Abydos, but after he left for Lesbos, the command had fallen to Polemon in the absence of any other senior officer there. I think Polemon's temporary appointment had also to do with attracting me to the city. But, by the grace of Athena, I had been able to enter Abydos and come out alive in spite of their planning.

I was much alarmed, though, by the news of the monster and shared the contents of Demosthenes's note with Miletus, Agos, Zamos and Mazus. Mazus was alarmed too, for he feared that a monster on the side of the Macedonians would greatly reduce his chances of taking back Abydos from them, and this the Persian king would surely order him to do. The strange thing was that all of us were alarmed by the news without really knowing the nature and scope of this alleged beast.

Thus it was that I decided to proceed to Lesbos with three triremes, and Mazus added four more from his navy to take the total to seven. Though he sent his troops in the charge of Gophoredes, he told him to deploy them under my supervision. I intended to sort out the matter of the monster at Lesbos and then proceed immediately to Sardis to meet the Persian king, who was on tour there, without coming back to Abydos. I asked Mazus whether he could send an envoy with me to Lesbos, for I wished the envoy to accompany me to Sardis, where I would present the introductory letters of Demosthenes, King Aegis of Sparta and Mazus to the Persian king Artaxerxes in order to get the support that I desired.

Mazus readily agreed to do so and said he would ask Luminas whether she would consider going on the journey with me. I had hoped he would suggest this and was elated. When Luminas heard of it, she was overjoyed too, though she hid her feelings in front of Mazus and made many comments about how uncomfortable she felt on the sea.

Mazus, however, insisted on Luminas being accompanied by his personal bodyguard, a Mede by the name of Phanus. This Phanus had been on an errand to Troy when Mazus had entered Abydos and been held hostage, but had rejoined him after his rescue. He was a person of enormous strength and taller than anyone I had ever seen.

Zamos staffed the three triremes with Phoenician sailors, as they were the best in the world after the Athenians, and provided a total force of a hundred armed men, apart from the sailors. Gophoredes himself had one hundred and twenty Persian soldiers under his command, apart from the sailors. With this force we set off for the city of Methymyna in Lesbos, where Demosthenes had said the Macedonians would halt. It would be a journey of around sixty parasangs and would take us six days, as we would have to hug the coast and halt in the night. Zamos hired a captain for navigation who knew the coast well, particularly the places where we would halt at night.

Before departing, I gave instructions to Miletus and Zamos to start recruiting mercenaries at a fast pace and to develop plans in collaboration with the Persian officers to take back Abydos from the Macedonians. I also sent a secret message to Demosthenes that I had embarked with seven triremes to Lesbos to see what kind of monster the Macedonians had made their own, and intended to befriend it if possible, as I had been advised by a trusted seer by the name of Mistros that if I befriended the monster, victory would be mine. I also sent a message to Phormio to find out if it was true that Athele was with child, whether it was mine, and when the birth was due. After Boridas's treachery, I was not sure whether he had spoken the truth.

I also sent the Persian Alabanda back to Abydos and told him to come out and report to Miletus about matters in the city every three days, and if there was something very important, then he should come earlier as well. Both Mazus and I intended to utilize the tunnels in any future aggression against the Macedonians. The tunnel from the graveyard was, however, unsuitable for taking large numbers of people, as the passage was narrow and in many portions it was flooded with water. So I told Miletus to explore with Alabanda the other tunnel, which started from the bath where the Macedonian barracks were, and to see if it was in a better condition for the secret movements of troops. I also told him not to share this information about the tunnels with the Persians, for I never knew at what point our interest could clash with theirs and a conflict might arise. This foresight on my part proved to be a blessing as future events unfolded.

The journey to Lesbos was uneventful, except for the nights that Luminas spent with me in my tent. She used to enter my tent in a manner such that Phanus, the bodyguard, did not notice. The second night that we spent on the coast, she sent an attendant of hers – she was travelling with two – to flirt with Phanus, and Phanus, aroused with passion, took Luminas's attendant behind the dunes and proceeded to impose himself on her. Luminas then promptly made an appearance, as if by chance, and at that point the attendant started shouting that Phanus was forcing himself upon her.

'Phanus, how dare you!' she exclaimed. 'I will have you reported to Mazus and beheaded.'

This threat from Luminas scared Phanus no end and he prostrated himself before her, begging her not to report the incident to Mazus; the satrap would take great umbrage at the incident since bodyguards were forbidden to have any sexual relationship with the attendants. Mazus could have him sold as a slave or even have him executed for his indiscretion. After Luminas forgave him, she had Phanus pledge to her his loyalty forever. In this manner she ensured that even if he suspected something between Luminas and me, he would not talk about it to anybody.

On the morning of the seventh day, we made it to the island of Lesbos and beached many parasangs away from the city of Methymyna, in an uninhabited inlet that the captain knew about. We told all the soldiers to leave their weapons and armour on the lowest deck and pretend to be transporters of goods. In case the people of Lesbos spotted us, they would report our presence to the Macedonians, being strongly allied to them. The captain explained that it was very normal for transport ships to make use of the inlet to give the crew rest, and even if the inhabitants saw us, they wouldn't be alarmed, unless the Persians appeared in their battledress. Gophoredes was also advised by me to take the same precaution that we had taken. Then, along with ten of my men, including Agos and Dorian, I made my way to the harbour at Methymyna to discover what kind of monster the Macedonians had managed to capture and how they intended to use it against their enemies.

Dorian said that it could be a giant octopus, for it had eight arms and he had heard stories from sailors claiming that an octopus had gripped their ship with its arms and sunk it in the ocean. He could offer no explanation, however, for the ability of the Macedonians to control this creature of the sea. And whether the creature could operate on land as well.

Agos said the monster could be a creation of the priests, who might have taken the beast called the elephant, which existed in the east, in the land of India, and added elements to it after worship so that it could ravage men in battle. All of us had heard tales about this beast, which had a trunk and could trample anyone in front of it to death. Even the Persian king was rumoured to have these beasts in his armies and they could only be controlled by their Indian masters, who sat on their backs.

With speculation rife among us, we proceeded to Methymyna and there at the docks we saw the biggest ship we had ever seen. It had three masts for hanging sails and Macedonian soldiers lined the dock in a single file, guarding the ship, even as many local inhabitants watched the manoeuvres of the captain of the ship as he tried to turn it around in the dock. So disciplined were the soldiers that none of them looked back to see what the captain was up to; they just stared impassively at the onlookers. The local residents were as fascinated by the ship as they were by the stone-faced demeanour of these Macedonian soldiers who watched for any threats to their ship.

Dorian soon came with information from the local tavern that the ship would be docked at the port for ten days, as the Macedonians were waiting for another monster to come to Methymyna. The two were supposed to proceed together to Abydos.

After the ship had been turned around, Parmenio made an appearance and the onlookers cheered, as he was dressed in the uniform of a general and had plumes sticking out of his helmet. A group of Lesboans who had been waiting for him to emerge started shouting at him to let them see the monster and all the people lining the docks cheered the request. But the Macedonians behaved as if they heard nothing. This annoyed the Lesboans and so this group of twenty people, which had been shouting requests to Parmenio, put forward four who were the tallest and strongest amongst them and challenged the Macedonians to let their monster have a duel with them.

'Let them duel our lads, Parmenio, and we shall see whether your monster can stand up to the strongest we have on Lesbos,' they shouted from the docks.

Parmenio, however, didn't take the bait. The hecklers kept shouting at him while he was on the deck, but they stopped when he went below again. The Macedonians then started applying a paste to the sides of the ships – people said it was a compound that was resistant to fire. Getting bored with watching this, the crowd left the docks and I sent Agos to incite the group which was heckling Parmenio to go back and wait for him to come up again and to continue shouting at him. In this manner did I hope for him to commit some indiscretion.

So Agos and Dorian struck up a friendship with the Lesboans and bought them wine to drink from the tavern. Agos told them: 'We are from Athens, and if an Athenian like us had thrown a challenge like the one you threw at Parmenio, he would have had no option but to accede to the request, otherwise it would be a great loss of face for him. But you Lesboans seem to have no effect at all on Parmenio or the Macedonians, which means that they don't consider you worthy opponents.'

With these remarks did Agos get their ire up. So all of them went back again to the docks and started throwing challenges at Parmenio, even though he was not visible, and they kept at it till evening when some Lesboan officials came and told them to stop as the Macedonians had complained about their behaviour. This fact aggravated the locals even more, and through the night they planned for more of their own to come to the docks the next day and make a stronger appeal to Parmenio.

To avoid the attention of Lesboan officials, we roamed the marketplace in Methymyna in groups of three. It was a bustling port city and had sailors stopping over from as far away as Libya and Egypt. The Lesboans had a policy of encouraging trade in the region, for that was how they made a living.

That night, at the tavern in which Agos, Dorian and I had taken lodgings for the night, I met Cholargus, son of Megara, from Methymyna. Over a glass of wine, we got talking.

'I make a living through diving for pearls. While doing this, I discovered that the Macedonian ship carrying the monster extends six cubits below the water, which means that it can carry a cargo of more than seventy thousand minae, and so the monster inside must be a very huge and heavy one. It's very foolish of the Lesboans to want to fight the monster, as it appears to be three hundred times heavier than any human and could perhaps take on an entire army by itself,' said Cholargus.

Importantly, Cholargus also told me that he had sold a bag full of pearls to the queen of Lesbos two days back and she had told him that King Phaticidas of Lesbos was due to visit Parmenio soon. The Macedonians had agreed to show him the monster, as the king had been an useful ally and had granted them everything they required in their preparations for war against the Persians.

According to Cholargus, King Phaticidas had even asked his troops to vacate their barracks temporarily, so that the Macedonian soldiers could utilize them during their stay in Lesbos. This had caused resentment amongst the Lesboan soldiers as they had to sleep in tents, out in the open, causing many of them to fall sick.

I should tell you at this time that I happened to have met the wife of King Phaticidas during the adventures I had after leaving Attica. Since I am not writing about those adventures now, I will dwell only briefly upon how I knew her, since she too happened to come into my life without my intending it. To tell you the truth, one of the reasons I had been desirous of coming to Lesbos was that I hoped to meet her again.

Her name was Morai and hers was not a Greek name but Ethiopian, for she belonged to the tribe known as Caruti that lived on the border between Egypt and Ethiopia. The Caruti were of royal Ethiopian lineage but fell on bad times when their king, Fusango, was deposed by a rival and they were chased all the way to Egypt, where they accidentally met a nobleman from Lesbos. At that time, Lesbos was much in need of human beings, for they had just suffered a plague which had killed half the population. The Lesboans were inviting people to come from all over Greece to settle in Lesbos and make it their home. So this nobleman took a hundred of these Caruti to Lesbos as slaves, even though they were of royal lineage. When the king of Lesbos came to know of their royal status, he gave them their freedom and many acres of land in the south, near the city of Mitylene, and here the Caruti had settled fifty years ago. Morai was born on the island.

The Caruti, however, retained their distinct customs. One of them was that when a person married, he offered his wife for sexual intercourse to the special guests he invited for the celebrations, and each male guest was supposed to have intercourse with the new bride and leave a gift for her before he left her tent. It so happened that in my wanderings I was taken hostage by the Caruti, around the time that Morai was getting married and King Phaticidas was present as a guest of Morai's father, who was the chief of the Caruti in Lesbos. According to Caruti custom, Morai was offered first to the king by the groom, as he outranked all the males present, and Phaticidas took a liking for Morai. Though he didn't stop other guests from spending time with her, he had her husband killed in an expedition not long after and married her. All this Cholargus revealed to me now, thinking I knew nothing of the matter.

But I knew about Morai from that night, for even though I was just a hostage, Morai's father had released me from the tent where I was being held a prisoner and treated me like an honoured guest, for it was a custom among the Caruti to release all prisoners when the daughter of their chief got married. This was how I had escaped from the clutches of the pirates of Ionia, and since then I had often fantasized about Morai. But that day, after Phaticidas had left me with Morai in her tent, I did not have any sexual intercourse with her and only talked during my time with her, and she was very surprised.

'I find you the most beautiful princess I have ever seen, but it's not a custom amongst us Greeks to have their guests sleep with a new bride,' I had told Morai.

That was the last I had seen of her, and now when Cholargus told me that she was the wife of King Phaticidas, it came as a big surprise to me. This Cholargus was a man of many skills. In the day, he was a diver in the seas, looking for pearls, and in the night, he was the cook in a tavern and was renowned for making big banquets – he even knew how to cook rice, mixed with wine and raisins, inside a lamb's belly.

Cholargus had been summoned by Morai to cook a feast for the Macedonians at noon two days from now. Because of his proximity to her, he knew a great deal about how things stood between Lesbos and Macedonia. Morai had told him that Lesbos had been allowed to become a tribute ally by King Philip on the condition that it pay a sum of hundred talents every year to the Macedonians for protection against the Persians, who often raided their island. Though the real reason, according to Morai, was that otherwise the Macedonians would make impediments to the trade that the Lesboans had in the region.

Cholargus confided that Morai had told him that Parmenio had come with the monster to threaten Phaticidas and make him pay the amount, which was overdue.

'That is the real reason the Macedonians are here. They want to scare Phaticidas. And he is offering them a generous reception in order to make them happy as he has just thirty talents in his coffers to offer them. Parmenio, however, thinks that to receive such a low tribute would be an insult,' said Cholargus.

King Phaticidas, feeling threatened by the Macedonian force that was already in the port at Methymyna, was going to meet Parmenio the next day, and thereafter the Macedonians had been invited to a feast on the grounds of the temple of Athena. Cholargus said that Phaticidas was having sleepless nights, for he felt that Parmenio would set the monster loose in his city if they did not pay the hundred talents and everything would be lost.

This is how things were when Phaticidas asked Cholargus to spy on the ship and find out all that he could about the monster, and that's what Cholargus had been doing for the past three days. He was diving to the bottom of the docks and checking the hull of the ship for any clues. It was Cholargus, incidentally, who had first incited the group of hecklers to shout challenges at Parmenio for a fight with the monster, but with no success so far.

The next day, a bigger crowd gathered at the docks to watch the ship carrying the monster and people came from afar with their children, for they did not want to miss an event of this magnitude, which might never happen again in the history of Lesbos. They wanted their progeny to witness it so that they could tell their own children about it later. The hecklers gathered early at the instigation of Agos, who had also promised a prize of twenty drachmas to the one who managed to rile the Macedonians the most. This incentive propelled them to start shouting challenges to Parmenio even before he could be seen anywhere, and so a Macedonian soldier complained to a senior functionary of King Phaticidas. When this functionary came to quieten the crowd, they started shouting insults at him.

'Pig face,' they called him and he withdrew hastily from the port.

Phaticidas himself arrived at the port around noon and, seeing him, the hecklers stopped, for they were afraid of him. Parmenio received Phaticidas and led him to the deck of the ship containing the monster and Phaticidas's soldiers pushed the crowd back from the docks.

I then located Cholargus and told him to take me to Queen Morai, as she would be alone in the palace now. I told him that I needed to see Morai because I needed her to talk to Phaticidas about granting us a large piece of land in Lesbos to settle a colony of shipbuilders from Phoenicia. I bribed Cholargus with fifty drachmas for his efforts and so, with great alacrity, he took me to Queen Morai's palace, where the bodyguards then escorted me to her.

Queen Morai surprised me with her opening words. She said: 'It took you a long time to come here. I have been expecting you.'

She was crying and I thought, initially, that she had confused me with somebody else, as I had only met her for a short time in her tent and was a little in doubt whether she would recognize me from her wedding night. But Morai then told me an incredible story. She said that having been married to Sebasticus, a Greek from the south of Lesbos, and loving him with all her heart, she had hoped to be happily married to him forever, but she had been denied that when Sebasticus died in an expedition that Phaticidas had mounted against a settlement on the island of Chios. Needing money, Phaticidas had taken one thousand men from Lesbos on ten triremes and, landing at Chios at dawn, he had ravaged five prosperous villages and a small town and had stolen their grain and all the money and ornaments that they had. On the way back to their triremes, they had encountered a small army that the king of Chios had sent against them and, though Phaticidas defeated them, the fight cost the life of Sebasticus, who was struck by an arrow that went through his heart. His body remained at Chios.

'I later learned from bodyguards faithful to me that it was Phaticidas who had ordered the death of Sebasticus and the arrow that hit him had not been fired by any of Chios's men but by a mercenary Cretan archer in Phaticidas's pay. But by the time I learned this, Phaticidas had already asked for my hand from my father and, since I was a widow, he had seen no reason to object. And neither had I. But for a month now, I have been having a dream in which I keep seeing the destruction of Methymyna and I feel that it is Sebasticus seeking revenge on Phaticidas and Lesbos itself. In the dream, I see the port being ravaged by a monster of iron and wood and I can see Phaticidas nowhere. But the one face I see over and over again in my dreams is yours, Seleucus. That is why, when I saw you here, I told you that I was expecting you,' said Moria.

I must confess that this was the first time it had struck me that the monster could be a man-made contraption and not the living beast that we had all imagined. Morai started sobbing then and clutched my arm.

'I want you to promise me something, Seleucus,' said Morai.

'How can I promise you something before knowing what it is that you want me to do?' I asked her.

But she insisted and clutched both my arms and hugged me and asked me to promise first and, in a moment of weakness, I acceded to her request. Morai, though dark skinned, was a very beautiful woman. She had the most expressive eyes I had ever seen, and the way she spoke Greek was itself a seduction for most men.

I imagined that Morai's request would be related to some minor issue, but when she whispered that she wanted me to kill Phaticidas and make her the ruler of Lesbos, it came as a total shock to me, though I didn't let it show it on my face.

Said Morai: 'I have wanted to kill him ever since I came to know that he was responsible for Sebasticus's death. I hate it when he sleeps next to me at night, and now he wants a son. I would hate myself and my son if I had to give birth to him through seed that Phaticidas leaves in me.'

I came to know that Phaticidas had not only had Sebasticus killed, but also all the other guests of honour who had slept with Morai on the wedding night, though it was a legitimate custom amongst the Carutis

Phaticidas was intensely possessive of Morai and jealous even if she looked at another man. He couldn't tolerate the fact that these other men had all slept with his wife, even though she wasn't his wife but Sebasticus's when it happened.

Hearing all this from Morai, I became worried that Phaticidas might return any time now and recognize me from the wedding night.

'How do you expect me to do what you desire? Do you have a plan? Isn't Phaticidas surrounded by bodyguards at all times?' I asked her.

Morai then told me that Phaticidas had taken a gift of many pearls for Parmenio, hoping to corrupt him; the pearls had been bought by Morai herself from various divers, Cholargus amongst them. He had also taken a few tiger skins and the teeth of an elephant, which he had got from the cargo he had confiscated of a Phoenician trader. With these gifts he hoped that Parmenio would be persuaded to send a report to Philip to lessen his annual tribute to twenty talents, which sum he wanted to pay in three months.

'I know that he has more than four hundred talents in his treasury, but being a miser, he doesn't want to pay the hundred talents due to the Macedonians, as he thinks it is too large an amount. But if you kill him and hand over the kingdom to me, I would marry you and we could then rule Lesbos together,' said Morai.

'Queen Morai, though I might help you in becoming the ruler of Lesbos, I have no intention of staying here. You can rule on your own and select a husband on the basis of merit and value to the kingdom and yourself. There is no need for you to shower gratitude on me by marrying me,' I said.

Morai then said that Phaticidas was arranging a banquet for the Macedonians the next day and I could go too, as her guest, but I reminded her that Phaticidas might remember me from her wedding night and order me killed, and so she immediately corrected herself and asked me to come the following day to meet her in the evening, after the banquet. In the meantime, I was to think of a plan that she could implement to kill Phaticidas and take over his army.

After this rather unusual meeting, I left Morai and went back to the docks, where I came to know that Phaticidas had left the ship with his bodyguards, without having gone below deck. It was while he was there that the other ship which the Macedonians had been waiting for had arrived, and Parmenio and his admiral had gone aboard the new ship to examine its cargo. The new ship was as big as the first and the hecklers, after the departure of Phaticidas, had come back and were urging Parmenio to release the monster for a duel with the strongest men of Methymyna.

In the evening, I met Cholargus again and he told me that Phaticidas's meeting with Parmenio had not gone well. Cholargus said that, though Parmenio had accepted the gifts that Phaticidas had brought for him, he had refused to relent on the amount due to Macedonia and had given a two-day period to Phaticidas to come up with the hundred talents or face the consequences. All this Cholargus had learned from one of Phaticidas's bodyguards who had been present during the exchange. The name of this bodyguard was Amestipolos and he was Cholargus's brother-in-law. He told Cholargus that though Phaticidas had promised Parmenio that he would look into the matter speedily and borrow from a few rich traders so as to pay the tribute, he had no intention of doing so and was cooking up a scheme to attack the Macedonians and take over the two ships with the monsters. He intended to do this the next day, after the banquet.

This revelation from Cholargus planted the seeds of an idea in my mind, but I needed to consult Morai on it before I could proceed further, and so I sent Cholargus to her with a letter requesting her to meet me at the temple of Athena that night.

'Do you have access to Phaticidas's treasury?' I asked Morai when I met her.

'I do. Though Phaticidas thinks that I don't know where it is, I have watched him go there many times in the night, when he assumed that I was asleep. It is in an underground chamber that can only be accessed through a tunnel from the palace. After having the tunnel and the chambers built, Phaticidas had the masons murdered, so that they could tell no one of their existence,' said Morai.

When I heard this story, I had no sympathy left for Phaticidas. Morai then told me that one day in a week, the priests from the temple of Apollo, which was two parasangs from the city, came to Phaticidas's palace to perform a sheep sacrifice. She said that a seer had advised Phaticidas that as long as he honoured Apollo in this way, once a week, there would be no threat to his kingdom. The priests numbered ten in all and came in three wagons, for Phaticidas also provided them with produce and grain to take back to their village. He had given Morai the responsibility of looking after the needs of the priests since he was busy with affairs of state.

Seeing that they were supposed to come the next morning, Morai asked whether she should not halt their coming, for that way eight days would have passed without the sacrifice and Phaticidas's bad time would start. I was, however, thinking along different lines, which was to make my own men come into Phaticidas's mansion on wagons and horses, pretending to be priests from the Apollo temple, and steal Phaticidas's treasury so that a hundred talents from it could be provided to Parmenio and he could be asked to support Morai as the new ruler instead of Phaticidas. I asked Morai whether she was amenable to the scheme and she gave her consent immediately, as she desired vengeance against Phaticidas without any delay.

After obtaining from her information about the route the priests from the Apollo temple would take, I went back to where our seven triremes were and picked a team of ten men and explained to them that they were to reach the Apollo temple before dawn and take the priests hostage within the temple complex itself.

Then I chose another team of ten men, Agos, Dorian and Otanes amongst them, and gave them instructions that they were to follow at some distance the earlier team to the Apollo temple, so the people of Lesbos didn't get alarmed on seeing so many people proceeding together to the temple. Once the first team of ten men had made the priests captive, they were to don the attire of the priests and, taking their wagons, proceed to Phaticidas's palace, along the route that the priests usually took. This route they were to enquire from the priests themselves. They were to also bring the sheep that were meant for sacrifice.

Once they reached the palace of Phaticidas, they were to follow the instructions of Morai, who would lead them to the underground chamber where Phaticidas maintained his treasury. They would then transport the talents to the wagons outside, hiding the money amidst the produce that they were entitled to take with them, and thus hoodwink the guards. Once they got out of Phaticidas's palace, they were to take the talents to our ships as the money would be safest there, but leave a hundred talents in a spare wagon at Methymyna so that I could pay off Parmenio.

I intended to talk to Parmenio the next day after having successfully deprived Phaticidas of his treasury. Luminas, being alone for the past few days, had grown very anxious about my safety and entreated that I take Phanus with me to meet Parmenio the next day, but I didn't want to take him as he attracted a lot of attention because of his size. Not a single person from Lesbos would have seen a man of that size and they would all know that he was a foreigner and would want to know how he came to be in Methymyna. But Luminas insisted and so I gave instructions to the men to take Phanus, but to make sure that he always sat in the wagon, as then he would be less likely to draw the attention of the people. I also advised the Persian Gophoredes and the rest of the sailors to be on the ready so that we could depart without delay if events required us to do so.

In the morning, ten of my men and I reached Phaticidas's palace dressed as priests. Since Phaticidas was not in his residence at the time of our arrival, it was easy for all of us to get into the worship hall and seal it off from the prying eyes of the guards. There was nothing unusual in this as this was how Phaticidas's instructions stood about the weekly sacrifice. Apparently, the sacrifice was conducted in a manner that nobody other than the priests and the person for whose benefit the sheep were being sacrificed could watch it, so that the benefits of the sacrifice would accrue only to those paying for and organizing it.

It was from the worship hall that the tunnel started to the underground chamber, which had an entrance made of crafted wood with attached levers. A difficulty arose in the opening of the door, for not even Morai knew the exact sequence in which the levers had to be pulled in order for it to be opened. Since time was running out, I summoned Phanus from the wagon outside and he used his strength against the door to break the levers and push it open for us. If Phanus hadn't been there, it would have taken us longer to make our way past the door, for the confined space in the tunnel made it difficult for two people to stand together and use their strength simultaneously against the levers. Bringing Phanus certainly proved useful, though now the guards at Phaticidas's place were all intrigued about this giant of a priest who had emerged from the wagon and gone into the worship hall.

After the guards who had seen Phanus informed the others around the perimeter of Phaticidas's palace about the size of one of the priests, those of them who had not been able to see him huddled outside the worship hall for a glimpse of him.

It was at this point that Phaticidas returned to his residence, putting all our plans in jeopardy. I immediately advised Morai on how to proceed with him, and this is how events unfolded.

Queen Morai met him at the door and Phaticidas told her that he had suddenly remembered that today was the day of the weekly sacrifice and so he had left the scene of his inspection, though he was scheduled to talk to his top military officers.

'I wanted to be present for the sacrifice, as important matters of state are to take place over the next few days and I want the Gods to be on my side. After I finish participating in the sacrifice, I intend to go back to the hill from where the docks can be seen clearly, so that I can better plan certain military matters,' said Phaticidas.

'That is a good thought. But the priests are acting very secretively today. The head priest of the Apollo temple has been visited by a very respected seer from Erythria in Ionia and he says that there is grave danger hovering over Lesbos, which he intends to ward off by offering sacrifices and rituals in a certain manner. They are performing the ceremonies in the worship hall and have forbidden anybody to enter it, including you, my king, till it is over. The seer from Erythria is a giant of a man and he is himself supervising everything to align all the Gods in your favour,' Morai told him.

Phaticidas was much moved by the fact that the priests had discerned the danger hovering over Lesbos on their own, without him having briefed them, and this singular fact reassured him that the priests were knowledgeable about future matters.

'I will wait with you, Morai, till the ceremonies are over, for I seek guidance from the priests about something I intend to do this afternoon. I want an assurance from the priests that it will have the kind of result that I seek and not have any unintended consequences,' said Phaticidas.

'What is it that you want to consult the priests about? Confide in me, my king. The new priest who has come from Erythria has insisted that only I go inside to convey any questions that we might seek answers to, during the rituals. He has warned me that if anyone else comes, the results to you could be disastrous,' said Morai.

Phaticidas then whispered his plans to Morai.

'I intend to poison the Macedonians at the banquet I am arranging for Parmenio and the other senior Macedonian officers, and then I intend to use my soldiers to take over their two ships at the docks and thus gain possession of the two monsters. I want to know from the priests whether today is the right day to initiate my plan, for if I don't succeed, the Macedonians will cause immense harm to Lesbos and particularly to Methymyna. Even the priests at the Apollo temple will perhaps not be spared by them,' said Phaticidas.

Morai then proceeded to the worship hall to narrate to me all that Phaticidas had told her and waited for me to give her an answer to take back to him. She was trembling with fear, as she had not anticipated that he would arrive while we were emptying his treasury.

After discussing the matter with Agos and Dorian, I told Morai to take Phanus with her and let him answer Phaticidas's question. Then Agos and I briefed Phanus on what he had to say and how he was to say it. We also tutored him regarding replies to other questions that we thought Phaticidas might ask, and we warned him that if Phaticidas asked him anything to which he did not know the answer, he should simply say that he would reply after the ceremony was over and proceed back inside the hall to be instructed by us.

When Morai took Phanus outside to meet Phaticidas, he was amazed at Phanus's size, for let alone priests, he had never seen a soldier like him in all his travels in the Greek world.

With a grave face, Phanus then proceeded to answer Phaticidas's question: 'If the poison is delivered to the Macedonians in wine that is red, before they have eaten anything, and if it is consumed also by the officers in the army of Lesbos, then it shall take effect and weaken the Macedonians and aid your strategy. For I have discovered that if the Macedonians alone take it, then those of your officers who are in league with the Macedonians, unknown to you, and who seek to snatch power from you, will survive and strike a bond with those Macedonians in Lesbos who will not be at the banquet. Then, together, they will lay the blame for the deaths due to poisoning at your door and, thus allying together, they will put you to death. So, proceed without hesitation, for today being a full moon day, it will fulfil all your aspirations, and this act of yours will rescue Lesbos from the tyranny of the Macedonians, provided you do as I say.'

Phaticidas was shocked by what Phanus said, for he had not imagined that any of his officers were in league with the Macedonians. He was immensely grateful to Phanus for having warned him and took off one of the gold rings on his hand and gave it to Phanus as a gift. Phanus, not having been briefed on whether to accept a gift, if one was offered, immediately refused it and said that only after the completion of the ceremony would he decide whether to take any gift from Phaticidas, as he took directions on all matters from Apollo himself.

This act of Phanus impressed Phaticidas no end, for never in his life, so he told Morai, had he met a priest who had refused a gift and who had told him that he would accept one only on the directions of the God.

Added Phaticidas: 'I intend to ask this priest whether he can stay in Lesbos and not go back to Erythria, for I am tremendously impressed with his character and want to conduct my future reign in Lesbos under his guidance.'

Since Phaticidas remained at his residence, awaiting the end of the ceremony, we were in a quandary as to how to carry his treasures to the waiting wagons – the underground chamber was awash with silver talents, and it also had a small quantity of golden talents and precious stones.

Then I sent Phanus to him again, and this time he told Phaticidas to fetch a pitcher of water from the sea, for he intended to pour the water on the sacrificial fire and then determine from the smoke that came out the future of Lesbos under his leadership. My plan was to disappear from the palace once Phaticidas departed to fulfil this task. But destiny intervened favourably, for a big commotion was heard and two of Phaticidas's soldiers came to him with the message that the Macedonians were taking out the beasts from their ships and the whole of Methymyna had gathered to watch the event.

SEVENTEEN

On hearing that the monsters were to be brought out, Phaticidas immediately left and instructed Morai to have the priests wait till he was back, specially Phanus. He told Morai that he had to make new arrangements at the banquet, as the priests had told him that his own officers were in conspiracy with the Macedonians and he also wanted to observe the monsters from the hilltop.

That was how fate intervened and we were able to empty the treasury unobserved.

But I left Morai and Phanus behind, for I didn't want Phaticidas to come back to an empty house and rethink his plans for the banquet. I briefed Phanus on what he was to do once Phaticidas returned with water from the sea and I gave Agos instructions to collapse the tunnel to the treasury chamber so that Phaticidas would not know till he had the tunnel re-dug that his treasure was gone, in case he decided to visit his chamber that very day.

I also left two of my men with Phanus and told them to rescue Morai and take her to the ship if things went contrary to what I had planned. One of the men I left behind was Otanes, the same Otanes whom we had rescued along with Tyros and Menicus from the house of Mios in Attica when they were due to be sacrificed by Antipater.

Thereafter, while Agos and some men transferred Phaticidas's treasury to our ships, I proceeded with Agos to locate Cholargus at the docks amidst all the confusion that the Macedonians were creating by unveiling the two monsters on their ships.

The monsters turned out to be amazing. They stretched to the height of ten men standing one on top of the other. The Macedonians called them Lithobolos Ares and Lithobolos Philip. The hecklers had started making snide comments at Parmenio right from the morning and the Macedonian general, in irritation, had commanded his men to bring up the monsters. Once the upper decks of the ships opened and the monsters started being pulled up on ropes, the Lesboans were disappointed that they turned out to be contraptions of wood, iron and sinew and not giant living beasts that people had been boasting they were, which could jump five plethrons in one leap and had eight arms, each of which had the strength to uproot a tree.

Looking at them, nobody could tell what the monsters could do, and the residents of Methymyna who had collected at the docks started booing Parmenio, for they felt the monsters were a big disappointment and consisted just of wood which had been carpentered into an elaborate sculpture. Then the officers started barking orders to the soldiers on the deck and the long arms of the monsters were revealed, hinged by sinew and springs to a giant bow, which itself was no less than the size of five men. It took ten men to pull on the ropes to stretch the spring which bent the bow of the contraption, and then five men lifted a rounded piece of stone which must have weighed at least five hundred minae into position on the arms of each of the monsters. Parmenio then ordered the monsters to be turned to face the sea, and facing the crowd of hecklers, he shouted: 'Behold, you ignorant men of Lesbos, what Lithobolos Ares and Lithobolos Philip can do. Behold and fear them.'

Saying this, he waved his arm and two men lifted the levers on each of the monsters that released the bow. The stones travelled on the arms of the monsters and flew into the air almost at the same time, travelling at least two stadia before landing in the sea with a huge splash. After this display, there was a stunned silence, as none of the Lesboans had seen a monster of this kind which could throw a five hundred minae stone to a distance of not less than two and a quarter stadia. Parmenio then had the monsters recalibrated and placed stones of a lesser size on their arms. When they were released by the levers, they travelled four and a half stadia before falling into the sea. They went so far that you couldn't even see the splash they made.

Then Parmenio turned the arms of the monsters to face the crowd and the smiles vanished from people's faces and nearly all of them fled the docks while the Macedonians, including Parmenio, had a good laugh. I managed to locate Cholargus in the fleeing crowd and went up to him.

'Cholargus, can you get Amestipolos, the bodyguard of Phaticidas, to meet me immediately as it is a matter of great urgency?' I asked him.

'I don't know where Phaticidas is, but whreever he is, that is where Amestipolos will be too. I can help you find him,' answered Cholargus.

I told him that Phaticidas had gone to the hilltop overlooking the port and, since there was very little time, I too proceeded with Cholargus to the spot. I suggested to him that he enter Phaticidas's camp and escort Amestipolos outside to meet with me. I also instructed Dorian to give Cholargus a hundred drachmas then and there for his efforts and Cholargus, much pleased with this largesse, immediately accompanied us on horseback to where Phaticidas was. He soon returned with Amestipolos.

'Here are a hundred drachmas for you, Amestipolos,' I told him even before he could speak.

Amestipolos took the money from me without any hesitation, but with great distrust on his face. I continued before he could respond in words to me: 'I offer you this fee, for I wish you to render me some services. But before we come to that, I have something to tell you for your own safety. You are not to drink the red wine that will be offered at the banquet that Phaticidas will be arranging for the Macedonians. If the wine is offered to you in the presence of Phaticidas, you are to only make a pretence of drinking it,' I told him.

'I am amazed that a stranger should come and advise me thus. What are your intentions and where do you come from?' asked Amestipolos, even as he counted the drachmas that I had given him.

For a moment, I felt that I may have chosen the wrong way of communicating with Amestipolos and that he would go and report the matter to Phaticidas. But Cholargus helped me calm him down and told him that I intended to buy land in Lesbos for making triremes to sell to the navies in the region. This explanation satisfied him and he felt that I was a person of some standing, an impression he probably hadn't got earlier, seeing me to be so young. He asked me what was in the red wine and should he inform King Phaticidas. I told him that Phaticidas himself would kill him if he gave this news to him and then feeling, because of the paucity of time, that to tell the truth to Amestipolos and Cholargus might be my best option, I told them what I could.

'Your king intends to poison the Macedonians, as well as the top officers of his own army, at the banquet, for his priests have advised him that his officers are in conspiracy with the Macedonians. He intends to poison the red wine and serve it before the meal to all the Macedonians who come to the banquet, as well as to all his officers who have been in contact with the Macedonians. After that, he intends to attack the remaining Macedonians at the docks and take over the two ships with the monsters. Since his army of four thousand men outnumbers the Macedonians, Phaticidas hopes to crush them,' I explained.

Amestipolos was greatly alarmed and asked me how I had come by this piece of information. I lied to him that I had overheard Phaticidas conversing with his priests in the morning and had also heard Queen Morai pleading with him not to kill his own officers, but Phaticidas had been adamant. I told him that I was there to meet Phaticidas to get a grant of land near the docks to manufacture triremes and, since Cholargus had told me that his brother-in-law was a bodyguard of Phaticidas, I thought it my duty to warn both of them.

Amestipolos was now more understanding of my motives. But being out of his depth, he asked me what he was supposed to do. I then asked him for the names of the officers from Lesbos who had been in contact with the Macedonian army and, after he gave me twenty-odd names, I asked him to choose two names out of those twenty who might be said to be the leaders. He immediately took the names of Brachimon and Fachulus and said that he was very friendly with both of them.

Cholargus then took me aside.

'It's true what Amestipolos says. He is the lover of both,' he whispered to me.

Both these men, it appeared, were very upset with Phaticidas for having made them give up their barracks to the Macedonians while they had to sleep out in the open.

On coming to know that Amestipolos was a lover to both Brachimon and Fachulus, I told him to take them into confidence, as long as they kept it to themselves, and also told him to bring both men to meet me quickly even as I stood there, for I intended to take a decision after meeting them.

Amestipolos then returned the one hundred drachmas that I had given him, as he said that he had done nothing to earn it and, in fact, I had saved his life by telling him not to drink the poisoned wine. I was very impressed by his behaviour. When he brought Brachimon and Fachulus to meet me, he had already revealed to them the plans of Phaticidas. Both of them being much more experienced than Amestipolos, immediately understood it to be true, as Phaticidas had held a meeting of his commanders after he had seen the display of the monsters, and Brachimon and Fachulus had been surprised not to have been asked to attend the meeting. Only commanders who had been out at sea and had returned that very day had been invited.

At that time, Brachimon and Fachulus had thought it odd that Phaticidas should not involve them as only the previous day they had laid down plans together to overwhelm the Macedonians at the docks. They said my story that Phaticidas would poison those of his officers who were in contact with the Macedonians made sense as Phaticidas, since returning from his house after meeting the priests, had only talked to officers who had not directly interacted with the Macedonians and had sent a different group of officers to invite the Macedonians to the banquet.

I then told Brachimon, as he seemed a natural leader, to inform the officers who had gone to bring the Macedonians to the banquet not to drink the red wine and only to pretend to be drinking it, and in this manner they would save their lives while the Macedonian officers would die. I also warned him to tell his fellow officers not to speak of Phaticidas's plan to the Macedonians, for they would then unleash the monsters on the city and destroy Methymyna.

'You need not worry on that account since the soldiers of Lesbos hate the Macedonians, as they have been arrogant and have behaved like brutes towards them. Besides, they think themselves superior and took over our barracks. We would sooner see them poisoned than save their lives,' said Brachimon.

Fachulus and Brachimon, however, raised the issue that once the Macedonian soldiers started getting affected by the poison while none of his officers showed any signs of poisoning, Phaticidas might order their butchery. Also, all the other officers would be privy to the plot and would come to the conclusion that some conspiracy was afoot as none of the Lesboan officers being targeted were dying of the poison in the wine.

I assured him that I had a remedy to the problem.

'I have already told my man Dorian to mix a potion of weeds and ground pearl that will induce vomiting. All of your friends are to swallow it as soon as the wine is served and that will induce redness in your eyes, vomiting and convulsions. Phaticidas will think that the poison is having its effect. Your men will have to pretend to be dead or severely disabled as the same poison affects people differently, depending on their ability to resist its effects,' I explained.

With Parmenio and his officers dead, Phaticidas would lead his troops to the dock, where five hundred Macedonian troops and sailors needed to be subdued. They were to await the outcome of this battle, I told Brachimon and Fachulus. If the Macedonians won, which seemed unlikely as they were fewer in number, they could greet them as the saviours of Lesbos, and if Phaticidas won, which was more likely, seeing that he commanded four thousand troops, they could wait till he came back to the palace and then take him hostage as he would be accompanied by only his bodyguards.

After they took Phaticidas hostage, I told them, they could declare Queen Morai the new ruler. She would denounce him as a king who poisoned his own officers on a whim of the priests, though they had done no wrong. Then Morai would declare that she had herself prayed for their well-being and a new priest from Delphi had arrived who had summoned the Gods and the officers had thus been saved from the ill effects of the poison.

The miracle would make the bulk of Phaticidas's officers convert to the cause of Queen Morai, and Phaticidas could then be put on trial for his crimes. In this manner did I state my plan to Fachulus and Brachimon. I also promised both men high posts in Queen Morai's regime; I convinced them the queen was on their side. After advising them thus, I sent them to prepare the officers loyal to them for Phaticidas's banquet. I also gave them the potion that Dorian had prepared that would induce vomiting in any man who drank it, but would do them no other harm.

I then proceeded to meet Parmenio at the docks before Phaticidas's officers arrived there to escort him and his officers to the banquet. Though I had told Brachimon and Fachulus that we would take Phaticidas hostage once he returned victorious from battle, I was not sure whether taking him hostage would convert his own officers to Morai's cause, for she was not Greek, even though she spoke it, and she belonged to the Caruti tribe and her skin was not white.

Besides, my main objective was to seize the monsters, for if they reached Abydos, it would make the city impregnable. And if Abydos remained in Macedonian hands, Philip would find it easier to establish a bridgehead in Asia against the Persians. It was exactly the intention of Philip and Parmenio to pulverize and surprise the Persians at Abydos and elsewhere with their lithobolos. Therefore I reached the docks with Dorian, full fifty talents in our wagon, and asked to be given an audience with Parmenio after claiming myself to be a secret herald of Queen Morai, the wife of Phaticidas.

Since I had never met Parmenio and had only heard of him as Philip's most trusted general, I wasn't worried that he would recognize me as Seleucus, son of Nicanor. The guards ushered me to the deck where I awaited Parmenio, and once he arrived, I said that it wouldn't be advisable for me to be seen by the many Lesboans thronging the docks and that it would be prudent if he granted me an audience below deck, unseen from prying eyes. Parmenio, seeing that he had nothing to lose, granted the request and we descended below, next to the monster. I noticed that they had broken up the monster into several pieces, so that it would be easier to transport it.

When Parmenio motioned to me to speak, I said: 'Great leader, I come to you with greetings from Queen Morai, who seeks to apologize on behalf of Lesbos for not having paid the tribute of a hundred talents in time. To convey her good wishes, she sends you fifty talents. The rest of the tribute she will hand over tomorrow, unknown to King Phaticidas, with the condition that you help instal her on the throne of Lesbos, after helping her to depose Phaticidas. If you are agreeable to this condition, she seeks to warn you also about danger coming your way today, with the intention of preparing you the better for it.'

Saying this, I kept quiet and waited for Parmenio to respond. Parmenio looked at me for a long time and then asked from which part of the Greek world I was, as I didn't sound like I was from Lesbos.

'Sire, I am from Olympia and I came to these parts almost by accident. I was actually on my way to Ionia where some of my friends were headed. Our ship got lost at sea when we were caught in a storm, and we landed up on the southern part of Lesbos, where the Caruti nursed us to health,' I said. 'Queen Morai is of the Caruti, a royal tribe that came here all the way from Ethiopia, a long time ago.'

'And why is it that she seeks to overthrow Phaticidas, her own husband?' asked Parmenio.

'It is not for me, lord, to know the intentions of queens, but I can hazard a guess for your lordship if he wishes me to do so,' I replied.

Parmenio nodded for me to proceed and I said: 'King Phaticidas is her second husband. Her first, Sebasticus, was murdered by order of Phaticidas, and since Sebasticus was Queen Morai's real love, she hates him for it. Phaticidas is not loved by his people or his soldiers, as he's a tyrant, and Morai seeks to get rid of him for the sake of the people of Lesbos.'

'And how would you remove Phaticidas from his kingship if we choose to help Queen Morai in her mission?' asked Parmenio.

'There is a plan that Queen Morai has prepared, which she will share with you once you give your agreement to her proposal,' I said.

Parmenio smiled. 'And what if we don't give our consent to the proposal and place our faith in Phaticidas?'

'I am hardly one to advise your lordship, but if your lordship disagrees with the proposal of Queen Morai, consider the fifty talents that I have brought for you a gift from her to you and nothing more of this matter will be mentioned to anyone,' I said.

'And what is this danger you spoke about earlier, young man?' asked Parmenio.

'I have been authorized to talk about it only if your lordship agrees to the proposal of Queen Morai. Since your lordship has not said either yes or no, I am not at liberty to disclose the danger that comes your way, but suffice it to say that Queen Morai has nothing to do with it and desires no harm to come to the Macedonians. May I implore your lordship to decide quickly, for soon the officers of Phaticidas will be here to escort you to the banquet that King Phaticidas has arranged for you, and it's important that the plan Queen Morai has prepared for you be implemented before you leave, for your own safety,' I said.

'What do you suggest I do, son?' Parmenio asked me mischievously.

'I suggest you accept the offer of Queen Morai and help her, for you shall not be disappointed,' I said.

'Since a Greek from Olympia is advising me to do this, I shall. I have come to the conclusion that Phaticidas has no intention of honouring his commitments to Macedonia and he seeks to mollify me with gifts that I consider of no value,' said Parmenio.

'Many thanks, sire. Now listen carefully to what I have to tell you about the plans of the tyrant Phaticidas and how to counter them. He seeks to poison you and all your officers at the banquet today by mixing poison in the red wine that he will serve to his guests before the banquet begins. He also intends to kill all those officers in his own army who have interacted with your officers, for his priests tell him that they are to be suspected of treachery. It is his intention, after killing you and your senior officers and those of his own whom he falsely suspects of treachery, to storm the dock with his soldiers and capture all your remaining soldiers and sailors and take for himself the two monsters. He feels that possessing them will scare the Macedonians into not sending retaliatory force, since he would be able to use the monsters from the shore to pulverize their ships. He does all this in order to not have to pay the tribute agreed upon earlier, for he's a greedy tyrant,' I said.

Parmenio listened very carefully to all that I said without displaying any emotion, so I continued: 'Queen Morai therefore advises you not to drink any of the red wine that Phaticidas is going to offer you, and if you are pressed by his officers, she suggests that you only pretend to drink it. She has sent you a potion of seaweed and herbs which, if you swallow after the wine is served, will cause you to vomit and make Phaticidas think that the poison is having its effect. Queen Morai also ordered me to drink this potion in your presence to reassure you that it is no poison. Though Phaticidas's poison and Morai's potion have the same effects initially, the former is the venom of adders and will lead to certain death while the effects of the latter will be but momentary,' I said.

After finishing my speech, I ingested the potion in front of Parmenio and immediately started convulsing and vomiting out all that I had eaten in the morning. Such was the potency of the potion that Dorian had prepared for me. He had learned how to prepare it while working in an asclepeion when he was a teenager.

After suffering the convulsions, I handed over the potion to Parmenio and I could see that he was deeply impressed by my demonstration and words.

'And what happens after we survive the banquet and Phaticidas finds that we haven't died?' asked Parmenio.

'Sire, Phaticidas commands four thousand troops, out of which three thousand have come from the south and the bulk of them belong to the Caruti. It was with their help that Phaticidas deposed the earlier king who ruled from Methymyna. These troops will rally around Queen Morai the moment she announces taking over the leadership from Phaticidas. At the banquet, Queen Morai will announce that Phaticidas intended to poison his own men and thus induce his officers to revolt in her favour. I also entreat you to remove your monsters from the docks at Methymyna. I and my men will take your ships to a hidden cove two parasangs from here, where the triremes of the Caruti are berthed. There, they will be safe from any damage that Phaticidas's soldiers could cause them, for we hear they intend to send divers and soldiers armed with grapple hooks and other tools to board your ships as soon as the banquet starts. It will be better for you to give orders to your admiral to depart with the ships immediately, as that would save them from the assault and take Phaticidas by surprise,' I replied.

Alarmed now by my revelations, Parmenio summoned his admiral in great haste. His name was Malcipas, son of Dumetos. Parmenio asked Malcipas how soon he could get the ships to move and Malcipas, surprised by the question, said that it would take more than an hour. Parmenio told him that he had half that time and explained to him that Phaticidas might be sending a raiding party to grab the ships and he was to therefore take them to a cove two parasangs from here and send two runners back over land to await further orders. Malcipas was also told to withdraw quietly, without a fuss, and tell the people at the dock that the ships were moving out so that they could turn around and exchange berths with each other, as the ship on the other side needed some repairs. Parmenio told Malcipas to give their own sailors the same explanation so that they couldn't give the plan away. Only after the ships had cleared the docks were fresh instructions to be given to the sailors.

Parmenio then decided that he himself would not go to the banquet and told Agaemon, son of Hintas from Pella, who was the officer in charge of the soldiers on the triremes, to convey to Phaticidas that he was unwell and therefore unable to attend. He took Agaemon into confidence and briefed him about Phaticidas's plans and gave him my potion to be distributed to as many people as possible to induce vomiting. Parmenio told him to instruct his men to pretend they were drinking the wine. Those who were not good at acting were not to drink at all. Parmenio further instructed him to take all the soldiers into confidence before they left the ship for the dock. Those on guard duty at the harbour were to be summoned four at a time into the vessel and informed as well. Parmenio then briefed Agaemon that, though only fifty of the officers had been invited to the banquet, all three hundred and fifty were to go and wait outside the banquet place, for Parmenio intended for all his men to be at one place to be able to defend themselves if Phaticidas attacked them.

Agaemon himself was very confident that once Phaticidas discovered that his plans had failed and ordered his soldiers to attack the Macedonians at the banquet, he would be able to rout them. Said Agaemon: 'Each Macedonian soldier is worth five Lesboan soldiers. We are not only stronger and more disciplined, but now that we have been warned of Phaticidas's plans, we will prepare our soldiers in a manner such that no one will be able to surprise them.'

Parmenio then ordered Agaemon to back Queen Morai once she exposed the deeds of Phaticidas and do everything he could to give her sole authority over Lesbos.

Once Agaemon started informing his officers and soldiers about the plans of Phaticidas and how they were to behave at the banquet, I informed Dorian about all that had happened between Parmenio and me. I instructed him to send Otanes quickly with a message to the boats that they should be expecting us and that they should behave like friends. Otanes was to tell Gophoredes, the Persian commander, that he was to take his vessels out of sight and only when Parmenio had anchored his two ships off the coast and he saw our signal from the cliff was he to make his move. His approach was to be as non-threatening as possible, and the soldiers on the deck were to be dressed as Greeks and not Persians.

I also told Dorian to take a party of ten men, including Cholargus, to King Phaticidas's palace, and through him deliver a message to Queen Morai to leave quietly with them as her life was in danger. Once both Morai and Phanus were out of the palace of Phaticidas, he was to instruct Agos to take Morai quickly to where our ships were, for I wanted him back at the cove before fighting erupted between Parmenio's men and our mercenaries. I also told Dorian to send a man to the Apollo temple to instruct our men to release the priests who were being held captive and to warn them not to come to Methymyna for the next two days as I didn't want them to get hurt in the fighting.

In this manner did I plan and scheme as well as I could, using truths and lies and half-truths to gain possession of the two stone-throwing contraptions that I felt would aid my cause in Abydos after the winter passed.

As the two transport ships slowly moved out of the harbour, Parmenio and I remained below deck. I had put the fear into Parmenio that Phaticidas's army had a hundred Cretan mercenary archers who were hiding behind the cliffs that overlooked the harbour, and if they came to the conclusion that the ships were rowing out not to return, they might fire arrows on the deck. Soon we were away from the docks and I gave directions to Malcipas which way to proceed, as I knew that hugging the coastline outside the reefs would soon bring us to where our ships were.

I also kept engaging Parmenio in conversation, for fear that if I gave him time to ponder, he might ask me questions to which I would have no answers. I asked him whether he knew the story of Queen Morai and the wedding rituals of the Caruti. When he expressed ignorance, I told him how the new bride amongst the Caruti had to sleep with the guests who had been invited to the wedding and how King Phaticidas and I had been guests at her wedding and had been taken inside her tent and, as we departed, each of us had to leave a gift for the bride.

I also told him how Phaticidas had been enamoured of Queen Morai ever since and had had her husband Sebasticus murdered and thereafter married her himself. After that, he hunted down each of the men who had slept with her on her wedding night and murdered them.

'I am the only one alive from that ritual night,' I told Parmenio.

Parmenio was amazed to hear the story and wanted very much to meet Queen Morai.

'After Phaticidas is deposed, she is going to divorce him and put him on trial. The queen's personality is such that an eminent person like yourself would be an ideal suitor for her,' I said, trying to flatter Parmenio.

'I have no time for women. A war with Persia looms ahead and I have to get these two lithobolos to Abydos,' said a smiling Parmenio.

But Parmenio did ask me whether Morai was with child, and I said no. The two ships travelled very slowly. The one carrying Lithobolos Ares had fewer rowers than the ship carrying Lithobolos Philip. Since Parmenio wanted the two ships to travel together, he had the ship carrying Lithobolos Philip – and us – slow down so the other could stay abreast. Parmenio then told me how the two lithobolos had been put together on the island of Rhodes.

'It took more than six months to construct the lithobolos; they are the biggest that have ever been made by the experts in the city of Kimoros at Rhodes. I had them specially constructed to designs submitted by the great inventor Samocles. I had got wind of the fact that Samocles had prepared a lithobolos that could throw a rock to a distance of three plethrons and so I sent my chief engineer with twenty talents and commissioned him to design a lithobolos that could throw rocks even further, to a distance of more than one stade. I specified that the rocks should be around five hundred minae in weight, as only something that heavy can break down fortifications of all kinds and also inflict damage on armies laying seige to a town,' said Parmenio.

The inventor Samocles had accepted the challenge, though it took him many months to make and test a lithobolos that could perform to the specifications of Parmenio. Malcipas, an admiral in the Macedonian navy, had accompanied Parmenio to help bring the ships safely to Abydos. Parmenio had his sailors and soldiers trained under Samocles in the art of using the lithobolos, for an engineer could calculate the distance that the stone would travel, provided he knew the weight of the stone, and the inclination of the arms of the contraption. Samocles even suggested the use of the contraption at sea, though Parmenio said that it would be unwise as the sea wasn't always calm and the instability of the platform could cause inaccuracies, which could lead to the boat capsizing.

The best thing about the lithobolos was that they could be dismantled at the port and then packed in carts and taken to where the battle was. After telling me everything he could about the lithobolos, Parmenio started asking me questions about Olympia. To avoid answering them, I suggested that two sailors be put on the job of counting the fifty talents that Queen Morai had sent him. Parmenio immediately sent for two sailors and we watched them count the drachmas. Since a talent was equivalent to seven thousand drachmas, it would take them a long time. Parmenio put eight more sailors on the job and it still took a long time. It turned out that the entire sum was fifty-one talents and not fifty, and Parmenio was satisfied with the outcome.

I then told him that Queen Morai had sent a hundred talents more for him personally, which would be delivered to him at the place where we would anchor and where the triremes of the Caruti were lying in hiding. Parmenio was greatly pleased to hear this, though he was worried at the same time about the fate of his soldiers at Phaticidas's banquet. I assured him that as soon as we reached the shore, we would have news waiting for him about the deposing of Phaticidas, and Queen Morai would then remain a tribute-paying ally of Macedonia for a long time to come.

With these sentiments in the air did I sight our triremes in the cove, with their bows facing outward. Malcipas ordered the ship behind us, which was carrying Lithobolos Ares, to move into the creek and drop anchor. It took them a long time, though Agos and twenty other mercenaries on small ships helped to guide it in. Once Ares was in the cove, all the sailors were taken to the beach by Agos. Then Malcipas ordered for the ship with Parmenio and me to be taken alongside the first ship and the sailors started rowing accordingly.

Parmenio took me to the deck and had his soldiers break four bottles of wine on the bow. The Macedonian sailors told me it was his custom to offer wine to Poseidon after each safe journey and before the dropping of the anchor. Then the sailors brought another bottle and Parmenio himself poured wine in three cups and offered one each to Malcipas and me. It was at this moment, while he was handing me the cup of wine, that Parmenio saw the ring on my hand, the one that I had bought in Athens and which I had shown to Alexander himself, asking him to remember it, so that when the time came, he would remember that I had spared his life at the house of Mios. It was the ring of the great Spartan king, Leonidas.

Parmenio's face turned red when he saw my ring.

'Where did you get that?' he asked me, alarmed.

'It was my father's ring, he gifted it to me just before he died,' I said.

Parmenio, however, was not to be pacified by my answer.

'Stop the oarsmen immediately, Malcipas. And have this impostor arrested at once,' he shouted, moving towards me.

At first, Malcipas thought that Parmenio had spotted a reef which he feared the ship might run into. But when Parmenio shouted for me to be arrested as I was an impostor, he ran towards me with his arms outstretched. I had no option but to jump from the deck of the ship into the sea and start swimming towards the shore.

That was when Agos ordered the archers to fire their arrows on the deck of Parmenio's vessel – which carried Lithobolos Philip – as some sailors had gathered on the deck to throw javelins at me as I swam and the arrows made them scurry down below the deck. Otanes, who was stationed at the top of the cliff to wave to the Persian Gophoredes to come in with his ships after both the Macedonian ships had anchored, now saw that though one of the ships was in our hands, the other containing Parmenio sought to escape to the open seas. So he gave the predetermined signal to Gophoredes to approach the inlet at full speed and thwart the escape of the vessel carrying Parmenio.

But the Persians were not good sailors. Though Gophoredes with his four triremes could have attacked Parmenio's ship and overrun it with their superior numbers, I think the Persian officers with Gophoredes lost heart on seeing the size of the Macedonian ship. Three of the four triremes that Gophoredes was leading fell back as if the sailors rowing them had leaden hands.

Only Gophoredes's trireme moved towards Parmenio's ship at the highest speed possible because of the leadership of Gophoredes, but it was more than three plethrons in advance of the other triremes and Malcipas, spotting this weakness in the attack and the lack of a proper formation, attacked Gophoredes's ship. He managed by the momentum of his ship to shave off all the oars of Gophoredes's trireme. At the same time, he managed to safeguard the oars of his own vessel and because of the pikes fixed on the sides of his ship, he even succeeded in tearing a hole in the Persian trireme and caused it to take water.

Thus, Malcipas's ship reached the open seas and Parmenio escaped and I managed to capture just one of the monsters. After this incident, fearing that Alexander might have told the tale about my ring to many Macedonians, I took care to turn the top towards my palm to make it less noticeable.

We could have given chase to Parmenio, but Gophoredes's trireme capsized and the other Persian triremes got involved in rescuing the sailors on board. The personnel on the three other triremes were busy subduing the sailors on the monster ship we had managed to capture, for, seeing that they had been tricked, they rebelled and tried to escape over land. But short of a few, Agos's men managed to capture them all.

While we rested on the beach, Queen Morai and Phanus reached the inlet, along with Dorian, and they told me how events had unfolded at the banquet. Once it started and King Phaticidas had served everybody with wine, both his officers and the Macedonians had waited for the poison to take effect. While those of Phaticidas's officers who had been alerted by me pretended that the poison had started working on them, the Macedonians did no such thing. In fact, they didn't even drink the potion that I had provided them, so confident were they of controlling the situation! Perhaps they were also a little suspicious of the nature of the potion.

Fachulus and Brachimon first fed the wine to the dogs to watch the effect it had on them and, when the dogs went into convulsions, they had proof that Phaticidas intended to harm them. So they started an open revolt against Phaticidas. Phaticidas, seeing that his own officers were turning against him, looked to the Macedonians for help to quell the rebellion, but the Macedonians, being forewarned, took him into custody and ordered him to deliver his treasury to them as they sought to leave Lesbos with all of Phaticidas's wealth.

Phaticidas then led them to the tunnel which led to the treasury and, since that had already been collapsed by Agos and others, it took them many hours to remove the dirt and stones. Finally, when Phaticidas entered the treasury with the Macedonians, he found it empty. The Macedonians were angry when they saw that there was nothing in the underground chamber that Phaticidas had led them to and killed him on the spot and declared that Queen Morai was the new leader of Lesbos, which was what Parmenio had told them to say.

But since Phaticidas's officers led by Fachulus and Brachimon were not well disposed towards Morai becoming the new ruler as she was a woman and not Greek, though she spoke the tongue, a fight broke out between the Macedonians and the officers from Lesbos who wanted Brachimon to be the interim leader till the demos decided who was most suitable for the post. Thus it was that Brachimon turned against his own queen, with the backing of half the officers in Phaticidas's army. The other half, who supported Phaticidas, remained neutral, as after his death they knew not whose side to take.

All the officers in Phaticidas's army were, however, equally unwilling to go to war with the Macedonians, for even though they didn't like them, they feared their fighting abilities. So, shortly, a truce emerged to back Queen Morai. The Macedonians forced Brachimon and Fachulus to rein in the soldiers loyal to them after Queen Morai promised them ten talents, and they also vowed to leave Methymyna the moment they got the money.

Queen Morai, eager to have them leave the shores of Lesbos as quickly as possible, came in haste to where I was in order to repossess the treasury of Phaticidas which we had emptied out. It so happened that she had taken a great fancy to Phanus while they were together. Phanus now prostrated himself before Luminas, to ask for permission to stay with Queen Morai, as she being the new ruler of Lesbos needed a chief for her bodyguards and Phanus had been appointed to that position. Luminas granted him permission with great alacrity, as that would mean that Phanus would not accompany us on our journey through Persia to meet the king.

In this way did events unfold and Morai became the ruler of Lesbos. The Macedonian officers who helped her were given a bonus of one talent apiece. Ten talents went to Brachimon and Frachulus and they were told to leave quickly from the port at Methymyna. Morai feared that once they came to know how Parmenio had been duped and one of the monsters had been captured, they would renege on their deal and muster arms against her as they would conclude that she had initiated the entire conspiracy to become the ruler.

In order to hasten the departure of the Macedonians, a false message was fed to them that Parmenio had sent instructions for all of them to report at the island of Tenedos, where certain foreign mercenaries were causing trouble. Hearing this, the Macedonians under Agaemon, son of Hintas from Pella, hired a Phoenician trireme and paid the owner two talents to take all the Macedonian troops to Tenedos. Thus did the soldiers leave Lesbos and Queen Morai immediately improved the defences of the port, so that if the Macedonians came back, they would be better prepared to fight them.

EIGHTEEN

To tell you the truth, of all the events that took place at Lesbos, I was most exhilarated at the possibility of having Parmenio as my captive. He was the most experienced general Philip had and, with him missing, the Macedonians would have found it difficult to take on Persia. It would also have grievously damaged their morale if it had been discovered that Parmenio had been captured by none other than Seleucus, son of Nicanor.

However, too much time had already been consumed by the events at Lesbos and it was important for me to proceed to Persia.

After instructing Gophoredes to transport all the triremes as well as the ship carrying the monster to Dardanos and then over land to the Persian camp near Abydos, where Mazus was, I proceeded with Luminas over land to Babylon, where Artaxerxes, the Persian king, was wintering. Before leaving, I sent a messenger to Demosthenes, with a letter explaining all that had happened and giving him the happy news that one of the monsters had been captured and it was a stone-throwing catapult of the size of ten men and not an animal from the sea as everyone had imagined. I also sent a messenger to Mazus, who would reach him before Gophoredes did, detailing the events and how a monster catapult had been captured, which could be put to good use in recapturing the town of Abydos after the winter was over. Right now, the snow in Abydos was knee deep, making the movement of personnel and equipment very difficult. I requested Mazus to send a huge force to Dardanos to meet Gophoredes's vessel, as the cargo it carried was precious and the ship it was being carried on was five times the size of any ship the Persians had ever seen. I also informed Mazus that I was proceeding to Babylon with Luminas to meet the Persian king. I deliberately avoided mentioning that Phanus had stayed back at Lesbos with Queen Morai.

The journey from Lesbos to Babylon took eighty days. From Lesbos, we went in three triremes to Smyrna on the Ionian coast, and from there, to Sardis, to avail of the royal roads. If King Artaxerxes had been in Susa, it would have taken twenty days more of travel at about six parasangs a day. The royal road went from Lydia to Phrygia to Cilicia, and then to Armenia, Matiane and Kissia. There were more than one hundred and fifty rest stations along the royal road to Susa, and even more on the way to Persepolis.

Altogether, we were seventy people, ten of them part of Luminas's entourage. I had included fifteen Persians in the group, so that language would not pose a problem while travelling in these foreign parts. I also sent a message to Zamos to station men at appropriate places along the coast, who could take messages to Athens at great speed if the need arose.

Luminas, with her royal status, could send messages through the Pirradazzish, who were express messengers and consumed rations from the storehouses along the royal road. Though they were primarily for the use of the king, the Persian noblemen and satraps also used their services. But no messages could be given to them if they were carrying the king's message. Such was the rule. They travelled on fast horses and each royal resthouse catered for six riders, three each way, who rode like lightning to the next resthouse, where other messengers took over.

In Lydia, we encountered the chief of the Pirradazzish, who was a Persian by the name of Gotarzes and was the maternal uncle of Luminas. It was by the grace of Zeus that we met him so early in our journey or we would have had great misfortune later.

Gotarzes was very happy to see Luminas, whom he had not met since her marriage to Mazus. He clasped her to his bosom and told her that Mazus was in great danger and we should not proceed further on our journey. He was returning from Babylon himself and was in the court of King Artaxerxes.

Said Gotarzes: 'The interloper Mritphakes, who had come to Abydos to take over Mazus's satrapy, was thwarted in his designs by the rescue of Mazus from Abydos. He then went to Babylon and narrated many lies to King Artaxerxes. He told the king that Mazus had struck a deal with the Macedonians and that it was with Mazus's consent that the Macedonians had taken over Abydos! He told him that Mazus's capture and subsequent rescue had all been staged to fool his own people into believing that he had nothing to do with it. With these lies Mritphakes convinced Artaxerxes that Mazus was in league with Polemon, the Macedonian chief at Abydos, and he entreated him to take swift action or the Macedonians would take control over the entire Hellespont and it would be easier for King Philip to land his army on Persian soil, as he had been planning all along.'

'What lies he has spoken! The person who rescued us is here and his name is Seleucus. It was Mazus who requested me to take him to meet the king,' said Luminas.

'I know the whole tale, as indeed do all of Mazus's men. I only tell you what lies Mritphakes told Artaxerxes. The king summoned Mazus immediately from Abydos, without letting him know why it was that he was being summoned. The Pirrazzadish themselves arranged for his travel over land to Babylon. He travelled more than fifteen parasangs a day on horseback to reach Babylon. There, without hearing any explanations from him, Artaxerxes had him taken into custody. He then appointed Mritphakes as the new satrap of Mysia and sent a force with him to take over the operations at Abydos,' said Gotarzes.

Hearing this news, Luminas became agitated and insisted that she reach Babylon as quickly as possible, even though Gotarzes cautioned her not to proceed further. He feared that Artaxerxes might think that she herself was involved in the conspiracy with Mazus. But Luminas wanted to reach Nazafarish, the wife of Artaxerxes, through her aunt Artystone. In the Persian court, the king's wife and his mother had great persuasive powers over the king, and Luminas hoped that she could persuade her aunt, who owned an estate in Babylon, to talk to Nazafarish, who was her niece, and she would in turn persuade King Artaxerxes to release Mazus, as he was innocent of the charges that Mritphakes had brought against him.

I promised Luminas I would talk to Artaxerxes myself, as I was the secret emissary of both Athens and Sparta and I had letters from Demosthenes and Clonus to prove this. Gotarzes was reluctant to let Luminas proceed to Babylon, as he was sceptical of Artaxerxes's moods. According to him, Artaxerxes was easily swayed by conspiracy stories from his men and had a tendency to accept these as the truth. Mritphakes had first flattered him with gifts of elephant tusks much larger than any Artaxerxes had seen, and after that had lied to him about Mazus. Artaxerxes had believed everything, as he was greatly concerned about Philip's avowed intentions of invading Persia with an army.

After hearing of Mazus's arrest, I decided to reach Babylon independent of Luminas, reasoning that if Artaxerxes decided to exact vengeance on Mazus's wife, I might be in a position to rescue her.

With this in mind, I presented my credentials to Brazus, who was the Persian commander of Babylon. By virtue of this position, he controlled the forces around the palace where Artaxerxes stayed, protected by his Immortals, the ten thousand bodyguards who were always in a circle around the Persian king. Brazus was the nephew of Artaxerxes, around forty years of age, and it was to him that all the emissaries of the neighbouring countries reported. If he thought any matter worthwhile, he took the emissary personally to meet the king. It was a great privilege to meet with the king, and even Brazus met him only occasionally.

'I am the only governor to have dined personally with the king,' Brazus bragged to me at our first meeting.

Apparently, it was a great privilege to sit alongside the king while he had his meals. Even at big state banquets, when more than five thousand Persian nobles sat together to feast, the king's section was separate from the rest and nobody could see him dine, even though he sat amidst them. It was only the king's wife or his mother who was granted this privilege. But Brazus claimed that Artaxerxes had had him summoned to his place of dining and they had had a meal together. It is curious how a particular act is a mark of great privilege in one society but bears no significance in another. If a Greek dined with King Philip, it would not be something to brag about, but for a Persian to dine with his king meant that he and four generations after him would brag about the deed!

Of course, once I came to know about this Persian weakness, I understood that they would do anything to enjoy such a privilege, and so I presented a diamond brooch to Brazus, saying that it was a gift from Morai, the queen of Lesbos, for King Artaxerxes. I also added a dagger made of gold, which had diamonds embedded in its hilt, as a gift from Demosthenes for King Artaxerxes. These two gifts I gave Brazus to present to the king, and then I requested an audience with him on urgent matters that concerned Philip's invasion of Persia, which I had orders to convey to the ears of Artaxerxes and no other. To Brazus himself I presented an emerald, telling him that it was a personal gift that Queen Morai had given me, but seeing the eminence of Brazus, I felt that the stone suited him better.

Brazus had never been given a gift of this magnitude even by his king, let alone an emissary, nor had any emissary ever brought such sumptuous gifts to him to be conveyed to King Artaxerxes. So he was greatly pleased and saw it as an opportunity to have another meal with the king, which would be unprecedented and would raise his stature in the Persian court beyond that of a certain Omares, who was the commander of the foreign contingent in the Persian army. He had dined with Artaxerxes just two weeks back and had bragged about it to everybody.

By this time, I could understand spoken Persian, but at times I pretended that I couldn't, so that I could listen to what the Persians had to say amongst themselves, for if I spoke in Persian they would be happy, but would conduct their own conversations with caution. Now Brazus, thinking that I didn't understand Persian at all, instructed his men in my presence to find out all about me from the retinue that had accompanied me and also issued orders to find out if I had more such gifts in my possession, for he then wished to befriend me further.

Anticipating that Brazus would try and corrupt my staff for information about me, I had already sent back the Persians who had accompanied me to Abydos, as I didn't want them to reveal that Luminas had travelled with me from Abydos to Lesbos and now to Babylon, for that would compromise my position with Artaxerxes as a Greek emissary. With my own men, I had left strict instructions not to mention Luminas at all or any details of my journeys, except those that I wished others to know of. Even these details only Agos and Dorian were authorized to supply, and any curious Persian officer was to be taken to them. I had also given Agos and Dorian permission to speak about the monsters to stoke the Persians' curiosity.

Within one day of meeting Brazus, his officers had made contact with my contingent and taken them to dinner, during which Agos and Dorian told them about the monsters in a manner that made the Persians think that the information had been cajoled out of my men by their skilful tongues and not because my men wished to speak about these stone-throwing machines.

Once this information was conveyed to Brazus, he promptly conveyed it to Artaxerxes.

Such was the king's curiosity that he had me summoned immediately, along with Brazus, to hear more about the monsters. Thus, I found myself standing in front of King Artaxerxes at his court in Babylon, with all the Persian noblemen in attendance, just two days after my meeting with Brazus. After presenting introductory letters from Demosthenes of Athens and Clonus of Sparta, I narrated briefly my adventures since I had left Athens and asked forgiveness of the king for having taken such a long time to deliver the letters.

I ended my speech thus: 'And in this manner, great king, did I come to Abydos, and upon learning that the Macedonians had taken control of the city from Phicias, son of Sistos, I advised Governor Mazus to go to Abydos. But he was captured by Polemon, the scheming Macedonian in charge of Abydos, and it was only with great difficulty that he was rescued. But it was fortunate that this episode occurred, great king, because I discovered the Macedonian plan to summon monsters from Lesbos. Though initially I thought that these monsters were giants from the sea, which had been tamed by the Macedonians through the worship of Poseidon, they turned out to be something else altogether, and it was Mazus who instructed me to proceed with great speed to capture them if I could. I can say with authority that if it hadn't been for his foresight, the Macedonians would have managed to ship both the monsters to Abydos and we would then have found it difficult to recapture the town. But now, because of the ingenuity of Mazus, we have managed to capture one monster which we have shipped to a port near Abydos, where it will be unloaded and transported over land to be taken charge of by Mazus, who will make good use of it against the Macedonians.'

Saying this, I kept quiet, and Artaxerxes kept quiet too, and as no one spoke in his court unless addressed by the king himself, there was silence among the nobles as well. Finally, Artaxerxes spoke: 'What is this monster you speak of?'

'Great king, this monster is a huge contraption that fits into a trireme which is about four hundred cubits long, and it can be transported over land only after being dismantled. We carry its many parts to the spot where we wish to activate it, and there we reassemble it. It can throw stones weighing up to five hundred minae as far as four and a half stadia, with such force that it can destroy fortifications. And if the machine is within a fortification, it can throw stones at the besiegers and destroy their battering rams and other equipment which they intend to use against the walls,' I explained.

'Can you draw this monster for me?' asked Artaxerxes.

Complying with his order, I drew the monster for him on the floor with lime. Artaxerxes got up from his throne to watch as I drew and made gasping noises. Hearing him make these noises of astonishment, his noblemen also made similar noises, but none had the courage to come and stand near Artaxerxes to watch the drawing. They craned their necks to see as much as they could from where they were seated.

The more Artaxerxes asked about the monster and the more details I gave, the more amazed his noblemen became. Once, when Artaxerxes expressed his incredulity, his noblemen also whispered amongst themselves and looked at me with consternation. Such was the flattery that the noblemen indulged Artaxerxes with. At the end, having satisfied himself with my explanations, Artaxerxes asked whether I could have these monsters constructed for his army, and I said that it could be done, but it would cost about two thousand talents for each monster, as the craftsmen guarded their secrets very closely. They got parts of the monster made on different islands and no one knew where a particular part was made, except the master engineer. Hence, only he could assemble the whole thing.

I had mentioned an exorbitant sum in order to dissuade Artaxerxes from ordering me to procure a few monsters for him. But it had the opposite effect. Not wanting to appear a miser in front of his noblemen, he ordered me to assist in building four contraptions like the ones I had just drawn. Not anticipating this turn of events, I mentioned to him that I would need some more money to hire two thousand mercenaries. I would also need to have ten triremes at my disposal, besides building four triremes of a special size to transport the stone throwers from the islands. Artaxerxes then instructed the noble Omares to fulfil all my needs from the treasury and moved to dismiss me from his presence.

Alarmed that the larger problem had not been resolved, I made the submission to Artaxerxes with bowed head that I had two more things to discuss with the great king, and one of them was for his ears alone, as it concerned his well-being.

Artaxerxes signalled to all the noblemen to leave and asked me to speak. And this is what I told him, to his increasing concern: 'Great king, I have information that King Philip of Macedonia has dispatched a hundred assassins trained in martial arts and gymnastics to assassinate you before his forces land at Abydos, so that the Persians are pushed into disarray and it will be easier for his army to gain victory. The assassins were trained in Pella, and while just five had crossed the Hellespont into Asia till two months ago, the rest are waiting to cross over. This information was given to me by my spy in the Macedonian camp, and it was confirmed when my men captured one of the assassins in Abydos. This man I will display before you, so that you can understand the extent of their skills and take adequate precautions against them. Rather than mete out punishment to him for daring to plan the assassination of the great king, I have convinced him of the error of his ways and in turn plan for him to get back to Pella and assassinate both Philip and Alexander and thus destroy the Macedonian ambition of conquering Persia, for I must tell you, great king, that the Atheneums do not like the Macedonians at all and consider them barbaric. But such is the power of the Macedonian army that it yokes all the people to servitude under them. This assassin, however, by the name of Cicero, I can produce before you. He is both deaf and mute and communicates only through sign language, but his physical skills are amazing.'

Artaxerxes was only too eager to see Cicero. After surrounding himself with twenty bodyguards, he ordered me to produce him. This Cicero was one of two messengers sent to me by Miletus, the commander of my mercenary troops, from Abydos. He had carried written tidings that two thousand mercenaries had been recruited by Pythagoras and sought to cross the seas from the harbour at Pirea. Cicero had been born deaf and mute and was now a personal servant to Miletus, who knew how to communicate with him in a sign language that nobody else understood. Agos had, however, learned to communicate with him because he had camped with him at Abydos.

Agos was the one who had suggested Cicero's name to me as the right person to be presented before Artaxerxes as one of the assassins, as he was a great gymnast and could even move along walls as fast as a spider and could throw a knife accurately from a distance. Agos had explained to Cicero what he was to do in front of Artaxerxes, confident that there was no need to give him the real explanation, as nobody could interrogate him in any language. And so, this Cicero was brought forward by me with his hands and legs tied. Artaxerxes then gave permission to untie him.

Thereafter, a wooden board was erected and the command from Artaxerxes was awaited. I had told Artaxerxes that all the assassins recruited by Philip possessed the same skills and some of them were exceptionally talented. Artaxerxes, fearing something extraordinary, called for twenty more Immortals to surround him and then, after making himself impregnable, he gave the command for Cicero to proceed and this command was conveyed by Agos to him.

Cicero immediately leaped up on one of the pillars like a cat and climbed to the top in no time at all and then, swinging from there, he aimed his knife at the wooden board. It went in two fingers deep, to everybody's amazement. Then, from the top of the first pillar, he leaped to the second and third and fourth till the twentieth, hanging from his fingers, and at last he slithered down like a snake, and doing many somersaults, he reached the board and pulled out the knife from there. He then walked forty paces away from the board and swung around and flung the knife straight at it, and this time it went in three fingers. I could hear even Artaxerxes gasp, though he was scarcely visible behind his bodyguards.

After Cicero completed his demonstration, I quickly had him bound once again and sent out of the court under the supervision of Agos, as I didn't want Artaxerxes to take him into custody. Artaxerxes then dismissed the Immortals who surrounded him and asked me what I intended to do with Cicero.

'Great king, I intend to train ten more men in the manner of Cicero, the person whose physical abilities you just saw. I will then bribe a few Macedonian noblemen, so that these men can achieve close proximity to Philip and Alexander and assassinate them. We in Athens and Sparta don't like the dominance of the Macedonians in our affairs,' I explained.

Artaxerxes looked very pleased with my answer.

'I offer you one thousand talents to help with your planning and a reward of twenty thousand talents if you succeed in assassinating Philip,' he declared to me in the presence of his noblemen. At this juncture, seeing him suitably inclined, I broached the subject of raising a mercenary army to counter the army of Philip if it did arrive in Asia, for, as I explained to Artaxerxes, we couldn't depend wholly on the assassins to do the job for us.

Artaxerxes answered that his governors had already employed several thousand mercenaries, to which I countered that the mercenaries I recruited would know all the tactics of the Macedonian army and could defeat them at their own game. Besides, they would be aided by their hatred of the Macedonians, as no Greek liked to live as a slave to another power. I also explained that the army thus raised could be sent to Sparta, so that the Macedonians would be bogged down in Ionia and would expend their resources there. This was what King Aegis of Sparta had in mind and for this project he had personally sought assistance from the Persian king. Hearing this, Artaxerxes instructed Omares to sanction an appropriate sum from the treasury in coordination with Spithridates, the governor of Lydia, who employed the maximum number of mercenaries.

Since Artaxerxes hadn't brought up the subject of Mazus in spite of my mentioning him very laudably in the beginning, I introduced his name once again by asking if I could summon two thousand mercenaries immediately for the siege at Abydos to aid Mazus, the governor there.

This time, Artaxerxes sat upright on his throne and asked me what I knew about Mazus and whether the news had reached me that he had been replaced by Mritphakes. I expressed ignorance in the matter and showed considerable surprise at such a development, then asked whether Mazus was in good health because if it weren't for him, we would not have been able to arrest Cicero and discover the plot of the assassins.

On hearing this, Artaxerxes expressed great surprise and asked me what I thought of Mazus. 'He is a great governor, as he always has the interests of the great king at heart. Even when I rescued him and he was in great personal danger, all he had in mind was not to let down the trust you reposed in him,' I replied.

Hearing this, Artaxerxes seemed pleased, but he maintained his silence. Feeling that it would not be appropriate to press the matter further, I waited to be dismissed from his presence and, bowing down, left the palace with Brazus in tow.

Brazus had been silent the entire time we were in the court, but once we got out, he started flattering me like I was his chief and took me straight to Omares. Both of them mentioned to me that they had never seen Artaxerxes in such a generous mood with respect to his finances. Brazus asked me with great incredulity how I could have taken Mazus's name in front of the king, knowing that he had been deposed and replaced by Mritphakes. I answered that I was not then aware of the fact.

Omares, however, was more frightened of me than incredulous, for to him, it was unthinkable that a person could talk to the king as candidly as I had. He suspected that I had some special powers. Agos had told him that I had single-handedly won over a monster from the great general Parmenio himself. After having heard of these exaggerated exploits from Agos, he was in the mood to negotiate my demand for recruiting mercenaries for the siege at Abydos. He mentioned to me that Mritphakes, the new governor in place of Mazus, was of the view that he could push the Macedonians away from Abydos without the help of any Greek mercenaries and so desired to have no contact with Miletus and his men. Mritphakes, of course, thought that Miletus was an independent Greek mercenary who employed many hundred Greeks to fight for him.

Mritphakes, instead, had asked for fresh troops from the garrison at Sardis and Spithridates, the governor of Lydia who was his uncle as well, had promised him ten thousand men from his own employ for a period of six months. Mritphakes's plan was to proceed against Abydos in winter itself so as to demonstrate to King Artaxerxes his superior generalship, even though his subordinates were against such an adventure. But such was Mritphakes's stubbornness that he intended to start his campaign with the fresh troops from Spithridates as soon as he reached Abydos, without even trying to assess the strengths and weaknesses of the Macedonians inside the city.

After hearing about Mritphakes's plans from Omares, I dispatched an express messenger to Miletus, stating that he had to disable the monster I had captured and sent on for the aid of Mazus, so that Mritphakes wasn't able to use it in his siege. And if the monster was already up and running, he was to sabotage it in such a way that none of the Persian engineers would be able to fix it, but if we wanted to utilize it, we could fix it in no time at all. He was to also ensure that none of these actions of sabotage were traceable to him or to the men he commanded, all of whom were in my employ, but should be blamed on a raid by the Macedonians.

Simultaneously, I asked Omares to send a message to Mritphakes to dismantle the monster and have it shipped to Babylon, as the great king was desirous of seeing it work. Omares, eager to please me and believing that Artaxerxes's command to me to bring him four stone throwers implied that the one captured by me at Lesbos was included, sent the message immediately to Mritphakes to pack the monster and send it by land to Babylon.

It so happened that while we were sitting in the office of Brazus, word came to him that Mazus's wife Luminas had met Artaxerxes after us, with the help of her aunt, and the king had ordered his release from custody. He had intended to reappoint him as the governor in place of Mritphakes, but it was revealed to him that thirty days in custody had deranged Mazus's mind and he was no longer the man that he once was, being prone to bouts of madness, during which he heard voices and imagined people in the room even when nobody was there. He also banged his head against the wall, impervious to the injuries this caused him.

Thus ended the story of Mazus. Luminas, whom I tried to convince to come back with me to Abydos and beyond, suddenly felt that Mazus had come to his ruin because of her infidelity to him. She also started imagining that she brought bad luck to people and believed that, if she spent more time with me, I too would be afflicted by her ill luck in due course of time. So she decided to take Mazus to his birthplace in Nineyeh and nurse him back to health. Only after she had done that, would she consider my proposal to participate in my travels, for she wanted the Gods to be pleased with her before she catered to her own desires.

That was the last I saw of her for a long, long time.

Part Four

NINETEEN

The next day was a public holiday and I was informed by Omares that the great king had invited me to dine with him. Omares said that Artaxerxes also wanted the deaf and mute assassin, Cicero, to give a demonstration in the great hall in front of all the noblemen and his Immortals, the ten-thousand strong contingent that guarded Artaxerxes.

Fearing that Artaxerxes might change his mind about Cicero and have him imprisoned, I had already dispatched him with Agos and a few other men back to Abydos. I told Omares that Cicero was supposed to wait for me there, for I had plans for him regarding certain activities in Greece.

Hearing this, Omares started shivering with fear. For a Persian, not being able to fulfil the wish of his king is a frightening thing, even if it isn't in his control.

'I will be flogged if I cannot find him, Seleucus. Seven days back, Artaxerxes ordered the lashing of the nobleman in charge of the logistics of the palace because a consignment of purple robes had been delayed by two days, coming as it was from faraway Egypt,' said Omares.

He then prostrated himself at my feet and pleaded with me to summon Cicero back somehow, or he would be disgraced. When I said that I didn't have the means to summon him back, as he had left more than eight hours ago, he said that he would issue all the monies for the mercenaries that I intended to recruit in advance and even advise the minder of the treasury, a person by the name of Cecod, to release the funds for the four monsters and give me an escort to transport this huge sum all the way to Abydos.

Omares somehow thought that it was still within my powers to summon Cicero or maybe he didn't understand me fully. But at this moment, something unexpected happened. I saw Agos returning with Cicero, escorted by a Persian guard! Apparently, they had been unable to leave Babylon as a guard at the gate had recognized Cicero, having seen him from afar at the palace. Since Cicero had made such an impression, he wasn't sure whether he was leaving legally or illegally. So after detaining them the whole night, he had produced them before Brazus to check what he was to do. Brazus sent them on to me in the morning, as he had no orders in the matter.

Omares, seeing Cicero, was tremendously relieved and he kissed my cheeks and Cicero's as well. He then took us to his house and gave us white tunics to wear after we had bathed in perfumed waters. Some of his concubines offered to take us to the bath and bathe us, much to the delight of Cicero, but I refused the offer.

While there was a special table at the dining hall for foreigners who could attend in their country's attire, all the Persians had to be dressed in white. There were two big rooms in the hall. One, where the king dined with his immediate family, which included his mother and wife, and the other, where the nobles sat. The two rooms were divided by a special curtain, whereby Artaxerxes could see everybody in the two halls, but people in the hall for noblemen couldn't see Artaxerxes. Just four noblemen would have the honour of dining with Artaxerxes's family and they would be sent private invitations just before the dinner began. It was considered the greatest honour for any Persian to dine with the king in his personal room on the day of a public dinner. It marked the closeness between these noblemen and the king and usually meant that they were to be awarded a higher post soon.

Both Brazus and Omares expected to be one of the four men to be dining with Artaxerxes, along with Spithridates, the governor of Lydia, who was in Babylon to discuss matters of state with the king, and Tabalus, the head of the Immortals. Tabalus had enjoyed this privilege the previous year too and, subsequently, Artaxerxes had solemnized the marriage of one of his nieces with him.

Once Brazus came to know that Artaxerxes had asked for Cicero to give a demonstration of his skills in the hall just before dinner, he was pleased that he could take the credit for having stopped him from getting out of Babylon. And since he was the one who had taken my gifts to Artaxerxes and also escorted me to his presence, he felt that it was his right to escort us again to the great dining hall and, by virtue of this, earn the privilege of dining with Artaxerxes in the king's private hall.

So, when Brazus came to know that Omares had whisked us away to his house and was preparing to escort Cicero and me to the great dining hall, he immediately came to Omares's house and demanded that we be handed over to him, as it was his duty to escort us to the dinner. But Omares claimed that since the direction to escort Cicero and me had come to him, he was not going to award the job to somebody else. So, in this manner they fought till Tabulus, the chief of the Immortals, came with his guards to Omares's house and said that Artaxerxes intended to have a private audience with Cicero and me before the dinner started and he requested me to accompany him. As Tabulus outranked both Brazus and Omares, they kept quiet, but each was happy that the other had been denied the privilege of escorting us.

Since only Agos could communicate with Cicero, I insisted on taking him along as well. And so Agos also had to take a perfumed bath and dress in white. While he did that, I took Omares aside and asked him whether he could make sure that the talents that Artaxerxes had promised me for the four monsters and the recruiting of the mercenaries could be provided to me the next day, so that I could embark on the project of the great king as quickly as possible. I also handed over a golden dagger to him as a memento of our meeting and gave him two purple tunics as gifts to be conveyed to Cecod, the head of the treasury of the Persian empire. Omares accepted the gifts with alacrity.

'I will also try, by a stratagem, to get you invited to the private dining room of Artaxerxes,' I informed him.

Hearing this, Omares's face lit up like the sun.

'If you can achieve that for me, you can count on my support for as long as I live,' said he.

So, when Tabulus presented me before Artaxerxes again, I had in my mind a scheme to help Omares which, if I had told him earlier, he would have heard with great consternation.

Artaxerxes told me that his wish was that Cicero give an extensive demonstration of his talents to all the ten thousand Immortals who guarded him, so that each one of them would be familiar with the skills of the assassins whom the murderous King Philip had unleashed against him. Once the physical prowess of the assassins was made clear to his bodyguards, Artaxerxes felt that they would be better prepared to protect him.

I immediately commended Artaxerxes on his foresight, but expressed a small misgiving.

'Have you, great king, considered the ramifications of the whole world coming to know of Cicero's skills? If you decide to expose the talents of Cicero to all your bodyguards, then surely some talk of it will reach the Macedonians and they will come to know that one of their assassins has been caught by the Persians and they will accordingly change their plans and perhaps teach their assassins new skills of which we would be unaware. But if we limit Cicero's demonstration to the two hundred officers amongst the Immortals and other noblemen of the Persian court, the matter will in all probability remain secret from the Macedonians. And, the officers who witness the tricks of Cicero could then instruct the soldiers, so that their ability to counter the Macedonian assassins is developed. In this way, both purposes would be served,' I said.

Artaxerxes listened carefully to what I had to say and Tabulus kept his counsel, wanting to be on the side of his king's opinion when it came. Artaxerxes finally spoke. He said: 'I find merit in your argument. Therefore Tabulus here will summon all the officers of the Immortals and, in front of them, this assassin here will display his physical accomplishments, so that my men may be better prepared for the evil machinations of Philip. I am told that the Persian Amorges has taken refuge with the Macedonians and advises them on all our methods and educates the generals of Philip's army about our weaknesses as he sees them. You will therefore instruct Cicero to display the whole range of his physical prowess so that no trick of his is held back.'

Artaxerxes ordered for the whole hall to be vacated and only the officers to be present. As Cicero prepared his body by stretching his limbs, I spoke to Artaxerxes once again in private and told him that there was a particular display that I wanted him to see, but which was best performed in the small hall which was his dining area and it required the presence of Omares, as only a person with a calm disposition such as his would be able to stay still as Cicero launched fifty knives, one by one, towards him as he stood against a pillar. The knives would take the outline of Omares's body without touching Omares.

'And Cicero will do all this blindfolded. The reason it can't be performed in the bigger hall is that even a small gust of wind could deflect the knives and cause grievous harm to Omares, whereas the smaller hall is protected from the wind on all sides, having no windows,' I said.

'I am amazed that this can be done. I have never seen anybody do it, nor even heard of anybody with this kind of prowess,' said Artaxerxes.

And though this skill of Cicero was real and not made up by me – in his early youth, he had picked up knife-throwing skills in Syracuse – he had not practised it in recent times because of his travels with us. But Cicero had expressed confidence to Agos that he would be able to pull off this feat without any prior practice as his skills were intact.

Before Cicero's demonstration in the main hall, Artaxerxes called for Omares and told him that he had been chosen for a special duty. When he arrived, Omares was told to armour himself and proceed to the king's dining hall. Once Omares was suitably dressed, Artaxerxes put on Egyptian breast plates, as was the custom of all Persian noblemen when they proceeded to battle, and sat in his place in the dining hall, surrounded by his bodyguards, so that even if Cicero threw a knife at him, it could not reach him.

Omares, on the other hand, was so pleased at being present in the king's dining room that he kept smiling at everybody and particularly at me, for he knew that I had done something to fulfil his desire. When he was told to stand up against a wooden pillar, he promptly did so. Artaxerxes then ordered for Omares to be blindfolded. He was worried that Omares might move out of fright when the knives came his way and thus provoke an accident.

But while Omares was being blindfolded, his mood changed, for he thought that there had been a complaint against him, as a result of which he was being executed in the king's own dining room, the biggest insult of all. His face blanched.

'What is my fault, great king, that I am to receive such a fate, here in your presence?' asked Omares with a bowed head.

Artaxerxes laughed loudly, hearing Omares speak thus. Hearing him laugh, Tabulus and the other officers of the Immortals laughed too and Omares looked at me with great anger, believing that I had something to do with this unexpected turn of events.

He then proclaimed to Artaxerxes that he was not to believe the lies of a foreign emissary, whatever they were, for he had not plotted against the king or indulged in any rebellion. Hearing Omares speak thus, Artaxerxes laughed even louder and all the nobles laughed as long as he laughed and became silent when he stopped. Believing that all was lost and that he was being insulted even by the minor officers amongst the Immortals, Omares became quiet and resigned himself to his fate. He began to mumble prayers and said loudly to Artaxerxes: 'I know not why you desire that I should leave the world. But if that is your desire, I shall not protest, for the great king knows best.'

Once the guards had blindfolded Omeres, Cicero was provided with knives of two different types. One was a short Persian dagger and the other was longer by two fingers and had a curved handle.

The Persians, as you might know, pray to a God called Ahura Mazda and they worship the sun as well. Omares prayed loudly to his Gods as he was blindfolded and stood against the pillar. Soldiers, meanwhile, counted out fifty knives for Cicero, and since the noblemen present knew nothing of what was about to take place, they also presumed that Omares was going to be executed by Cicero with fifty knives and, believing this to be the case, all of them fell silent.

Then I gave Agos the task of blindfolding Cicero and there was a collective gasp from all the noblemen, as they thought that Artaxerxes was evening the odds by doing so and was having fun in the midst of an execution.

But Cicero threw his knives so fast that you couldn't see his throwing arm and the knives pinned the entire tunic of Omares to the pillar! A stunned silence followed as everybody realized that it was a demonstration of skill and that Cicero had outlined with knives the figure of Omares on the pillar. Agos then walked up to Omares and pulled out all the knives and removed the blindfold from his eyes and there was much cheering. As the noise died, I addressed Artaxerxes thus: 'Great king, each one of the assassins of Philip is as skilful as this man Cicero, and I have been told that a few of the assassins are women and they are the most dangerous, as no man expects a woman to possess this degree of skill. Instead of knives, they use hairpins. But even pins can pierce the heart and cause death.'

Artaxerxes listened carefully to my words and then he turned to Omares, who was shaking with relief, to say: 'You conducted yourself most admirably, Omares, and for this display of courage, even though you thought that you were being executed for some fault of yours, on every public holiday you shall have the privilege of dining with me in my private chamber and I confer on you a personal gift of one hundred talents.'

Hearing this, Omares wept with joy and, bowing before the great king, said: 'I will continue to serve you to the best of my ability and may I die the day I stop doing so.'

Hearing his words, Artaxerxes smiled, but I could detect envy in Tabulus, Spithridates and the other nobles; I was told later that this kind of dining privilege had never been extended to anybody by any Persian king.

After this display with knives, Cicero gave a demonstration like the one he had given earlier in the big hall, and this time it was even better than before. He swung on a rope suspended from the ceiling and, with great gymnastic prowess, jumped from pillar to pillar, even as everybody gasped and thought he would fall straight to the ground. Then, when Tabulus's attention was diverted, he leaped straight from a pillar next to him and, before Tabulus's guards could react, he put his knife to his throat. Then disengaging, he bowed towards Artaxerxes and retreated to where I stood with Agos.

Seeing Tabulus enraged at this act of Cicero, I tried to soothe his temper with these words: 'My lord Tabulus, it was on my instructions, to show the capability of such assassins, that Cicero put a knife to your throat. In future, your bodyguards will be alert to this possibility, as will you, and assassins like Cicero will never be able to achieve what they desire. And now I seek the leave of the great king to proceed with what we discussed earlier, for any delay in the matter could have dire consequences.'

Artaxerxes gestured that I could leave, but Tabulus stopped me at the gate of the great hall and desired that Cicero be left in his private charge, for he felt that he was the best person to train the Immortals. But I responded thus: 'That cannot be for the time being, my lord, for he is the only one I have who can recognize the other assassins and I intend to catch them at the coast, as they don't yet know that one of their own now works for Athens and Persia. I also need him for some urgent work in Macedonia, and I urge your lordship not to press your request, seeing that the larger good of Persia would be served if he travels with me.' Seeing that Tabulus hadn't understood all the ramifications of the matter, I explained further, 'The Macedonians have sent many men like Cicero to Persia to attempt the assassination of the great king; Cicero was one of them. I now intend to locate and kill the remaining assassins. Of course, I would request you to keep this information confidential, as it could affect the security of your king.'

'Of course,' said Tabulus. 'The king himself told me about the assassins. But none of them will be able to get past the vigilance of the Immortals, this much I can assure you. If you need any help in your task of capturing the assassins, do not hesitate to ask me.'

I assured Tabulus that I would. From his demeanour, however, I could make out that Artaxerxes had not told him anything about the assassins, but since it would be a great loss of face to admit this, he had to pretend that, being the chief of the Immortals, he was privy to all such matters.

By now, Omares had joined me and he hugged me to his bosom, much to the surprise of Tabulus, for he didn't know how Omares had got into Artaxerxes's dining room in the first place. After I begged leave of Tabulus, Omares took me to his house and kissed my hand and even had his wife wash my feet, much to my embarrassment. His wife was even more relieved than he was. She had been informed by Omares's brother, an Immortal, that her husband had nearly been executed. Now that luck had turned in his favour and he had permanent dining privileges with the great king, she was beside herself with joy and asked Omares to provide me with a Persian wife. I politely declined the offer, even though I was tempted!

Over the next two days, with Omares's help, I got all the talents I needed from Cecod, the chief treasurer of the Persian court, to procure the four monsters. Cecod, who had heard about the events of the previous day, was more than eager to help me, as he imagined that I could be persuaded to help him get dining privileges from Artaxerxes also. This I promised to organize for him during my next trip to Babylon; I told him that I would be returning soon with the monsters.

Cecod, with Omares's help, provided me with two thousand talents to raise a mercenary force which could be used by the Spartans and by me to counter the Macedonians. Omares then took me to meet Spithridates, who came to the door of his dwelling to receive him, such was his high status now. Spithridates promised to provide a contingent of troops to accompany me all the way to Abydos and then to Sardis, where I was to take the monster that I had captured from Parmenio in Lesbos.

Artaxerxes had instructed Spithridates to bring the monster to Sardis, as Babylon was too far away and he intended to travel to Sardis himself in the next few months to observe the workings of the monster. Spithridates now asked Omares whether he could himself head the troops that would go to Abydos to get the monster back and Omares, thinking that if he managed to get the monster from Abydos to Sardis, it would add to his prestige, accepted the suggestion of Spithridates. It pleased me as well, for now I would have a Persian nobleman with me who could put some fear into Mritphakes.

Once Omares and I reached Abydos from Babylon – I am not now dwelling on the events that overtook us on the way to Abydos – we discovered the extent of the mess that Mritphakes had created Spithridates had sent twenty thousand troops to help him in the assault on Abydos, but he had insisted on attacking through winter and had suffered huge losses of men.

The snow was fairly deep and Miletus, the leader of my mercenaries, had camped with his troops two parasangs away from Abydos to avoid the possibility of Mritphakes summoning his men to battle. Miletus had received my message to sabotage the monster and said that Mritphakes at first couldn't understand the significance of the monster and gave no importance to it, specially as it had allegedly been captured by me, a person whom he considered a stooge of Mazus. Therefore he continued to launch attacks on the walls of Abydos, even though his men were slow through the snow and became easy targets of the archers from within the walls of Abydos.

Parmenio, meanwhile, had managed to bring Lithobolos Philip to the port of Abydos. The Macedonians had dug a big trench in which they had located the lithobolos and once, when Mritphakes ordered an infantry attack at night, Parmenio rained stones on them the size of carts and killed a thousand men. The Persians, having never seen anything like this, were amazed, thinking that the Macedonians had help from Zeus or certainly some other divinity. It was only after Miletus explained to Mritphakes that the Macedonians were using a machine that they had got from Rhodes and that one of these had been captured and sent on to Abydos by me that Mritphakes realized the treasure he had been sitting on.

Intending to do to the Macedonians what they had done to him, Mritphakes ordered Miletus to assemble the monster as soon as he could. Miletus, having been forwarded written instructions by me from Lesbos, quickly assembled the monster and threw some stones towards Abydos, which created gaping holes in the fortifications. But because the snow was deep and the soldiers' morale low, no assault could be organized to take advantage of the breach, which was soon mended.

It was at this stage that my message reached Miletus that he was to sabotage the monster in such a way that no blame could be apportioned to him or my men. After receiving these instructions, Miletus replaced the special sinews that wound down the arm of the monster with locally made sinews which looked the same but didn't have the same power. The stones therefore travelled a distance of only three plethrons before falling to the ground.

Mritphakes blamed the debacle on one of Mazus's officers, Gophoredes, the same person whom Mazus had sent with me to Lesbos with one hundred and twenty Persian soldiers. Gophoredes, after returning to Larisa with Lithobolos Ares, had come to know of the arrest of Mazus and the appointment of Mritphakes in his place. He had consequently escaped to the employ of Spithridates. But once the lithobolos failed, Mritphakes saw it as an opportunity to blame Gophoredes. Using his good relations with the officers of Spithridates, he had him arrested. And even though Gophoredes had no role to play in sabotaging the lithobolos, he was tortured to reveal how he had caused damage to it.

This was the state of affairs in Abydos when I arrived. Once Omares served Mritphakes with orders to place the monster in his custody, as he had to transport it to Babylon for Artaxerxes's inspection, Mritphakes became undecided. Thinking that the monster had to be of some importance for Omares to have been sent all the way from Babylon to ensure its successful transport, he sought to emphasize that he needed the machinery to breach the fortifications of Abydos, but when Omares insisted he comply with orders immediately, he caved in and gave instructions for the monster to be handed over to Omares's men, who were soldiers that Spithridates had sent on the king's behalf.

Once the monster was in the possession of Omares's men, Miletus replaced the original sinews and Omares had his men understand the workings of the monster, so that they would be able to reassemble it at Sardis.

Around this time, a herald arrived from the Macedonians at Abydos. This was a great surprise for all of us. The Macedonians under Polemon had hitherto refused to talk with the Persians. But now, with Parmenio as their new chief, things had changed.

The herald brought with him strange gifts. At Mritphakes's feet he dropped six arrows. On five of them lay pierced a pigeon, a rat, a dog, a fish and a duck respectively, while the sixth arrow had nothing. The herald, after laying out the objects, gathered up his horse and began to leave, when Mritphakes asked him what it all meant.

'My master has forbidden me to speak. My only instructions were to deliver the objects,' said the herald. Saying this, he rode away, leaving the Persian camp to puzzle over the meaning of the gifts.

Omares felt that the Macedonians wanted to issue a warning that any Persian who attempted to take over Abydos would meet with the same fate as the dead creatures. But then, what was the need of sending the sixth arrow? Since nobody could give a satisfactory answer, Mritphakes enquired if there were any wise men in the region. Some of the Persian officers, having heard of the seer Mistros in Larisa, who was a shepherd and who had also told me certain things, forcibly transported him overnight to Abydos to meet Mritphakes. He placed the objects that the Macedonian herald had brought before him and asked Mistros to interpret the message.

Mistros, who by nature was quiet and spoke his prophecies while holding the palm of the person who wished for answers, asked Mritphakes to place his palm in his own and, after Mritphakes had done so, he studied the arrows placed before him.

Having considered the objects, Mistros said: 'The Macedonians wish to convey that the Persians will not succeed in retaking Abydos even if they come by air, as represented by the pigeon, or from under the ground, as represented by the rat, or over the ground, as represented by the dog, or if they come by sea, as represented by the fish, or even if they came by both sea and land, as represented by the duck. The sixth arrow means that the Persians will not have any success even if they devise some new way of approaching Abydos that does not involve the air, land or sea, for that arrow would take care of it,' said Mistros.

Having said this much, Mistros let go of Mritphakes's hand and prepared to go. Since his explanation made sense, Mritphakes was satisfied, but then he bade Mistros to stop.

'When do you think Abydos will fall to my army?' asked Mritphakes.

'I could hold your hand to find out, but I don't know if my ancestors will give me the answer or whether, after giving me the answer, they will allow my tongue to speak,' said Mistros.

Mritphakes then gave Mistros five hundred drachmas.

'Your tongue had better speak now or I will have it pulled out,' he said threateningly.

The Persian officers were aghast at this attitude of Mritphakes and warned him privately how a nobleman from Larisa had once taken unnecessary offence at Mistros, only to lose his leg in battle the next day. They warned Mritphakes that Mistros had powers bestowed on him by the Persian God Ahura Mazda himself and therefore he should not seek to harm him in any way. But Mritphakes dismissed them with great disdain and repeated his threat.

Mistros didn't display any fear or anger, but only said that he would submit to whatever fate the Gods had in store for him. Then, holding Mritphakes's hand again, he said: 'My ancestors tell me that the leader who desires the fall of Abydos will be dead within two days and the fate of Abydos will be decided by another person present here and it will not be through either land, or sea or air.'

Saying this, Mistros released Mritphakes's hand and started to leave. But, shaken by his words, Mritphakes had Mistros arrested.

'You will be under arrest for two days and then we will know what big liars your ancestors are and how you yourself are a big impostor. If I survive more than two days, I will personally cut off your head,' shouted Mritphakes.

Saying this, Mritphakes increased the guard outside his camp four-fold and brought all the troops in his command to surround his camp so that not even a cat could get through, and in this manner he sought to pass two days. He also put on the outer perimeter any person whom he had ever had a disagreement with and decided to shift the tents of his wives and concubines far from his dwelling, for he thought that trouble might also come from that direction. With these precautions he thought he could survive two days and override the prophecy of Mistros.

Mistros too was kept well guarded. Feeling for him and intending to rescue him from the fate of being beheaded by Mritphakes, specially since the prophecies he had made for me had all come true, I sent him a message through Boriphon, the Cretan archer who was in my pay, that we would be mounting an attack shortly on his guards to free him from the clutches of Mritphakes. But Mistros refused any attempts at rescue.

Said Mistros to Boriphon: 'If Seleucus and you insist on freeing me, I will have no option but to take my own life, as my ancestors have instructed me to stay where I am.'

Boriphon came back disappointed and told me what Mistros had said and I decided to abide by his wishes, as I did not want to be instrumental in him taking his own life.

After the hour passed at which Mritphakes was to declare the end of two days, a Persian soldier by the name of Atos came running to me and told me the most amazing story I have ever heard. Mistros himself became a bigger legend thereafter.

Atos, who was keeping watch for us in Mritphakes's camp, said that, at the appointed time, when the sun was at a certain height, Mritphakes declared that the prophecy of Mistros was wrong. And with great glee he changed his robes and donned the clothes of a Persian nobleman at war, complete with a cuirass. Exactly at that moment, a big noise started behind the tent of Mritphakes. It turned out to be a dog and a cat, barking and mewling at the sight of a serpent, which was hissing at them both. Since a serpent was rare in the region, Mritphakes's men started betting on whether it would survive the dog and the cat and Mritphakes himself forgot for a moment that he was due to proceed to behead Mistros, so engrossed was he in watching the serpent dart here and there, trying to escape the dog and the cat. Both the animals had buried their differences to fight the serpent, which was three and a half cubits in length.

When it looked like the animals had lost their appetite and the serpent had successfully warded them off, an eagle that had been circling above swooped down and clawed the serpent up into the air and, since it was so unexpected, everybody's jaws dropped in disbelief. The serpent was too long and lively for the eagle to hold on to for long and it eventually dropped it from the sky. Just then, Mritphakes remembered that he was supposed to proceed to where Mistros was and started walking in that direction and, lo and behold, the serpent fell on Mritphakes's head and bit him on his neck. The poison from its fangs was so strong that Mritphakes started frothing at the mouth within minutes and his body convulsed. His face turned blue and his breathing became laboured and slowly his breath ran out. As for the serpent, it escaped after biting Mritphakes.

This then was the amazing tale I heard from Atos. I went to the Persian camp to hear it again from the other Persian soldiers. They all narrated to me the same story, with minor variations. Some said that the eagle came down purposefully and dropped the serpent on Mritphakes's neck while some said that it dropped it because it couldn't hold it in its claws any longer and still others said that the eagle then perched on a tree and watched till Mritphakes was dead before flying away.

In this manner did Mritphakes die and all the Persians agreed that Mritphakes died before the two days were up, for in his hurry to declare the failure of the prophecy of Mistros, he had come out of his dwelling before time. The Persian officers who had forcibly brought Mistros to Abydos prostrated themselves before him and asked forgiveness not only of him but also of his ancestors and Mistros, being a simple person without an ego, readily granted it.

That day in the evening, Mistros came by my dwelling, having heard from Atos that I planned to cross the seas for Greece shortly. And the moment he saw me, he said: 'Finish your business in Abydos before sailing west. You will think that your business is over, but an event will occur which will shake you up. After you sail west, return to Asia with your loved ones once the king is dead or you will come to grief.'

Mistros said this even without holding my hand or being asked a question. After he made his prophecy, he asked me to make a sacrifice to Poseidon before I left the shores of Asia and then he asked for my help to reach Larisa as quickly as possible, for when the Persian officers had dragged him to Abydos, his daughter had been sick and he was worried for her.

When I asked him what business I had to finish in Abydos, as there was none in my mind, and which king was supposed to be dead, he said that I was a clever Hellene and would figure out his words as he himself didn't know what they meant, being only a conduit for what his ancestors wished to convey. Having said this, he refused to speak any further.

I had Dorian escort Mistros all the way to Larisa, with ten of my mercenaries to keep a watch for brigands, for the Persians had given him some money for his prophecy, even though it had led to the death of their commander.

The truth was that Mritphakes was not liked by his men and they were happy that he was dead. The first thing they did after his death was to release Gophoredes, who had been put under arrest by Mritphakes on the false charge of sabotaging the monster. Gophoredes came to meet me sometime after he was released.

Said Gophoredes: 'My men have seized a person called Automa near the port of Larisa. This Automa claims to be an inhabitant of Rhodes. He says Parmenio had brought him to Abydos to reassemble the monster. He says Parmenio released him after he had assembled and made some repairs to the monster and paid him the amount that was due to his father. But Automa claims that the sum of money he received was less than what had been agreed upon. In fact, it was significantly less. Fuming with anger at having been cheated by the Macedonians, he now wants to exact revenge. Though Parmenio had arranged a passenger transport to take him to Rhodes, Automa disembarked at Lesbos, giving the excuse of wanting to meet his mother's brother, who was at Methymyna. And he waited there for a while and boarded another trireme to come to Larisa with the intention of meeting the Persians, as he knew that another monster his father had helped manufacture had been hijacked and had made its way behind the Persian lines. He has so far refused to reveal his purpose to the Persian guards whom he approached at Larisa and has declared his wish, instead, to meet the highest person in authority,' reported Gophoredes.

Since Mritphakes was dead, the Persians had approached Gophoredes, as he was part of the team that had been responsible for stealing the monster from the Macedonians. Gophoredes immediately brought this information to me and requested that I in turn use my influence with Omares, who was due to leave the next day for Sardis, to have him appointed as the temporary chief of the Persian forces till such time as a new governor was appointed by King Artaxerxes.

I went to Omares and requested him to appoint Gophoredes as the temporary chief of the region. Omares said that he didn't have the authority to do so, but if all the senior Persian officers came to him with the request, he would do it anyway, since a war was being fought, and he would then send a messenger to Artaxerxes asking for instructions in the matter.

Gophoredes therefore arranged for the senior officers to speak to Omares. A number of them were confidantes of the late Mritphakes who had transferred their allegiance to Gophoredes, as they didn't want to be singled out for vengeance by the officers whom Mritphakes had persecuted for no reason at all.

After they all called for Gophoredes to take over the army until Artaxerxes sent a replacement, Omares pronounced him chief, as he was the seniormost Persian official present. Gophoredes then brought Automa to my dwelling and there I came to know that he was the son of Samocles from the city of Kimoros. The same Samocles who Parmenio himself had told me had designed the monsters and knew all their secrets.

Overjoyed at this development, but hiding my feelings from Automa, I asked him what his motive was in seeking out the Persians. Automa said that he sought our help to rescue his wife Fouma from within Abydos. The Macedonians, he said, were holding her captive and had told him that she would be released only after a replacement engineer was sent by

Automa or his father Samocles. They believed that the Persians would launch an offensive in the summer and they wanted an engineer around in case the monster needed repairs during that time.

In this manner did I realize what Mistros meant when he instructed me to finish my business in Abydos first before sailing west. I was not only amazed by Mritphakes's death, but also by the fact that it had brought Gophoredes back into reckoning and he had then brought me the story of Atutoma. If any one of these three events had not happened, the matter would not have developed to my advantage.

I had actually been thinking of sailing the very next day to Athens, and from there to Rhodes, to meet Samocles to place an order for the monsters. If Automa had come to me even a day later, I would no longer have been in Asia. I had been getting impatient to proceed to Athens, as I wanted to meet Athele. I had not seen her for a long time, and a messenger had come, saying that she had given birth to a boy.

'If we rescue your wife, what are you willing to do for us?' I asked Automa.

'I am willing to do anything you ask of me,' he said sincerely.

So I extracted a promise from him to build us four monsters at Rhodes with the help of his father Samocles and also to introduce us to the Phoenicians who had built the big triremes to transport the monsters. Automa said that though it was his father who had designed and built the monster, he had taught him everything, and if his father had a problem in helping the Persians (for the Macedonians had made him take an oath not to build a similar machine for anybody else), he was confident of executing the task with the help of his brothers.

I had these conversations with Automa in the absence of Gophoredes, whom I had sent out under the pretext of calling my partner Zamos, the brother of my business partner Phormio, who was managing things for me in Asia. Zamos had just come to Abydos from Athens with a contingent of two thousand mercenaries. It was on one of his vessels that I had intended to go back to Athens, but now the rescue of Fouma had to be arranged, so I instructed Miletus to prepare a plan that would enable us to do so.

Miletus quickly came up with a plan for my approval. He said that Fouma shared quarters with a concubine of Parmenio, who used to be Polemon's concubine but had switched allegiances when Polemon fell into disfavour after Parmenio's return from Lesbos. These quarters were near the barracks of the Macedonian soldiers, right next to the public bath, which had a tunnel under it, unknown to the Macedonians. There were still two tunnels unknown to the Macedonians, as you might remember – one which we had used to escape with Mazus and which started from under the aristocrats' graveyard under a tombstone, and the other which started from under the bath. The one that we had used to meet Alabanda, which began in the docks, had been blocked off by Agos with stones. Miletus said that, while I had been away, he had met Alabanda twice, though the last time was nearly a month ago, when Alabanda had required some provisions, as food supplies had dried up temporarily in Abydos because of the siege.

Alabanda had told Miletus that the Macedonians had put in place many precautionary measures that would make it impossible to launch a rescue attempt by boat, like we had done for Mazus. They had installed gates at the harbour and lines of rope that would isolate any trireme if it were suspected of bringing in a rescue party. They also had divers who accompanied triremes inside the port and it was their job to see that no person left the triremes unwatched. They also had sentries moving around the harbour in boats at all times.

Alabanda told Miletus that the Macedonians had been frightened when the lithobolos we had captured started throwing stones into the city of Abydos, for they felt that an accurate use of the machine would destroy the outer walls. The Persians, Scythians and Medes inside the city, who had been reduced to slavery by the Macedonians, were hoping that the monster would mean the end of the siege for them and, even though a few stones fell on their houses and destroyed them, they were hoping for the success of the enemy's monster. Alabanda, in fact, had provided a detailed map with Macedonian positions that would make it easier for us to target the stones thrown by the monster.

But now the monster had been taken by Omares to Sardis. The maps, however, allowed Miletus to plan the rescue. He intended to take in a party of seven people, three of whom would be Persian women dressed in a manner similar to the captive women inside the city but who in reality were women well versed in the art of warfare and were under Gophoredes's command. Some Persian satraps trained a small contingent of women in archery, horse riding and swordsmanship, and Miletus intended to choose three from amongst them. The rest would be men dressed as Macedonian soldiers, so it would appear that the women were in their custody. That was how the captive women generally moved within Abydos, escorted by Macedonian soldiers. The truth was that the soldiers had seized some of the women of the city as concubines for themselves and were scared that, if they let the women go on errands alone, they could be seized by some of the other soldiers to work as their concubines!

These seven people were to approach the quarters of Parmenio's concubine and there identify Fouma and bring her back through one of the tunnels. Miletus was still undecided as to which tunnel to use and had sent Agos to meet Alabanda to assist in the plans, for without him to guide the rescue party through the streets, it would be difficult for them to reach their destination.

Agos returned with the information that Alabanda preferred the use of the tunnel that emerged at the graveyard inside Abydos. The one that emerged under the bath had been flooded by an army of rats and, since the women would be nervous of rats, Miletus decided to use the tunnel which had been used before, even though it was a little longer, according to Alabanda.

The party of four men, one of whom was Miletus, was selected on the basis of how well they spoke Greek in the Macedonian accent and, though I spoke the best since my father had been Macedonian, I did not include myself in the party, nor did I allow Agos and Dorian to go, as I did not want to risk the safety of my best men in the operation. Miletus, of course, went because a senior person to take decisions was needed, but I told him not to take undue risks and not persist in the attempt if he felt that it was impossible.

Zamos felt that I should not send Miletus in the party, as he was far too important for the operations in Asia, but Miletus insisted on going. I asked Agos to find out the reason for his insistence and it emerged that one of the Persian women of the three sent by Gophoredes for the operation was his concubine! Miletus, being lonely in Abydos, had been secretly seeing this Persian woman, imagining that nobody would find out and now, worried for her safety or for some other reason, he was insisting on accompanying the rescue party. In the end, therefore, the party of men included Miletus, Cicero, Tyros and Otanes. Menicus wanted to be included too, but Miletus rejected him as he was too tall for the tunnels.

We kept the departure of the rescue party a secret from all the Persians, except, of course, Gophoredes and the women who were helping us. I remember the name of just one of those three. It was Farisa and she was short but elegant.

I must tell you here that something else was preying on my mind. Though I hadn't intended to go after Polemon right then, for weightier matters had surfaced, I began to think that it couldn't just be the rescue of Fouma that the seer Mistros had hinted at when he said that I was to finish my business in Abydos first before proceeding to the west. After I came to know that Fouma stayed with a concubine who had been with Polemon but had switched her affections to Parmenio, I saw it as an opportunity to capture Polemon!

Besides, I had heard no news of the murderers Argus, Zeferino and Menechus and thought that, if I captured Polemon, I could get to know of their whereabouts as well. To tell the truth, I hated Argus the most. It was his ambition to win the four-horse chariot race in Olympia that, in many ways, was responsible for the chain of events that led to the death of my parents and even the deaths of Pindar, Harmodius and, later, Zanylos. And for my present situation as well.

There had been moments during my various journeys when I thought that I had lost my desire for revenge, but I think it never went away. It just transformed itself into setting up obstacles in the way of the Macedonians, so that they would become weak and Greece could raise the banner of freedom. Somewhere along the way, I had realized that if I served the larger role of an emissary, which Demosthenes and Clonus had conferred on me, I could exact the sort of revenge on Macedonians and Macedonia which would far outweigh the satisfaction of killing all the individuals involved.

Also, apart from the all-consuming hunger for revenge, the truth was that I was getting addicted to travelling and seeing foreign lands, for they brought me adventures that come to very few in the short life of a man. And I must admit that, on a few occasions, I woke up in the morning totally free of any impulse of revenge but, on the other hand, there were many more times when I would wake up sweating in the night, aching for the blood of Argus, Polemon, Menechus and Clearchus. For, though I had let go of Clearchus after he gave me the information about the Macedonian treasury, I now regretted the decision as I thought it dishonourable on my part. So I had decided to hunt down Clearchus too. And even Alexander, for when I had spared his life at Mios's house, he hadn't killed Zanylos yet. I had thought then and continue to think now that his desire to kill me so soon after I had spared his life was unworthy of a prince.

Agos had brought me the information I had desired from Alabanda, which I had instructed him not to reveal to Miletus. The facts that Alabanda revealed were these: Polemon still desired his earlier concubine, who was now with Parmenio, but because Parmenio was the new chief, he was unable to do anything about it. Alabanda also found out through the servants of the concubine that the reason Parmenio had allowed Automa to leave Abydos was because he desired his wife Fouma! That was the reason Automa was so worried about her.

Around this time, Miletus's conduct started bothering me. First I was annoyed that he hadn't spoken the truth to me that the reason he wanted to join the rescue party was because he wanted to protect his concubine. Second, and more dangerous, I found out from Zamos that Miletus had come to know that I was a secret emissary of Demosthenes and that I had met the Persian king on a secret errand. Unknowingly, Omares had also talked to Miletus about how Cicero was one of the assassins that I had discovered who had been sent by King Philip to murder Artaxerxes. This fact amused him no end, though he kept his counsel in Omares's presence. Later, though, he revealed to Zamos (living in proximity with Zamos in my absence had made him erroneously believe that Zamos was closer to him than to me) after drinking wine, that I was too young for the job I was doing and, since I did not have the experience of years, he proposed that Zamos and he take over the mercenaries and intercede with Demosthenes that they were more suited to the job at hand.

Zamos reported this matter to me and, since I had become extra careful after the treachery of the Theban Boridas, I now looked for an opportunity to be rid of Miletus, for I couldn't afford somebody in so senior a position in my ranks to be nursing rebellion against me. But I wanted this to happen in a manner that the mercenaries, some of whom he had recruited himself and who loved him, wouldn't suspect me of having any hand in his departure.

Accordingly, I told Agos to take Tyros and Otanes into confidence, for both of them owed their life to me and had sworn a lifelong allegiance and I trusted them. I excluded Cicero from the plan as he had been Miletus's servant and, though he had come close to Agos and me in our journeys and earned rewards from us, I wasn't sure he would maintain secrecy where Miletus was involved. That was because Miletus had known him for many years and he stayed in a tent next to Miletus's, performing tasks for him. But since Cicero's skills were required for the rescue, he was included.

The plan that Miletus proposed was for four men dressed as Macedonian soldiers to escort the three Persian women, one of whom was Farisa, to the abode of Parmenio's concubine, where Fouma was. There they were to get in forcibly and hold the concubine while Fouma packed her belongings. Then they were to bind the concubine with rope, so that she wouldn't be able to raise an alarm, and make their way back to the graveyard and escape through the tunnel by which they had come. Automa had given them a necklace of his, which Miletus was supposed to show to Fouma so that she had no doubt that they had been sent by her husband to rescue her from Abydos. Farisa was given the job of clothing Fouma like a Mede concubine, so that none of Parmenio's soldiers would recognize her. Alabanda was to meet the party at the graveyard at the appointed time and lead them to the dwelling of Parmenio's concubine.

Agos, however, objected to this plan as it worked against our strategy to leave Miletus behind. He proposed a plan to Miletus based on his discussions with Alabanda. He said that Alabanda had discovered certain facts after observing the dwelling of the concubine. Parmenio's soldiers, not always the same ones, came at an appointed hour in the night to convey her to Parmenio's dwelling. Agos suggested that it would be safer for the four men of the rescue party to announce to the concubine that they had come to take her to Parmenio. Since it wasn't the same soldiers who came every day to escort her, Agos felt that she would have no reason to suspect that they were impostors.

Alabanda would then take them all to an empty dwelling; everyone living in the house had been killed by the Macedonians and it had acquired a desolate look, being overgrown with shrubbery. There, the three Persian women would hold the concubine while the men left again to get Fouma. Miletus would then show Fouma the necklace that Automa had sent and escort her to the graveyard. While Tyros and Otanes took her through the tunnel, Miletus and Cicero would go back to get the three Persian women, as women couldn't travel alone in the city. They would leave the concubine tied up in the house, so she couldn't raise an alarm. Alabanda would go back and release her later, so that she wouldn't die unnoticed.

This plan was endorsed by me and Miletus was made to accept it, though he didn't look very happy. The real plan, however, unknown to Miletus, was to use the concubine as bait to snare Polemon. The concubine was very vengeful towards Polemon because she had been led to believe by Alabanda that Polemon had been responsible for the killing of her husband. Her husband was the same Mede who had tended the graveyard and whom Alabanda himself had killed!

Since Polemon still thought that the concubine liked him, as before, Alabanda proposed to send a message to him through a beggar that she awaited his companionship at the desolate house, the only place where they could meet without detection. He was to proceed there without his guards – else, his movements might be reported to Parmenio.

Of course, all this would happen without Miletus's knowledge. Once the four men returned to the graveyard with Fouma (with Miletus and Cicero thinking that she was being escorted out by Tyros and Otanes), she would be transferred instead to Agos and Dorian, who would be waiting at the tunnel mouth, unknown to Miletus. They would take custody of Fouma and bring her through the tunnel, as it would need a lot of courage on her part to go on her own. Miletus and Cicero, on the other hand, would proceed to where the Persian women and the concubine were.

But before they got there, Tyros and Otanes would have returned to the desolate house by a short cut explained to them by Alabanda. They would do so unknown to Miletus and Cicero, who would be delayed by Alabanda on some pretext. Then Alabanda would leave Miletus and Cicero at a particular place and tell them to stay there until a Macedonian patrol, which was visible in the distance, went back to its barracks, and that would give time to Tyros, Otanes, the Persian women led by Farisa, and Alabanda to seize Polemon and knock him unconscious. They would then put him in a sack and Tyros and Otanes would carry him back to the graveyard and escape with the Persian women through the tunnel, dragging Polemon with them. As for the concubine, who was the property of Parmenio now, she would be given the choice of remaining there or leaving Abydos with them. For I didn't want any harm to come to a woman who had done us no harm.

The beggar whom Alabanda used to send the message to Polemeon would also be used by him to take a message to the Macedonian soldiers, informing them about the whereabouts of Miletus and Cicero. As the Macedonians were all the time looking for infiltrators who they thought came in by climbing the walls at night, they would pounce on the two of them. I figured that while Cicero would escape, it would not be possible for Miletus to do so, and that was my objective. The capture of Miletus would resolve my apprehensions about him.

This was the plan and, after briefing Tyros and Otanes properly and taking Farisa into confidence, the rescue party was dispatched. Things went according to plan in the beginning. The men arrived at the concubine's quarters before the time that she normally expected them, but since Parmenio's men often did that, she was not suspicious. She left readily with them, presuming she was being escorted to Parmenio's dwelling, but they took her to the desolate house instead and, after leaving her tied up there for the benefit of Miletus and Cicero, the men returned to the concubine's house to reveal their real identity to Fouma and take her to the tunnel.

But this was where things deviated from the plan. Fouma turned out to be an unwilling participant in the escape, especially after Miletus showed her the necklace from her husband! This came as a surprise to everyone, including Alabanda.

These were Fouma's exact words: 'I have no wish to leave Abydos for my husband Automa. I don't consider him my husband any more as he ill treats me when drunk. I prefer to spend my time here in Abydos and travel to Pella with a Macedonian friend who promises to take care of me much better than Automa did.'

This was reported to me later by Otanes. Since this was an eventuality that had not been planned for, Miletus, who thought himself the leader of the rescue party, was at a loss. For, to him, the real purpose of the rescue was to bring back Fouma and, since she balked and desired not to come with them, Miletus consulted with Tyros and Otanes on how best to proceed further. While they discussed the matter, Fouma raised an alarm that frightened all the four men, for they knew that in the dwelling nearby were some Thracians who had come to Abydos with sixty horses to be delivered to Parmenio.

Since Alabanda was keeping watch outside, he defused the situation by telling the Thracians that Parmenio's concubine and her friend were having a fight and the Thracians laughed about it. Alabanda then entered the concubine's quarters and put a knife to the throat of Fouma to silence her and, after she was sufficiently frightened, he asked her why she was resisting. But Fouma remained resolutely silent and so Alabanda tied her mouth swiftly with cloth and then bound her hands and legs with rope and put her body in a sack, which was easy as she was frail and small. He and Tyros and Otanes took turns carrying the sack on their way to the graveyard.

Apart from this, the rest of the events followed as planned. After depositing Fouma at the tunnel, Alabanda returned with Miletus and Cicero by a different route on which he knew Macedonian patrols abounded. Therefore he had a legitimate excuse for abandoning them both behind some shrubbery by claiming that a Macedonian patrol was approaching. From there, he proceeded alone to the desolate house.

They waited at the house for the beggar who had gone to Polemon with a message from the concubine who he was enamoured of – or so Polemon would be told. The beggar soon came back and told them that Polemon was delighted when he got the message and said that he was coming forthwith to meet her.

Here the concubine recognized Alabanda as one of her kidnappers and, since she knew him from before as her late husband's friend – she had no idea that Alabanda was responsible for murdering her husband – she asked him what the matter was and why she was being kept in confinement.

'To tell you the truth, we are using you as bait to lure Polemon to us. We have some business with him,' Alabanda confided to her.

'If you had told me your objective before, I would have helped you willingly. You need not have resorted to kidnapping me to achieve your purpose,' she said.

Upon hearing this, Alabanda untied her.

Tyros then asked the concubine, as they waited for Polemon to arrive, whether Fouma, whom she boarded with, had taken a new lover. For Tyros could think of no other explanation for Fouma's behaviour and that was what Fouma herself had told them. But at the mere mention of Fouma's name, the concubine started cursing her.

'That whore! Parmenio saw her accidentally once and had her summoned to his residence. And such was Fouma's low character that she immediately grew infatuated with him and lost all affection for her husband,' claimed the concubine.

The concubine's jealousy, however, appeared to emanate from the fact that Parmenio had been showering Fouma with more presents than he gave to her. She claimed that it was Fouma who had schemed with Parmenio to get rid of her husband Automa from Abydos.

At this point, Tyros offered to rescue the concubine from the Macedonians and told her that they intended to escape through a secret tunnel. She accepted the offer and declared that she knew which tunnel they were talking about as her late husband had been its custodian during the reign of King Phicias. She said that she had never told the Macedonians about the tunnel and had intended to use it herself, except that when she came to explore it, she found that the entrance had been hidden with earth and rocks and she was unable to remove all of it.

After she revealed her knowledge of the tunnel, Tyros had no option but to take her along as well, as he couldn't risk leaving her behind for fear that she would reveal the existence of the tunnel to the Macedonians and jeopardize any future need of ours to use it.

Polemon arrived at the appointed place at the time he had been told, with no suspicion of a plot. And as Tyros, Otanes, Alabanda and the Persian women led by Farisa watched, he pounced on the concubine passionately. It was only when all of them emerged from the shadows that he pushed the concubine away from him, realizing that it was a trap.

'At whose behest did you call me here, you vile woman?' Polemon asked the concubine.

'Your own fate is tired of your actions, Polemon, and seeks revenge,' replied the concubine.

By this time, all the men had come forward and seized Polemon, but since my instructions to Otanes and Tyros had been to bring him alive, no harm was caused to him. But once his arms and legs were tied and his mouth covered with cloth, the concubine approached him with accusations of having murdered her husband and, before any of the rescue party could realize what was in her mind, she stabbed Polemon many times with a dagger she snatched from Alabanda's waist.

'Take this, you son of a Macedonian maggot,' the concubine shouted, as she stabbed him repeatedly in his belly. And before Farisa could step in and stop her, Polemon's tunic was all covered with blood.

So it was a bleeding and incoherent Polemon whom they dragged through the tunnel with as much care as they could to stop his bleeding, but the wounds were deep and, when he was produced before me, his consciousness had gone and the anticipation of exacting revenge that had been building up in me was left unsatisfied, as the act of retribution on a person who is dying and who doesn't recognize the victor is in many ways hollow. The glint of fear and loss in the eyes of Polemon were essential to the squaring up of his past misdeeds against my family.

So my thirst for revenge remained unabated, even though Polemon died in front of my eyes from the wounds given to him by the concubine. He died before I could ask him about the whereabouts of Argus, Zeferino, Menechus and Clearchus, a task that I had planned with great relish but which was now of no consequence. It was a strange will of the Gods that a man who had outsmarted the Spartan Spiticos and survived many wars ultimately died at the hands of a Mede concubine. In this, I thought, there was great irony.

TWENTY

The concubine was left to her own fate in Abydos by Tyros and Otanes, as they were angry with her for having stabbed Polemon, but they left five hundred drachmas with her, which they had taken with them in case some unforeseen circumstance required them to pay a bribe. Alabanda never went back to where Miletus and Cicero awaited him and, instead, gave the beggar twenty drachmas to inform the authorities that two Persians, dressed in the uniform of Macedonian soldiers, were plotting something vile behind the shrubbery near the temple of the Medes.

It was Cicero who later explained to Agos what happened after he escaped from Abydos on his own. He said that Miletus and he waited a long time for Alabanda to come back, as they didn't know the paths around Abydos and they were afraid to move around on their own since they were in Macedonian uniform. They feared that the Macedonian soldiers had found out about the desolate house and everybody had been arrested. All this they discussed in sign language. Miletus then dispatched Cicero to the desolate house on his own; because of his climbing skills, he could move along the roofs and trees and thus avoid the soldiers and other residents on the streets. But by the time Cicero reached the desolate house, everybody had left and even the concubine had returned to her dwelling. Cicero's sharp eyes noticed the blood on the floor, though, which hadn't been there earlier in the night.

Cicero then returned to where Miletus was, but he saw that a contingent of Macedonian soldiers was already there and had surrounded Miletus and was asking him the password for the night. All the Macedonian soldiers in Abydos were given new passwords every night, so that the soldiers could distinguish between friend and foe. Since Miletus spoke Greek, they were a little hesitant to arrest him, but they were suspicious because none of the soldiers had seen him before and so they repeatedly asked him for the password and Miletus kept saying he had forgotten it. They then asked him to which unit he belonged and, when he kept silent, they seized him. Miletus didn't put up any resistance, as any skirmish would have been futile. He had, however, seen Cicero and warned him to keep away by making signs, and the Macedonian soldiers, seeing Miletus make weird gestures with his hands, thought that he was deranged in the mind.

After the soldiers took Miletus away to the barracks, Cicero returned to the graveyard on his own and searched for the grave below which the tunnel started. Just then, some dogs started barking and chased him and so he had to leave the graveyard. He then scouted for a section of the fortifications which would be easy to climb over. After identifying a section, he waited till the soldiers patrolling the top of the walls came down to warm themselves at a log fire. Then he climbed the walls swiftly, descended on the other side and ran to safety behind the shrubs and reached the Persian lines from where the men of Gophoredes conveyed him to Agos.

This then was the story of how Miletus was seized by the Macedonians, and how Cicero escaped, as I had thought he would. The story with Fouma, however, became more curious by the day. As soon as she was brought to the other side of the tunnel and conducted to Automa's tent, she turned into a devoted wife and embraced him with great affection. Tyros and Otanes, who had witnessed her conduct at the concubine's house, were amazed at the transformation that came over her. But I sensed that all was not well with her conduct and I was determined to get to the bottom of it, for Automa was important to me if I had to deliver the monsters that King Artaxerxes wanted.

The very next night, Fouma fled, unknown to the guards, and when a distressed Automa pleaded with Agos for a search party for his wife and a search was launched, she was discovered on horseback near Larisa. The horse had been provided to her by Farisa, not for escape but as a loan for a few days till Automa left for Rhodes.

This time, it was I who confronted Fouma alone in her tent and, since the events of the past few days had broken her spirit, she cried in front of me and confessed that she had intended to reach Larisa and catch a boat back for Abydos.

'I intended to elope with my lover, who has promised to take me to Pella in Macedonia for a new life. I am not attracted to Automa any more and, while I don't wish him any harm, I cannot continue living with him as my heart is elsewhere,' confessed Fouma to me.

This lover of hers turned out to be Modius, son of Phisinus, and a cousin of Olympias, the queen of Macedonia and wife of King Philip!

Modius had come to Abydos to deliver a hundred mounts and to seek employment under Parmenio. But because of Olympias's closeness to him and his sense of being a part of the Macedonian nobility, he was haughty in the manner in which he met Parmenio. His arrogance so angered Parmenio that, to teach him a lesson, he imposed a false charge of misappropriation of funds on him and had him arrested, but because of his status as nobility, he could do him no further harm except send him back to Pella after the imposition of a fine of ten talents, double the amount of money that had allegedly been misappropriated.

Modius was now waiting for his men to arrange a loan of ten talents to pay off Parmenio's fine and attain freedom once again. His men had gone to Olympias to plead his case and were due to return in ten days' time. It was while he was imprisoned in his own dwelling that he had fallen sick and Parmenio had arranged for Fouma to take care of him. The two had become intimate and Parmenio lost the affections of Fouma, who transferred them to Modius after he declared his intention to take her with him to Pella to live on his land and bear him children. Whether Modius intended to have her as his wife or concubine, I didn't know yet, but I saw this as an opportunity to befriend him, to fulfil the idea that I had impressed King Artaxerxes with – namely, the death of Philip.

After Mistros's prophecy, which had alluded to the death of a king, I had begun to think that the king he alluded to was none other than the Macedonian king, and this fell in well with my own plans. Mistros's next prophecy in front of Mritphakes, who had provoked him to challenge his ancestors, had been: 'My ancestors tell me that the leader who desires the fall of Abydos will be dead within two days and the fate of Abydos will be decided by another person present here and it will not be through either land or sea or air.'

I felt that Mistros had referred to me when he said 'another person present here'. And as to his prediction that it would be neither through land or sea or air that Abydos would fall, I concluded, after a lot of thought, that if Philip were assassinated, the Macedonians would of their own accord pull out of Abydos, as it was Philip who had the ambition to invade Persia.

Since I had decided to proceed to Macedonia myself to work towards the assassination of Philip, I saw in Modius a possible ally, specially since I had heard that Philip had taken on another wife by the name of

Eurydice, who had borne him a son and thus rendered Olympias furious. I intended to use this disaffection in the supporters of Olympias and Alexander to further the objectives of Athens.

In view of all this, I made an offer to Fouma. I told her that I would send an envoy to Abydos to pay off the fine imposed by Parmenio on Modius. The envoy would bring him back by boat to Larisa and she could join Modius there.

'You can even claim to Modius that you arranged the talents by stealing from your own husband, who had been given an advance by a Persian satrap to manufacture another war catapult. But in return for this favour, you are to introduce me to Modius as the person who helped you steal Automa's money and, earlier, rescued you from Abydos,' I suggested to Fouma.

'I would be more than happy to do that and will give you my undying support if you help me thus,' answered Fouma.

Since Agos hadn't revealed to Automa that his wife had been found near Larisa, it was told to him that she had gone for a ride on a horse and the horse had gone mad after a dog bit it and it had then run off a cliff and his wife had thus perished in the sea, along with the horse. Agos produced a shepherd as a witness, who in turn produced a scarf of Fouma that had fallen off her shoulders as the horse ran out of control and, seeing the scarf, Automa grieved all the more.

But in two days, the cloud of suffering lifted from his shoulders and he came to me declaring that he wished to proceed to Rhodes and get to work on making the monsters and the triremes that would transport them. I therefore gave one hundred and fifty talents to Zamos and put two transport ships at his disposal, with a hundred armed men, not including the sailors, and told him to escort Automa to the island where his father Samocles and his other brothers would help manufacture four monsters for us. Automa said that it would take nearly eight months to make the monsters, apart from the time taken to travel to the islands. I then gave Zamos a letter of introduction to Queen Moria at Methymyna, in case the need arose for him to seek her help in any way.

In this manner did I dispatch Zamos to Rhodes along with Automa, telling him to periodically send messages of progress to Pythagoras and Phormio in Athens, as they would know where to forward those tidings to me. Once the monsters were within two months of completion, he was to await my message on where to sail with them. I also made Zamos understand how important the monsters were, as they would decide the war in favour of whoever owned them. Impressed with the importance of his mission, Zamos selected a hundred men from among the mercenaries to undertake the journey and requested me to spare Dorian to be his second in command. I readily agreed.

After bidding farewell to Zamos and Dorian at Larisa, I proceeded to send a carefully chosen envoy to Abydos. Nearchus, son of Andromitus, was a Macedonian who had been exiled by Philip on account of his being a friend of Alexander. Alexander had become openly hostile to Philip, like his mother Olympias, after Philip married Eurydice, and Philip, in order to teach Alexander and Olympias a lesson, had exiled all of his friends. Besides Nearchus, Harpalus, son of Machatas, Naxos, son of Lagus, Erigyius, son of Larichus, and his brother Laomedon all incurred Philip's wrath and were exiled from Macedonia.

All these people first reached Athens and upon learning that Pythagoras, the famous charioteer, was recruiting mercenaries to employ in Persian lands, they came to him for help. They desired respectable placements in Asia till such time that the anger of Philip had subsided. Demosthenes, seeing the opportunity, advised Pythagoras to help them, and he sent them over to Zamos to be recruited into the mercenary army, which they were told was just a small army that sought employment with different Persian satraps and helped maintain law and order. Pythagoras recruited them at thirty drachmas a day, and this allowed them to recruit servants, for that was the life they were used to back in Macedonia.

I selected Nearchus from amongst these exiles when I learned that he knew Parmenio. Even though he was an exile, I knew that he would be greeted with warmth by Parmenio if he entered Abydos through the harbour. I never met the exiles directly, for I was worried that they might recognize me as Nicanor's son. Therefore I dealt with them through Agos and it was announced to the troops that Agos would be their chief until Zamos came back from his journey to Rhodes. The men had been told that Miletus had been captured by the Macedonians and, though some of them were upset by the fact, no one suspected any treachery. None of the men offered to launch a rescue mission for Miletus, either.

Agos briefed Nearchus. 'You are to get to Abydos in a boat that will have a Phoenician crew,' he said to him. 'Upon reaching, you must announce that you are there on a mission to meet Parmenio, the garrison commander. Since you know Parmenio, you will gain easy access. Upon meeting him, you will tell him that you have been sent on a secret errand by Olympias, the queen of Macedonia, requesting the release of Modius.

If Parmenio asks for any written communication from the queen, you are to say that the queen prefers the matter to remain secret. Since she has been forbidden by Philip to interfere in matters of state, she is in no position to send a sealed letter. This is what you are to say.

'You must then declare that you have brought with you a sum of ten talents to be paid as a fine for the transgression of Modius – if it is required. And that Modius is to be released without delay and handed over to you. You are to say that you will be taking Modius to Larisa, from where he would be sent by ship to the coast of Greece and thence to the oracle of Delphi, where Olympias desires him to be for a particular task. All this you will tell Parmenio, and no more. You will have to be careful, for if Parmenio gets wind of the fact that you come from the camp of the mercenaries, he might arrest you on suspicion alone,' said Agos to Nearchus.

'You need not worry. I will do as you say and Modius will be with you soon,' said Nearchus.

Agos promised Nearchus a sum of one talent if he brought Modius to Larisa. He was then given ten talents, which he was to hand over to Parmenio only if Parmenio would not release Modius without the payment of the fine.

After Nearchus had been dispatched to Abydos, I undertook the worship of Poseidon as Mistros had advised me, for I now intended to leave for Macedonia to organize the assassination of Philip. I rode in a vessel beyond the harbour of Larisa and sacrificed a bull on the high seas as Ionian priests chanted verses to the glory of the sea God. The blood was poured into the seas and everybody present drank a cup. After the sacrifice, an eagle appeared from nowhere and sat on the mast of the vessel and the priests said that it was a good sign, though when I asked why, they offered no satisfactory explanation, except the story that they had once performed a similar sacrifice for the tyrant of Palestine and an eagle had come and perched on the mast after it was done. And the priests said that the tyrant had left on a journey to Sicily with five ships of corn and olive oil, and though pirates attacked his fleet, they were unable to board a single ship.

This story was cited by the priests as proof that if an eagle perched on a ship after a sacrifice, it was a sign that Poseidon had accepted the sacrifice in good spirit and no harm would befall the person at whose behest it had been undertaken.

Two days after the sacrifice, Nearchus returned with Modius. He said that Parmenio had insisted on the ten talents and therefore he had had to part with the sum. Parmenio had also told him that a search was on for a Macedonian commander called Polemon, who had disappeared. The Macedonians feared that he had gone over to the Persian side, with all the secrets of their fortifications, as he had been the commander before Parmenio and was not on good terms with him after having been replaced.

Nearchus also told Agos that Parmenio had warned him to stay away from a mercenary known as 'Seleucus, son of Nicanor'. He was said to be very dangerous and responsible for having seized one of the stone-throwing monsters from Parmenio's possession at Lesbos by a deception of grand proportions. Parmenio was apparently ready to pay any price for the head of this Seleucus and had told Nearchus to inform him immediately if he came to know anything about his whereabouts. Nearchus then asked Agos if he knew anything about Nicanor's son and if he could use any of his men to search for him, as Parmenio had promised a reward of up to thirty talents for any person who captured Nicanor's son, dead or alive. Parmenio suspected that Nicanor's son was somewhere near Abydos and that he had brought the monster which he had snatched from them all the way from Lesbos to Larisa to sell it to the Persians. Only, he couldn't figure out why the Persians weren't using the monster to batter the city; for if he had been the Persian commander, that was what he would have done.

Nearchus also revealed that the Macedonians had in custody Miletus, whom Nearchus had met briefly after he came to Larisa, and he was curious as to how the Macedonians had got hold of him. Agos told him that Miletus had been captured by the Macedonians at night when he was answering nature's call, and he told Nearchus to be careful, as Parmenio was not to be trusted.

Later, when Agos talked to the Phoenician sailors who had taken Nearchus to the port at Abydos, he was told that Nearchus had never unloaded the bags that he had taken with him. But on the way back from Abydos, a vessel had met them at sea and Nearchus had then offloaded all the bags into that vessel. After this, Nearchus had given the crew two hundred drachmas each and told them not to reveal the matter to Agos and the sailors had happily given their word. They had then resolved not to reveal the story to Agos voluntarily, unless Agos himself found some cause for suspicion and asked them about what had happened. The Phoenicians were scared of Zamos and Agos, as they were strict taskmasters. And since they wanted to preserve their relationship with Zamos and the rest of the mercenaries, they spoke the truth to Agos.

As a fine for not telling him earlier, Agos asked each of the sailors to return the two hundred drachmas they had received from Nearchus and also told them that they wouldn't be paid for the trip to Abydos. The sailors were relieved that they had been let off lightly. One of them came up to him and said: 'The vessel into which Nearchus offloaded the bags has sailed into Larisa now and the sailors on it are probably expecting Nearchus to come and collect his property.'

After receiving this information, Agos promptly sent Tyros and Otanes, along with five men, to the vessel in the port. After searching the boat, they discovered the bags, but they found that four talents were missing. They seized the bags, then enquired from the sailors as to how they came about the money, but the sailors said that they never knew what the bags contained, though they guessed that it could be money. They revealed that they had been hired by Nearchus at the docks of Abydos and he had told them to follow his vessel till they were halfway to Larisa, at which point he desired to shift some cargo from his vessel to theirs. They were to follow half a day later to Larisa, so no one would suspect that they were carrying his cargo.

Nearchus had told them that he wasn't transferring the cargo in Abydos itself as he didn't want the Macedonians to see what was inside the bags. They also said that four Greeks had come to their vessel and each had taken three bags from the cargo, and they had assumed that they were Nearchus's men. The sailors said that they didn't know these men, but could identify them if they saw them again.

Agos then came back and told me all that he had discovered and asked how he should proceed with Nearchus, now that it was clear that he hadn't paid a single drachma to Parmenio as claimed. I told him to arrest Nearchus and confront him with the truth and then order his execution, as he was in our pay when the task was given to him and, instead of complying with our instructions, he had indulged in deceit and greed. Agos also said that he suspected that the rest of the Macedonian exiles had been in on the plot and it was they who had taken one talent each from the bags that Nearchus had brought back.

When Agos confronted Nearchus with all the facts, he broke down.

'Yes, Agos, I confess that I lied. I did it so that my friends and I could have a life of respectability while in exile. In Macedonia, we all had big estates and employed many servants, but in Asia, we are worthless mercenaries. The truth is that Parmenio had Modius released immediately, once I told him that I had come to him with a message from Olympias herself, requesting the immediate release of Modius as she needed his services at Delphi,' confessed Nearchus.

Agos then summoned all the other Macedonian exiles and asked them whether they had been party to the plot of Nearchus to keep the money for themselves and all of them initially said that they knew nothing about it. But Tyros then came and revealed to Agos that the sailors had identified the Macedonian exiles from afar. Harpalus, Naxos, Erigyius and Laomedon had indeed collected the bags of money.

The exiles, realizing that they had been caught in the act, confessed to their crime and said that they were only helping Nearchus and thought that the money was his. But under my instructions, Agos seized them and made an announcement that they would all be executed the next day at dawn. Being mercenaries, they had to stick to a higher form of discipline, and executing them would set an example for all the men, so that such a thing never happened again. Hearing this, they were all alarmed and begged Agos for forgiveness, for they thought he was the sole master now that Zamos was away. But Agos had them roped and gagged and placed them in a stable, and the rest of the Greek mercenaries were happy as they had resented the fact that the Macedonian exiles were being paid much more than they were for the same job.

Even as Agos confronted the Macedonian exiles, Menicus had taken Modius, the Macedonian who had been brought from Abydos by Nearchus, to meet Fouma. Modius was so surprised to see her that he became speechless and, when she told him that it was she who had arranged for money to be offered to Parmenio for his release by robbing her husband Automa, he started crying, for he saw it as evidence of her love for him. He promised her undying affection for the rest of his life and cursed Nearchus and the rest of the Macedonians for trying to rob her of the money she had robbed from Automa. She then introduced me to Modius as the person who had helped her to steal from her husband. He readily agreed to help me in whatever way he could, back in Macedonia, where I intended to send him. He was even more helpful after I told him that I intended to gift him two talents, so that he could spend the sum on a lavish wedding at Pella, and if he didn't have any objections, I intended them to travel with me to Macedonia on my vessel. I told him I was going there to explore trading opportunities.

But Modius was so greedy that he first wanted to know whether he could approach the chief of the mercenaries and get the ten talents that had been seized from the exiles since it was Automa's property, which now belonged to Fouma. I was unhappy that Modius had come to know about this incident after overhearing some loose talk amongst the mercenaries. I told him that the money would be returned to Automa, as it was his and not Fouma's, and we had only stolen it for his release. Now that his freedom had come about, it was only right that the money should go back to its owner. With this answer was he silenced, though I told him that I would loan him another talent if he was in such great need for resources. Modius immediately agreed to receiving the loan and promised to return it within a year, though I was certain he had no intention of doing so.

I then sent Modius and Fouma to live together in a house in Larisa till further travel could be organized and instructed Menicus to post a guard there and ensure that they had no contact with any other person.

Agos then asked me whether I actually intended to execute the Macedonian exiles next day at dawn and I confided to him that it was a ploy to win the confidence of the Macedonians, so that they looked upon me as a saviour and became beholden to me for saving their lives.

Accordingly, the next day, they were brought forward for their execution in front of a select crowd and Agos read out the charges they were guilty of. He then asked them whether they had anything to say about the matter and Nearchus, speaking for everybody, said: 'We think that the punishment of execution is too great for the offence under consideration, and if at all anybody has to be executed, it should be just me and the rest of my friends should be released, as they had only minor roles to play in the whole episode. They became involved only after I brought the money back from Abydos.'

The rest of the exiles kept quiet when Nearchus said this, as if they agreed with him, and it showed them in a bad light. But Agos remained unmoved in front of them and said that nothing had changed since the previous day and he saw no reason to let them live, specially as they had confessed to their crime.

Ordered Agos: 'Tyros and Otanes, you will begin with the execution of Harpalus, son of Machatas, as he offered resistance while being arrested, whereas the others ceded peacefully to authority. You may show no mercy while cutting off his head.'

Tyros and Otanes then dragged an unwilling Harpalus outside the stable and he could be heard by all, saying his prayers to Zeus. Then there was the sound of a sword coming down and the thud of a head falling to the ground. Tyros and Otanes returned to the stable with a bloody sword and Agos asked for Naxos, son of Logus, to be taken next.

All the Macedonian exiles broke down then, presuming that Harpalus had been executed. Nearchus, Naxos, Erigyius and Laomedon fell on their knees and begged Agos for forgiveness. They declared to him that they had in their possession their personal seals and they would sign away on paper the ownership of all their estates in Macedonia and Agos could recover as a fine all the lands that they owned there. In return, they just wanted to be spared death. Agos responded by asking them what good their estates in Macedonia were to him as he was in Asia and didn't desire to live on their estates in Pella.

At this point, I spoke from amidst the crowd, introducing myself as Demetrius, a trader from Eubea who roamed all of Greece and Asia.

'May I speak in your presence?' I asked Agos.

'Yes, you may, Demetrius. What is it that you want to say at a time when we are busy getting rid of some rats?'

'I think, my lord, that the punishment you deliver far outweighs the crime they have committed. If it pleases you, I am willing to pay a fine of ten talents on behalf of all the exiles. This was the sum they had intended to steal, but ultimately couldn't. In return, I would be satisfied with ownership of the estates, provided they put their seals to the deeds,' I said.

Agos challenged me to produce ten talents first or keep my mouth shut. 'Demetrius, you don't look like a person who could arrange a hundred drachmas,' he said, 'let alone ten talents!'

There was laughter at these words, but I had already arranged to have ten talents outside in a wagon with the help of Menicus and had it produced by five of his men. Agos dropped his jaw for everybody's benefit and the gathering fell silent and the exiles viewed me with great hope.

'Here are ten talents. Your treasurer can count them – they will not be a drachma short. These men are lucky, for I am just returning from a very fruitful business transaction in Thebes and happened to be carrying my profits,' I announced to the gathering.

Agos then turned to the exiles and asked: 'So, tell me, do you prefer death or do you prefer what Demetrius here is suggesting?'

All the exiles unanimously agreed to do what was desired by me in order to stay alive and Agos smiled and granted them their wish. They fell on the ground and wept with joy and came up to me and kissed my hands and said that they would pray for me till the end of their lives.

The exiles then requested that Harpalus's body be delivered to them so that they could give him a proper burial, but Agos refused the request, saying that the body had already been thrown off the cliff and traitors in the mercenary camp were not given the privilege of a burial.

Of course, as you may have guessed, Harpalus had been gagged by Tyros and Otanes behind the stable as he finished his prayers and the head of a sheep had been cut instead. Harpalus himself was taken to a dwelling far away from the mercenaries and was told that the date of his execution had been postponed and the priests would be consulted for an appropriate date. So, though Harpalus was relieved for the moment and kept touching and kissing the many lucky charms on his body, which had been provided to him by the priest at the temple of Zeus in his village, his despondency didn't leave him. He felt that he had achieved only a temporary reprieve.

The other four exiles, Nearchus, Naxos, Erigyius and his brother Laomedon huddled next to me, anxious not to let me out of their sight. Being in a foreign land for the first time in their lives and thinking they had just escaped execution at the hands of the mercenaries, they didn't want Agos to have a change of heart. I lied to them that a Macedonian had once saved my life and I was only returning a favour to his countrymen. I told them that it was only by chance that I was travelling that way and, hearing at the tavern that some Macedonian exiles were being executed, I had made my way to the stable to watch the proceedings.

'I am also desirous of doing business in Macedonia with King Phillip, but right now, I have no way of approaching him. I desire his help in buying a large tract of land in Thebes. As Philip is the virtual ruler of all of Greece, except Sparta, I desire his intervention in the matter, for the Thebans are reluctant to part with their land, though I offer a fair price,' I added.

Nearchus replied that they had been exiled by Philip for being close to his son and the king distrusted them. They could not therefore intercede on my behalf directly with hum. But they could provide me with letters of introduction to their relatives, who were close to King Philip and who could arrange a meeting with him for the matter to be resolved in my favour. Naxos said: 'I will provide you with a letter of introduction to Alexander himself and his close friend Hepasthion, and they will intercede on your behalf with the Thebans, even if Philip doesn't.'

They then talked about the politics of their land and told me that Olympias, the wife of Philip and the mother of Alexander, was furious that Philip had married another woman. She worried that the family of the new wife might make the succession of Alexander difficult in the event that Philip died. In this manner did I learn all about the families that were allied with Philip and those that nursed a grudge against him because of his marriage with Eurydice. I also learned that Philip was hosting his annual boar hunt a month from now and it would last a full two weeks. After that, there would be a meeting of the war council, which would decide the best way to proceed in the invasion of Persia. The exiles confided that they had come to Asia to learn more about the landscape, so that when Philip arrived here, as he had promised to, he would find their knowledge of the Persian language and customs useful enough to forgive them and welcome them back into his fold.

After several hours of conversation with them, when they were sufficiently drunk, Erigyius revealed the real reason for their exile. Said Erigyius: 'Philip came to know that we were plotting to murder Eurydice during the boar hunt, with the help of Donios, her former lover, who was much aggrieved that she had been given to Philip in marriage rather than to him as promised by her father. But Philip had become enamoured of Eurydice after seeing her at the wedding celebrations of Naxos, and Eurydice's father had broken the engagement gladly, seeing that his daughter would be marrying the king of Macedonia.

'Olympias, however, became upset because she heard that Eurydice's father had extracted a promise from Philip that should Eurydice bear him a son and Philip lived to see him grow to sixteen years of age, the throne would fall to him and not to Alexander after his death. But no one really knew whether Philip had made this promise or whether he meant it in jest. Olympias, however, believed the story to be true and desired the murder of Eurydice before she even gave birth to a child, but she had not succeeded in this. When Philip confronted her, she promptly denied it, but her resolve hardened even further and she involved Harpalus, Naxos, Nearchus, myself and my brother Laomedon in the matter. We succeeded in exciting Donios to such an extent that, without worrying about any consequences, he entered the household of Eurydice when she visited her father and nearly managed to kill her, but the guards intervened and saved her life.

'Eurydice's father swore his daughter to secrecy about the incident, for if Philip learned about it, he might even have had him executed for exposing her to such danger. Donios, by then, had grown repentant and had gone into hiding in the estate of Naxos to avoid the men of Eurydice's father who hunted him. Philip was only told that Donios had been insulting to Eurydice at the behest of his friends, and for that alone he exiled all of us.'

Even though Nearchus and Naxos were not as drunk as Erigyius, they didn't stop him from revealing these secrets to me, for they thought that, having saved them from death, I desired no harm to them. In the next two days, I obtained as many introductory letters from them as possible and also letters handing over their estates to me because of a debt they had incurred overseas. They also wrote instructions to the managers of their estates to do as I desired as the new owner. I gave them five talents each for the estates they handed over to me and they were overjoyed at this gesture on my part, as some of their estates weren't of that value and either way the money would allow them to live like noblemen in Asia. Since I desired their friendship, I also gave instructions to Agos to use their services in training the mercenaries.

Elated at this turn of events, Nearchus and Naxos wrote a letter of introduction to Olympias, detailing how I had saved their lives. When I thought I had their confidence, I revealed to the two of them that I had heard that the king of Persia sought help to assassinate Philip and was willing to give a huge reward to anybody who helped plan the act. I told them that if they had any ideas about how it could be done, I could introduce them to a Persian who was looking into the matter.

The two men, seeing some profit from this disclosure, immediately wished to be introduced to the Persian. I told them that he had gone to Sardis and would be back soon, but before I introduced them to him, they had better reveal their ideas to me so that I could judge them on their 'merit' as I was a friend who was interested in their well-being. The concerned Persian, I told them, was a very impatient sort of person and would not tolerate any infantile ideas.

Said Nearchus: 'I assure you that our ideas are not infantile. It was not for nothing that Philip had us exiled. I have a foolproof plan to get rid of him, and it is only because Alexander did not approve of it that I did not implement my idea.'

Naxos, not willing to be left behind, added: 'I too had thought of a plan to do away with Philip, but I was afraid of discussing it with Alexander after Nearchus's plan was dismissed by him with great anger. He forbade us to even contemplate the assassination of his father.'

'Our only purpose in getting Philip assassinated was to get Alexander to be king, so that we ourselves could acquire positions of authority in the kingdom. My plan was to use an Illyrian named Gerochus, whose family had been put to the sword by Philip and who now only nurses thoughts of revenge against the king. He came close to committing the act at the Congress in Corinth, but he was discovered by Philip's bodyguards, Trillimachus and Machatas, who stay with him at all times, except when he retires to his bedroom in the night. I offered money to Gerochus to commit the act, but he returned the money, saying that he didn't need the motivation of a few minae to kill Philip, he intended to do it for free. But the problem is that the bodyguards of Philip are always on the lookout for Gerochus, as they recognize him. The advantage of using Gerochus is that the blame for the assassination would not fall on Olympias or Alexander, though they would be the ones to immediately benefit from the act. I convinced Gerochus to work in concert with me, so that it would be easier for him to exact his revenge. He is even now waiting for my instructions in a small town in Thessaly, where he works as a carpenter,' said Nearchus.

Naxos claimed that his plan was better, as it didn't involve a person like Gerochus, who would be easily recognized by the bodyguards of Philip. He then told me such an incredible story that my mouth fell open even listening to it. Said Naxos: 'I bought ten adders from an Egyptian trader in Lolcos, who was on his way back to Egypt. He was the master of three transports and carried the adders with him wherever he went, to scare his crew and keep them under control. If one of those adders bit a man, he would die within one hour. I once arranged for a dog to be bitten and it died even before the hour had passed. I have left the adders with my servant on my estate in Apollonia, which is east of Pella and three riding days away. My servant keeps them alive on a diet of rats, lizards and small birds and the room where they are kept is heated in winter so that they don't die. I had hoped they would reproduce, but they haven't so far; I don't even know how many of them are male and how many female. Maybe all of them are male and that's why they don't reproduce. But whether male or female, they have the same deadly poison in their fangs. And it will be easy to smuggle the adders into Philip's bed with the help of his pages, who are not checked by the bodyguards. If the adders bite Philip even once, he cannot be saved.'

'I think, Naxos, that a king deserves a better death than by the bite of an adder. To die by the dagger or the sword is more honourable,' countered Nearchus.

'I just brought it up as a plan that Demetrius could inform his Persian friend about. He might think it a good proposition. The people of Egypt frequently use adders for such things. There is no need to get into the ethics of the act, Nearchus, for murder is murder, whether it arrives in the form of steel or the fangs of an adder,' said Naxos.

When I asked them whether Erigyius or Laomedon had any plans that they wished to talk about, both Naxos and Nearchus started laughing and confided to me in a whisper that Erigyius was the lover of Olympias and Philip had exiled him when he came to know of this. Naxos also laughingly added that Erigyius was just one lover Philip had come to know about and there were many others. In fact, Philip had married Eurydice to get back at Olympias for her infidelities. When I asked them who the others were, Nearchus said that he suspected Antipater as well, but didn't have any evidence. He said that the animosity between Antipater and Olympias was only a recent occurrence, after Antipater had spurned her amorous attentions for fear of Philip.

I stood up then to take my leave of them. 'It was good listening to you both. I will await the return of my Persian friend from Sardis to brief him on what the two of you have told me and, depending on his reaction, I will introduce you to him. In the meantime, I am proceeding on a journey to Athens and will meet you after I return,' I told them.

I gave strict instructions to Agos that the Macedonian exiles were to be watched at all times and were not to be given access to any messenger who was going to Macedonia, as I feared that, on thinking deeply, they might be able to see through my ruse and warn people in Macedonia of my intentions.

I also contacted Harpalus at this point. After having faked his execution in front of the other exiles and kept him in isolation, I approached him to determine what he had to offer that would aid me in my mission. But I found that Harpalus had by then become mentally unsound through worrying about his impending execution. Some people have a huge fear of death and Harpalus seemed to be one of them. Agos said that he didn't speak at all to his guards and didn't remember whether he had eaten his meals and demanded food at all times by banging his food bowl on the ground. He also looked at every person with great suspicion, as if they were coming to do him harm. In this manner did he look at me too and ran as far away from me as he could, as if escaping a wild boar. I decided that, till his mental faculties recovered, he would be of no use to me and instructed Agos to have some Persian doctor treat him.

After this interaction with Harpalus, I had a vessel readied to take me to the coast of Anthemus. From there, I intended to proceed to Pella. Since Zamos had taken Dorian with him, I had to leave Agos behind to mind the mercenaries. I, however, took the decision to take with me Tyros, Otanes and Menicus, who were all bound by oath to serve me.

Since we would be leaving Asia and crossing the open seas to get to the Anthemus coast, the sailors packed the vessel with onions and salted fish wrapped in fig leaves since we couldn't cook on the sea for fear of starting a fire. It was on the evening of the day before we were supposed to leave that I distinctly remember thinking about Mistros's prediction: 'Finish your business in Abydos before sailing west. You will think that your business is over, but an event will occur which will shake you up. After you sail west, return to Asia with your loved ones once the king is dead, or you will come to grief.'

I thought that the rescue of Fouma from Abydos and Polemon's death was the business that Mistros had meant me to finish and the event that had occurred after that was the bringing back of Modius from detention by Parmenio. Therefore I could now consider my business in Abydos over and could proceed to the west to Macedonia, as I had earlier planned.

TWENTY-ONE

At this point, something happened which caused a great commotion, but discussing it now will take me away from the main thread of my narration, so I will desist.

Suffice it to say that the incident involved the treachery of Gophoredes, who had taken over from Mritphakes in Abydos. It also brought to light certain dealings between Mritphakes, when he was still alive, and Parmenio, and led to a naval engagement between Gophoredes's forces and my own, which ended in his death. The forces of Parmenio were involved as well, and I think it was this event that Mistros was referring to when he said that an event would occur that would shake me up. I will talk about this episode in the second edition of my histories, if I am granted enough time and well-being. For now, all I will mention is that Miletus, instead of being put to death by Parmenio, was befriended by him. I suspect it was because he revealed his usefulness to him by telling him some of my secrets.

Modius and Fouma travelled with me on my vessel to Macedonia and Modius promised me many times that he would help me in my objectives, whatever they were, as he had the ear of Olympias. He started building up his importance in Macedonia for fear that I might consider him unimportant and therefore disregard him along the way. As for Fouma, she kept talking to me whenever Modius was below deck and kept reassuring me that she would influence Modius to do whatever I desired and that she would be more loyal to me than even to Modius!

After a journey of twenty days over sea and land, we reached Bottiaea in the north-west, where Nearchus's estate was. Modius was our guide for the entire journey. I had chosen Nearchus's estate as my base in Macedonia because, being a bachelor, he had no family staying on his estate. This gave me the freedom to plan and implement what I had in mind.

After handing over Nearchus's letters to his estate manager, whose name was Gobyras, and claiming Nearchus's estate, I assured Gobyras that he would continue to be employed by me at double the salary he presently received and this made him very happy, as he had not got any salary at all from Nearchus for the past one year and lived on what he could make off the land. At this point, Modius took my leave, along with Fouma, to proceed to his estate in Pella to meet his brothers and sisters and introduce Fouma to them. He promised to return in ten days.

I utilized the following week to take over the estates of Naxos, Erigyius and his brother Laomedon. Menicus, Tyros and Otanes went to each of their estates and took them over, and where there were families involved, I paid them three thousand drachmas each to take up new lodgings. Initially they were resistant, but they agreed when Menicus offered them the money, though legally all the payment had been made to the owners themselves in Larisa and I had documents to that effect.

After obtaining possession of the estates, I enquired from Menicus which of them was the most beautiful and desirable and without hesitation he replied that the estate of Laomedon was situated between two hills and had a great pasture for grazing cattle, as well as natural beauty, and it was an estate where Olympias had spent time in her childhood before destiny made her queen of Macedonia. It was also the nearest to Pella.

Whereupon, I sent Tyros and Otanes to Modius, even before he could return to Bottiaea, to tell him to arrange an audience for me with Olympias. Modius arrived three days later, saying that he had met Olympias and acquainted her with my request and she had invited me to visit her the following week during the boar hunt festival when everybody, except she, would be in the countryside and she would have time to listen to me.

Modius said: 'I told her how you helped in my release from Parmenio and also how, if it hadn't been for you, Naxos, Nearchus, Erigyius and his brother Laomedon would have been executed. All the Macedonian exiles being friends of Olympias, she exhibited an immediate interest in meeting you.'

Two days before the date of my audience with Olympias, I sent Gobyras to Pella with Menicus to ascertain whether Antipater, Alexander, the charioteer Argus, Clearchus, Menechus or Zeferino were in Pella, for they were the ones who would immediately recognize me as Seleucus, son of Nicanor, and I could find myself in great danger. Gobyras came back and said that he could uncover details of only three people on my list. They were Antipater, Alexander and Argus, and all three were in Philip's entourage six hundred stadia from Pella, in the forests of Crestonia, where boar abounded, and would come back only two weeks later for the beginning of summer festivities in Pella. Fifty members of the Corinthian league would also be present at these festivities and Philip was due to ask them for various facilities for his Persian campaign.

Argus was the son of Damaris, the chief maid of Olympias, as I have revealed earlier, and against him my desire for revenge remained unabated. Menicus told me that the news of the disappearance of Polemon had reached Pella, for he had overheard gossip in the market square about how Alexander had lost his temper when he was told by Parmenio's son Philotas that Polemon had disappeared from Abydos and Parmenio feared that Nicanor's son had something to do with his disappearance. This had subsequently been confirmed by the capture of Miletus, a mercenary who worked for Nicanor's son. This Miletus, according to the gossip, had sworn to get the head of Seleucus for Parmenio and he had forgiven him his crimes for this determination. And as Miletus knew the ways of Seleucus, Parmenio was confident of catching him soon.

I was surprised that news of Miletus had travelled to Pella.

In the absence of Gobyras, Tyros commented: 'It would have been better to have slit Miletus's throat than to hope that the Macedonians would execute him.'

'Yes. I had not forseen this. I will learn to weigh my decisions better in the future,' I responded.

For the audience with Olympias, I took the letters of introduction from Nearchus and Naxos and the gifts that I had carried from Larisa specially for her. They included a golden Persian horn used in special ceremonies and the skin of a white tiger, so rare that Persian nobles were willing to pay up to three talents for it. Many people, upon seeing the skin, refused to believe that it belonged to a white tiger, thinking instead that a regular tiger skin had somehow been whitened. These tigers were hunted by the Scythians after travelling thirty days north of their country. Once they brought the skins to their lands, they traded with the Medes for gold and silver, for they knew not yet how to mine these metals.

It was Damaris, the chief maid of Olympias, who ushered Modius and me into Olympias's presence. The letters from the exiles that I handed to the queen introduced me as Demetrius.

I had already instructed Modius to leave after the introductions. So, after greetings had been exchanged, he asked to be excused by Olympias, stating that he had to go back urgently to his estate to see if he could eradicate the blight that afflicted the corn in his fields. Olympias gestured for him to leave.

It was not at Philip's residence that Olympias met me but in a residence where she had removed herself after Eurydice was declared the new wife of Philip and he insisted on putting her up in his palace as an affront to Olympias, with whom his relations had deteriorated. Here, she plotted with everything at her disposal to ensure that her son Alexander got what was due to him.

Upon receiving the presents of the tiger skin and horn, Olympias was delighted. When I further sought to present her the estate of Laomedon, where she had spent time in her childhood, she was overwhelmed and initially refused, but after I insisted and flattered her by saying that her kind of beauty would look best against the beauty of that estate, she relented and agreed to accept it, provided I asked for something in return.

Since Damaris was present by her side and was listening to everything, I told Olympias that it would not be proper for me to ask for something at our very first meeting, but if the queen graced me with an audience again, I would reveal to her my heart. Hearing this, she invited me for dinner the next day.

The next day, after we had dined, we went for a walk in the garden. Olympias asked me again what I wished and I replied that I would accept whatever she wished with regard to me. Hearing this, she expressed her dissatisfaction and again asked me to reveal what lay in my heart. This time, I said that I would like nothing better than to see her son Alexander crowned as the king of Macedonia. She looked up at me sharply then and asked whether I had been sent to her by Philip to assess the leaning of her mind. Surprised by this question, I assured her that I had never met Philip in my whole life and only venerated her after hearing stories about her from Nearchus, Naxos and Erigyius.

Hearing Erigyius's name, her face lightened up again and she said: 'Now, what may Erigyius have said about me to you?'

'He said that you were the most beautiful woman in the whole world when you were young,' I replied.

'Only when young? What do you think of me now?' she asked.

'I think he was wrong. I think your beauty enhances with age. And I mean that with all my heart,' I said.

'You lie like all men do,' said Olympias, though I could see that she was pleased with my answer. I think she was a little sharp with me initially because she had no idea what Nearchus and Naxos had revealed to me about her. Then, suddenly, she said something that made me very nervous. 'I would like you to meet Prince Alexander when he comes back from the boar hunt, for he will be greatly educated by your experience in Asia and it will help him prepare for the Persian campaign.'

Seeing me hesitate, she asked: 'Don't you want to meet the prince?'

'My queen, if you insist on my meeting him, I will do so, but I am a very private person and it was only your strength of character and the stories of your beauty that enthralled me from afar and brought me here. Now that I have seen you, I desire to leave shortly, convinced that no woman rivals you in beauty or wisdom. I wouldn't want to waste the time of the prince with my idle talk and experiences, which he is unlikely to be interested in,' I said.

'I desire that he become king quickly and that woman Eurydice is removed from Pella,' said Olympias with quiet determination.

'Whatever the queen desires will happen, for the Gods will listen to you,' I said. 'And if the Gods don't, my queen, I will.'

In this manner did proximity develop between us, and if you were to ask me at what point she trusted me enough to start conspiring with me, I would tell you it was the point when she confessed to me that she wanted Alexander to become king quickly and wanted Eurydice removed from Pella.

I came to know later that Olympias suspected every man who met her to be Philip's agent. Only when she was certain that he was not did she open her heart to him. The chief maid Damaris confessed to Modius later that she had never seen Olympias take to a stranger like she took to me and she asked Modius if he knew for certain that I was not an agent of Philip.

I suspected that Modius, by saying all this, was trying to increase his own importance as the person who had introduced Olympias to me. After finding out that I had gifted Laomedon's estate to Olympias, he had become greedy and expected that I would do something similar for him as well.

Seeing his greed grow, I asked him to take a gift to Damaris from me and convince her that I wasn't an agent of Philip. Modius said that he had already done that, but a present wouldn't harm anybody. So I gave him a golden necklace to take to Damaris, knowing full well that he wouldn't and would gift it to Fouma instead. Though no priest had conducted rites for the ceremony of their marriage, Modius called Fouma his bride.

When I was next with Olympias, she was seated with a man who seemed much distressed. His name was Mindarus and I shall remember his face for as long as I live. He was weeping as he told his tale to Olympias.

While returning to Macedonia from the temple of Athena, where Mindarus and his brother had gone on a pilgrimage to gain wisdom to solve a property dispute between themselves, they had taken shelter in a field outside Athens. There, some bandits had attacked them and robbed them of their mounts and provisions and, rendered penniless, they had asked for help from the Macedonian garrison on the Theban border. The officer there had given them shelter and credit of twenty drachmas to help them return to Pella.

The following night, while they slept in a field, they heard voices. Thinking some robbers were again intending to rob them, they shouted out a challenge and, becoming very fearful, threw their spears in the dark in the direction of the voices. They heard shouts of pain and, when they rushed to the spot, they saw that their spears had hit two boys aged around twelve. Hearing the commotion, a crowd of Thebans gathered, for they were still in Theban territory, and they accused the Macedonians of murder and attempted to execute them on the spot.

Fearing death, Mindarus told the crowd that it was his brother who had thrown both the spears and therefore they should deal with his brother and let him go. Now this was a straight lie, as each of the brothers had thrown a spear, but Mindarus wanted to live so badly that he was willing to put all the blame on his younger brother Hecatomanus. Hecatomanus, when he heard his elder brother lie, said nothing at all, and the crowd assumed that it was indeed he who had thrown both the spears and, since the mothers of the two dead boys had come on the scene and were wailing uncontrollably and demanding of the crowd why the two men were still alive, the crowd lynched Hecatomanus and then deliberated amongst themselves on how to proceed with Mindarus.

Just then, the chief of the Macedonian garrison, who had lent twenty drachmas to the two brothers, reached the spot after having heard of the incident. At the same time, a shepherd who had seen the whole incident from afar told the crowd that Mindarus had thrown one of the spears, but Mindarus stoutly defended his lie in front of the crowd and, seeing the arrival of the Macedonian garrison chief they quietly left, leaving behind the grieving mothers and their families. For they knew that they could be charged with the murder of Hecatomanus, as they had taken the law into their own hands instead of approaching a magistrate with the matter.

The garrison chief, meanwhile, arranged for the burial of Hecatomanus and Mindarus was inconsolable the whole time, and confessed at last to the chief of his cowardice in putting the whole blame on his brother.

'I understand the guilt that possesses you. But it is better that one of you has survived, as now you can not only take care of your family but your brother's as well, whereas if both of you had died, there would have been none to take care of them. I urge you to be calm, Mindarus, and proceed to Pella,' said the chief.

But deep inside, the chief himself was disgusted by the behaviour of Mindarus and mentioned it to a Macedonian priest called Caldemus, who was returning to Macedonia after a pilgrimage to Olympia. When Caldemus returned to Pella, he spread the word about what had really happened. And when Hecatomanus's wife heard about the cowardice of the elder brother of her dead husband, she came in front of Mindarus's house and hurled abuses at him and everybody in his village shunned him like the plague. Even Mindarus's wife, unable to bear the ignominy, left for her parents' house, saying that she would have preferred to become a widow rather than live with this shame.

Mindarus had then made his way to Olympias, as he had once worked as a manager on one of her estates, with the request that she help him in his purification. It appeared that many years ago, when King Philip had been imprisoned in Thebes in his younger days, he had become a devotee of Zeus and, through special prayers, he had developed the power of purification, whereby if somebody sought to atone for certain acts that he may have committed, Philip could pray to the Gods and purify his heart. But since it involved absolution, the person who performed the purification rites had to take upon himself the consequences of the acts of the person who sought the purification. The purifier mitigated the harshness of the consequences to himself through prayer and the powers that he had attained through his devotion to Zeus.

Olympias went into introspection after Mindarus cried in front of her and I watched, sitting in a corner. After a long time, she got up and addressed Mindarus thus: 'I see the pain in your heart, and if you do as I say, you will be purified. The day Philip returns to Pella from the boar hunt, fifteen days from now, you must be the first person to accost him as he proceeds to the Pella Zeus. On the temple steps, you shall prostrate yourself at the feet of Philip and beg for purification. You will, however, not tell him right then for what act you need purification. After the king has finished his prayers, he will come and seek you out. The fact is, the king cannot refuse your request if you make it to him on the temple steps as he is on his way to sacrifice; he would see your being there as a signal from Zeus to take care of your problems. I know this secret because I have performed purification myself, but yours is something that Philip alone can take care of. From now until Philip's return, go every day to the Pella Zeus and seek his blessings so that Philip might take up your cause when he returns from the boar hunt.'

After saying this, she dismissed him from her presence and smiling wickedly at me, said: 'You bring me good luck, Demetrius. I have waited for a purification like that of Mindarus's for a long time.'

She did not engage with me beyond these words that day, but I found out from Gobyras, who strangely turned out to be a cousin of the priest Caldemus, who was one of the ten priests at the Pella Zeus, that Philip had stopped the ritual of purification for the last five years, as he felt that he did not have a balance of stored prayers to mitigate the ill effects of a purification, specially if it involved murder.

Said Gobyras: 'Since Philip has been busy with his campaigns, he has not been able to observe the specific rituals that the purification rites demand, and if he were to engage in purification of a heinous crime, then calamity would surely befall him. All this, Caldemus told me.'

It was after learning this fact that I understood the villainy of Olympias and how astutely she was planning the demise of Philip, hoping that he would take on the purification of Mindarus, who had not only committed a murder out of fear but also placed the blame for it on his younger brother. Because the sin of Mindarus was immense and Olympias knew that the power of purification that Philip possessed had weakened over time, she calculated that if Philip took on the task of purifying Mindarus, it would be his end.

But I found the whole aspect of purification illogical. How could one person's crime be heaped on another human being? I looked at the plan of Olympias with great scepticism and immediately put in motion my own, for I did not want to waste any time hoping that hers would find fruition. I had already sent Menicus to locate the Illyrian Gerochus, whom Nearchus had cultivated and who had already made an attempt on Philip's life, only to be thwarted by his bodyguards Machatas and Trillimachus. Nearchus had said that Gerochus had fled to Thessaly, where he now worked as a carpenter.

Naxos's story about the adders he had purchased also turned out to be true, for on his estate in Apollonia there were indeed eight adders; two had died. Each adder was about three cubits in length and had to be handled very carefully. Phaselis, who looked after them, told Tyros that they had already claimed the life of his brother who, while feeding them, had been bitten by two adders together on his left hand, and the poison had made him die a terrible death within the hour. Since then, Phaselis was very careful while feeding the adders and even covered his hands with leather clothing, so that if he made a mistake and the adder's fangs reached him, they would not penetrate to his skin.

I now sent one of my men to Athens with a secret message to Demosthenes, which I took pains to hide inside the body of a whole salted fish, so that even if the messenger was searched by Macedonian soldiers on the way, they would not find anything.

In the message to Demosthenes, I mentioned all that had happened since my meeting with King Artaxerxes and how I was now in Pella to plot the assassination of Philip. I urged him to initiate a rebellion in Hellas the moment he heard of Philip's death, as I was determined to be successful. I told him to be prepared for the eventuality or he would be unable to utilize the opportunity that Philip's death would present, and that he should have the satisfaction of knowing that it was the emissary from Athens, whom he had appointed, who had achieved the deed. I also mentioned all the other triumphs that had been achieved by me, like the advance received from King Artaxerxes for the monsters and the recruiting of mercenaries. I asked him whether he or Clonus the Spartan were in need of any urgent finances to plan the rebellion post the death of Philip, for all the exiles of the entire Hellenic world would have to be motivated at once to plot against the Macedonians for the rebellion to be successful.

After having sent the missive to Demosthenes in Athens, I began to furiously think of a plan. It was around this time that Olympias's chief maid Damaris approached me through Modius, seeking employment for a person named Telephus on my estate, which was once the estate of Nearchus. This Telephus was the nephew of Damaris, and when I came to know that his wife was the chambermaid of Eurydice, Philip's new wife, I promptly gave him employment, even though I guessed that he was Olympias's spy, sent to learn more about me.

It was the coming of Telephus to work on my estate and the fact that his wife worked for Eurydice that made me decide that Naxos's plan of using the adders against Philip had great merit, since his wife could be made an accomplice in getting access to Philip's private quarters. Therefore I set Otanes the task of finding out any weakness of Telephus.

Otanes came back with this report within two days: 'Telephus has gambling debts of two hundred drachmas. He owes them to a Macedonian cavalry officer. The officer was willing to sell his debt for one hundred and fifty drachmas, so I immediately bought it.'

Otanes then sent one of our men to threaten Telephus to come good on two hundred drachmas or face his wrath. Telephus, greatly surprised by this development, came as a supplicant to me to ask for a loan and I wriggled an oath of loyalty out of him and even made him confess that it was Damaris who had insisted that he seek employment on my estate so that Olympias could be informed of all that was happening. I told him that, henceforth, he would convey only what I wished him to. He readily agreed to the condition, as he was afraid of the consequences of not being able to pay two hundred drachmas to his new debtor.

After this, I sent Cicero, who had travelled with me, even though it was Agos who could best communicate with him, to be an assistant to Phaselis, Naxos's manager who looked after the adders, so that he could learn as much as possible about handling the creatures. This was because Cicero was most swift with his hands and least fearful of the reptiles.

Then, one day, after Cicero had gained a level of confidence and expertise with the adders – he could pick them up by the tail and keep the head away with a stick – I approached Telephus and asked whether he could introduce Cicero to his wife as a doctor who could cure various ailments, specially growths on the chest, which skill he had learned by spending time with Persian doctors. I had learned that the uncle of Eurydice, whose name was Attalus and who was a general in Philip's army and poised to proceed to Abydos to help Parmenio in retaining the city, had an abscess on his back, which the doctors in Pella couldn't treat. Attalus was willing to pay a sum of five talents to any doctor who cured him, as he was in great agony. And Cicero, I knew, had picked up considerable medicinal knowledge from the doctors in Persia.

Attalus, as Philip's uncle-in-law, had offered a toast at the wedding banquet of Philip and Eurydice. 'May the union between Philip and Eurydice bring a legitimate heir to the throne,' he had said. And Alexander, insulted by the toast, had thrown his goblet at Attalus, whereupon Philip had become so enraged that he had drawn his sword and intended to strike Alexander, but having consumed too much wine, he had fallen between the tables and had not been able to accomplish the act.

At that point, both Alexander and Olympias had fallen out with Philip. Olympias had gone to her brother's kingdom in Epirus while Alexander had fled to Illyria. But Philip had soon sought to mend his relationship with the Epirots and given in marriage his daughter Catherine to the king of Epirus, Alexander the Molossian, who was also her uncle, being Olympias's brother.

Thereafter, truce was declared and Olympias came back to Pella and Alexander accompanied Philip on the boar hunt. After Philip returned from the boar hunt, the wedding of Catherine with Alexander the Molossian would take place in Aegae, accompanied by three days of celebrations in the city. It was also widely known that Philip had taken the decision to leave Alexander behind in Macedonia as regent while he proceeded on his Persian campaign.

But Attalus was unhappy with Philip's decision, as it would bring Olympias back into the centre of things. Therefore he had incited Pixodarus, the king of Caria, to offer his daughter in marriage to Arrihidaeus, the mentally retarded brother of Alexander, in the hope that Philip would then nominally bestow the regency on Arrihidaeus and he, Attalus, would manage things in his name. But after inciting Pixodarus to offer his daughter, Attalus had become incapacitated by the abscess on his back and sought an urgent cure to be able to receive Philip when he returned from the boar hunt.

This was where the skills of Cicero came in. Once Telephus told his wife, who was the chambermaid of Eurydice, about him, he was promptly summoned by Eurydice for help in treating her uncle, as she depended greatly on him to protect her and her child Caranus from the machinations of Olympias.

Cicero therefore gained immediate access to Attalus, who had been staying at Philip's residence since the beginning of his sickness, and he took Otanes with him as an interpreter. Both Eurydice and Attalus were impressed by Cicero. By applying certain herbs which he carried in his bag, he managed to decrease the pain that Attalus had been suffering.

Through several gestures, Cicero promised to cure him in three weeks' time and Attalus was joyous when he heard this.

A few days after this breakthrough in the household of Eurydice, Menicus returned with Gerochus from Thessaly and I saw this as a good omen, for it proved that Nearchus was not lying and providence was helping us. I lodged Gerochus in the former estate of Naxos in Apollonia, for if he stayed with me, Telephus might recognize him and inform the authorities. I got Menicus to interrogate him thoroughly and ask him whether his desire to assassinate Philip still burned fast and strong in him. He was so enraged at having his motivation questioned that he made a wound on his chest with a dagger and on that blood he swore that just so would Philip's blood flow one day and if any man questioned his hatred, he would die a similar death.

This gesture convinced Menicus of Gerochus's determination. The plan that emerged in my head then was to install Gerochus in a position where he could launch an attack with a dagger on Philip, for that was the weapon he was most comfortable with. If Philip escaped the attack, I would have Cicero and Otanes place the adders in his bedroom since they now had access to his residence through Attalus.

But around this time, Otanes reported to me an event that made me rethink my strategy. He told me that Attalus had taken Cicero and him to the Pella residence of Pixodarus, the king of Caria, and in their presence the bodyguards of Attalus had dragged in Pausanias, whom Attalus referred to as the scorned lover of Philip. This Pausanias was a childhood friend of Philip. Together they had been held hostage in Thebes in their youth and that was when they had become lovers. But recently, Philip had taken a new lover and discarded Pausanias and, since Attalus had many years ago been slighted by Pausanias, he saw this as the perfect time to seek revenge on him, as he was no longer under the protection of Philip.

Therefore Attalus had Pausanias called to the residence of Pixodarus on a pretext and there he had his hands and legs bound and had him sodomized by his bodyguards and those of Pixodarus, all the while taunting him about Philip, who was not there to protect him. After the molestation, which lasted several hours, they released him and left him unconscious outside Pixodarus's residence. Otanes, taking pity on him, carried Pausanias to his lodging on my estate, which was Nearchus's former estate. He did this unobserved by any of the guards of Attalus or Pixodarus.

Since I was sleeping at the time, he didn't ask my permission, but far from rebuking him, I lauded him for the opportunity he had brought. Once Pausanias regained consciousness after the administration of various salts, he expressed great gratitude towards Otanes for having taken care of him and, coming to know that I was the owner of the estate, he thanked me for my hospitality. He kept mumbling: 'I have been betrayed by the highest authority in the land of Macedonia.'

Initially, he did not take the name of Philip, but when the pangs of jealousy rose, he did. He was bitter specially at the fact that Philip no longer accorded him his protection, in spite of their having been lovers for long, and he considered this a great betrayal. He also took the name of one Oxyrides, who he claimed had betrayed him. Oxyrides had been his servant and Philip had become infatuated with him. Philip had subsequently broken off all contact with Pausanias and had taken Oxyrides with him on the boar hunt. This was Pausanias's biggest lament – that Philip had ignored him for the boar hunt and for a month before that had refused to meet him, and had him insulted by his bodyguards Trillimachus and Machatas. He also cursed the day that he had taken Oxyrides into his employ.

On my instructions, Otanes took good care of him, all the while inserting the seed of revenge in his mind by talking about the 'insolence' and 'betrayal' of Philip and how it didn't suit a king to behave in this manner. He also spoke of how such behaviour was always avenged by the Gods. Since such language was music to Pausanias's ears, gradually he also started talking like Otanes.

Then I went to him one day and said: 'Pausanias, I had a dream in which you were covered with blood and so was Philip. My dream didn't tell me, however, how the blood came about.'

Pausanias listened intently to the story of my dream and remarked quietly that he too had been having dreams of a similar nature and had seen the same dream thrice already. I don't know whether he really saw those dreams or made them up like I had. He continued: 'I want to know whether I have your trust, so that I can confide a certain decision of mine to you. You have taken good care of me and I owe you a great deal. As the consequences of my decision would be enormous, I want to sufficiently warn you, so that all of you can prepare your flight in advance.'

Otanes and I reassured him that, whatever his decision, we would fully back him.

'You should not worry about consequences to us, for, being mere travellers in Macedonia, we will be leaving the country shortly. Our trading requires us to be in Ionia,' I told him.

After he had been pacified by these assurances, Pausanias confided that he had made up his mind to kill King Philip at Aegae, during the celebrations that would accompany Catherine's wedding to the king of Epirus.

Half expecting some adverse reaction from us to his announcement, he put his hand on his dagger.

'If that is your decision, we welcome it, as we do not like Philip either, being from Athens. We dislike the fact that he has put the entire Greek people under his yoke and clamped down upon their freedom,' said Otanes.

'I even promise to provide you all the help that you will need for committing this act. I could also arrange for your escape to Thebes, where no one will look for you,' I said.

Hearing me say this, he grew in confidence and told me that games had been organized for the celebration in Aegae on the second day of the marriage and he had been appointed one of the three judges of the equestrian events. This would involve being in the same enclosure as Philip.

Pausanias reasoned that, since he had earlier been a bodyguard of Philip, no one would suspect him of any untoward intentions and, once he got close enough to Philip, he would use his dagger to stab him to death. Said he: 'My only worry is how to get past the two main bodyguards of the king, Trillimachus and Machatas. Philip himself does not at his age possess the strength to resist me, specially since surprise will be on my side. Besides, in our youth, I always won the wrestling bouts between us.'

'You need not worry about how to get past Trillimachus and Machatas. I will arrange a diversion with a person by the name of Gerochus, who himself harbours thoughts of revenge against Philip,' I said to Pausanias, as though the thought had only just occurred to me.

'Of course, I have heard about Gerochus! If that is the case, my revenge will soon be real,' said Pausanias.

Pausanias then drew a diagram on the sand for me and explained the layout of the place where the celebrations were to be held. The best time for him to attack Philip, he said, would be as they got out from an archway into the stand where Eurydice and Attalus sat. He said that, at that point, the other bodyguards would not be in a position to help Philip, as they would be ahead of him. He himself, however, would be sitting in his position at the judges' table next to the archway and would therefore be between Philip's bodyguards and Philip.

On my part, I told Pausanias that I would have two horses waiting for him at the entrance of the venue of the celebrations to aid his escape. But he would have to get there somehow before the guards recovered from the shock of his deed.

This was how I bolstered the confidence of Pausanias. However, I was under no illusion that Pausanias could escape after assassinating Philip or that he would even be able to leave the venue. But I feared that if I spoke my mind, Pausanias might lose heart and decide not to go ahead.

I now forbade Pausanias to leave the estate, as I was worried that he would speak to somebody else about his intentions and jeopardize the whole plot. He agreed, but said he was worried for his two sons, who ran an estate in Bisaltia.

'I promise to send two talents to your sons to make sure that they are well looked after in the event that something happens to you. But I don't think that anything will, as surprise will be on your side,' I assured him.

Pausanias was overwhelmed by this generosity, but asked: 'What interest do you have though, Demetrius, to help me on such a dangerous mission?'

'I follow whatever I see in my dreams, as I have observed over time that if I don't, Goddess Athena punishes me severely. So, even if a particular course of action seems arduous and impossible, I never lose heart as the Goddess always shows me the way and protects me from danger,' I said.

Pausanias was highly pleased with my answer, thinking that if that was the case, Athena would surely protect him as well and, believing this, he had no more questions and waited for the day when he would journey to Aegae to enact his revenge.

TWENTY-TWO

The day after King Philip returned from the boar hunt to Pella, as was the custom, he bathed very early and proceeded to the Pella Zeus and there he was accosted by Mindarus, who prostrated himself at his feet and asked for the rites of purification.

As I watched from the crowd, Philip helped Mindarus get up and asked his name. He then asked him what crime he had committed that he should need purification, but since Mindarus had been warned by Olympias not to state the nature of his crime before Philip gave his word, Mindarus burst forth into a lamentation.

'I am a cursed and helpless man and only you, great king, can be my saviour or I will have no option but to take my life, as the guilt in my heart is all pervasive,' lamented Mindarus.

As Philip made to go without answering him, Mindarus clutched his robe in desperation and Machatas and Trillimachus moved to strike Mindarus down, but Philip forbade them and addressed Mindarus thus: 'Go, Mindarus, your wish shall be fulfilled. Meet me tomorrow at dawn at my residence and I will do your purification. And tell Olympias, to whom you surely went for advice, for only she would know that I would not refuse a request on the steps of the Pella Zeus, that Philip will not shirk from the purification, no matter how serious your crime. For it is only by the will of Zeus that you could have made this intervention, and if his will holds, your purification will be done.'

Speaking thus in front of everybody, he proceeded inside the temple and there the priest Caldemus, who had seen everything from the top of the temple steps, came with a face of horror to Philip and made him aware of the crimes of Mindarus, as it was he who had heard of his cowardice first, and he implored Philip not to go ahead with the purification. But Philip struck him aside and said: 'Purification is not for the faint-hearted, Caldemus. I have given my word and so it shall be.'

I must say that there was admiration in my heart for Philip at the way he treated the whole episode with Mindarus. Even though he was a despot, he had a lion's heart and believed that his word, when given, could not be changed.

The next day, I got the details from Otanes on how Philip received Mindarus in the morning and proceeded to purify him.

Said Otanes: 'Philip seated Mindarus in front of the altar to Zeus and, after lighting some incense, he started saying prayers. After he finished his prayers, he started chanting hymns in the glory of Zeus and, after he had done that for sometime, he went into prayer again. He then lit ten lamps in front of the deity and put his hands on Mindarus's head. Mindarus started shivering violently and his eyes closed and he started uttering words which were in a foreign tongue and they came out in a torrent. This went on for a long time and it appeared that something from inside Mindarus was coming out and going into Philip, for his eyes were closed and it appeared that he was controlling some kind of pain. At the end of it, Philip pushed Mindarus away, having absorbed all of his guilt, and Mindarus smiled as if a burden had lifted from his shoulders. Without speaking to Mindarus, Philip gestured for him to leave and then he sat quietly in prayer for some more time before getting up. He looked haggard and tired from his exertions.'

'All of us learn of strange things every day, Otanes, but this is one of the strangest,' I said.

At this point, Otanes asked me something very strange and I mention it here because it will have great relevance later.

'Why did you take the risk of coming to Philip's residence while he was administering the purification rites to Mindarus?' asked Otanes.

I was taken aback because I had not stepped out of my estate that day.

'I did not. I did not even step outside my room all morning,' I said.

Otanes, however, smiled and didn't believe me. I then called Telephus in and asked him in Otanes's presence whether I had left the estate at all during the day.

'Not at all, sire,' declared Telephus.

Hearing this from Telephus, Otanes was a little confused and then, after Telephus had left, Otanes told me that a person who looked exactly like me had come to Philip's residence and had a long talk with Attalus, and when Otanes waved to him, he offered no sign of recognition and instead glared at him, which surprised Otanes. He had come to the conclusion that I was plotting something significant and did not want to be recognized. He also said that this person who looked like me talked to another person called Argus. Otanes, however, said that he was not sure whether he was the same Argus that I hunted or another one. And the few people in Philip's household he was familiar with because of his duties towards Attalus knew nothing about this Argus and so his enquiries remained fruitless.

I was puzzled by this revelation of Otanes and could find no explanation for it. In the end, I came to the conclusion that Otanes was overstating things. The person might have looked a little similar to me, but to say that he looked exactly like me was unbelievable. I did question Otanes closely about the appearance of the Argus he spoke of, but his description of him did not match the Argus that I sought revenge against.

The matter slipped out of my mind when, the next day, Olympias sent word through Telephus that she intended to pay a visit to my estate the following day. I sent an appropriate missive of welcome and it turned out that she had come to invite me for her daughter Catherine's wedding to Alexander the Molossian at Aegae. She stressed that she would see to it that I met Prince Alexander on the occasion, for she was keen that the two of us meet.

'I will of course be present at the wedding,' I promised her, as I had no other option.

'Now you must tell me, Demetrius, whether you have a woman in your life,' said Olympias to me.

'I have a woman who has borne me a child. She lives in Athens, where I shall head shortly, and from there to Asia where my business lies,' I confessed to her.

'Oh, I am surprised to hear that you have a woman in Athens. I had thought that you would make a good husband for a niece of mine. But since you have a wife, I will not press you further on the matter,' said Olympias.

She did, however, bring up the subject of her discomfiture that I hadn't asked for something in return for the estate I had gifted her and I told her that her coming to visit me was honour enough. She then took an emerald ring off her finger and gifted it to me, saying that she was pleased with my behaviour.

Said Olympias: 'This ring has been on my hand for many years and my son Alexander has been instructed by me not to refuse the request of anybody who shows him this ring. Look at its inside. It bears an inscription of my name. It was gifted to me by my brother at the time of my marriage to Philip.'

I gladly accepted the gift, though surprise was evident on my face and Olympias, reading my expression, said that she had gifted such a precious heirloom to me because she was in a good mood after Philip had done the purification of Mindarus and, with the omens being so good, she was confident that Alexander's star was on the ascendancy. So saying, she allowed me to kiss her hand and left my estate, and I never met her again.

I must confess that immediately after she left, I had the ring washed and the water fed to a dog, for I had an apprehension that it might have been laced with some kind of poison, but that was not the case. It was only after this that I came to believe that it was a genuine gift. But I speak of this act of mine to illustrate how Olympias inspired an element of fear in all men because of the way she was and her single-minded determination in working with complete ruthlessness towards what she wanted. In fact, the more I think about it, the more firmly I am persuaded that it was her prayers that had brought me to Macedonia in the first place and it was her will that used me as an instrument for Philip's death. Of this I am convinced, though Demosthenes, to whom I once confided this belief, dismissed my view by saying that Olympias was just a jealous queen and a strong mother and no claims of extraordinariness should be imputed to her conduct or her persona. But I disagreed, for Demosthenes had never set eyes on Olympias, nor had he looked deep into her eyes and felt that she could read all of your deepest thoughts.

At Aegae, it was noon when Pausanias thrust his dagger into Philip's heart.

The day before the assassination, I had asked Phaselis from Naxos's former estate to bring all the adders to Pella, for in the evening, Cicero and Otanes intended to carry them in a wicker basket to Philip's house, where they would store the basket in the room provided to them by Eurydice while they took care of Attalus.

But my purpose in calling Phaselis to Pella was to ask him whether he could extract the venom of the adders into a glass and he said that his brother, who had died of an adder's bite, had done it once by catching an adder by its neck and taking its fangs close to a bowl. The adder had instinctively bitten the bowl and the poison had flowed out of its fangs and into the bowl. That was the first time he had seen the colour of the poison and it was dark brown. I asked him whether he could extract the poison in the same way for me, as I needed a portion of it for a particular task. I told him that I would pay him one talent if he did this for me.

When Phaselis heard about the reward, he immediately agreed to do it, though he took many precautions, such as wrapping his hands with thick cloth and choosing an adder that was less aggressive than the others, and he did exactly what he had seen his brother do. The adder bit the bowl in great fury and about ten drops of venom collected in it. But Phaselis didn't release the adder quickly enough and I think he also failed to catch its neck with sufficient force. The creature turned its neck and bit him on his wrist before he could shrug it free. Phaselis howled in pain.

'By Zeus, I have been bitten, Demetrius. My hand is burning,' he lamented.

After some time, he started shaking. 'I appeal to you to take care of my wife and two small children who live in the village of Parmemnum, south of Pella,' said Phaselis.

'I promise I will take care of them,' I said, holding him, and it consoled him somewhat.

But soon his agony grew unbearable and his breathing became laboured. His hand turned blue and he started frothing at the mouth. And then he requested Cicero, who was watching impassively, to kill him with his sword. Since Cicero couldn't understand what he was saying, Phaselis turned to me.

'Kill me, Demetrius. The agony is too much. Better to die by the sword than in this manner,' Phaselis begged me.

I took pity on him. Taking Cicero's sword, I thrust it into the heart of Phaselis and stopped his agony.

The death of Phaselis was unexpected and it haunted me for many nights. However, after I had him buried on the estate, I told Pausanias that his death was a good omen and it had removed all danger from his path. I had to tell him the lie as he had become agitated after witnessing the death of Phaselis and thereafter spoke in pessimistic terms about the obstacles that could arise in Aegae. But my explanation calmed him a bit and then I told him to give me his dagger, for I intended to perform a special ceremony to increase its power in the night, before we got up early in the morning to travel to Aegae, and Pausanias readily handed it over to me.

That night I made Tyros inscribe the words 'Seleucus, son of Nicanor' on the blade of the dagger and, after I did that, I applied the venom of the adder to the sides of the dagger and on its surface and then slid it back into its scabbard. When I gave the dagger back to Pausanias, I warned him, 'You are not to draw the dagger until you are close to Philip and in a position to stab him. If you take it out of its scabbard before that, all its powers will dissipate and you will fail in your objective. All the omens are in your favour. If you maintain this last bit of discipline before the final act, our preparations won't go to waste,' I said.

I was worried that Pausanias would take the dagger out and cut himself on the skin and the poison would then affect him instead of Philip and Phaselis's accidental death would be in vain.

But Pausanias vowed to do as I said and hid the dagger in his tunic. The night before Philip's assassination, I sent the treasure that I had carried with me from Asia on to Pythagoras in Athens and sent the majority of the mercenaries who had come with me in the same convoy. They went dressed as traders who were returning with wagonloads of ash wood, which was found in abundance in Macedonia and was used for making weapons. To Tyros I gave the task of delivering one silver talent to the family of Phaselis and two talents to the family of Pausanias, to do as they wished, without giving any explanations.

Menicus was to take care of our getaway horses, which would be stationed two and a half stadia from the celebration venue at Aegae. Two other horses would be stationed directly opposite the venue and would be managed by Modius's servant. Since Modius too had been invited to the celebrations, I had requested him for assistance in managing two horses and they were placed there for Pausanias to use after his deed.

Though I never for a moment thought that Pausanias would get to ride those horses, I placed them there so that, when he entered the venue, he would look at them and believe that escape was possible. I didn't place any of my own men near those horses. I knew that the first thing the Macedonians would do after the deed would be to arrest the servant handling Pausanias's horses.

Cicero and Otanes would watch the proceedings from where Attalus was and, if Pausanias was successful, they were to quietly slip out and walk to the place where Menicus held the horses. If Pausanias failed, they were to proceed to Eurydice's home immediately and place the adders at all points in Philip's room where he was likely to go after he returned. Philip's bodyguards would not be at the house while Philip himself was at the celebrations and Cicero and Otanes would have all the time in the world to place the adders in his bed and amongst his tunics and even where he kept his weapons.

Gerochus had been brought by Menicus to Aegae and had been positioned inside the venue of the celebrations. Before he left to supervise the getaway horses and right at the moment when Philip entered the venue, Menicus walked up to Trillimachus and Machastas, the chief bodyguards of Philip, and informed them that the assassin Gerochus waited with a dagger at the end of the tunnel.

Both of them, being alarmed by this news, left Philip's side as he walked flanked by Prince Alexander and Alexander the Molossian. As a consequence, when Philip entered the arena where the games were to be held, his bodyguards were dealing with Gerochus. This gave Pausanias the chance to rush at him while he was standing alone and, as he stabbed Philip, he shouted, 'Glory be to Macedonia' and before Alexander the Molossian could detach him from Philip, he had managed to stab him four times through the heart.

Though I could see Philip mouthing some words, I could not make them out.

The crowd had just got up to give Philip a loud acclaim when Pausanias stabbed him. Though some of the Macedonian guards present immediately rushed up and ran their swords through Pausanias's chest, none of them was able to stop him from committing the act itself. And just at this moment, as I stood near the exit of the theatre with a clear view of Olympias, I saw her turn her face to me and smile like she was thanking me for the deed.

Until today, I know not how she could have known where I was or whether I was there at all, and how she could have known that I was responsible for the assassination. I mention this particularly because I know that there are many who will say that I impute too much to the gaze of a woman and she might only have been looking at me perchance. But I insist that it was not so and that the look she gave me was not one of surprise or revulsion or sadness, but of great gratitude and understanding. There was absolutely no shock in her eyes.

After Pausanias stabbed Philip, I saw Trillimachus and Machatas rushing to his side, but I think the king was dead by then. I left the theatre soon after, elated at the success of my plan, and rushed to where Menicus stood with the horses. There, we waited for Cicero and Otanes. When finally they arrived, Otanes told me that the amphitheatre was crowded with people and it had taken them a long time to get out. But he confirmed the death of both Philip and Pausanias.

Said Otanes: 'Hepasthion and a few other Macedonian nobles have already declared Alexander as the new king and his first order was to kill Gerochus after his interrogation. The Macedonians feel that Gerochus and Pausanias worked as a team. Alexander has also ordered a hundred horsemen from among Philip's bodyguards to comb the roads leading to Aegae for any suspicious looking men. They presume that Pausanias had some external support and so the unit is advancing on the road to Athens, believing that any troublemakers would have originated from that part of Greece. But the road to the Anthemus coast is still without danger, and if you take the decision to go back to Asia, it will be safer than proceeding onwards to Athens.'

But even though I remembered the warning of Mistros at this point, 'to proceed back to Asia after the death of a king', I thought that I would follow his advice after visiting Athens. This decision of mine set off a series of events over which I soon lost control.

But for now, I told Otanes to go back to Pella and obtain information on the movement of the Macedonian soldiery, so we could move unhindered to Athens, using certain paths not used by them. Since I had engraved Pausanias's dagger with my name, I reasoned correctly that once the Macedonians read the inscription and brought it to Alexander's notice, he would unleash the forces at his command to hunt me down. And though I was not scared at the prospect and relished the challenge, I did not want to be captured at the moment of my biggest triumph.

I told Otanes to collect as much information as he could and then to team up with Tyros when he returned from meeting the families of Pausanias and Phaselis. Together, they were to meet me at a predetermined point in Elimea, where we would wait for all the information they brought and then proceed accordingly. If I had fled soon after I reached Menicus and the horses, I would have been ahead by now of any Macedonian party, but having lost that time, I could not be sure that the Macedonians were not ahead of me, for they knew the country much better than I did and I lacked a local guide.

Otanes then said that he would like to go with Cicero, for he was afraid of going back alone to Aegae and Pella. I agreed to his proposal and departed with Menicus for Elimea and told Otanes to join me there on the fifth day from today. I also told Menicus to ride up ahead as fast as he could to Elimea and see if he could locate our main party, which was on its way to Athens.

'If you catch up with them, you are to depute one amongst them as a messenger to rush to Athens and carry the message to Demosthenes that Philip has been assassinated and Alexander is the new king. After doing that, you are to await my arrival in Elimea,' I instructed Menicus.

It took me three days to get to Elimea. I rode in the wagon of a carpenter from Elimea after befriending him on the way. I hitched my horse behind his wagon as I figured that I might draw more attention travelling alone than with a local from these parts. Also, I needed a local guide. The carpenter had been called to Aegae to help in the construction of the podium at the theatre and he was in great sorrow over Philip's death. By the time we reached Elimea, we had crossed two Macedonian patrols, but they let us past without any problem because they knew the carpenter. But they stopped and searched other strangers on the way.

I was relieved to see Menicus waiting for me in Elimea. He had successfully located our main party and sent two amongst them, and not one, to Athens as fast as they could go, with the message for Demosthenes. Menicus said that none of them was willing to travel alone, as they felt that if even a small unit of Macedonians surrounded them, they had a better chance of escaping with a partner at their side. Therefore he took the decision to send a party of two.

Menicus and I waited for five days at Elimea at the carpenter's house, for he had offered us his hospitality and we had decided that it would be safer to stay in a house than in a tavern. By the fifth day, Otanes, Tyros and Cicero had still not arrived. So we decided to wait three more days. Then, on the eighth day, just when we had decided that it would be dangerous to wait beyond that night, Otanes and Tyros made it to Elimea without Cicero.

Otanes narrated their experiences thus:

'When we went back to Aegae, we met Attalus at the marketplace, accidentally. The general was terrified that Alexander would immediately have him arrested, for he had insulted him at the wedding of Philip and Eurydice and, even more than Alexander, he was terrified of Olympias. When we were standing with Attalus thus, a messenger came from Eurydice, saying that her house was infested with reptiles and her son Caranus had been bitten. She asked for immediate help from him to locate Cicero and bring him to her residence to try and save Caranus's life. But as soon as Attalus heard this, he panicked. For he thought that it was Olympias who had arranged this manner of hideous death for Caranus and, thinking he would be next on the list, he left promptly for lower Macedonia, without even visiting Eurydice or collecting his personal effects!

'Then I came to know that the Macedonians had arrested Mobius and his servant, who had held the horses for Pausanias at the celebration venue. After coming to know this, Cicero and I decided not to proceed to the estate where we had been staying, as we thought that Mobius would take the Macedonians there.

'When Philip's body was prepared for burial and the performance of his last rites, the priest Caldemus pulled out the dagger from his body, where strangely it had remained since his death. While wrapping it in cloth, he saw the inscription "Seleucus, son of Nicanor" on the blade and presumed that Nicanor was the name of Pausanias's father. He then passed on the blade to Alexander's companion, Hepasthion. When Alexander learned of the inscription on the blade, he was furious beyond belief and sent a thousand soldiers to scour the countryside for Nicanor's son, whose description he gave personally to all his soldiers. All this I overheard from priests at the Pella Zeus, who were officiating at the funeral of Philip.

'By this time, Pausanias's body had been strung up on the street in front of Aegae and people were throwing stones at it. But the next day, everyone was amazed to see that somebody had placed a golden crown on his head. When I rushed to see whether this was true, I found that some Macedonian soldiers had taken the crown down and were holding it in their hands.

'From that point, rumours were rampant that it was Olympias who had placed the crown on Pausanias's head and even hung a garland around his neck in the night, and many people whispered of Alexander himself being involved with Olympias in planning the deed. The discovery of adders in the house of Eurydice was cited by them as evidence of the hand of both Olympias and Alexander. For they all said that adders were not found in Macedonia and someone had taken the trouble of getting them all the way from Asia or Egypt.

'But the priest Caldemus was by now telling whoever cared to listen that it was Philip's purification of Mindarus that had led to the event, as the sins of Mindarus had flowed to Philip and destroyed the merit he had built with pious acts and offerings and no one should look at other reasons for his death. Then the people who loved Philip dearly, specially his bodyguards, caught hold of Mindarus and killed him on the spot, without a trial, for they all felt that Caldemus was right in making such an assertion.

'However, even amidst this confusion, the Macedonians continued with their investigations and soon Mobius told them that he had come back to Macedonia in a trireme with a trader whose name was Demetrius and they had all disembarked off the coast of Anthemus and stayed at the estate of Nearchus, which was not his estate any longer. He told them that Demetrius had been introduced by him to Olympias, for he was a trader of repute and, having travelled all over Asia and Greece, he had desired to have an audience with the queen to present her with some articles that he had acquired in his travels. Mobius, however, proclaimed vigorously that this Demetrius had absolutely no links with Philip's death! He told the Macedonians that though Demetrius was not traceable at the moment, it could be that he had left on urgent business and would be back soon. Since Mobius could offer no satisfactory explanation for how his servant came to be holding the horses of Pausanias, his claims were closely examined.

'At this time, I cultivated the priest Caldemus by hiring him to conduct a sacrifice for Zeus. I even gave him an advance of a hundred drachmas. Caldemus promised to conduct the sacrifice after he had finished all his duties concerning the burial of Philip and the ten-day rituals that followed. He then proceeded to reveal to me many things that had happened post the assassination.

'He told me that he had received strict instructions from Hepasthion to deny that any inscription was found on the dagger and to call it a rumour spread by the Persians, even though there were very few of them there and all who were there were exiles from the Persian court. Caldemus also said that he had been instructed by Hepasthion to tell everyone he met that it was only Pausanias's jealousy of Oxyrides, who was Philip's new lover, that had made his former bodyguard kill him.

'He also explained to me that this was done so the people would stop blaming Olympias and Alexander for Philip's murder, for Alexander was worried that the loyalists of Philip might launch a rebellion if they believed that he was responsible for his father's death. They even released Mobius, for his detention would have implied that Olympias was in some way involved, as he was her cousin. Modius, however, was so shattered by the experience of having been suspected of being an accomplice in Philip's murder that he put the blame for it on Fouma! He reasoned that all manner of ill luck had come to him ever since he met her, starting from the time that Parmenio had put him in detention in Abydos. Modius subsequently abandoned Fouma to her own devices, and I saw her begging on the streets of Pella. I did not have the courage to help her for fear of attracting attention to myself.

'It was after I discovered these things that Tyros returned from his errands. He was surprised to see both Cicero and me still in Pella, for he had presumed that he would have to travel alone all the way to Elimea. He informed me that after he had compensated the families of Phaselis and Pausanias, news came to him on the road that the Macedonians had arrested Pausanias's elder son and confiscated a part of the money given to him by Tyros – the other portion had been taken away by Pausanias's younger son and they had failed to catch him. They questioned him at length on how he came to have the money. Tyros heard this story from a stranger whom he befriended on his way back, for he had first stopped to meet Pausanias's family and then gone on ahead in the same direction to complete his errand regarding the family of Phaselis. Not having till then known about Philip's death, or his father's hand in it, Pausanias's son told the authorities that somebody had come a few days back to give them this fortune, which he claimed had been sent to them by their father, who in turn had got a gift from Philip. It was the exact story that Tyros had told him.

'After hearing this from Pausanias's son and determining that he was innocent of his father's crime, a tremendous manhunt was launched for the man who had come with the silver talents to Pausanias's place in a wagon. It didn't worry Tyros, however, for he had long since discarded the wagon and was now travelling on horseback. Since the Macedonians had not known of Phaselis, they never reached his home and Tyros never told his family that Phaselis had died, for then they would have demanded an explanation for his death and may have caused further trouble.

'But things changed drastically at this point. After Tyros, Cicero and I made plans to leave Pella for Elimea, I went to visit Caldemus for the last time. There I saw Miletus on the temple steps! He was there along with four other Macedonian soldiers, talking to Caldemus. I immediately took evasive action, so Miletus couldn't see me. After Miletus and the soldiers departed, I went and met Caldemus and came to know that an Athenian named Miletus had come to meet him, escorted by soldiers from Parmenio's unit in Asia.

'Caldemus told me that they had arrived just a day before Philip's assassination and intended to warn Philip about the arrival in Macedonia of Seleucus, son of Nicanor. Miletus told Caldemus that Philip knew about the activities of this Seleucus from after the war at Chaeronea, though neither Antipater nor Alexander had apprised him about his later exploits.

'Miletus had come to Caldemus to know what had been written on the blade of the dagger which Pausanias had used to kill Philip and which Caldemus had pulled out from his ribs. Caldemus told the party that "Seleucus, son of Nicanor" was all that he could see and if they wished to know more, they would have to go to Hepasthion to obtain the blade and examine it, for the dagger was no longer with him.

'But, according to procedure, they could check the blade only after the succession of Alexander to the throne, as it was considered to be a bad omen for the son if the weapon used in his father's murder was washed before all the ceremonies were over. And, in this case, because the son was succeeding the father as king, the ceremonies would include the crowning ceremony and the celebrations thereof. All this, Caldemus informed Miletus and the Macedonians.

'Miletus then explained to Caldemus how he happened to be there: he had come to know that Nicanor's son had crossed the seas to come to the Anthemus and also that he had recently consulted Mistros, a soothsayer fom Larisa in Asia. So he and the Macedonian soldiers with him made their way to Mistros and tortured him till he told them what he had said to Seleucus and came to know that he had told him to "return to Asia after the death of the king". Miletus guessed that the king could only mean Philip and informed Parmenio about it. Parmenio immediately gave him an escort and a fast vessel and they landed on the Anthemus coast to warn Philip, but before they could do so, it was all over.

'I then took leave of Caldemus, but as I was coming out of the temple, Miletus saw me and raised an alarm. I had to run quickly to my horse and ride speedily to where Cicero and Tyros were waiting for me. But Miletus and the Macedonians chased us and Cicero, when he saw Miletus, was caught in two minds.

'For Miletus had been Cicero's master and had brought him to Asia to join the mercenaries and the two had gone to Abydos together, where Miletus had been caught but Cicero had escaped. While Tyros and I escaped by riding hard as our horses were fresh, Cicero's heart was not in it and he lagged behind. I suspect that he deliberately held back in order for Miletus to catch up with him, for Miletus kept gesticulating at him and making signs and Cicero kept turning back to see what Miletus was telling him. And thus we lost him.

'After riding hard the entire day, we exchanged our horses at a loss with a Macedonian trader. This was so we could obtain horses of a different colour than the ones we had been seen on by Miletus and the Macedonians. We also came by the longest and hardest possible route, hoping that the Macedonians would not follow us on such an arduous route. That's what delayed us.'

Hearing these facts from Otanes, I was extremely surprised at Miletus turning up in the most unexpected of places. I was also very sad that Miletus had tortured Mistros and I felt great anger towards him. I asked Tyros, Otanes and Menicus whether any of them would consider going back to Pella and Aegae voluntarily and stay there till the celebrations being planned for Alexander's succession were over and then report the events to me at Pythagoras's house in Athens. I told them that this time they would have to be very careful and cultivate new informers, and stay away from all those who knew them, as the interrogation of Mobius would possibly have led the Macedonians to Telephus and also to Damaris.

After Tyros, Otanes and Menicus consulted amongst themselves, Tyros said that since all three of them owed their life to me, they would all be happy to do whatever I wished and it was for me to suggest who I considered the most worthy of staying back in Macedonia. I then chose Menicus as he was tall like the Macedonians and it would be easy for him to pretend that he was one of them. I made him shave his head to better disguise himself and left him with enough resources. Bidding him goodbye, the rest of us left for Athens, deciding to travel only in the night, to avoid being observed.

Thus did the episode of the assassination of Philip of Macedon conclude. He was felled by his former lover Pausanias, in the year that Pythodelus was the archon of Athens.

Part Five

TWENTY-THREE

It was after four weeks that Menicus returned to Athens. Before that, I united with Athele, who had borne me a son who was now six months old. I also gave the report of my wanderings to both Demosthenes and Clonus, who travelled all the way from Sparta to meet me. Both were amazed at my adventures and the extent of my achievement. That I had brought back a sum of one hundred talents for them to spend as they saw fit further enhanced my status. As for Athele, she was always pressing me to narrate my adventures and I told her about everything except my relationship with Mazus's wife Luminas and Queen Morai of Lesbos.

Demosthenes and Clonus congratulated each other on how their choice of emissary had paid them rich dividends. Demosthenes arranged a feast for a thousand people to celebrate the death of Philip and entreated Lycargus, the controller of the festival fund, to confer on me the golden crown at the next festival of Dionysus. But I disagreed with Demosthenes and told him that I didn't hanker for any award. Besides, I said, honouring me with the golden crown would motivate Alexander to move his armies into Athens and unnecessarily drag it into a conflict which it could ill afford.

But Demosthenes insisted and said that the money I had brought would allow them to recruit a strong army, and if Alexander did travel to Athens with his forces, he would get a fitting reply. But I still refused and, as a compromise, it was decided to offer me the golden crown in complete secrecy and so, six witnesses were arranged. They were Demosthenes, Lycargus, Pythagoras, Mios, Calliphus, and the archon Pythodelus.

It was the archon who placed the crown on my head and Demosthenes gave a speech. Said he: 'Rarely do people get to honour one so young. In the history of all of Hellas, I cannot think of anyone who was the recipient of the crown at so young an age. Or, if there was, we have not read about it in the histories that have come down to us from ancient times. But even if we are honouring him at a young age, it is not merely our affection for him that is urging us to bestow the honour. He has shaped events in a manner that no one before him has. One of the functions of an emissary is to pursue the interests of his state at all times and, in his case, even though he was devoid of the benefit of our advice and judgment on many issues, since the distance between us was too great for messages to fly back and forth frequently, he managed to grasp every opportunity that came his way and pursued the interests of not only Athens, but all of Greece.

'We are only sorry that what we confer on him today is less than what should be. For we are only expressing the gratitude of Athens, whereas we should be conferring on him an award from the leagues. Sadly, the leagues are controlled by Macedonia and the yoke on us also has its genesis in Amphipolis. In the death of Philip, we have achieved what a dozen wars couldn't have achieved for us. For, in statecraft, assassinations have a pertinent place, particularly if it is tyrants who fall to the blade. Used as we are to our independence, the yoke of Macedonia hangs on our necks like a plough on bulls. In eliminating Philip, he has given us a chance to throw the yoke off and once again strive to regain our greatness as the pre-eminent nation in Hellas, which we were for a long time and which we will be again.

'Not only did Seleucus achieve that, he convinced Artaxerxes to give us the talents to create a small mercenary army and to harass the Macedonians if they chose to go to Persia. And when I alerted him about the stone-throwing monsters, he made an adventure to Lesbos and outsmarted the smartest Macedonian general Parmenio and made off with a lithobolos and had it conveyed to Artaxerxes. He has harassed the Macedonians at Abydos and made it hard for them to hold on to the city, which they need to should they decide to cross the Hellespont into Asia. He has achieved all this at an age when the rest of us were busy chasing women and drinking and making fools of ourselves. It's a pity that we cannot honour his achievements in a public forum, where thousands would know of his deeds and dream to be of service to Athens in the manner that he has been.'

Demosthenes spoke a great deal more, but this was the essence of what he said, and then the others spoke one by one and Pythagoras and Calliphus spoke about how they first met me and Pythodelus expressed surprise that I was the same Nicanor's son who had achieved fame at Olympia. Then Demosthenes swore them all to secrecy again about the golden crown and Pythodelus wrote a statement explaining the circumstances that led to their awarding it to me in secrecy and all the six people present signed it. It is still one of my most precious possessions.

Afterwards, I spoke briefly, and this is what I said: 'People of Athens – I shall call you that even though here you are just six, for you represent all that we cherish about the Hellenes – I stand before you, the same man that some of you first met nearly two years ago, only considerably wiser. I thank you for the honour you have bestowed on me and, though it sits on my head, I must emphasize that it's only because of the blood and sacrifice of several of my friends such as Pindar, Harmodius and Zanylos that I stand before you today. I should also mention that it would not have been possible for me to achieve success without the guidance of soothsayers such as Pythadorus from Pylos; Harmodius, who died a martyr's death at Chaeronea; and Mistros, the soothsayer from Persia. I would not have achieved what you may think I have achieved without their help and that of others. Or indeed, without the confidence shown in me by Demosthenes, for how many are wise enough to see potential in boys who are not yet men? But my work is not complete and I still thirst for vengeance against those who killed my family and were responsible for the death of my friends. To that list I have to add all the enemies of Athens now, for more than any other nation, it is she who inspires me, for I have seen tyrannies and despots in Asia and even in the Hellenes, and would not like our people to suffer under them.'

After I finished speaking, a big argument broke out. Menicus had just arrived and his reports, which I shared with all present, sparked the squabble. He brought news that Alexander had approached the Thessalian league for confirmation of himself as its leader. He intended to cement his position as the chief of the league of Corinth by getting the Thessalian league to endorse him, as well as the Amphictyonic league at Delphi, besides other states in the Peloponnese. He also intended to pursue Philip's dream of a Persian campaign and was eager that the states in the Peloponnese give him peace so that he could proceed on his conquest without any domestic distraction and, to that end, he desired to be announced as the hegemon of the Corinthian league.

Menicus then gave us accounts of the celebrations that had ensued on Alexander's coronation. He said that he personally saw Olympias offer libation at the spot where Pausanias was hung on the day he murdered Philip. Two brothers of Alexander of Lyncestis were executed for allegedly collaborating with Pausanias: the brothers had apparently had a dispute with Olympias over an estate. And it was also declared that there were other collaborators whose names would be revealed in due course to all of Macedonia.

Menicus then narrated to us the strange account of the death of Miletus.

'After the priest Caldemus informed Miletus that it was Hepasthion who had the dagger that Pausanias used to kill Philip, he went to him along with the Macedonian officers investigating the murder of Philip. Apparently, right at that moment, there was a priest from Pellagonia with Hepasthion, also examining the dagger. He could apparently divinate the future by observing the bloodstains on a blade after a person had been stabbed. But he could do so only after two weeks had elapsed from the date that the blood had been shed. This priest from Pellagonia told Hepasthion, in the presence of Miletus and other officers, that a great military campaign was in the offing and it would be a series of victories and no defeats for the Macedonians if they were led by Alexander.

'Hepasthion interrupted the priest rudely and asked him to tell him something he did not know, and then the priest said two things. He said Alexander would defeat all living beings except one, and that one person would be from Hellas, and then he said that the dagger had it in it to take one more life. And when he said that, Hepasthion was highly amused and asked him whose life he thought the dagger would take, and the priest said that it would be someone who had travelled recently from afar.

'Hepasthion dismissed the priest and gave the dagger, still wrapped in cloth, to Miletus to examine and, while he was examining the dagger, it fell from his hands and, the point pierced his thigh and he started bleeding. Nothing happened in the beginning, but soon Miletus started shivering and started having difficulty in breathing and, by night, he died, even though all the best doctors in Pella came to attend on him.

'Everybody was amazed at his death, for it was just a mere cut that he had received. Menicus said that Hepasthion called back the priest from Pellagonia and introduced him to Alexander and told him about his predictions. Alexander then asked the priest who this person was that he wouldn't be able to defeat and the priest said that it would be the same person who was responsible for Philip's death.

'Then Alexander commented that it was Pausanias who was responsible for Philip's death and asked how, if he was already died, he could defeat him. The priest replied that Pausanias was just the bow and arrow – and just as we don't blame a bow and arrow for a death but the person who pulls the bowstring and discharges the arrow, in the same way the blame should not be put on Pausanias.

'Alexander then asked the priest for a solution to find and eradicate this person, who he said would be the only person to defeat him, and the priest said that Alexander would get the chance within one year from that day, but not after that. And when Alexander asked him how he could be so precise, he said that the manner in which Philip's blood had congealed on the blade and made patterns was how he saw the future and he spoke only what he saw, without fear or favour.

'I learned all the above things from Hepasthion's servant, whom I befriended in Pella at a tavern. This was in the period when Olympias had made wine free for four days after Alexander's coronation, and it was rumoured that all the wine in the country finished in those four days and everybody got sick from drinking in excess.'

I never told the Athenian elders how I thought Miletus had died. But I was surprised that the poison from the adder could stay so long on the blade and that a simple cut on the thigh was enough to poison his blood.

After hearing Menicus, Demosthenes said that the time was right to organize a rebellion across the whole of Hellas against Alexander. Lycargus, however, advised caution, as the Macedonian army was 'as strong under Alexander as it was under Philip'. Pythagoras agreed with Lycargus, but suggested that rebellion be stoked in states other than Athens to see what reaction it provoked from Alexander and to then gauge how he compared with his father Philip. The priest Calliphus prophesied that Alexander wouldn't last long, as he did not have Philip's acumen in warfare or governance, and Pythodelus also felt the same and added that Alexander was too young to act wisely and his hot-headedness would be his downfall. But Mios said quietly that it would be unwise to disregard Alexander's capabilities.

Noticing my silence, Lycargus turned to me and asked me what I thought.

'I think everything depends on how strongly Alexander intends to execute Philip's desire for a military campaign in Persia. If he nurtures his father's dream to take his army to Asia, then he will seek endorsement for his project from all the leagues. He will be afraid to leave behind a rebellious population, as that will cut him off from his own territory.

Therefore Alexander will seek to quell all rebellion in his lands first if he thirsts to conquer Persia like Philip did,' I said.

Everybody remained quiet after hearing my assessment and Menicus added that the exiles from Asia – Naxos, Nearchus, Erigyius, Laodemon and Harpalus – had made their way to Macedonia after coming to know of Philip's death and they had already met Alexander and he had made them his companions. Now they were actively engaged in planning the logistics of crossing the Hellespont. How they had managed to give Agos the slip, I didn't know. I was surprised most of all by Harpalus's escape, as he had become mentally unsound.

I explained to Demosthenes how I had scared the exiles in order to buy their estates in Macedonia, so that I could have a base for my operations, and how I had gifted Laodemon's estate to Olympias to be in her good books, but had later not utilized her help in the plot to assassinate Philip. I also told him that I felt she knew all about what I was doing, without me or any of those in my employ telling her about my plans. And I stated that I thought she was not of this world. But Demosthenes disagreed with me and said, as I have mentioned earlier, that Olympias was nothing more than a jealous wife and a protective mother.

Pythagoras then asked me how I thought Athens should proceed.

'Though I don't have the wisdom that all else in this room have, I feel that Athens should secretly organize all the rebels in the different territories, particularly Thebes, as she would be important in any rebellion, and also send secret messages to the exiles of the different nations who have been exiled because of their unfavourable views of Philip and Macedonia. At the same time, Athens should be cautious about doing anything openly that will annoy Alexander and give him a pretext to move against the city. If at some time you feel that there is an opportunity for disavowing Alexander and Macedonia, you should exercise it, but before you do that, you should prepare yourselves thoroughly so that you don't blunder into anything,' I advised.

Everybody liked this approach, as it satisfied those who wanted to plan rebellion and also those who advised caution. Demosthenes suggested that I proceed to Delphi and Thebes and see if I could provoke unease in the governing councils there and urge them not to endorse Alexander as the chief of the Corinthian league, as that would be a big setback for him. But Lycargus warned that any such adventure would have to be carried out skilfully, so that the Macedonians couldn't point a finger at Athens, for Menicus had also revealed that Alexander intended to travel to all parts of Hellas, including Athens, to formally seek their endorsement for the war against Persia and, when he came, it would be difficult not to accede to his request.

After this, the meeting for conferring the golden crown on me ended and it was sworn by all to keep my identity a secret, for that would best serve the interests of Athens. Thereafter, everybody departed to their homes.

Menicus then came up to me and revealed more. He said that he had met Nearchus on the last day, taking the risk that he would not alert the authorities to his presence, and had been welcomed with open arms by him. He had enquired about me with great concern and sought to know from him whether the person who was his master was 'Seleucus, son of Nicanor' as Hepasthion and Alexander now declared or was he just the trader Demetrius without any connection to this Seleucus.

Continued Menicus: 'I assured Nearchus the best I could that the person he knew as Demetrius and who had saved his life in Asia had nothing to do with this Seleucus, son of Nicanor. I told him that it was all a clever rumour manufactured by Hepasthion and Alexander to hide their own devious plots.

'Nearchus then told me that Alexander himself had doubts about his mother Olympias's role in Philip's death and suspected that the person who went by the name of Demetrius in Macedonia and had bought the estates of the exiles was, in fact, none other than Seleucus, son of Nicanor. Alexander had also come to know that this Demetrius had met his mother several times. He had, by decree, given back the estates of Nearchus, Naxos and Erigyius and compensated Laodemon with land elsewhere since his estate was now the property of Olympias.

'Nearchus told me that he and the other exiles were amazed when Harpalus joined them at the dock in Larisa. They smuggled him into the vessel that was taking them to the port at Amphipolis, unknown to Agos and the other mercenaries. According to Nearchus, Harpalus had been spared by Agos and only a sheep had been executed, though all of them had thought that Otanes and Tyros had executed Harpalus!

'Nearchus told me how he couldn't fathom why Agos had pretended to have executed Harpalus, but he said that he was grateful for it anyway, as it had moved Demetrius to come to their rescue! Nearchus surmised that perhaps Agos had wished to use Harpalus for some other purpose. According to Nearchus, Harpalus had only pretended to be insane because he thought that the mercenaries still harboured a desire to kill him and were only consulting the priests for an appropriate date.

'After pretending to be insane for many days, he noticed that the mercenaries guarding him had lost interest in him as they thought him to be harmless. That was when he plotted his escape and made his way to the docks. Luckily, it was the same day that the exiles were boarding a vessel to go to Asia after having escaped Agos. Together, they sailed for the Anthemus.

'After hearing what Nearchus had to say, I again defended Demetrius and said that he could rest assured that Demetrius was not Seleucus and that, though he had met Olympias, he had met her at the insistence of Mobius and not for any reason of his own. I also emphasized to Nearchus that since there was no link between Agos and Demetrius, there could be no link between the reappearance of Harpalus and Demetrius. I told him that to connect the two matters would be terribly farfetched.'

'That was good thinking on your part, Menicus,' I said.

Menicus had also found out that the five exiles were not happy with Alexander. Although he had welcomed them with open arms, seeing that they had borne the brunt of Philip's anger for having helped him, he had still not given them the importance that he reserved for Hepasthion and the others, and had bestowed on those others lands far in excess of their own after his coronation. Nearchus told Menicus that, even after Naxos told Alexander that it was he who had brought the adders which had been discovered at Eurydice's home, one of which had caused the death of her son Caranus, Alexander refused to believe him as Naxos could not offer any evidence except the statement of Nearchus supporting him, which also Alexander disregarded.

Menicus then told Nearchus that, in his opinion, there was no person called 'Seleucus, son of Nicanor' as he and his master Demetrius had never met anybody of that name in all their travels. He added that the person had been invented by Alexander and Antipater to divert attention from their own conspiracies. Menicus then smiled and told me that Nearchus was convinced by this theory of his, as he believed that it was Olympias and Alexander who had plotted the death of Philip and now sought to blame an imaginary person to hide their crime.

Nearchus also told Menicus that a disgraced former Olympian called Argus, who was the son of Damaris, the chief maid of Olympias, had been given the task of hunting this 'son of Nicanor' down and he had gone ahead and employed Erigyius, Laodemon and Harpalus as he believed, based on what Miletus had told him and certain letters of Parmenio, that Nicanor's son was the person who had swindled them by terrorizing them and then buying their estates.

Argus's claims had been further bolstered by the escape of Harpalus, when everybody had thought him dead. Since nobody had explained this mystery satisfactorily, the exiles who joined Argus believed that it was Demetrius who had acted in consort with Agos to fool them. And since Argus had also seen Nicanor's son and his description of him matched what the exiles said I looked like, it was assumed by Erigyius, Laodemon and Harpalus that Argus was right in his theory.

Nearchus told Menicus that Argus had been given sufficient resources by Hepasthion to track down Seleucus, wherever he was, and bring him or his head to Alexander. Nearchus, however, felt that all this was an effort to convince the troops loyal to Philip that somebody other than Olympias and Alexander was responsible for the death of Philip, so that Attalus and the other nobles couldn't exploit their anger to stoke a rebellion.

Nearchus added to Menicus that Argus had even arrested one Ptolemy from Amphipolis, claiming that he was Nicanor's son and everybody rejoiced, even though this said Ptolemy kept denying the charge. Then some doubts surfaced when Ptolemy's mother started blaming Hepasthion for wanting to murder her son and, alarmed at this charge, Hepasthion ordered an investigation and it was discovered that Ptolemy was indeed just a nobleman from Amphipolis and had come to be deployed in Alexander's army that was heading to Persia, with thirty of his mounts. Besides, he had known Philip very well and was even friendly with Alexander. Nearchus also added that he had heard reports that Argus had been tailing Ptolemy from before the death of Philip, believing he was Seleucus, son of Nicanor. But Hepasthion and others put down the error to Argus's obsession with Nicanor's son, after losing the quadragi to him at Olympia.

Once the confusion had been sorted out and Argus reprimanded, Alexander summoned Ptolemy to his presence, as he had not seen him for many years and, observing him closely, he agreed with Argus that there indeed was a resemblance and Argus could not entirely be faulted for the error.

Said Menicus: 'Nearchus then told me that Naxos and he thought the whole exercise had been staged by Hepasthion to convince the admirers of Philip that there indeed was a "son of Nicanor", though in reality there was none! After obtaining all this information, I took Nearchus's leave, but promised to come back to him with tidings from Demetrius, that is you, in the near future.'

TWENTY-FOUR

When I heard from Menicus that Argus had been given the task of hunting me out, my desire for revenge resurfaced strongly and I cursed myself for not having done all that I could to avenge the death of my parents and friends. I must confess that after coming back to Athens and being united with Athele and my son, I was happier than I had ever been and all thoughts of revenge had been pushed to the back of my mind.

I will not here waste time in narrating details of my personal life, for I intend to write the history of our times, keeping in mind how my actions impacted the big events of the day and how the course of history would have been different without me. I have no desire for self-glorification, but the truth is that the life I chose was enmeshed with the violence of the times, as also with the leadership of Hellas and Persia, for I was the chief emissary of Athens. Besides, I seek here to give the real story behind the events recorded in history, so that future generations might judge these times by the truth of what happened rather than what they infer through improper representations.

Therefore all I will say here regarding my life with Athele and my son – whom I named Zanylos in honour of the friend who sacrificed his life to save me – is that, till the time Menicus took the name of Argus, I was enjoying a peaceful reunion with Athele, but hearing that name poisoned my mind again and I became restless. The next day, I visited the Athena temple at the Parthenon and shaved off all my hair, offering it to the Goddess as penance for not having killed Argus earlier, for I saw it as my failure. I vowed not to grow my hair back till Argus had been killed.

I noticed that with the hair shaved off my head, my own men at first failed to recognize me, even if I stood next to them. And when Phormio, my Phoenician partner, came to meet me, he didn't recognize me either until he looked into my eyes. Phormio had been away recruiting mercenaries in Argos when I arrived in Athens and he brought the news, which Clonus had already conveyed to me, that the Spartans under King Aegis would oppose the leadership of the Macedonians in the war against the Persians, as their constitution did not allow for anybody other than their king to lead them in war. But if the Macedonians agreed to King Aegis leading the armies, they would participate in the war against Persia with all their heart. Since the Macedonians would never agree to King Aegis leading the army, the Spartans thought they could not be faulted for not joining the war.

Around this time, there came a message from Agos that all the exiles had escaped from Abydos after they heard of the death of Philip. And they had been helped by Parmenio, as he realized that with Alexander becoming the new king, the exiles would be back in favour.

Agos made another important revelation: the Persian king Artaxerxes had died and his place had been taken by King Darius. Though Artaxerxes had watched the demonstration of the monster at Sardis, which Omares had shown him and he had been very elated at seeing its capabilities, a sudden illness had seized him and he died on the way back to his capital. But at Sardis, he had appointed Omares the commander of Mysia and that included Abydos and so, in effect, Omares was now in charge of the campaign against the city of Abydos. With the news of the sudden death of Artaxerxes, every one of his satraps in the provinces had become anxious, as they didn't know whether his successor would replace them with his own men. Omares too was in great sadness, for after having achieved the privilege of dining with the great king at all major public festivals, he would have to earn the privilege all over again with the new king.

When I had sent a message to Demosthenes about the assassination of Philip, I had also sent a secret instruction to Pythagoras to send a message to Agos in Asia, detailing the death of Philip, for I intended the news to reach Artaxerxes as soon as possible. He had promised a gift of twenty thousand talents for the assassination of Philip, and I had intended to claim it as soon as I could, before he changed his mind. Now Agos wrote that he had conveyed the message of Philip's death to Artaxerxes when he was in Sardis and the king, according to Omares, had been highly pleased. Artaxerxes himself had bragged to Omares that the death of Philip had been ordered by him and Omares had rejoiced more at the fact that the king had bragged to him than at the news of the death of Philip!

I hadn't told Demosthenes or Clonus about the arrangement between Artaxerxes and me, for I intended to give them the good news only when it happened. I had thought that, with this money, Athens would be immensely strengthened and could then afford to raise a large army and navy to defend itself adequately against Macedonia, and perhaps even defeat it. But now, with the death of Artaxerxes, I was not sure. Agos said that he had reminded Omares to politely request Artaxerxes to pay the amount promised and Omares had done that. Artaxerxes had told Omares to convey to me that the amount would be released from the treasury once he got back to Susa, as he never forgot a promise he had made. Things had changed after his death, however.

Still, I sent another message to Agos and told him to request Omares to proceed to the new king, Darius, and remind him of the promise Artaxerxes had made and tell him that, since it was at the behest of Persia that I had committed the act, the amount promised by Artaxerxes in the event of Philip's assassination should be paid to me in all fairness. I added that I would proceed to Asia shortly, after settling some matters at Delphi, and that Agos was to send to me the response of Omares immediately, so that I could plan for the future. I also told Agos to promise Omares five thousand talents out of the twenty thousand that Artaxerxes had promised me, so that he had an incentive to pursue the matter forthwith.

At this point, a dispute broke out between Demosthenes and Clonus on how to adequately share the two hundred talents that I had brought for their use from Asia. While Demosthenes claimed one hundred and fifty talents from the sum, Clonus wanted it to be split in equal proportion. But Demosthenes claimed that the profits had come because he had taken the decision to appoint me as the emissary, and because it was his foresight that had resulted in the profit, he demanded a larger share. But Clonus disagreed and said that both of them had together appointed me and, in fact, he had known me longer than Demosthenes knew me, and if it hadn't been for his help, I would still be a prisoner of King Zetomandus in Sparta.

Besides, said Clonus, they were the only Greek state opposing the Macedonians openly, even though a Macedonian garrison was posted in Argos to keep a watch on them. The two then called upon me to adjudicate between them. I told them that, at this juncture, confronted as we were by larger problems, we should maintain unity and it was best that they resolve the distribution amicably, otherwise it would be to the advantage of Alexander. I added that they shouldn't look upon me to settle the dispute as I was the emissary of both Athens and Sparta and under their command, and didn't have the wisdom of either of them, let alone both of them together.

The two then mutually resolved to put the decision to Pythagoras since both trusted him to be fair. Pythagoras suggested that they keep seventy-five talents each and hold the remaining fifty talents in reserve, to go to the one that needed it more, depending upon the circumstances. I then gave the suggestion that the fifty talents in reserve be handed back to me, as I intended to use the money to bribe the members of the Amphyctionic league in Delphi to vote against Alexander being declared the chief of the Corinthian league. Both Demosthenes and Clonus agreed to this solution, though Demosthenes did so less readily than Clonus.

Later, when Clonus reported the matter to King Aegis, he found fault with the arrangement and ordered Clonus to give written instructions to Demosthenes and to me that I would henceforth cease to be Sparta's secret emissary to Persia and that I should not presume to act in Sparta's interests in the future. Clonus explained to me privately that King Aegis used the pretext of the sharing of the profit to remove me from the post as he now wished to take Sparta's case himself to King Darius, having met him in Sardis a few years back, when Darius was a governor there. He presumed that he could convince Darius to make him the focal point of the rebellion against Alexander, and not Demosthenes. In this way did I cease to become the emissary of Sparta and remain that of Athens.

Two days later, another message arrived from Agos, and this time he sent word that Parmenio had received orders to pull out of Abydos and the Macedonians had rented vessels from the Phoenicians and from other Ionian states to begin the evacuation of the three thousand troops they had there. According to Agos, a Macedonian soldier who had deserted his army out of love for a girl from Lemnos had told him that Alexander wanted the troops back home to be sent to counter the Illyrians, who were proving to be a nuisance to him.

Since Alexander had taken refuge with the Illyrians to escape the wrath of Philip after he had thrown a cup of wine at Attalus during the wedding banquet of Philip, the Illyrians thought that Alexander owed them a favour and, thinking that he would ignore their acts of aggression, they had moved against the Paeonians and, after ravaging some of their land, had made off with their cattle. The Paeonians had come complaining to Alexander and he had ordered the Illyrians to return the cattle, but the Illyrians had ignored his orders and had insulted the heralds of Alexander. All this, Agos mentioned in his message, and it was strange that I got this news from Asia rather than from Macedonia.

Immediately afterwards, I sent a message to Agos, telling him to inform Omares and the other Persians – in the event that my message reached him before the Macedonians began their withdrawal from Abydos – that I was creating trouble for Alexander in the territory of the Illyrians, as a result of which he was ordering his forces out of Abydos. I wanted our mercenaries to claim credit for Parmenio's departure from Abydos in order to impress the new king, Darius.

When I informed Demosthenes about Agos's message, he was perturbed.

Said Demosthenes: 'I assume that if Parmenio is withdrawing from Abydos, it means that Alexander does not want to proceed on his Persian campaign. Yet, Alexander's main objective in pursuing the leagues has been to get an endorsement to head the Persian campaign and for them to join it.'

'Maybe Alexander has delayed his campaign to settle matters with the neighbouring states and get an endorsement from the leagues,' I said.

'You may be right, but the message from your man Agos has given Athens its strategy: to tell the members of the league that Alexander has no intention of proceeding to Persia, as he has pulled his units out from Abydos in Asia. We should tell the members that Alexander desired to get an endorsement from the league to proceed to Persia only as a ruse to get himself appointed as the captain-general of the league,' said Demosthenes.

I found merit in this explanation of Demosthenes and, the next day, I left for Delphi with Menicus, Tyros, Otanes, my wife Athele and my son Zanylos.

I sent Otanes ahead to establish contact with the chief priest at Delphi. He was a person by the name of Busiris, son of Micon, and was as fat as a buffalo. Otanes was to go to Busiris and tell him that his master was arriving shortly from Olympia with his infant son and wished for the priest to bless him and make an oracle.

'Otanes, you will then gift Busiris two hundred drachmas to make all necessary arrangements for the blessing ceremony and establish a friendship with him and, while doing so, learn everything possible about the names of the persons in the Amphictyonic league at Delphi.

Tyros will then reach you and together you will try to locate the Pythia at Delphi. Every month on the seventh, which is now ten days away, the Pythia makes oracles to people who seek her guidance from all over Hellas,' I instructed Otanes.

A new temple was being constructed on the Delphian site by three architects from Corinth, whose names were Spintharos, Xenodoros and Agathon. They were constructing the temple in lieu of the one that had been destroyed by an earthquake several years earlier. That temple had been built more than three hundred years ago by an Athenian family and was called the Temple of Alcmenidae, in remembrance of the family which had funded its construction. But a dispute had arisen between the descendants of the family who now lived in Delphi and the new funders of the temple over what the new one would be called. The new funders were a Macedonian family from Pella, from the house of Agamboros, and they had agreed to fund the construction after Philip had emerged as the ruler in Macedonia. There had been rumours earlier that it was Philip himself who was funding the construction by using the family of Agamboros as a front, for after he had defiled the temple and appropriated certain historic offerings for personal use, there had been a major outcry.

Since people from all over the Hellenic world regarded the Apollo temple at Delphi to be supreme among oracles and had become used to calling it the Temple of Alcmenidae, there was a strong resistance to renaming it the 'Temple of Agamboros'. A big conference was being held on the eighth day of the month to resolve this issue, a day before the Amphictyonic league met to discuss the proposal to support Alexander's campaign in Persia. Thus, there were parties from all over Hellas, and even further, who had come to ask for the oracle's advice on the seventh day. There were also parties who had come to attend the conference on the eighth, which was to decide the naming of the temple, and also delegations that had come to attend the meeting of the league on the ninth day.

The Pythia, by tradition, was a woman over fifty years of age and she was selected on the basis of her spiritual disposition and her ability to go into trances and lead a life of solitude. On the seventh day of every month, the priestess would bathe in the spring of Castalia and, after purifying herself with barley smoke and the smoke from burning laurel leaves, she would enter the temple of Apollo and seat herself over the fissures from where hot gases emanated from the centre of the earth. After seating herself thus, she would begin to eat laurel leaves.

While some said that it was the hot gases from the centre of the earth that made the Pythia go into her trance, others said it was the combination of the gases plus the chewing of the laurel leaves which induced the trance; the deeper her trance, the more accurate her oracles were supposed to be. Nobody was allowed to view the Pythia when she was in her trance, except the priests, but people were allowed to hear her. And only the priests could understand what she was saying and put her wisdom into verse, which they read out in front of everybody. If a king or another person of stature arrived at Delphi, his oracle was not to be read in public if he so wished, but the priests later gossiped to the people anyway and nothing remained a secret for long.

In Delphi, Tyros and Otanes told me that the present Pythia was fifty-five years old.

Said Tyros: 'The Pythia is not allowed to meet anybody for ten days before the oracle. But we have found out the names and dwellings of two of her sons who stay in Delphi itself. While one is a trader in horses, the other works as a wrestling instructor at the Delphi gymnasium, training athletes for the Pythian Games, and his name is Aradus.'

Added Otanes: 'The king of Siphnos has come with great tribute to add to the treasury of the Siphnians. This time, he is dedicating ten rams made of gold to Delphi; part of it is atonement for not having presented a dedication for the last five years. As a result of not doing that, the gold mines on their island have been flooded with water.'

The Siphnians had dedicated their treasury to Delphi more than two hundred years ago, and theirs was the most splendid of all treasuries, rivalling even the one constructed by the Athenians. It was made entirely from marble imported from the island of Paros. Since all the treasuries were built to commemorate victories and to express gratitude to the Pythia for her advice, without which the victories may not have happened, the Athenians had dedicated shields of their martyrs from different victories and even those of their vanquished opponents, specially the Persians whom they had defeated on the plains of Marathon.

Monimus, the king of Siphnos, was an ally of the Athenians and Siphnos itself was a signatory to the twelve-member Delphian league that had been created after the first Sacred War to control the sanctuary at Delphi because its treasures were being coveted by the neighbouring towns. Then, when fire destroyed the temple, funds were raised from the entire Greek world and even beyond, from as far as the city of Massalia. The Massalians, in fact, were dedicating another statue of Athena this year, which they had brought all the way from their city, and they intended it to replace the stolen statue of Athena Pronoia, which had been robbed two years ago.

The Massalians, however, went into dispute with Spintharos, Xenodoros and Agathon, the three architects of the new temple being funded by the Agamboros family from Macedonia. While the architects insisted that the Massalians place the statue at a place different from where it was earlier, the Massalians wanted to place it at the same spot where their ancestors had placed it, and in this their leader was being supported by the majority. The architects, on the other hand, insisted that the new spot would protect the statue better from landfalls. But this argument was perceived to be specious by many as the incline nearby was devoid of rocks, though the temple had indeed been saved from being raided by the Persians by virtue of a landfall and it was this story that the architects cited in their defence.

Otanes further enlightened me: 'A dispute has also emerged between Monimus, the king of the Siphnians, and the Massalians. Both are insisting on dedicating their objects on the day of the oracle, but the chief priest Busiris will grant permission to only one of the parties to dedicate their objects on that day, or it will result in a huge crowd on the premises. Busiris says that the last time such a crowd gathered, it led to many objects being stolen from the treasuries.

'But the biggest controversy that has arisen is the decision of the Macedonians to dedicate to Delphi the three hundred spears which they say belonged to the warriors of the Theban Sacred Band and which they claim to have collected from the battlefield at Chaorenea. The Macedonians intend to place the spears in their newly constructed treasury to remind all of Hellas, particularly the Athenians and the Thebans, of their military supremacy. While the states are allowed to keep what they wish in their treasuries, the Athenians and Thebans and their allies perceive this Macedonian intent as an insult to them.'

Tyros added: 'Besides, the Athenians and Thebans are saying that it would be an insult to the dead warriors of the Sacred Band and Hellenic culture does not allow them to disrespect the dead unless they are from a culture different from their own. There are others who are saying that the Macedonians had collected spears from all over the battlefield and are claiming falsely that they belonged to the Sacred Band. You must know too, Seleucus, as you were there. Wasn't the battle so furious that nearly all the spears of the Sacred Band broke before their deaths?'

'Yes, the battle was furious, Tyros. And I didn't see anybody collecting spears on the battlefield. I am determined to oppose this Macedonian perfidy the best I can. The Helots in the Sacred Band fought till death to protect me,' I said.

I sent Tyros to all the delegates from twelve members of the league – in which Macedonia had inserted itself only after Philip's intervention in the Sacred Wars – except Macedonia, to speak against the Macedonian intention. Since each member state had two votes, there were twenty-four delegates in all, though the states could send more delegates based on their contribution to the resources of the league. The league met every six months in spring and autumn; the last meeting had been in Thermopylae, but that was when Philip was alive. This time, the league was meeting at Delphi in autumn, for the first time since the death of Philip.

Tyros approached the members as a merchant from Lemnos which, though not a member of the league, contributed generously to the upkeep of the temple. One by one, he approached the Oeteans, the Thebans, the Dolopes, the Dorians from Sparta, the Malians and the Pythians of Delphi, who were also members, apart from the others. But he didn't approach the Macedonians, who had taken the place of the Phocians after their expulsion from the league. The Phocians, though, were allowed to visit the sanctuary and had some of the largest delegations and they spoke freely against the Macedonians.

The vote of the Pythians was exercised by the current Pythia through the priest Busiris, and when Tyros went to him to solicit support against the Macedonian decision, he pointed out that the matter was outside the jurisdiction of the league, as any member state could dedicate what they wished to their own treasury and therefore the matter would not be taken up at the meeting of the league. The Thebans, Athenians and Spartans, however, felt that the matter could be taken up at the meeting and intended to raise the issue.

Busiris told Tyros privately that the Macedonians had already dedicated the spears to Delphi, and the final ceremony of 'appearance', wherein bundles of spears would be kept in front of Apollo for his blessings, was due to be completed two days later. After that, the spears would be housed in the Macedonian treasury. Thus, he said: 'A league meeting on the matter after the event to revoke this decision of the

Macedonians is pointless, as there is no provision in the constitution to revoke a dedication already made. Only Apollo can revoke it, not the league. That is the way the law stands.'

Receiving this information from Tyros, I was tremendously agitated and resolved to defeat this purpose of the Macedonians. Otanes brought word that, the next day, the Macedonians were putting up a drama for the people in the theatre at Delphi. They had brought a troupe from Macedonia and the play was an enactment of the battle at Chaeronea and the Macedonians intended to use fifty of the three hundred spears that they claimed belonged to the dead warriors of the Sacred Band during the play. Wielding those fifty would be the local Delphians who had been recruited for the purpose and who would take on the role of Thebans from the Sacred Band. They would be defeated and slaughtered by the Macedonians and have their spears taken away.

Amongst these Delphian recruits was Aradus the wrestler, who was the son of the Pythia and who worked as an instructor at the gymnasium. Each of the fifty Delphians had been recruited for the sum of one drachma a day for rehearsals and two drachmas for each day of the performance. Since people came from all parts of Hellas to seek advice from the oracle on the seventh of every month and there was a representation from twelve states, besides other states which had sent their dedications, the Macedonians intended to establish before them all their supremacy through the medium of theatre.

Coming to know that Aradus was being paid by the Macedonians for the play, I sent Menicus to him, pretending to be the younger brother of one of the Sacred Band whose spears the Macedonians claimed to have in their possession, and he asked Aradus how he would feel if his brother had died and his spear was being used to make fun of him.

'I would break the legs of the person who dared to do that,' said Aradus.

'Then why are you continuing to rehearse thus with the Macedonians, knowing that they will be using the actual spears on the day that the play is staged in front of five thousand people?' asked Menicus.

Aradus looked him straight in the eye and answered: 'None of my brothers was in the Sacred Band and therefore the question doesn't apply to me. But I concede that you have a point. Please spell out what is in your mind and whether any profit lies in it for me.'

Menicus, seeing that Aradus spoke so openly, asked him whether he had any influence over the rest of the Delphians who were participating in the Macedonian play. Aradus said that all of them were from his gymnasium and would do what he desired, provided it was not the taking of a life and each one of them got a profit out of the deed.

Menicus promptly proposed to Aradus his strategy: 'I will pay each one of your colleagues fifty drachmas for breaking the spears on their thighs and singing odes to the Macedonian soldiers as they charge at them on the stage. That way, you will convert an action drama into a farce and, at the same time, deny the Macedonians the pleasure of dedicating all the three hundred spears to their treasury.'

'Consider it done. But I want the price to be increased to seventy-five drachmas per person,' demanded Aradus.

Menicus bargained with him and brought down the amount to sixty drachmas. He paid him half the sum in advance, with a promise to pay the other half after the deed was done, and Aradus walked away with great pleasure at having concluded a profitable transaction.

The next day, when the Macedonians staged the play, a big crowd of invitees gathered – except the Thebans, who had refused to attend – which included the Macedonian delegation to the league, which was twenty strong. Thymondas, the Thessalian writer of the play from Pluto's academy, was also present. The fifty Delphians did as Menicus had instructed and, right when the Macedonians charged them on horses – the actors wore masks – the Delphians turned their backs to them in unison and broke the spears. Then, keeping them on the ground, they started singing in loud voices, which so baffled the Macedonians that they didn't know how to proceed next. Everybody started laughing and most thought that the whole thing was part of the original play that the playright had written and therefore turned to look at him with admiration.

But Thymondas himself was petrified by what had happened and got up quickly to go backstage and ascertain what had gone wrong. The Macedonians in the play did not know how to proceed further as all the hired Delphians were singing non-stop in praise of Apollo. So Thymondas immediately ordered the play to be stopped. Thereafter, some jugglers and gymnasts entertained the invitees. The Delphians demanded their pay from the Macedonians, but Thymondas refused to pay them, saying that the play had been sabotaged, and he wanted to know who had done it since, in the rehearsals, everybody had acted in accordance with the script.

The Macedonian delegation too went backstage and a quarrel broke out between some of them and the Delphians. The Macedonians wanted to beat up the Delphians for having broken fifty of the spears which had been brought for the dedication. But the Delphians maintained that it was part of the play and they had done only what Thymondas had told them to do, and when they said this with such conviction, some of the Macedonians started suspecting that Thymondas had sabotaged the proceedings after being bribed by the Thebans, and one of them began to beat up Thymondas, till the leader of the Macedonian delegation intervened.

In this manner was the Macedonian dedication to their treasury sabotaged. The next day, Aradus spread the story that all the spears that the Macedonians were claiming to be of the Sacred Band, had actually been manufactured in Thessaly and had been transported by the Thessalian delegation. Though the story was not true, everybody believed it and criticized the Macedonians for lying at Delphi and urged them not to continue with the dedication.

The Macedonians maintained complete silence as to their intentions. But the priests observed that they had withdrawn from the ceremony where the spears were to make their 'appearance' in front of Apollo. They had told the priests that they would think about dedicating the spears later, in Alexander's presence, but that never happened.

Sometime later, Menicus found out that Aradus had only given the rest of his Delphian colleagues sums they would in any case have got from the Macedonians and kept the remainder for himself. When he confronted Aradus, he first denied it and then, when Menicus told him the exact sums he had paid to the others, he became sheepish and confessed to his greed and offered to correct his behaviour. But Menicus assured him that what he did with the money was his concern and he only needed one more errand done, and in this way did Menicus get a hold over Aradus.

'I want you to take me to your mother, who is the Pythia, for a secret meeting,' said Menicus.

'Many people have come to me with this request, but I have refused everybody,' said Aradus.

'I am not everybody. I have a specific purpose in meeting her, which will be for the good of all of Hellas,' said Menicus.

'What is your purpose and how do you have so many drachmas to spend?' asked Aradus.

'Apart from being the brother of a dead soldier of the Sacred Band, I am also a secret herald of Monimus, the king of Siphnos. He employs me, even though I am a Theban, for he trusts me,' said Menicus.

Menicus further told Aradus that it was common knowledge that Monimus had brought ten rams made of gold to dedicate to the Siphnian treasury. The ostensible reason being that it was an offering to Apollo to atone for not having dedicated anything of value for the last many years, and also to ward off the kind of floods they had had this year in the gold mines of Siphnos. But the real reason was something different.

Aradus's curiousity was aroused and Menicus swore him to secrecy before telling him that Monimus had had a vision, wherein he was instructed to dedicate ten golden rams at Delphi and Apollo had then revealed to him that each of the ten rams would achieve a separate goal. Of the ten goals, Menicus himself had been told of only four goals. The other six goals remained a secret.

Aradus then asked Menicus what were the four goals he knew, and Menicus said they were: the continuance of the importance of Delphi as the principal oracle in all of Greece; the restoration of Athens as the principal power in all of Greece; the sending of a colonizing force to Libya, where Monimus had discovered silver mines that no one knew about; and the opposition of Alexander as the captain-general of the league.

Aradus listened avidly.

'Who will select the men who will proceed to Libya to exploit the silver mines? Will these men be entitled to any bounty?' asked Aradus.

'The selection of the men will be done by me and I intend to recruit only the best and brightest. Men who have the intelligence to achieve great things and are tough enough to bear hardship. Since the exploitation of the mines would require at least a thousand men over three years, the pay has been settled at two drachmas a day and five drachmas each for the five leaders who will be selected and who will work under the supreme leader. The supreme leader of the expedition has already been appointed and he was in Delphi trying to identify leaders for the expedition from amongst several aspirants because, apart from the pay, there is also a starting gift of a hundred drachmas for each leader,' said Menicus.

'Can you introduce me to the supreme leader and endorse my candidacy?' asked Aradus.

'I can, provided you ask your mother, the Pythia, to air certain oracles on the seventh that would suit Monimus. If you can do that, I will not only introduce you to him but also ensure that you are made one of the leaders of the expedition,' said Menicus.

Aradus pondered for a while and said that he would go and talk to his mother who, at the moment, was in seclusion in a cave. But he knew of a way to enter the cave without being detected and would consult her on the subject.

He then wanted to know what Monimus wished to ask the Pythia on the seventh. And Menicus said, 'Monimus will ask her whether the temple's name should be changed from the Temple of Alcmenidae to the Temple of Agamboros, and she will have to say in whatever manner she sees fit that the earlier name of Alcmenidae should be retained, as the people have more faith in that name. The next thing that Monimus will ask is whether Alexander should be made captain-general of the Delphian league and to this I would like the answer, in the Pythia's own way, that he should not be made captain, or blood will flow in Hellas and women will lose their husbands in war. If the Pythia does this, then I will arrange for you to be made a leader of the expedition to Libya and also recommend to Monimus that you deserve a special gift from the Siphnians,' explained Menicus.

Hearing this, Aradus was tremendously excited and promised to go and talk to his mother. He was confident that she would listen to him, as she was weary of being the Pythia, but the chief priest Busiris was not letting her proceed into retirement since the people had more faith in the current Pythia than the one earlier who gave predictions of harvests that never happened and plagues that occurred in spite of offerings to the Gods.

The next day, he came back after meeting the Pythia and said that she had readily agreed to do as Monimus desired, provided he fulfil certain of her own conditions.

Said Aradus: 'Monimus is to pay her ten talents, as the Macedonians have also approached her with requests and they want her to say that Alexander is capable of leading the Delphian league and that there would be huge victories for him if he proceeds to Persia. Monimus is also to insist to the priest Busiris that he wants his session with the Pythia to be a private one and he is to declare that he will dedicate one talent of gold for the upkeep of the establishment where food is provided free to all the poor pilgrims. The Pythia also wants the entire sum of ten talents before she makes any pronouncements since Monimus might go back on his word, leaving her helpless.'

Menicus was not in favour of this, but Aradus said the Pythia would not have it any other way. So, finally, after consulting me, he gave Aradus the entire sum demanded.

'Now I will facilitate your becoming a leader in the expedition to Libya, but after the league meets, as I have other important matters to attend to now. However, if the Pythia does not do as expected, Monimus will see to it that grievous harm comes to her and you and your entire family. And I will not then be able to intercede in the matter,' warned Menicus.

'Monimus will have no reason to trouble us. The Pythia will do as he bids,' said Aradus.

After securing the Pythia and Aradus in this manner, I approached Monimus as a biannual pilgrim to Delphi for twenty years and told him that a group of people, of whom I was chief, hated the Massalians and intended to help Monimus in his plan of dedicating his golden rams on the day of the oracle. Monimus was pleased to hear this, but then I told him that there was a major obstacle in his path, as the Pythia and Busiris had taken money from the Massalians to deny the Siphnians this privilege. If Monimus did not exceed the sum they had offered, he would lose out to the Massalians and that would be an insult to him personally, as the Siphnian treasury was one of the oldest and certainly the best at Delphi.

Monimus was alarmed by this news.

'How much have the Massalians paid for this favour to be achieved?' asked Monimus.

'They have paid a sum of forty talents to all the priests and attendants at the oracle, as well as the Pythia, but how they have distributed the money internally, I don't know. However, if you bribed them with fifty talents, I could make the Delphian staff renege on their agreement with the Massalians; not only would their money not be returned to them by the priests and the Pythia, but they would not achieve their objectives either,' I said to Monimus.

Hearing this, King Monimus's face lit up at the thought that he would get to dedicate the rams on the day he desired. And since the Massalians had insulted him personally in their arguments to buttress their case, he was eager for them to incur a loss of both money and prestige.

Monimus therefore agreed to fund the enterprise and asked where he was to deliver the fifty talents and I told him that he had to deliver only half the sum now and the other half later, as I was a personal friend of the priests and they trusted me to keep my word. Monimus was even more pleased when he heard this, for it assured him that he was not being cheated by the priests.

But then I told him that he would have to ask a few questions of the Pythia. One, whether the newly renovated temple should retain the name of the Temple of Alcmenidae or should it be changed to the Temple of Agamboros, as the new funders desired. Two, whether Alexander should be named the chief of the Delphian league and should the league endorse his decision to proceed on his Persian campaign.

Monimus was a little alarmed on hearing that he had to ask these questions, but agreed when I convinced him that it was necessary because on the correct answer hinged a positive outcome. And when he failed to see the connection, I explained the following.

I said that if the Pythia gave her consent for the temple to be called the Temple of Alcmenidae, which was the current name, it would be beneficial for him, as it would mean that the land in front of the Siphnian treasury would continue to be empty. And that was the land where he intended to perform the ceremony of his offerings. However, if the name of the temple was changed to the Temple of the Agamboros, the land would be taken over by the architects and they would shift the new statue of Athena that the Massalians had brought to that spot. The Massalians might well argue that, since the statue was there, the plot of land should be under their control and they would therefore deny the Siphnians the right to conduct their offering there.

Monimus agreed immediately to ask the question about the change of name on hearing this. But he expressed doubts about the other question.

'With regard to Alexander's fitness to lead the league and to undertake the Persian campaign, I fear that my asking that question will annoy the Macedonians,' said Monimus.

'It will not, as nearly all the delegates plan to ask the same question and, in any case, nobody can blame you for what the Pythia says,' I countered.

My logic comforted Monimus and he agreed to the plan.

I then sent Otanes to the priest Busiris since he had already established contact with him. Otanes told him that his master was on his way to Delphi and wanted to conduct an offering on the day of the oracle and he intended to pay Busiris two talents for the upkeep of the establishment where free food was provided to the poor pilgrims.

'I have been authorized by my master to pass on the funds to you immediately if you agree to the proposal,' said Otanes.

Busiris agreed at once and Otanes then had the sum delivered to his dwelling. That evening, Otanes went to his dwelling again and asked whether he could arrange for the dedication ceremony to be done outside the area where the Pythia sat and where the pilgrims came and asked their questions as his master has received a communication in a dream that his offering will be best received if it is made at that spot.

Busiris answered: 'Any offering at that spot will not be possible, as it is the area limited to private audiences which the Pythia has with the many kings assembled in Delphi. It would be hard for me to fulfil the request unless your master can dress in the garb of a priest. Then all the pilgrims would think that he is part of the temple staff and would therefore not complain. But to achieve this, I will have to bribe the other priests at the temple and would need an extra amount of a thousand drachmas for the task to be accomplished without a scandal.'

Otanes immediately agreed and had a thousand drachmas delivered to Busiris without any delay.

Then Otanes went to Busiris a third time and said that his master had another favour to ask of him, which was that the Massalian request to instal the new Athena statue at the original spot be granted and, for this, his master was willing to pay a sum of two talents more to Busiris. Busiris was overjoyed that Apollo had sent him such a wealthy devotee and said that, if the amount could be raised to three talents, he would bribe the architects with two talents and keep one for himself.

Otanes agreed immediately and Busiris went and talked to the architects and came back to say that they had agreed to withdraw their objection, provided the Massalians agreed to climb the hill and remove the rocks that most threatened to slide down the slope and cause destruction to the statue of Athena, for if the statue was robbed again or destroyed by rocks, a calamity would befall the Apollo temple.

Otanes immediately agreed to the condition of the architects on behalf of the Massalians, thinking that, even if they could not be persuaded, he would personally organize and pay a team of Delphians to do the needful. Finally, Busiris set the condition that the Massalians would have to choose another date for the installation, as their insistence to instal the statue on the day of the oracle would encourage thieves and robbers and it would be difficult to keep an eye on every person in the complex. Otanes agreed to this as well.

After having thus managed Busiris, I approached the Massalians and asked them what favour they could do me if I convinced the new architects and the temple authorities to allow them to instal the statue of Athena at the spot that they wished. They said that I would have their undying gratitude. I pointed out to them that gratitude was not something one could eat or drink and asked them if they had something else which was more valuable. They then said that they would give in marriage a daughter of their village to me. To this I replied that I already had a woman and did not seek another, no matter how beautiful she was. Then the leader of the Massalians spoke to me. He said: 'We will offer our lives in any adventure which you might plan in the future, for such is our devotion to Athena and our desire to instal the statue at the old place that we are prepared to do all that is possible for us to achieve our objectives. We lack the resources to offer bribes or we would have tried that too.'

I then told them that, seeing their devotion to Athena, I had decided to pay the bribes on their behalf and would see to it that their view prevailed. I asked them what they desired more: to instal Athena's statue at the old place, but on a date different from the day of the oracle, or have the statue installed at the place the architects were suggesting, on the date of the oracle. The Massalians thought about this for a while and then said that it was more important to have the statue installed at the same spot. They said that it didn't bother them what date was allotted to them for the dedication and that they had become involved in a dispute with Monimus about conducting the ceremony on the day of the oracle, as they thought that he was a pompous old fool who was conceited because of his wealth and they wanted to teach him a lesson.

I then urged them to withdraw their plea to have their dedication on the day of the oracle, as I would ensure that they got the spot they wanted to instal the statue. They agreed, provided such intimation was first provided to them by the temple authorities and the architects.

I said, at last, that they would have what they wanted and gifted them five talents for use on the journey back, for they had suffered many hardships to come from their land and the journey had taken them more than a month. For the five talents, I told them they would have to ensure that the slopes above the statue of Athena were cleared of all rocks.

The Massalians were astonished by my gift and told me that they were greatly in debt to me. Their chief, who had been silent for a while, then got up and said that, in return for this gift, they would leave two of their best men behind with me, who were bachelors and could therefore stay back without any worries. He brought the two men forward. Their names were Nautaca and Myndus and they were both twenty-five years of age and could speak the local tongue fluently, having spent a lot of time in Delphi.

Though I said that there was no need for them to do such a thing, the Massalians said that their honour would not allow a gift to go unreturned and they were therefore offering the services of two of their best men for a period of eight years, after which they were free to return to their lands if they so desired. In this manner did Nautaca and Myndus enter my employment, and they proved their worth in the days to come.

On the seventh day, the day of the oracle, I entered the inner sanctum early in the morning with Athele and my son Zanylos, for it was considered auspicious to enter the sanctum before dawn. After receiving the priest's blessing, I sent them back home under the protection of Nautaca. Otanes, who was with me, introduced me to Busiris as his master and he gave me the clothing of a priest and, donning this, I sat next to him as he conducted the oracle for the others.

I had made it a point to sit there as I wanted to listen to the questions asked by those who wished their oracles to remain private, for I knew there would be a lot to learn from the questions they asked. I also wanted to hear the oracle of the Pythia concerning Monimus, for her answers to his questions would reveal whether Aradus and she had kept their end of the bargain. We knew that if the Pythia answered as we wished, it would create a big controversy and the Macedonians would face the ire of the public.

When Monimus entered the sanctum sanctorum, with all his thousand followers waiting outside, he asked Busiris for a private audience and the request was granted. He then asked the questions I had instructed him to ask. He first asked whether the temple should be renamed the Temple of Agamboros. Busiris was surprised at the question and, in all likelihood, he had not prepared the Pythia for it, or so I thought. After the question was passed to the Pythia, the answer came before Busiris could intervene. The other priests interpreted her mystical utterings thus:

From an old shell a new shell is born.
Does the father not give the seed for the son?
Does the son then deny his name?
Even a son sired out of wedlock
Does the seed of his father use.

Monimus then went out to his followers and repeated the verse and, after much discussion, the throng came to the conclusion that the Pythia had spoken for the old name of Alcmenidae to be retained and a big thrill went through them as the majority wanted it that way.

Then Monimus entered the sanctorum again and asked his second question: should Alexander be made the chief of the Delphian league and should the Hellas support his Persian campaign? Busiris became extremely alarmed when Monimus asked this question and rushed inside to the Pythia, followed by the other priests. When the question was conveyed to the Pythia, loud noises came from her throat and she started muttering and shouting and Monimus listened in awe and, finally, after much heated argument between the other priests and Busiris, the following verses were read:

Blood will flow and widows will be made
If a man rules whose father suffered the blade;
He will lead Hellas to doom
And many thousands will lie in tombs.
The men be warned and the priests pray
That Hellas be not led astray.

The face of Monimus turned red after he heard the verses and he didn't know what to do and Busiris looked crestfallen. Then one of the priests, who looked most elated, ran up to the crowd and whispered to one of Monimus's men how the Pythia had responded to the second question and he repeated it to the Siphnians around him and they to some others. By the time Monimus came out, nearly everybody knew what the Pythia had said, but still they waited for Monimus to tell them.

Besides the Siphnians, the Thebans, the Athenians and even the Phocians, who hated the Macedonians, had gathered there, and when the Pythia's words were repeated to them, they were joyous beyond belief and urged Monimus to reveal all. Not having any other option, he repeated the Pythia's words and there was a roar from the crowd and the news spread like fire.

After listening to the oracle, Monimus asked Busiris whether he could proceed to his treasury to dedicate the golden rams and Busiris told him to give him some time to consult the architects and the Massalians, so Monimus waited in the sanctorum. Then, after giving the impression that he was deliberating with the architects, Busiris came and declared that Monimus could proceed to dedicate the golden rams to the treasury immediately. To the crowd, Busiris announced that the architects had consented to let the Massalians use the old spot to dedicate the statue of Athena. Hearing this, a roar erupted from the Massalians and they blew the trumpets they had brought and broke into song and dance.

Busiris then told the Massalians to conduct their dedication the next day and they agreed. After the end of the oracle, Monimus was very thankful to me and said that the rest of the twenty-five talents due to me would be given after his dedication ceremony was over and he requested me to attend the ceremony, but I politely refused as I had to go back to listen to the questions that the people asked the Pythia privately.

Many people sent their representatives to ask questions on their behalf as they couldn't make the journey themselves. A representative came from Illyria who asked whether their state should go to war with Macedonia, now that Philip had died, but Busiris turned away the representative on the pretext that he wasn't carrying any credentials to show that he was from Illyria. When he protested, Busiris had him thrown out by the temple guards. The questions that Monimus had asked and the answers that he had received from the Pythia had stoked the ire of the Macedonians, and a delegation from them visited Busiris. After that, if any pilgrim asked a political question, he would try and deflect it on some pretext or the other, particularly if the person who asked the question didn't seem to possess any authority.

In this manner did he turn away a representative of King Pistoris, the tyrant of Lemnos, who asked whether the island should entertain vessels from Macedonia, as he was afraid that Philip would send his forces to capture the island and they would come on ships. The representative from Lemnos clearly didn't know that Philip had died and hadn't bothered to educate himself on the way, and Busiris ordered the guards to throw him out of the temple premises.

But there were representatives of formidable appearance, who came with guards for protection, and when they asked political questions,

Busiris was not able to do much about it. One such representative came from Cyprus and he asked if their king, by name of Lemonos – not to be confused with the island – could enter into a matrimonial alliance with the daughter of King Aegis of Sparta and whether such an alliance would bear fruit and the Pythia replied:

The womb is ripe, the journey lengthy,
But he who questions is brittle ice.
Good for the man, but the pleasure short,
And doom for the woman as she will be a barren lot.

After hearing this, the representative of Cyprus asked Busiris what it meant and he said that they just translated the words of the Pythia and King Lemonos would have to find the meaning through his own wisdom. This answer so infuriated the representative that he threw his shoe at Busiris and the priest darted inside to escape his wrath.

After sitting in the sanctorum for so long, I was beginning to feel that the exercise was a waste of time, when two representatives arrived quickly, one after the other. One of them, from the island of Rhodes, asked the Pythia whether they could supply stone-throwing monsters to a Greek mercenary party that had arrived from near Abydos in Asia and the Pythia answered:

Let the monsters go
And make them fast,
Or bad weather will tear the mast.
Another danger lurks with men on a vessel
Coming to steal, but fear them not,
For in the sea they will rot.

After memorizing these words with great care, the representative left and I gave instructions to Menicus to go and detain the person and question him. The next representative turned out to be a Macedonian and Busiris treated him with great respect. He asked the Pythia how to go about capturing a person from Olympia called 'Seleucus, son of Nicanor' who roamed all of Hellas and caused grief to the Macedonians. Since the representative had requested a private audience and he had four Macedonian hoplites with him, Busiris had turned away most of the temple priests from the room while he awaited the Pythia's answer. And the Pythia answered thus:

He will be like wind between your fingers,
Like the fire no one can drink.
But here he is, in Delphian rule.
And he who asks the question
Shall wither before ten suns are past.

There was much consultation amongst the Macedonians to understand the meaning behind the Pythia's words. Some felt that it was positive, for it put the location of Nicanor's son in Delphi, and others were not too enthusiastic, as they felt that even if he was here, the Pythia had said in the first line that it would be difficult to catch him as he was as slippery as the wind.

As they left the sanctorum, I instructed Nautaca and Myndus to follow them around the whole day and bring me tidings of what they did and said.

In the afternoon, Menicus came to me, bringing with him the man from Rhodes. The man told me that two persons called Zamos and Dorian had arrived in Rhodes in two vessels and with many mercenaries. He said that they were also accompanied by a person called Automa, whom they knew. He said that Zamos, their leader, desired them to make stone-throwing monsters of a size which they alone had the knowledge to build. And their chief had agreed to do so, for Zamos offered them double the price they had quoted if the monsters could be readied in four months for them to take back. So work had started on two triremes to transport the four monsters, triremes of a size the like of which had never been made; for them to be stable in the seas, their keel had to be made in a unique way.

But, continued the representative from Rhodes, after the work had started, Automa came to them one day when he was drunk and revealed that the monsters were meant for Persia and not Macedonia, as they had originally been told by Zamos. They confronted Zamos with what Automa had said, but he denied his assertions and maintained that the monsters were meant for Macedonia.

The representative said that Samocles, the manufacturer of the monsters, was a personal friend of General Parmenio and the Macedonian had forbidden him to sell the monsters to any other power.

Therefore, on hearing Automa, they had started to suspect that Zamos was lying and hence a representative had been sent to Delphi to enquire from the Pythia whether they could supply the monsters to the Greek mercenaries without anything untoward happening. If the Pythia gave a positive prophecy, he was supposed to go back to Rhodes, and if the Pythia gave a negative prophecy, he was supposed to go to the Macedonians and seek their advice on the matter.

The representative was, however, happy at the advice he had received from the oracle and intended to proceed back to Rhodes via Pireus in Attica. But I feared that he would change his mind and seek an opinion from the Macedonians, in which case they might think in terms of jeopardizing the project. Therefore I sent Menicus to escort him all the way to the Pireus harbour and then on to one of our vessels to Rhodes, so that he didn't get a chance to talk to the Macedonians, even if he so wished.

At Pireus, Menicus was to explain to my partner Phormio how we had intercepted the representative from Rhodes and he was to then select somebody from amongst our own men to escort him all the way to Rhodes, with a secret message for Zamos and Dorian, explaining all that had happened, so they would be more alert.

I even arranged for a gift of a golden horn for the representative and assured him that the prophecy of the oracle was in their favour and they should go ahead with the production of the monsters at an increased pace. Since I was in priestly attire, the representative thought that my advice was part of the Delphian process and was glad that so much care was being taken of him. After making sure from him that there weren't any more representatives from Rhodes with him, I sent him to Pireus and instructed Menicus to return as soon as he could.

After Menicus and the representative left, I expressed gratitude to the Gods for having planted in my mind the idea of listening to the questions of the pilgrims, for if I hadn't done that, I wouldn't have come to know about the last two queries – the one from Rhodes, and the other concerning Nicanor's son.

TWENTY-FIVE

In the evening, Nautaca and Myndus reported to me that the Macedonians whom I had sent them to follow had encamped behind the gymnasium and there they discussed amongst themselves the meaning of the oracle's words. They were able to get close to them because they were with hundreds of other pilgrims from Hellas who had also chosen that spot for their encampment. Nautaca found out by talking to one of the Macedonian guards that this particular group was different from the one which had come with the delegates, for they had come to Delphi at the behest of a certain Argus, who wanted oracular guidance on his hunt for a certain 'Nicanor's son', who was a thug and a brigand, they had been told.

Myndus, on the other hand, found out that the Macedonians were upset that the Pythia had spoken against the new temple being called the Temple of the Agamboros, and in the meeting of the pilgrims the next day, they expected that it would be difficult for the Macedonians to win support for the new name, as the pilgrims put great faith in what the Pythia prophesied.

Tyros, who had also followed them, but at a distance, for fear that one of the Macedonians might recognize him from his travels in Macedonia, found out from a group of Thessalian pilgrims that the Macedonians had given them the task of finding out who was behind extracting the prophecy from the Pythia about continuing with the old name of the temple, for they refused to believe that it was an honest oracle. Privately, they had confided to the Thessalians that they themselves had tried to bribe the priests and the Pythia to enable a certain prophecy to be made about Alexander, but had not been successful as the Pythia had demanded an exorbitant amount of money and they had considered the price too high for the favours they asked. They were certain therefore that the Pythia had been bribed a larger amount to give adverse predictions on issues that concerned them.

The Thessalians, though, thought that the Macedonians were making up the story to hide their disappointment about the Pythia's predictions, for their investigations had not yielded any cause for suspicion. They also told Tyros that, as allies of the Macedonians, they had heard of Nicanor's son before and one of their own generals, Parmenio, had dealt with him earlier, in Asia, and vanquished him from Abydos. But the Macedonians were now saying that, after his departure from Asia, he had ventured into Pella and was one of the party that had conspired to have Philip murdered and now, according to the Pythia, he could be in Delphi itself!

Since Tyros had introduced himself to them as a Greek who had come to Delphi all the way from a small colony in Egypt, they were more open to talking to him as they considered him harmless, specially as Tyros professed neutrality in the affairs of Hellas.

After they came to know that he had travelled from Egypt, the Thessalians wanted to recruit Tyros for an errand. They asked him to go to the chief priest Busiris and other assistant priests, as well as any other person he felt would be useful to find out if the Pythia was engaged in a conspiracy against the Macedonians, and also if he could find out anything about Seleucus, son of Nicanor. They claimed that, being Thessalians, everybody identified them as allies of the Macedonians and didn't speak to them out of fear, whereas once they came to know that Tyros had travelled from Egypt, they might lower their guard and reveal to him something of significance in their gossip. When Tyros agreed to do their bidding, they gave him a sum of ten drachmas and promised him five more if he brought some information of value.

After coming to know that it was Argus who had sent the group of Macedonians who had come to the oracle asking about Nicanor's son, I decided to lay a trap for him. I told Tyros to go back in the night to the Thessalians and tell them that he had overheard a pilgrim asking at the oracle whether it would be safe for Seleucus, son of Nicanor, to appear at the installation ceremony of the statue of Goddess Athena, which the Massalians were conducting the next day.

I said to Tyrus: 'You are to tell them that the Pythia had answered that it would be fraught with risk, but if his devotion to Athena was true, then nothing would happen to him. You should then say that you followed the pilgrim to the camp of the Phocians and that was possibly where Nicanor's son was hiding.'

Though the Macedonians had taken over the voting rights of the Phocians in the Delphian league after defeating them in battle, they couldn't stop individual Phocian pilgrims from coming to Delphi during the time of the oracle. And this time, about a thousand Phocians had come to Delphi; all of them hated the Macedonians.

So Tyros returned to the Thessalians in the night and narrated the lie, and the Thessalians were so pleased with the information that they paid him fifteen drachmas and immediately went to the Macedonians with the information, claiming it to be the result of their own efforts. The Macedonians, who had been full of despondency at the events of the day, became enthusiastic and despatched three spies to the Phocian camp.

Anticipating this, I had told Otanes to spread rumours in the Phocian camp that five Macedonians were expected to enter their camp at night and spy on them. Therefore their entire contingent of pilgrims was on guard and prepared to single out any person who wasn't from their state. When the three Macedonians arrived, dressed as peasants, the Phocians leapt on them and, declaring them to be robbers, gave them a thrashing before submitting them to the Delphian authorities, who released them after their identities were established. When the Delphians asked them what they were doing in the camp of the Phocians, they replied that they had lost their spears in the day and had gone to look for them, but nobody believed their story. Once the Macedonian camp came to know about their spies had been beaten up, they cited it as evidence amongst themselves of Nicanor's son being in the camp of the Phocians. The Thessalians urged them to surround the Phocian camp with soldiers and ask for Nicanor's son to be given over.

But the Macedonian officers were reminded that the rules of the league did not permit the entry of soldiers into Delphi and even Alexander, who was said to be attending the league meeting on the ninth day of the month, would have to leave his two thousand soldiers at the outskirts of the town and enter only with the fifty bodyguards permitted to the chief of the league. And the Delphians could raise objections to that as well, for Alexander was not yet the chief of the league.

Otanes then brought information that the Macedonian soldiers who were outside Delphi were considering entering the city as ordinary men, after leaving behind their weapons and armour. Since the Phocians were not armed either, except for the few weapons they were allowed to prevent brigandry and theft, the Macedonians hoped to surround them as pilgrims and press matters.

But the Phocians got wind of this in the night and alerted the Thebans and the Athenians and they all decided to come to the aid of the

Phocians by staying together, so that their number would go up by three times and the Macedonians would not have the courage to execute their plans. And so, after lighting fires all over the camp to protect them from the chill, the Phocians, Thebans and Athenians huddled together, and in this manner they passed the night.

The next day, I sent Athele and my son Zanylos to Thebes so that, even if things went wrong for me, nobody could take them hostage. This act provided me with great relief and the courage to attend the pilgrims' meeting, which was to decide the new name of the temple. Once the dedicated pilgrims from each state present had made their way to the Delphi theatre, Busiris called the meeting to attention and started the proceedings. The descendants of the Alcmenidae family spoke first and said that, for two hundred years, the temple had been called the Temple of Alcmenidae. To change the name now would be to disrespect the family. There was tremendous applause when they sat down and then the chief of the Agamboros clan stood up and spoke.

Said he: 'We funded the construction of the temple after the earthquake, and had it not been for us, the temple would still be in ruins, as the devastation was so huge that nobody was willing to come forward to fund the reconstruction. Keeping this in mind, it is only fair that our clan be remembered for this deed and, since we are not asking for anything more than what is normal in these circumstances, we hope that everybody will vote for honouring our service to the temple by calling it the Temple of Agamboros.'

His argument was sound and there were no disparaging remarks, except from the Phocians, who disliked everything the Macedonians did or said. But when the proposition was put to the vote, the pilgrims voted overwhelmingly in favour of the retention of the old name and, since this decision had not been left to the league but to the pilgrims, there was nothing the Macedonians could do about it. The Agamboros clan was disappointed beyond belief and the playwright Thymondas and the three architects Spintharos, Xenodoros and Agathon consoled them by saying that, for the Gods, the deeds counted and not the name. But that was small consolation for the clan.

The Macedonians were upset by this decision of the pilgrims and opined that had it not been for the oracle of the Pythia, the pilgrims would have voted for the renaming of the temple, as that was the way it had been done by their ancestors. So they pressurized the Delphians to start looking for a new Pythia and instal her before the seventh of the next month and they wished to delay the decision to continue with the old name till such time that the new Pythia was in place. They felt that an oracle in their favour might make the pilgrims vote for them. They also aspired to pass this decision to the league by an amendment of the constitution, so that the matter was decided by voting by the delegates. They were certain that, there, the Macedonian view would prevail.

But the Delphians were obstinate and said that once a decision had been taken by the pilgrims, it could not be countermanded, and a new Pythia could be installed only if the current Pythia forfeited the faith of the pilgrims by some act that disgraced her, but such a thing had not happened. So they wouldn't start looking for a new Pythia, or Apollo's curse would be on them. In this manner they resisted the Macedonians.

After the meeting of the pilgrims, I sent Tyros once again to the Thessalians to tell them that Nicanor's son was determined to make it to the Massalian dedication ceremony to Athena and he had bribed the Phocians to surround the ceremonial space in a manner that would make it too crowded for the Macedonians to locate him, should they come looking for him there. Tyros then added: 'I also learned from a Phocian that each one of them had received half a drachma to attend the Massalian ceremony, so that it could be much grander than the Siphnian one, which boasted more wealth but fewer pilgrims.'

Before Tyros went to the Thessalians with this story, I gave a thousand drachmas to some Massalians, who were brought to me by Myndus and Nautaca, with instructions to distribute one drachma each amongst the Phocians. They were to tell them that it was a bribe to come to the Massalian dedication and make it much bigger than the Siphnian one. The Phocians were delighted with this largesse from the Massalians and agreed to even bring some friends and relatives. When the Thessalians and Macedonians made their own enquiries, it confirmed what Tyros had said and they trusted him even more and paid him ten drachmas for this information.

Tyros then returned to them much before the Massalian ceremony began and, this time, he told them that Nicanor's son would be one of the twenty people in masks who would be throwing flowers and incense sticks at the pilgrims as they made their way in a procession to the grounds of the dedication. He was making this guess, he said, after hearing some Massalians argue that there should be no foreigners amongst the people throwing flowers, but their chief had said that they would have to make an exception for the man who was funding their dedication. The Thessalians, convinced of Tyros's logic, went ahead and convinced the Macedonians and told them that it was they who had discovered the information. And whatever information came to them from their allies, the Macedonians accepted in good faith.

I then sent word to the chief of the Massalians that I intended to send some of my followers to throw flowers in the procession, wearing masks of Athena, and the chief was more than happy to oblige me. After his agreement to my proposal, I had Otanes recruit twenty people from the Delphi gymnasium and theatre. He provided a mask of Athena to each one of them – these were readily available at the shops in Delphi – and gave them tunics which covered their body in such a manner that it was difficult to guess, specially after they had donned their masks and caps, whether they were men or women. And among the twenty people Otanes recruited, there were ten women whose height and deportment were similar to that of the men. After paying them two drachmas each for following the procession and throwing flowers at the pilgrims, Otanes bade them goodbye and told them to go to the Massalian camp.

With the Phocians thronging the Massalian camp, and the Athenians and Thebans also joining them, the length of the procession grew. The masked Delphians Otanes had recruited ran about throwing flowers at everyone and the Massalian musicians played the flute and horn and other instruments and produced music which was unlike the music of Hellas, and this caused more people to come out and join the procession as it made its way to the temple.

After the Massalians started their dedication with great pomp and show, the Thessalians and Macedonians, along with a few of their allies from other states, started arriving in great numbers; they concentrated on the area where the masked men and women were throwing flowers at the pilgrims. Once the statue of Athena had been erected and all the rituals completed, the pilgrims made their way slowly in a line to the statue and put offerings at the feet of Athena and the Massalian priests then distributed sweets to everybody present.

When the ceremonies were over and the crowd was about to disperse, the Macedonians and Thessalians pounced on the twenty masked Delphians in groups of three and four and a big commotion ensued. Everyone thought that they had been caught stealing from the offerings, but the masked Delphians who managed to escape raised their voices and shouted that they were being assaulted and they took off their masks and half of them turned out to be women.

The pilgrims then thought that the Macedonians and Thessalians were brigands trying to kidnap the women of Delphi, and a loud roar ensued from the crowd and everyone pounced on the men who were trying to wrestle with the masked figures. It soon came to light that the men conducting the assault were Macedonians and the first to give them a fight were the Massalians. The Phocians joined the Massalians, and so did the Athenians and the Thebans. Together, they captured ten of the assaulters while the rest fled.

Unfortunately, there were just two Macedonians amongst the ten assaulters; the rest were Thessalians, who were more enthusiastic than the Macedonians about trying to nab Seleucus. But since nobody hated the Thessalians as much as they hated the Macedonians, all ten were let free after an interrogation, during which they claimed that they were looking for Nicanor's son amongst the masked men. When they were asked how they had thought that the women could be men, they said they had been deceived by the masks and taken the women for men. In this manner did the Macedonians and Thessalians make fools of themselves.

But after this incident, the Macedonian soldiers at the edge of Delphi entered the town in big numbers and, though they didn't outwardly carry arms, the Delphians claimed their swords were hidden in their tunics. The leader of the Macedonian delegation, a person by the name of Thapsacus, son of Odon, declared that the Macedonians had come to guard the delegates from the twelve different states, so that no untoward incident happened in Delphi before the voting of the delegates on the ninth. It was rumoured that Alexander too was coming to attend the meeting.

After the Macedonians planted themselves in front of the dwellings of the delegates, they grew very fearful and my efforts of getting Tyros and Otanes to each of the delegates to convince them to vote against Alexander bore no fruit, as each one of them had come with instructions from their state not to annoy the Macedonians. Now, with the Macedonian soldiers posted outside their dwellings, they even feared for their lives if they voted against Alexander.

At this time, when Tyros went to the dwelling where the delegates from Aetolia had taken refuge, the Macedonian guards became privy to the conversation he was having with them and arrested him, demanding to know on whose behalf he had approached the Aetolians and asked them to vote against Alexander. Hearing the commotion, the Thessalians too came to the place and one of them recognized Tyros as the person who had brought to them the information that Nicanor's son would be one of the masked persons in the procession of the Massalians and that he had earlier provided information that Nicanor's son was in the Phocian camp. When the Macedonians heard this, they were very upset with the Thessalians for having claimed earlier that they had got the information through their own efforts, for now it was clear that Tyros had been misleading them.

Tyros, being surrounded by the Macedonians and Thessalians, claimed that he was a Greek who lived in Egypt and that on his own initiative he had been meeting the delegates to warn them that they would lose their independence to the Macedonians who sought to subjugate them as slaves. He further claimed that it was Athena who had come to him in his dreams and had told him to proceed with these actions. He also denied that he had ever offered any information to the Thessalians and accused them of lying.

At this charge, the Thessalians grew agitated and attacked Tyros, which attracted a large group of Delphians and Phocians to his defence. The Delphian authorities informed the Macedonians that they had no authority to arrest a person on their land and, even if Tyros was trying to convince the delegates to vote against Alexander, he was not breaking any law and was acting well within the rules of the league. The Delphian authorities said that if the delegates were so easily swayed from their purpose after listening to the arguments of a citizen from Egypt, then it was the fault of the delegates and not Tyros, and the Macedonians had to let him go. But the Macedonians attached two spies to him to report his activities back to them and therefore Tyros went to the quarter of the whores and spent time with some women there to get the Macedonians off his back.

Around this time, King Monimus of Siphnos sent word to me to collect from his camp the remaining sum he owed me. Deciding against laying a trap for Argus in Delphi, I had decided to leave the place after collecting the money I was owed by Monimus. Thus, I proceeded to the dwelling Monimus had hired from a Delphian aristocrat for the duration of his stay, leaving Otanes outside with Myndus and Nautaca to keep a discreet watch. I told them that if I didn't come out of Monimus's dwelling within a short while and signal that all was well, they should presume that a conspiracy was afoot, and they were to then proceed to the Massalian chief and request for help and also to report the matter to Lycargus, who had come to Delphi as head of the Athenian delegation.

If neither of them was in a position to offer assistance, they were to send a messenger to Athens and inform Phormio and Pythagoras.

Monimus greeted me effusively and showered me with great praise for my help in arranging the dedication of the golden rams to the Siphnian treasury. He said that the act would benefit his mines and increase production, as that was what the oracle on their island had said and he had never been wrong. He then said that some old friends of his wished to make my acquaintance to get the advantage of my advice on a matter related to Delphi and that he personally would be greatly obliged if I could offer them some assistance. Then he got up and left the room and his guards came in and blocked the only exit from the room and, before I could realize that it was a trap, more guards entered the room and, pointing a sword at me, they took away the dagger that I always carried under my tunic.

Then into the room walked Argus, Harpalus and Erigyius, Monimus behind them.

TWENTY-SIX

In this manner did Monimus deceive me. After the guards assured them that I was not armed any more, Argus came and examined me closely and made me take off the top of my tunic, which covered my head as well, and though he had some doubt in his mind initially whether I was Seleucus, son of Nicanor, after examining my eyes closely, he nodded his head with great pleasure and proclaimed that I was indeed Seleucus. And then Harpalus too identified me as Seleucus, though I had met him just once, when he was pretending to be insane. And Erigyius, who had interacted extensively with me in Asia and whose estate I had bought, said: 'He is the person to whom all of us sold our properties. The person who pretended to be Demetrius the trader.'

Argus was delighted that he had finally caught me.

'I wouldn't have recognized him if he had walked past me in Delphi,' said Argus.

Harpalus and Erigyius also claimed that my appearance had changed even from the time I had met them in Asia. Then each of them started claiming credit for having caught me, saying that Alexander would be pleased to learn the next day that the chief conspirator in the death of Philip had been captured. Monimus, who only then understood the importance of my capture, gasped on hearing this.

'If this is indeed the case and Seleucus is responsible for the death of Philip, then I will personally hand him over to Alexander, as it is through my efforts that he has been trapped,' proclaimed Monimus.

'No, I shall take him to the Macedonian encampment immediately, for I fear that Seleucus has accomplices who will try to rescue him. We can keep him most secure amongst the Macedonian soldiers,' said Argus.

But Monimus opposed this course of action, presumably because he thought that the entire credit for capturing me alive would go to Argus and so would any reward from Alexander. Therefore he proposed that I stay in his custody till Alexander arrived the next day to attend the meeting of the Delphian league and then he would proceed with a heavy escort of bodyguards to Alexander's dwelling and hand me over. This proposition of his met with stiff resistance from Argus and an argument ensued, during the course of which they impressed on each other the pivotal role each had played in my capture. This was how I learned of the manner in which I had been captured.

When Argus first approached Delphi, he decided not to enter the town for fear of being seen by me. He sent Harpalus instead, to enquire of Monimus why he had asked the questions that he had of the Pythia. The first time, Monimus sent him away, saying that he didn't answer the questions of strangers. The second time, Argus sent Harpalus with a letter from Thapacus, son of Odon, who was the leader of the Macedonian delegation to the Delphian league, asking for an explanation as to why the golden talents that he had offered to the temple of Apollo on the day of his offering had turned out to be deficient.

Apparently, the coins of Monimus, which were supposed to be minted in pure gold, had lost their lustre and it had become apparent that Monimus had only got the coins plated on the outside with gold. Thapacus demanded an explanation for this from Monimus. Seeing that he had been exposed, Monimus begged forgiveness, as he knew that if the news got out, the Siphnians and he would never be trusted again in Delphi and their treasuries would be under scrutiny for fraud.

It was the chief priest Busiris who had informed Thapacus about this matter and he in turn had passed on the information to Argus, knowing that he was investigating the conduct of Monimus with the oracle. Monimus had then told Harpalus that he had paid a bribe to the Pythia and the authorities through a person who called himself Demetrius and that the person had then made it possible for him to make his dedication on the day of the oracle and he still owed this person twenty-five talents. Argus, suspecting that Demetrius and Seleucus were the same, arrived at Monimus's dwelling and asked him what I looked like and how I spoke, and Monimus's answers convinced him that I was the person he was looking for.

He then instructed Monimus to send a message to me to come and collect the remainder of the sum I was owed. And when I arrived, they watched me initially through a hole in the wall and, convinced that it was I and not one of my staff, they revealed themselves. This was how I had been captured.

But I personally think that my fault lay not in having examined the talents that Monimus had given me as an advance more closely, for that would have revealed to me that the talents he was distributing were fake and alerted me to his character. Monimus boasted to Argus that, for all my smartness, he had fooled me by delivering a worthless advance to me, consisting of bronze talents plated with gold. When Argus asked him whether the golden rams he had offered as dedication were also of a similar nature, Monimus insisted that they were of pure gold and only as much metal was mixed in them as was necessary to give gold the required hardness. In this manner did they continue talking till it was well past the time that I was expected outside by my men, who thus came to the conclusion that I had been deceived and trapped.

To prolong my stay at Monimus's dwelling, I addressed him thus: 'King of Siphnos, I have no quarrel with you. But if you aid the Macedonians in their evil plans, the wrath of Apollo will be upon you, for you deceived the temple with your offering. And even the wrath of Athena will be upon you because you hindered the Massalians in their intent to instal the statue of Athena on the day of the oracle. You also deceived me without cause and, though I forgive you, these people from Macedonia whom you now consider your friends will always think of you as someone they cannot trust, seeing how easily you deceive the Gods and betray the people whom you make pacts with. Therefore I entreat you to let me go and not heed Argus, for he is a murderer. Look at the choices you have. If you let me go, you will have done the right thing, but if you help these men, you will have the momentary satisfaction of having helped King Alexander. Believe me, the only reward you will get is the reward of being enslaved under his rule. Look at Erigyius, whom Argus has brought along to hunt for me. I saved him in Asia when he was to be executed by a mercenary chief for having betrayed the people who paid his wages. I then paid him a handsome sum to purchase his estate in Macedonia, which I was under no obligation to do, as they had agreed to hand over the claims to their estates free of charge to me. Now, this very man is partnering the murderer Argus, who killed my father through deceit, to hand me over to Alexander, so they can win his favour and obtain gifts. Therefore think, great king, and do what your heart tells you to do.'

Argus then asked Erigyius whether it was true that I had bought his estate and, since I looked intently at him, he couldn't lie, but he said that the documents were signed by him under duress, for he and the other exiles had feared for their lives. But he agreed that I had helped him and the other exiles and taken care of their needs as noblemen and done more for them than could be expected from a total stranger.

But, he also added, at that time, he had no idea that I was Alexander's sworn enemy and was Nicanor's son. He ended by saying that once he and the other exiles, except for Nearchus and Naxos, had come to know that I was involved in the conspiracy behind the assassination of Philip, they had offered their services to Alexander to track me down under the leadership of Argus.

Then, to keep Monimus confused, I turned on Erigyius.

'I accuse you, Erigyius, of being the lover of Olympias and of having planned the assassination of Philip with the help of Harpalus. And I challenge you to deny that you are not a cousin of Olympias and a lover of hers since many years,' I said.

Hearing this truth, the face of Erigyius turned red and he was rendered speechless.

Then Argus, sensing that events were going differently from what he intended, interrupted by hitting me on my head with the handle of his sword and saying: 'Stop your lies, you impudent stooge of Athens, or you will lose your head this instance and I shall myself present it to Alexander with great pleasure. As for you, Monimus, I am losing patience now and order you to let us go with this assassin or I shall report your conduct to Thapacus and King Alexander and their wrath will be more damaging to you than anything I would do.'

It was a mistake on Argus's part to have addressed Monimus thus, for he was the king of the Siphnians and his bodyguards were listening to all that was being said. Monimus asked Erigyius first whether it was true that he was a lover of Olympias, for the fact intrigued and amused him. Erigyius did not reply, though his face conceded that there was truth in my accusation. Harpalus, seeing Erigyius discomfited, said that the relationship between Olympias and Erigyius was their private matter and had nothing to do with the present circumstances.

At this moment, the bodyguards of Monimus informed him that two envoys had come from Lycargus and sought to convey a message regarding the delegate meeting of the Delphian council. Monimus ordered them in and, before Argus could hide me from the envoys, they entered the room. And they were Phanus and Phormio himself!

Though I was surprised to see them both, I didn't let the surprise show. Phanus, you will remember, was the bodyguard of Mazus who had accompanied Luminas and me to Lesbos and had stayed back in Lesbos to help Queen Morai. Monimus and the Macedonians were amazed at his size. Phanus was a Persian, but so long as he did not speak, he looked like a Greek from one of the Ionian cities. Phormio, my partner, addressed Monimus thus: 'Great king of Siphnos, the message that I carry from Lycargus is that your treasury at the temple has been robbed and the golden rams have disappeared. However, Athenian hoplites have caught the robbers and have recovered six of the ten rams, besides other artefacts. Lycargus requests your presence at his camp to examine the recovered objects immediately and claim what is yours.'

When Monimus heard Phormio speak thus, he turned ashen and cursed the robbers and decided to proceed immediately to the Athenian camp. But then Phormio said: 'Lycargus also advises that, though you are welcome to come, it might be more prudent to send a man who recognizes your treasures best, along with as many guards as you can send, for the robbers who have been caught claim that the rest of the loot is in a wood not far from here. Lycarugus suggests that, though he could provide you with guides, it is best that you send your own forces to recover your goods. For, he says, the Siphnians will strive harder for their own property than people of other states. Also, if you went yourself, my lord, word might get out about the robbery and others might lay their hands on the treasures the robbers have stolen.'

Monimus thought over what Phormio had said and, agreeing with Lycargus's advice, he ordered twenty of his bodyguards to leave for the Athenian camp immediately and report to Lycargus. When they had left and only four guards remained with Monimus – the others being in a camp a little way off – Phormio unsheathed his sword with great speed and placed it at Monimus's throat.

'Have Seleucus released or your neck will soon be without a head,' said Phormio.

Surprised by this sudden manoeuvre of Phormio, the remaining four bodyguards of Monimus took out their swords and started circling him. 'Watch him, watch him,' muttered Monimus to his bodyguards. He was getting very nervous.

At a certain point, Argus started to draw his sword. But Phanus proved too quick for him. He hit him a blow across his chest and Argus sprawled on the floor.

Seeing the physical strength of Phanus, Harpalus and Erigyius ran to hide behind Monimus's bodyguards, who drew their swords and started circling both Phormio and Phanus.

As no one threatened me now, I snatched Argus's sword from his waist and slashed him across his face and he started howling. Then I addressed Monimus thus: 'I had told you, great king, that you would come to grief if you assisted these Macedonian dogs. Call off your guards and you might still live.'

Monimus motioned for his guards to make way for me. Phanus then grabbed a spear from one of the guards and impaled Harpalus on it, and the spear went through his heart and lungs, for he started vomiting blood and was dead almost instantaneously. He then pulled the spear out from Harpalus's chest and the Macedonian slumped to the ground. Seeing this, Erigyius put down his sword and begged forgiveness, even though he hid behind Monimus's guards. These guards were tall and strong and only held back because Phormio's sword was at the throat of their king, and if they tried to harm us, they knew Monimus would surely die. Also, the size of Phanus had put fear in all the guards and Monimus himself. After he killed Harpalus so effortlessly, the guards had moved back ten paces from him.

I then stood over Argus, who lay on the floor clutching his face, and addressed him thus: 'Argus, you shall die at my hands shortly. Let Monimus be witness to your death and let him carry the news to Alexander and tell him that I have a long memory. Let Monimus tell him that you died like a dog at my feet and there was nothing that the great Alexander could do to save you. I kill you now, for having murdered my father Nicanor, as I have killed Leon, Alcidas and Polemon. If you have to say anything in your defence, then say it now and I shall listen.'

As I stood over him, Argus suddenly moved with great speed and, taking out a dagger from under his tunic, he dug it deep into my left thigh. Phanus, seeing the movement, impaled Argus with his spear before he could strike me another time. He ran the spear through him and picked him up in the air and stuck the point of the spear on a wall.

Even though I was in great pain myself and was losing blood, I remember shouting at Argus. He was twitching on the spear, and the more he twitched, the more blood flowed from his wound.

'Like you, your friends too shall die the death of dogs,' I said to him.

Argus made as if to say something, but he didn't have the strength. His blood dripped on the floor and mingled with the blood flowing rapidly from my thigh. That is the last I remember of the incident, for after that I lost consciousness. I learned later that Phormio carried me on his back out of Monimus's dwelling, even as the rest of my men gathered around me and formed a defence. In this manner they got me out of Delphi and to Thebes.

TWENTY-SEVEN

My escape from Monimus and Argus was miraculous for a variety of reasons. There was the unanticipated presence of Phanus in Delphi. He had been sent there from Lesbos by Queen Morai to seek an oracle from the Pythia about a rebellion brewing in her territories. Phormio himself was coming from Athens to Delphi, carrying a message from Agos for me. And it was while Otanes was proceeding to seek the help of the Massalian chief to have me rescued that he chanced upon both and, after introducing them to each other, he advised Phormio of my predicament. Phormio, realizing the gravity of the situation, made the plan for my rescue in consultation with Menicus and Otanes. It was Menicus who came up with the idea of saying that the Siphnian treasury had been robbed, to entice the bulk of Monimus's bodyguards away from his dwelling.

When I regained consciousness, I was in a wagon on my way to Thebes with a physician from the camp of the Massalians tending to me. As the path was uneven, every jolt travelled to my thigh and caused me to moan in pain. Phormio explained to me that the blade of Argus's dagger had broken off in my thigh and the physician had removed it. As a result, I had lost more blood. But they were now taking me to Thebes as there was a famous female physician there by the name of Agnodice who was an expert in treating wounds caused by weapons.

When I reached Thebes, they took me to where Athele and my son Zanylos were staying and Athele started crying when she saw me, for my body was burning with fever and I had turned weak due to the loss of blood. Phormio said that there was iron still in my thigh. When Agnodice arrived, she opened up my wound again while four people held me still, and with her deft fingers she removed the piece of iron. Then she cauterized the wound with burning iron, as she said that merely stitching it up could cause a swelling and perhaps the only way out then would be amputating the leg. She applied herbs like one would on a burn and applied some potions and then gave me wine with opium to mitigate the pain.

In this manner did she treat me for a month, by applying salves and herbs that hastened the healing of the wound. Agnodice said that if I had delayed in coming to her by even one day, I would have lost the use of my leg, as the wound would have festered and then no herb could have cured it.

My strength returned soon, however, and I was able to deal with matters that required my attention while lying in bed. Agos had sent a message that Brazus, the commander of Babylon, and Tabulus, the chief of the Immortals, had joined hands against Omares. They had been jealous when Omares achieved dining privileges with Artaxerxes and now, fearful that he would get close to the new king, Darius, they had come together to conspire against him. Among other things, they had denied to Darius that twenty thousand talents had been promised to Seleucus, son of Nicanor, for the killing of Philip of Macedonia. However, Agos mentioned in his message that Darius awaited the arrival of the monsters that Artaxerxes had ordered and the demonstration of which the former king had seen at Sardis just before he was taken ill and died. Darius had expressed a desire to watch the demonstration too, when he was next in Sardis.

Upon reaching Thebes, I had sent Menicus to Macedonia, so that he could keep me updated with news of Alexander, and messages flew back and forth between us in the following weeks. In the spring, he sent word that Alexander was proceeding to Illyria with his armies. After successfully visiting Delphi and later Athens, he had called for a meeting of representatives to Corinth and was appointed captain-general of the league. There, he had formally requested all the assembled Greeks for the right to command the campaign against Persia. The only people who refused his request were the Lacedaemonians since their tradition prohibited them from serving under a commander of another state.

Alexander first moved against the Illyrians and the Triballi, as he desired to secure the troublesome kingdoms bordering Macedonia before he ventured onward for his Persian campaign.

Agos had already sent word from Asia that he had claimed credit on my behalf for the Macedonians' departure from Abydos. And Omares had claimed an even bigger share of the credit by launching an attack just when the Macedonians under Parmenio were leaving Abydos, and everyone then got the impression that they had left because of the ferocity of his attack. When news of this reached Darius, he commended Omares for his bravery and that was when Omares requested again that old commitments made by Artaxerxes be fulfilled by the new king, as otherwise 'those that Persia employed for the security of her realm' would lose faith in the empire.

Darius then sanctioned five thousand talents as payment for the assassination of Philip, which Omares finally convinced him had been the handiwork of the secret emissary from Athens, that is, Seleucus, son of Nicanor. Out of the five thousand talents, Omares kept two thousand for himself and turned over the rest to Agos. Darius also expressed the desire to see me, but was informed that I was recovering from injuries and would come as soon as my health permitted.

As reports from Menicus came frequently, brought by messengers who went back and forth, it became apparent that Alexander was an even better commander than Philip as far as ingenuity was concerned and his men were beginning to look up to him with increasing confidence. After Illyria, he proceeded against the Triballians and then the Getae, who inhabited the land across the Danube.

On the banks of the Danube, Alexander offered sacrifices to Zeus the saviour and Heracles and thanked the river for allowing him passage. In this, he was different from Philip, for though Philip worshipped the Gods and offered sacrifices, they were few and far between, whereas Alexander made it a point to honour the Gods before every engagement, big or small. Sometimes he offered libations in the privacy of his tent and sometimes, to boost the morale of his troops, he offered them in full view of his soldiers.

Alexander also established the policy of distributing spoils at a very early stage. In the campaign against the Thracians, he ordered his officers to take all the booty captured to the coastal towns and there have it distributed. When it came to women, the policy was that the officers would choose first from amongst the women who had been captured, and after they had done so, the hoplites could take their pick in a hierarchical manner, the choice first falling to the unit whose bravery had most helped achieve victory. And the men who captured the women were supposed to make provisions for them out of their own pay. Because of this, the men kept only as many women as they could afford in their travelling retinue.

A few weeks later, Menicus sent a message that he had been wounded by an arrow and was therefore resting in Thrace, but he had heard from a traveller who claimed to be certain of the fact that Alexander had been grievously wounded in battle by the Taulantians and had died two days later. I conveyed this message immediately to Demosthenes by an express messenger on horseback, with a cautionary note that he should wait till the news was confirmed by the Macedonians themselves or some other source. But Demosthenes pounced on the information and announced the death of Alexander in his northern campaign as an irrefutable fact. In Thebes, this provoked the leaders of the Theban exiles, Orchimandus and Thamotus, to lead a rebellion against the government, of which Amyntas and Timolaus were the main representatives.

Orchimandus and Thamotus slipped into the city at night and murdered Amyntas and Timolaus and then surrounded the Cadmeia, which housed the Macedonian garrison. After they had done this, they announced to the Theban assembly the news of the death of Alexander and incited them to throw off the Macedonian yoke from Thebes and all of Greece. Having aroused the assembly into a lust for freedom, they sent messages soliciting support from the Aetolians, Acarnanians, Ambraciots, Athenians, Arcadians, Eleians and the Argives.

Demosthenes at this time conveyed to me that he had received a secret letter of support from the Macedonian general Attalus, confirming the death of Alexander and encouraging him to organize a revolt in Athens and wherever else he was capable of, and assuring him that Attalus himself would then move against Antipater in Pella and open a front in the rear of Alexander's army! Since the death of Philip, rebellion had secretly been brewing in the Greek states, and with the news of Alexander's death travelling like fire, all the forces who hated the Macedonian rule began the task of recovering their freedom.

The Thebans locked all the gates of the city and forbade people to leave unless they were messengers of the state and, even though I had desired to leave the city with Athele, Zanylos and my men, I was told to go back to my dwelling and test my fate with the rest of the city's population. The Thebans feared that if people started deserting the city, there would be no one left to defend it.

Orchimandus and Thamotus then organized the digging of trenches and heavy stockades all around the Cadmeia. The Macedonians in the Cadmeia under Philotas, observing the preparations of the Thebans, thickened the walls of their fortifications and collected all manner of objects that they could use as missiles.

On the second day after the murder of Amyntas and Timolaus, I went to meet Orchimandus and said to him that confrontation with the

Macedonians may not be the best way forward. I said to him: 'It may not be wise to adopt such a course of confrontation with the Macedonians, for wisdom does not lie in fighting for freedom in a situation where, even if we defeat a Macedonian contingent, we would have won just one battle and the Macedonians could summon reserves swiftly. And if we lose, it won't be just the lives of the soldiers that we forfeit, but also those of our families and our dependants, besides our homes and hearth and all else that we hold dear in this city.'

For, I argued, if the Macedonians won, they would fall upon the city with all their wrath and make an example of it. Therefore, I said, prudence lay in preparing for a battle away from Thebes, so that even if it didn't go according to plan, they could at least retreat to the shelter of their city and make a second stand if needed. I ended by saying that Orchimandus should not mistake my arguments for lack of courage, for I hated the Macedonians as much as the Thebans did, if not more, and I had fought alongside the Sacred Band at Chaeronea. Orchimandus, of course, thought me to be an ordinary citizen of Eleia who now worked in Athens and had business in Asia. Fearing the Macedonian spies, I was lying low while recuperating and was going by the name of Demetrius.

But Orchimandus was not influenced by what I told him, being blinded by the news of Alexander's death and his success against Amyntas and Timolaus. Instead, he questioned my antecedents and rebuked me for spreading a mood of pessimism in the city.

After Orchimandus rejected my arguments and insisted on proceeding on the path to doom, I approached Thamotus, hoping that if I managed to convince him of my reasoning, he would overrule Orchimandus. But Thamotus, after giving me a patient hearing, compared notes with Orchimandus and concluded that I was an agent of the Macedonians trying to subvert their preparations for war. They then made enquiries about me and confined my wife Athele and son Zanylos in the precincts of the Theban Zeus, so that I would stand up and fight alongside them, knowing that otherwise it would be the death of my family.

So, shortly after I had sent the message to Demosthenes informing him of the demise of Alexander, all these unexpected events occurred. At this time, I was also bereft of help, for the Thebans had commissioned all the aliens and refugees present in Thebes to man the palisades around the Cadmeia. They had set up guards at crucial points around the fortifications and also perimeter defences away from the city, which they themselves manned. Tyros and Otanes had been drafted by the forces around the Cadmeia for digging trenches – they spared me since I was still limping from the wound in my thigh, though I had been gaining strength by exercising in the gymnasium.

The Thebans were currently blinded by their hatred of the Macedonians, specially since the Macedonian garrison based at the Cadmeia and headed by Philotas had performed many high-handed acts during the past few months, such as settling property disputes in favour of the Macedonian partisans, and thus alienated the entire population. Keeping this in mind, I realized that I had to think of ways to increase the efficiency of the forces within Thebes, so that they were better able to face the Macedonian assault, which I saw as inevitable even without Alexander. Therefore I approached Uranus, a Theban hoplite with some say in matters, whom I had befriended by gifting some equipment to the gymnasium of which he was manager. I asked him to convey a message from me to Demosthenes and Pythagoras in Athens.

He was to tell Pythagoras to send as many weapons and heavy armour as he could to Thebes, as a significant number of men were still without proper weaponry. Then I told him to tell Demosthenes to muster as many Athenian men as he could to come to Thebes to fight alongside the Thebans, for, without a sizeable army, Thebes was doomed. I told him to tell the Athenians that the Theban exiles had exhorted the population to make war at all costs and needed to be supported.

I then stamped my personal seal on both the messages, so that Demosthenes and Pythagoras would not doubt their genuineness. Uranus, convinced of the merit of the messages, at once set forth with another instructor, though Orchimandus and Thamotus objected to his leaving, alleging that he was slipping away from Thebes under the guise of getting aid from Athens. They could do nothing about it, however, as Uranus had a substantial and powerful following amongst the Theban athletes.

Two days later, Uranus returned from Athens and reported that Pythagoras had furnished him with heavy armour and weapons to equip over a thousand hoplites. Pythagoras had diverted to Thebes supplies meant for the mercenaries in Asia and Uranus had brought the armoury in twenty wagons that Pythagoras provided. The Thebans were overjoyed when they received this armour, for it allowed them to increase their manpower. When Uranus informed his athletes that it was my initiative and personal funding that had made the weapons and armour possible, they were quick to honour me, but this annoyed Orchimandus and

Thamotus, who, apart from giving speeches, had not done anything of substance so far.

After Demosthenes got my letter, he produced a soldier in Athens who claimed that he had been injured in the same battle at Illyria in which Alexander had been fatally wounded. He also claimed that the Macedonians had kept this news secret while they pursued other enemies in the north to prevent any rebellion in the Greek territories. After this, more support was garnered for the Thebans in their revolt, as the Athenians felt safer to come to the aid of Thebes once they were assured that Alexander was dead. All this, Uranus witnessed and informed me. Where Demosthenes suddenly produced this soldier from, I don't know, but I certainly doubted his story because the message I had got from Menicus had stated that Alexander had been wounded in the battle againt the Tautalians and not the Illyrians.

After Demosthenes made his speeches exhorting the Athenians to seize the opportunity and strike a blow against Macedonian hegemony, another Athenian orator by the name of Phocion advised prudence. He said that it would be better for Athens to collect all its soldiery at one place and wait to see the outcome of the Theban rebellion and advance to the aid of Thebes only when they were sure that the Thebans had the upper hand. The Athenian assembly then came to the conclusion, specially since Pythodelus, the archon of Athens, also supported Phocion's position, that they would just wait and watch and not proceed directly to the aid of Thebes.

When the soldiers from the Peloponnese came to know of the Athenian position, they too sent their hoplites only as far as the Isthmus and told them to await further orders. In this way did two major allies apply caution and desert Thebes.

At this time, I got news that overturned Menicus's earlier message. In this message, he said that Alexander was very much alive and, learning of the Theban revolt, was travelling with his armies to Thebes to oversee matters himself, apprehensive that the other Greek states might start taking inspiration from Thebes to create trouble for him all over Hellas. Menicus apologized for his original message and said that he had been deceived about Alexander's death and, in his excitement to deliver the news quickly to me in Thebes, he had not checked the veracity of the report. He said that he was still recovering from his injury and so was travelling slowly behind the army of Alexander, which had already crossed Boeotia. They were headed for Onchestus and were looking for a place with water for their army to camp, he said.

Alarmed by the news, I immediately went to Orchimandus and Thamotus and apprised them of this new development. Not wanting them to disregard me this time, I took Uranus and his athletes along with me. When they heard that Alexander was not only alive but marching towards Thebes, they immediately dismissed the information as false. They said that my messengers must have been misled by the fact that a man by the name of Alexander had taken over the armies of Macedonia, but that was Alexander, son of Aerop. When Uranus asked them how they had come by this information and, more importantly, why they had not shared it with the rest of the citizens, they said that they had themselves just heard the news and were waiting to announce it at the assembly!

At the assembly, the Theban exiles again roused the members with big words like 'liberty' and 'autonomy' and spread the lie that the Alexander heading towards them was Aerop's son and not the son of Philip. In this manner did they manage to get a resolution passed unanimously that the city would fight the Macedonians for its freedom.

But when news came that Alexander had passed Thermopylae and was headed towards Iolaus, the Thebans started having doubts. Seeing them flag in confidence a little and fearing that there would be total annihilation if they persisted in pursuing bravery instead of wisdom, I turned to a person by the name of Euriphides, who was the father of one of the athletes in Uranus's gymnasium. This athlete had drawn my attention to the fact that his father had predicted, before the ancestral oracle at Thebes had done so, that the spider's web in the southern part of the temple of Demeter, on which no spider had been seen for two months, indicated a big future loss for the city. It was only after he had spoken thus that the oracle at Thebes had said: 'The woven web is bane to one, to one a boon.'

While the oracular response had come after the Theban exiles took over the city, Euriphides had made his prediction two month ago, said the athlete. So I went out to meet Euriphides with the intention of getting Uranus to produce him before the assembly to counterbalance the foolish epidemic of bravery, which was devoid of all rationality.

Euriphides turned out to be a hoplite who had been blinded at the battle in Chaeronea and since then had developed powers to divinate. He clutched my hands once he heard my voice and, before I could ask him anything, he said: 'There will be blood everywhere and I am glad that I am blind so I will be spared the sights of plunder and ravaging. If, in the next forty-eight hours, a delegation is not sent to Alexander expressing remorse, the city will be razed to the ground.'

Hearing these dire predictions, Uranus was terrified and so was I. Euriphides had earlier asked his son, the athlete, to check the colours of the spider's web when light first touched the insides of the temple in the morning. He wished to know if the web took on the colours of a rainbow. And when his son had gone and observed the phenomenon the next day, he had found that the spider's web did indeed adopt the colours of a rainbow. So, now, Euriphides told us that the colouration implied that troubles of different hues would afflict Thebes and the fact that no spider could be located on the web meant that even animals would desert the place after disaster struck.

Uranus immediately took Euriphides to the assembly and he repeated his prediction based on what he had been told. He also said that every morning, for the past three days, he had felt a heaviness of the heart, similar to how he had felt on the morning of the battle of Chaeronea, and it implied that a big disaster loomed for everyone around him. After he spoke thus, Orchimandus and Thamotus were upset with Uranus for having produced Euriphides before the assembly without their permission, but Uranus scolded them by saying that everyone had a right to put forward their views before the assembly.

At this point, a group of Thebans came forward. They had just returned from Delphi and they claimed to have seen bloodstains on the roof of the temple which the Thebans had dedicated there. They said the bloodstains could be seen even from the hillside and, when one of them got on the roof and rubbed with his fingers, it was ascertained that they were genuine bloodstains. They washed the stains away on the instruction of the priests, but the next day they reappeared and the oracle at Delphi then said that those whose blood the Thebans had shed and whose property they had displayed in the temple as spoils of war would soon seek their revenge along with some others. This, the group told the assembly and, as they finished their story, a youth came running to the assembly and shouted that all the statues in the marketplace at Thebes were sweating. Euriphides, who was still there, said with great calm that this signified that overwhelming disaster would befall the city.

Hearing these portents all at once, the elders in the assembly opined that the fate of Thebes should not be risked on the battlefield. A more prudent approach should be taken and a dialogue should be initiated with Alexander and his pardon sought. But Orchimandus and Thamotus and the other exiles stood up and said with great certainty that matters had progressed too far and a pardon could not be expected from Alexander. In their opinion, no humane treatment could be expected from the Macedonian king at this point.

The exiles felt that even if Thebes offered terms of truce and apologized for its rebellion, Alexander would still demand their heads for having started the uprising. They then started beating drums and cymbals and blowing horns and played all kinds of rousing music, exhorting the populace to prepare for war against Alexander. They recalled the Theban victories at Leuctra and Manitea and the exploits of the Sacred Band and their great general Epamonidas and said that all the portents that seemed to prophecy the destruction of Thebes signalled, in fact, the end of Alexander. In this manner they marshalled the emotions of the populace and the city decided to go to war.

Seeing that there was no way out, except war, I pleaded with the exiles to let my wife and son leave the city, but they flatly refused permission, as they wanted all hands to man the palisades. They repeated that even if one woman or child left the city, it could create an epidemic of departures. Besides, they claimed that men would fight best knowing that if they lost, their families would be slaughtered.

When I enquired from the exiles how many of them had families in Thebes, they kept quiet, and it was later revealed to me by Uranus that the majority of them had sent their families to Athens when they were first exiled by the Macedonian partisans.

The atmosphere in the city was getting foul and, though the Thebans had not lost courage, there was an impending sense of doom, as if they battled the Gods themselves. Though they would do the best that they could to defend their city, they felt now that it would not be enough. That was when Tyros brought news that while he had been posted at the outermost perimeter defences in full view of the Macedonian camp, he had seen Piros enter the Macedonian camp with ten soldiers and with them, as prisoner, was Menicus. He was sure that it was Menicus because when he shouted a greeting, Menicus looked at him and nodded, but he was taken away inside the camp quickly.

Now, if you remember, this Piros was the same Macedonian who had been in Antipater's employ and managed his treasury. He had been helping Antipater to conduct a human sacrifice at the instructions of the

Egyptian priests and it was from there that I had rescued Menicus, Tyros and Otanes. I suspected that while Menicus was following Alexander's army, Piros must have spotted him and, as he was not in the best of health, had seized him as a prisoner. I was disturbed by this news, as I was worried that Alexander would have Menicus tortured to find out where I was. And once he knew that I was in Thebes, he would discard any conciliatory approach towards the city and might even force the Thebans to give me up in return for pardoning them.

In the morning, things took a turn for the worse. The Macedonians hung up the body of Menicus outside the outermost palisade and proclaimed that he was a Theban agent working on behalf of his master Seleucus, better known as the son of Nicanor. A herald then approached the Theban lines and announced on behalf of Alexander that he was prepared to forgive the rebellion of the Thebans if they handed over Orchimandus, Thamotus and Seleucus, son of Nicanor, to them.

The Thebans conferred animatedly amongst themselves as to who this 'son of Nicanor' was. The elders to whom everyone turned for an answer said that they wouldn't hand over either Orchimandus or Thamotus to the Macedonians, as that would be a betrayal, and since the two had only voiced what all of them felt, it would be unfair to single them out for punishment. Besides, they said, knowing how untrustworthy the Macedonians were, even if their demands were fulfilled, they might still attack the city.

A herald was then sent to the outer palisade and he announced to the Macedonians that if they wanted Orchimandus and Thamotus, they would have to come and get them. He further said that as for 'the son of Nicanor', they had no idea who he was.

After a brief pause, a Macedonian herald got up on one of their siege machines and announced that Alexander would be satisfied with just the 'son of Nicanor' and that the Thebans could keep Orchimandus and Thamotus, provided they were exiled from Thebes. If they did that, the herald finished, Alexander was willing to pardon all. On hearing this message, the Thebans again huddled together and discussed whether anybody knew anything about this 'son of Nicanor' and speculated whether it was the same person who had won the quadragi in Olympia.

At this point, a Theban got up and, pointing at me, said that I was Seleucus, son of Nicanor, and everyone turned and looked at me with great curiosity. I remembered the Theban as one of Boridas's men who had helped us in the raid at Antipater's house.

To tell you the truth, I was getting to the point where I would have announced my real identity to the Thebans, but now that one of Boridas's men had done so, I kept quiet and waited patiently for whatever fate had in store for me. The man then went on to say that I was the one who had planned a raid at Antipater's dwelling in Athens, along with Boridas, who had later disappeared. Hearing this, the audience burst into applause and Orchimandus, fearing that elements in the crowd might again point to Thamotus and him as the principal architects of the danger they were in, proceeded to say that the Thebans would not be so cowardly as to hand over somebody so brave. Then he admonished me for not having revealed my identity earlier to them.

Getting a chance to speak in front of everyone, I spoke thus: 'Thebans, I value your friendship and, as your well-wisher, I advise you to hand me over to Alexander, for I think that will assuage his anger. I shall willingly go over to the Macedonians, provided you let my men escort my wife and child out of Thebes, for my only worry is about their safety. Though I might appear young, I am old between the ears and have troubled the Macedonians more than any man alive and Alexander desires revenge against me for the various wrongs I have committed against them for over two years. The man that they have hung beyond the palisades is Menicus, a loyal friend of mine. It was Alexander's thirst for revenge that made him kill Menicus and now, having come to know that I reside in Thebes, he seeks me and nobody else. Therefore allow me to go to him as he wishes.'

Before the elders could respond to what I had said, Uranus got up and countered my argument thus: 'Seleucus, or son of Nicanor, or whatever name you go by, we appreciate your spirit of sacrifice but make no mistake, we do not wish to avoid a battle with the Macedonians. We would not want peace with the Macedonians at the cost of continued subjugation. And so, do not blame yourself or feel that you have brought this upon us, for we have travelled this road with open eyes and in spite of the portents that warned us of dire consequences. We cannot agree to your going over to the Macedonians, for we cannot have it said that the mighty Thebans, with soldiers as fearless as the Sacred Band, hid behind a single man when the Macedonians marched upon them. We do not promise that we can protect your life if you fight with us, but we certainly will not send you to your death to save our own skins.'

When Uranus finished speaking, the rest of the Thebans endorsed his view and the elders said that no one except Demosthenes could have spoken better. And then someone cursed Demosthenes for not having sent soldiers as promised. Afterwards, the Theban herald replied in this manner to the Macedonians: 'Although Seleucus, son of Nicanor, is with us and wishes to walk across and meet Alexander, we, the Thebans, will not let it be said that we gave up a person who never harmed us to save our own lives. Therefore do what you will.'

A hushed silence fell, which was broken by the Macedonian herald, who addressed the Thebans thus across the palisades: 'King Alexander wishes to say that he is disappointed at the Theban refusal to hand over Seleucus, son of Nicanor. He also announces that any Theban who wishes to have his life spared can now walk across and live in peace like the rest of the Greeks. The others will face dire consequences.'

The Theban herald responded spiritedly on the instruction of the elders: 'The Thebans wish to announce that any Macedonian who desires to get rid of his king and free Greece of its tyrant is welcome to join us.'

Apparently, Alexander became furious at this statement and came to the conclusion that the Thebans despised him beyond the possibility of reconciliation. But even before he could order any action, Perdicass, a Macedonian officer of the Guards, driven to rage by what the Theban herald had said, signalled the assault on Thebes on his own initiative, without waiting for Alexander's signal.

Thus began the ruin of Thebes.

TWENTY-EIGHT

Initially, when hostilities broke out against the Macedonians, the Thebans stationed me at the main gate beyond the second palisade. The men at the first palisade capitulated to the speed and brutality of the first attack, but by the time the Macedonian officer Perdicass arrived at the second palisade with his men, Uranus had rushed to fill the breach with his wrestlers, and here the two lines clashed with great vigour until Uranus speared Perdicass and his men became more concerned with saving him than in fighting their way forward. Orchimandus, intending to prevent the safe return of Perdicass to the Macedonian lines, moved forward with the exiles and cut off their route of exit. It was at this point that the Macedonian Amyntas came to the rescue of Perdicass by charging down the first palisade with his unit and engaging the Theban exiles, but though this diverted the attention of Orchimandus and his men from Perdicass, they soon started getting the better of Amyntas and that was when Alexander ordered the main body of his troops to move towards the gate to rescue both Perdicass and Amyntas.

The Cretan archers, led by their chief Eurybotas, then moved in along with the Agrianes, who were the most dangerous; they were the swiftest troops I had ever seen. The Thebans unleashed their missiles on the main body of the archers to stop their advance and the Macedonians took heavy casualties. A few of the Thebans ran and picked up bows and as many arrows as they could from the dead Cretans and rushed back to the gate, from where they started firing arrows at the leaders of the Macedonian units, aiming particularly at Eurybotas. Very soon, an arrow pierced the neck of Eurybotas and, seeing him fall, a thrill went through the Thebans and for a while they believed that they could win.

The Cretan archers were severely demoralized by the death of Eurybotas. All this while, Tyros, Otanes and I had stayed at the gate, throwing javelins at the Macedonians, but when the Theban elder who led the troops at the gate died from being struck by a javelin, I took over the gate. Summoning as many Thebans as I could, I set them the dangerous task of going to the front lines to collect javelins, those which were lying on the ground as well as those which had found their mark. For the Macedonians were so numerous that if it had not been for the barrage of javelins, they would have pressed forward with great speed and force.

With the recovered javelins, a fresh defence was mounted at the gates and it staved off the Macedonians and created some space for the Thebans to push forward with their reserve. This small reserve forced the Macedonians beyond the first palisade and, thus, whatever ground Perdicass had gained was won back by the Thebans. By then, more Macedonians had been killed than Thebans, and Alexander, watching this reversal and observing the retreat of the Macedonian phalanx, pressed forward his reserves in large numbers to replace the returning troops. This drew taunts from the Theban exiles, which not only infuriated the Macedonians but Alexander himself and, being thus provoked, he joined in the fray.

It was when I saw Alexander at the front that I rushed forward myself, in spite of my injury, to where Uranus stood with his wrestlers; both Tyros and Otanes tried to stop me, but just then, a fresh wave of Macedonian troops surged forward and an exhausted Uranus was felled before I could reach him. When I look back now on the events of that day, if I had to pick the turning point in the battle, it would be the death of Uranus. For it was his wrestlers who bore the brunt of the Macedonian phalanx and suddenly, with Uranus dead, they became rudderless and moved in different directions. This presented an opportunity for the Macedonian troops, already charged up because of Alexander's presence, and since they were not professional troops and had never been in battle, the wrestlers started to falter.

The Theban war veterans, who had been posted elsewhere as part of the cavalry, turned to rush back into the city when they came to know that the Macedonians had entered through the postern gate and, as they swept past, one of their horses knocked me unconscious. Tyros and Otanes managed to carry me with great difficulty to safety at a house near the main gate and threw water on my face to revive me, but when I remained unconscious, Tyros seized a horse from a Theban and, placing me in the middle, with Otanes at the back, he proceeded towards the rear of the city, where the Macedonians had not made their way yet, and escaped into the woods.

The Macedonians, rather than chase the Theban cavalry and infantry into the woods, fell upon the civilians and started a bloodbath in the city. The people of Thebes, bereft of the support of their soldiers and other fighting power, still harboured hopes of a victory and confronted their aggressors with broken swords or damaged spears or sticks – whatever they could lay their hands on – but it was a lost cause. The Macedonians did not spare even the women and children clinging to the statues of Gods and Goddesses. So determined were they to make Thebes an example for all of Greece that even infants were not spared. Yet, the Thebans showed remarkable character and not one man was seen begging for mercy for himself or his family. In the end, more than seven thousand Thebans were slaughtered and the Macedonians realized a sum of four hundred and twenty talents from selling thirty thousand Thebans into slavery.

Athele and Zanylos escaped the massacre with the help of the physician Agnodice, and for that I shall remain eternally grateful to her. She gave them shelter in the poet Pindar's house, where about twenty refugees had gathered, including members of Pindar's family, who were friends of Alexander. But when everyone was rounded up, the Macedonians spared Pindar's house from any retribution and also his family, but segregated the others and took them to the marketplace where slaves were being sold. Though they spared Agnodice the fate of a slave, as they needed her to treat their wounded, they disregarded her pleas on behalf of Athele and Zanylos.

In the meantime, the leader of the exiles, Orchimandus, was captured and brought before Alexander. Alexander blamed him for all that had happened and ordered his execution and instead of bearing his fate manfully, Orchimandus told Alexander that it would be a mistake to have him killed, as he knew where the family of Seleucus, son of Nicanor, was. When Alexander heard this, he wanted to know more and bade his men stay the execution.

But Orchimandus demanded that Alexander first promise him his life, and Alexander swallowed his revulsion for Orchimandus and gave him his word. Then Orchimandus was taken to the market square where all the Theban women were, and there he identified Athele and Zanylos like the coward that he was.

Alexander then had Athele brought forward and asked her who her husband was. She was too scared to speak, so he asked Philotas to interrogate her and he also told him to bring Zanylos to him.

He examined Zanylos closely, trying to determine if there was any resemblance to what he remembered of me from the time I had him under my sword.

Before any conclusion could be reached, however, Alexander asked Athele directly whether she was the wife of Seleucus, son of Nicanor, and Athele proudly replied that she was. Since the matter was settled, Alexander gave Orchimandus his freedom, but exiled him to Asia.

After Athele disclosed her identity, Alexander told Philotas to let her rejoin the Thessalians who had paid for her, but he whispered something in his ear and Philotas then carried Zanylos in his arms and took him to the Macedonian encampment. When she saw this, Athele started hurling abuses at Alexander for snatching her son away from her and even called him the son of a pig. The Thessalian who had bought her then dragged her by her hair to a nearby house and there Philotas and some other Macedonians ravaged her. When they had thus satisfied their lust, they took her to the well of Pindar's house and pushed her into it. Agnodice, who was there, cursed them all but they couldn't do anything to her, for not only had she got Alexander's pardon but she was also treating the wounds of Perdicass.

In this manner did the events at Thebes unfold. And in spite of all my efforts, I could get no information about Zanylos, my son – I didn't know whether he lived or died. All I knew was that it was Philotas who had taken him to the Macedonian encampment when Alexander's army was in Thebes.

TWENTY-NINE

After Alexander's departure from Greece, I waited till my leg had healed fully and then I returned with great haste to Abydos in Asia so that I would be there before Alexander's armies crossed the Hellspont, the strip of water that separates Europe from Asia. I intended to look for an opportunity to kill him after he set foot in Asia. However, there was no opportunity to kill him in Abydos as he never entered the city.

The soldiers said that Alexander slaughtered a bull halfway over the Hellespont and let the blood drip into the sea as an offering to Poseidon. From a golden cup he poured wine into the sea to keep the Nereids in good humour. Then, being in the first trireme, he threw his spear on the shore to claim Asia and, having donned full armour, he was the first person to disembark on the soil of Asia. At the exact point that he got out, he dedicated an altar to Zeus, Athena and Heracles, having made a similar altar at the place where he had left Sestus in Europe.

All this I heard the soldiers speak of at Alabanda's house in Abydos. I waited in the tunnel below for them to leave, standing next to the skeleton of Boridas. His clothes were rotting but still on him – I recognized him by the dagger that lay next to him. The rats had not disturbed it. There were three skeletons lying next to each other and more, perhaps, at the entrance of the tunnel near the port. After the soldiers left the house above, I lifted the trapdoor and emerged with Agos.

Agos and I had counted two hundred vessels sailing into Abydos. But the city itself was unoccupied. Parmenio had ravaged it when he left it after Philip's death and the Persians had not reoccupied it as it was infested with plague.

Alexander's soldiers had moved into the city to see if there was something left to pillage. Those soldiers who had been there before with Parmenio and Polemon took a detour through the city out of curiosity and narrated accounts of battles that had taken place within its fortifications to the new arrivals.

From Abydos, Alexander marched inland to Troy and the seer Mistros saw him there. After Miletus, son of Megacles, had taken his eyes out, Mistros had settled in Troy. I had known that Miletus had tortured Mistros for information about me, but not that he had blinded him.

At Troy, Alexander offered prayers and a sacrifice to Athena, who was the patron goddess of the city, and gave as a gift the suit of armour that he had donned when he set foot in Asia. The priests then offered him the shield of Achilles which still hung on the walls. Whether it was indeed the shield of Achilles, I do not know, for that war took place many hundreds of years ago, but since he claimed descent from Neoptolemus on his mother's side, Alexander was happy to receive the gift. He had it carried ahead of him in battle, and it was thus that he fought on the banks of the river Granicus. But that was some days later.

Alexander had noticed the blind Mistros while offering a sacrifice to Athena in the temple at Troy and asked the priests about his identity. He was told that he was a seer who had been blinded by order of Polemon for having helped Seleucus, son of Nicanor. This piqued his curiosity. The priests then told him that Mistros's gift of divination remained in spite of having been blinded and people came from far and near to ask him questions. Alexander then addressed Mistros directly and asked him how he came to be so and what vision he had regarding his life.

Mistros replied thus: 'I am thus by the will of Athena. And even though I am denied the sight of the world, I can see in my mind that Alexander, son of Philip, will be the harbinger of much blood.'

'Whose blood?' asked Alexander with great concern.

'Those that Athena will send in your opposition, King Alexander, and also those who travel with you now,' replied Mistros.

But Alexander was not impressed by this answer and lost interest in Mistros. He went on to lay flowers on the tomb of Achilles and called him a lucky man, for Achilles had had a poet like Homer to pen his brave deeds while he himself had none yet.

I met Mistros after Alexander and his armies had left Troy. Before I could even announce myself, he said: 'You come back in much sorrow, Seleucus. I had told you to leave for Asia once the king was dead, but you disregarded my advice. If you had listened, you would not be greaving thus.'

It was true. Mistros had told me to head east once the king had died, but I had ignored his advice because of my desire to visit my family in Athens before returning to Asia. That decision had started the chain of events leading to the massacre at Thebes.

'I am a mere mortal, Mistros. But I seek to know from you where my son Zanylos is, for he is being held by the Macedonians. I know not whether he lives or dies,' I said.

Mistros kept quiet. Then he said: 'A battle will come soon, next to a river, and your life will change again. He whom you seek will become your master. Things will change later, but for now it is better that you let him become your master.'

After this, he refused to say any more, but when I pressed him he added: 'Your questions will be answered by he who will come to you on top of a beast. Have patience.'

I mulled over Mistros's words as I proceeded to locate Omares. For many days, I had been seeking a meeting with Memnon of Rhodes after King Darius had appointed him the commander of the coast and the islands of the Aegean Sea that were in alliance with Persia, but he had been elusive. Now, however, the Persian satraps had called a meeting at Zeleia and Memnon would be present there. So Omares had informed me through Farisa, the Persian woman who had been on the mission with me to capture Polemon.

Farisa had brought a portion of my treasury, which had been kept in safe custody in Sardis, to pay the twenty thousand Greek mercenaries who were now headed by the Persian Omares. Their recruitment had been done at great speed and four thousand of them were Thebans who ached for revenge against Alexander's troops. But in spite of their numbers, I had no great hopes from them, as very few of them had battle experience similar to the troops of Alexander and the few who did had always been on the losing side. Hence, their instincts could not be relied upon in the battlefield.

But Zamos insisted that Pythagoras had trained them well before dispatching them. I had sent for Zamos once I arrived in Abydos and he had come with the news that Dorian would arrive with the monsters at Lesbos within three weeks and there he would await my instructions. At Lesbos, they would have the sanctuary of Queen Morai and the Persians had little influence there, even though they controlled the seas. Meanwhile, the Greek states waited anxiously for Alexander's first defeat, so that they could muster up the courage to rebel against Macedonia.

After Alexander had obtained leadership of the Corinthian league for his Persian campaign, King Darius had sent word stating his intention to recruit ten times the number of mercenaries that the Persians currently had with them. And after Darius had seen the demonstration of the monster arranged for him at Sardis by Omares, he had seen the possibilities of the weapon and harboured hopes of getting more before the coming battle with Alexander. For the successes of the Macedonian king in the northern campaign had removed doubts regarding his leadership and Darius too had come to the conclusion that he was a worthy son of Philip and not an upstart.

At the town of Zeleia, Memnon of Rhodes advised the Persian commanders that, rather than risk an engagement with Alexander before their armies could be organized properly, it would be better to burn all the crops, destroy the horse feeds, poison the wells and burn the towns in the region to make it difficult for Alexander to feed his men and horses. But Arsites, the satrap of northern Phrygia, said that he would not endorse the razing of even one single house in his domain and the Persian commanders Spithridates, Petines and Rhemithres agreed with his view. Omares was silent and so was the commander Arasmes. Memnon of Rhodes then countered that the other point not in favour of an engagement was the absence of Darius himself – for his bravery was well known in battle – specially as Alexander was himself present to boost the morale of his troops.

But Arsites dismissed this opinion of Memnon and so did Spithridates and Petines, for they suspected Memnon of wanting to hold on to his position for as long as he could by delaying the war. Memnon's motive was different, though: he believed that an engagement with Alexander would result in victory for the Macedonians and some of the blame for that would fall on him. The others, however, imagined that it would be easy to defeat Alexander.

After the meeting, Memnon of Rhodes sought me out and asked my opinion on the issue, even though it would not change the decision already taken. I told him that I would have waited till the monsters arrived and, after properly securing them, I would have sought out Alexander for an engagement. Alexander would not be able to counter the monsters with his phalanx; on the contrary, they would smash his phalanx to bits.

When Memnon heard of the monsters, he was impressed and desired to take them over. Believing Mistros's prophecy to mean that Memnon would be my new master since he was the one I had been seeking for the last month, I told him that my man Dorian was due to arrive in Methymyna in three weeks' time and, once the cargo arrived, we could think of where to land the monsters in Asia.

Though I had no desire to answer to Memnon, I had great trust in what Mistros had told me. Besides, he was the only Persian, apart from Darius, who had access to resources and it was he, through Omares, who paid for the mercenaries on behalf of Darius. And the different states on the coast paid an annual tribute to the Persian king through him.

My business with Memnon was to extract a higher price for the monsters as I had been told by Omares that there was no record in Darius's court of the exorbitant sum that King Artaxerxes had paid in advance for them. Omares had already propositioned Memnon of Rhodes for an additional sum of a thousand talents for the monsters to be paid to Zamos, who worked for me. Memnon promised to pay the sum on delivery of the monsters, but he wanted a favour done first. He wanted Spithridates, Arasmes and Petines to be killed by the Greek mercenaries during the first battle with Alexander and he promised me five hundred talents for achieving this. His request didn't surprise me. Having expressed his opposition to the engagement, he wanted the others to lose since that would strengthen his position in the Persian camp and he would be second only to Darius.

When I asked him why he wanted to spare Arsites and Rhemithres, he said that he needed witnesses to survive the battle, who would then report to Darius about the folly of their ways and his opposition to the same, thereby earning the trust of the king. Memnon was convinced that the Persians under Arasmes would lose the battle and, though he would fight alongside them, he did not want to be blamed for the defeat.

I was surprised at the confidence Memnon displayed in me at this, our first meeting, and at that time I took it as another sign of what Mistros had foretold: that I would have a new master after a battle next to a river. I strongly believed that Memnon was destined to be that, for I had been seeking him relentlessly after returning to Asia. If I was to fulfil my obligation of being the chief emissary of Athens, I needed Memnon on my side.

Therefore I instructed Agos to brief Hesiod, son of Strabo, who was the battle chief of the mercenaries, to prepare a strategy for deployment if an engagement did take place with Alexander, so that Spithridates, Arasmes and Petines would suffer the worst of it. Hesiod himself was a

Theban whom Spithridates had insulted two days ago for not standing up when he walked past him – but Hesiod's contention had been that he was employed by Zamos, not Spithridates, and it was Zamos he was obliged to salute and not him.

This had infuriated Spithridates and Petines, who was his junior, had then confronted Hesiod and called him an insolent Theban. Hesiod had laughed at Petines and said that it was the best compliment that a Persian had paid him and Petines had then struck Hesiod in the face, and if Zamos had not intervened to calm things down, Petines would have been killed by Hesiod and his men at that very instant.

Hesiod was therefore delighted when Agos briefed him on what was to be done regarding Spithridates, Arasmes and Petines. Since the mercenaries would hold the centre in any engagement, as the Persians were not confident of their own infantry matching up to the Macedonian phalanx, it would provide many opportunities to Hesiod to fulfil Memnon's brief.

Around this time, the Persian Autophradates came with information about three Greeks who had been spotted in the town of Tamare, not far from where the Persian army was. Though they were pretending to be mercenaries under Zamos, he was sure that they weren't, for they had been discovered asking all kinds of questions, such as only spies would ask. Upon being confronted, the three had confessed that they were not part of the mercenary troops yet, but intended to be recruited.

But when the Persians decided to escort them to Zamos, they confessed that they had been sent by the orator Phocion from Athens. Hearing Phocion's name, I requested Autophradates to give the men into my custody so that I could investigate the matter further. For Phocion was a stooge of Alexander and one of the leaders of the camp in opposition to Demosthenes.

Agos interrogated the three Athenians and discovered that they had indeed been sent by Phocion to Alexander's camp with information about how Demosthenes and Lycargus had been aiding the recruitment of the mercenaries in the Pelopponnese. The names of the three men captured by us were Magas, Himmeras and Cleops. They added, after Agos threatened them with death, that a plot was afoot to get Demosthenes to travel to Delphi and, once he was outside Attica, to have him murdered. They claimed it might already have happened and, learning of this from Agos, I immediately sent a messenger to Athens, warning Demosthenes of the plot.

Agos felt that the three Athenians were hiding something more and so he continued to interrogate them till he got the whole truth out of them. The three Greeks, it appeared, had actually come in advance of a hundred mercenaries whom they had recruited on behalf of the Paeonians and the Lancers in Alexander's army. Some men from the units of the Lancers and the Paeonians had developed disputes with their masters in the Macedonian army over pay and had left and the two units had thus become understaffed. The leader of the Lancers, a man called Platulus, son of Sidarus, had sought Phocion's help to organize replenishments from Lemnos, as that would be quicker.

Platulus knew that Phocion had some influence over Lemnos because he was the son-in-law of King Pistoris, the tyrant there. At Phocion's request, Pistoris agreed to send eighty men; the remaining twenty Phocion was organizing from within Attica itself. Cleops, Magas and Himmeras had come to Asia ahead of the twenty men whom Phocion was sending from Attica to join the eighty men in Lemnos, and together they would be joining the Paeonians and Lancers in Alexander's army in three weeks' time.

When Cleops, Magas and Himmeras reported to Platulus, the chief of the Lancers, and conveyed to him that they were the vanguard of the hundred troops being arranged by his friend Phocion, he took them to meet Philotas, Parmenio's son. Philotas had then sent them here, behind the Persian lines, on a spying mission to find out how many mercenaries the Persians commanded and who their leaders were.

That was when they were captured by my men. They said Philotas particularly wanted them to find out if 'Seleucus, son of Nicanor' was the leader of the mercenaries, as this was the information that Alexander desired most. When Agos asked them what they had been able to find out, they replied that they had discovered that the mercenaries were led by the Theban Hesiod and they were twenty thousand in number. They added that they were supposed to report back to Philotas within thirty-six hours with the information and he had given them the password 'the cobwebs of Demeter' to cross the Macedonian lines.

Agos then posed this question to them: 'Do you wish to live or die? If you wish to live, you will have to join the mercenaries who are going to fight on the side of the Persians. If you refuse, we are going to kill you immediately.'

The three quickly took an oath to join the mercenaries and to never speak to the Macedonians again.

In this fortuitous manner did I manage to encounter the three Athenians who had been sent by Phocion to join Alexander's army, I took it as a sign that the Goddess Athena looked at me again with favour. Having taken a vow to kill Alexander, I saw the capture of the Athenian spies as an act of divine intervention in my favour and therefore I immediately plotted to use the information given by them to enter the Macedonian camp and fulfil my objective.

At this time, a message came from Tyros, behind the enemy lines, that the town of Priapus had surrendered to Alexander and his advance scouts had reported to him the presence of the Persian army beyond the river Granicus. The message said that Alexander was now marching towards the Granicus in battle order.

When Hesiod communicated this message to the Persian commander Arasmes, he ordered his troops to prepare to occupy the river bank furthest from the approaching Macedonian troops, and he ordered a rich meal for his soldiers, so that they might be better prepared for the battle the next day. The speed with which these events occurred took me by surprise, as I had imagined that Alexander would proceed first to Sardis before engaging with the enemy. But now that he was marching towards the Granicus to engage with the Persians, very little time was left for me to penetrate their lines.

So I summoned Zamos and Agos and told them of my plan to penetrate the Macedonian lines and fight alongside the Lancers and against the Persians in the hope of coming close to the Companion Cavalry and getting an opportunity to launch a surprise attack on Alexander.

Both Zamos and Agos expressed their disagreement with my plan, saying that the risks were too great and they would rather I sent an assassin than risk my life. Agos also argued that the battle order was not yet known and my plan would work only if Alexander was on the same wing as the Lancers and the Paeonians. But then, seeing that my mind was made up, Agos made one last plea: 'I would like to accompany you behind the Macedonian lines. I will not let you go alone.'

Then Zamos asked: 'Can I take Hesiod into confidence about your scheme, so that he can depute a hundred mercenaries to protect you if you desire to change sides during the course of the battle?'

But I did not grant him permission, as I didn't want any one except Zamos to know our whereabouts, and I also expressly forbade him to speak of the matter with the Persians. I then extracted from him a promise to continue searching for my son Zanylos in the event of my death and to not spare Philotas or Alexander if it was within his powers to harm them. This pledge he readily took.

Then I instructed Zamos to locate as many men as he could amongst the Persians whose height and build were similar to mine and persuade them to wear heavy armour and such other paraphernalia that would make it difficult for anybody to identify them in battle. These men were to be mounted on white horses and positioned amidst the advance Persian cavalry on their left wing. But I gave no explanation to Zamos for such an order.

After this, Agos and I departed for Priapus with the intention of breaching the Macedonian lines and joining the Lancers under Platulus; the thought of settling scores with both Alexander and Philotas made me proceed at a brisk pace. One parasang short of Priapus, we encountered scouts of the Macedonian army under Hegelochus, and when we demanded to cross the lines, he asked us what the password was and when we said 'the cobwebs of Demeter', he deputed two men to escort us all the way to the Macedonian lines, without asking any further questions. This increased our confidence, as we were now assured that Himmeras, Magas and Cleops had spoken the truth.

My own appearance had changed beyond recognition after the battle at Thebes and there were scars on my face and body and a ruggedness in my appearance that had not been there before. Besides, I had grown my hair, whereas, in Thebes, I had been clean shaven. Because of these changes, I was confident that the few Macedonians who knew me would find it difficult to recognize me.

When we finally reported to Platulus, he was surprised that we weren't the men he had been expecting. Then Agos addressed him thus: 'The investigations of Magas, Himmeras and Cleops are not complete yet. They have sent the two of us to convey to you whatever facts they managed to obtain. The mercenaries are about twenty thousand in number and are led by a person called Seleucus, son of Nicanor. It is this man who will lead them from the left flank, ahead of even the Persians.'

Platulus absorbed this informaton carefully, as he sensed it was of importance to both Philotas and Alexander himself.

Agos then added: 'Magas also came to know that in order to disguise himself even from his own men, Seleucus has arranged for many soldiers to be dressed like him and each one of them will be mounted on a white steed. With such an arrangement, Seleucus intends to deceive the

Macedonians as to his whereabouts and even those in his own camp who are his enemies and are plotting to harm him.'

Platulus immediately took Agos with him to meet Philotas and he made Agos repeat all that he had told him and Philotas, excited by the information, went straight to Alexander with it. He instructed Platulus and Agos to wait nearby in case Alexander wanted to talk directly to them. So Agos waited nervously near Alexander's tent for, while he had never met Alexander, there were other Macedonians whom he had been to battle with at Lesbos, and if they recognized him, his fate would be sealed.

Philotas emerged smiling from Alexander's tent and said that the king would shortly be giving orders to march to the Granicus to engage with the Persians. Later, it came to be known that Parmenio had advised Alexander to halt on the side of the river opposite the Persians, for to attempt the crossing in the present circumstances was fraught with risk. Parmenio argued with Alexander that, the river being deep in places and the opposite bank steep, the men would have to cross in loose order and on a broad front and this would give the Persian cavalry an opportunity to attack them as they emerged unorganized on the other side. And that, Parmnenio pointed out, would be a great disadvantage to them and could cause their failure in the very first battle.

But Alexander, having been briefed by Philotas about the presence of Seleucus across the Granicus, was blinded by vengeance and not amenable to reason. Yet, his answer to Parmenio displayed none of his hidden motives, for he spoke to him thus: 'Yes, Parmenio, you advise well. But people would say that Alexander, son of Philip, having crossed the Hellespont without difficulty, felt afraid to cross a mere trickle like the Granicus. The delay in crossing the river would be interpreted by our enemies as a sign of fear and it would damage our fighting reputation. This would give the Persians confidence and they would start thinking that they are as good as us. But if we launch into the river and emerge on the other side and defeat them, it will be made clear that the Macedonians are fearless. And it would shatter the confidence of the Persians.'

Before Platulus escorted us to where the Lancers were, Philotas came and spoke again with Agos. He asked him whether he recognized Seleucus and Agos said that he did. Hearing this, he was pleased and told Platulus not to position Agos in the initial assault party, as he wanted him alive to identify Nicanor's son and, saying this, he laughed and went away to be at the head of the Companion Cavalry. Platulus then turned to me and told me to position myself next to Agos.

I heard later that Zamos had spread the word through a mercenary that a prophecy had come that those riding a white horse would survive the first battle at Granicus. Many of the mercenaries crowded around him, asking for white horses, and when the rich Persian nobles enquired what the commotion was about, they were told that there was a prophecy from Mistros that riding white horses would augur well for the battle and bring victory to the Persians. When the Persians heard this, there was a huge rush for white horses, but only ten horses could be found for the right wing, the rest having been appropriated by the nobles on the left wing. The nobles on the right wing, including Spithridates and Petines, bought white horses for themselves at an extravagant price, for they had great faith in Mistros, having witnessed the power of his predictions in the past.

Arasmes, though in the centre, also bought a white mare and positioned himself in the centre of the cavalry, from where he directed all the operations. There were some Persian nobles who exchanged horses with other noblemen who had white horses and paid them large sums of money for the exchange. Omares, who had also exchanged his black horse for the white horse of one of his bodyguards, had to reluctantly give it away to Mithridates, the son-in-law of Darius, who had not managed to get one for himself.

Since Omares was an important ally for us, Zamos was relieved to see him give up the white mare, else Zamos would have had to devise a way to get rid of it, possibly by laming him; he didn't want Omares to be targeted by Alexander or his men. Though I had not disclosed to Zamos my motive in issuing such instructions, he had arrived at a conclusion on his own – that I would be disclosing to Alexander's camp that the leaders of the enemy soldiers would be on white horses.

Though that was not exactly what I had told Philotas, it served the purpose of Memnon of Rhodes, for the nobles he wanted eliminated were all on white horses. After that, Zamos spread the rumour that it wasn't just white horses that Mistros had talked about; he had also sent Byzantine helmets to Omares to be distributed to those whom the Gods had decided would live, for these helmets had been blessed by both the Persian and the Greek Gods. After spreading the rumour, he had some helmets delivered to Omares's tent. All the nobles who heard about this immediately came to Omares's tent on some pretext or the other and asked if he had kept a helmet for them.

Omares, on hearing the commotion, found out from his servants that a cartload of Byzantine helmets had been delivered at his tent by some men, who had left immediately, saying that Mistros had sent them for the Persians to use. Since there were more helmets than white horses, every nobleman who had managed to acquire a white horse also got the Byzantine helmet with a visor, while those who were feeling unlucky at not having been able to acquire a white horse were now happy that they had at least acquired a helmet which would bring them luck.

And so the two great armies faced each other across the Granicus. The bugles were sounded and the trumpets blared and voices sang odes to the God of war.

Platulus placed Agos and me at the rear of the Lancers. It was Amyntas who led the advance scouts into the river, followed by the cavalry squadron of Socrates. Alexander followed soon after, with his Royal Guards, who were three hundred in number, and Platulus followed behind them. The troops forded the river at an oblique angle to the flow and were met by arrows and javelins once they were halfway across, which they tried to fend off the best they could with their shields, protecting their horses as well as themselves. But most of the missiles were discharged from high ground by the Persians and it became difficult to protect both men and horses at the same time. Philotas then ordered the archers to come halfway into the river, so that the Persians would come under fire themselves and it would reduce the number of missiles they discharged at the Macedonians.

But the leading column of the squadron led by Socrates was cut down immediately by the Persians and the men who followed had not only to face the missiles but also to climb over the bodies of the men and horses that had been cut down. The bank of the Granicus turned red with blood, but the Macedonians soldiered on and two columns occupied a portion of the opposite bank in spite of the concerted efforts of the Persians to deny them the bridgehead. As men on horses jostled with each other, the Macedonian pikes began to have an advantage, as they could engage with the enemy from a greater distance than the Persians could with their lances. As the columns of troops came up the river, they added mass to the cavalry already perched on the opposite bank, and the added momentum made the Persians cede more territory. Soon, the volume of missiles being fired at the leading Macedonian columns dropped, as the

Persians were scared of injuring their own men. In this way the battle continued for a while, with the two armies jostling for space on the river bank. Then into this melee Alexander launched himself with his Guards and so ferocious was their assault that they started pushing the Persians back relentlessly, a few plethrons at a time.

Shortly, the determined Macedonian assault, their large pikes and their tactics and bravery made the Persians give up ground and they lost the defensive advantage they had enjoyed at the start of the battle. Once the battle moved to the plains beyond the banks of the river, the advantage was frittered away entirely by the Persian commander Arasmes, who had moved his position from the centre to the left wing.

In this confusion, Agos and I managed to get close to the Royal Guards. Most of the soldiers were caked in mud and it was impossible to know who was from which regiment; only Alexander was distinguishable by the plume on his helmet.

Agos and I managed to injure the horses of several of the Macedonians, forcing them to dismount, even though we fought alongside them. We defended ourselves the best we could from the Persian missiles, which targeted the Macedonians and us in equal measure. I sent Agos to Philotas, who was near us, to point out the white horses with the Persian nobles mounted on them and, seeing them, Philotas rode rapidly to Alexander. The two of them then galloped purposefully towards the nearest rider on a white horse. He happened to be Petines and, in the fight that ensued, Alexander broke his spear. Whereupon Philotas lent him his; if he hadn't done that in time, Petines would have grievously injured Alexander.

But Philotas was left without a weapon and, though earlier I had decided to kill him at the first opportunity, I weakened in my resolve when the thought came to my mind that he was one of the two people who knew where Zanylos was and I needed him alive. As a result, I let the opportunity pass, but then a group of four Persians fell upon us and Agos and I had to kill all four to survive. Then four of their friends, who had seen them getting slaughtered by us, also came to engage us, and it was with some difficulty that we managed to fight them off.

By this time, after having killed Petines and discovered that it wasn't Seleucus, Alexander had moved to the next person he could see on a white horse and that happened to be Mithridates, the son-in-law of Darius, who was riding towards him ahead of his troops. Though the Persian nobles had jostled to get white mounts and helmets, they were at heart brave souls who did not want to be labelled as cowards in front of their men. So, even though they took all the precautions they could, they also fought bravely against the Macedonians. Even Memnon of Rhodes fought with his many sons and I could see him from a distance, but whoever I could recognize I stayed away from as, on the battlefield, they would take me for a Macedonian and I would have no option but to kill them to survive. And so I stayed away from Omares as he bravely fought Philotas and it was with great sorrow that I saw him die at Philotas's hands. I was sorry that I could do nothing to help him, but I took a vow then and there that Philotas would die a painful death at my hands if I survived the battle.

It was the skirmish with the four Persians who engaged Agos and me that prevented me from catching up with Alexander and his Guards, but I could see them galloping towards Mithridates. As Alexander galloped faster than his guards, he was the first to reach Mithridates, knocking him off his horse with his spear. He then dismounted and struck Mithridates a few more times and Mithridates, even though mortally wounded, caught the spear with his two hands and prevented Alexander from pulling it from his chest. And seeing Alexander defenceless once again and enraged that Mithridates had thus been mortally wounded, Rhoesaces, a Persian nobleman who was related to the former king Artaxerxes, rushed at him with great speed and struck Alexander on his head with his lance. And from afar it looked as if Rhoesaces had cut off Alexander's head and every Macedonian fighting in the vicinity halted his actions to observe whether Alexander was alive. For a long moment, it did look like Rhoesaces had killed the king, but all he had done was cut a portion of his helmet along with the plume. It was Alexander's helmet which absorbed the blow to his head. Although shaken, Alexander caught hold of Rhoesaces's hand when he swung his lance again and pulled him down from his horse and with his own lance speared him through his cuirass and the Macedonians, relieved that their king was alive, fell with greater ferocity upon the enemy.

After Rhoesaces was killed by Alexander, Spithridates, the satrap of Lydia, rushed at Alexander from behind, intending to take him by surprise. If it hadn't been for Clietus, the son of Dropidas, who chopped off Spithridates's right arm with one blow, Alexander would have been in trouble once again. To the credit of Spithridates, he had galloped to the left wing of his army from the right wing, seeing that there was trouble. But all he met was death.

Having witnessed the death of Petines, Mithridates, Rhoesaces and Spithridates, the commander of the Persians, Arasmes himself rushed towards Alexander. He was joined by Arbuphales, the nephew of King Darius. But by now the Royal Guards had created a protective ring around Alexander and they killed both with ease. With the death of Arasmes, the morale of the Persian cavalry was crushed. Arsites, the governor of northern Phyrgia, who had originally opposed the policy Memnon had advocated of laying bare the land, fled behind the mercenaries who had been stationed at the rear of the Persian battle formation. And thus the Persian cavalry, suddenly bereft of leadership, caved in at the centre.

The Persians were further dispirited after the Royal Guards cut off the heads of each of the Persian nobles who had fought sitting on a white horse and held them up in front of the Persian army. Alexander examined each of the heads and concluded that the head of Petines was that of Seleucus. At first he had discounted this possibility, but I think he changed his mind because Petines was about my age, and since injuries scarred his face, a proper identification was not possible.

After the rout of the Persian cavalry, they fled in every direction, and even Memnon of Rhodes fled with his few surviving sons. And since the collapse of the Persians was so sudden, the Greek mercenaries were as shocked as the Persians themselves. Deprived now of cavalry protection on both their flanks, the Persians were at the mercy of the Macedonians. At this point, one of Hesiod's mercenaries snatched the head of Petines, which Philotas had been holding aloft, and made off with it to the mercenary ranks.

Alexander was chasing the retreating Persian cavalry, inflicting as many losses as possible, but seeing Petines's head being whisked away by the unknown mercenary and believing it to be the head of Nicanor's son, he wheeled around and diverted his attention to the twenty thousand mercenaries who had scarcely moved from the spot that Arasmes had ordered them to be in. Even if he hadn't been fully convinced of Petines being Nicanor's son, after the unknown mercenary rushed away with Petine's head, Alexander was convinced that it was indeed Seleucus whom he had killed. Whereupon he exploded with rage and ordered his troops to surround the mercenaries who, in fact, had already been circled by Parmenio's left wing. Parmenio's section had had an easier crossing at the Granicus because the bulk of the Persian forces had been concentrating on thwarting the battalions of Amyntas and the Royal Guards.

I found out later that it was Hesiod who had instructed the unknown mercenary to snatch Petines's head from Philotas's hand to claim to Zamos that it was his mercenaries who had killed Petines and not the Macedonians as was evident to all those present. Hesiod, perhaps hoping that Zamos was not in a position to observe what was happening, was not guided by any reason. And in this petty error lay the seed for the Macedonian brutality that followed.

For what happened was that, with Platulus dead, there was no one in Alexander's army who recognized Agos and me since we had been enlisted into the Lancers just before the battle. Except, of course, Philotas, who recognized only Agos, having spoken to him at the commencement of the battle. But Philotas had been deputed by Alexander to reach the Persian baggage train before the Thessalians did so, for Parmenio's men were notorious for not sharing any loot with the central treasury.

A section of the Royal Guards then mistook us to be mercenaries in the employ of the Persians and started encircling us. Slowly, we backed into the only gap available, which led into the midst of the mercenaries who were themselves being attacked by the Macedonians from almost all directions, except the one from where we joined them. Thus, instead of fighting our way out and escaping into the woods which lay at a distance of one parasang, we ended up amidst the mercenaries, who assumed that we were one of their party and welcomed us gladly.

As we dismounted from our horses to mingle with the mercenaries, the battle raged fast and furious around us. At one point, as I swerved and dipped and rose again to confront yet another Macedonian soldier, it seemed to me that it would never end. That day, the Macedonians spared no one and only two thousand survived of the twenty thousand. Agos and I were among them. Hesiod died a particularly violent death, decapitated by Perdicass in front of the mercenaries who survived.

But just before we became prisoners, I sustained a blow to my head; when I awoke, there was nothing that I remembered about myself.

THIRTY

Before I proceed further in my tale, let me confide to you my predicament as I dictate these words to Agos. It is some years now after the battle of Granicus. And though I have time on my hands right now and some amount of freedom, even in captivity, I do not know how long this will last. For danger lurks.

The battle of Granicus shaped my life in an unexpected direction. In fact, you could call Granicus the halfway point of my tale. I don't claim to be a historian of the standing of Thucydides and Herodotus, whose works I became familiar with when Persepolis was burned down and some Persians came to me with a request for help in preserving many important manuscripts. But it was while reading their works that the desire had sprouted in me to write my own story.

You could say that the only profession I ever specialized in was that of an emissary, which does not in any way qualify me to record important historical events for posterity. You could also say that I am not learned enough to comment on events of great importance. I have only one thing to say to all those who think this way: the bulk of my writings comprises a narration of actual events and very rarely do I delve into the motives of men and why they do the things they do, for I believe that if you place the facts accurately before the readers, they have the ability and insight to form an opinion on their own. And since there can be no imagination attached to the narration of facts, I am confident that my approach is a worthy one.

When I came to consciousness those many days after the battle of Granicus, the first person I saw was a man they called Strabo, son of Ochello, who was feeding me crushed mustard flowers in red wine to purge me of the venomous bile in my system.

I had bandages on my body and the man called Strabo kept addressing me by the name of Ptolemy, though I had no recollection of the name or anything else. It was in this condition that King Alexander came to visit me. My head was bandaged and only one eye was visible. He enquired after my health and I answered deliriously, for a fever enveloped me and my head throbbed continuously from the wound it had received.

The physician Ortemis attended on me personally and bled me from the head and neck to dilute the build up of bad blood in my body. He also made potions of herbs which Strabo made me drink regularly.

I was visited twice by Alexander and more often by Hepasthion, who kept asking me a single question: 'Where are the hundred and twenty talents, Ptolemy?'

Apparently, there had been a hundred and twenty talents in my possession and these were being transported in a wagon behind the baggage train, having got delayed by two days at the city of Priapus.

Strabo answered Hepasthion the first time the question was asked. He said: 'My master and I were attacked by the Persians as we repaired our wagon. They captured our wagon, the talents and him. Though I searched for him in the neighbouring area and tried to locate the Persian brigands, I was unsuccessful. By the time I rejoined the army from Priapus, the battle of Granicus had already taken place. It was while I was examining the men who were injured or sick to see if there were any soldiers known to me who might be in need of assistance that I discovered my master again. It is my belief that he must have escaped on his own from the Persians who had captured him, and made his way to the battlefield to join the battle. He must have not been able to report quickly enough to the Companions and therefore fought near the scouts. But once he was injured, he was mistaken for a mercenary and arrested along with two thousand others. It was fortunate that I spotted him, or else he would be on his way to hard labour in Macedonia along with the rest of the prisoners, for he was so grievously injured that he couldn't have spoken for himself. When I found him, he was being tended to by a soldier named Agos, whose life he had apparently saved on the battlefield and this person was now determined to nurse him to health out of gratitude.'

Strabo kept repeating this story to everyone who came to meet me while I was recuperating.

This Ptolemy, who they thought I was and who I believed for a time I was, was apparently responsible for the treasury. That was why Hepasthion visited me regularly to see if I had come out of my delirium, so that he could hear the story of my escape and find out about the group of Persians who had waylaid me at Priapus when Ptolemy's wagon had broken down. He suspected that the residents of Priapus had something to do with the incident. But I didn't confirm or deny his hypothesis, semi-conscious that I was.

I discovered later that Agos had been identified by the Macedonian Philotas as the person who had joined the Lancers before the battle began on the banks of the Granicus, and so he had been separated from the group of mercenaries being sent for hard labour to the mines in Macedonia. It was his good fortune and mine that none of the captured mercenaries identified him as being one of their own.

Agos had removed the ring of Leonidas that I wore, for fear that Alexander would recognize it. He also removed the emerald ring that Olympias had given me, for he remembered what I had told him – that Alexander had been sworn by her not to refuse a favour to a person bearing the ring – and he felt it could be used at an appropriate occasion. He also made sure that the amulet around my neck was not stolen by anybody. For, having been given to me by my mother, I had the belief that no wrong would visit me as long as I wore it.

Agos told Strabo and Philotas that I had saved his life on the battlefield by lending him my own spear when his was broken, and it was as a result of this that I had suffered the blow to my head and he was feeling guilty about it. And so he had decided to nurse me till I got well and then offer himself to my employ if I so desired. All these lies he told the Macedonians to stay close to me and watch for any danger.

It was after a few weeks of coming to consciousness that I got back my memory – or rather, a substantial part of it. It happened while I was on my way to Sardis in the baggage train. I fell from the wagon in my sleep and bruised my skull again. Agos says it brought back my memory that same night. I was fortunate that Strabo was not around when I came to my senses and it was Agos who sat beside me.

After Agos explained the entire circumstances of my survival to me and about the Macedonians having mistaken me for a certain Ptolemy, he asked for further instructions.

'I think we should escape from here as soon as possible. We don't know how long they are going to mistake you for this Ptolemy. Once your face heals and your bandages come off, they will realize their error,' said Agos.

The night my memory came back, Alexander visited me again and I will not shirk from saying that I was grasped by fear. But he was very cordial; apparently, this Ptolemy and he shared a friendship of some kind. In his presence, I pretended to be in delirium once again.

'I see little progress, Ortemis,' Alexander rebuked my physician. 'Guards, I want Ptolemy shifted closer to my tents. He will be better taken care of there and will be in more comfort.'

Once they shifted me near his tents, only Strabo was allowed to have access to me. The rest of the men, including Agos, were denied entry by the pages.

Now, when I look back, I realize that it was to my benefit that my memory was restored before Alexander took me to his tents, as it prepared me better to face him. I can explain this stroke of destiny only by acknowledging that the Goddess Athena watched over me. For if he had taken me under his wing even a day earlier, it is entirely possible that I would have regained my memory in his presence and, seeing him there, I might have thought that I was in captivity and reacted accordingly.

Alexander boasted to me about the injuries he had got at the battle of Granicus. His own personal physician, Phillip of Acarnania, attended to his wounds in my presence and then he bade Phillip examine me in detail to see why I continued to be in delirium. Of course, my delirium now was deliberate, as I feared getting into conversation with him lest he ask me something, the answer to which would reveal that I was an impostor.

Then, one day, Phillip, after removing the bandages on my face, refused to put on fresh bandages as he said that my wounds would heal faster if they got more air. And when Alexander saw me without the bandages for the first time and still didn't doubt that I was Ptolemy, I grew in confidence. When I got a chance to view myself in a mirror after he had gone, I saw why. There were deep scars on my face and I looked different even to myself.

It was this incident that gave me the confidence to come out of the delirium I had been faking and once word spread that I was in my senses, I was visited in my convalescent state by a man known as Theron. He had, apparently, been in the party of men led by me, that is Ptolemy, when we had been attacked near Priapus. After waiting long enough for Strabo to go on an errand, he began to speak.

'Where is my share of talents, Ptolemy? I need to know.' From his manner of asking, it seemed as though Ptolemy and Theron were together in some kind of conspiracy and further revelations from Theron confirmed this. He winked and added: 'Both Hepasthion and Alexander have been fooled. Because of the injuries you have sustained, you can keep a larger share than decided earlier, but I want at least ten talents for myself. Tell me where you have hoarded the treasure, for then I could go there myself and retrieve my share without having to bother you.'

'We have been double-crossed, Theron. We lost a lot of the talents,' I replied. I had to say something.

This came as a big shock to him. 'By whom, Ptolemy?' he asked.

'By the person whom you never trusted much,' I answered.

'That would be Geronochus. I didn't trust him from the beginning. Has he disappeared with the talents?' asked Theron.

'He came to me saying that he himself had been ambushed later and could save only half the treasure given to his custody,' I answered.

Theron made a face and said that he didn't trust this Geronochus one bit and that we should capture him wherever he was and torture him for the truth.

'The difficulty is that we do not know where he is and even the talents he claimed he had managed to save from the ambush, he has not delivered yet. For all we know, he may have died in the war. Maybe his body is rotting in some place where nobody has cared to look,' I told Theron.

Theron pondered this possibility, but dismissed it saying that Geronochus was too clever to have been killed in the war, for he knew how to save his own skin by preferring safety to bravery of any kind. I got rid of him then, by asking him to make secret enquiries if anybody had seen Geronochus.

After the visit of Theron, I was visited by a person called Callisthenes, who was the official historian of Alexander and travelled with his armies on a pay of five drachmas a day. I had heard of him before as the nephew of the great Aristotle, who was tutor to Alexander himself. As soon as he saw me, Callisthenes spoke in a voice that was half pleading and half threatening. 'Please give me the five hundred drachmas for having kept your secret,' he said.

Not knowing what this secret of Ptolemy's was, I demanded to know whether anybody had approached him to reveal what he knew. And he said that Theron had already come to him, wanting to know where Geronochus was.

Said Callisthenes: 'The scoundrel is hiding in my wagon at your request. Of course, I refused to divulge this to Theron in spite of his threats. But if you don't pay me quickly, I am going to reveal all, and you cannot blame me.'

I then told Strabo to take Callisthenes to Agos and instruct him to pay five hundred drachmas to him as soon as he could. And before Callisthenes left, I told him to write down details of all the transactions that had taken place between us so that there could be no misunderstanding in the future. Callisthenes agreed to my demand after an assurance from me that his handwritten document would remain with me in strict confidence.

That same night, Strabo asked me: 'Sire, do you want me to bring Analisa to your tent? She came to me to say that she was worried for you, and having heard that you are back in your senses, she cannot resist visiting you in the night, specially since Perdicass is occupied with negotiations with the Persian Mithrines, who commands the inner fortress in Sardis. For my part, I am convinced that your recovery is due to the prayers of Analisa, as she fasted and made offerings to Zeus daily for your recovery and, even before that, when she heard the news of your capture in the ambush at Priapus.'

I told Strabo that he could bring her that night. I had not had a woman for a long time and I was curious about this Analisa. However, I was also afraid that she might sense that I was not Ptolemy and so I decided not to discard my clothes or light a lamp, hoping that the darkness would deceive her. Women are very astute and Analisa would have been used to a certain behaviour from Ptolemy.

But I need not have worried, for Analisa was too much in love with Ptolemy to examine me properly. She kissed my wounds and applied the herbs herself and bathed me and did everything that a wife does, except she was the mistress of Perdicass. The same Perdicass who was the officer in charge of the Cadmeia when the Thebans laid siege to it.

Analisa left early in the morning, clothed in a tunic that went over her head so the guards posted at the baggage train would not recognize her, and since Strabo was her escort, they dared not question her.

The next day brought Callisthenes again to my tent, with a note detailing all the transactions between him and me – that is, Ptolemy. From this note, it appeared that Callisthenes had been a persistent blackmailer of Ptolemy, having managed to discover many of his secrets, and had recently turned accomplice in his various projects of thievery. He had marked a hundred drachmas for not revealing the fact that he had seen Ptolemy in confabulation with Attalus four times before the death of Philip. He had marked one hundred and fifty drachmas for not revealing the fact that Ptolemy was the lover of Alexander's sister Catherine before her marriage to Alexander the Molossian, king of Epirus. And another fifty drachmas for not revealing that he was the lover of Arrihidaeus's wife, who was the daughter of Pixodarus, the king of Caria – Arrihidaeus was the mentally retarded brother of Alexander. In this manner did Callisthenes lay charges against the character of Ptolemy and after I read the whole list, I discovered there was also a charge of fifty drachmas for not revealing the fact that Ptolemy had lamed Hepasthion's horse in one of Alexander's battles against the northern tribes.

Ptolemy appeared to be a serial offender of some kind. This, however, was only a listing of the amounts due to Callisthenes from Ptolemy. There was also a list he had prepared for the amounts that he had already received for the tasks that Ptolemy had instructed him to do, which came to a total of two thousand drachmas. The biggest charge of five hundred drachmas in the list related to a payment made for starting a rumour after the death of Philip that Olympias had briefed the assassin Pausanias and offered him a bribe for killing Philip, and that the two people who had witnessed the event had been murdered by Hepasthion.

There was also a payment of four hundred drachmas for not revealing that the son of Philip and Eurydice had not died in the manner made out in the beginning, that is, from the bite of an adder. He had instead been whisked away to Ptolemy's house to be kept away from all prying eyes, for Attalus and Eurydice feared that Olympias would have the child killed. Callisthenes had stumbled upon this fact when he visited Ptolemy's house in Pella.

After Callisthenes disclosed the association between Ptolemy and Attalus, I was entirely convinced that this Ptolemy was indeed the same person whom Tyros had seen at Eurydice's house, where Cicero was treating Attalus for his abscess, and mistaken for me. If you remember, I had mentioned earlier that a very peculiar event had occurred when I was at Pella. While Cicero was at Attalus's residence, trying to cure the growth on his body, Tyros had seen a person in shape and size who was exactly like me. And, in fact, he had become so confused that he had asked me what I had been doing in the house of Attalus. And I had to explain to him, though I was equally puzzled, that it hadn't been me.

There was also the incident I had been made aware of when Argus had captured a certain Ptolemy, suspecting that it was me, but he had been proved wrong as that Ptolemy had turned out to be a Macedonian nobleman who was a friend of both Philip and Alexander. And Alexander had even examined him for his resemblance to Seleucus, that is, me. I was now sure that it was this same Ptolemy they were mistaking me for.

That night, as I lay musing in my bed, something floated up from the back of my mind. Something my mother had said to me before she left for her brother's house, that last time I had seen her. She had told me that I had been found as an infant on the steps leading up to the temple of Zeus in Olympia. My father Nicanor had found me there, and since both he and my mother had been in prayer to Zeus for a son for many years, they saw it as a sign from the God to adopt the child. And the priests of the temple agreed to the adoption as nobody could locate the mother of the child.

But ten days later, a note had arrived at our house, addressed to my father, saying that the person writing the note was my mother. The letter said I was one of the twins she had conceived out of wedlock when her husband had been away at sea for two years. She did not disclose her name or who the father of the twins was, but said that the other twin had been taken in by a Macedonian family who had come to attend the Games at Olympia and the family had later returned or was on their way back to Pella.

This she mentioned just by way of information, and she said that she was happy that one of the twins had been adopted by Nicanor, as she had found out that he was a person observant of his duties to men and the Gods and had a pious and beautiful wife. She assured him in the letter that she too was of noble lineage and would not at any time come to reclaim the child, in case my father harboured such a fear.

After receiving the letter, my father Nicanor made a journey on the road to Pella as fast as his horse would permit, hoping to overtake the family who had the other twin and convince them to hand him over so that the two brothers could be raised together as one family. But he could never locate them. He made enquiries at the temples of Pella, Dium and Apollonia about any family in the knowledge of the priests who had come to Olympia for some religious ritual (for people often combined a visit to the Games with a pilgrimage), and upon being given some names, he visited each one of their estates, though they were at tremendous distances. But at no estate could he find any infant boy of my age. Therefore, after spending two months in Macedonia, he returned to Olympia disappointed and raised me the best he could.

Thinking back upon all this, I became convinced that Ptolemy of Lagus was my brother, and I was determined to find him if he was still alive. When my mother told me this story, I had dismissed it, but now circumstances had pushed me into pretending to be my own brother.

You must understand that I came to know about the tale of my twin only at the time when I was about to depart from Olympia, pursued by Polemon and his accomplices. It had sounded very strange to me at the time and subsequent events had taken my mind away from the words of my mother. But now, I was glad that she'd had the foresight to tell me all this before we parted, for otherwise I might not have known of the tale at all and the matter of Ptolemy and our similarity would forever have been a mystery to me.

As I recollect these bygone events, I think it is material that I put in a brief word here about Agos, the person to whom I narrate all these stories, and who writes down all that I say with great diligence. Agos has been with me through much of what I speak about and he fills in the gaps at points where my memory proves erroneous. Unlike the many historians travelling with Alexander, whose brief it is to portray the Macedonian in a light he does not deserve, Agos and I recall every little detail with clarity and accuracy and take the greatest care to write about events exactly the way they happened. We do not embellish our tale with facts that show us in a better light in the way Alexander has his historians do – but that is the prerogative of wealth and power.

The history that I narrate I have decided to divide in two parts. The first part, which will shortly draw to a close, I shall smuggle out with Otanes. He will soon be proceeding down river on the Indus, aboard one of the ships headed for the mouth of the river, from where it will turn to follow the coast to Babylon. For that is the geographical assessment of Admiral Nearchus, and to him Alexander has entrusted the command of his ships while he himself seeks to march through the Gedrosian desert.

I will make two copies of the first part of my histories and while one copy I will smuggle out in the possession of Otanes, the second I will hide amidst Alexander's goods, for he travels with many manuscripts though he rarely has the time to read them, involved as he is with managing his conquered territories.

But let me return to my account now, for I am always conscious that time is not something I have control over. Once I was persuaded that Ptolemy was my brother, I sent a message to Zamos to send some of my men to Macedonia to discover as much about the family of Ptolemy of Lagus as they could. They were to also find out everything about his friends and the layout of his estate, for, if I were to continue being Ptolemy of Lagus, I had to know all about myself! I also strictly forbade him to tell the Persians where I was. He was only to tell them, if asked, that I was on my way to Lesbos to take charge of the monsters.

In the afternoon, Callisthenes came into my tent again and this time he was very agitated. He said that Theron's partners in the expedition had rejoined the baggage trail and they were threatening him with dire consequences if he did not reveal where Geronochus was. Callisthenes said that he suspected it was Theron who had instigated them. He said that they had issued an ultimatum to him – to either find Geronochus within ten days or hand over the share that was due to them.

I then asked Callisthenes the names of these men and how much of a share they demanded. And he looked at me with great surprise and asked: 'Why do you ask me something you already know?'

'I just want to be sure, Callisthenes, that it's the same men and not others,' I said feebly.

'Well, there's that dog Zeferino, and the one-eyed Menechus and Clearchus, the person whom you once complained about to Perdicass,' said Callisthenes.

'Yes, I know,' I said quietly.

'The three always move as a group, watching each other's back. Theron once told me that they had made an enemy of Seleucus, son of Nicanor, the Greek who won the quadragi in Olympia, and are worried that he hunts them. This Seleucus was the person that Argus had suspected you to be till Hepasthion reprimanded him and the matter was settled,' said Callisthenes.

'I know,' I repeated. 'How many talents do they want as their share?'

'They are asking for five talents in all. Zeferino further said that if Geronochus was not found and, as a consequence, their share was not made available to them within ten days, they would take the matter first to Perdicass and then to Hepasthion. For they feel that if they told the whole tale to Hepasthion, he would certainly forgive them, but he wouldn't forgive you. That's what Zeferino said. I asked them to talk to you directly, but they said that since they had only dealt with me, they did not feel comfortable approaching you,' said Callisthenes.

I then feigned a bout of sickness and asked Callisthenes to write down in detail all the tasks that Theron and his partners had done for us at Priapus and before. Then I told him that he was not to worry about them and once the entire episode was clear in my mind after reading all the details that he would provide, I would take care of the matter within ten days.

'I will do that,' said Callisthenes. 'But I find it strange that you should ask me to write about this matter as well, considering that you asked for me to keep it secret from everybody. Besides, it was you who issued all the orders and who plotted the entire ambush – you know all the details better than I do.'

'Of course I do, Callisthenes. But I seek to know all that you know and how you implemented my orders so that there is no detail that I miss out and I can grasp the matter in its entirety and so identify where the mistakes were made,' I said.

'If that is the purpose, I will do as you say,' replied Callisthenes.

Before he left, I also asked him to meet Agos in the evening and take him to where Geronochus was hidden and I told him to proceed in the matter only after making sure that he was not being followed by Theron or the others who threatened him.

After the departure of Callisthenes, I immediately asked Strabo to bring Agos to me, wherever he was. Once Agos arrived, I explained the entire matter to him and he was amazed to hear the story and both of us thanked Athena for bringing to us the three murderers we hunted. We also expressed incredulity at the nature of the plot that my brother Ptolemy had been the author of and were full of admiration for him.

I confided to Agos the certainty I felt about the missing Ptolemy being my twin and Agos was confounded when he heard the story from me. It was only after hearing it that he saw some merit in my decision to stick it out in the Macedonian camp. 'Though I must admit that I am frightened at the prospect that the real Ptolemy might enter the camp any time and you might be exposed,' he said.

To be honest, I wasn't worried at all about Ptolemy discovering me, as I was eager to meet my brother. In fact, after reading the transaction list of Callisthenes, I had become enamoured of Ptolemy, my brother whom I had never met, and was tempted to remain in my new identity.

The next day, Hepasthion walked into my tent unannounced.

Said he: 'Alexander has decided to build a temple to the Olympian Zeus at the spot where the Persian acropolis stood and where their garrison had been stationed in Sardis. You should be happy about it.'

I lacked the courage to ask him why he thought I should be happy about it, but when Strabo asked me later why I was not pursuing my morning ablutions to Zeus any more, I reasoned that Hepasthion must have had the devotion of Ptolemy to Zeus in mind.

Hepasthion also asked me to get ready to proceed with Alexander the next day for Ephesus, as some Greek mercenaries led by Amyntas, son of Antiochus, were in control there. Hepasthion said that since Amyntas did not like Alexander, I would be useful in negotiating a peaceful settlement, seeing that I knew him since childhood.

In dealing with Hepasthion, from the very first day, I had realized that he did not like to be counselled against any particular view that he might have taken or anything Alexander wanted executed in a particular way. So now, I quietly agreed to do as he wished. My desire for revenge against Alexander had not disappeared after I regained my memory, but I think the weakness in my body and the fact that I had still to recover from my wounds had instilled a sense of prudence in me. Also, the fact that my plan to kill Alexander during the battle had backfired made me less confident. The only thing in my favour was the fact that Alexander thought Seleucus had died in the battle of Granicus.

So, though I can say with certainty that my hatred for Alexander and the Macedonians had not diminished, I have to admit that my strategy regarding how to obtain my vengeance changed around this time, and that had something to do with the circumstances I found myself in. For, though pretending to be Ptolemy was dangerous for me, it was also exhilarating as it put me in a position of importance amidst my enemies. Being so close to them made me think that my privileged position was ordained by Athena, and the thought developed in me to learn the ways of my enemies so as to be able to direct their destruction better from within their ranks.

It was these thoughts which dominated my mind as I started my journey the next day with Alexander for Ephesus. It took us four days to reach Ephesus with a force of four thousand soldiers (the rest of Alexander's army rested in Sardis for a few days) and, after camping outside the city, Alexander sent me alone on horseback to talk to Amyntas, even though he was convinced that Amyntas would fight, since he was angry at the way the mercenaries had been slaughtered at Granicus.

Amyntas was, however, pleased to see me. He was more afraid than angry and took my offer of a safe passage for himself and the mercenary troops he commanded the moment I offered it to him. He also revealed something of significance to me: 'I am proceeding to meet Memnon of Rhodes, for the Persian has offered me employment to handle some monstrous stone throwers in Lesbos which have been recently constructed by them.'

Amyntas also mentioned that he had been offered a considerable sum by Memnon of Rhodes to identify officers in Alexander's army who could be bribed to start a rebellion against Alexander. He said that Memnon was willing to pay five talents to each officer who decided to defect from Alexander's army and one talent to every soldier. Amyntas then moved closer to me and said that since I had always talked about supporting Arrihidaeus, the demented brother of Alexander, who had been my childhood friend till his mental afflictions started, now was the time to prove my loyalty.

Not wanting to burn bridges with Amyntas, I told him that I would be in regular touch with him, but told him to depart from Ephseus as soon as his warships could take him, as Alexander desired nothing better than to put him and the other mercenaries to death. This pushed him to move swiftly and leave Ephesus with his troops. When I came back and reported their departure to Alexander, he was surprised, as he hadn't expected Amyntas to give in so easily.

I told Alexander that Amyntas had lost all heart for battle after he failed to sway me to his side, in spite of the bribe he offered me of ten talents. This impressed Alexander considerably, just as I had intended.

The next day, Alexander called me to his presence and then he made an announcement in front of Hepasthion and the others.

Said Alexander: 'Ptolemy of Lagus, I hereby appoint you an emissary in my army. You are to work directly under me, though from the offices of Eumenes, son of Calliphos, who is the chief of my spies. Your knowledge of Persian uniquely qualifies you to the new post and it would be your task to go and offer my terms of truce to the rulers of the kingdoms my army travels to. In this manner my armies could subjugate more kingdoms without any bloodshed. And where a battle becomes unavoidable, it will be your duty to bring information that could help us defeat the enemy.'

In this manner did I, Seleucus, son of Nicanor, mistaken to be Ptolemy of Lagus, get promoted to emissary in the armies of Alexander. And thus did the prophecy of Mistros come to be true. For Mistros had said, 'A battle will come soon, next to a river, and your life will change again. He whom you seek will become your master. Things will change later, but for now it is better that you let him become your master.'

I had thought then that Mistros was referring to Memnon of Rhodes as the man who would become my new master, as I had been trying to contact him at that point. But I had missed the larger truth, that the person I sought above all was Alexander!

To tell you the truth, it was Mistros's prophecy more than my own weaknesses and temptations that moved me to accept Alexander as my master. For his prophecies had never failed me and I took courage from his last words to me. For he had also said: 'Your questions will be answered by he who will come to you on top of a beast. Have patience.'

So I had to accept my situation till I met the man who would come into my life on top of a beast. Until then, I would wait patiently for the time when the wheel turned again, for turn it had to.

But more urgent matters were to be dealt with first. Agos brought word that Zeferino, Menechus and Clearchus had followed Callisthenes without his knowledge and seized Geronochus. And from Geronochus they had got information which they intended to reveal to Hepasthion unless Ptolemy, the master of Callisthenes, paid them fifteen talents for their silence, over and above the sum due to them for their services.

Then, one day, Alexander called me to his tent and brought to my attention a story that surprised me no end. He wanted me to investigate the truth of it. He said, in the presence of Hepasthion: 'Ptolemy, a Helot, a Spartan and an Athenian have narrated a story to Hepasthion that I find alarming. I am therefore giving you the responsibility of investigating the truth of their assertions and find out if Seleucus, son of Nicanor, is still alive and whether he is in our camp. I thought that it was his head that the mercenaries ran away with at Granicus, but apparently it is not so.'

It had so happened that Cnidus, the Helot in whose house we had stayed in Sparta and who had informed against Harmodius and me at the Spartan Gerousia, had teamed up with Masicus, the Spartan whose wife Petra had eloped with Cnidus, and Alcibiades, the Athenian who had betrayed me in Athens after getting friendly with Carmene, the sister of Athele!

After Cnidus had run away with Petra when she was with child, Masicus had hunted them down in Athens around the time that Thebes had fallen. By that time, Cnidus had become disillusioned with Petra because she had turned out to be a nag and he was also unhappy that he was raising Masicus's son and not his own. Masicus himself, after having his jaw broken by the husband of Eudora the whore and losing his boat to us, had come to know eventually that it was Seleucus, son of Nicanor, who had escaped using his boat. He then set about looking for his wife Petra, as he had become the laughing stock of his friends in Sparta, and he intended to bring her back, specially as he was aware that she had been with child when she left. So he visited every town and went to the wine shops, for he assumed that Cnidus would start a similar business anywhere he settled, as he knew little else.

In this assessment he was right. He reached Athens and finally found Cnidus and his wife Petra running a tavern in the city. But by the time he found Petra, he had grown out of his love for her and found that he bore no ill-will towards Cnidus either. Strangely, the two men became friends and together berated Petra for the manner in which she had ill-treated them both! Then Cnidus, during a drunken bout, suddenly put the blame for their predicament on Seleucus, as he felt that he had been the reason for his falling on bad times. Masicus also felt that Nicanor's son had played foul with him, by stealing his boat and putting him up to a needless fight with Eudora's husband. Therefore the two decided to hunt down Seleucus and teach him a lesson.

In this frame of mind they visited the Athena temple at the Parthenon to seek her blessings before they embarked on their mission. There, they bumped into Alcibiades, who, after being released by Aumides the jailor, had started working as a servant in the temple. If you remember, the Macedonian Paucinias, who had been the chief of staff of Antipater, had caught Himerius thinking he was Seleucus, son of Nicanor. And it was Alcibiades who had led Paucinias to Himerius and had turned from a villain to a hero after the rumour started that he had duped the Macedonians of ten talents.

Alcibiades, incidentally, had also been nursing a grudge against me for a long time, even though he himself had betrayed me. Coming to know of the objectives of Cnidus and Masicus, he decided to befriend them and together the three came to Asia, looking for employment as mercenaries. And they were recruited by Pythagoras himself, as he had never met them earlier and had no knowledge of their past.

They had landed on the coast just a few days before the battle of Granicus and had been given the task by Zamos to procure the Byzantine helmets that he was distributing to the Persian nobles. Zamos too knew nothing of their history, as he had never been in Athens with us. It was after the battle, when the three had the good fortune to escape the battlefield, that they spied Memnon of Rhodes passing on some talents to Zamos for having arranged the killing of the Persian nobles in the battle.

They also overheard Zamos boasting to Memnon of Rhodes that it had been the idea of Seleucus, son of Nicanor, to have Alexander think that one of the men riding a white horse was Seleucus himself. With this story the three then defected to the Macedonian camp and were led first to Eumenes, who, after hearing their story, took them to Hepasthion and Alexander. The men informed them that the head which Alexander had thought to be of Nicanor's son was not his but that of Petines, a Persian nobleman.

After hearing this story, Alexander admitted to the possibility that he had been mistaken in his belief that the head belonged to Nicanor's son. He said the head had been too disfigured for him to examine properly.

Alexander was now angry at the possibility of Nicanor's son being alive and even more angry at the possibility that he could be in the Macedonian camp in disguise! For Alcibiades had also told him that they had overheard Zamos boasting to Memnon of Rhodes that Seleucus was in fact in the Macedonian camp, looking for an appropriate moment to kill first Philotas and then Alexander himself.

And even though Hepasthion dismissed this bit of information as a mere boast on Zamos's part to impress the Persians, Alexander wanted to get to the bottom of it. Thus it was that he summoned me. I was lucky that the three men had left his presence when I reached him, but I was instructed to meet them by Alexander himself, so that I could gauge the veracity of their information and start my investigation into the matter. Added Alexander: 'If you find this Seleucus, son of Nicanor, and produce him alive before me, I will make you a general in my army, Ptolemy.'

These then were the complications that I faced as Alexander marched towards the port town of Miletus. After two years of relentless pursuit, the men I sought were nearly within my grasp: Zeferino, Menechus, Clearchus, and of course, Alexander. There was also Philotas, who was the only link between me and my son Zanylos. And the words of Mistros travelled with me wherever I went. He had said: 'Your questions will be answered by he who will come to you on top of a beast. Have patience.'

It was the year when Pythodelus was still the archon of Athens. And I, Seleucus, was not only the son of Nicanor, I was also Ptolemy from Lagus, an emissary of King Alexander the Great.

CAST OF CHARACTERS

Aegis:	The new king of Sparta
Aeschines:	Rival of Demosthenes
Aeschylus:	Famous Athenian orator
Agaemon:	Officer in charge of soldiers of the Macedonian triremes
Agathon:	Corinthian architect in Delphi
Agnodice:	Famous female physician of Thebes
Agos:	Soldier and accomplice of Seleucus
Ahinadab:	Phoenician pirate
Alabanda:	Persian accomplice of Agos in Abydos
Alcibiades:	Athenian captured at Chaeronea
Alcidas:	Macedonian soldier under Polemon
Alexander:	Prince, and later king, of Macedonia; son of Philip
Alexander the Molossian:	King of Epirus
Amestipolos:	Bodyguard of Phaticidas; brother-in-law of Cholargus
Amorges:	Persian exile in the court of Alexander
Amyntas:	Macedonian soldier
Analisa:	Lover of Ptolemy; mistress of Perdicass
Anos:	Athenian herald at the Spartan Gerousia
Antipater:	General in King Philip's army
Aradus:	Wrestling instructor at the Delphi gymnasium
Argus:	Macedonian charioteer
Aristos:	Macedonian soldier in Pylos
Aristotle:	Tutor of Alexander
Arnos:	Helot labourer in Pylos
Arrihidaeus:	Mentally unsound brother of Alexander
Arasmes:	Commander of Persian forces at Granicus
Arsites:	Satrap of northern Phrygia
Artaxerxes:	King of Persia
Asidamus:	Spartan soldier; father of Spiticos

Asmetus:	Former governor of Abydos; father of Mazus
Astyochus:	Port commander of Las
Athele:	Athenian widow; wife of Seleucus
Atos:	Persian informer appointed by Seleucus
Attalus:	Macedonian general; uncle of Eurydice
Augusta:	Priest at temple of Apollo in Sparta
Aumides:	Athenian jailor
Automa:	Son of Samocles; husband of Fouma
Boridas:	Leader of Theban exiles
Boriphon:	Leader of Cretan archers in Seleucus's employ
Brachimon:	Leader of Phaticidis's army in Lesbos
Brasidas:	Patient at Ganymede's asclepeion
Brazus:	Persian commander; nephew of Artaxerxes
Brunic:	Euboean scout at Chaeronea
Busemon:	Flag bearer of the Macedonian cavalry at Chaeronea
Buserne:	Persian exile in the court of Alexander
Busiris:	Chief priest at Delphi
Caldemus:	Macedonian priest
Calliphus:	Priest at temple of Athena in Athens
Callisthenes:	Official historian of Alexander
Cannus:	Brother of Spiticos
Caranus:	Son of Eurydice and Philip
Carinus:	Nobleman; friend of Alexander
Carmene:	Widowed sister of Athele
Carmus:	Chief of the village of Dramos
Catherine:	Daughter of Philip
Cecod:	Head of the Persian treasury
Chares:	Athenian general
Cholargus:	Diver in Methymyna
Cicero:	Deaf and mute employee of Seleucus
Cimon:	Helot collaborator of the Macedonians
Clearchus:	Macedonian soldier
Cleomenes:	Athenian soldier in jailor Aumides's unit
Clonus:	Spartan charioteer, later ephor
Cnidus:	Wine-seller in Sparta
Connidas:	Patient at Ganymede's asclepeion in Pylos
Corcyra:	Son of Kozma, chief metallurgist of the Olympic Games
Cynisca:	Legendary Spartan charioteer
Damaris:	Chief maid of Olympias

Darius: King of Persia after Artaxerxes
Democles: Legendary charioteer
Demosthenes: Famous Athenian orator
Dominos: Spartan herald
Donios: Former lover of Eurydice
Dorian: Helot escapee from Sparta; employee of Seleucus
Dradocotus: Page of Alexander
Epamonidas: Theban general
Erigyius: Macedonian exile; friend of Alexander
Eudora: Helot woman in Zeros
Euriphides: Father of Uranus; divinator
Eurybotas: Chief of Cretan archers in Theban war
Eurydice: Queen of Macedonia; second wife of Philip
Fachulus: Officer in Phaticidas's army
Farisa: Concubine of Gophoredes
Fouma: Wife of Automa
Gamyetus: Spartan ephor
Ganymede: Physician in Pylos
Gelon: Tavern owner in Athens
Gerochus: Illyrian nobleman
Geronochus: Accomplice of Ptolemy
Gobyras: Manager of Nearchus's estate
Gongylus: Euboean prisoner captured at Chaeronea
Gophoredes: Officer in the Persian army
Gotarzes: Maternal uncle of Luminas
Harmodius: Helot rower with powers of prophecy
Harmos: Brother of Carmus; new chief of the village of Dramos
Harpalus: Macedonian exile; friend of Alexander.
Hecatomanus: Brother of Mindarus
Helen: Wife of Minos
Helena: Wife of Polemon
Himerius: Athenian delinquent
Hepasthion: Companion of Alexander
Hesiod: Veteran soldier from Thebes
Hypereides: Leading citizen of Athens
Kelos: Chief controller of the Olympic Games
Lamachus: Euboean captured at Chaeronea
Laomedon: Macedonian exile; brother of Erigyius
Larcinus: Helot woman from Zeros

Lasimodus:	Rower and companion of Harmodius
Lemonos:	King of Cyprus
Leon:	Macedonian soldier under Polemon
Leonidas:	Legendary Spartan king
Luminas:	Wife of Persian governor Mazus
Lycargus:	Controller of festival fund in Athens
Machatas:	Bodyguard of Philip
Malcipas:	Admiral in Macedonian navy
Masicus:	Spartan boatman; husband of Petra
Mazus:	Governor of Mysia
Megabos:	General in Mazus's army
Memnon of Rhodes:	Commander in the Persian army
Memphios:	Mercenary in the employ of Seleucus
Menechus:	Macedonian soldier under Polemon
Menicus:	Athenian rescued by Seleucus
Menelus:	Athenian wagon driver
Mestacles:	Seer at Pelops
Miletus:	Veteran soldier from Athens
Mindarus:	Macedonian citizen
Minos:	Ionian chief of delegation to Athens
Mios:	Athenian aristocrat
Mistros:	Persian seer from Larisa
Mithridates:	Son-in-law of Darius
Modius:	Cousin of Olympias; lover of Fouma
Monimus:	King of Siphnos
Morai:	Wife of Phaticidas; queen of Lesbos
Mritphakes:	Persian noble
Myndus:	Massalian accomplice of Seleucus
Nautaca:	Messalian accomplice of Seleucus
Naxos:	Macedonian exile; friend of Alexander
Nazafarish:	Wife of Artaxerxes
Nearchus:	Macedonian exile; friend of Alexander
Nicanor:	Macedonian charioteer in Olympia; father of Seleucus
Nicias:	Timber merchant; uncle of Seleucus
Olympias:	Queen of Macedonia; mother of Alexander
Omares:	Commander of the foreign contingent in Persian army
Orchimandus:	Theban exile
Otanes:	Athenian rescued by Seleucus

Oxyrides: Lover of Philip
Parmenio: Macedonian general
Patromos: Legendary Spartan charioteer
Paucinias: Macedonian chief of staff
Pausanias: Scorned lover of Philip
Perdicass: Macedonian officer of the Guards
Petines: Commander in the Persian army
Petra: Wife of Masicus
Phanus: Personal bodyguard of Mazus
Phaselis: Employee of Naxos
Phaticidas: King of Lesbos
Phicias: Governor of Abydos
Philip: King of Macedonia
Phillip: Physician of Alexander
Philotas: Son of Parmenio
Phisias: Athenian moneylender
Phocion: Athenian orator
Phormio: Merchant sailor from Lesbos
Pindar: Friend of Seleucus in Olympia
Piros: Macedonian in charge of Antipater's treasury
Pistoris: Tyrant king of Lemnos
Pixodarus: King of Caria
Platulus: Commander of Lancers at Granicus
Polemon: Manager of Macedonian delegation in Olympia
Ptolemy: Nobleman from Amphipolis
Pythadorus: Priest at temple of Apollo in Pylos
Pythagoras: Athenian charioteer
Pythodelus: Archon of Athens
Rhoesaces: Persian nobleman
Samocles: Carioteer from Thebes
Samocles: Inventor from Kimoros
Samcottus: Helot on Spiticos's ship
Samthos: Charioteer from Corinth
Scion: Helot soldier
Sebasticus: Former Greek husband of Morai
Seleucus: Macedonian from Olympia; son of Nicanor
Spintharos: Corinthian architect in Delphi
Spithridates: Persian governor of Lydia
Spitos: Thessalian charioteer

Stella: Mother of Seleucus; wife of Nicanor
Strabo: Servant of Ptolemy
Tabalus: Head of the Persian Immortals
Telephus: Nephew of Damaris
Telos: Physician in Olympia
Tepidas: Leader of the Theban Sacred Band
Thamotus: Theban exile
Thasidomus: Former Periokoi commander of Pylos; father of Harmodius
Themistocles: King of Eleia
Theron: Macedonian accomplice of Ptolemy
Thucydides: Leading citizen of Sparta
Thymondas: Thessalian playwright
Timines: Athenian aristocrat and lawyer
Timos: Famous Athenian orator
Trachomus: Military commander of Las
Trillimachus: Bodyguard of Philip
Trilomachus: Helot servant of Cnidus
Tymos: Soldier in Sacred Band; lover of Tepidas
Tyros: Athenian rescued by Seleucus
Uranus: Manager of gymnasium in Thebes
Xenodoros: Corinthian architect in Delphi
Zamos: Brother of Phormio
Zandimus: Spartan hoplite
Zanus: Servant of Kelos, later of Polemon
Zanylos: Helot servant of Ganymede
Zanylos: Son of Seleucus
Zeferino: Nobleman and chief organizer of bets in Olympia
Zetomandus: King of Sparta
Zicos: Helot sailor
Zymindas: Helot friend of Zanylos
Zumidos: Helot leader appointed by Zatomandus

CHRONOLOGY OF EVENTS

359 BC: The regent head of Macedonia, Philip II, crowns himself king in the most difficult times, with the neighbouring Thracians, Illyrians and Greeks invading and plundering the country.

358 BC: Philip subdues the Paeonians and the Thracians, who had invaded the eastern regions of Macedonia.

356 BC: Alexander is born to Philip and Olympia, at Pella.

354 BC: Philip captures city of Methone, loses an eye in battle.

346 BC: Philip's ten-year conflict with Athens temporarily ends and peace is sworn at Thessaly. Key Greek cities submit to Macedonian control, except Sparta.

338 BC: Battle of Chaeronea. Philip destroys the combined armies of Athens and Thebes and reasserts supremacy over Greek territories; Alexander commands cavalry, Sacred Band of Thebes annihilated in battle.
Philip marches into Thebes, instals Macedonian garrison.
Artaxerxes IV assumes throne as king of Persia.

337 BC: Philip establishes league of Corinth, a confederation of Greek cities, to facilitate the use of military forces in his war against Persia. He is authorized by the league, as Hegemon of Greece, to initiate a sacred war of vengeance against the Persians for desecrating Athenian temples in the Second Persian War (480-479 BC).

336 BC: Assassination of Philip, Alexander assumes the crown.
Darius III crowned as king of Persia.

335 BC: Macedonian garrison in Thebes besieged.
League orders city of Thebes to be razed to the ground by Hegemon Alexander, to instil fear among rebels.

334 BC: Alexander invades Asia Minor, backed by the league and a combined Greek army.
Battle of Granicus, Alexander defeats Persian army for the first time.

333 BC: Battle of Issus, Alexander defeats the Persian army, captures Persian royal family.
Persian King Darius III abandons army and flees.
Alexander gains control over southern Asia Minor.

332 BC: Alexander invades Egypt and is enthroned as Pharoah at Memphis.

331 BC: Battle of Guagamela, final defeat of King Darius III.
Alexander conquers Babylon, Susa and Persian capital Persepolis.

330 BC: Bessus, a Persian kinsman in Bactria, stabs Darius III and declares himself Artaxerxes V.

329 BC: Alexander crosses Hindu Kush into Central Asia, invades Bactria.
Artaxerxes V, usurper of Persian throne, arrested.

327 BC: Invasion of India begins at Taxila.

326 BC: Battle of River Hydaspes, Alexander defeats Indian king Porus.

325 BC: Alexander leaves India.

323 BC: Death of Alexander in Babylon.
Ptolemy I Soter, General under Alexander, assumes the throne.

BIBLIOGRAPHY

Arrian, *The Campaigns of Alexander*, ed. J.R. Hamilton, tr. Aubrey De Selincourt, London: Penguin, 1976.

———*Anabasis of Alexander* and *Indica*, tr. P.A. Brunt, 2 volumes, Loeb Classical Library, Cambridge: Harvard University Press, 1989.

Brosius, Maria, *The Persians: An Introduction*, New York: Routledge, 2006.

Curtis, John and Nigel Tallis ed., *Forgotten Empire: The World of Ancient Persia*, Berkeley: University of California Press, 2005.

Farrokh, Kaveh, *Shadows in the Desert: Ancient Persia at War*, UK: Osprey, 2007.

Fields, Nic, *Ancient Greek Warship (500–322 B.C.)*, UK: Osprey, 2007.

Secunda, Nick, *Greek Hoplite (480–323 B.C.): Weapons, Armour, Tactics*, UK: Osprey, 2000.

———*The Army of Alexander the Great*, UK: Osprey, 1992.

———*The Persian Army (560–330 BC)*, UK: Osprey 1992.

Strassler, Robert B. ed., *The Landmark Thucydides: A Comprehensive Guide to the Peloponnesian War*, New York: Free Press, 1996.

———*The Landmark Herodotus: The Histories*, New York: Pantheon Books, 2007.

Warry, John, *Warfare in the Classical World*, New York: Barnes & Noble, 2000

ACKNOWLEDGEMENTS

Novelists craft their novels in solitude. A mind not at peace cannot perhaps write anything of any significance. I have to thank several people for helping me with the creation of this seeming bubble of quiet.

I must thank Lakshmi and Dada for their constant, benevolent urging; Ashish Kacholia, for his generous spirit; Vibhav, for his hospitality and friendship in faraway places; Monu, for his conversations; Somesh, for his wit and big-heartedness; Guruji, for his ever-present optimism; Sudhir Varma, for his number crunching and Uday Shankar, for providing opportunities every now and then.

For constant literary feedback, I have to thank my agent Gillon Aitken. For helping me edit my rather voluminous output, I have to thank Karthika, my editor at HarperCollins, and my favourite former teacher of English from Allahabad, Amrita Chatterjee. For getting me going, indirectly, on my Greek project, I have to thank Sir V.S. Naipaul; he advised me many years ago to read a lot of history. I am not sure I took his advise in the way it was intended, for my first brush with history of any sort was to read the ancient Greek authors and there it has remained on pause. I read the works of Herodotus, Arrian, Thucydides and a few others and opened up for myself a fascinating new world. This novel is the consequence.

I am immensely grateful to those who have helped me navigate the various judicial processes in which I have been involved and who keep me going, relatively unscathed, in the face of the prosecutorial venom of the Indian state. I thank Siddhartha Luthra, Kevin Gulati, Prashant Bhushan, Dushyant Dave, Akhil Sibal, Harish Salve, Raian Karanjawala, Pramod Dubey, Manish Tewari, Satyanarain, Meet Malhotra, Pradeep, Rishabh Jain, Arundhati Katju, Ruby Ahuja, Meenakshi Grover and others at their offices. They may be lawyers, but they are friends first.

I have to thank all the founders and members of the Foundation for Media Professionals, for dreaming big and helping craft a family away from home. We are still travelling and are a work in progress, but we hope to be somewhere significant eventually. For being on this journey together, I thank Madhu Trehan, Manoj Mitta, Vivian Fernandes, Vineet Narain, Shashi Shekhar, Srinivasan Seetharaman, Ashutosh, Sanjay Pugalia, Amitabh, Harpal Singh, Vipul Mudgal, Sanjay Salil, Shivani Sharma Dasmahapatra, Shalini Singh, Amit Goel, Dalip Singh, Deepak Sharma, Sandhya Sridhar, Masumi Bhattacharya, Paranjoy Guha Thakurta, Saikat Datta and all others. Of course, Rajeshwar Dayal, Anja Minnaert, Vinoo, Debashish and others at the Friedrich Ebert Stiftung Foundation as well.

The former, present and honorary Cobrapost family I have a special affection for. Most remain in touch and are nostalgic about the work we did together. I must specially mention Disha Mehra, Suhasini Raj, Anju Juneja, Amitabh, K. Ashish, Arnab Datta, Ruchi Bharti, Neeraj, Anuranjan Jha, Rakesh, Satyashree Gandham, Harish, Himanshu, Nitin, Syed, Vineet, Rakesh Johri, Manoj, Digvijay and Kapil.

For keeping me grounded, I have to thank the larger Allahabadi bunch that is a constant presence in my life. To single out people here would be opening a can of worms. Still: Biswadeep Moitra, Ashish Chopra, Neeraj Roy, Sameer Shah, Atul Mehra, Nitin Khanna, Amit Sehgal, Ashish Abrol, Ashish Gupta, Mohit Mehrotra, Anuj Srivastava, Ajit Sahi, Bala Subramanian, Adil Syed Khan, Vivek Srivastava, Amit Bhagat, Rakesh Trivedi, Pankaj Bhola, Tighmanshu Dhulia, Sandeep Chandra, Prabhat Shanglu, Devesh Sahay (wherever he is), Sanjay Banerjee, Rishadat Kabir and Sameer Sharma.

Many thanks to Ketaki Goswami, Nooraine Fazal, Rahul Johri, Rajdeep Sardesai, Aravind Adiga, Milind Deora, Vinutha Mallya, Tarun Tejpal, Shekhar Bhatia, Mahesh Bhatt, Arundhati Roy, Vandana Singh, Shazi Zaman, Livleen Sharma, Tomita San, Nambu San, Vipul Patel, Sonal Ladwa, Vani Tripathi, Krishna Prasad, Amitava Kumar, Sagarika Ghose, Dr Sanjeev Dhavan, Dr Sanjay Bhatnagar, Adam Dunn, Dr Brij Bhushan Agarwal, Leena Ali, Beena Sarwar, Ruchi, Indrajit Banerjee, Maheshwar Perry, Peali Datta, Madhu, Ranjit Bhushan, Rhonda Baughman, Prahlad Kakkar, Virat Bhatia, Chiki Sarkar, Sruti Debi, Fayaz Rizvi, Piyush Jain, Sunil Khosla, George Varghese, Poonam Saxena, Jaggi Panda, Sunil Khosla, Eric Burnand, Manu Joseph, Chantal Thevenoz, Nishi Mallick, Mohammed Shaqeel, Rohini Sharma Killough and Stephen Farrell, for their presence and continuous support. Many thanks also to the dozens of constables from the CISF who have been my constant companions over five years. And a big thank you to

Haider and Ashutosh at Inosoft, and the team at HarperCollins, specially Pradipta Sarkar, Natasha Puri, Shantanu Ray Chaudhuri, Shuka Jain, Neelini Sarkar, Lipika Bhushan and P.M. Sukumar for all their help.

Finally, none of my fictional forays would have been possible without the loving presence of my wife Reema and my two daughters Rhea and Esha, and their patient understanding when I insist on inhabiting ancient and contemporary worlds.